THE WALKING DEAD

BOOK THREE

a continuing story of survival horror.

created by Robert Kirkman

image comics presents

The Walking Dead

book three

ROBERT KIRKMAN
creator, writer

CHARLIE ADLARD
penciler, inker, cover

CLIFF RATHBURN
gray tones

RUS WOOTON
letterer

Original series covers by
CHARLIE ADLARD & CLIFF RATHBURN

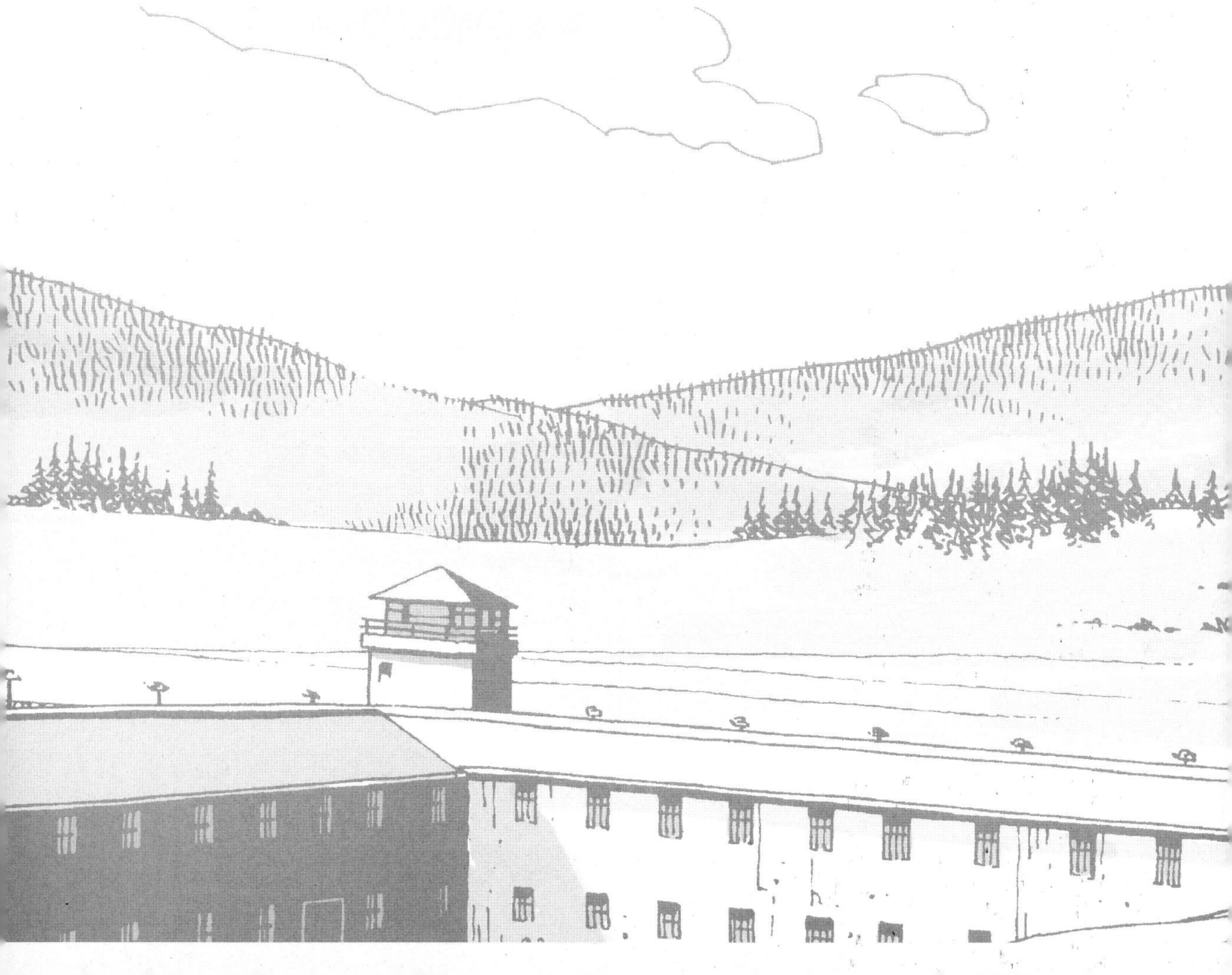

Robert Kirkman
chief executive officer

J.J. Didde
president

www.skybound.com

Robert Kirkman
chief operating officer

Erik Larsen
chief financial officer

Todd McFarlane
president

Marc Silvestri
chief executive officer

Jim Valentino
vice-president

Sina Grace
editorial director

Shawn Kirkham
director of business development

Tim Daniel
digital content manager

Eric Stephenson
publisher

Todd Martinez
sales & licensing coordinator

Jennifer deGuzman
pr & marketing coordinator

Branwyn Bigglestone
accounts manager

Emily Miller
administrative assistant

Jamie Parreno
marketing assistant

Sarah deLaine
events coordinator

Chad Manion
assistant to mr. grace

Sydney Pennington
assistant to mr. kirkham

**Feldman Public
Relations LA**
public relations

Kevin Yuen
digital rights coordinator

Tyler Shainline
production manager

Drew Gill
art director

Jonathan Chan
senior production artist

Monica Garcia
production artist

Vincent Kukua
production artist

Jana Cook
production artist

www.imagecomics.com

Chapter Five:
The Best Defense

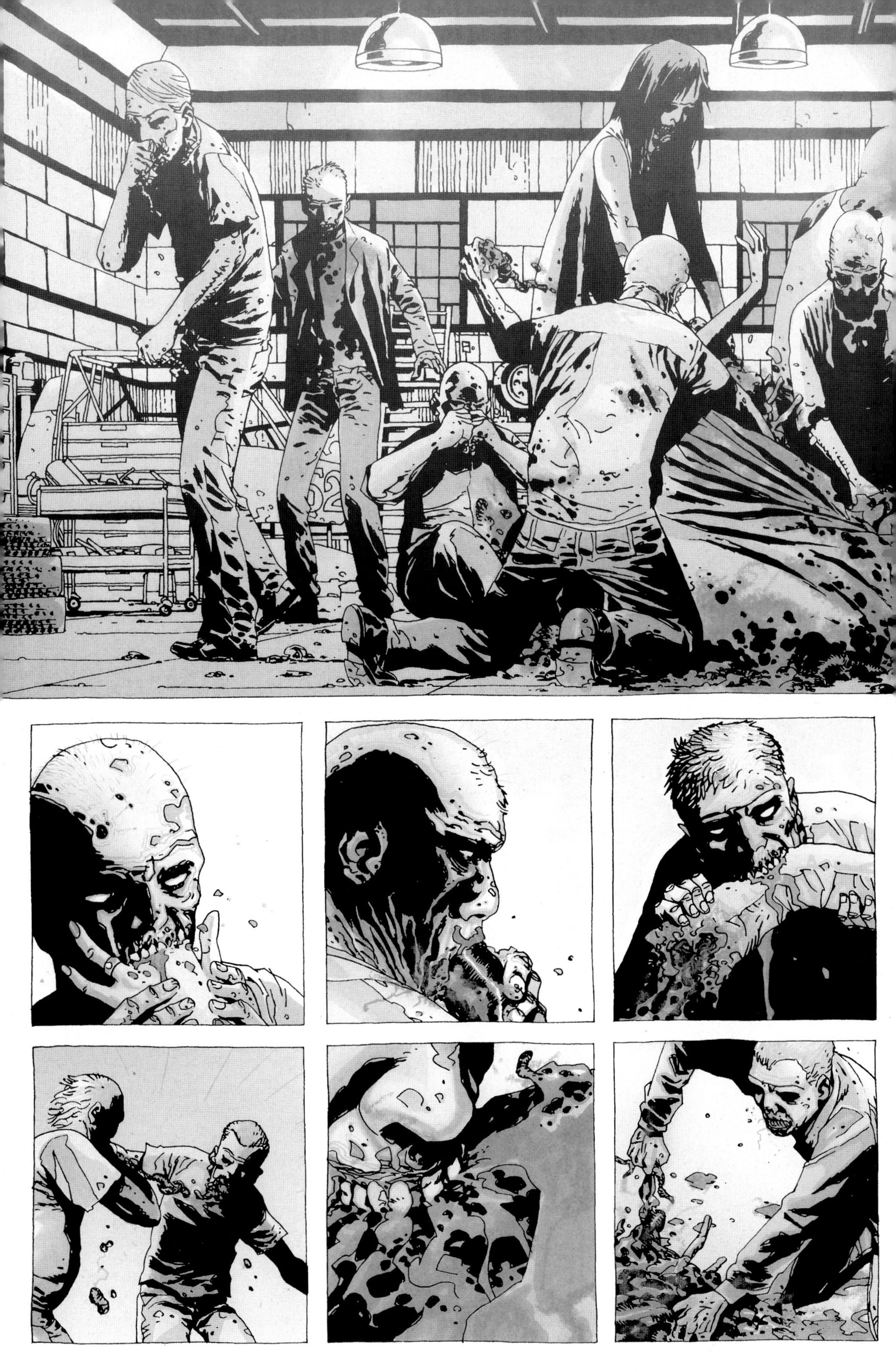

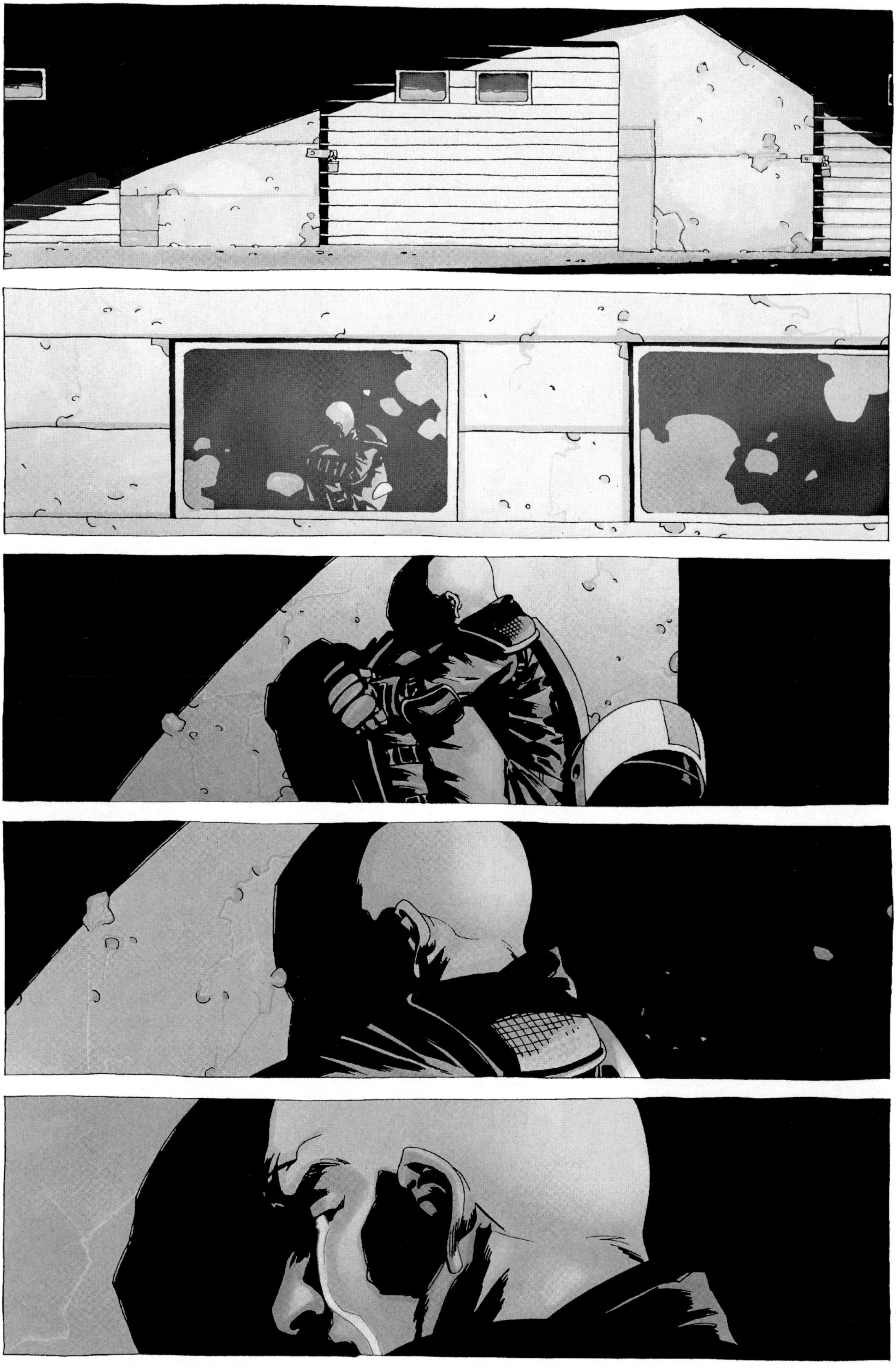

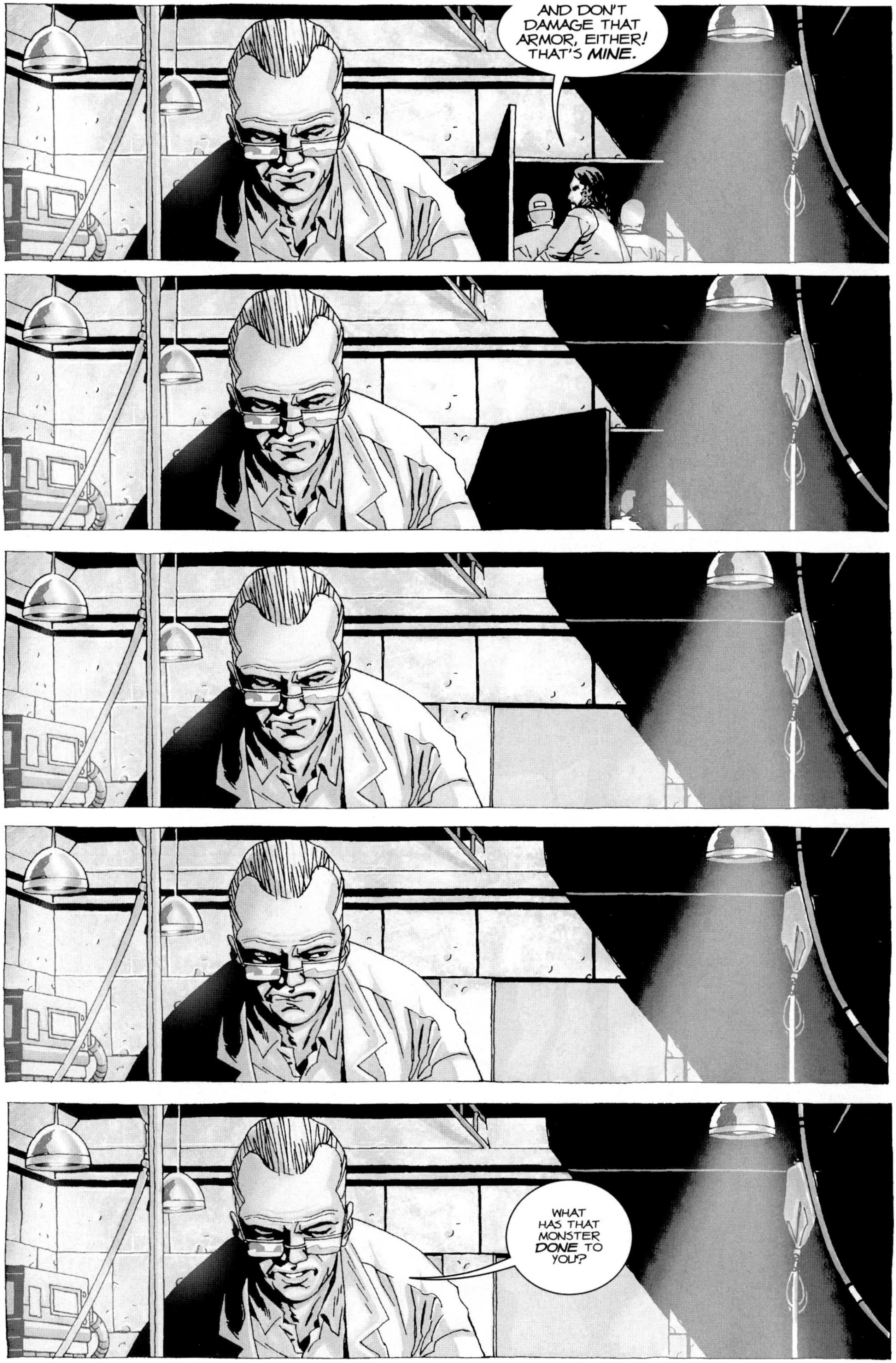
AND DON'T DAMAGE THAT ARMOR, EITHER! THAT'S *MINE.*
WHAT HAS THAT MONSTER *DONE* TO YOU!?

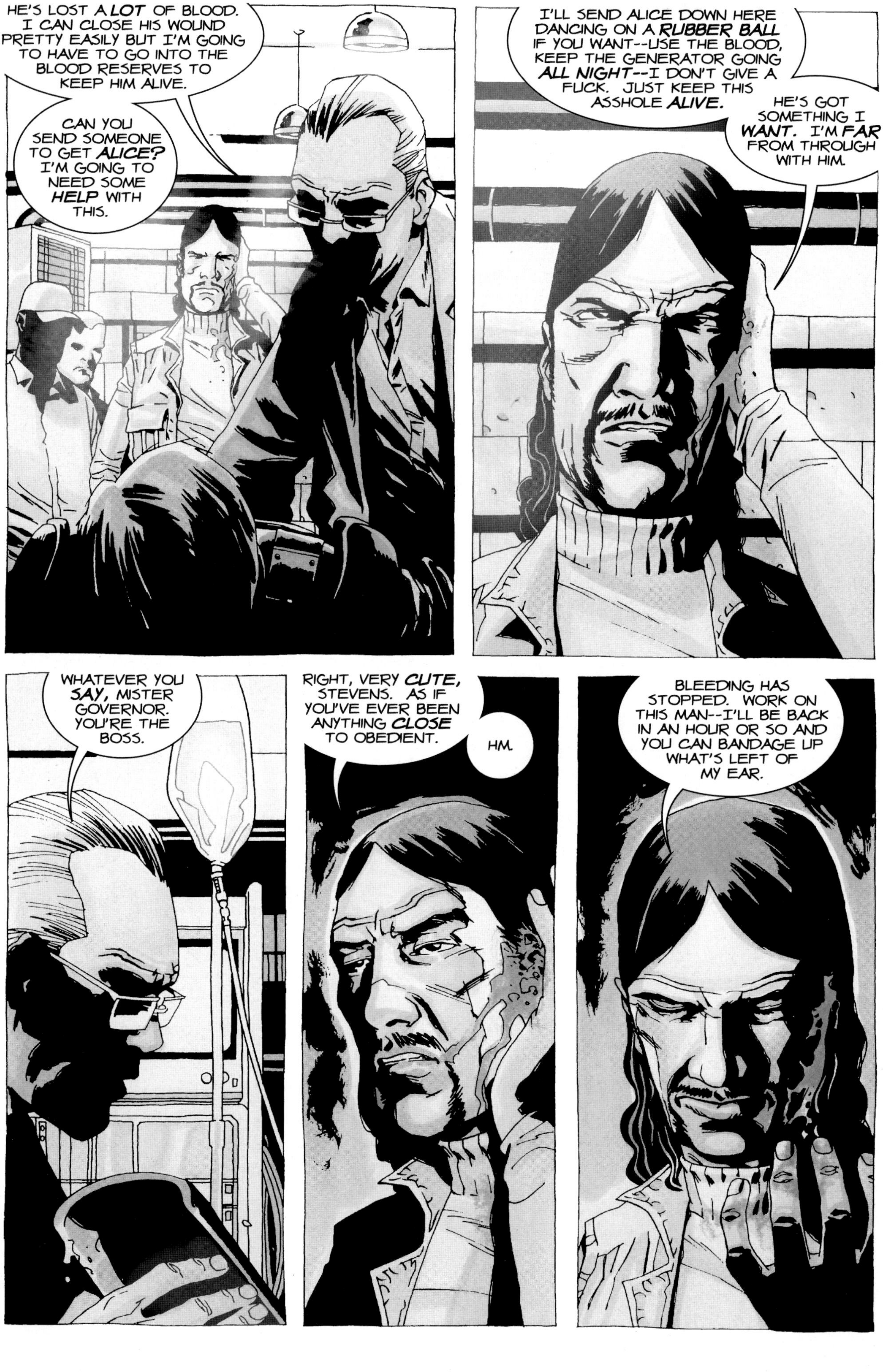
HE'S LOST A LOT OF BLOOD. I CAN CLOSE HIS WOUND PRETTY EASILY BUT I'M GOING TO HAVE TO GO INTO THE BLOOD RESERVES TO KEEP HIM ALIVE.
CAN YOU SEND SOMEONE TO GET ALICE? I'M GOING TO NEED SOME HELP WITH THIS.
I'LL SEND ALICE DOWN HERE DANCING ON A RUBBER BALL IF YOU WANT--USE THE BLOOD, KEEP THE GENERATOR GOING ALL NIGHT--I DON'T GIVE A FUCK. JUST KEEP THIS ASSHOLE ALIVE.
HE'S GOT SOMETHING I WANT. I'M FAR FROM THROUGH WITH HIM.
WHATEVER YOU SAY, MISTER GOVERNOR. YOU'RE THE BOSS.
RIGHT, VERY CUTE, STEVENS. AS IF YOU'VE EVER BEEN ANYTHING CLOSE TO OBEDIENT.
HM.
BLEEDING HAS STOPPED. WORK ON THIS MAN--I'LL BE BACK IN AN HOUR OR SO AND YOU CAN BANDAGE UP WHAT'S LEFT OF MY EAR.

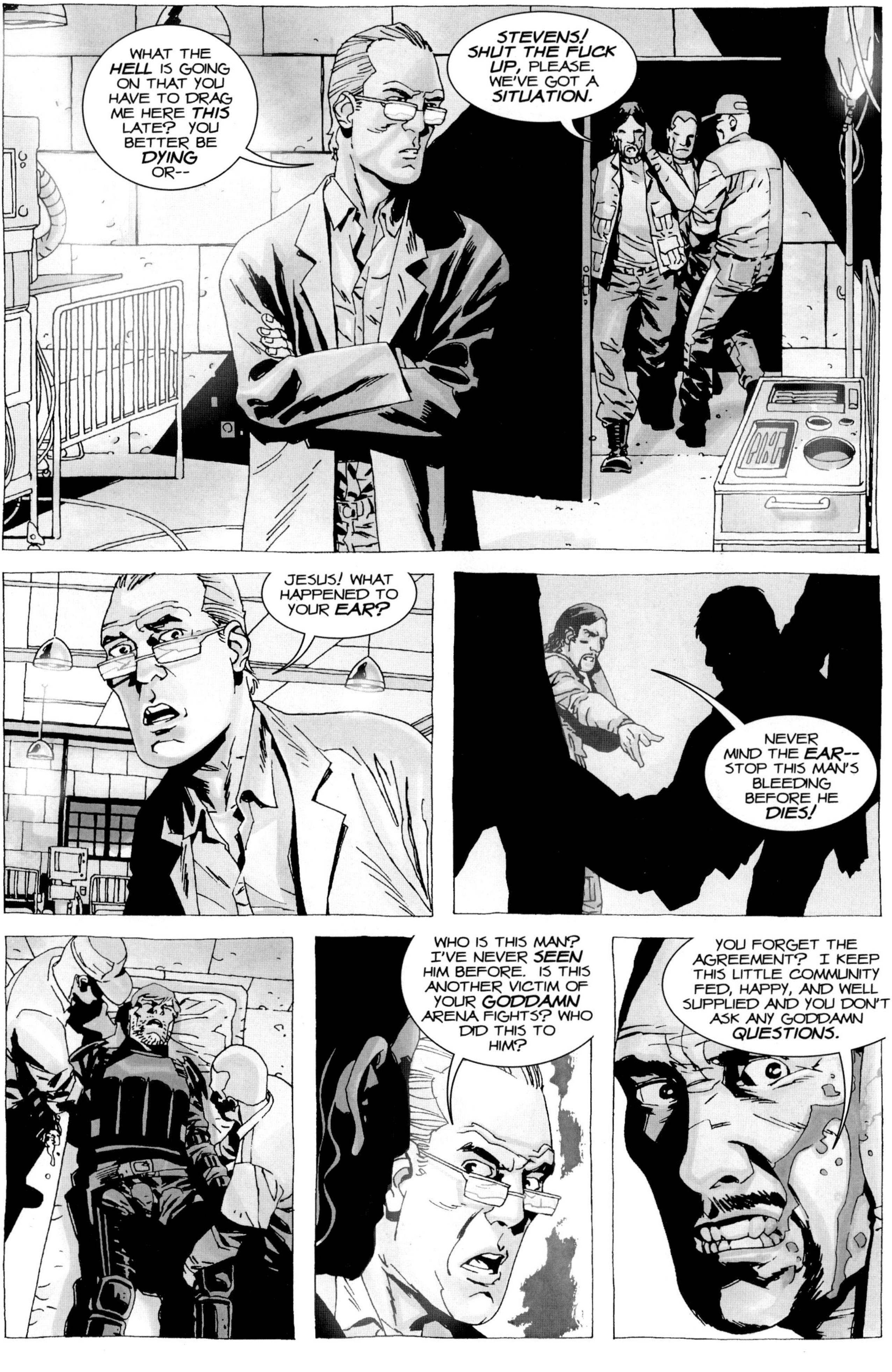
WHAT THE HELL IS GOING ON THAT YOU HAVE TO DRAG ME HERE THIS LATE? YOU BETTER BE DYING OR--
STEVENS! SHUT THE FUCK UP, PLEASE. WE'VE GOT A SITUATION.
JESUS! WHAT HAPPENED TO YOUR EAR?
NEVER MIND THE EAR-- STOP THIS MAN'S BLEEDING BEFORE HE DIES!
WHO IS THIS MAN? I'VE NEVER SEEN HIM BEFORE. IS THIS ANOTHER VICTIM OF YOUR GODDAMN ARENA FIGHTS? WHO DID THIS TO HIM?
YOU FORGET THE AGREEMENT? I KEEP THIS LITTLE COMMUNITY FED, HAPPY, AND WELL SUPPLIED AND YOU DON'T ASK ANY GODDAMN QUESTIONS.

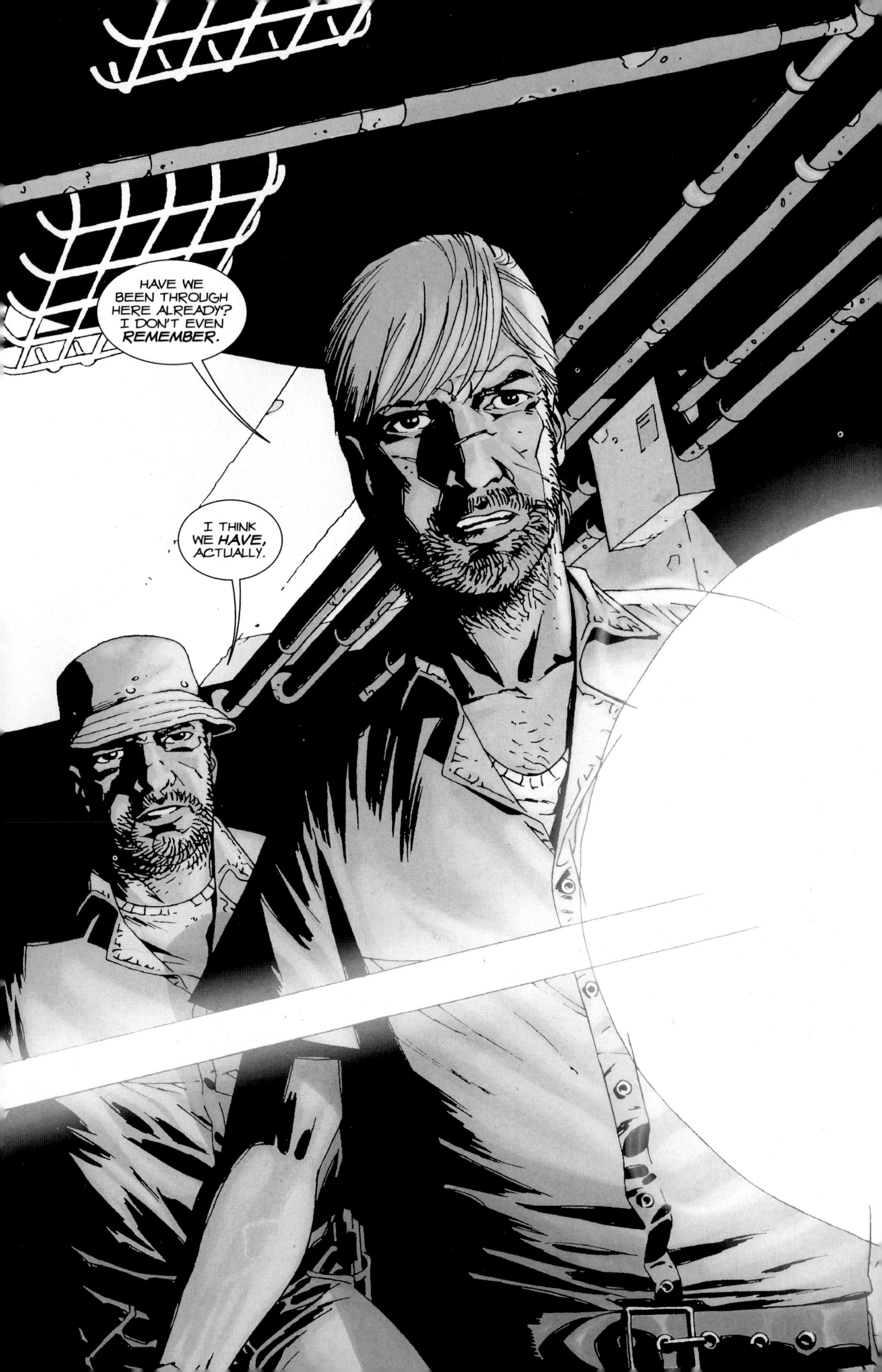
HAVE WE BEEN THROUGH HERE ALREADY? I DON'T EVEN *REMEMBER*.
I THINK WE *HAVE*, ACTUALLY.

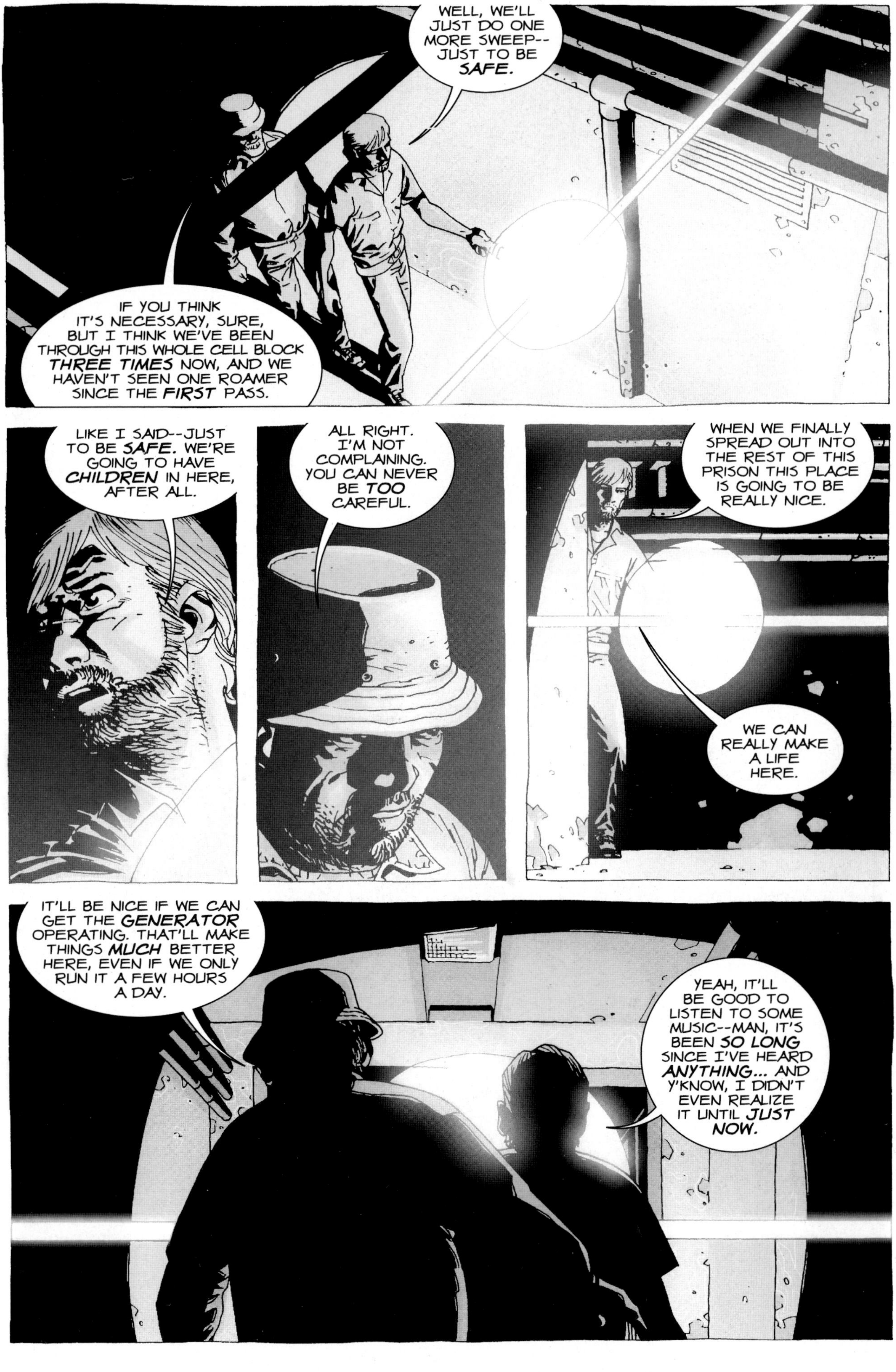
WELL, WE'LL JUST DO ONE MORE SWEEP-- JUST TO BE SAFE.
IF YOU THINK IT'S NECESSARY, SURE, BUT I THINK WE'VE BEEN THROUGH THIS WHOLE CELL BLOCK THREE TIMES NOW, AND WE HAVEN'T SEEN ONE ROAMER SINCE THE FIRST PASS.
LIKE I SAID--JUST TO BE SAFE. WE'RE GOING TO HAVE CHILDREN IN HERE, AFTER ALL.
ALL RIGHT. I'M NOT COMPLAINING. YOU CAN NEVER BE TOO CAREFUL.
WHEN WE FINALLY SPREAD OUT INTO THE REST OF THIS PRISON THIS PLACE IS GOING TO BE REALLY NICE.
WE CAN REALLY MAKE A LIFE HERE.
IT'LL BE NICE IF WE CAN GET THE GENERATOR OPERATING. THAT'LL MAKE THINGS MUCH BETTER HERE, EVEN IF WE ONLY RUN IT A FEW HOURS A DAY.
YEAH, IT'LL BE GOOD TO LISTEN TO SOME MUSIC--MAN, IT'S BEEN SO LONG SINCE I'VE HEARD ANYTHING... AND Y'KNOW, I DIDN'T EVEN REALIZE IT UNTIL JUST NOW.

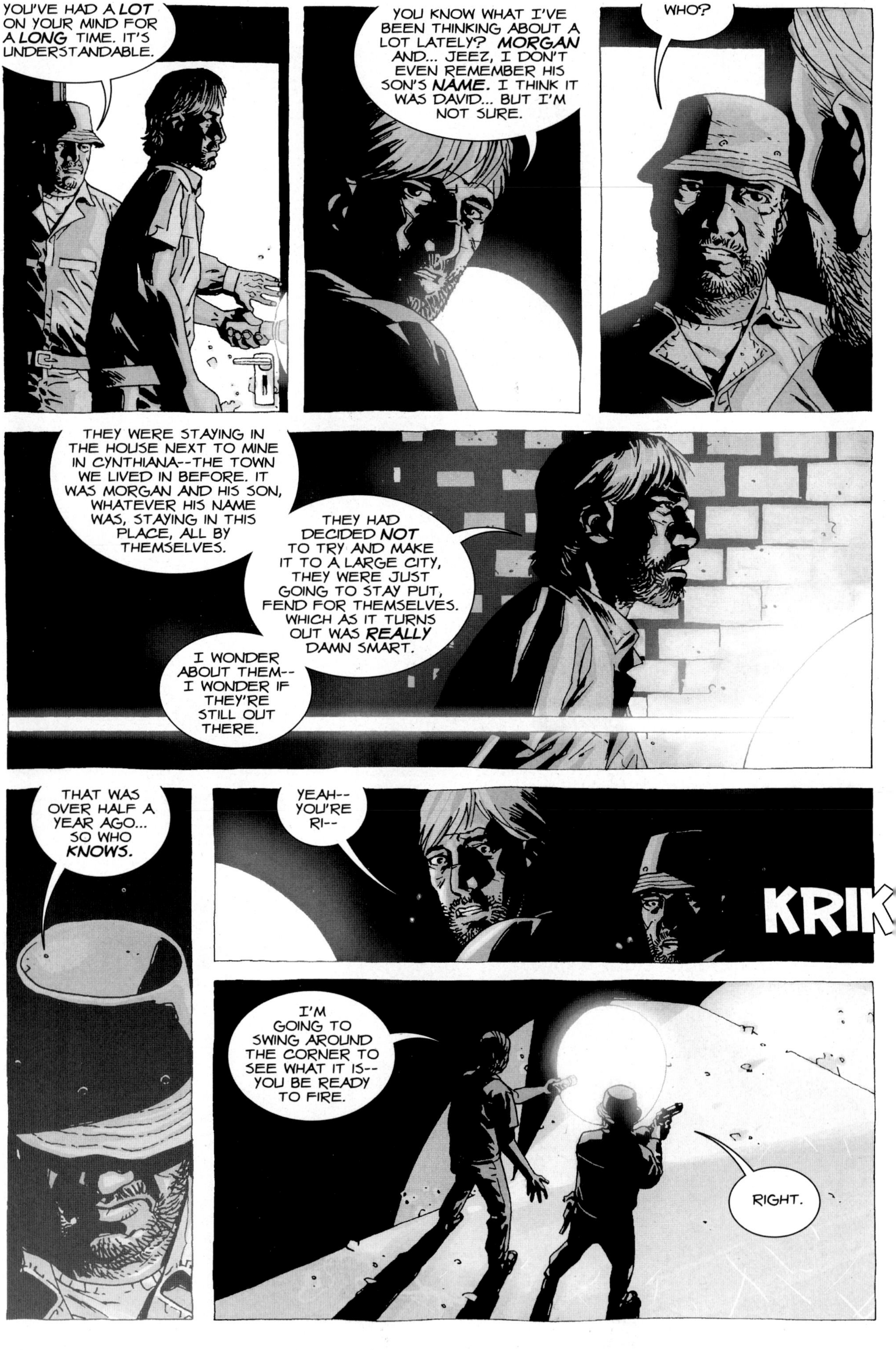
YOU'VE HAD A LOT ON YOUR MIND FOR A LONG TIME. IT'S UNDERSTANDABLE.
YOU KNOW WHAT I'VE BEEN THINKING ABOUT A LOT LATELY? MORGAN AND... JEEZ, I DON'T EVEN REMEMBER HIS SON'S NAME. I THINK IT WAS DAVID... BUT I'M NOT SURE.
WHO?
THEY WERE STAYING IN THE HOUSE NEXT TO MINE IN CYNTHIANA--THE TOWN WE LIVED IN BEFORE. IT WAS MORGAN AND HIS SON, WHATEVER HIS NAME WAS, STAYING IN THIS PLACE, ALL BY THEMSELVES.
THEY HAD DECIDED NOT TO TRY AND MAKE IT TO A LARGE CITY, THEY WERE JUST GOING TO STAY PUT, FEND FOR THEMSELVES. WHICH AS IT TURNS OUT WAS REALLY DAMN SMART.
I WONDER ABOUT THEM-- I WONDER IF THEY'RE STILL OUT THERE.
THAT WAS OVER HALF A YEAR AGO... SO WHO KNOWS.
YEAH-- YOU'RE RI--
KRIK
I'M GOING TO SWING AROUND THE CORNER TO SEE WHAT IT IS-- YOU BE READY TO FIRE.
RIGHT.

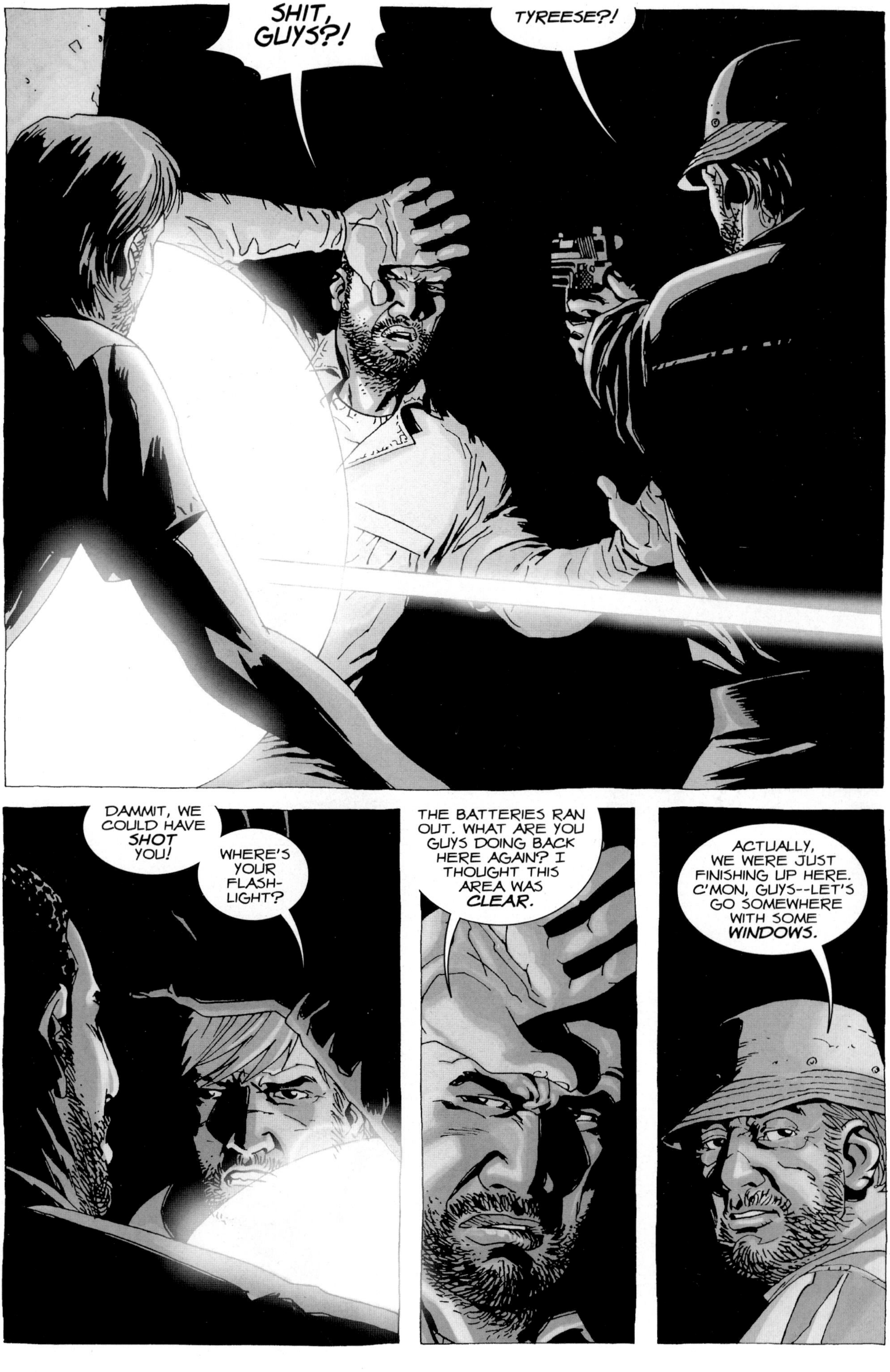
SHIT, GUYS?!
TYREESE?!
DAMMIT, WE COULD HAVE SHOT YOU!
WHERE'S YOUR FLASH-LIGHT?
THE BATTERIES RAN OUT. WHAT ARE YOU GUYS DOING BACK HERE AGAIN? I THOUGHT THIS AREA WAS CLEAR.
ACTUALLY, WE WERE JUST FINISHING UP HERE. C'MON, GUYS--LET'S GO SOMEWHERE WITH SOME WINDOWS.

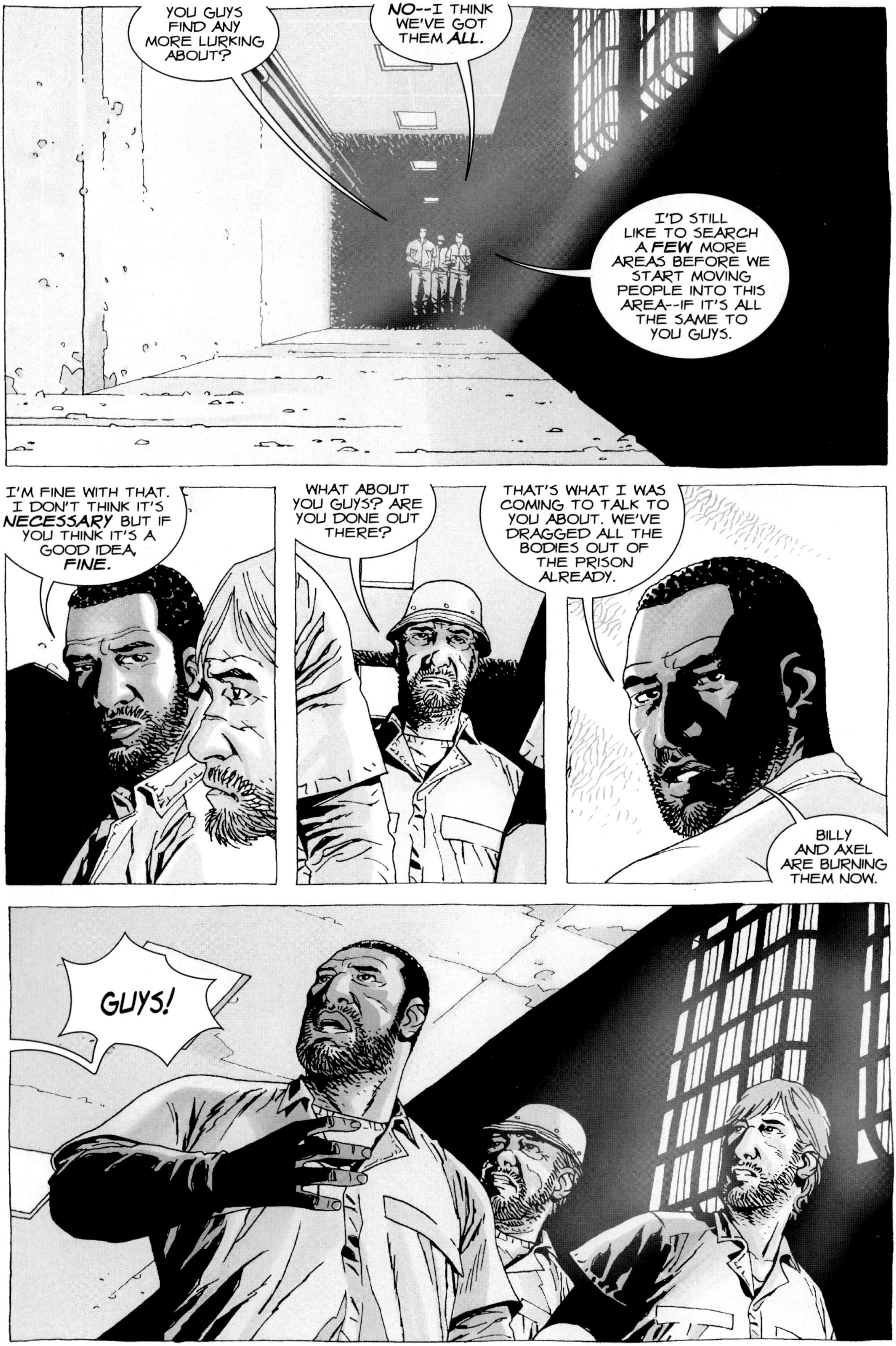
YOU GUYS FIND ANY MORE LURKING ABOUT?
NO--I THINK WE'VE GOT THEM ALL.
I'D STILL LIKE TO SEARCH A FEW MORE AREAS BEFORE WE START MOVING PEOPLE INTO THIS AREA--IF IT'S ALL THE SAME TO YOU GUYS.
I'M FINE WITH THAT. I DON'T THINK IT'S NECESSARY BUT IF YOU THINK IT'S A GOOD IDEA, FINE.
WHAT ABOUT YOU GUYS? ARE YOU DONE OUT THERE?
THAT'S WHAT I WAS COMING TO TALK TO YOU ABOUT. WE'VE DRAGGED ALL THE BODIES OUT OF THE PRISON ALREADY.
BILLY AND AXEL ARE BURNING THEM NOW.
GUYS!

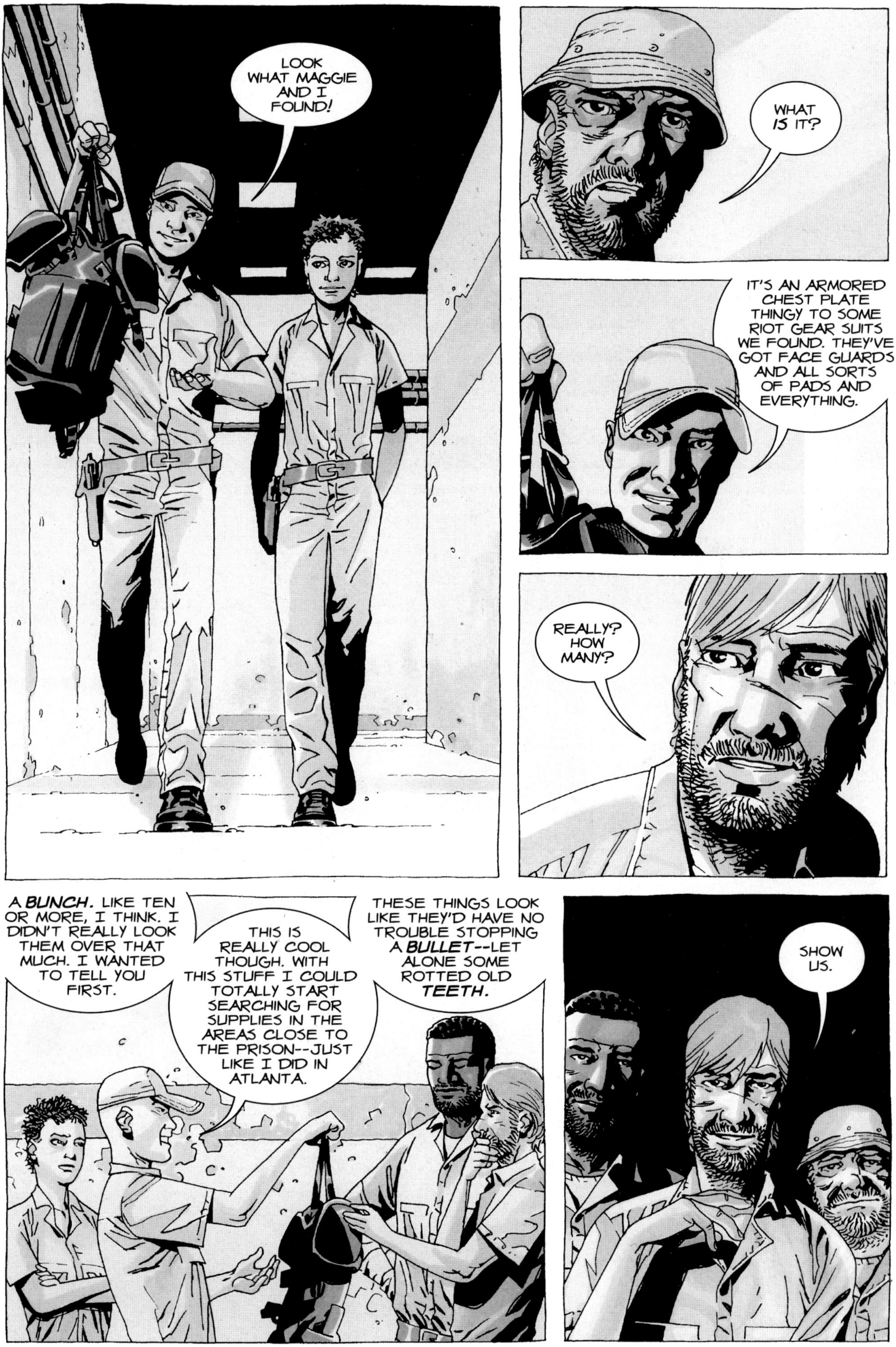
LOOK WHAT MAGGIE AND I FOUND!
WHAT IS IT?
IT'S AN ARMORED CHEST PLATE THINGY TO SOME RIOT GEAR SUITS WE FOUND. THEY'VE GOT FACE GUARDS AND ALL SORTS OF PADS AND EVERYTHING.
REALLY? HOW MANY?
A BUNCH. LIKE TEN OR MORE, I THINK. I DIDN'T REALLY LOOK THEM OVER THAT MUCH. I WANTED TO TELL YOU FIRST.
THIS IS REALLY COOL THOUGH. WITH THIS STUFF I COULD TOTALLY START SEARCHING FOR SUPPLIES IN THE AREAS CLOSE TO THE PRISON--JUST LIKE I DID IN ATLANTA.
THESE THINGS LOOK LIKE THEY'D HAVE NO TROUBLE STOPPING A BULLET--LET ALONE SOME ROTTED OLD TEETH.
SHOW US.

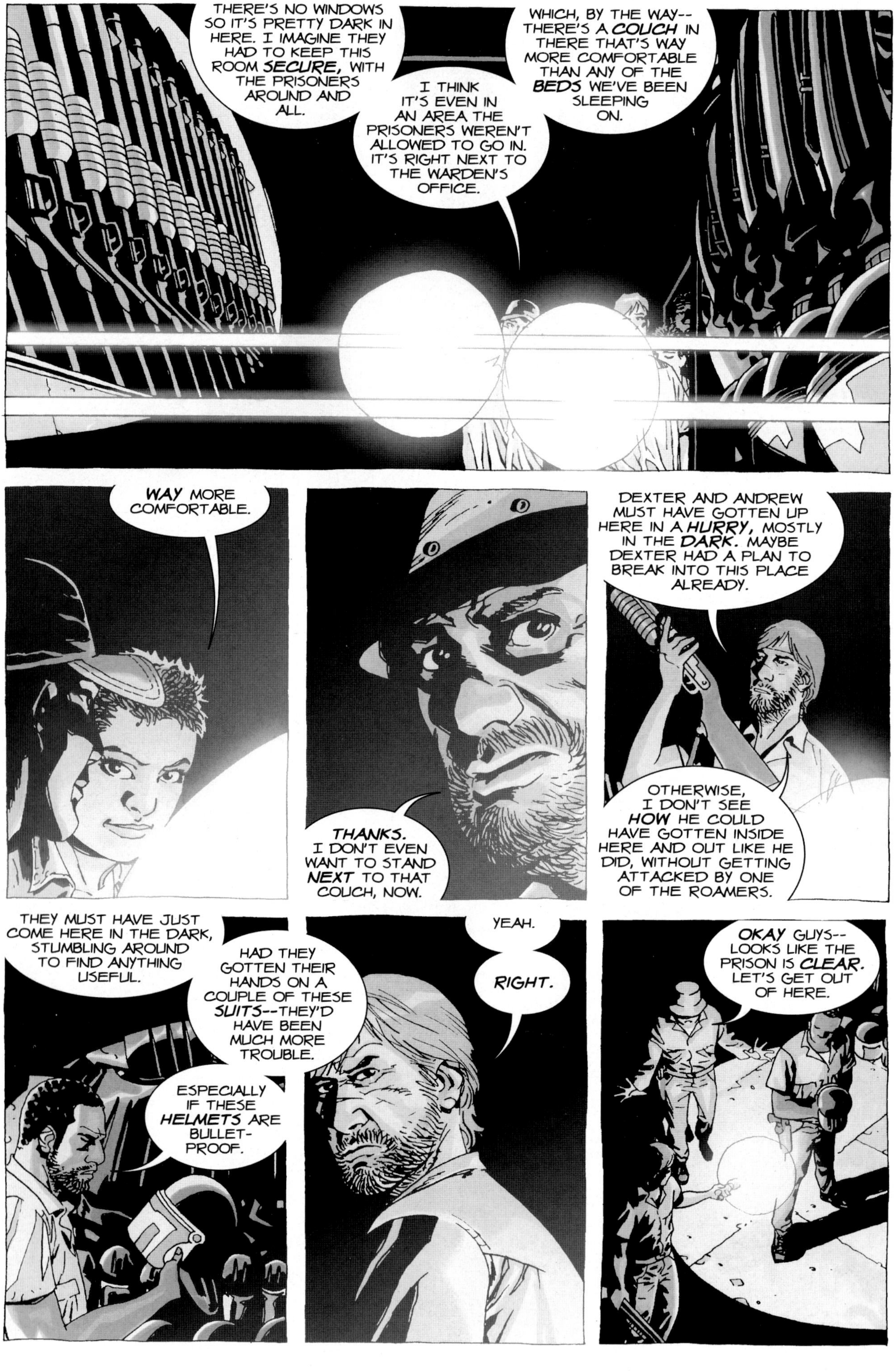
THERE'S NO WINDOWS SO IT'S PRETTY DARK IN HERE. I IMAGINE THEY HAD TO KEEP THIS ROOM SECURE, WITH THE PRISONERS AROUND AND ALL.
I THINK IT'S EVEN IN AN AREA THE PRISONERS WEREN'T ALLOWED TO GO IN. IT'S RIGHT NEXT TO THE WARDEN'S OFFICE.
WHICH, BY THE WAY-- THERE'S A COUCH IN THERE THAT'S WAY MORE COMFORTABLE THAN ANY OF THE BEDS WE'VE BEEN SLEEPING ON.
WAY MORE COMFORTABLE.
THANKS. I DON'T EVEN WANT TO STAND NEXT TO THAT COUCH, NOW.
DEXTER AND ANDREW MUST HAVE GOTTEN UP HERE IN A HURRY, MOSTLY IN THE DARK. MAYBE DEXTER HAD A PLAN TO BREAK INTO THIS PLACE ALREADY.
OTHERWISE, I DON'T SEE HOW HE COULD HAVE GOTTEN INSIDE HERE AND OUT LIKE HE DID, WITHOUT GETTING ATTACKED BY ONE OF THE ROAMERS.
THEY MUST HAVE JUST COME HERE IN THE DARK, STUMBLING AROUND TO FIND ANYTHING USEFUL.
HAD THEY GOTTEN THEIR HANDS ON A COUPLE OF THESE SUITS--THEY'D HAVE BEEN MUCH MORE TROUBLE.
ESPECIALLY IF THESE HELMETS ARE BULLET-PROOF.
YEAH.
RIGHT.
OKAY GUYS-- LOOKS LIKE THE PRISON IS CLEAR. LET'S GET OUT OF HERE.

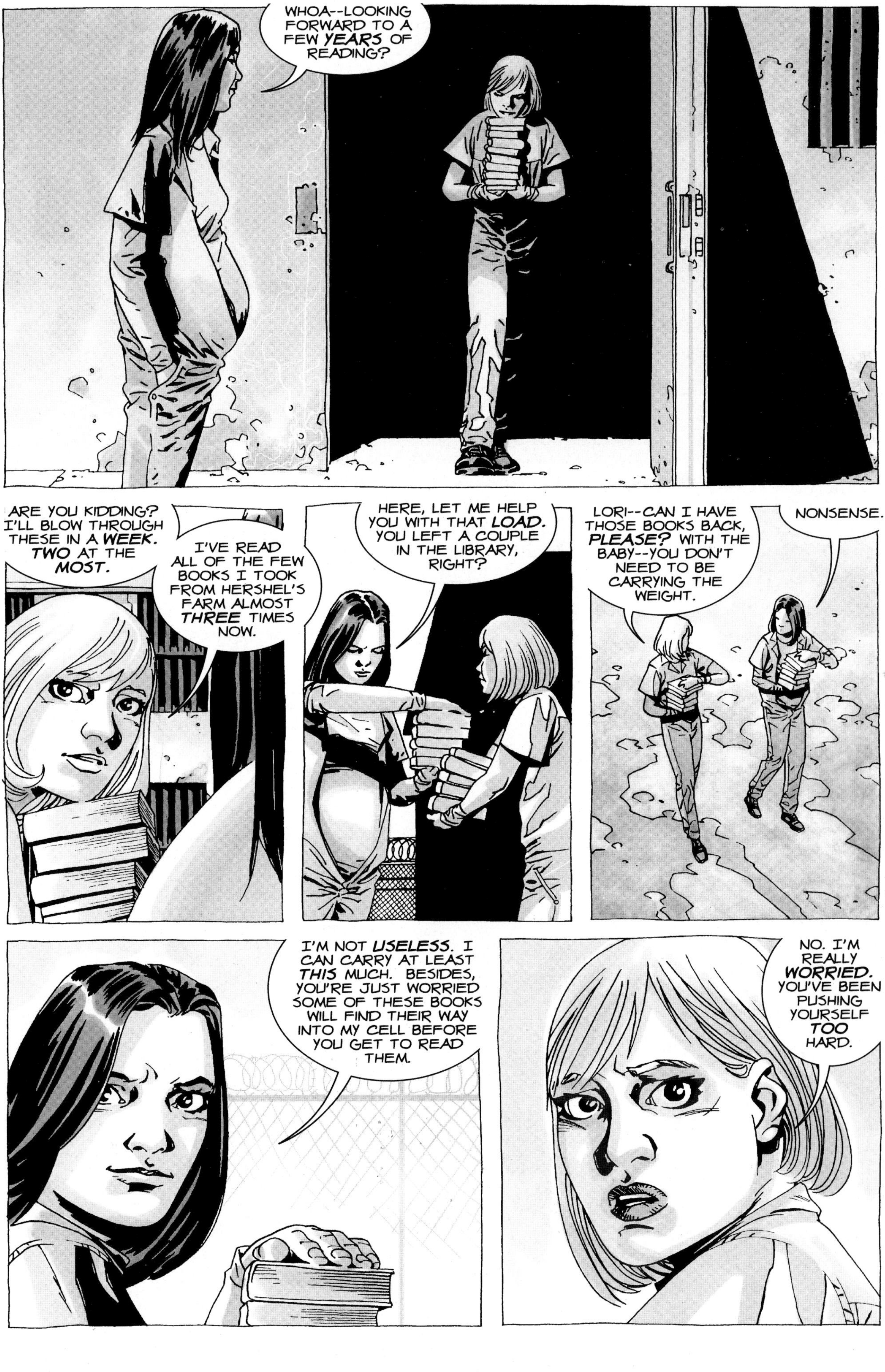
WHOA--LOOKING FORWARD TO A FEW YEARS OF READING?
ARE YOU KIDDING? I'LL BLOW THROUGH THESE IN A WEEK. TWO AT THE MOST.
I'VE READ ALL OF THE FEW BOOKS I TOOK FROM HERSHEL'S FARM ALMOST THREE TIMES NOW.
HERE, LET ME HELP YOU WITH THAT LOAD. YOU LEFT A COUPLE IN THE LIBRARY, RIGHT?
LORI--CAN I HAVE THOSE BOOKS BACK, PLEASE? WITH THE BABY--YOU DON'T NEED TO BE CARRYING THE WEIGHT.
NONSENSE.
I'M NOT USELESS. I CAN CARRY AT LEAST THIS MUCH. BESIDES, YOU'RE JUST WORRIED SOME OF THESE BOOKS WILL FIND THEIR WAY INTO MY CELL BEFORE YOU GET TO READ THEM.
NO. I'M REALLY WORRIED. YOU'VE BEEN PUSHING YOURSELF TOO HARD.

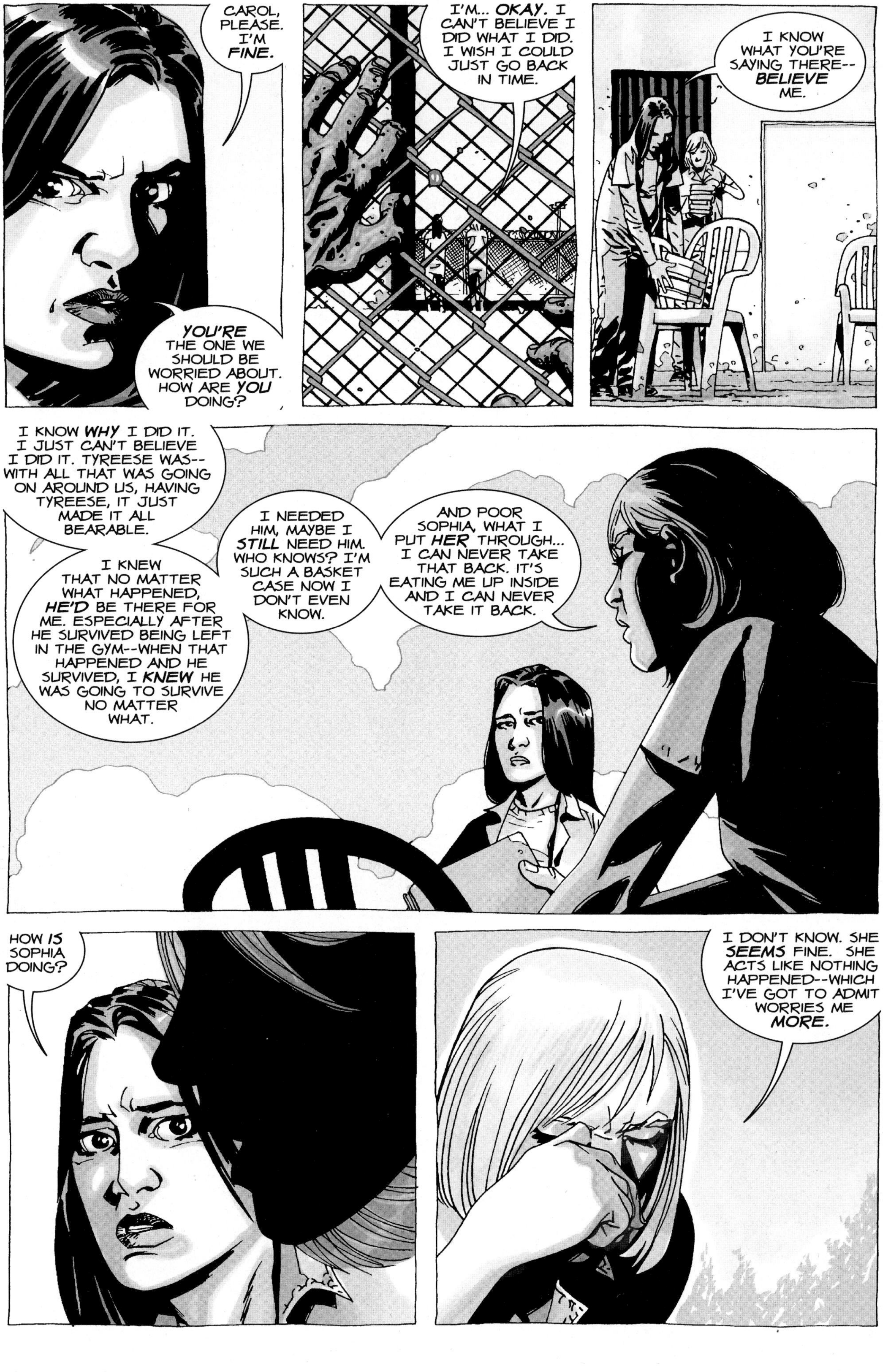
CAROL, PLEASE. I'M *FINE.*
YOU'RE THE ONE WE SHOULD BE WORRIED ABOUT. HOW ARE *YOU* DOING?
I'M... *OKAY.* I CAN'T BELIEVE I DID WHAT I DID. I WISH I COULD JUST GO BACK IN TIME.
I KNOW WHAT YOU'RE SAYING THERE-- *BELIEVE* ME.
I KNOW *WHY* I DID IT. I JUST CAN'T BELIEVE I DID IT. TYREESE WAS-- WITH ALL THAT WAS GOING ON AROUND US, HAVING TYREESE, IT JUST MADE IT ALL BEARABLE.
I KNEW THAT NO MATTER WHAT HAPPENED, *HE'D* BE THERE FOR ME. ESPECIALLY AFTER HE SURVIVED BEING LEFT IN THE GYM--WHEN THAT HAPPENED AND HE SURVIVED, I *KNEW* HE WAS GOING TO SURVIVE NO MATTER WHAT.
I NEEDED HIM, MAYBE I *STILL* NEED HIM. WHO KNOWS? I'M SUCH A BASKET CASE NOW I DON'T EVEN KNOW.
AND POOR SOPHIA, WHAT I PUT *HER* THROUGH... I CAN NEVER TAKE THAT BACK. IT'S EATING ME UP INSIDE AND I CAN NEVER TAKE IT BACK.
HOW *IS* SOPHIA DOING?
I DON'T KNOW. SHE *SEEMS* FINE. SHE ACTS LIKE NOTHING HAPPENED--WHICH I'VE GOT TO ADMIT WORRIES ME *MORE.*

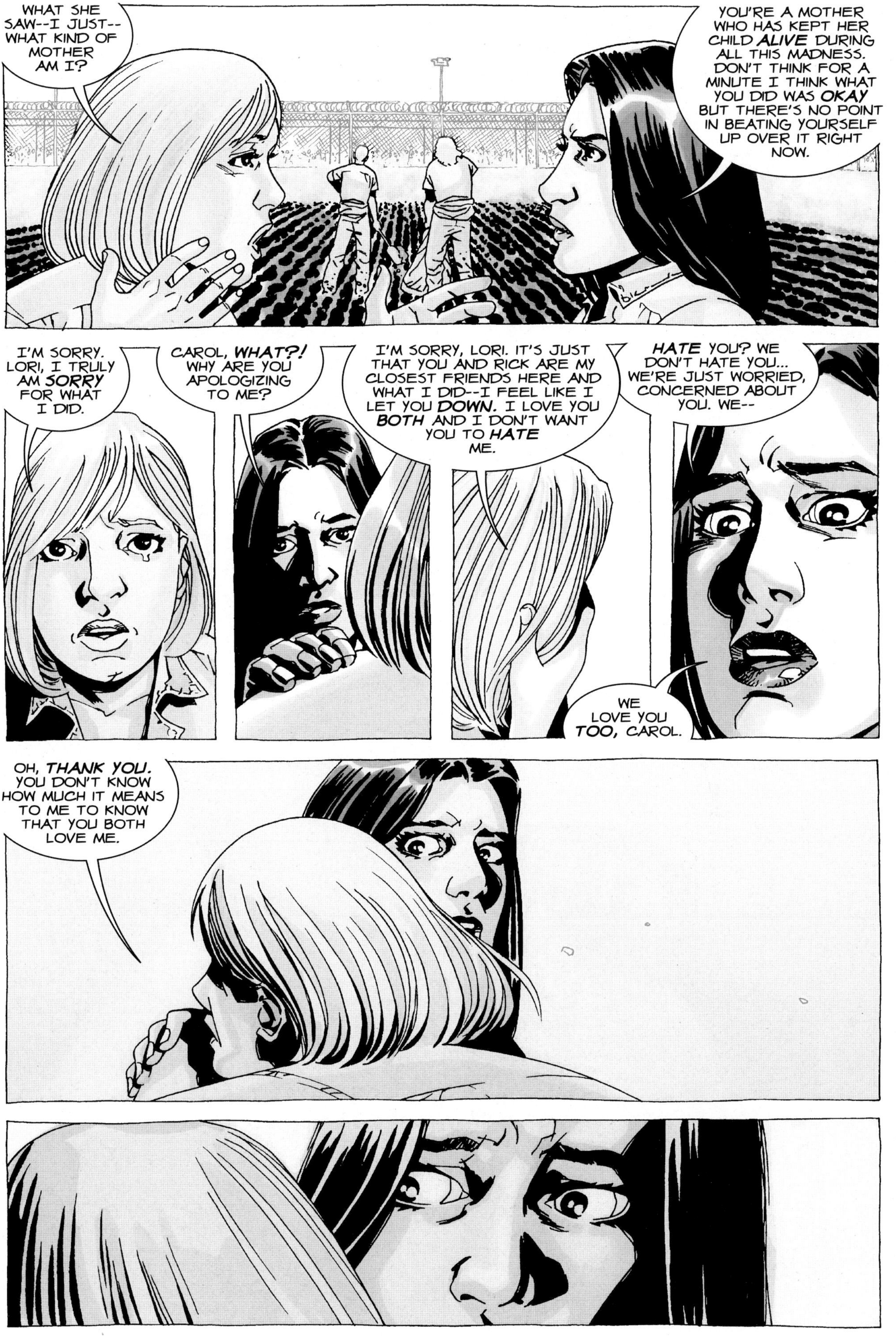
WHAT SHE SAW--I JUST--WHAT KIND OF MOTHER AM I?
YOU'RE A MOTHER WHO HAS KEPT HER CHILD ALIVE DURING ALL THIS MADNESS. DON'T THINK FOR A MINUTE I THINK WHAT YOU DID WAS OKAY BUT THERE'S NO POINT IN BEATING YOURSELF UP OVER IT RIGHT NOW.
I'M SORRY. LORI, I TRULY AM SORRY FOR WHAT I DID.
CAROL, WHAT?! WHY ARE YOU APOLOGIZING TO ME?
I'M SORRY, LORI. IT'S JUST THAT YOU AND RICK ARE MY CLOSEST FRIENDS HERE AND WHAT I DID--I FEEL LIKE I LET YOU DOWN. I LOVE YOU BOTH AND I DON'T WANT YOU TO HATE ME.
HATE YOU? WE DON'T HATE YOU... WE'RE JUST WORRIED, CONCERNED ABOUT YOU. WE--
WE LOVE YOU TOO, CAROL.
OH, THANK YOU. YOU DON'T KNOW HOW MUCH IT MEANS TO ME TO KNOW THAT YOU BOTH LOVE ME.

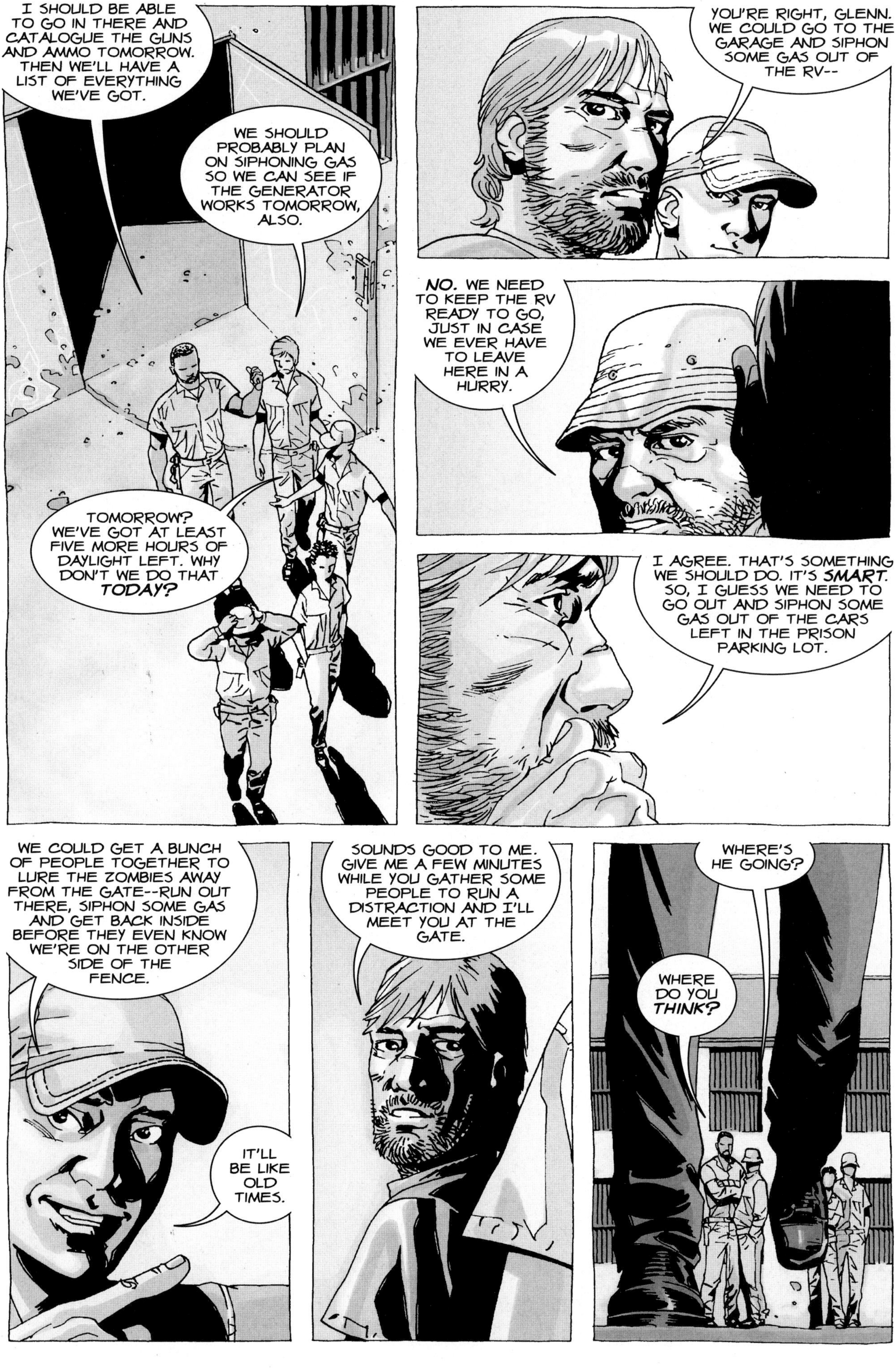
I SHOULD BE ABLE TO GO IN THERE AND CATALOGUE THE GUNS AND AMMO TOMORROW. THEN WE'LL HAVE A LIST OF EVERYTHING WE'VE GOT.
WE SHOULD PROBABLY PLAN ON SIPHONING GAS SO WE CAN SEE IF THE GENERATOR WORKS TOMORROW, ALSO.
TOMORROW? WE'VE GOT AT LEAST FIVE MORE HOURS OF DAYLIGHT LEFT. WHY DON'T WE DO THAT *TODAY?*
YOU'RE RIGHT, GLENN. WE COULD GO TO THE GARAGE AND SIPHON SOME GAS OUT OF THE RV--
NO. WE NEED TO KEEP THE RV READY TO GO, JUST IN CASE WE EVER HAVE TO LEAVE HERE IN A HURRY.
I AGREE. THAT'S SOMETHING WE SHOULD DO. IT'S *SMART.* SO, I GUESS WE NEED TO GO OUT AND SIPHON SOME GAS OUT OF THE CARS LEFT IN THE PRISON PARKING LOT.
WE COULD GET A BUNCH OF PEOPLE TOGETHER TO LURE THE ZOMBIES AWAY FROM THE GATE--RUN OUT THERE, SIPHON SOME GAS AND GET BACK INSIDE BEFORE THEY EVEN KNOW WE'RE ON THE OTHER SIDE OF THE FENCE.
IT'LL BE LIKE OLD TIMES.
SOUNDS GOOD TO ME. GIVE ME A FEW MINUTES WHILE YOU GATHER SOME PEOPLE TO RUN A DISTRACTION AND I'LL MEET YOU AT THE GATE.
WHERE'S HE GOING?
WHERE DO YOU *THINK?*

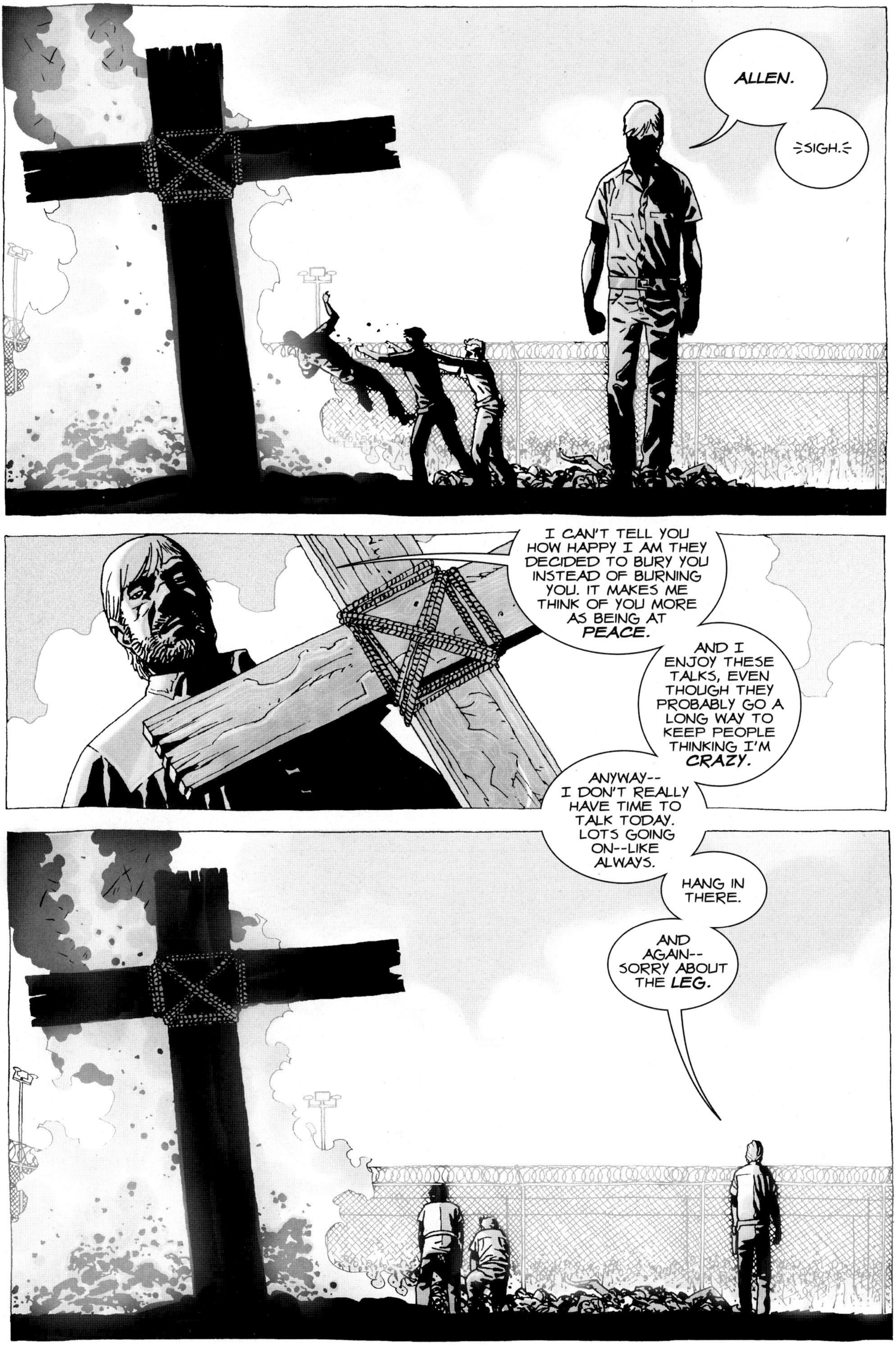
ALLEN.
SIGH.
I CAN'T TELL YOU HOW HAPPY I AM THEY DECIDED TO BURY YOU INSTEAD OF BURNING YOU. IT MAKES ME THINK OF YOU MORE AS BEING AT PEACE.
AND I ENJOY THESE TALKS, EVEN THOUGH THEY PROBABLY GO A LONG WAY TO KEEP PEOPLE THINKING I'M CRAZY.
ANYWAY-- I DON'T REALLY HAVE TIME TO TALK TODAY. LOTS GOING ON--LIKE ALWAYS.
HANG IN THERE.
AND AGAIN-- SORRY ABOUT THE LEG.

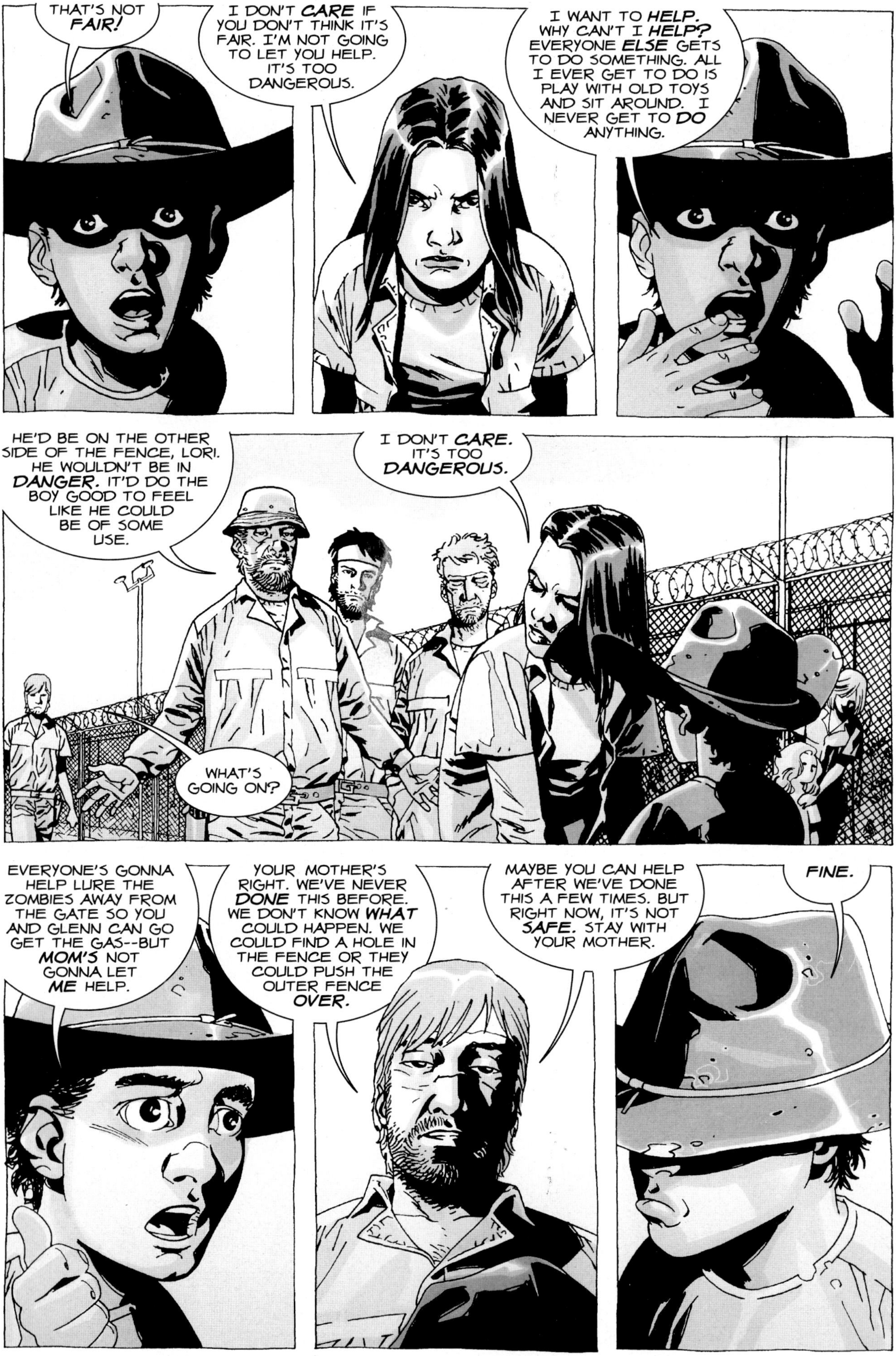
THAT'S NOT FAIR!
I DON'T CARE IF YOU DON'T THINK IT'S FAIR. I'M NOT GOING TO LET YOU HELP. IT'S TOO DANGEROUS.
I WANT TO HELP. WHY CAN'T I HELP? EVERYONE ELSE GETS TO DO SOMETHING. ALL I EVER GET TO DO IS PLAY WITH OLD TOYS AND SIT AROUND. I NEVER GET TO DO ANYTHING.
HE'D BE ON THE OTHER SIDE OF THE FENCE, LORI. HE WOULDN'T BE IN DANGER. IT'D DO THE BOY GOOD TO FEEL LIKE HE COULD BE OF SOME USE.
I DON'T CARE. IT'S TOO DANGEROUS.
WHAT'S GOING ON?
EVERYONE'S GONNA HELP LURE THE ZOMBIES AWAY FROM THE GATE SO YOU AND GLENN CAN GO GET THE GAS--BUT MOM'S NOT GONNA LET ME HELP.
YOUR MOTHER'S RIGHT. WE'VE NEVER DONE THIS BEFORE. WE DON'T KNOW WHAT COULD HAPPEN. WE COULD FIND A HOLE IN THE FENCE OR THEY COULD PUSH THE OUTER FENCE OVER.
MAYBE YOU CAN HELP AFTER WE'VE DONE THIS A FEW TIMES. BUT RIGHT NOW, IT'S NOT SAFE. STAY WITH YOUR MOTHER.
FINE.

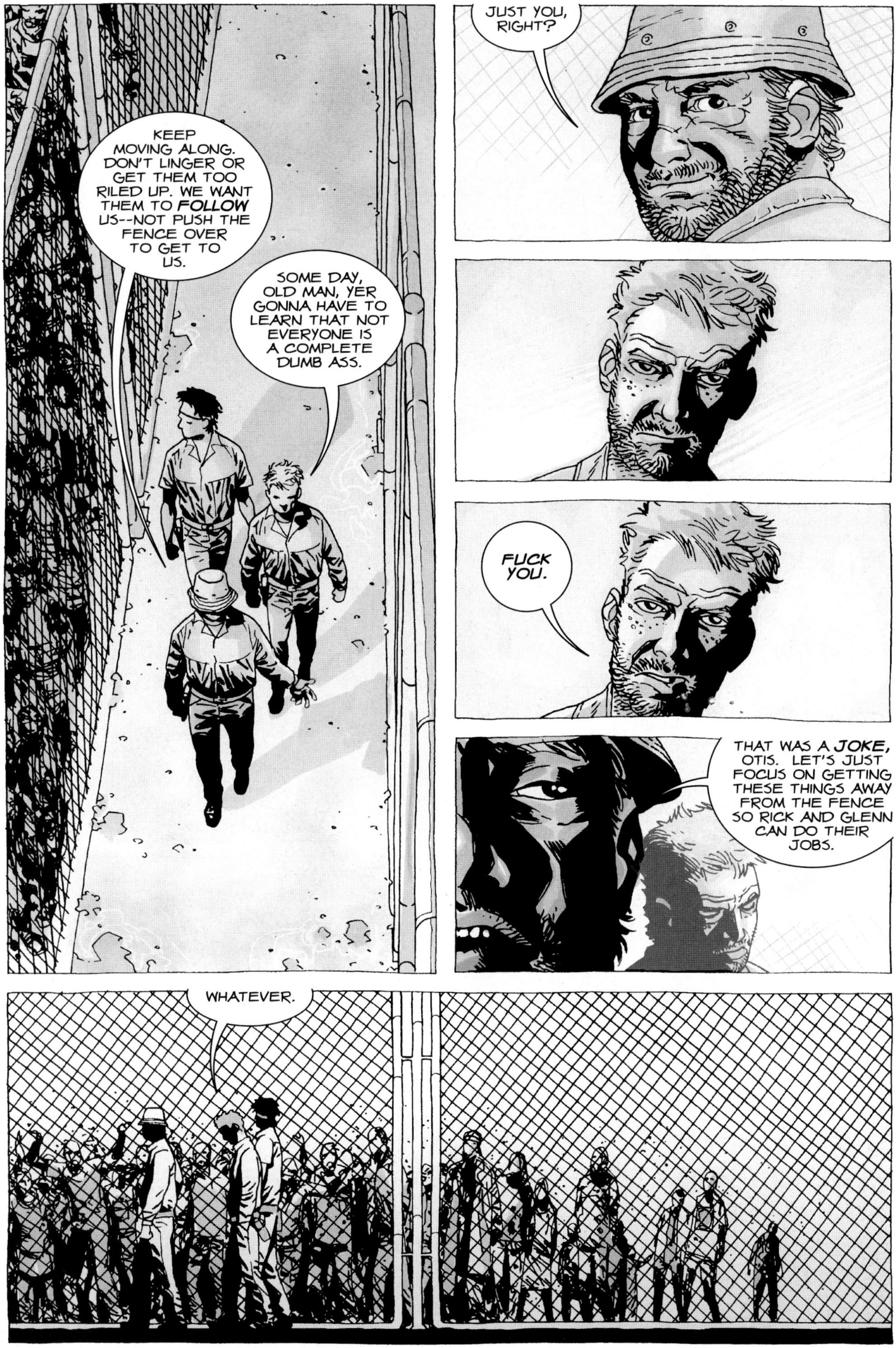
KEEP MOVING ALONG. DON'T LINGER OR GET THEM TOO RILED UP. WE WANT THEM TO FOLLOW US--NOT PUSH THE FENCE OVER TO GET TO US.
SOME DAY, OLD MAN, YER GONNA HAVE TO LEARN THAT NOT EVERYONE IS A COMPLETE DUMB ASS.
JUST YOU, RIGHT?
FUCK YOU.
THAT WAS A JOKE, OTIS. LET'S JUST FOCUS ON GETTING THESE THINGS AWAY FROM THE FENCE SO RICK AND GLENN CAN DO THEIR JOBS.
WHATEVER.

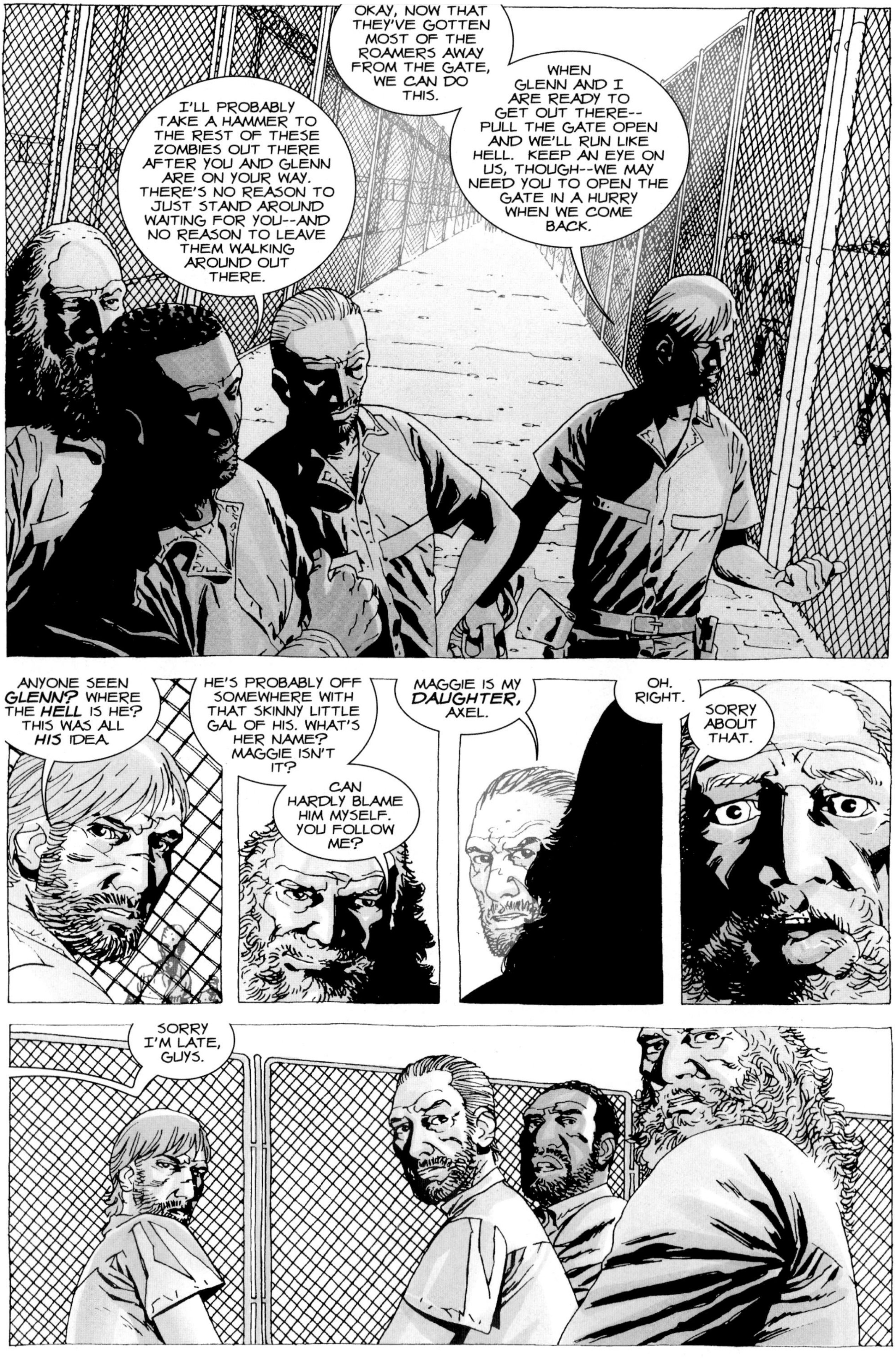
I'LL PROBABLY TAKE A HAMMER TO THE REST OF THESE ZOMBIES OUT THERE AFTER YOU AND GLENN ARE ON YOUR WAY. THERE'S NO REASON TO JUST STAND AROUND WAITING FOR YOU--AND NO REASON TO LEAVE THEM WALKING AROUND OUT THERE.
OKAY, NOW THAT THEY'VE GOTTEN MOST OF THE ROAMERS AWAY FROM THE GATE, WE CAN DO THIS.
WHEN GLENN AND I ARE READY TO GET OUT THERE-- PULL THE GATE OPEN AND WE'LL RUN LIKE HELL. KEEP AN EYE ON US, THOUGH--WE MAY NEED YOU TO OPEN THE GATE IN A HURRY WHEN WE COME BACK.
ANYONE SEEN GLENN? WHERE THE HELL IS HE? THIS WAS ALL HIS IDEA.
HE'S PROBABLY OFF SOMEWHERE WITH THAT SKINNY LITTLE GAL OF HIS. WHAT'S HER NAME? MAGGIE ISN'T IT?
CAN HARDLY BLAME HIM MYSELF. YOU FOLLOW ME?
MAGGIE IS MY DAUGHTER, AXEL.
OH. RIGHT.
SORRY ABOUT THAT.
SORRY I'M LATE, GUYS.

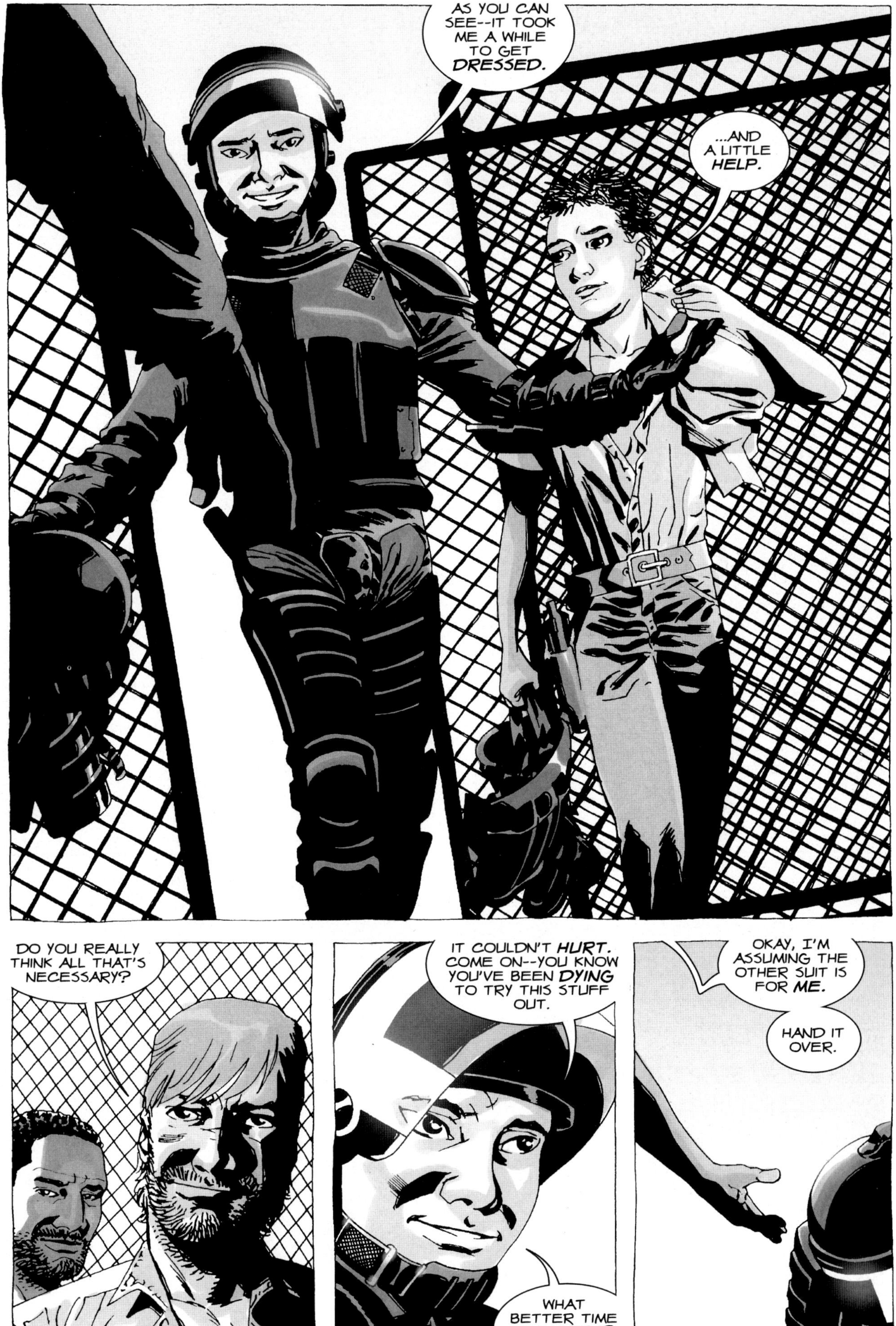
AS YOU CAN SEE--IT TOOK ME A WHILE TO GET DRESSED.
...AND A LITTLE HELP.
DO YOU REALLY THINK ALL THAT'S NECESSARY?
IT COULDN'T HURT. COME ON--YOU KNOW YOU'VE BEEN DYING TO TRY THIS STUFF OUT.
WHAT BETTER TIME THAN NOW?
OKAY, I'M ASSUMING THE OTHER SUIT IS FOR ME.
HAND IT OVER.

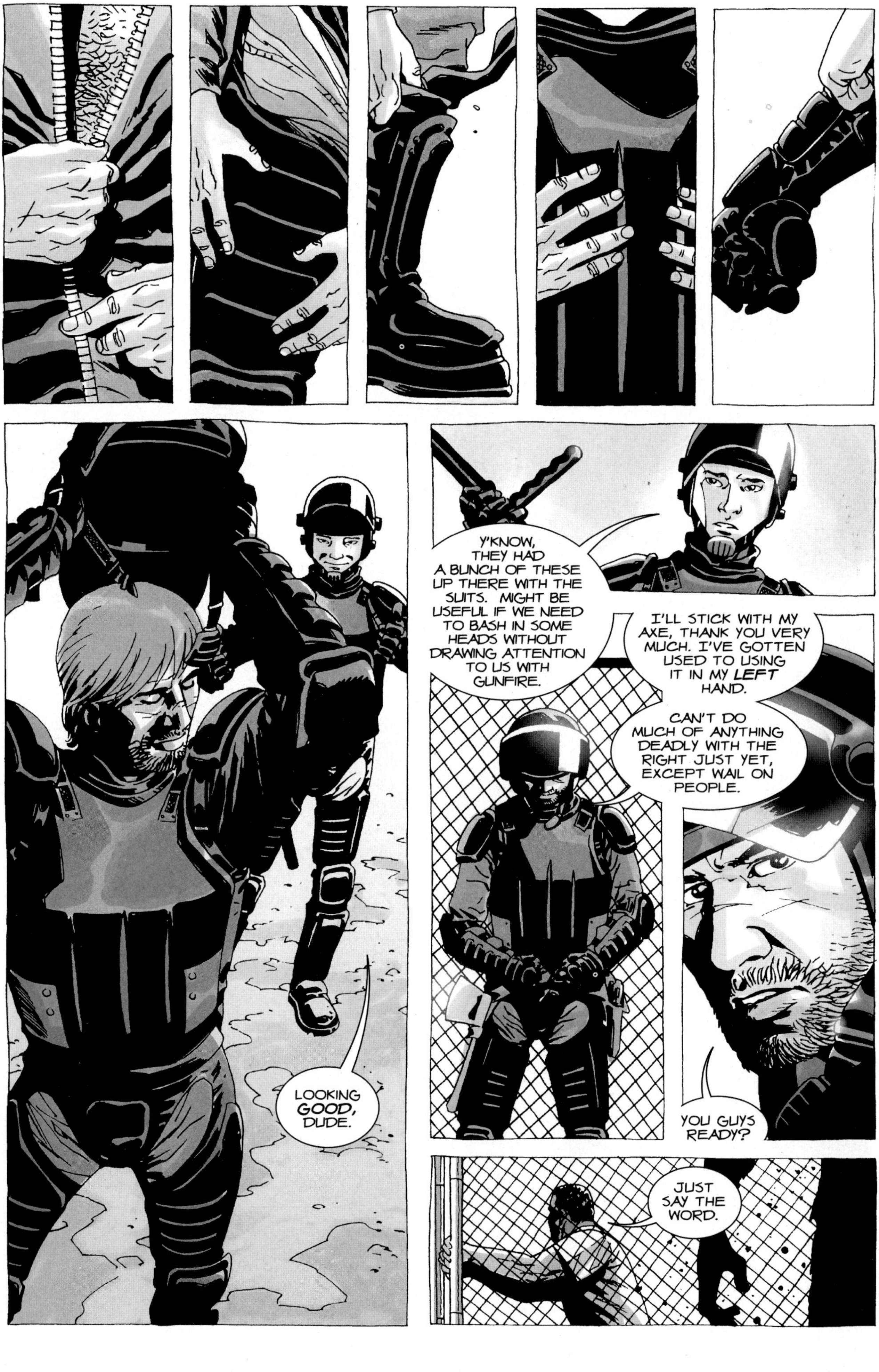
LOOKING GOOD, DUDE.
Y'KNOW, THEY HAD A BUNCH OF THESE UP THERE WITH THE SUITS. MIGHT BE USEFUL IF WE NEED TO BASH IN SOME HEADS WITHOUT DRAWING ATTENTION TO US WITH GUNFIRE.
I'LL STICK WITH MY AXE, THANK YOU VERY MUCH. I'VE GOTTEN USED TO USING IT IN MY LEFT HAND.
CAN'T DO MUCH OF ANYTHING DEADLY WITH THE RIGHT JUST YET, EXCEPT WAIL ON PEOPLE.
YOU GUYS READY?
JUST SAY THE WORD.

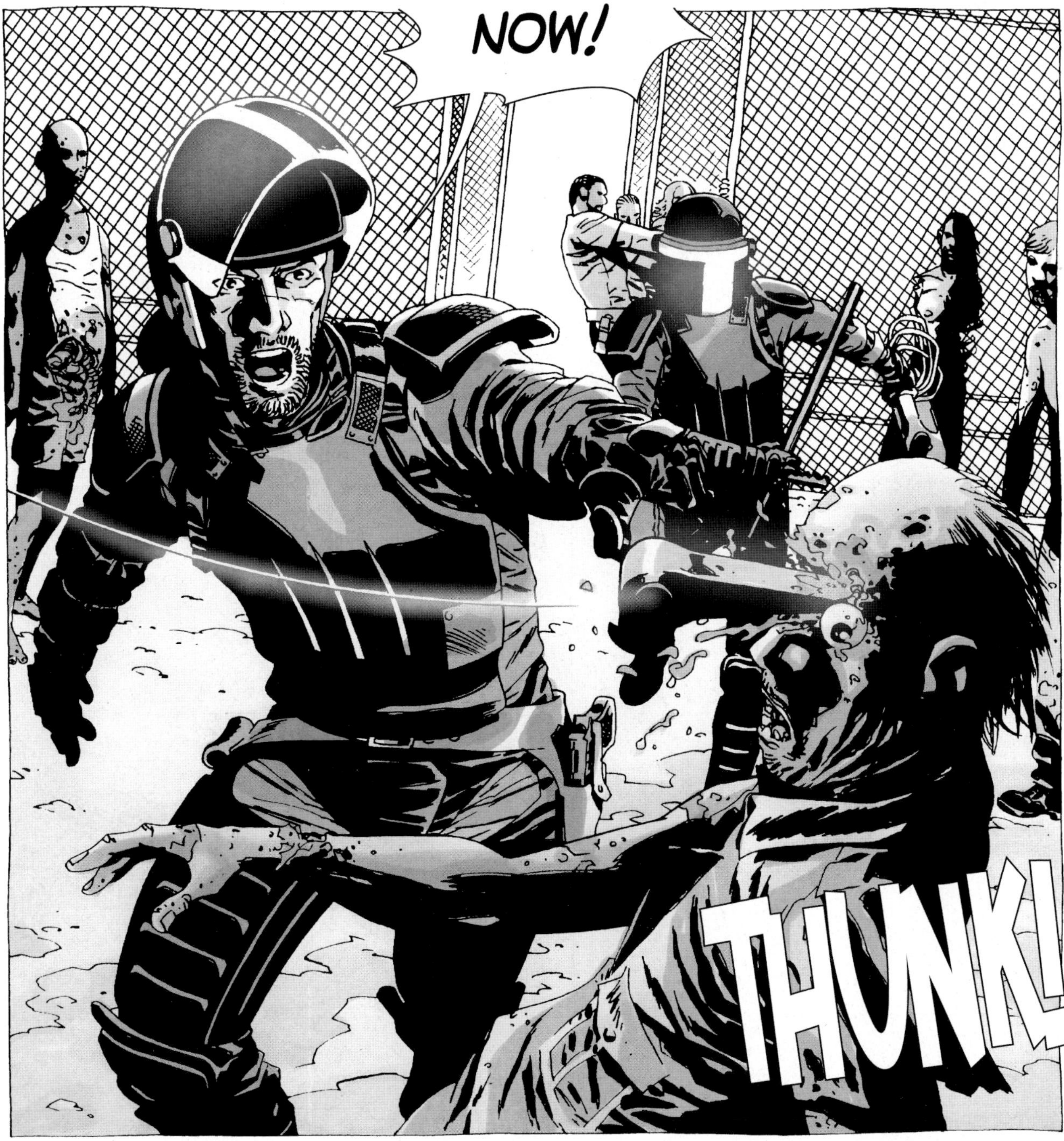
NOW!
THUNK!

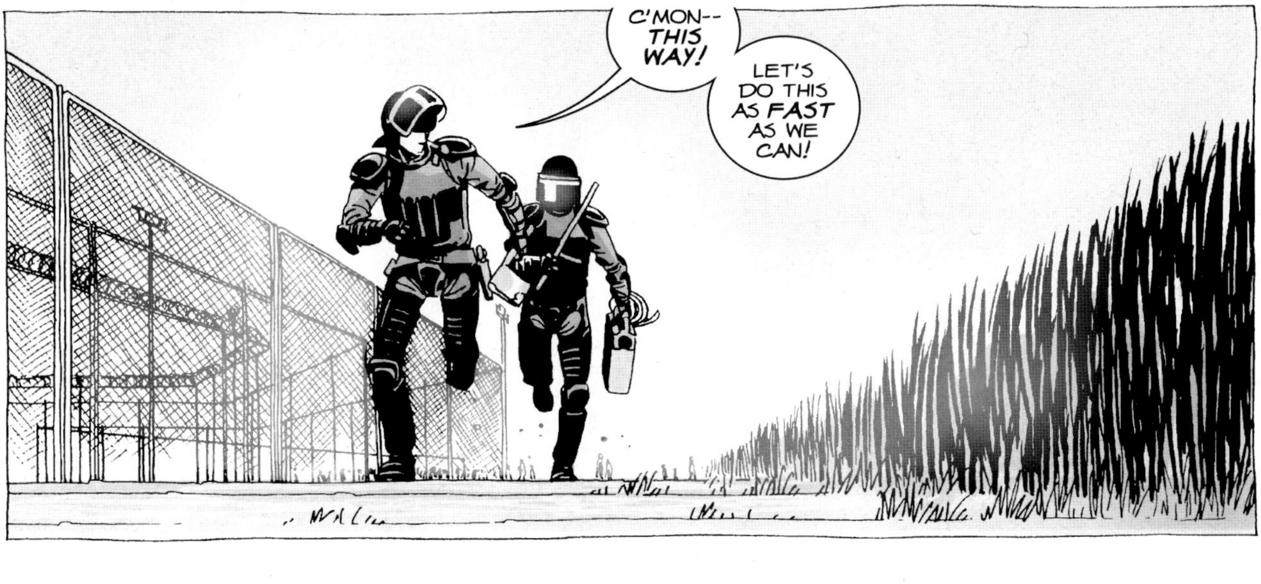
C'MON-- THIS WAY!
LET'S DO THIS AS FAST AS WE CAN!

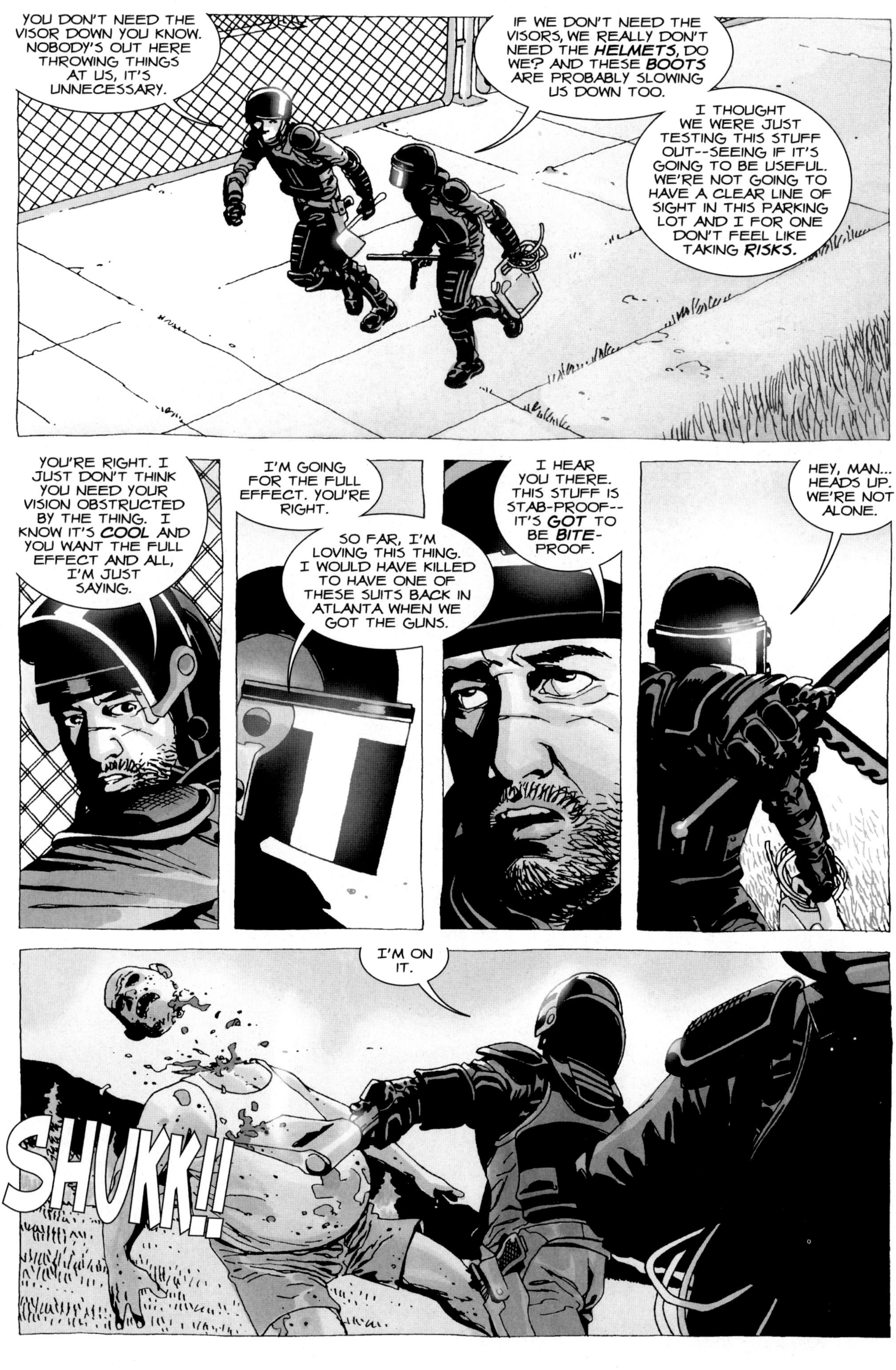

YOU DON'T NEED THE VISOR DOWN YOU KNOW. NOBODY'S OUT HERE THROWING THINGS AT US, IT'S UNNECESSARY.
IF WE DON'T NEED THE VISORS, WE REALLY DON'T NEED THE HELMETS, DO WE? AND THESE BOOTS ARE PROBABLY SLOWING US DOWN TOO.
I THOUGHT WE WERE JUST TESTING THIS STUFF OUT--SEEING IF IT'S GOING TO BE USEFUL. WE'RE NOT GOING TO HAVE A CLEAR LINE OF SIGHT IN THIS PARKING LOT AND I FOR ONE DON'T FEEL LIKE TAKING RISKS.
YOU'RE RIGHT. I JUST DON'T THINK YOU NEED YOUR VISION OBSTRUCTED BY THE THING. I KNOW IT'S COOL AND YOU WANT THE FULL EFFECT AND ALL, I'M JUST SAYING.
I'M GOING FOR THE FULL EFFECT. YOU'RE RIGHT.
SO FAR, I'M LOVING THIS THING. I WOULD HAVE KILLED TO HAVE ONE OF THESE SUITS BACK IN ATLANTA WHEN WE GOT THE GUNS.
I HEAR YOU THERE. THIS STUFF IS STAB-PROOF-- IT'S GOT TO BE BITE-PROOF.
HEY, MAN... HEADS UP. WE'RE NOT ALONE.
I'M ON IT.
SHUKK!!

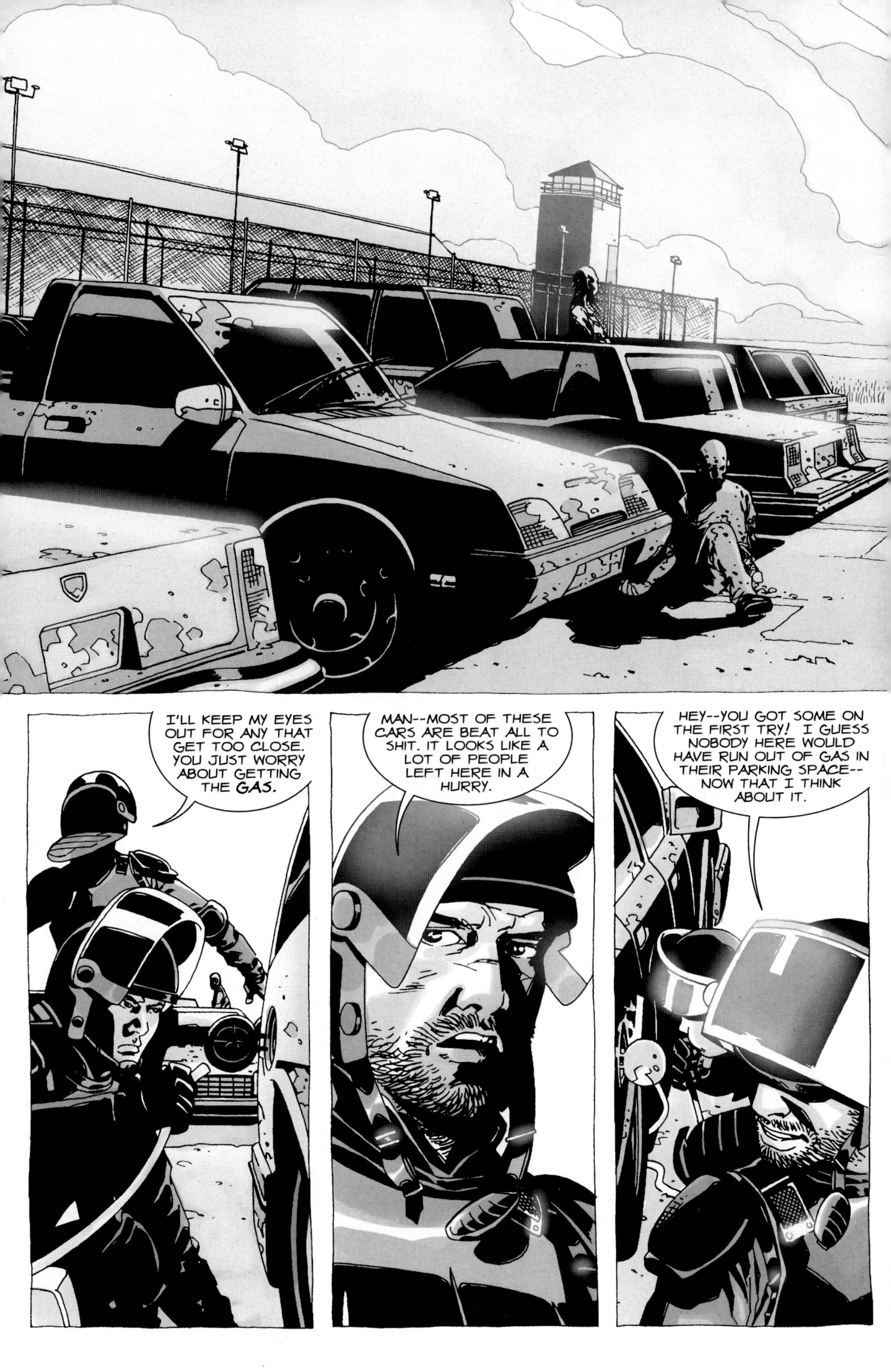
I'LL KEEP MY EYES OUT FOR ANY THAT GET TOO CLOSE. YOU JUST WORRY ABOUT GETTING THE GAS.
MAN--MOST OF THESE CARS ARE BEAT ALL TO SHIT. IT LOOKS LIKE A LOT OF PEOPLE LEFT HERE IN A HURRY.
HEY--YOU GOT SOME ON THE FIRST TRY! I GUESS NOBODY HERE WOULD HAVE RUN OUT OF GAS IN THEIR PARKING SPACE-- NOW THAT I THINK ABOUT IT.

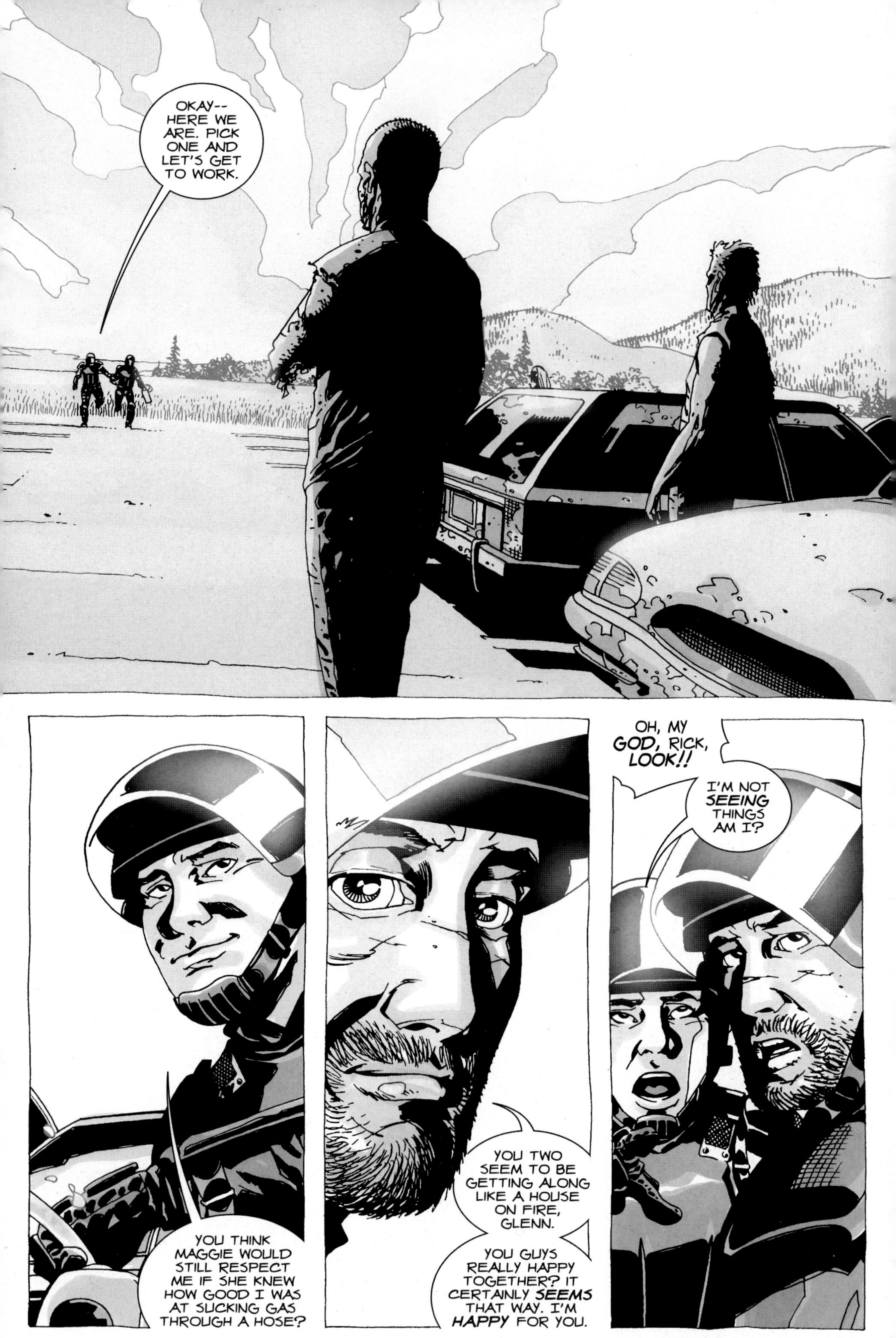
OKAY-- HERE WE ARE. PICK ONE AND LET'S GET TO WORK.
YOU THINK MAGGIE WOULD STILL RESPECT ME IF SHE KNEW HOW GOOD I WAS AT SUCKING GAS THROUGH A HOSE?
YOU TWO SEEM TO BE GETTING ALONG LIKE A HOUSE ON FIRE, GLENN.
YOU GUYS REALLY HAPPY TOGETHER? IT CERTAINLY SEEMS THAT WAY. I'M HAPPY FOR YOU.
OH, MY GOD, RICK, LOOK!!
I'M NOT SEEING THINGS AM I?

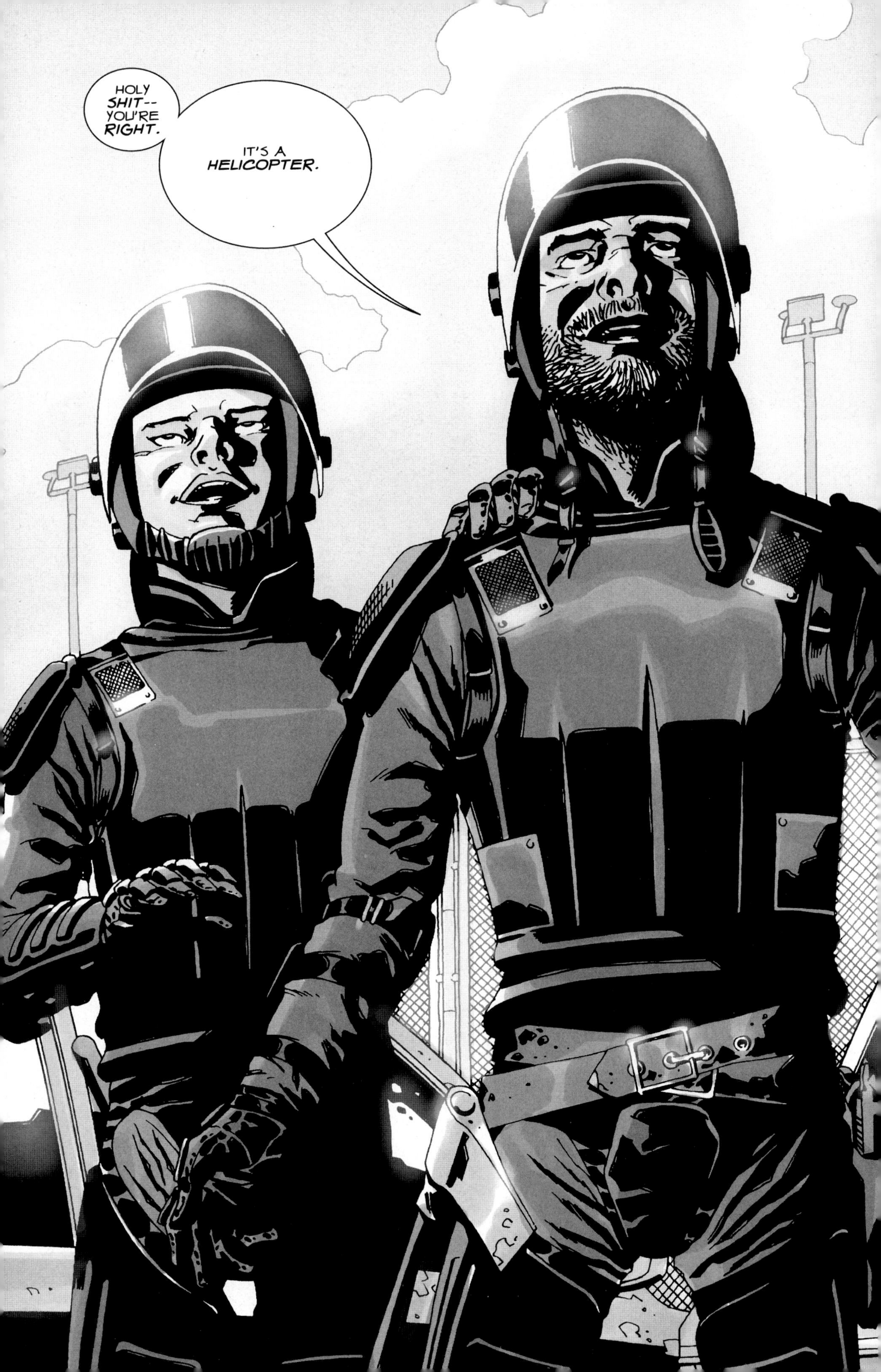
HOLY SHIT-- YOU'RE RIGHT.
IT'S A HELICOPTER.

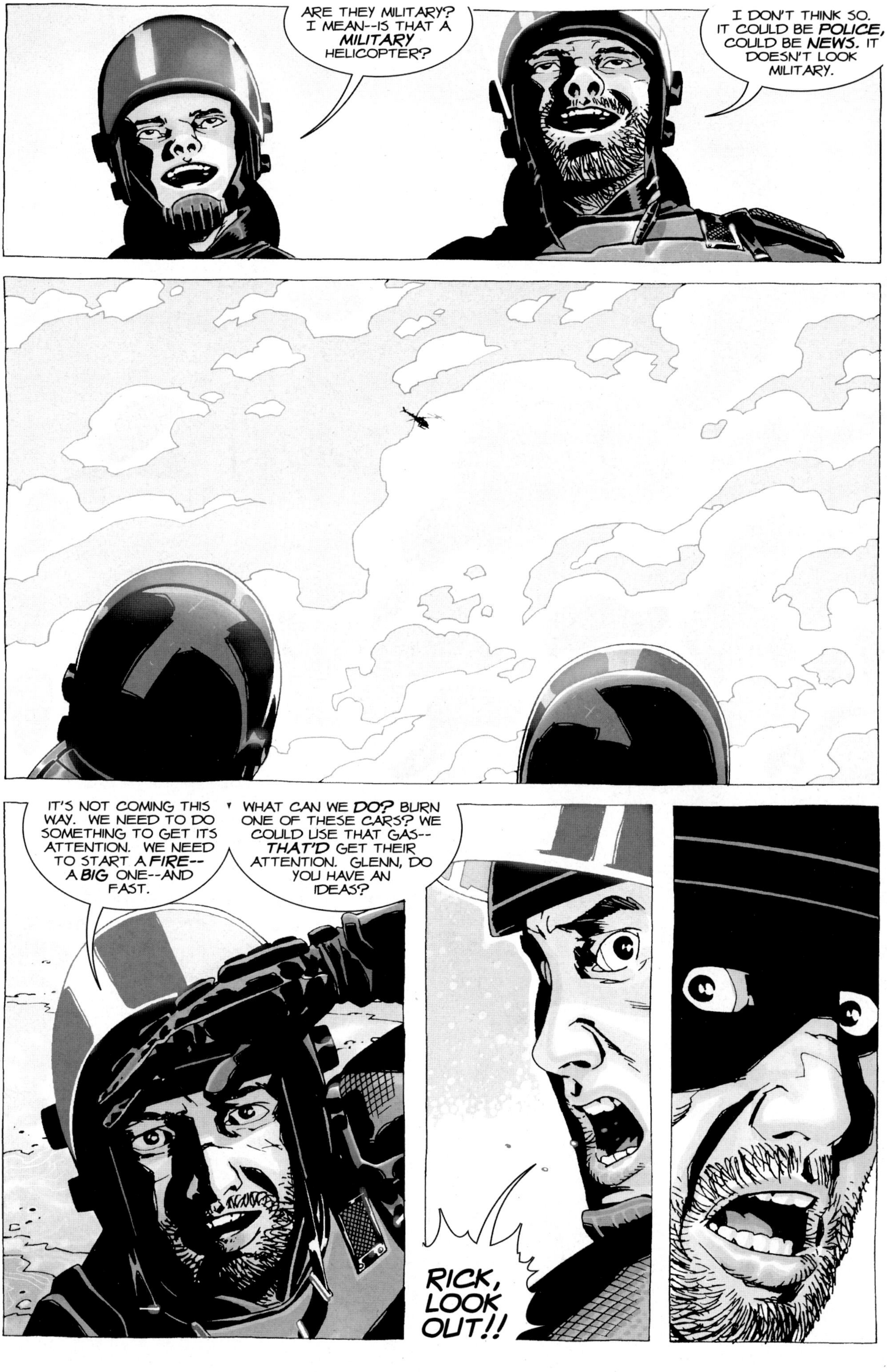
ARE THEY MILITARY? I MEAN--IS THAT A MILITARY HELICOPTER?
I DON'T THINK SO. IT COULD BE POLICE, COULD BE NEWS. IT DOESN'T LOOK MILITARY.
IT'S NOT COMING THIS WAY. WE NEED TO DO SOMETHING TO GET ITS ATTENTION. WE NEED TO START A FIRE-- A BIG ONE--AND FAST.
WHAT CAN WE DO? BURN ONE OF THESE CARS? WE COULD USE THAT GAS-- THAT'D GET THEIR ATTENTION. GLENN, DO YOU HAVE AN IDEAS?
RICK, LOOK OUT!!

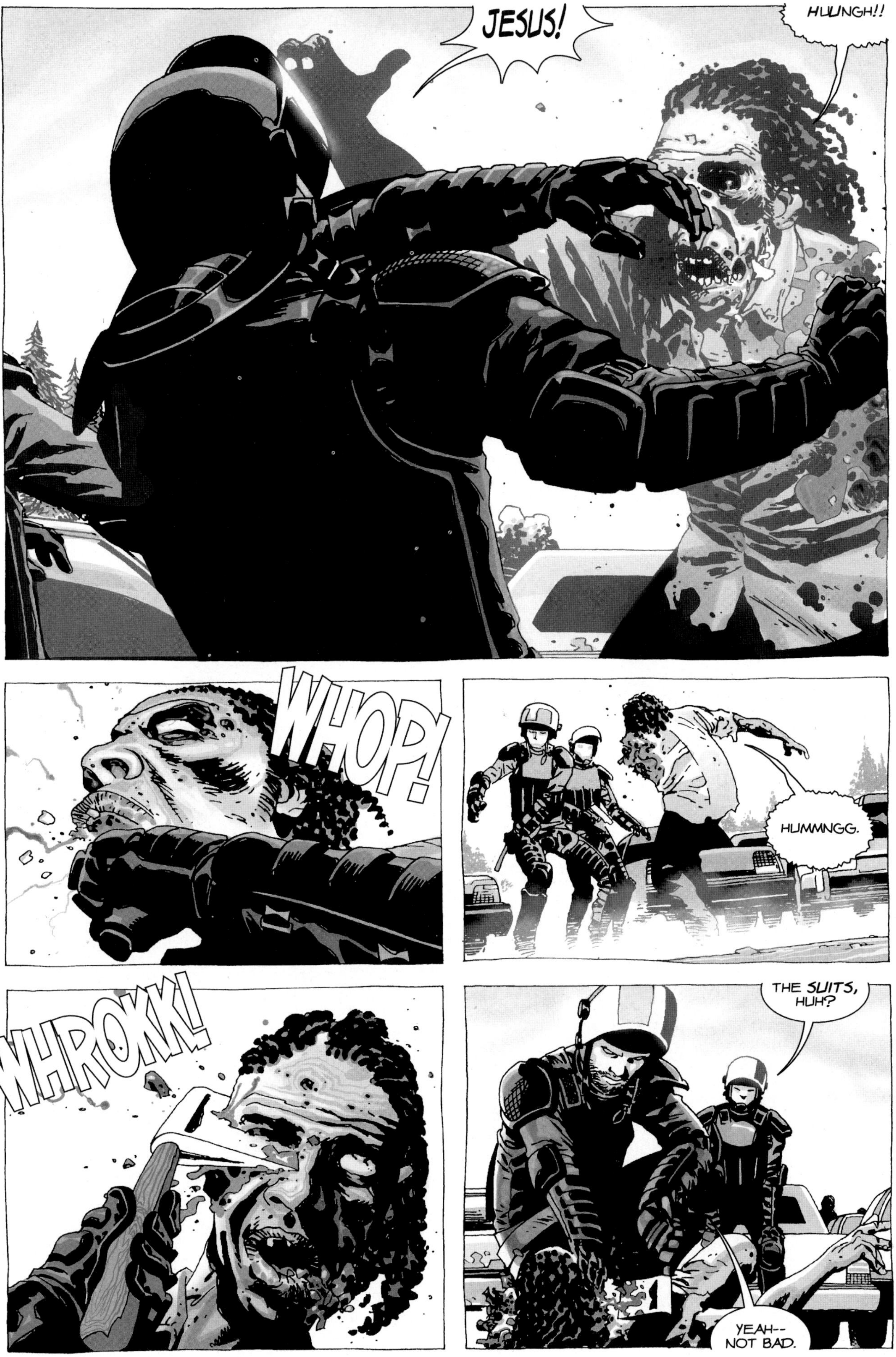
JESUS!
HUUNGH!!
WHOP!
HUMMNGG.
WHROKK!
THE SUITS, HUH?
YEAH-- NOT BAD.

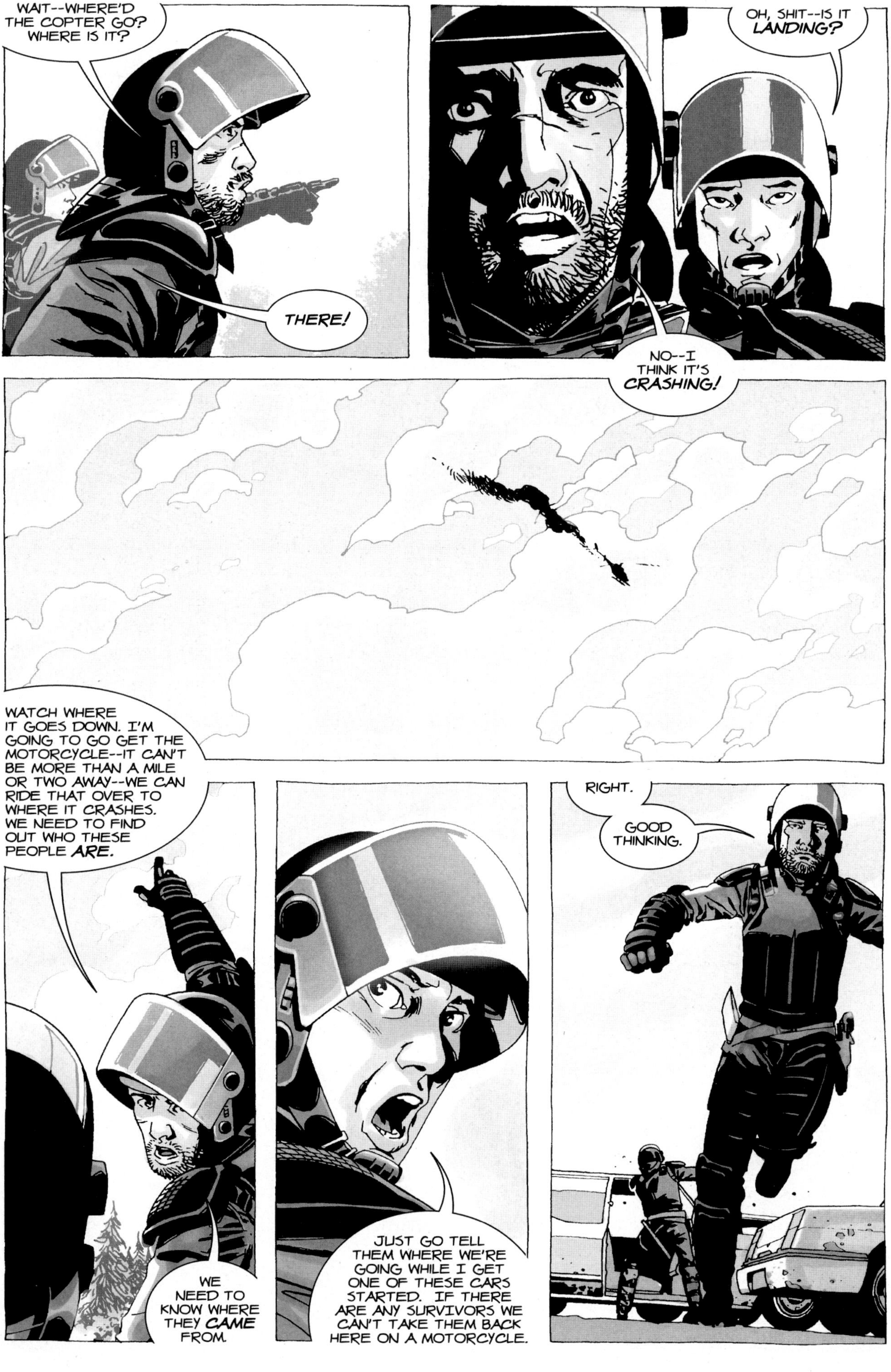
WAIT--WHERE'D THE COPTER GO? WHERE IS IT?
THERE!
OH, SHIT--IS IT LANDING?
NO--I THINK IT'S CRASHING!
WATCH WHERE IT GOES DOWN. I'M GOING TO GO GET THE MOTORCYCLE--IT CAN'T BE MORE THAN A MILE OR TWO AWAY--WE CAN RIDE THAT OVER TO WHERE IT CRASHES. WE NEED TO FIND OUT WHO THESE PEOPLE ARE.
WE NEED TO KNOW WHERE THEY CAME FROM.
JUST GO TELL THEM WHERE WE'RE GOING WHILE I GET ONE OF THESE CARS STARTED. IF THERE ARE ANY SURVIVORS WE CAN'T TAKE THEM BACK HERE ON A MOTORCYCLE.
RIGHT.
GOOD THINKING.

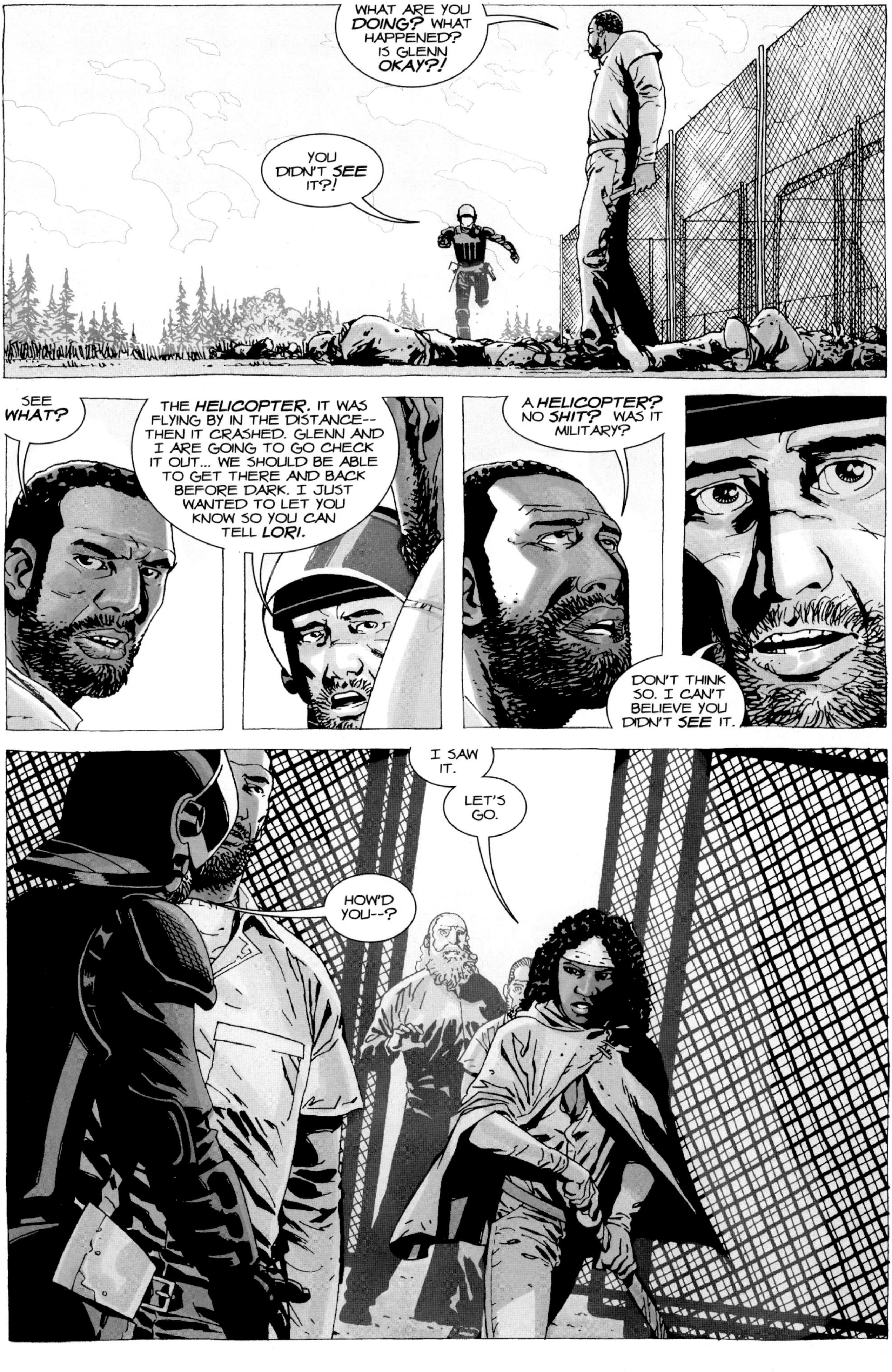
WHAT ARE YOU DOING? WHAT HAPPENED? IS GLENN OKAY?!
YOU DIDN'T SEE IT?!
SEE WHAT?
THE HELICOPTER. IT WAS FLYING BY IN THE DISTANCE-- THEN IT CRASHED. GLENN AND I ARE GOING TO GO CHECK IT OUT... WE SHOULD BE ABLE TO GET THERE AND BACK BEFORE DARK. I JUST WANTED TO LET YOU KNOW SO YOU CAN TELL LORI.
A HELICOPTER? NO SHIT? WAS IT MILITARY?
DON'T THINK SO. I CAN'T BELIEVE YOU DIDN'T SEE IT.
I SAW IT.
LET'S GO.
HOW'D YOU--?

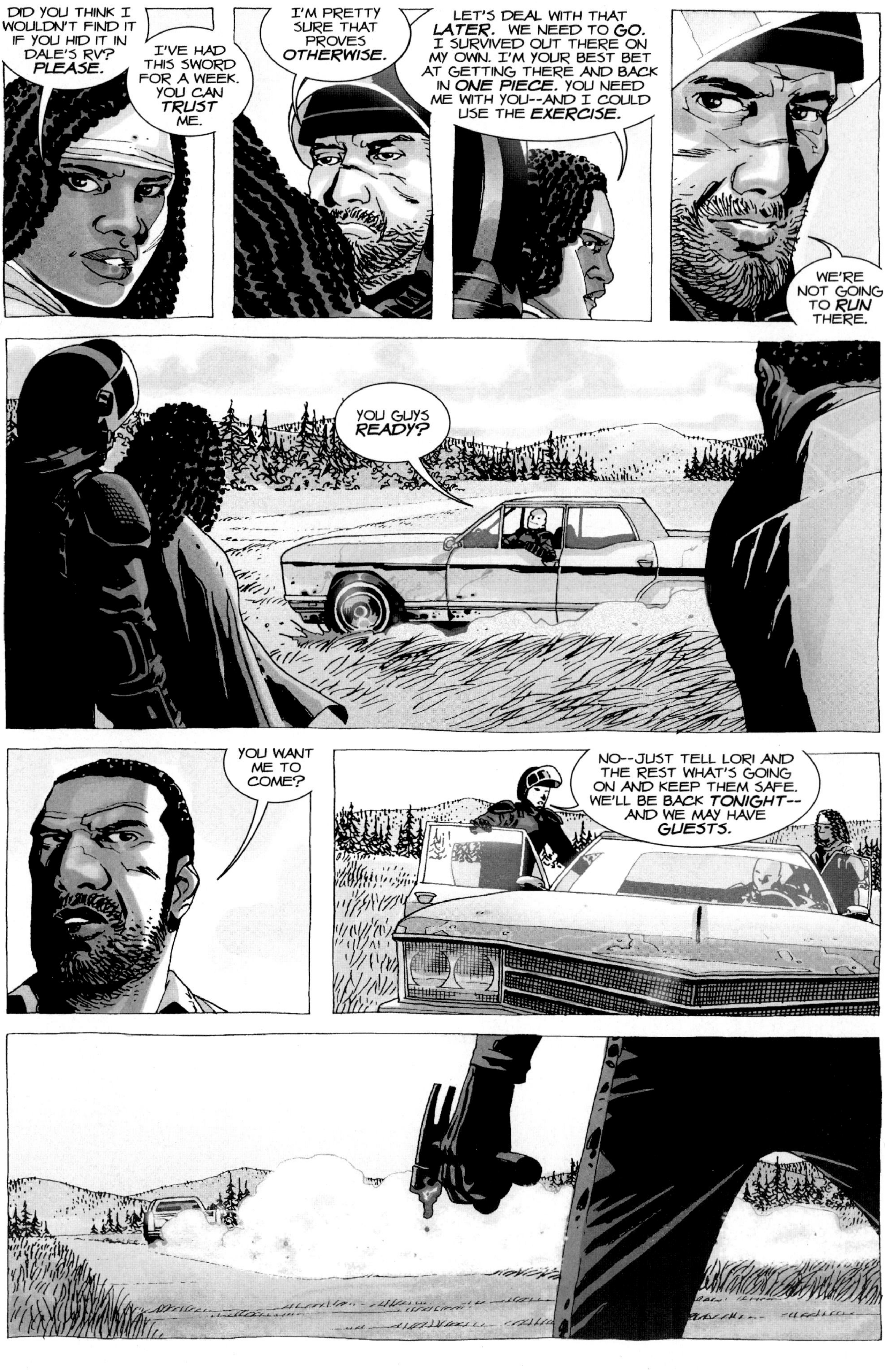
DID YOU THINK I WOULDN'T FIND IT IF YOU HID IT IN DALE'S RV? *PLEASE.*
I'VE HAD THIS SWORD FOR A WEEK. YOU CAN *TRUST* ME.
I'M PRETTY SURE THAT PROVES *OTHERWISE.*
LET'S DEAL WITH THAT *LATER.* WE NEED TO *GO.* I SURVIVED OUT THERE ON MY OWN. I'M YOUR BEST BET AT GETTING THERE AND BACK IN *ONE PIECE.* YOU NEED ME WITH YOU--AND I COULD USE THE *EXERCISE.*
WE'RE NOT GOING TO *RUN* THERE.
YOU GUYS *READY?*
YOU WANT ME TO COME?
NO--JUST TELL LORI AND THE REST WHAT'S GOING ON AND KEEP THEM SAFE. WE'LL BE BACK *TONIGHT*-- AND WE MAY HAVE *GUESTS.*

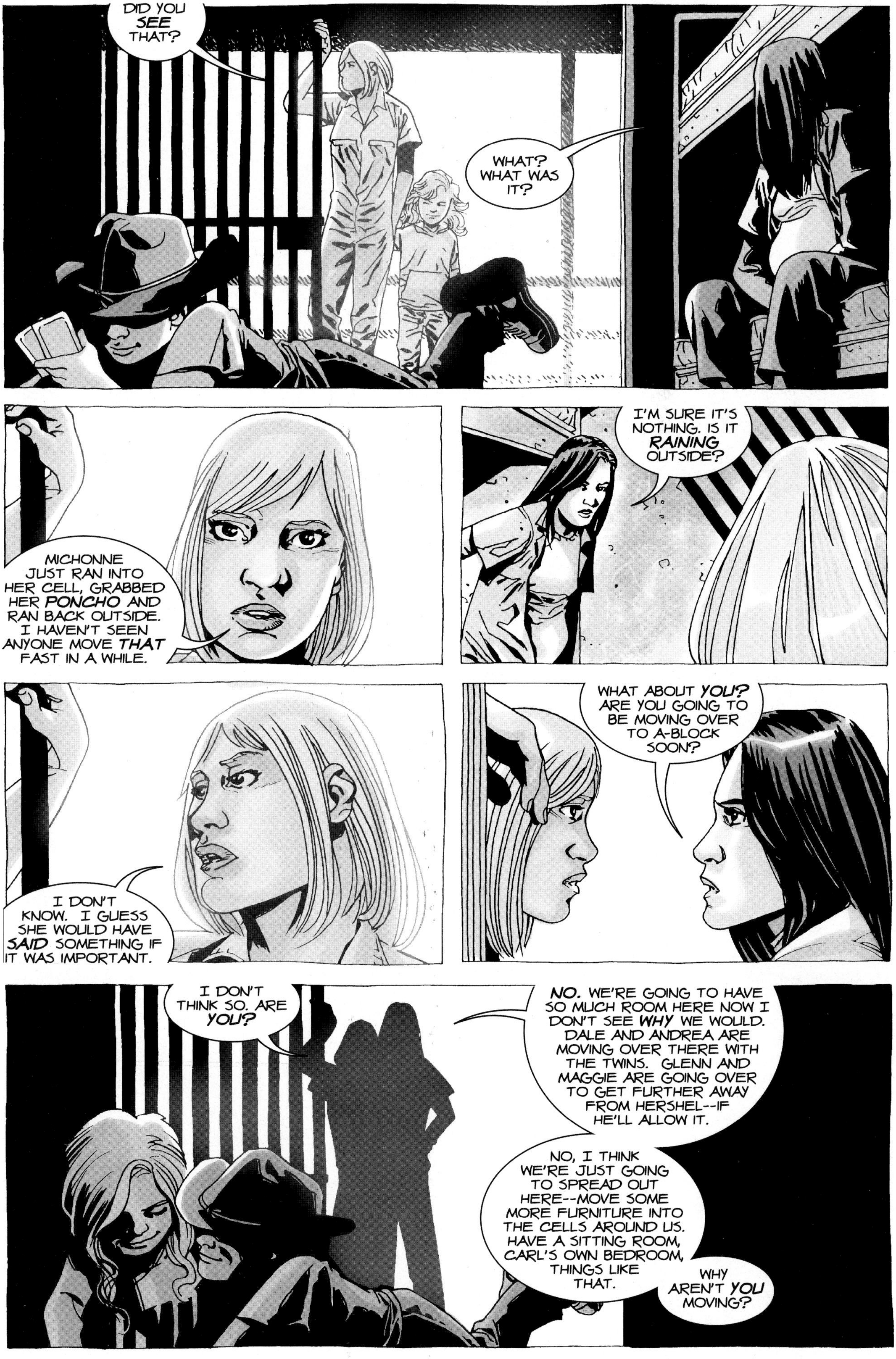
DID YOU SEE THAT?
WHAT? WHAT WAS IT?
MICHONNE JUST RAN INTO HER CELL, GRABBED HER PONCHO AND RAN BACK OUTSIDE. I HAVEN'T SEEN ANYONE MOVE THAT FAST IN A WHILE.
I'M SURE IT'S NOTHING. IS IT RAINING OUTSIDE?
I DON'T KNOW. I GUESS SHE WOULD HAVE SAID SOMETHING IF IT WAS IMPORTANT.
WHAT ABOUT YOU? ARE YOU GOING TO BE MOVING OVER TO A-BLOCK SOON?
I DON'T THINK SO. ARE YOU?
NO. WE'RE GOING TO HAVE SO MUCH ROOM HERE NOW I DON'T SEE WHY WE WOULD. DALE AND ANDREA ARE MOVING OVER THERE WITH THE TWINS. GLENN AND MAGGIE ARE GOING OVER TO GET FURTHER AWAY FROM HERSHEL--IF HE'LL ALLOW IT.
NO, I THINK WE'RE JUST GOING TO SPREAD OUT HERE--MOVE SOME MORE FURNITURE INTO THE CELLS AROUND US. HAVE A SITTING ROOM, CARL'S OWN BEDROOM, THINGS LIKE THAT.
WHY AREN'T YOU MOVING?

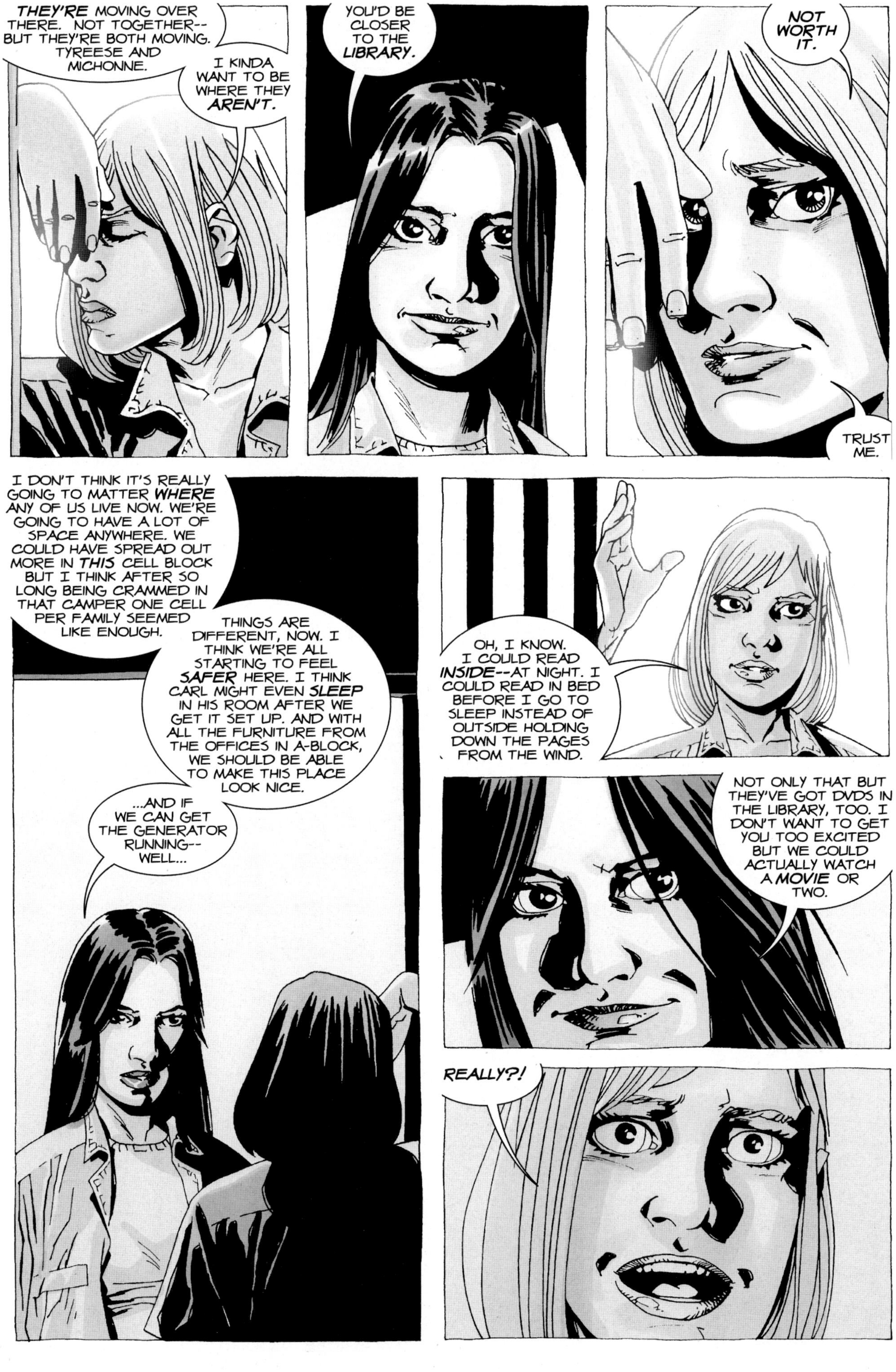
THEY'RE MOVING OVER THERE. NOT TOGETHER-- BUT THEY'RE BOTH MOVING. TYREESE AND MICHONNE.
I KINDA WANT TO BE WHERE THEY AREN'T.
YOU'D BE CLOSER TO THE LIBRARY.
NOT WORTH IT.
TRUST ME.
I DON'T THINK IT'S REALLY GOING TO MATTER WHERE ANY OF US LIVE NOW. WE'RE GOING TO HAVE A LOT OF SPACE ANYWHERE. WE COULD HAVE SPREAD OUT MORE IN THIS CELL BLOCK BUT I THINK AFTER SO LONG BEING CRAMMED IN THAT CAMPER ONE CELL PER FAMILY SEEMED LIKE ENOUGH.
THINGS ARE DIFFERENT, NOW. I THINK WE'RE ALL STARTING TO FEEL SAFER HERE. I THINK CARL MIGHT EVEN SLEEP IN HIS ROOM AFTER WE GET IT SET UP. AND WITH ALL THE FURNITURE FROM THE OFFICES IN A-BLOCK, WE SHOULD BE ABLE TO MAKE THIS PLACE LOOK NICE.
...AND IF WE CAN GET THE GENERATOR RUNNING-- WELL...
OH, I KNOW. I COULD READ INSIDE--AT NIGHT. I COULD READ IN BED BEFORE I GO TO SLEEP INSTEAD OF OUTSIDE HOLDING DOWN THE PAGES FROM THE WIND.
NOT ONLY THAT BUT THEY'VE GOT DVDS IN THE LIBRARY, TOO. I DON'T WANT TO GET YOU TOO EXCITED BUT WE COULD ACTUALLY WATCH A MOVIE OR TWO.
REALLY?!

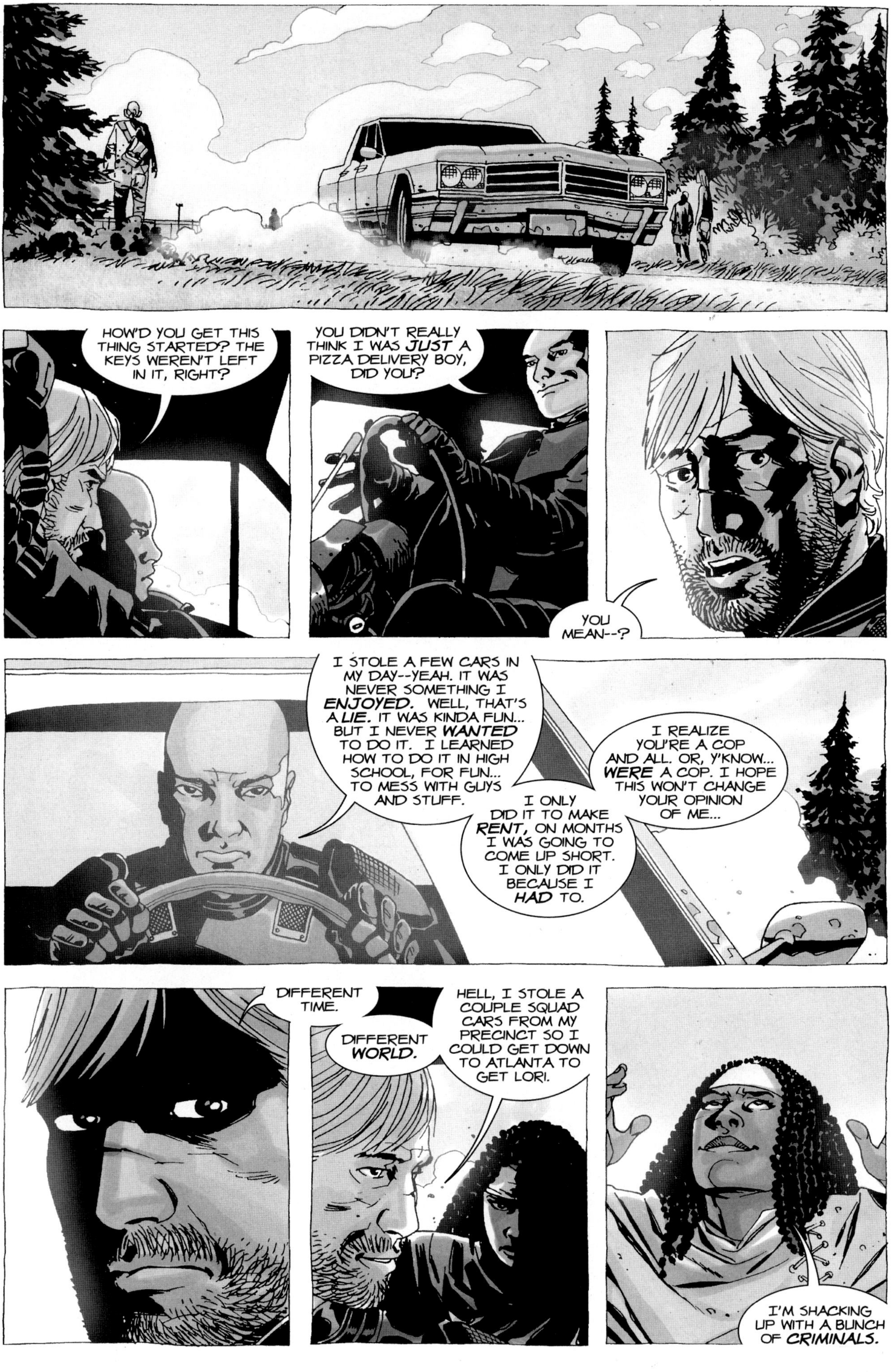
HOW'D YOU GET THIS THING STARTED? THE KEYS WEREN'T LEFT IN IT, RIGHT?
YOU DIDN'T REALLY THINK I WAS JUST A PIZZA DELIVERY BOY, DID YOU?
YOU MEAN--?
I STOLE A FEW CARS IN MY DAY--YEAH. IT WAS NEVER SOMETHING I ENJOYED. WELL, THAT'S A LIE. IT WAS KINDA FUN... BUT I NEVER WANTED TO DO IT. I LEARNED HOW TO DO IT IN HIGH SCHOOL, FOR FUN... TO MESS WITH GUYS AND STUFF.
I ONLY DID IT TO MAKE RENT, ON MONTHS I WAS GOING TO COME UP SHORT. I ONLY DID IT BECAUSE I HAD TO.
I REALIZE YOU'RE A COP AND ALL. OR, Y'KNOW... WERE A COP. I HOPE THIS WON'T CHANGE YOUR OPINION OF ME...
DIFFERENT TIME.
DIFFERENT WORLD.
HELL, I STOLE A COUPLE SQUAD CARS FROM MY PRECINCT SO I COULD GET DOWN TO ATLANTA TO GET LORI.
I'M SHACKING UP WITH A BUNCH OF CRIMINALS.

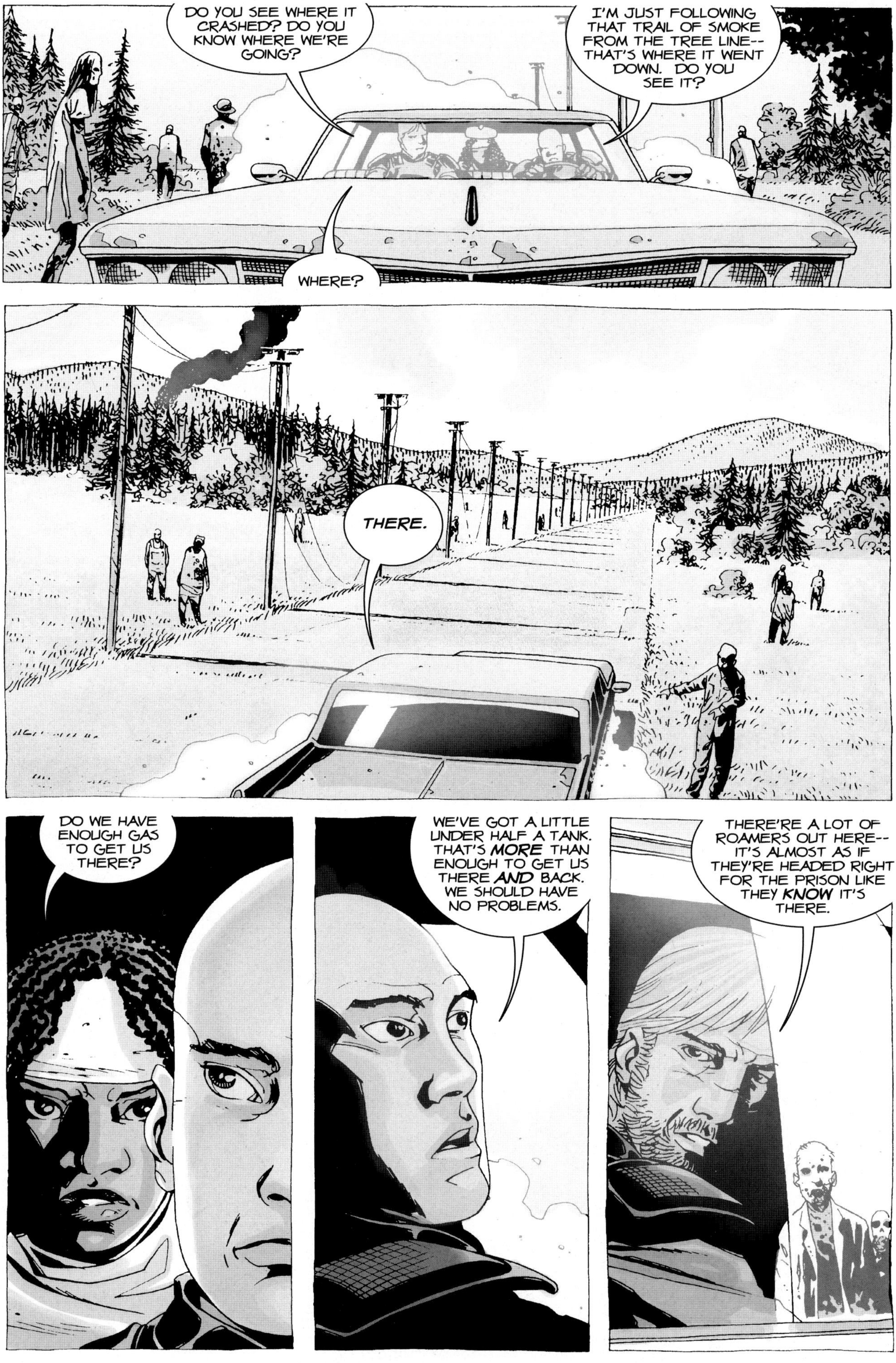
DO YOU SEE WHERE IT CRASHED? DO YOU KNOW WHERE WE'RE GOING?
I'M JUST FOLLOWING THAT TRAIL OF SMOKE FROM THE TREE LINE-- THAT'S WHERE IT WENT DOWN. DO YOU SEE IT?
WHERE?
THERE.
DO WE HAVE ENOUGH GAS TO GET US THERE?
WE'VE GOT A LITTLE UNDER HALF A TANK. THAT'S MORE THAN ENOUGH TO GET US THERE AND BACK. WE SHOULD HAVE NO PROBLEMS.
THERE'RE A LOT OF ROAMERS OUT HERE-- IT'S ALMOST AS IF THEY'RE HEADED RIGHT FOR THE PRISON LIKE THEY KNOW IT'S THERE.

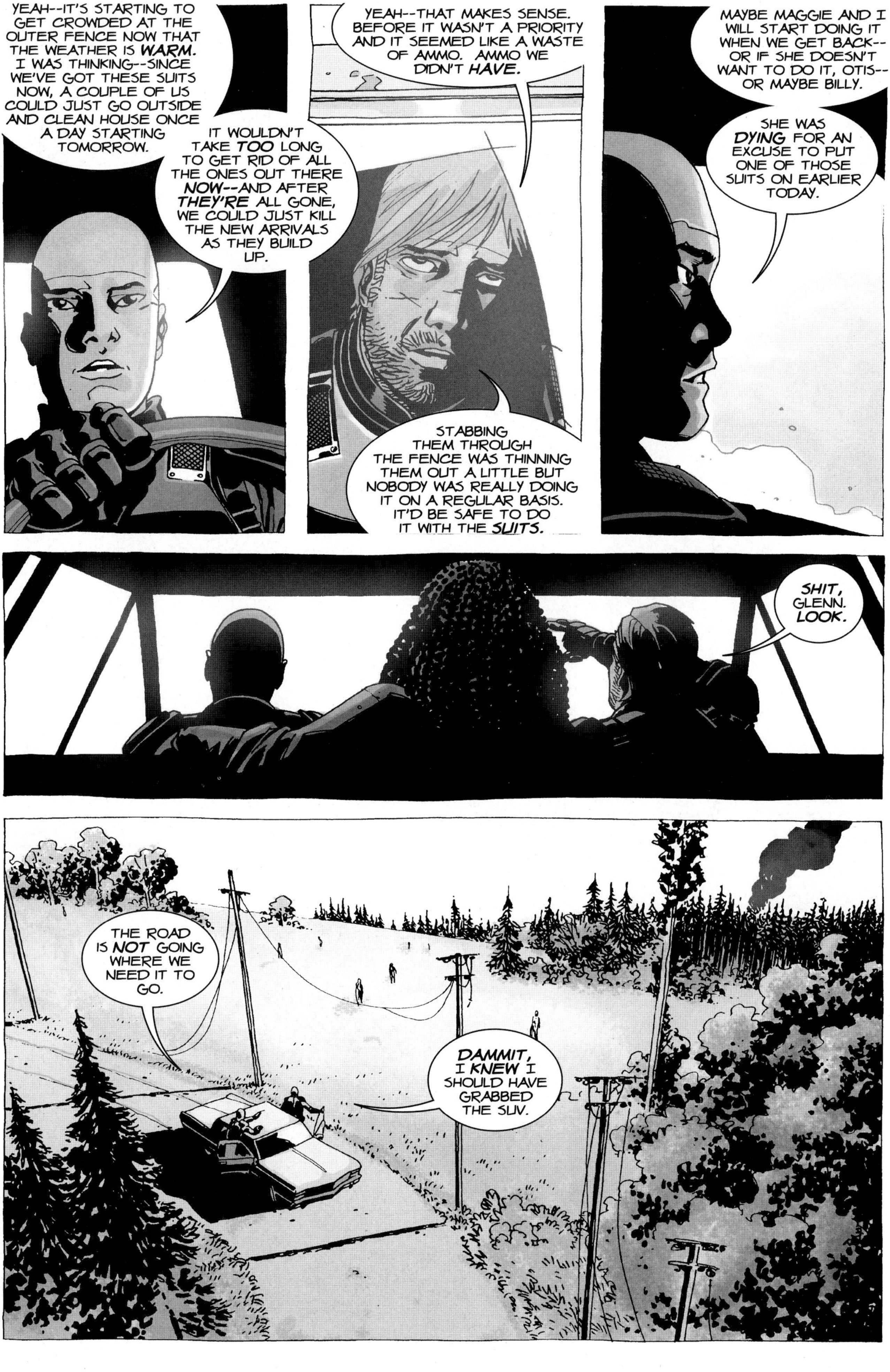
YEAH--IT'S STARTING TO GET CROWDED AT THE OUTER FENCE NOW THAT THE WEATHER IS WARM. I WAS THINKING--SINCE WE'VE GOT THESE SUITS NOW, A COUPLE OF US COULD JUST GO OUTSIDE AND CLEAN HOUSE ONCE A DAY STARTING TOMORROW.
IT WOULDN'T TAKE TOO LONG TO GET RID OF ALL THE ONES OUT THERE NOW--AND AFTER THEY'RE ALL GONE, WE COULD JUST KILL THE NEW ARRIVALS AS THEY BUILD UP.
YEAH--THAT MAKES SENSE. BEFORE IT WASN'T A PRIORITY AND IT SEEMED LIKE A WASTE OF AMMO. AMMO WE DIDN'T HAVE.
STABBING THEM THROUGH THE FENCE WAS THINNING THEM OUT A LITTLE BUT NOBODY WAS REALLY DOING IT ON A REGULAR BASIS. IT'D BE SAFE TO DO IT WITH THE SUITS.
MAYBE MAGGIE AND I WILL START DOING IT WHEN WE GET BACK--OR IF SHE DOESN'T WANT TO DO IT, OTIS--OR MAYBE BILLY.
SHE WAS DYING FOR AN EXCUSE TO PUT ONE OF THOSE SUITS ON EARLIER TODAY.
SHIT, GLENN. LOOK.
THE ROAD IS NOT GOING WHERE WE NEED IT TO GO.
DAMMIT, I KNEW I SHOULD HAVE GRABBED THE SUV.

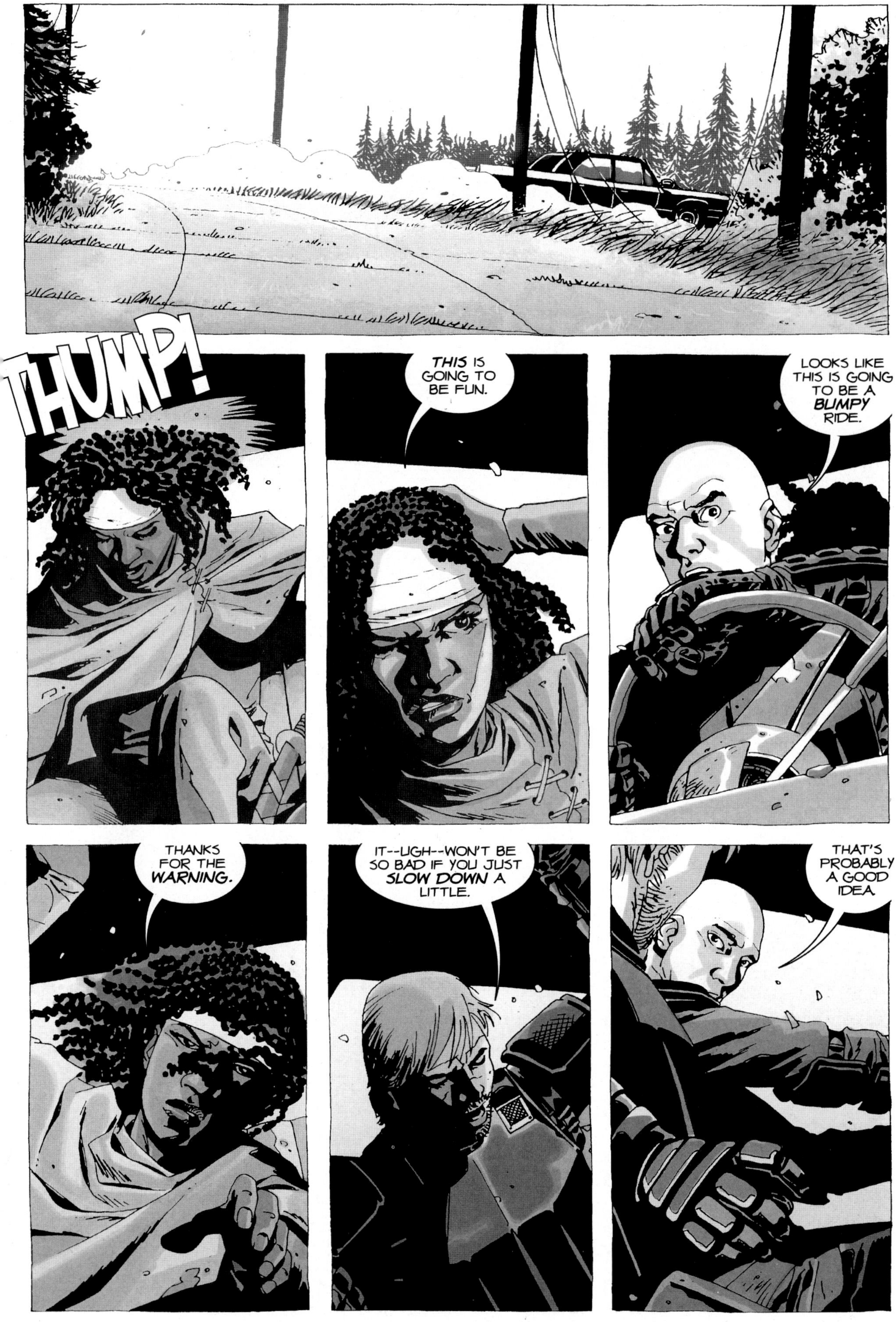
THUMP!
THIS IS GOING TO BE FUN.
LOOKS LIKE THIS IS GOING TO BE A BUMPY RIDE.
THANKS FOR THE WARNING.
IT--UGH--WON'T BE SO BAD IF YOU JUST SLOW DOWN A LITTLE.
THAT'S PROBABLY A GOOD IDEA.

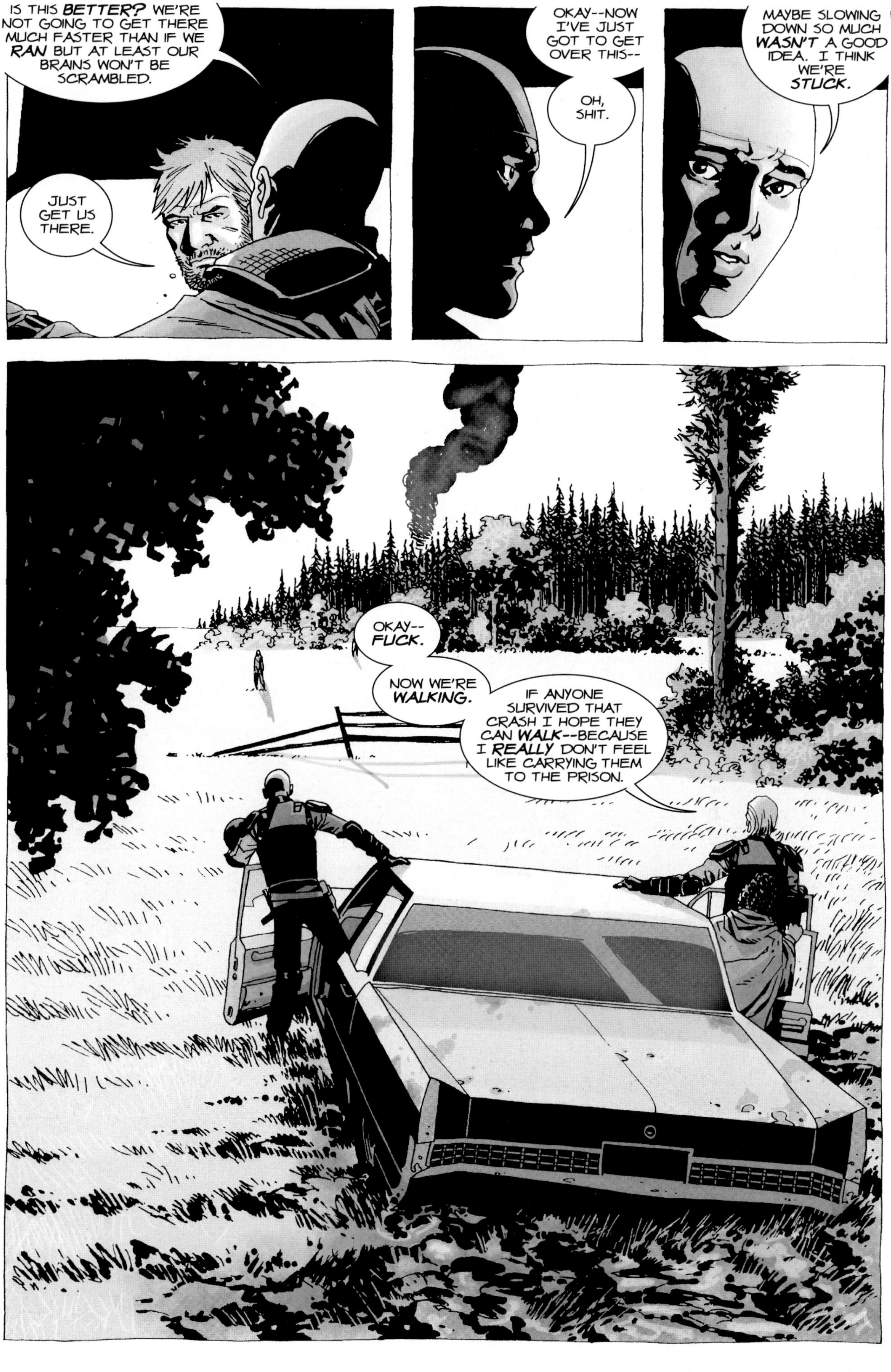
IS THIS BETTER? WE'RE NOT GOING TO GET THERE MUCH FASTER THAN IF WE RAN BUT AT LEAST OUR BRAINS WON'T BE SCRAMBLED.
JUST GET US THERE.
OKAY--NOW I'VE JUST GOT TO GET OVER THIS--
OH, SHIT.
MAYBE SLOWING DOWN SO MUCH WASN'T A GOOD IDEA. I THINK WE'RE STUCK.
OKAY-- FUCK.
NOW WE'RE WALKING.
IF ANYONE SURVIVED THAT CRASH I HOPE THEY CAN WALK--BECAUSE I REALLY DON'T FEEL LIKE CARRYING THEM TO THE PRISON.

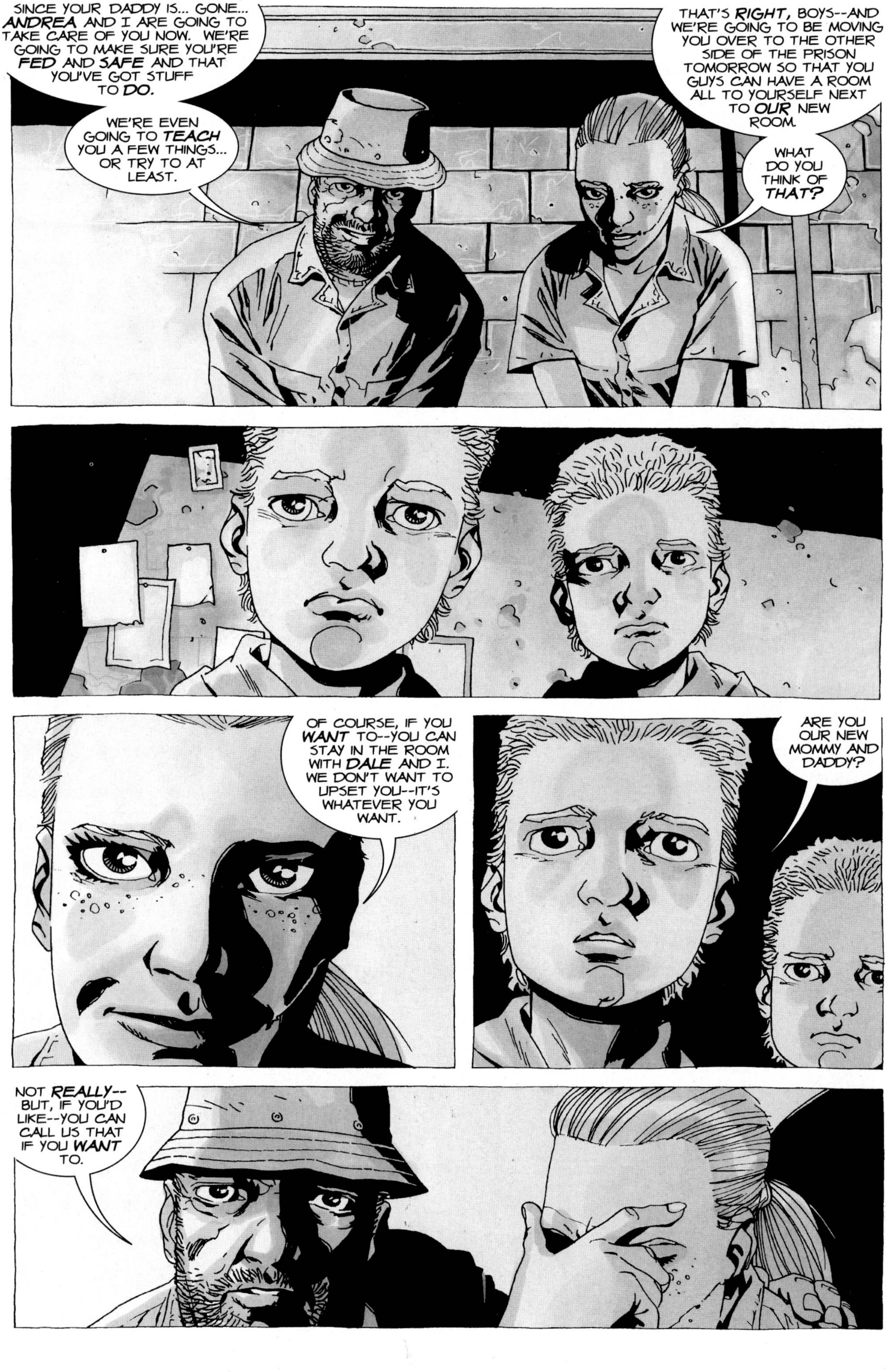
SINCE YOUR DADDY IS... GONE... ANDREA AND I ARE GOING TO TAKE CARE OF YOU NOW. WE'RE GOING TO MAKE SURE YOU'RE FED AND SAFE AND THAT YOU'VE GOT STUFF TO DO.
WE'RE EVEN GOING TO TEACH YOU A FEW THINGS... OR TRY TO AT LEAST.
THAT'S RIGHT, BOYS--AND WE'RE GOING TO BE MOVING YOU OVER TO THE OTHER SIDE OF THE PRISON TOMORROW SO THAT YOU GUYS CAN HAVE A ROOM ALL TO YOURSELF NEXT TO OUR NEW ROOM.
WHAT DO YOU THINK OF THAT?
OF COURSE, IF YOU WANT TO--YOU CAN STAY IN THE ROOM WITH DALE AND I. WE DON'T WANT TO UPSET YOU--IT'S WHATEVER YOU WANT.
ARE YOU OUR NEW MOMMY AND DADDY?
NOT REALLY-- BUT, IF YOU'D LIKE--YOU CAN CALL US THAT IF YOU WANT TO.

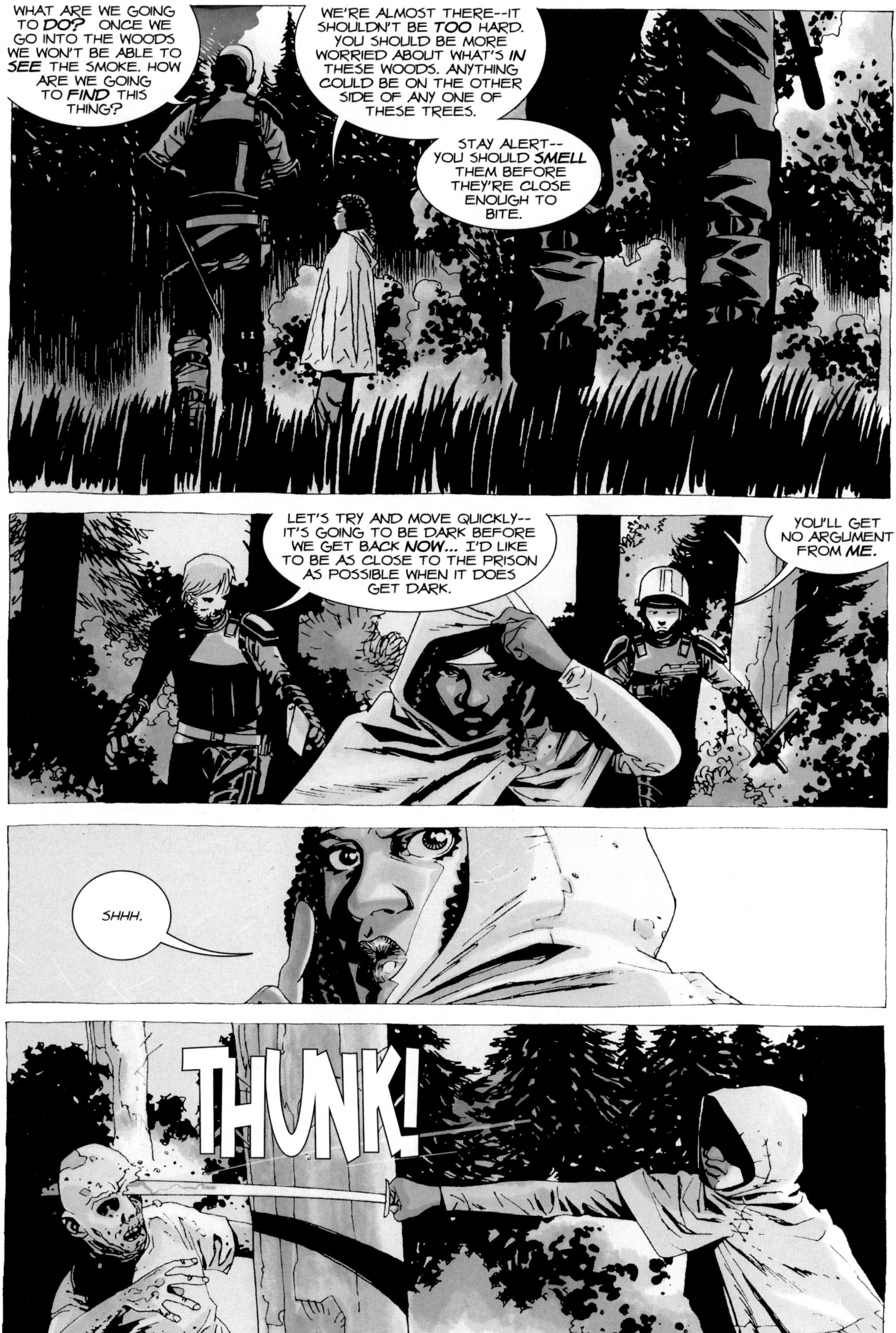

WHAT ARE WE GOING TO DO? ONCE WE GO INTO THE WOODS WE WON'T BE ABLE TO SEE THE SMOKE. HOW ARE WE GOING TO FIND THIS THING?
WE'RE ALMOST THERE--IT SHOULDN'T BE TOO HARD. YOU SHOULD BE MORE WORRIED ABOUT WHAT'S IN THESE WOODS. ANYTHING COULD BE ON THE OTHER SIDE OF ANY ONE OF THESE TREES.
STAY ALERT-- YOU SHOULD SMELL THEM BEFORE THEY'RE CLOSE ENOUGH TO BITE.
LET'S TRY AND MOVE QUICKLY-- IT'S GOING TO BE DARK BEFORE WE GET BACK NOW... I'D LIKE TO BE AS CLOSE TO THE PRISON AS POSSIBLE WHEN IT DOES GET DARK.
YOU'LL GET NO ARGUMENT FROM ME.
SHHH.
THUNK!

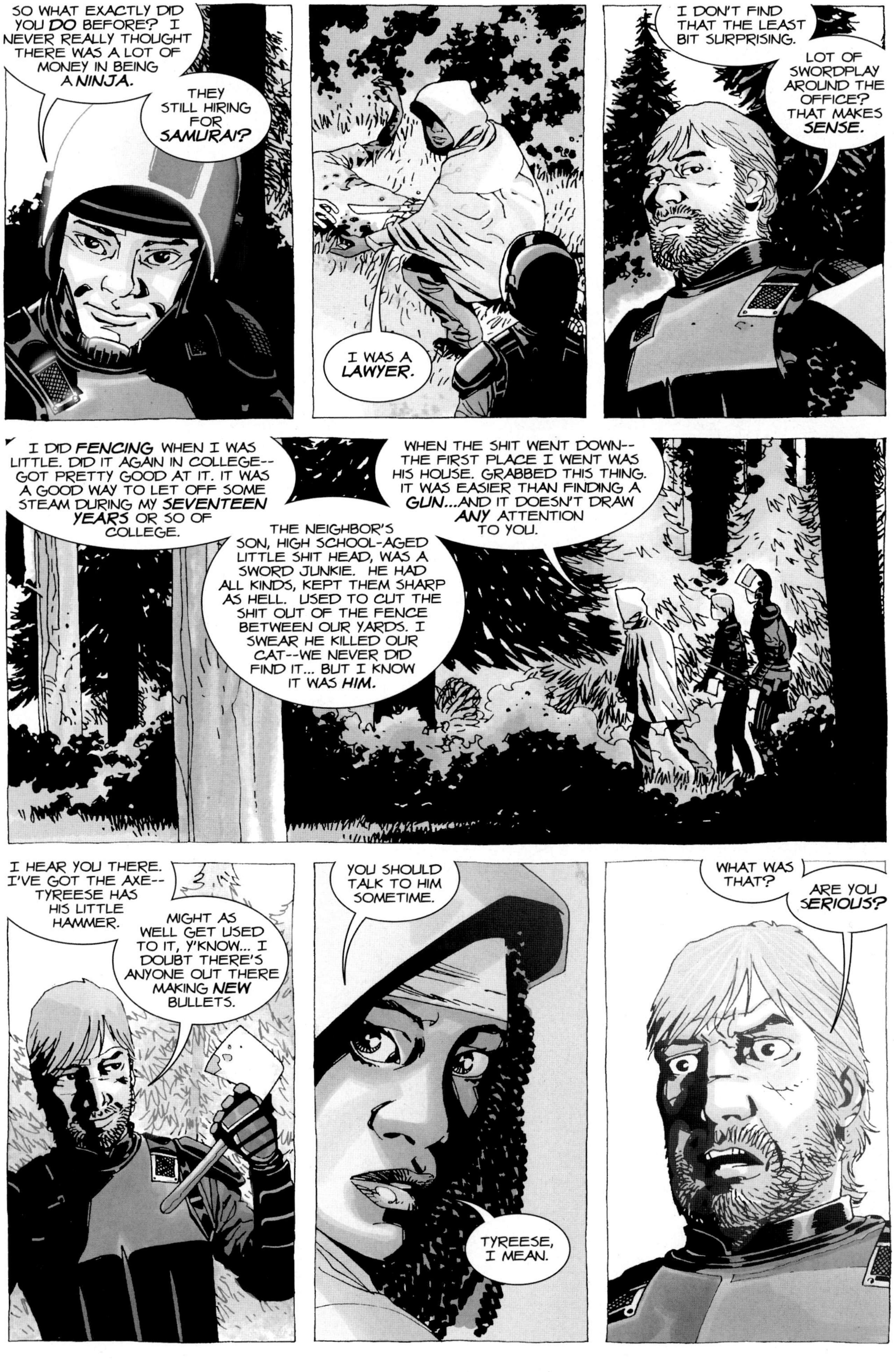
SO WHAT EXACTLY DID YOU DO BEFORE? I NEVER REALLY THOUGHT THERE WAS A LOT OF MONEY IN BEING A NINJA.
THEY STILL HIRING FOR SAMURAI?
I WAS A LAWYER.
I DON'T FIND THAT THE LEAST BIT SURPRISING.
LOT OF SWORDPLAY AROUND THE OFFICE? THAT MAKES SENSE.
I DID FENCING WHEN I WAS LITTLE. DID IT AGAIN IN COLLEGE-- GOT PRETTY GOOD AT IT. IT WAS A GOOD WAY TO LET OFF SOME STEAM DURING MY SEVENTEEN YEARS OR SO OF COLLEGE.
THE NEIGHBOR'S SON, HIGH SCHOOL-AGED LITTLE SHIT HEAD, WAS A SWORD JUNKIE. HE HAD ALL KINDS, KEPT THEM SHARP AS HELL. USED TO CUT THE SHIT OUT OF THE FENCE BETWEEN OUR YARDS. I SWEAR HE KILLED OUR CAT--WE NEVER DID FIND IT... BUT I KNOW IT WAS HIM.
WHEN THE SHIT WENT DOWN-- THE FIRST PLACE I WENT WAS HIS HOUSE. GRABBED THIS THING. IT WAS EASIER THAN FINDING A GUN...AND IT DOESN'T DRAW ANY ATTENTION TO YOU.
I HEAR YOU THERE. I'VE GOT THE AXE-- TYREESE HAS HIS LITTLE HAMMER.
MIGHT AS WELL GET USED TO IT, Y'KNOW... I DOUBT THERE'S ANYONE OUT THERE MAKING NEW BULLETS.
YOU SHOULD TALK TO HIM SOMETIME.
TYREESE, I MEAN.
WHAT WAS THAT?
ARE YOU SERIOUS?

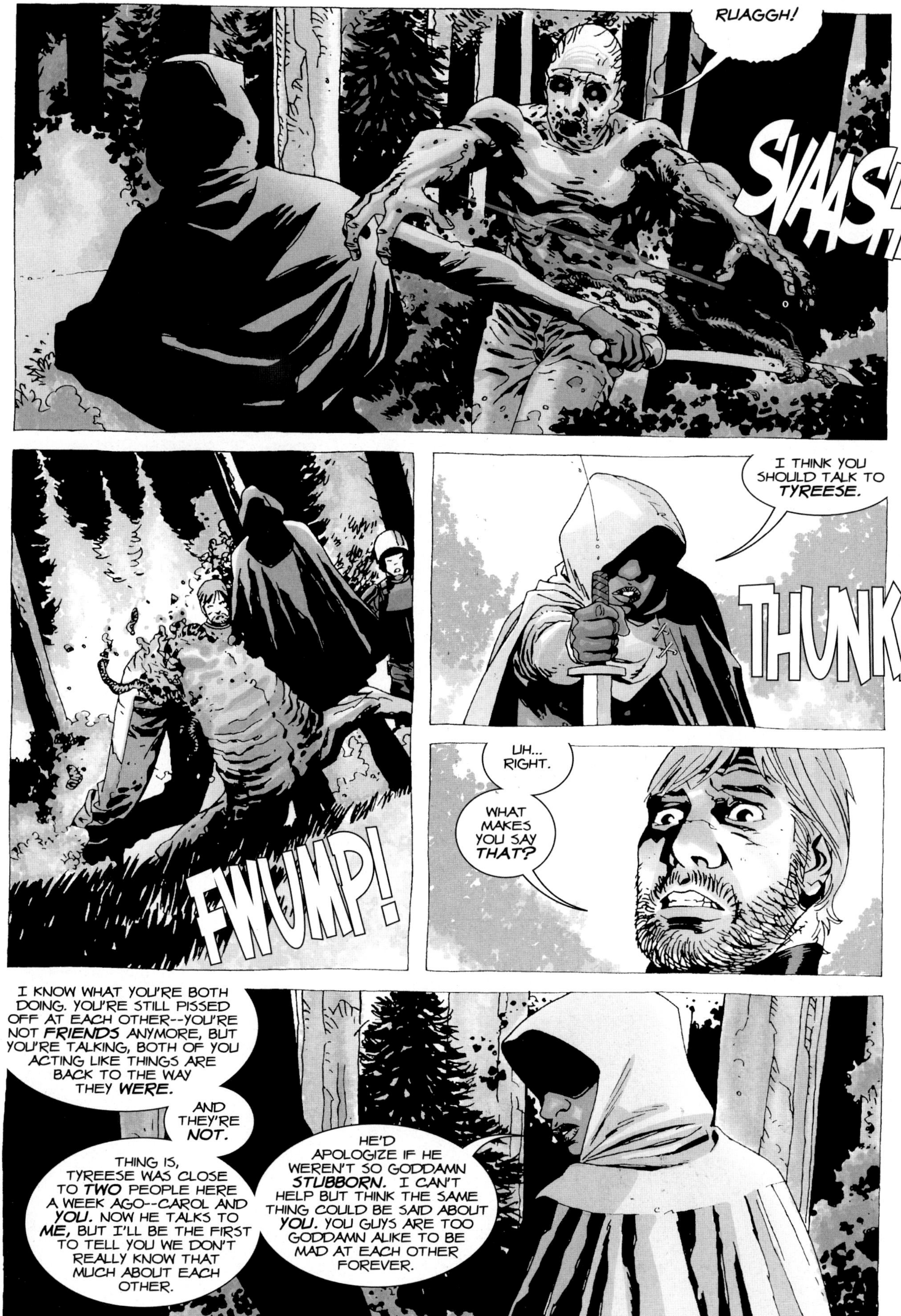
RUAGGH!
SVAASH!
FWUMP!
I THINK YOU SHOULD TALK TO TYREESE.
THUNK!
UH... RIGHT.
WHAT MAKES YOU SAY THAT?
I KNOW WHAT YOU'RE BOTH DOING. YOU'RE STILL PISSED OFF AT EACH OTHER--YOU'RE NOT FRIENDS ANYMORE, BUT YOU'RE TALKING, BOTH OF YOU ACTING LIKE THINGS ARE BACK TO THE WAY THEY WERE.
AND THEY'RE NOT.
THING IS, TYREESE WAS CLOSE TO TWO PEOPLE HERE A WEEK AGO--CAROL AND YOU. NOW HE TALKS TO ME, BUT I'LL BE THE FIRST TO TELL YOU WE DON'T REALLY KNOW THAT MUCH ABOUT EACH OTHER.
HE'D APOLOGIZE IF HE WEREN'T SO GODDAMN STUBBORN. I CAN'T HELP BUT THINK THE SAME THING COULD BE SAID ABOUT YOU. YOU GUYS ARE TOO GODDAMN ALIKE TO BE MAD AT EACH OTHER FOREVER.

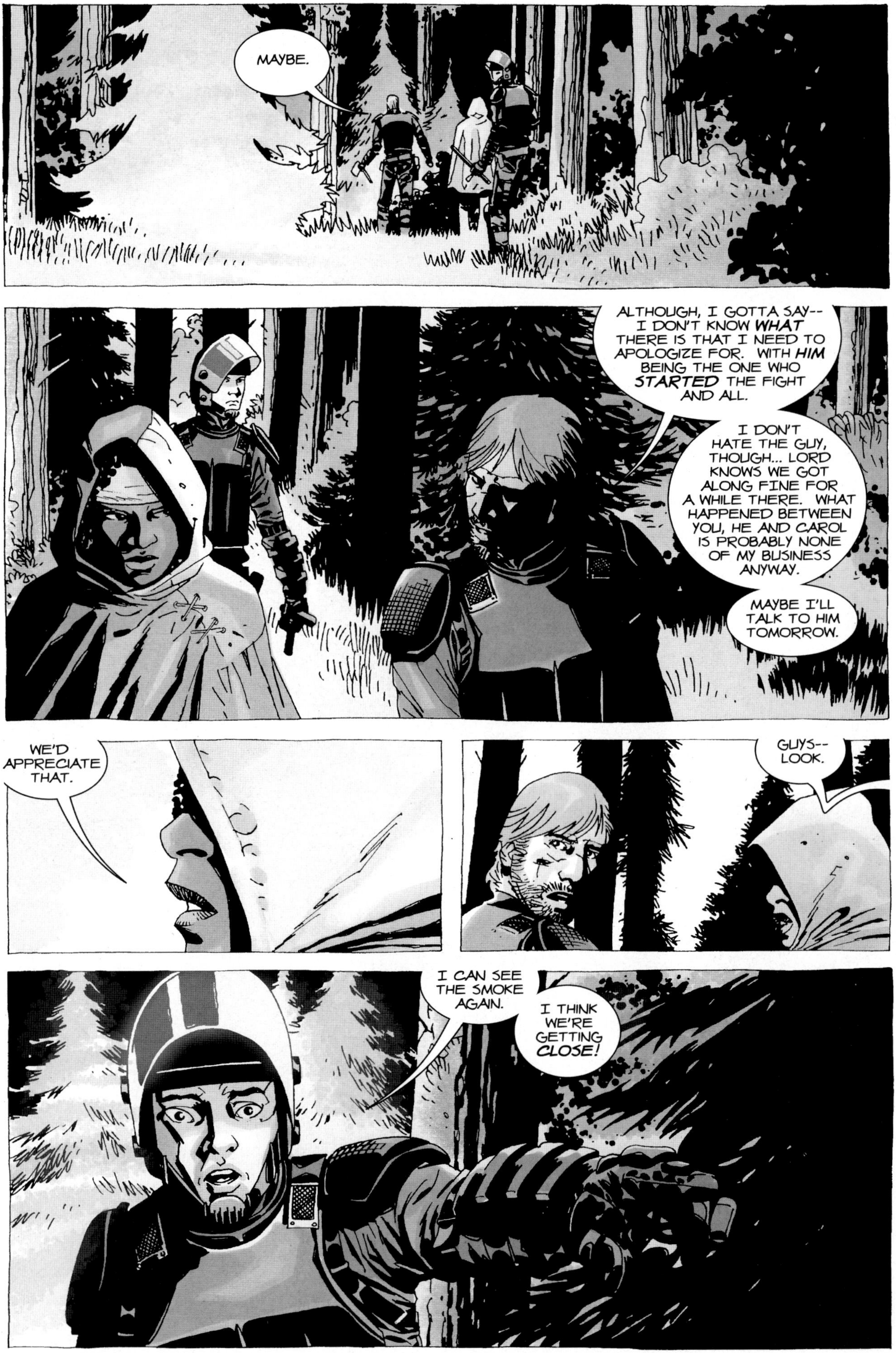
MAYBE.
ALTHOUGH, I GOTTA SAY-- I DON'T KNOW WHAT THERE IS THAT I NEED TO APOLOGIZE FOR. WITH HIM BEING THE ONE WHO STARTED THE FIGHT AND ALL.
I DON'T HATE THE GUY, THOUGH... LORD KNOWS WE GOT ALONG FINE FOR A WHILE THERE. WHAT HAPPENED BETWEEN YOU, HE AND CAROL IS PROBABLY NONE OF MY BUSINESS ANYWAY.
MAYBE I'LL TALK TO HIM TOMORROW.
WE'D APPRECIATE THAT.
GUYS-- LOOK.
I CAN SEE THE SMOKE AGAIN.
I THINK WE'RE GETTING CLOSE!

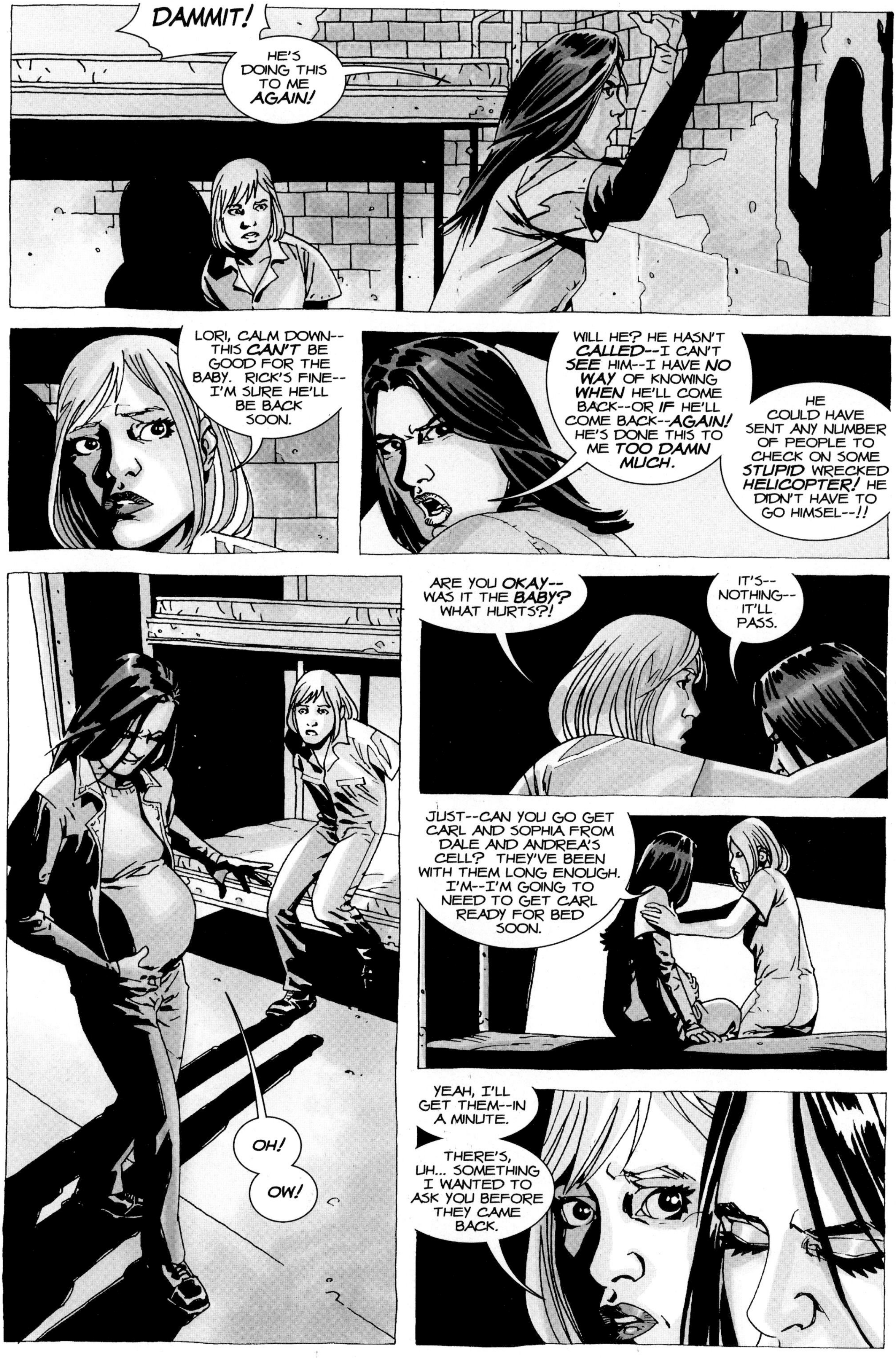
DAMMIT!
HE'S DOING THIS TO ME AGAIN!
LORI, CALM DOWN--THIS CAN'T BE GOOD FOR THE BABY. RICK'S FINE--I'M SURE HE'LL BE BACK SOON.
WILL HE? HE HASN'T CALLED--I CAN'T SEE HIM--I HAVE NO WAY OF KNOWING WHEN HE'LL COME BACK--OR IF HE'LL COME BACK--AGAIN! HE'S DONE THIS TO ME TOO DAMN MUCH.
HE COULD HAVE SENT ANY NUMBER OF PEOPLE TO CHECK ON SOME STUPID WRECKED HELICOPTER! HE DIDN'T HAVE TO GO HIMSEL--!!
OH!
OW!
ARE YOU OKAY--WAS IT THE BABY? WHAT HURTS?!
IT'S--NOTHING--IT'LL PASS.
JUST--CAN YOU GO GET CARL AND SOPHIA FROM DALE AND ANDREA'S CELL? THEY'VE BEEN WITH THEM LONG ENOUGH. I'M--I'M GOING TO NEED TO GET CARL READY FOR BED SOON.
YEAH, I'LL GET THEM--IN A MINUTE.
THERE'S, UH... SOMETHING I WANTED TO ASK YOU BEFORE THEY CAME BACK.

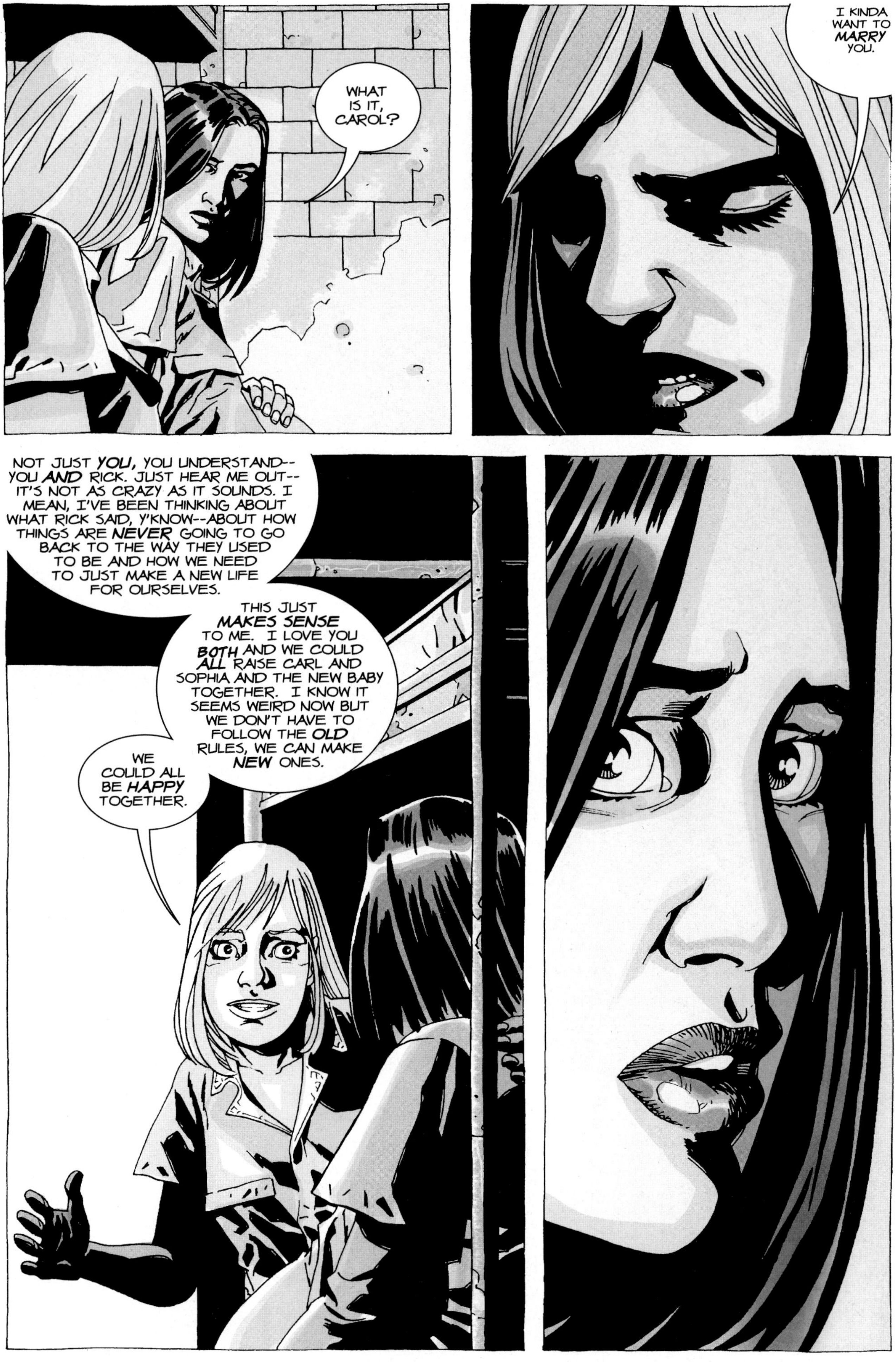
WHAT IS IT, CAROL?
I KINDA WANT TO MARRY YOU.
NOT JUST YOU, YOU UNDERSTAND-- YOU AND RICK. JUST HEAR ME OUT-- IT'S NOT AS CRAZY AS IT SOUNDS. I MEAN, I'VE BEEN THINKING ABOUT WHAT RICK SAID, Y'KNOW--ABOUT HOW THINGS ARE NEVER GOING TO GO BACK TO THE WAY THEY USED TO BE AND HOW WE NEED TO JUST MAKE A NEW LIFE FOR OURSELVES.
THIS JUST MAKES SENSE TO ME. I LOVE YOU BOTH AND WE COULD ALL RAISE CARL AND SOPHIA AND THE NEW BABY TOGETHER. I KNOW IT SEEMS WEIRD NOW BUT WE DON'T HAVE TO FOLLOW THE OLD RULES, WE CAN MAKE NEW ONES.
WE COULD ALL BE HAPPY TOGETHER.

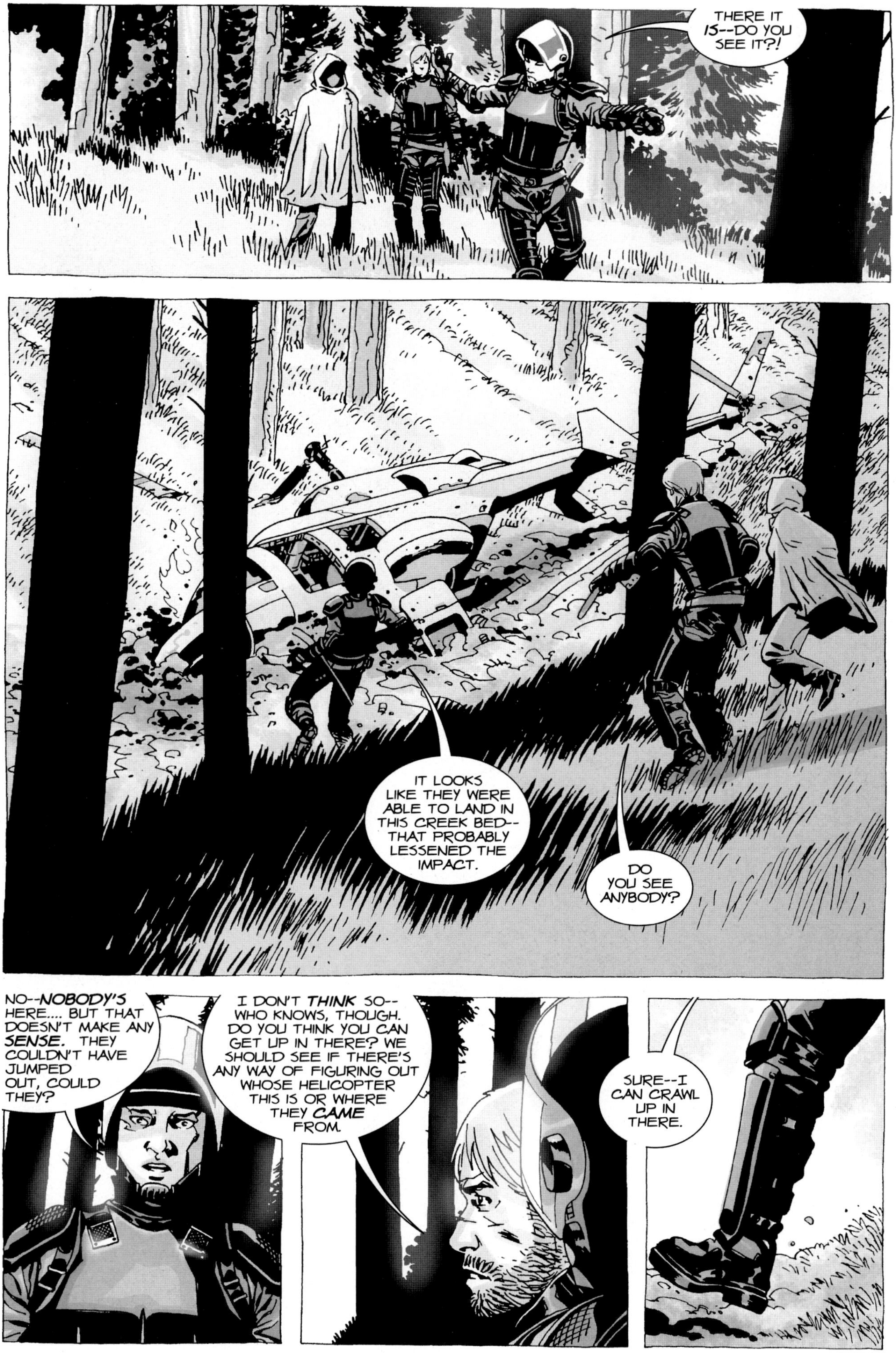
THERE IT IS--DO YOU SEE IT?!
IT LOOKS LIKE THEY WERE ABLE TO LAND IN THIS CREEK BED--THAT PROBABLY LESSENED THE IMPACT.
DO YOU SEE ANYBODY?
NO--NOBODY'S HERE.... BUT THAT DOESN'T MAKE ANY SENSE. THEY COULDN'T HAVE JUMPED OUT, COULD THEY?
I DON'T THINK SO--WHO KNOWS, THOUGH. DO YOU THINK YOU CAN GET UP IN THERE? WE SHOULD SEE IF THERE'S ANY WAY OF FIGURING OUT WHOSE HELICOPTER THIS IS OR WHERE THEY CAME FROM.
SURE--I CAN CRAWL UP IN THERE.

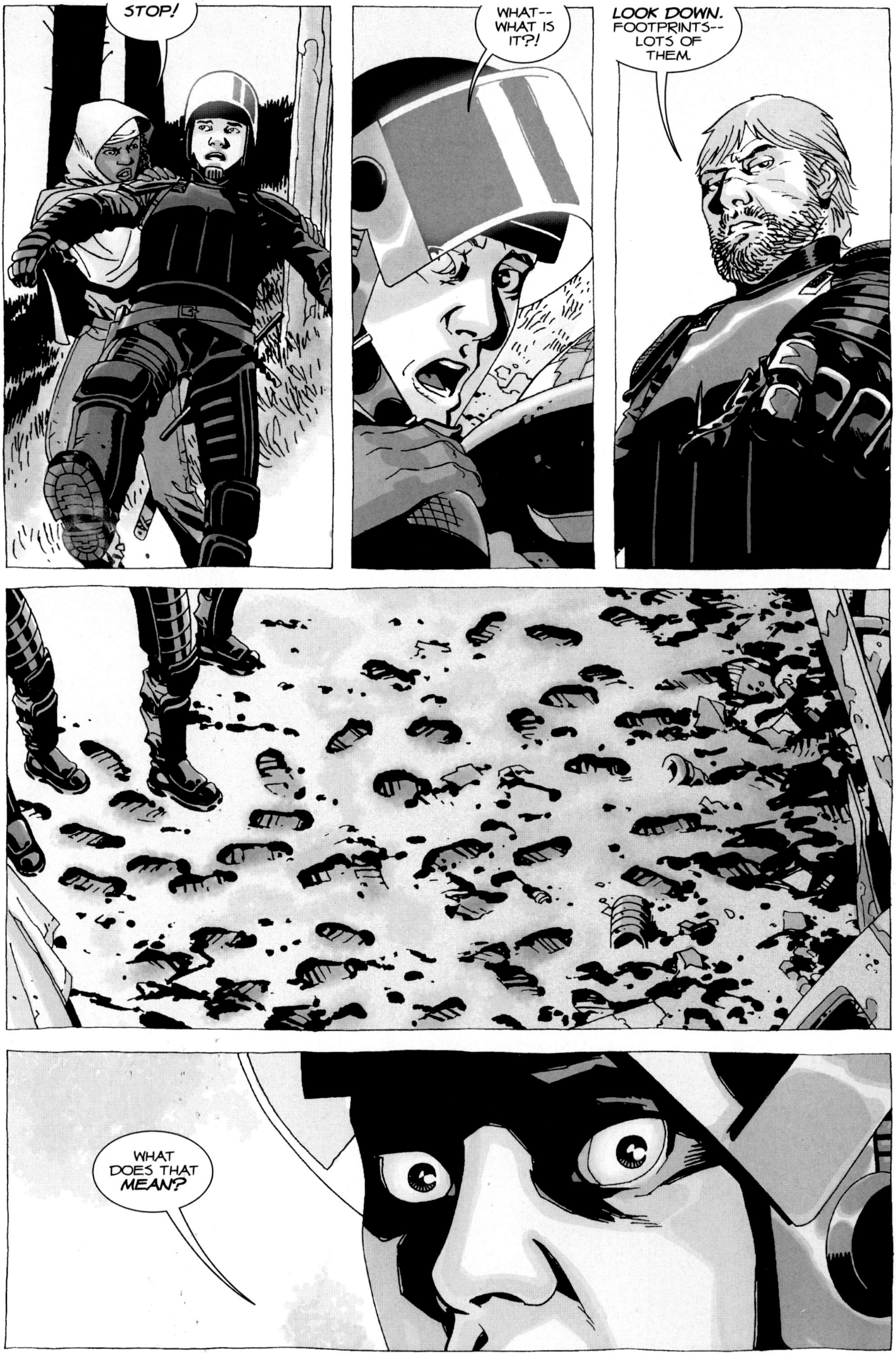

STOP!
WHAT-- WHAT IS IT?!
LOOK DOWN. FOOTPRINTS-- LOTS OF THEM.
WHAT DOES THAT MEAN?

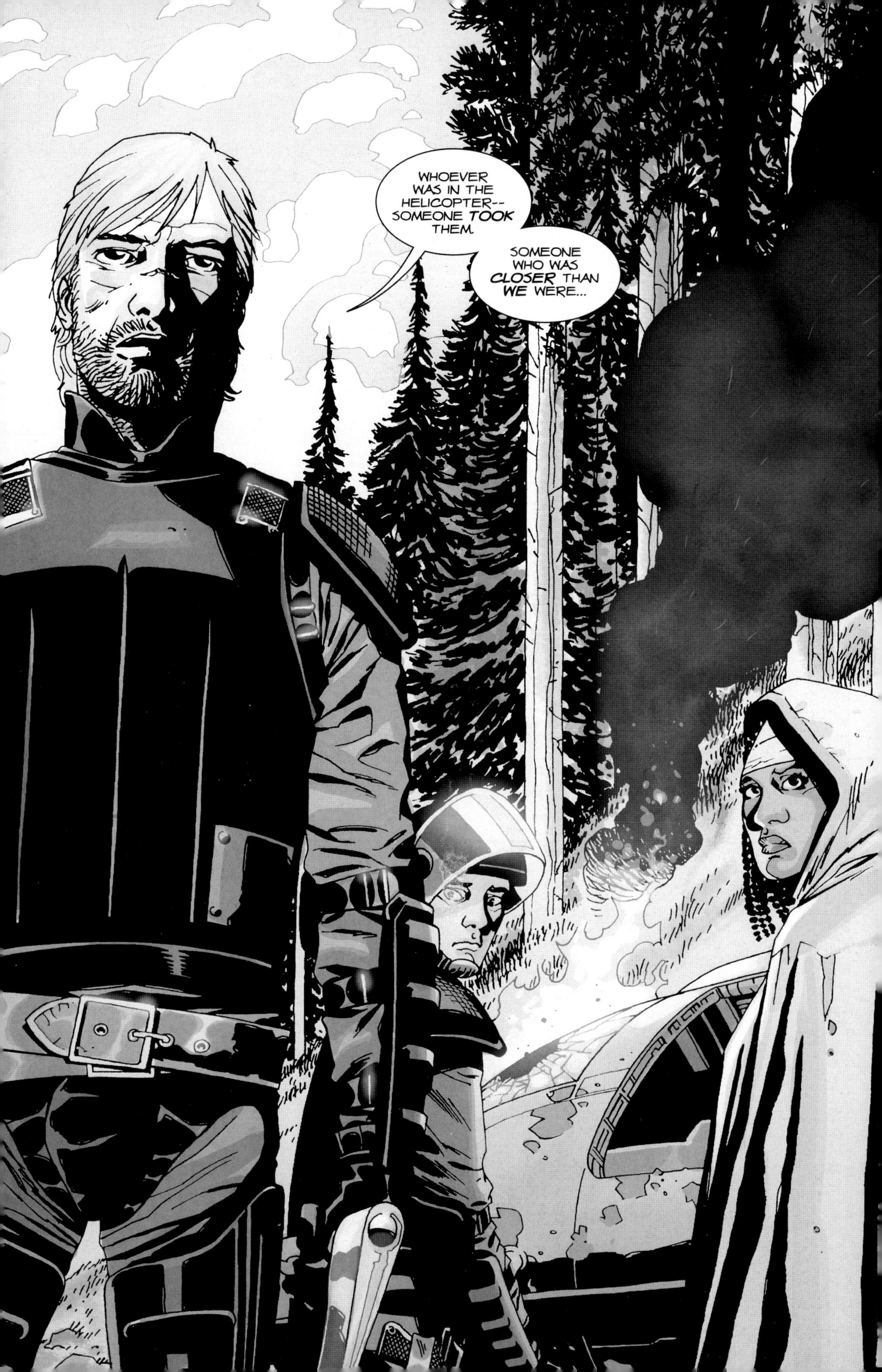
WHOEVER WAS IN THE HELICOPTER-- SOMEONE TOOK THEM.
SOMEONE WHO WAS CLOSER THAN WE WERE...

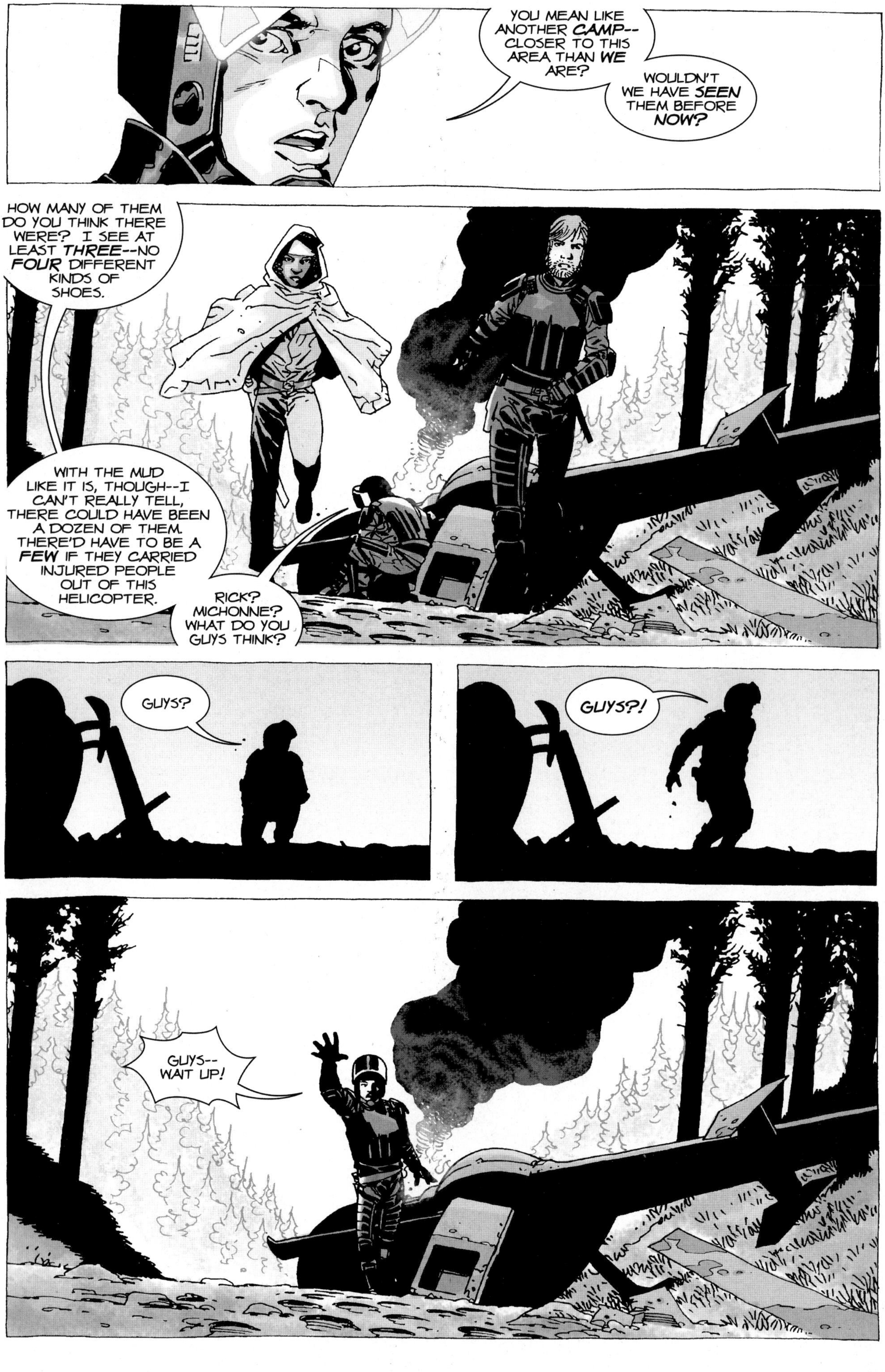

YOU MEAN LIKE ANOTHER CAMP-- CLOSER TO THIS AREA THAN WE ARE?
WOULDN'T WE HAVE SEEN THEM BEFORE NOW?
HOW MANY OF THEM DO YOU THINK THERE WERE? I SEE AT LEAST THREE--NO FOUR DIFFERENT KINDS OF SHOES.
WITH THE MUD LIKE IT IS, THOUGH--I CAN'T REALLY TELL, THERE COULD HAVE BEEN A DOZEN OF THEM. THERE'D HAVE TO BE A FEW IF THEY CARRIED INJURED PEOPLE OUT OF THIS HELICOPTER.
RICK? MICHONNE? WHAT DO YOU GUYS THINK?
GUYS?
GUYS?!
GUYS-- WAIT UP!

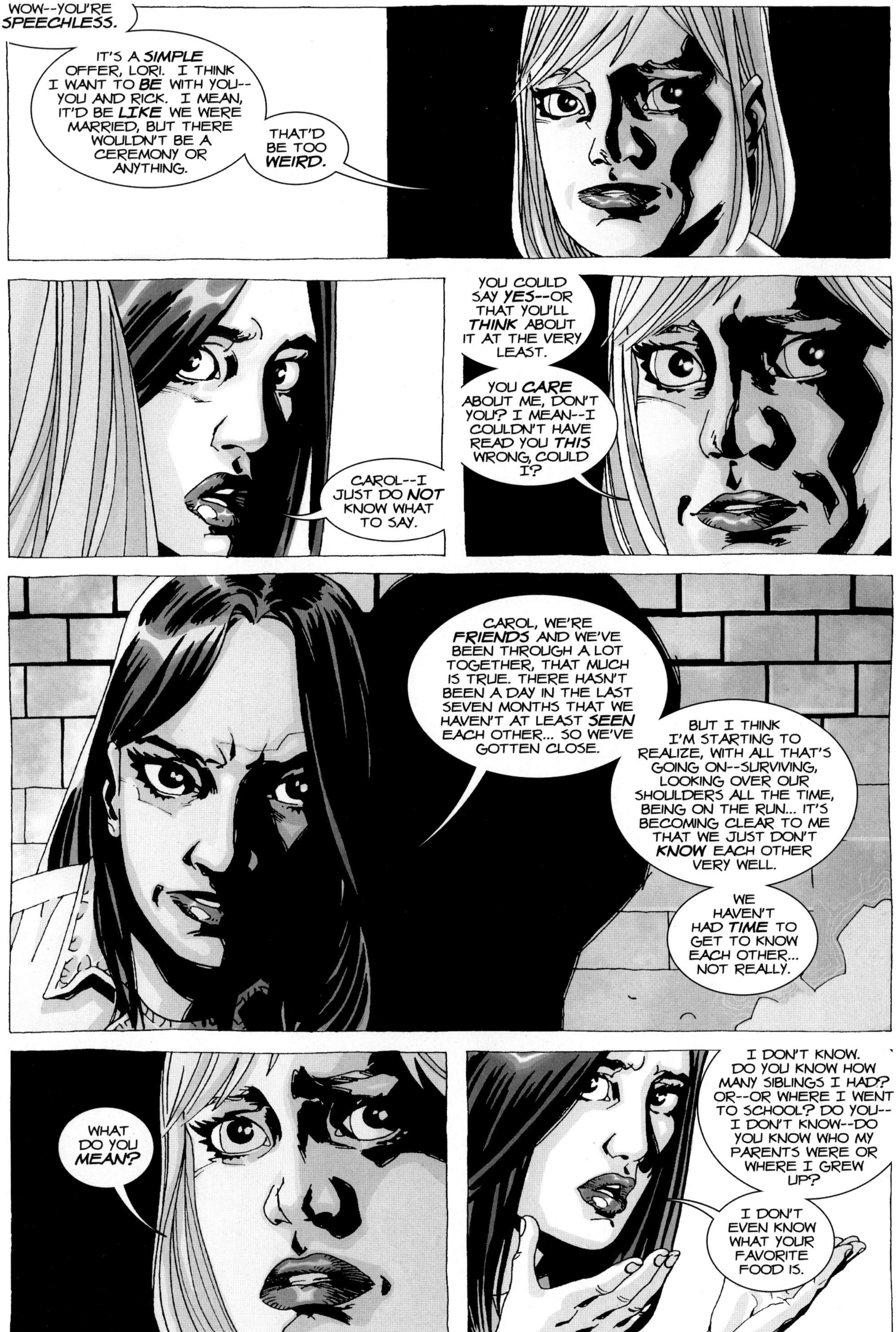
WOW--YOU'RE SPEECHLESS.
IT'S A SIMPLE OFFER, LORI. I THINK I WANT TO BE WITH YOU-- YOU AND RICK. I MEAN, IT'D BE LIKE WE WERE MARRIED, BUT THERE WOULDN'T BE A CEREMONY OR ANYTHING.
THAT'D BE TOO WEIRD.
CAROL--I JUST DO NOT KNOW WHAT TO SAY.
YOU COULD SAY YES--OR THAT YOU'LL THINK ABOUT IT AT THE VERY LEAST.
YOU CARE ABOUT ME, DON'T YOU? I MEAN--I COULDN'T HAVE READ YOU THIS WRONG, COULD I?
CAROL, WE'RE FRIENDS AND WE'VE BEEN THROUGH A LOT TOGETHER, THAT MUCH IS TRUE. THERE HASN'T BEEN A DAY IN THE LAST SEVEN MONTHS THAT WE HAVEN'T AT LEAST SEEN EACH OTHER... SO WE'VE GOTTEN CLOSE.
BUT I THINK I'M STARTING TO REALIZE, WITH ALL THAT'S GOING ON--SURVIVING, LOOKING OVER OUR SHOULDERS ALL THE TIME, BEING ON THE RUN... IT'S BECOMING CLEAR TO ME THAT WE JUST DON'T KNOW EACH OTHER VERY WELL.
WE HAVEN'T HAD TIME TO GET TO KNOW EACH OTHER... NOT REALLY.
WHAT DO YOU MEAN?
I DON'T KNOW. DO YOU KNOW HOW MANY SIBLINGS I HAD? OR--OR WHERE I WENT TO SCHOOL? DO YOU-- I DON'T KNOW--DO YOU KNOW WHO MY PARENTS WERE OR WHERE I GREW UP?
I DON'T EVEN KNOW WHAT YOUR FAVORITE FOOD IS.

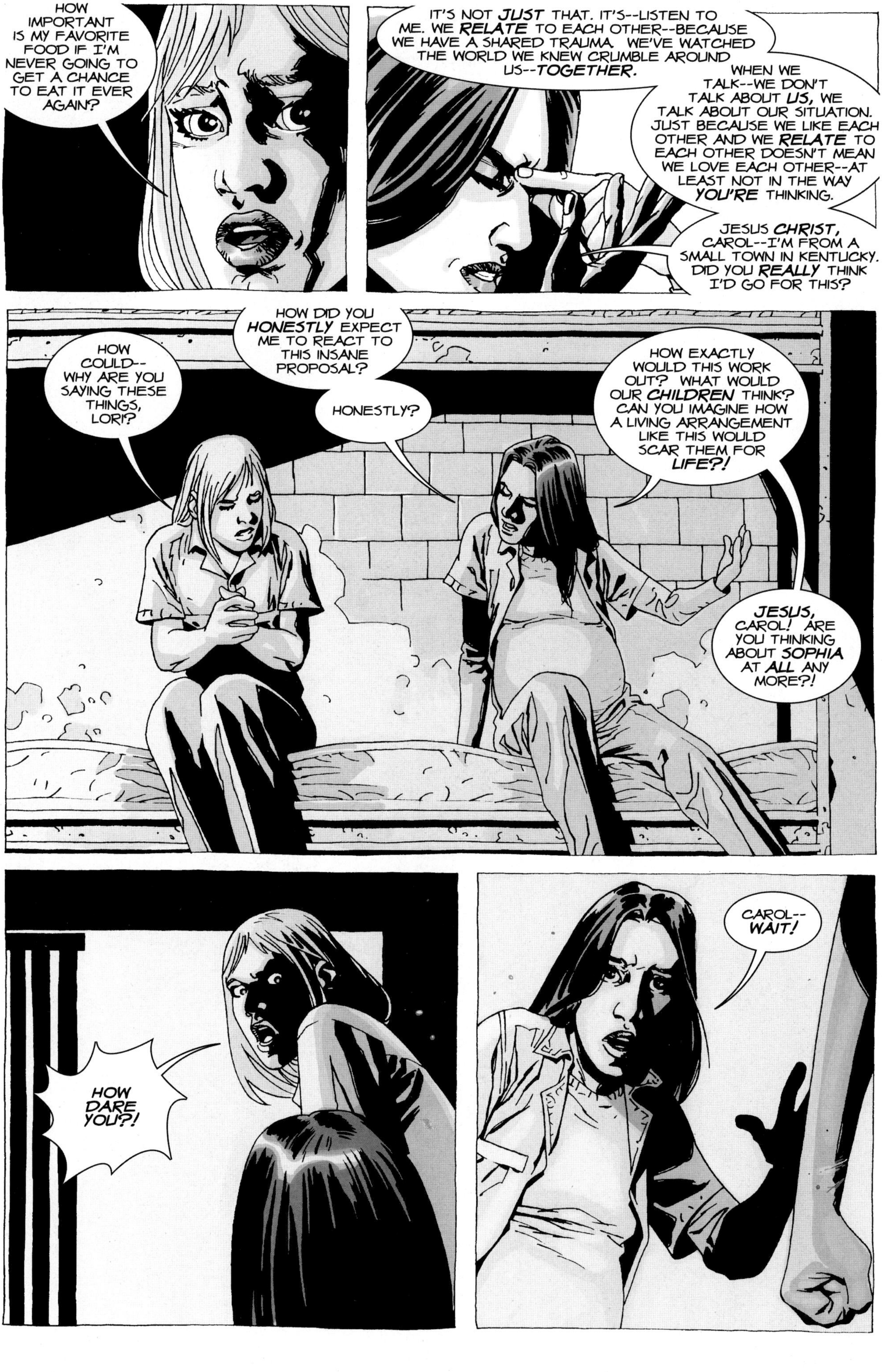
HOW IMPORTANT IS MY FAVORITE FOOD IF I'M NEVER GOING TO GET A CHANCE TO EAT IT EVER AGAIN?
IT'S NOT JUST THAT. IT'S--LISTEN TO ME. WE RELATE TO EACH OTHER--BECAUSE WE HAVE A SHARED TRAUMA. WE'VE WATCHED THE WORLD WE KNEW CRUMBLE AROUND US--TOGETHER.
WHEN WE TALK--WE DON'T TALK ABOUT US, WE TALK ABOUT OUR SITUATION. JUST BECAUSE WE LIKE EACH OTHER AND WE RELATE TO EACH OTHER DOESN'T MEAN WE LOVE EACH OTHER--AT LEAST NOT IN THE WAY YOU'RE THINKING.
JESUS CHRIST, CAROL--I'M FROM A SMALL TOWN IN KENTUCKY. DID YOU REALLY THINK I'D GO FOR THIS?
HOW COULD-- WHY ARE YOU SAYING THESE THINGS, LORI?
HOW DID YOU HONESTLY EXPECT ME TO REACT TO THIS INSANE PROPOSAL?
HONESTLY?
HOW EXACTLY WOULD THIS WORK OUT? WHAT WOULD OUR CHILDREN THINK? CAN YOU IMAGINE HOW A LIVING ARRANGEMENT LIKE THIS WOULD SCAR THEM FOR LIFE?!
JESUS, CAROL! ARE YOU THINKING ABOUT SOPHIA AT ALL ANY MORE?!
HOW DARE YOU?!
CAROL-- WAIT!

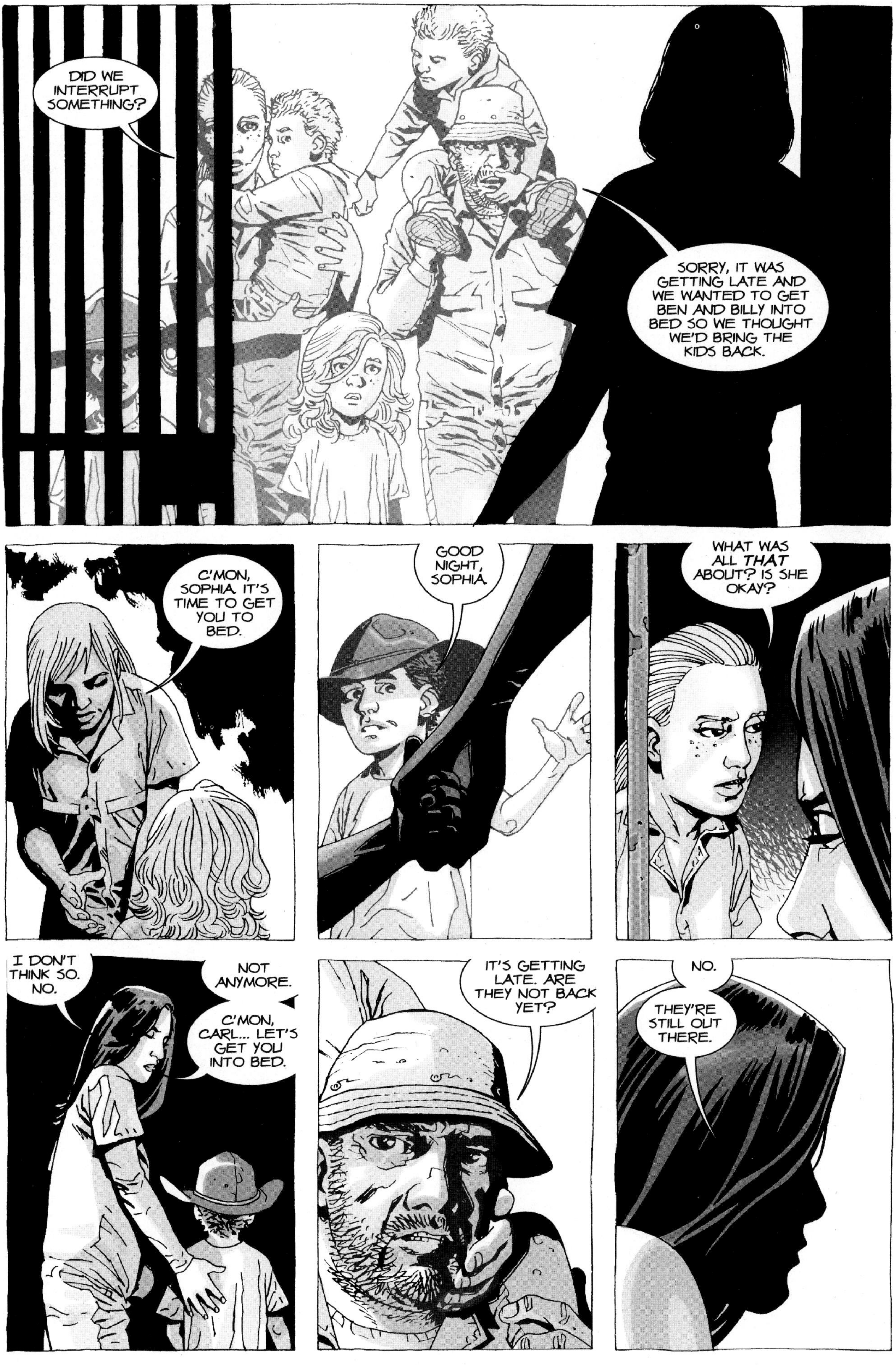
DID WE INTERRUPT SOMETHING?
SORRY, IT WAS GETTING LATE AND WE WANTED TO GET BEN AND BILLY INTO BED SO WE THOUGHT WE'D BRING THE KIDS BACK.
C'MON, SOPHIA. IT'S TIME TO GET YOU TO BED.
GOOD NIGHT, SOPHIA.
WHAT WAS ALL *THAT* ABOUT? IS SHE OKAY?
I DON'T THINK SO. NO.
NOT ANYMORE.
C'MON, CARL... LET'S GET YOU INTO BED.
IT'S GETTING LATE. ARE THEY NOT BACK YET?
NO.
THEY'RE STILL OUT THERE.

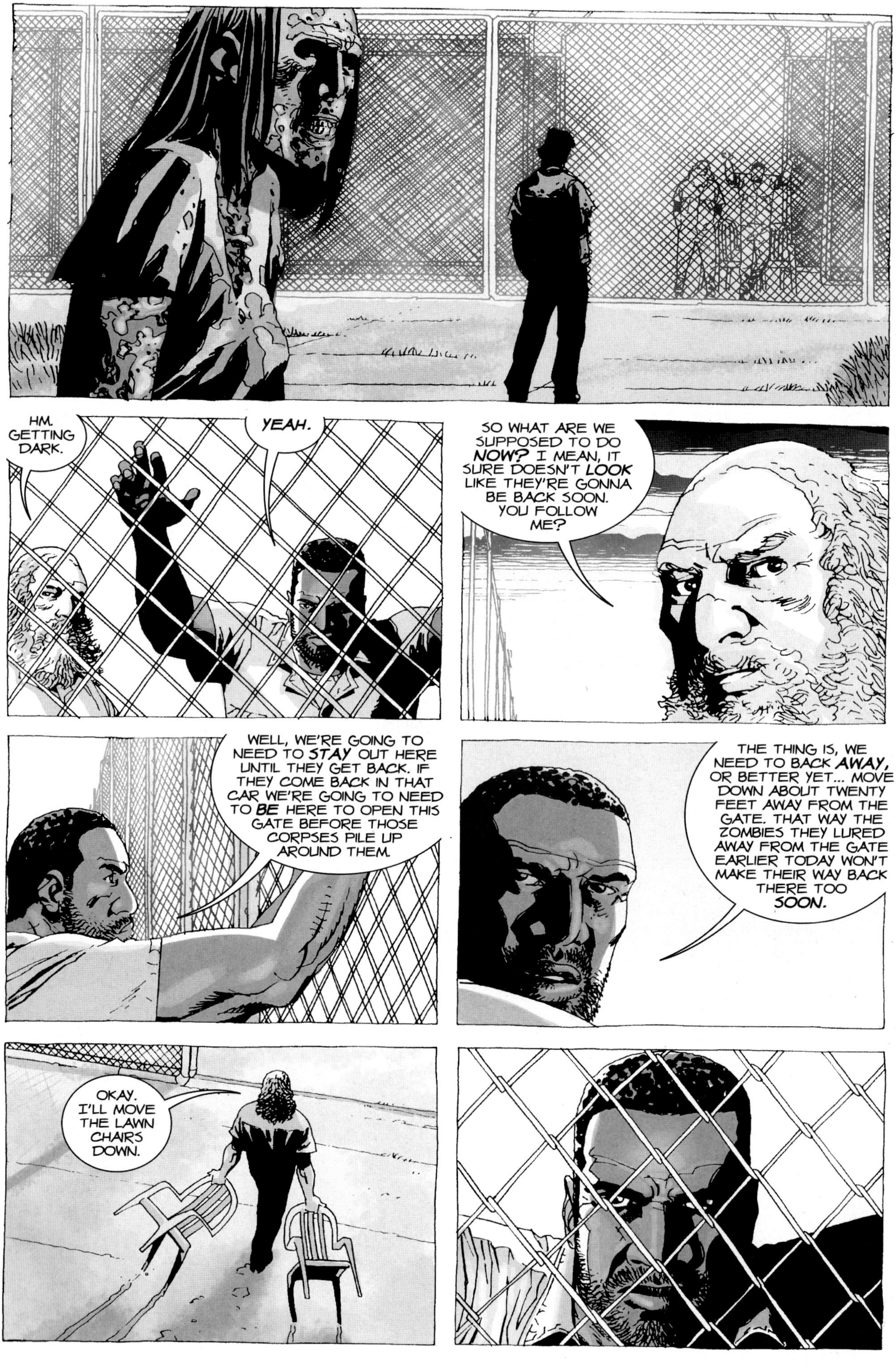
HM. GETTING DARK.
YEAH.
SO WHAT ARE WE SUPPOSED TO DO NOW? I MEAN, IT SURE DOESN'T LOOK LIKE THEY'RE GONNA BE BACK SOON. YOU FOLLOW ME?
WELL, WE'RE GOING TO NEED TO STAY OUT HERE UNTIL THEY GET BACK. IF THEY COME BACK IN THAT CAR WE'RE GOING TO NEED TO BE HERE TO OPEN THIS GATE BEFORE THOSE CORPSES PILE UP AROUND THEM.
THE THING IS, WE NEED TO BACK AWAY, OR BETTER YET... MOVE DOWN ABOUT TWENTY FEET AWAY FROM THE GATE. THAT WAY THE ZOMBIES THEY LURED AWAY FROM THE GATE EARLIER TODAY WON'T MAKE THEIR WAY BACK THERE TOO SOON.
OKAY. I'LL MOVE THE LAWN CHAIRS DOWN.

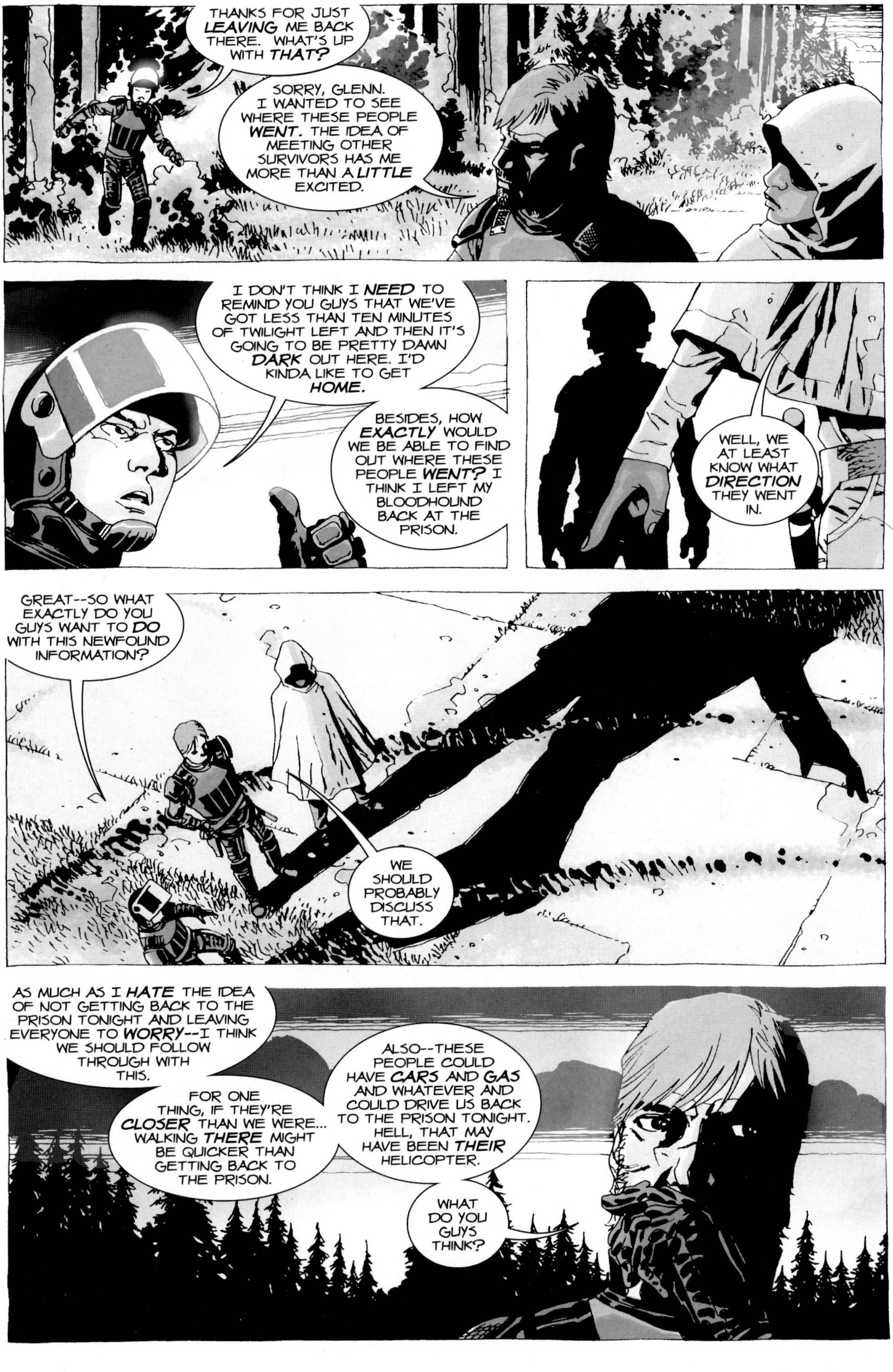
THANKS FOR JUST LEAVING ME BACK THERE. WHAT'S UP WITH THAT?
SORRY, GLENN. I WANTED TO SEE WHERE THESE PEOPLE WENT. THE IDEA OF MEETING OTHER SURVIVORS HAS ME MORE THAN A LITTLE EXCITED.
I DON'T THINK I NEED TO REMIND YOU GUYS THAT WE'VE GOT LESS THAN TEN MINUTES OF TWILIGHT LEFT AND THEN IT'S GOING TO BE PRETTY DAMN DARK OUT HERE. I'D KINDA LIKE TO GET HOME.
BESIDES, HOW EXACTLY WOULD WE BE ABLE TO FIND OUT WHERE THESE PEOPLE WENT? I THINK I LEFT MY BLOODHOUND BACK AT THE PRISON.
WELL, WE AT LEAST KNOW WHAT DIRECTION THEY WENT IN.
GREAT--SO WHAT EXACTLY DO YOU GUYS WANT TO DO WITH THIS NEWFOUND INFORMATION?
WE SHOULD PROBABLY DISCUSS THAT.
AS MUCH AS I HATE THE IDEA OF NOT GETTING BACK TO THE PRISON TONIGHT AND LEAVING EVERYONE TO WORRY--I THINK WE SHOULD FOLLOW THROUGH WITH THIS.
FOR ONE THING, IF THEY'RE CLOSER THAN WE WERE... WALKING THERE MIGHT BE QUICKER THAN GETTING BACK TO THE PRISON.
ALSO--THESE PEOPLE COULD HAVE CARS AND GAS AND WHATEVER AND COULD DRIVE US BACK TO THE PRISON TONIGHT. HELL, THAT MAY HAVE BEEN THEIR HELICOPTER.
WHAT DO YOU GUYS THINK?

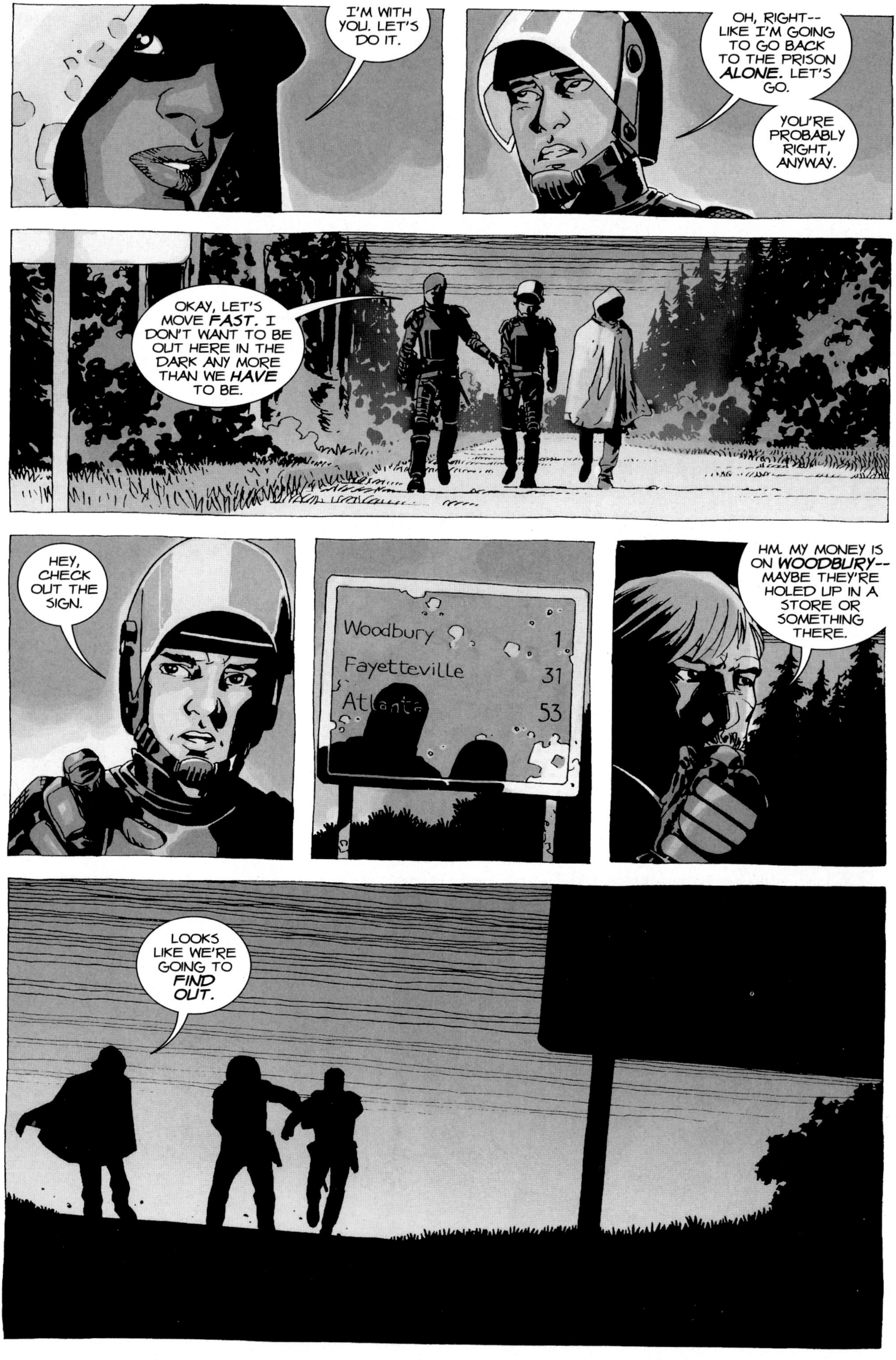
I'M WITH YOU. LET'S DO IT.
OH, RIGHT-- LIKE I'M GOING TO GO BACK TO THE PRISON ALONE. LET'S GO.
YOU'RE PROBABLY RIGHT, ANYWAY.
OKAY, LET'S MOVE FAST. I DON'T WANT TO BE OUT HERE IN THE DARK ANY MORE THAN WE HAVE TO BE.
HEY, CHECK OUT THE SIGN.
Woodbury 1
Fayetteville 31
Atlanta 53
HM. MY MONEY IS ON WOODBURY-- MAYBE THEY'RE HOLED UP IN A STORE OR SOMETHING THERE.
LOOKS LIKE WE'RE GOING TO FIND OUT.

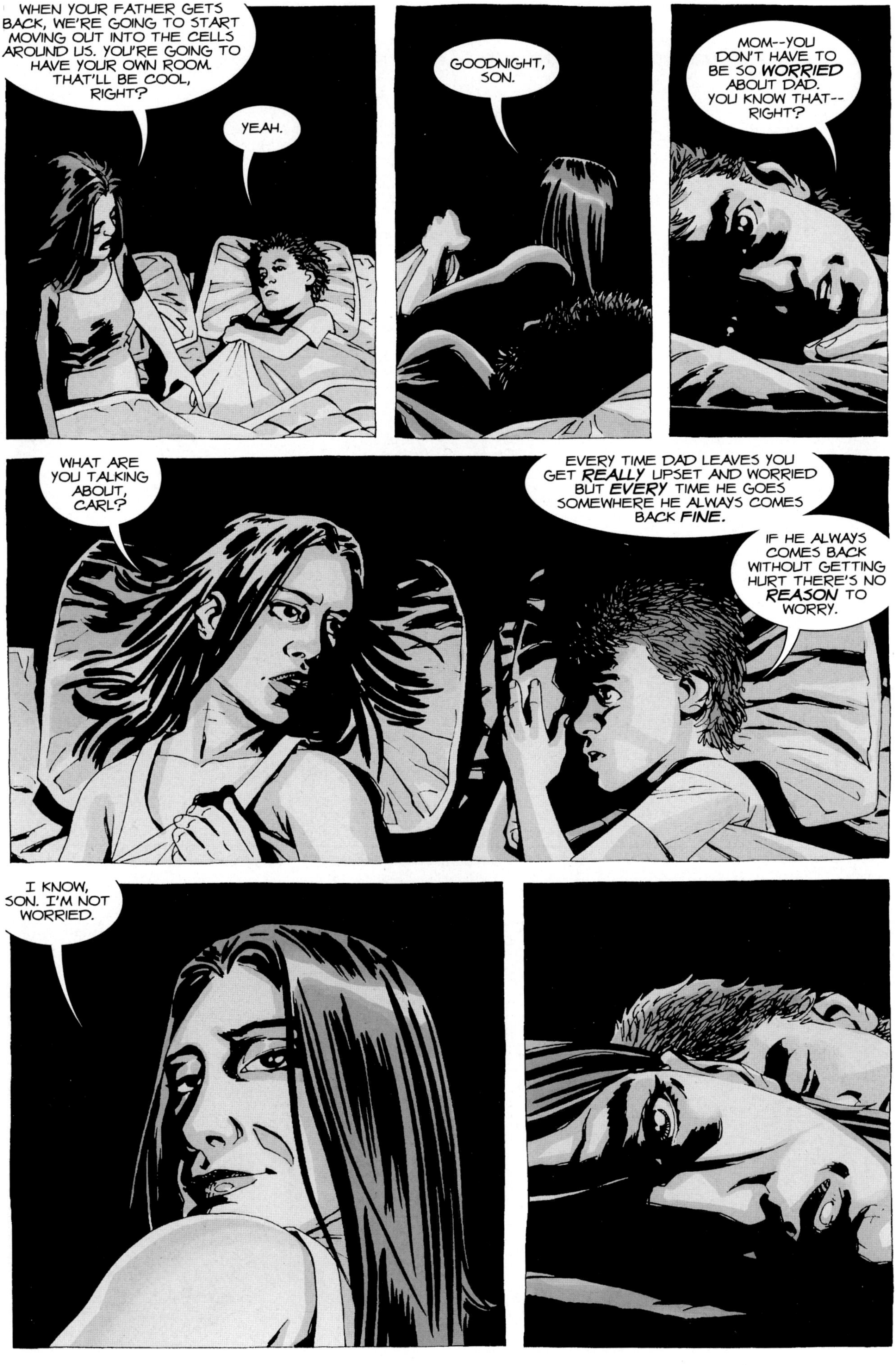
WHEN YOUR FATHER GETS BACK, WE'RE GOING TO START MOVING OUT INTO THE CELLS AROUND US. YOU'RE GOING TO HAVE YOUR OWN ROOM. THAT'LL BE COOL, RIGHT?
YEAH.
GOODNIGHT, SON.
MOM--YOU DON'T HAVE TO BE SO WORRIED ABOUT DAD. YOU KNOW THAT--RIGHT?
WHAT ARE YOU TALKING ABOUT, CARL?
EVERY TIME DAD LEAVES YOU GET REALLY UPSET AND WORRIED BUT EVERY TIME HE GOES SOMEWHERE HE ALWAYS COMES BACK FINE.
IF HE ALWAYS COMES BACK WITHOUT GETTING HURT THERE'S NO REASON TO WORRY.
I KNOW, SON. I'M NOT WORRIED.

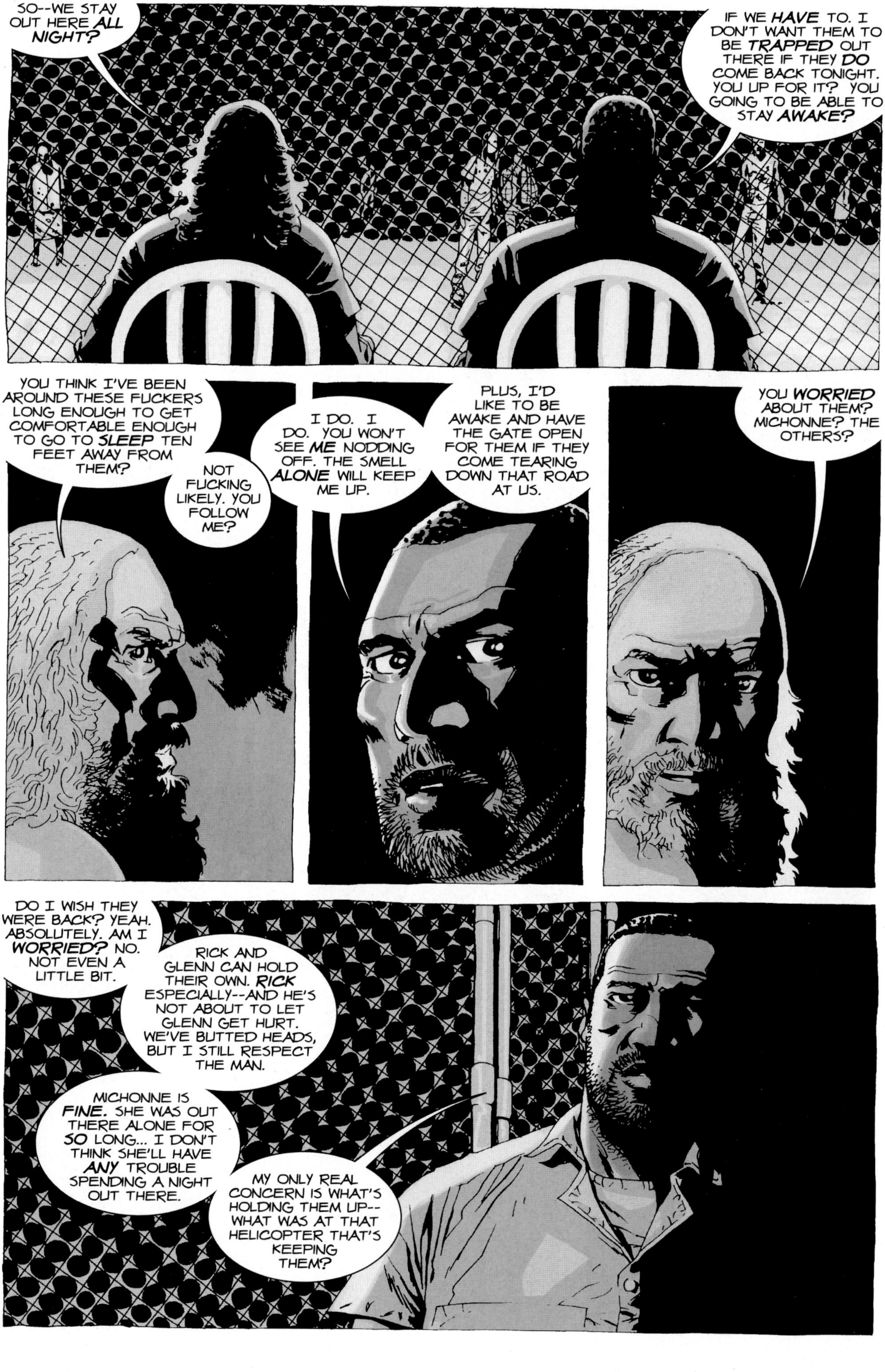
SO--WE STAY OUT HERE ALL NIGHT?
IF WE HAVE TO. I DON'T WANT THEM TO BE TRAPPED OUT THERE IF THEY DO COME BACK TONIGHT. YOU UP FOR IT? YOU GOING TO BE ABLE TO STAY AWAKE?
YOU THINK I'VE BEEN AROUND THESE FUCKERS LONG ENOUGH TO GET COMFORTABLE ENOUGH TO GO TO SLEEP TEN FEET AWAY FROM THEM?
NOT FUCKING LIKELY. YOU FOLLOW ME?
I DO. I DO. YOU WON'T SEE ME NODDING OFF. THE SMELL ALONE WILL KEEP ME UP.
PLUS, I'D LIKE TO BE AWAKE AND HAVE THE GATE OPEN FOR THEM IF THEY COME TEARING DOWN THAT ROAD AT US.
YOU WORRIED ABOUT THEM? MICHONNE? THE OTHERS?
DO I WISH THEY WERE BACK? YEAH. ABSOLUTELY. AM I WORRIED? NO. NOT EVEN A LITTLE BIT.
RICK AND GLENN CAN HOLD THEIR OWN. RICK ESPECIALLY--AND HE'S NOT ABOUT TO LET GLENN GET HURT. WE'VE BUTTED HEADS, BUT I STILL RESPECT THE MAN.
MICHONNE IS FINE. SHE WAS OUT THERE ALONE FOR SO LONG... I DON'T THINK SHE'LL HAVE ANY TROUBLE SPENDING A NIGHT OUT THERE.
MY ONLY REAL CONCERN IS WHAT'S HOLDING THEM UP-- WHAT WAS AT THAT HELICOPTER THAT'S KEEPING THEM?

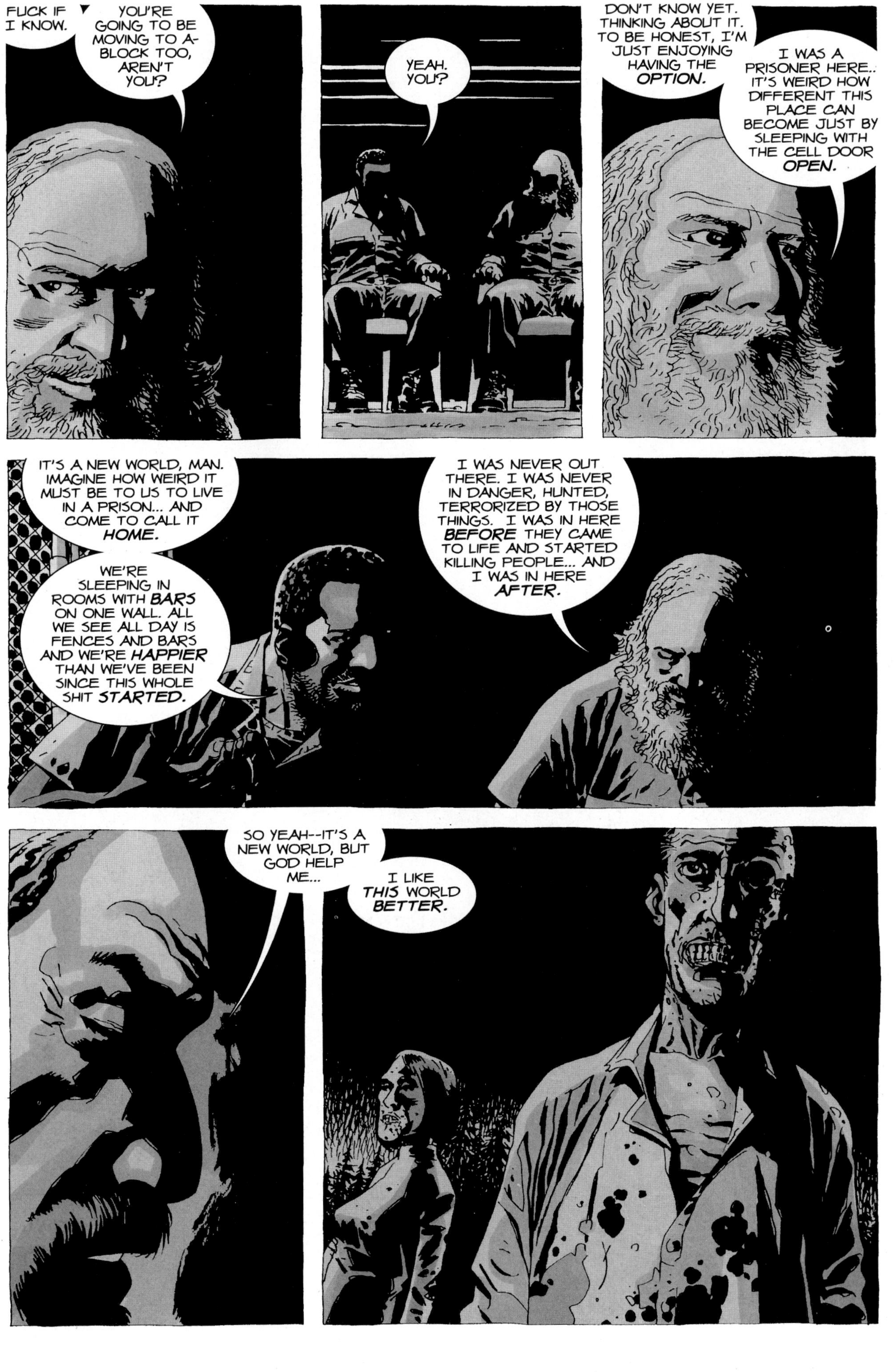
FUCK IF I KNOW.
YOU'RE GOING TO BE MOVING TO A-BLOCK TOO, AREN'T YOU?
YEAH. YOU?
DON'T KNOW YET. THINKING ABOUT IT. TO BE HONEST, I'M JUST ENJOYING HAVING THE OPTION.
I WAS A PRISONER HERE.. IT'S WEIRD HOW DIFFERENT THIS PLACE CAN BECOME JUST BY SLEEPING WITH THE CELL DOOR OPEN.
IT'S A NEW WORLD, MAN. IMAGINE HOW WEIRD IT MUST BE TO US TO LIVE IN A PRISON... AND COME TO CALL IT HOME.
WE'RE SLEEPING IN ROOMS WITH BARS ON ONE WALL. ALL WE SEE ALL DAY IS FENCES AND BARS AND WE'RE HAPPIER THAN WE'VE BEEN SINCE THIS WHOLE SHIT STARTED.
I WAS NEVER OUT THERE. I WAS NEVER IN DANGER, HUNTED, TERRORIZED BY THOSE THINGS. I WAS IN HERE BEFORE THEY CAME TO LIFE AND STARTED KILLING PEOPLE... AND I WAS IN HERE AFTER.
SO YEAH--IT'S A NEW WORLD, BUT GOD HELP ME...
I LIKE THIS WORLD BETTER.

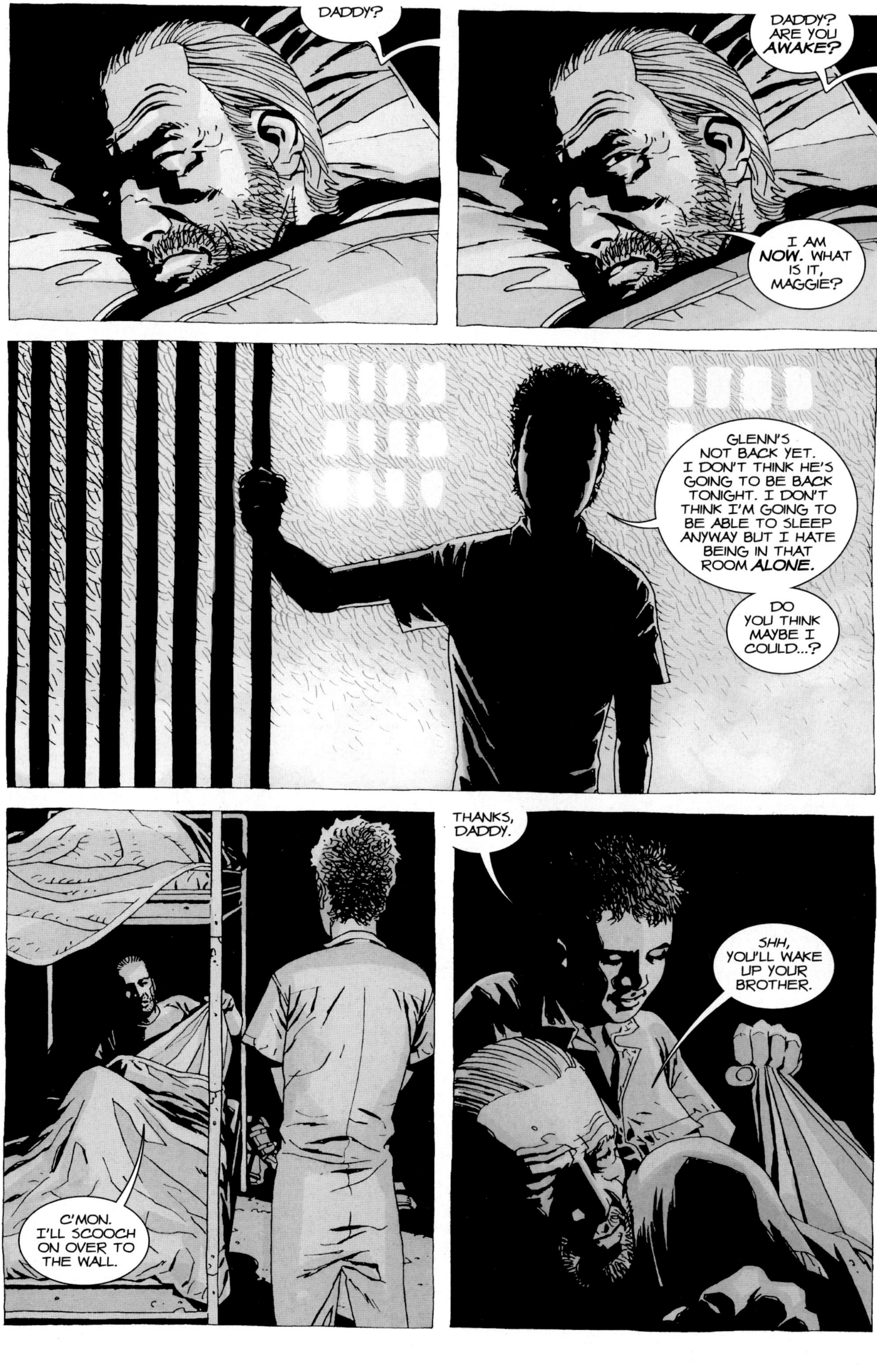
DADDY?
DADDY? ARE YOU AWAKE?
I AM NOW. WHAT IS IT, MAGGIE?
GLENN'S NOT BACK YET. I DON'T THINK HE'S GOING TO BE BACK TONIGHT. I DON'T THINK I'M GOING TO BE ABLE TO SLEEP ANYWAY BUT I HATE BEING IN THAT ROOM ALONE.
DO YOU THINK MAYBE I COULD...?
C'MON. I'LL SCOOCH ON OVER TO THE WALL.
THANKS, DADDY.
SHH, YOU'LL WAKE UP YOUR BROTHER.

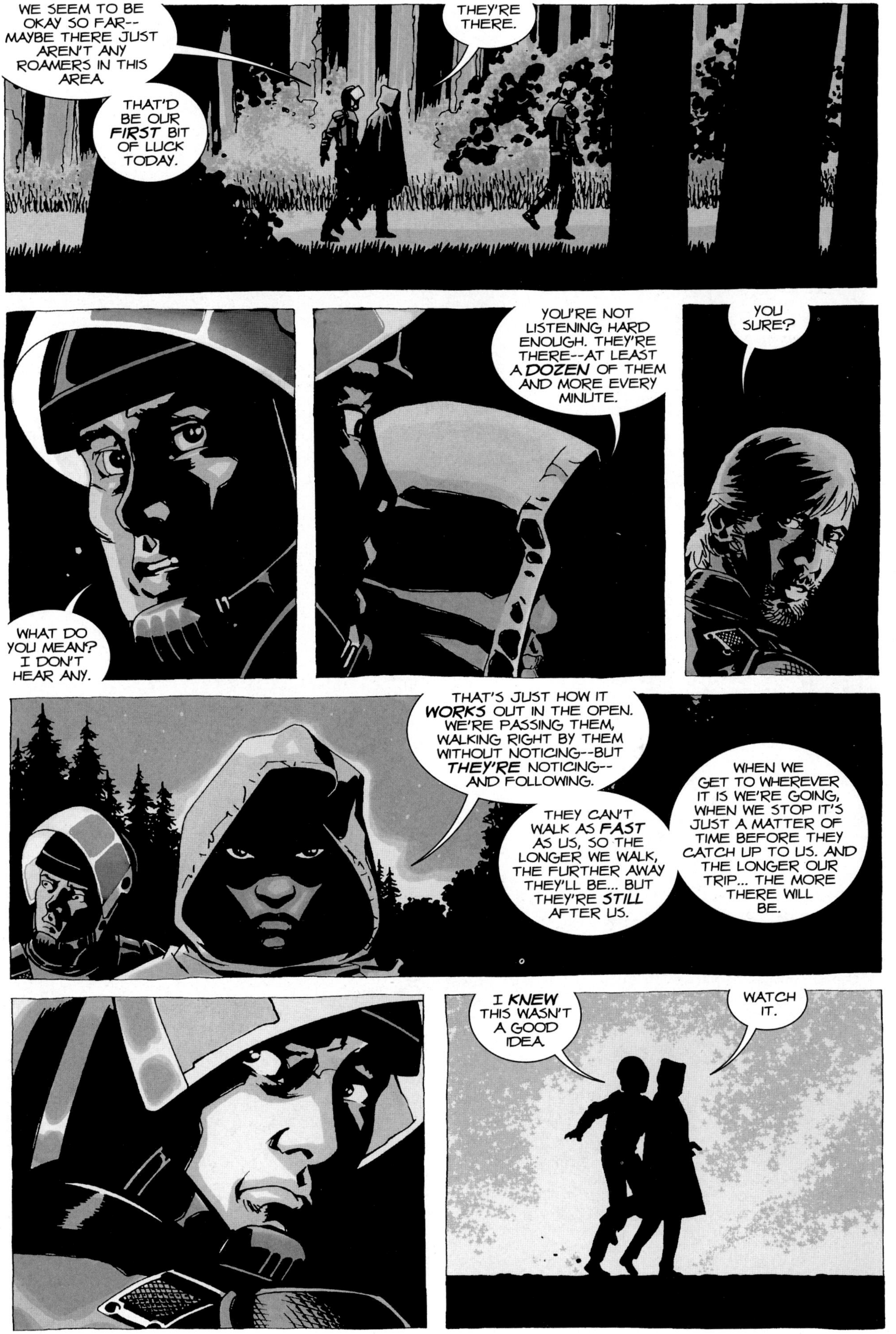
WE SEEM TO BE OKAY SO FAR-- MAYBE THERE JUST AREN'T ANY ROAMERS IN THIS AREA.
THAT'D BE OUR FIRST BIT OF LUCK TODAY.
THEY'RE THERE.
WHAT DO YOU MEAN? I DON'T HEAR ANY.
YOU'RE NOT LISTENING HARD ENOUGH. THEY'RE THERE--AT LEAST A DOZEN OF THEM AND MORE EVERY MINUTE.
YOU SURE?
THAT'S JUST HOW IT WORKS OUT IN THE OPEN. WE'RE PASSING THEM, WALKING RIGHT BY THEM WITHOUT NOTICING--BUT THEY'RE NOTICING-- AND FOLLOWING.
THEY CAN'T WALK AS FAST AS US, SO THE LONGER WE WALK, THE FURTHER AWAY THEY'LL BE... BUT THEY'RE STILL AFTER US.
WHEN WE GET TO WHEREVER IT IS WE'RE GOING, WHEN WE STOP IT'S JUST A MATTER OF TIME BEFORE THEY CATCH UP TO US. AND THE LONGER OUR TRIP... THE MORE THERE WILL BE.
I KNEW THIS WASN'T A GOOD IDEA.
WATCH IT.

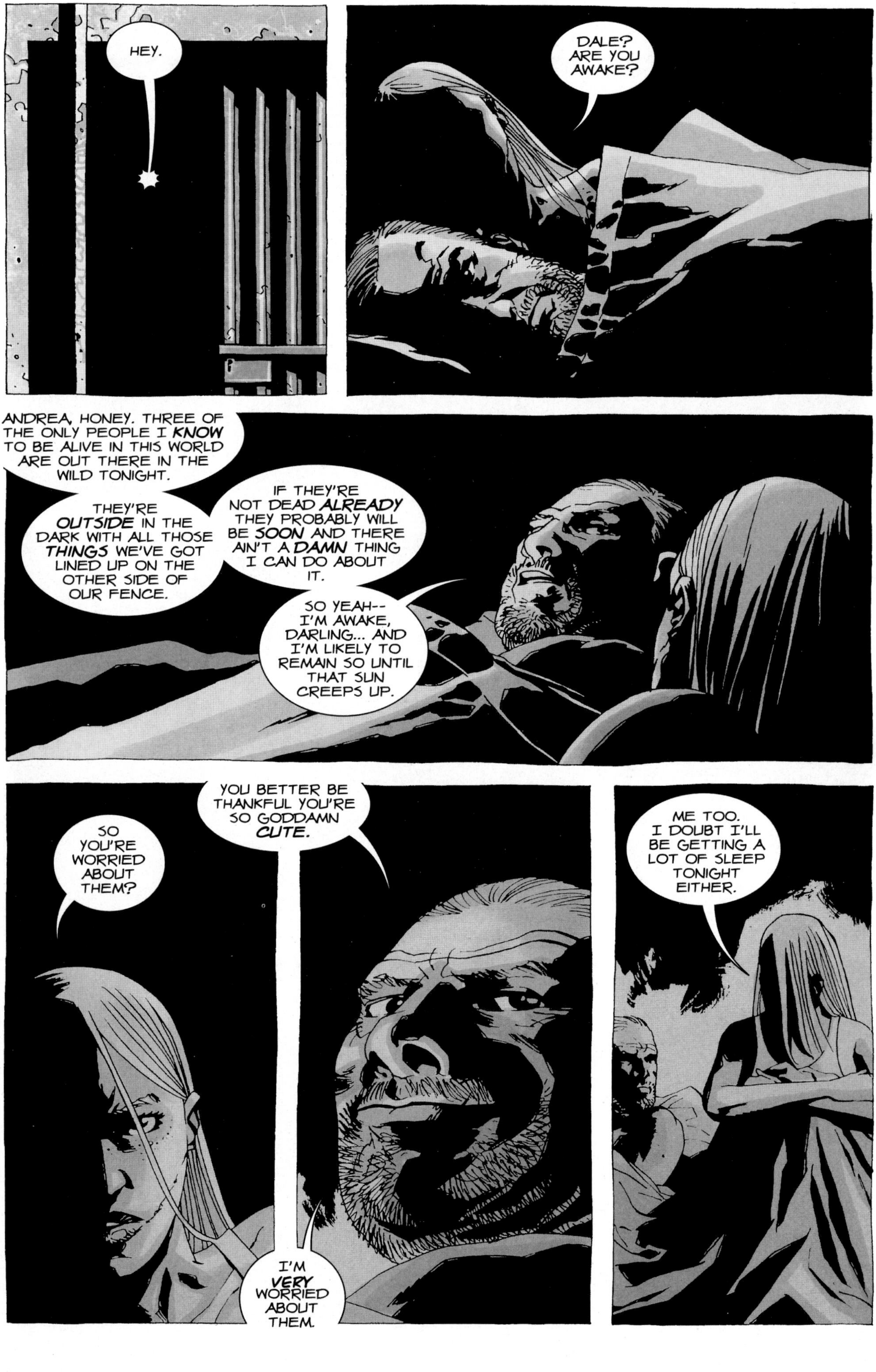
HEY.
DALE? ARE YOU AWAKE?
ANDREA, HONEY. THREE OF THE ONLY PEOPLE I KNOW TO BE ALIVE IN THIS WORLD ARE OUT THERE IN THE WILD TONIGHT.
THEY'RE OUTSIDE IN THE DARK WITH ALL THOSE THINGS WE'VE GOT LINED UP ON THE OTHER SIDE OF OUR FENCE.
IF THEY'RE NOT DEAD ALREADY THEY PROBABLY WILL BE SOON AND THERE AIN'T A DAMN THING I CAN DO ABOUT IT.
SO YEAH-- I'M AWAKE, DARLING... AND I'M LIKELY TO REMAIN SO UNTIL THAT SUN CREEPS UP.
SO YOU'RE WORRIED ABOUT THEM?
YOU BETTER BE THANKFUL YOU'RE SO GODDAMN CUTE.
I'M VERY WORRIED ABOUT THEM.
ME TOO. I DOUBT I'LL BE GETTING A LOT OF SLEEP TONIGHT EITHER.

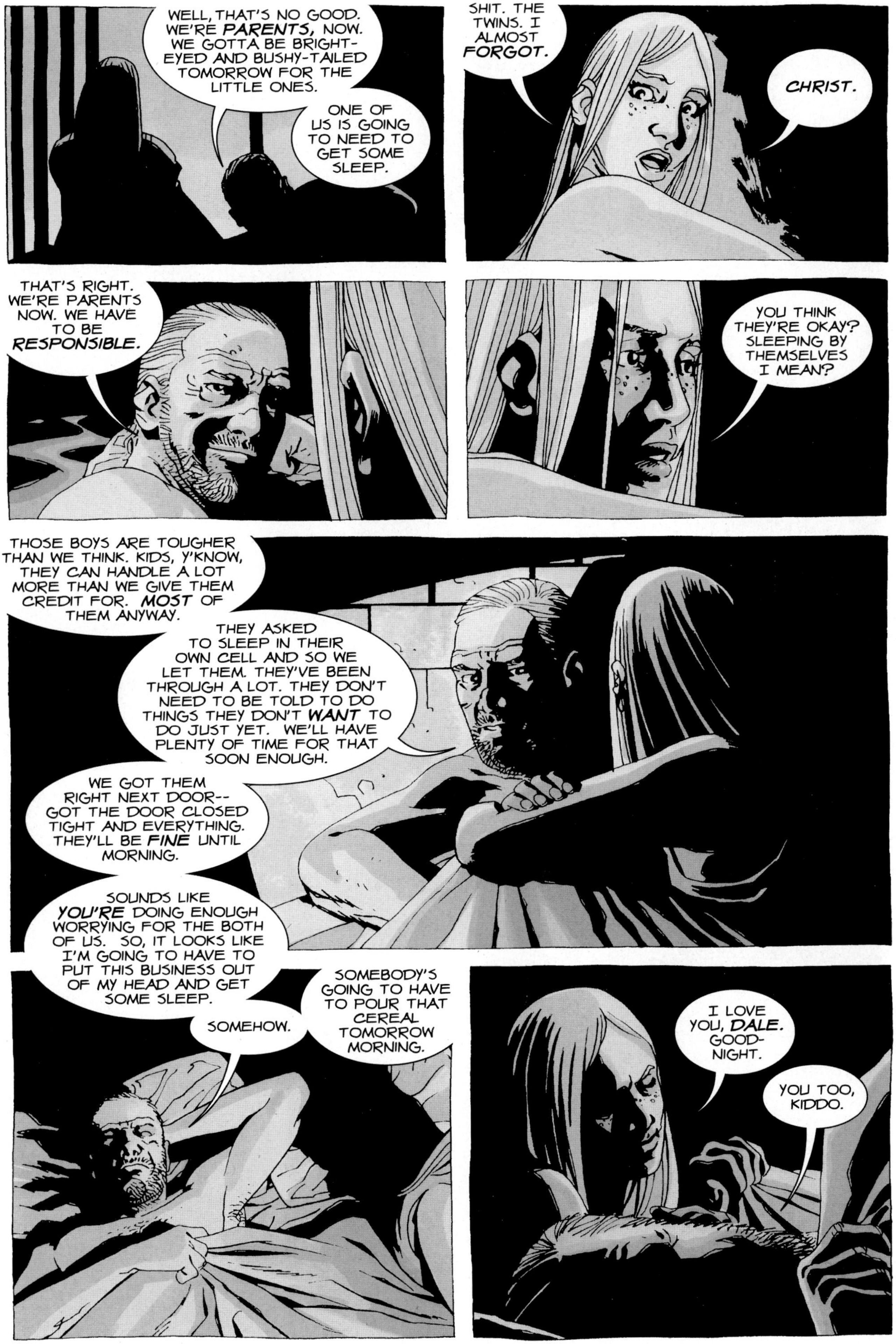
WELL, THAT'S NO GOOD. WE'RE PARENTS, NOW. WE GOTTA BE BRIGHT-EYED AND BUSHY-TAILED TOMORROW FOR THE LITTLE ONES.
ONE OF US IS GOING TO NEED TO GET SOME SLEEP.
SHIT. THE TWINS. I ALMOST FORGOT.
CHRIST.
THAT'S RIGHT. WE'RE PARENTS NOW. WE HAVE TO BE RESPONSIBLE.
YOU THINK THEY'RE OKAY? SLEEPING BY THEMSELVES I MEAN?
THOSE BOYS ARE TOUGHER THAN WE THINK. KIDS, Y'KNOW, THEY CAN HANDLE A LOT MORE THAN WE GIVE THEM CREDIT FOR. MOST OF THEM ANYWAY.
THEY ASKED TO SLEEP IN THEIR OWN CELL AND SO WE LET THEM. THEY'VE BEEN THROUGH A LOT. THEY DON'T NEED TO BE TOLD TO DO THINGS THEY DON'T WANT TO DO JUST YET. WE'LL HAVE PLENTY OF TIME FOR THAT SOON ENOUGH.
WE GOT THEM RIGHT NEXT DOOR-- GOT THE DOOR CLOSED TIGHT AND EVERYTHING. THEY'LL BE FINE UNTIL MORNING.
SOUNDS LIKE YOU'RE DOING ENOUGH WORRYING FOR THE BOTH OF US. SO, IT LOOKS LIKE I'M GOING TO HAVE TO PUT THIS BUSINESS OUT OF MY HEAD AND GET SOME SLEEP.
SOMEHOW.
SOMEBODY'S GOING TO HAVE TO POUR THAT CEREAL TOMORROW MORNING.
I LOVE YOU, DALE. GOOD-NIGHT.
YOU TOO, KIDDO.

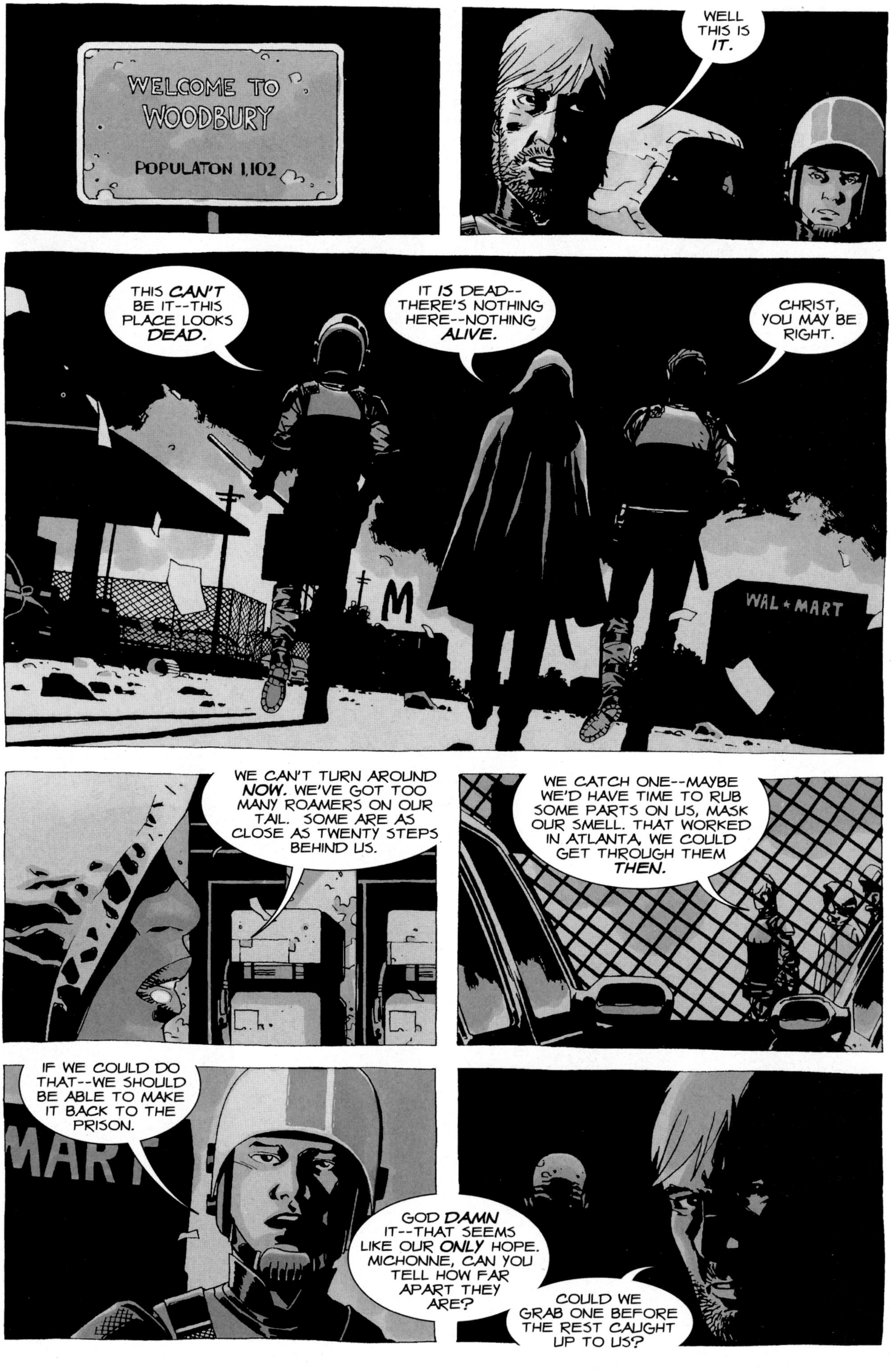

WELCOME TO WOODBURY
POPULATON 1,102
WELL THIS IS IT.
THIS CAN'T BE IT--THIS PLACE LOOKS DEAD.
IT IS DEAD-- THERE'S NOTHING HERE--NOTHING ALIVE.
CHRIST, YOU MAY BE RIGHT.
M
WAL★MART
WE CAN'T TURN AROUND NOW. WE'VE GOT TOO MANY ROAMERS ON OUR TAIL. SOME ARE AS CLOSE AS TWENTY STEPS BEHIND US.
WE CATCH ONE--MAYBE WE'D HAVE TIME TO RUB SOME PARTS ON US, MASK OUR SMELL. THAT WORKED IN ATLANTA, WE COULD GET THROUGH THEM THEN.
IF WE COULD DO THAT--WE SHOULD BE ABLE TO MAKE IT BACK TO THE PRISON.
MART
GOD DAMN IT--THAT SEEMS LIKE OUR ONLY HOPE. MICHONNE, CAN YOU TELL HOW FAR APART THEY ARE?
COULD WE GRAB ONE BEFORE THE REST CAUGHT UP TO US?

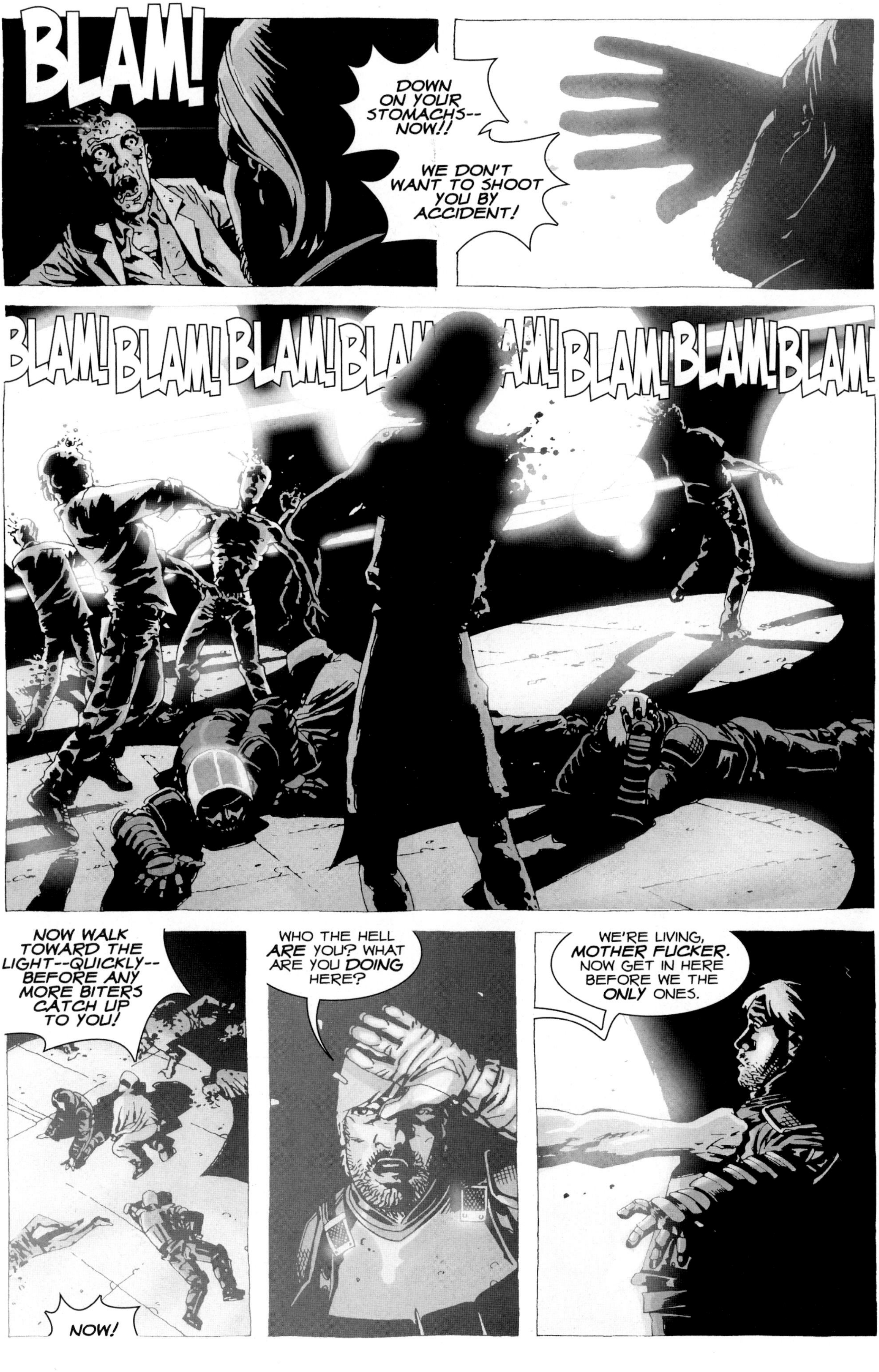
BLAM!
DOWN ON YOUR STOMACHS-- NOW!!
WE DON'T WANT TO SHOOT YOU BY ACCIDENT!
BLAM! BLAM! BLAM! BLAM! BLAM! BLAM! BLAM! BLAM!
NOW WALK TOWARD THE LIGHT--QUICKLY-- BEFORE ANY MORE BITERS CATCH UP TO YOU!
NOW!
WHO THE HELL ARE YOU? WHAT ARE YOU DOING HERE?
WE'RE LIVING, MOTHER FUCKER. NOW GET IN HERE BEFORE WE THE ONLY ONES.

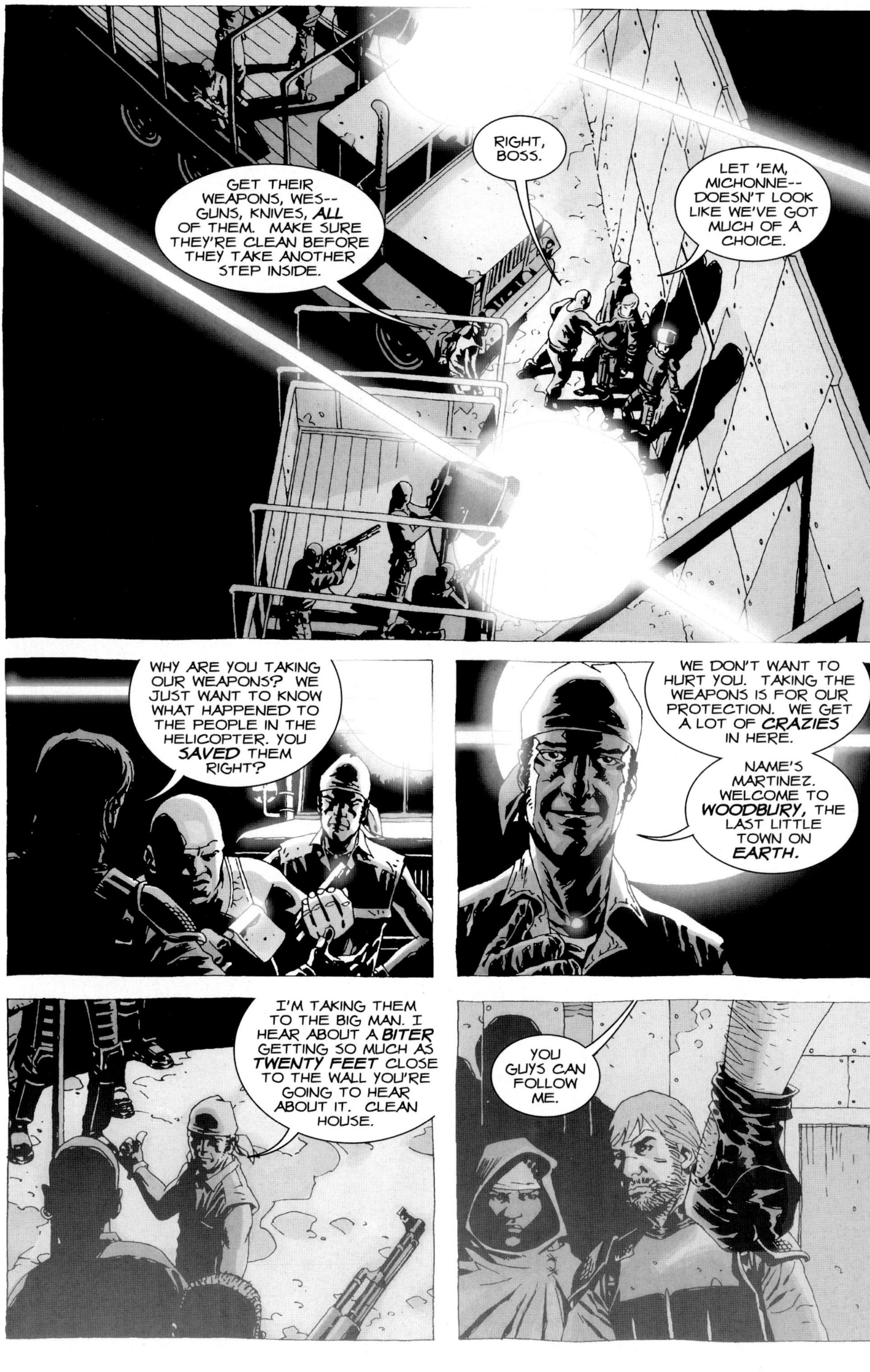
GET THEIR WEAPONS, WES-- GUNS, KNIVES, ALL OF THEM. MAKE SURE THEY'RE CLEAN BEFORE THEY TAKE ANOTHER STEP INSIDE.
RIGHT, BOSS.
LET 'EM, MICHONNE-- DOESN'T LOOK LIKE WE'VE GOT MUCH OF A CHOICE.
WHY ARE YOU TAKING OUR WEAPONS? WE JUST WANT TO KNOW WHAT HAPPENED TO THE PEOPLE IN THE HELICOPTER. YOU SAVED THEM RIGHT?
WE DON'T WANT TO HURT YOU. TAKING THE WEAPONS IS FOR OUR PROTECTION. WE GET A LOT OF CRAZIES IN HERE.
NAME'S MARTINEZ. WELCOME TO WOODBURY, THE LAST LITTLE TOWN ON EARTH.
I'M TAKING THEM TO THE BIG MAN. I HEAR ABOUT A BITER GETTING SO MUCH AS TWENTY FEET CLOSE TO THE WALL YOU'RE GOING TO HEAR ABOUT IT. CLEAN HOUSE.
YOU GUYS CAN FOLLOW ME.

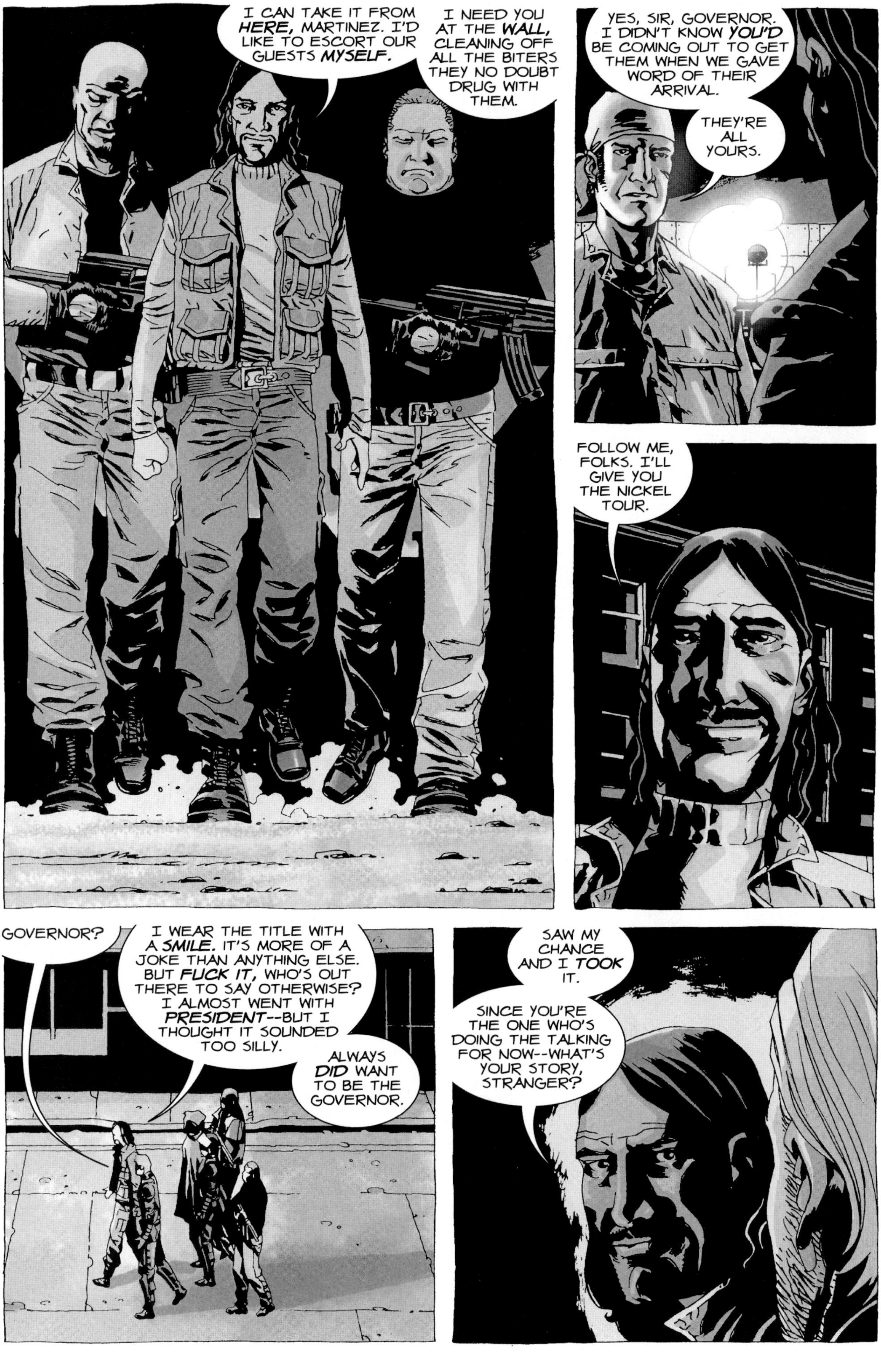
I CAN TAKE IT FROM HERE, MARTINEZ. I'D LIKE TO ESCORT OUR GUESTS MYSELF.
I NEED YOU AT THE WALL, CLEANING OFF ALL THE BITERS THEY NO DOUBT DRUG WITH THEM.
YES, SIR, GOVERNOR. I DIDN'T KNOW YOU'D BE COMING OUT TO GET THEM WHEN WE GAVE WORD OF THEIR ARRIVAL.
THEY'RE ALL YOURS.
FOLLOW ME, FOLKS. I'LL GIVE YOU THE NICKEL TOUR.
GOVERNOR?
I WEAR THE TITLE WITH A SMILE. IT'S MORE OF A JOKE THAN ANYTHING ELSE. BUT FUCK IT, WHO'S OUT THERE TO SAY OTHERWISE? I ALMOST WENT WITH PRESIDENT--BUT I THOUGHT IT SOUNDED TOO SILLY.
ALWAYS DID WANT TO BE THE GOVERNOR.
SAW MY CHANCE AND I TOOK IT.
SINCE YOU'RE THE ONE WHO'S DOING THE TALKING FOR NOW--WHAT'S YOUR STORY, STRANGER?

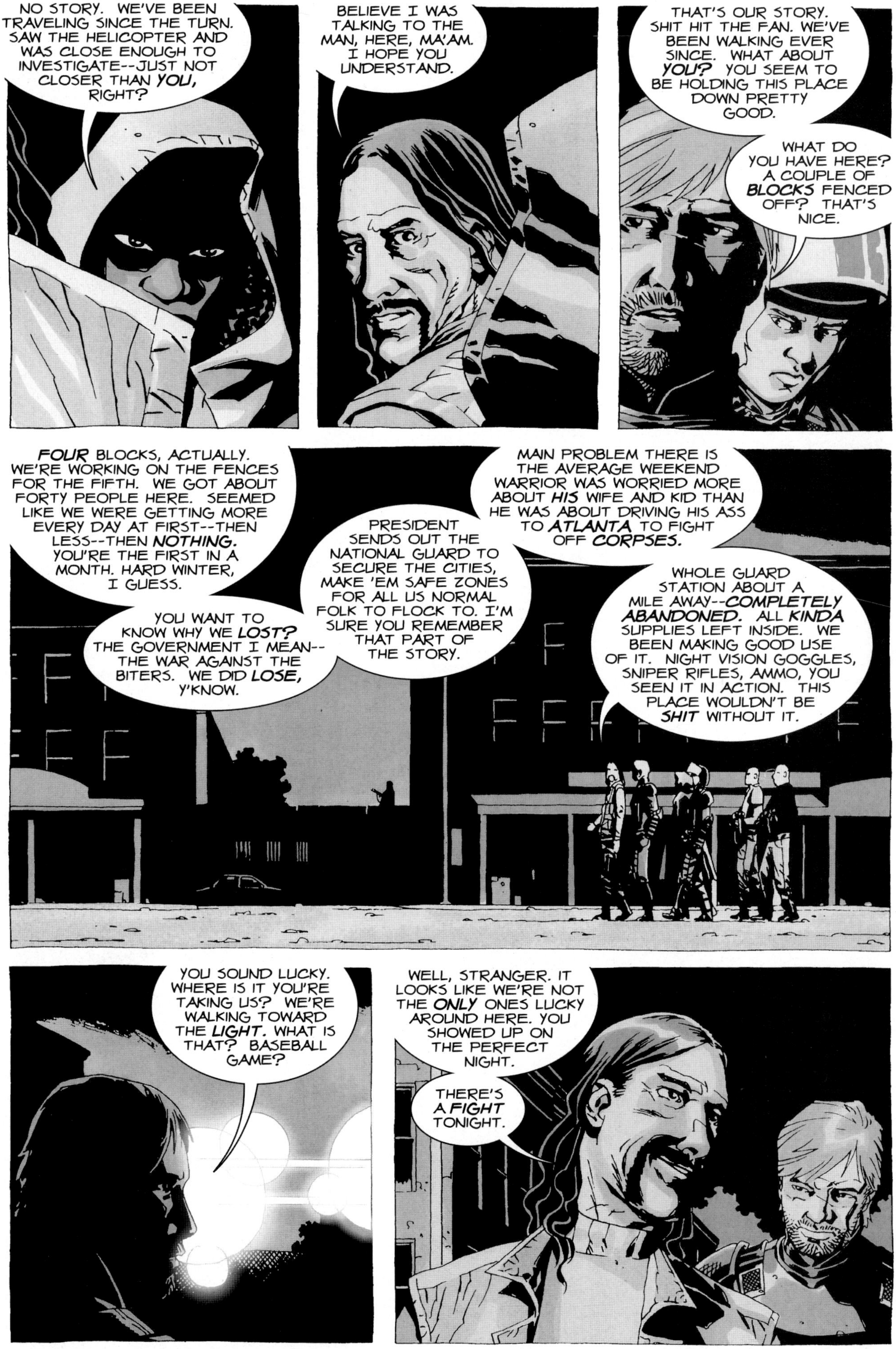
NO STORY. WE'VE BEEN TRAVELING SINCE THE TURN. SAW THE HELICOPTER AND WAS CLOSE ENOUGH TO INVESTIGATE--JUST NOT CLOSER THAN *YOU,* RIGHT?
BELIEVE I WAS TALKING TO THE MAN, HERE, MA'AM. I HOPE YOU UNDERSTAND.
THAT'S OUR STORY. SHIT HIT THE FAN. WE'VE BEEN WALKING EVER SINCE. WHAT ABOUT *YOU?* YOU SEEM TO BE HOLDING THIS PLACE DOWN PRETTY GOOD.
WHAT DO YOU HAVE HERE? A COUPLE OF *BLOCKS* FENCED OFF? THAT'S NICE.
FOUR BLOCKS, ACTUALLY. WE'RE WORKING ON THE FENCES FOR THE FIFTH. WE GOT ABOUT FORTY PEOPLE HERE. SEEMED LIKE WE WERE GETTING MORE EVERY DAY AT FIRST--THEN LESS--THEN *NOTHING.* YOU'RE THE FIRST IN A MONTH. HARD WINTER, I GUESS.
YOU WANT TO KNOW WHY WE *LOST?* THE GOVERNMENT I MEAN-- THE WAR AGAINST THE BITERS. WE DID *LOSE,* Y'KNOW.
PRESIDENT SENDS OUT THE NATIONAL GUARD TO SECURE THE CITIES, MAKE 'EM SAFE ZONES FOR ALL US NORMAL FOLK TO FLOCK TO. I'M SURE YOU REMEMBER THAT PART OF THE STORY.
MAIN PROBLEM THERE IS THE AVERAGE WEEKEND WARRIOR WAS WORRIED MORE ABOUT *HIS* WIFE AND KID THAN HE WAS ABOUT DRIVING HIS ASS TO *ATLANTA* TO FIGHT OFF *CORPSES.*
WHOLE GUARD STATION ABOUT A MILE AWAY--*COMPLETELY ABANDONED.* ALL *KINDA* SUPPLIES LEFT INSIDE. WE BEEN MAKING GOOD USE OF IT. NIGHT VISION GOGGLES, SNIPER RIFLES, AMMO, YOU SEEN IT IN ACTION. THIS PLACE WOULDN'T BE *SHIT* WITHOUT IT.
YOU SOUND LUCKY. WHERE IS IT YOU'RE TAKING US? WE'RE WALKING TOWARD THE *LIGHT.* WHAT IS THAT? BASEBALL GAME?
WELL, STRANGER. IT LOOKS LIKE WE'RE NOT THE *ONLY* ONES LUCKY AROUND HERE. YOU SHOWED UP ON THE PERFECT NIGHT.
THERE'S A *FIGHT* TONIGHT.

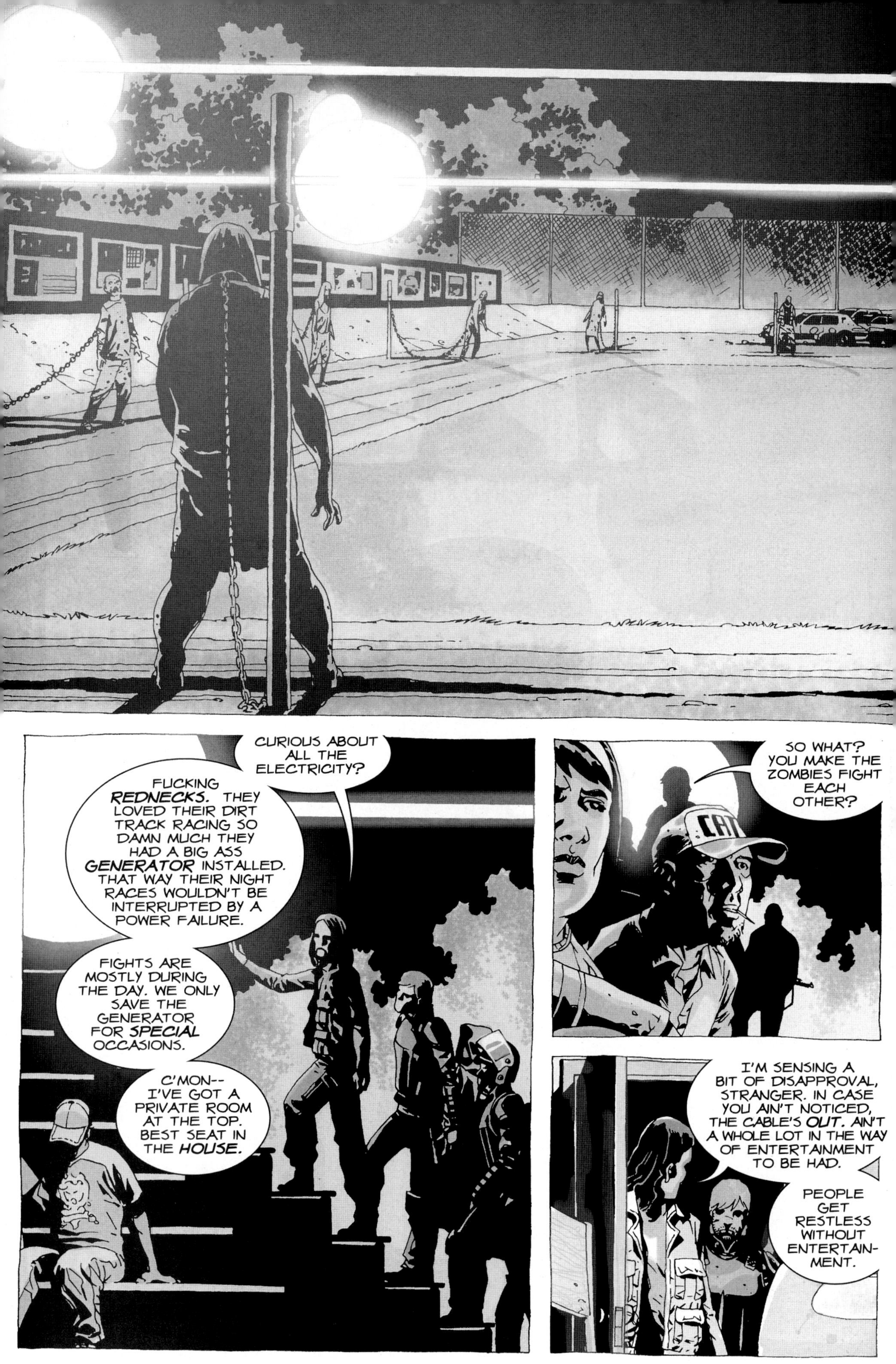
CURIOUS ABOUT ALL THE ELECTRICITY?
FUCKING REDNECKS. THEY LOVED THEIR DIRT TRACK RACING SO DAMN MUCH THEY HAD A BIG ASS GENERATOR INSTALLED. THAT WAY THEIR NIGHT RACES WOULDN'T BE INTERRUPTED BY A POWER FAILURE.
FIGHTS ARE MOSTLY DURING THE DAY. WE ONLY SAVE THE GENERATOR FOR SPECIAL OCCASIONS.
C'MON-- I'VE GOT A PRIVATE ROOM AT THE TOP. BEST SEAT IN THE HOUSE.
SO WHAT? YOU MAKE THE ZOMBIES FIGHT EACH OTHER?
CAT
I'M SENSING A BIT OF DISAPPROVAL, STRANGER. IN CASE YOU AIN'T NOTICED, THE CABLE'S OUT. AIN'T A WHOLE LOT IN THE WAY OF ENTERTAINMENT TO BE HAD.
PEOPLE GET RESTLESS WITHOUT ENTERTAIN-MENT.

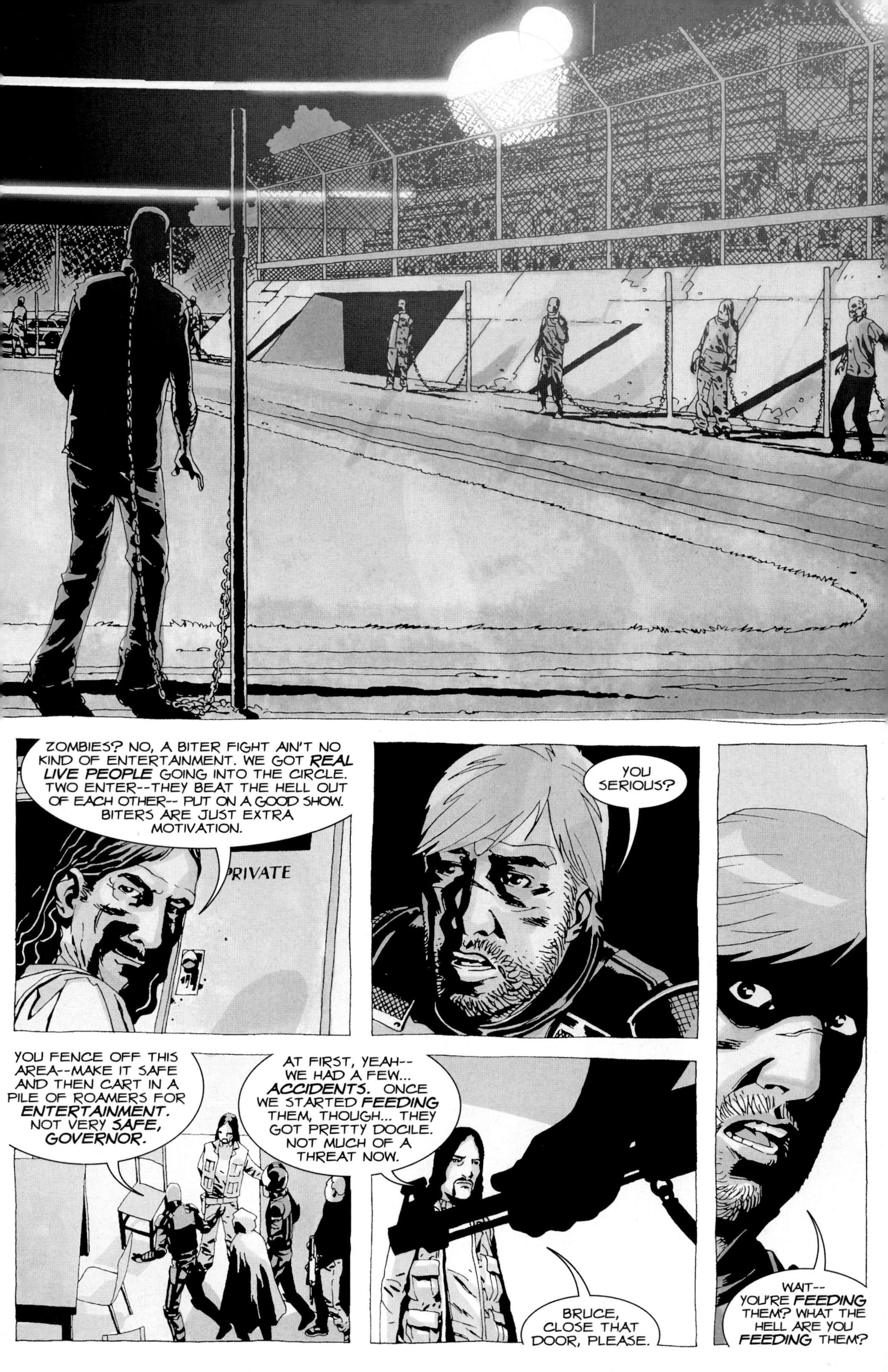
ZOMBIES? NO, A BITER FIGHT AIN'T NO KIND OF ENTERTAINMENT. WE GOT REAL LIVE PEOPLE GOING INTO THE CIRCLE. TWO ENTER--THEY BEAT THE HELL OUT OF EACH OTHER-- PUT ON A GOOD SHOW. BITERS ARE JUST EXTRA MOTIVATION.
PRIVATE
YOU SERIOUS?
YOU FENCE OFF THIS AREA--MAKE IT SAFE AND THEN CART IN A PILE OF ROAMERS FOR ENTERTAINMENT. NOT VERY SAFE, GOVERNOR.
AT FIRST, YEAH-- WE HAD A FEW... ACCIDENTS. ONCE WE STARTED FEEDING THEM, THOUGH... THEY GOT PRETTY DOCILE. NOT MUCH OF A THREAT NOW.
BRUCE, CLOSE THAT DOOR, PLEASE.
WAIT-- YOU'RE FEEDING THEM? WHAT THE HELL ARE YOU FEEDING THEM?

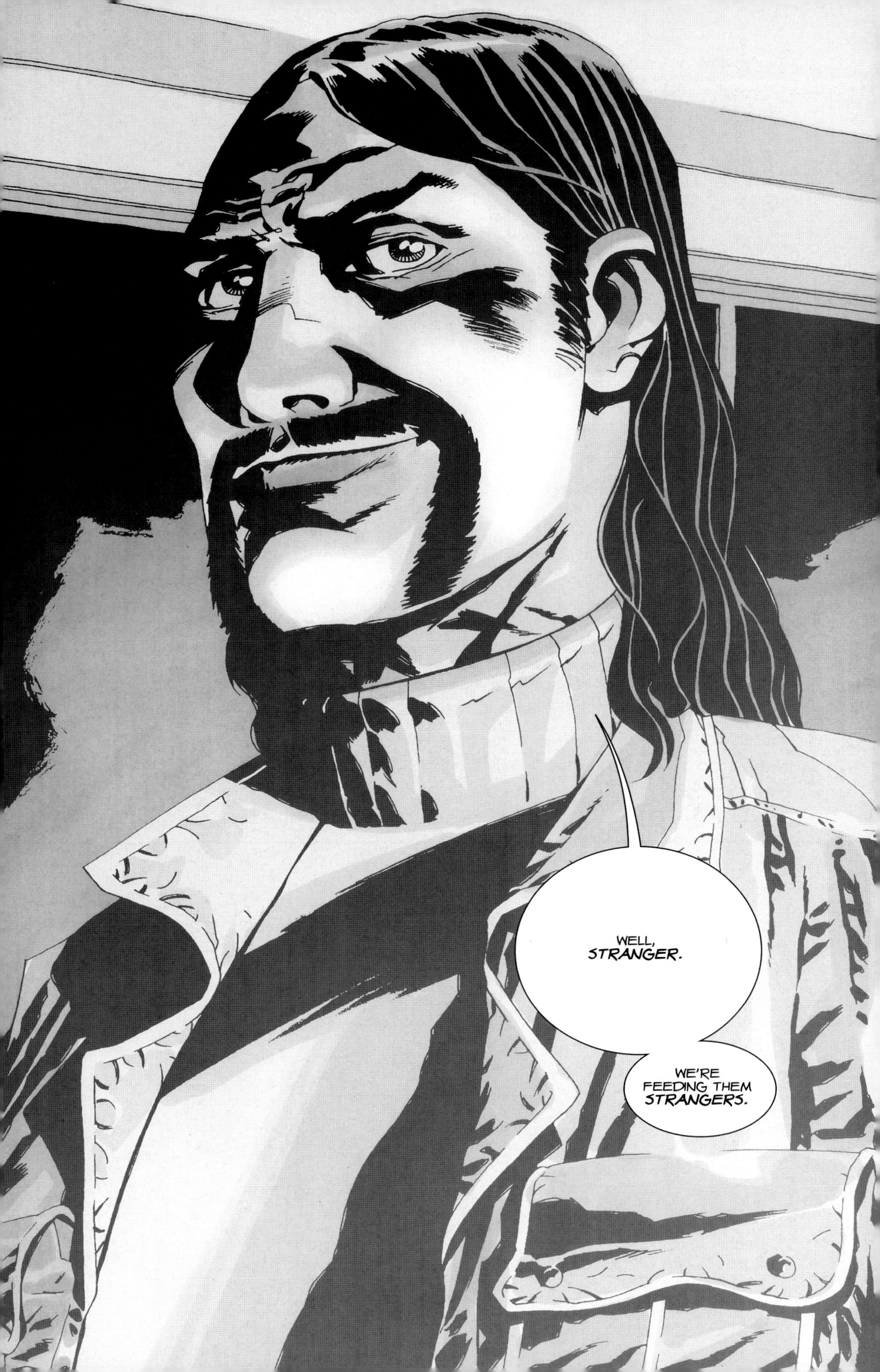
WELL, STRANGER.
WE'RE FEEDING THEM STRANGERS.

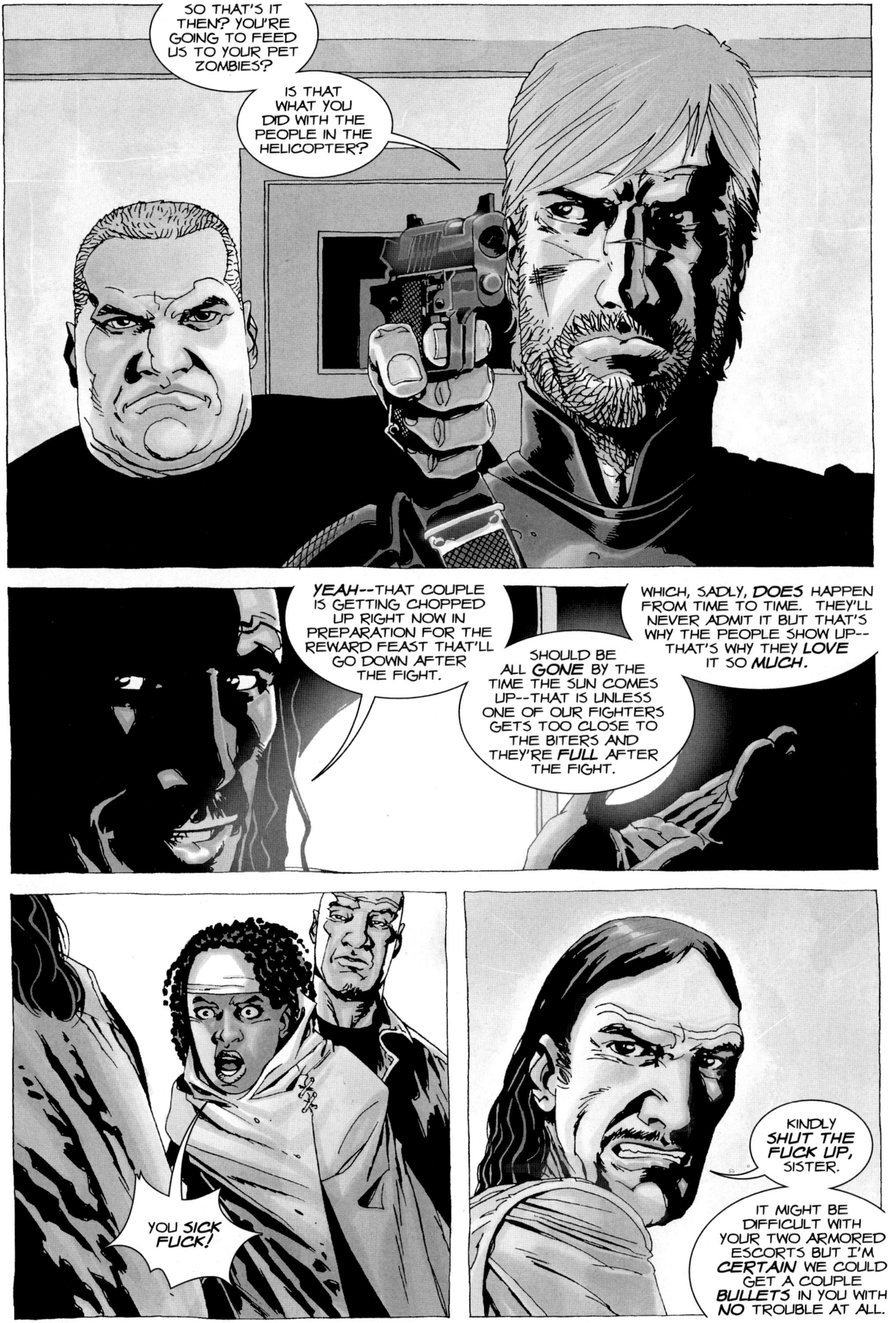
SO THAT'S IT THEN? YOU'RE GOING TO FEED US TO YOUR PET ZOMBIES?
IS THAT WHAT YOU DID WITH THE PEOPLE IN THE HELICOPTER?
YEAH--THAT COUPLE IS GETTING CHOPPED UP RIGHT NOW IN PREPARATION FOR THE REWARD FEAST THAT'LL GO DOWN AFTER THE FIGHT.
SHOULD BE ALL GONE BY THE TIME THE SUN COMES UP--THAT IS UNLESS ONE OF OUR FIGHTERS GETS TOO CLOSE TO THE BITERS AND THEY'RE FULL AFTER THE FIGHT.
WHICH, SADLY, DOES HAPPEN FROM TIME TO TIME. THEY'LL NEVER ADMIT IT BUT THAT'S WHY THE PEOPLE SHOW UP--THAT'S WHY THEY LOVE IT SO MUCH.
YOU SICK FUCK!
KINDLY SHUT THE FUCK UP, SISTER.
IT MIGHT BE DIFFICULT WITH YOUR TWO ARMORED ESCORTS BUT I'M CERTAIN WE COULD GET A COUPLE BULLETS IN YOU WITH NO TROUBLE AT ALL.

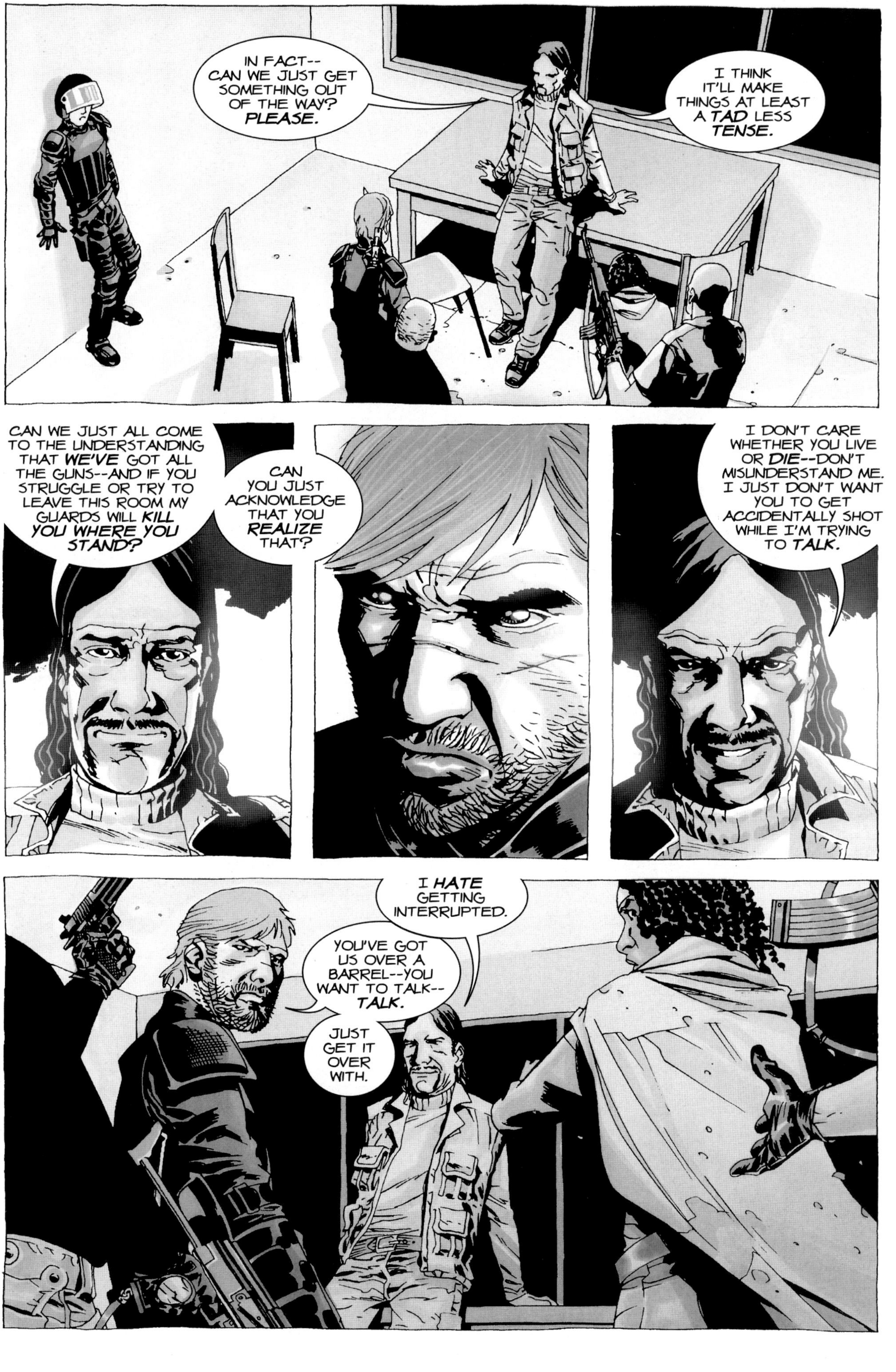

IN FACT-- CAN WE JUST GET SOMETHING OUT OF THE WAY? PLEASE.
I THINK IT'LL MAKE THINGS AT LEAST A TAD LESS TENSE.
CAN WE JUST ALL COME TO THE UNDERSTANDING THAT WE'VE GOT ALL THE GUNS--AND IF YOU STRUGGLE OR TRY TO LEAVE THIS ROOM MY GUARDS WILL KILL YOU WHERE YOU STAND?
CAN YOU JUST ACKNOWLEDGE THAT YOU REALIZE THAT?
I DON'T CARE WHETHER YOU LIVE OR DIE--DON'T MISUNDERSTAND ME. I JUST DON'T WANT YOU TO GET ACCIDENTALLY SHOT WHILE I'M TRYING TO TALK.
I HATE GETTING INTERRUPTED.
YOU'VE GOT US OVER A BARREL--YOU WANT TO TALK-- TALK.
JUST GET IT OVER WITH.

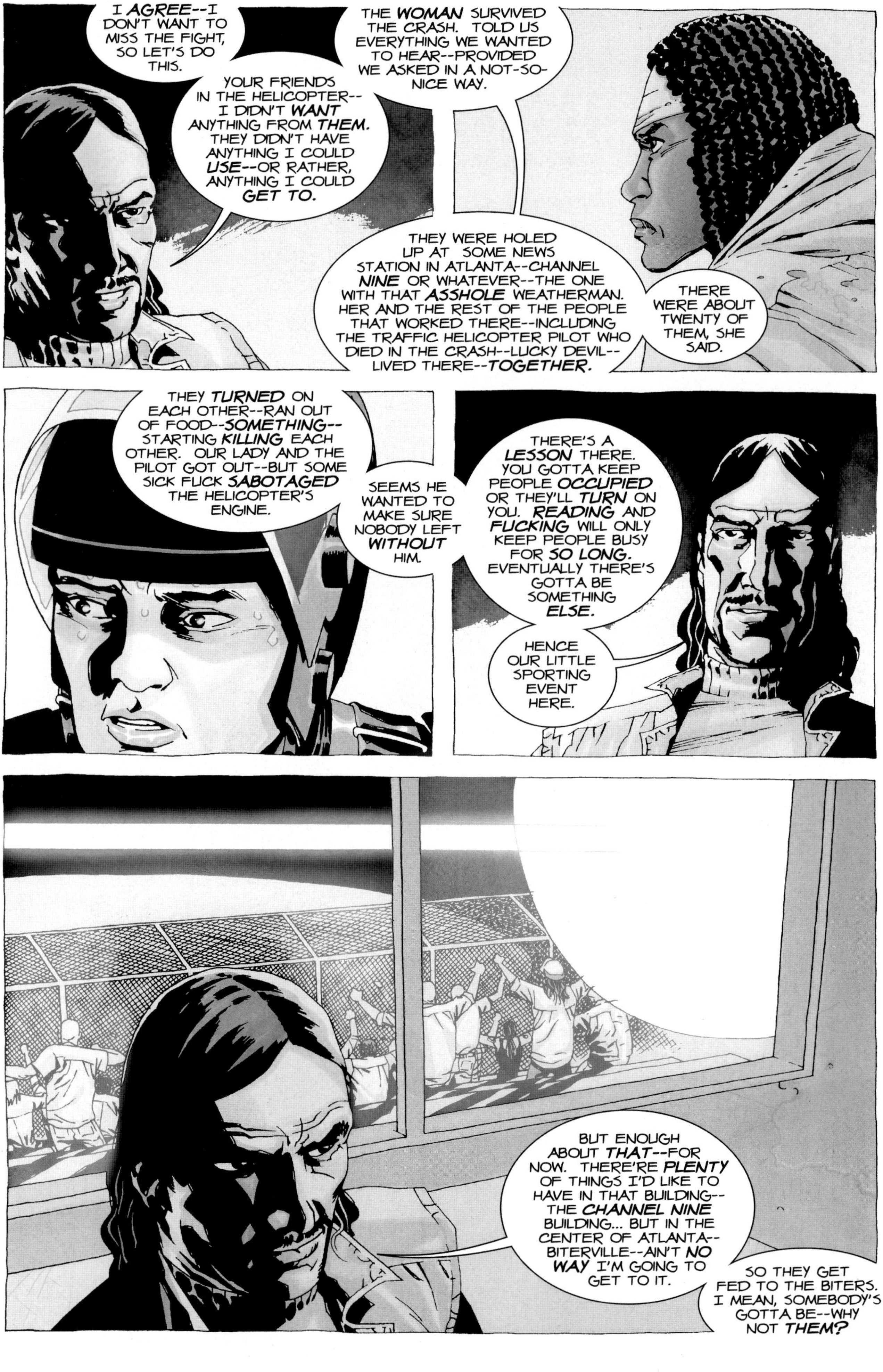
I AGREE--I DON'T WANT TO MISS THE FIGHT, SO LET'S DO THIS.
YOUR FRIENDS IN THE HELICOPTER-- I DIDN'T WANT ANYTHING FROM THEM. THEY DIDN'T HAVE ANYTHING I COULD USE--OR RATHER, ANYTHING I COULD GET TO.
THE WOMAN SURVIVED THE CRASH. TOLD US EVERYTHING WE WANTED TO HEAR--PROVIDED WE ASKED IN A NOT-SO-NICE WAY.
THEY WERE HOLED UP AT SOME NEWS STATION IN ATLANTA--CHANNEL NINE OR WHATEVER--THE ONE WITH THAT ASSHOLE WEATHERMAN. HER AND THE REST OF THE PEOPLE THAT WORKED THERE--INCLUDING THE TRAFFIC HELICOPTER PILOT WHO DIED IN THE CRASH--LUCKY DEVIL--LIVED THERE--TOGETHER.
THERE WERE ABOUT TWENTY OF THEM, SHE SAID.
THEY TURNED ON EACH OTHER--RAN OUT OF FOOD--SOMETHING--STARTING KILLING EACH OTHER. OUR LADY AND THE PILOT GOT OUT--BUT SOME SICK FUCK SABOTAGED THE HELICOPTER'S ENGINE.
SEEMS HE WANTED TO MAKE SURE NOBODY LEFT WITHOUT HIM.
THERE'S A LESSON THERE. YOU GOTTA KEEP PEOPLE OCCUPIED OR THEY'LL TURN ON YOU. READING AND FUCKING WILL ONLY KEEP PEOPLE BUSY FOR SO LONG. EVENTUALLY THERE'S GOTTA BE SOMETHING ELSE.
HENCE OUR LITTLE SPORTING EVENT HERE.
BUT ENOUGH ABOUT THAT--FOR NOW. THERE'RE PLENTY OF THINGS I'D LIKE TO HAVE IN THAT BUILDING--THE CHANNEL NINE BUILDING... BUT IN THE CENTER OF ATLANTA--BITERVILLE--AIN'T NO WAY I'M GOING TO GET TO IT.
SO THEY GET FED TO THE BITERS. I MEAN, SOMEBODY'S GOTTA BE--WHY NOT THEM?

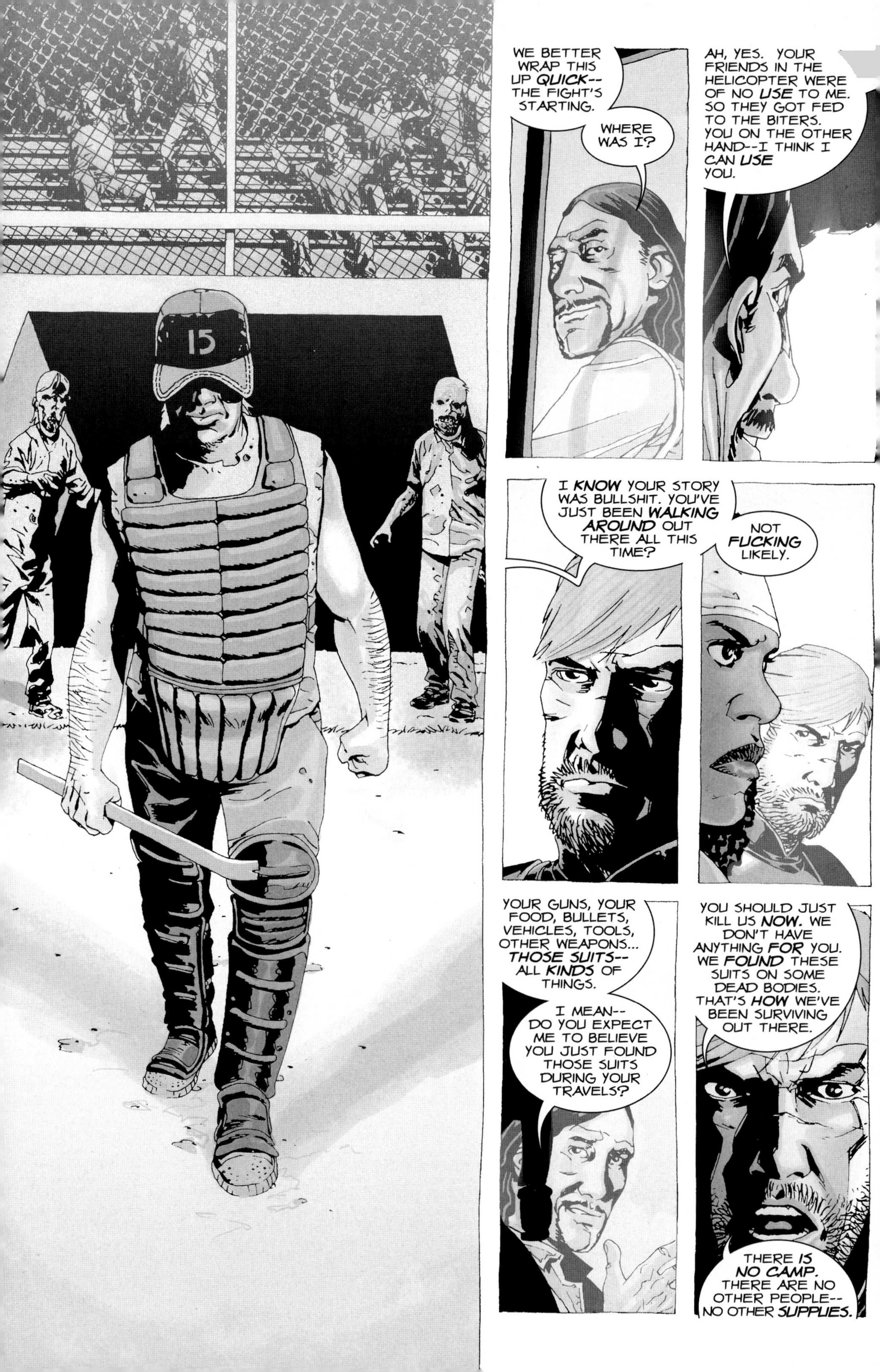

WE BETTER WRAP THIS UP QUICK-- THE FIGHT'S STARTING.
WHERE WAS I?
AH, YES. YOUR FRIENDS IN THE HELICOPTER WERE OF NO USE TO ME. SO THEY GOT FED TO THE BITERS. YOU ON THE OTHER HAND--I THINK I CAN USE YOU.
I KNOW YOUR STORY WAS BULLSHIT. YOU'VE JUST BEEN WALKING AROUND OUT THERE ALL THIS TIME?
NOT FUCKING LIKELY.
YOUR GUNS, YOUR FOOD, BULLETS, VEHICLES, TOOLS, OTHER WEAPONS... THOSE SUITS-- ALL KINDS OF THINGS.
I MEAN-- DO YOU EXPECT ME TO BELIEVE YOU JUST FOUND THOSE SUITS DURING YOUR TRAVELS?
YOU SHOULD JUST KILL US NOW. WE DON'T HAVE ANYTHING FOR YOU. WE FOUND THESE SUITS ON SOME DEAD BODIES. THAT'S HOW WE'VE BEEN SURVIVING OUT THERE.
THERE IS NO CAMP. THERE ARE NO OTHER PEOPLE-- NO OTHER SUPPLIES.

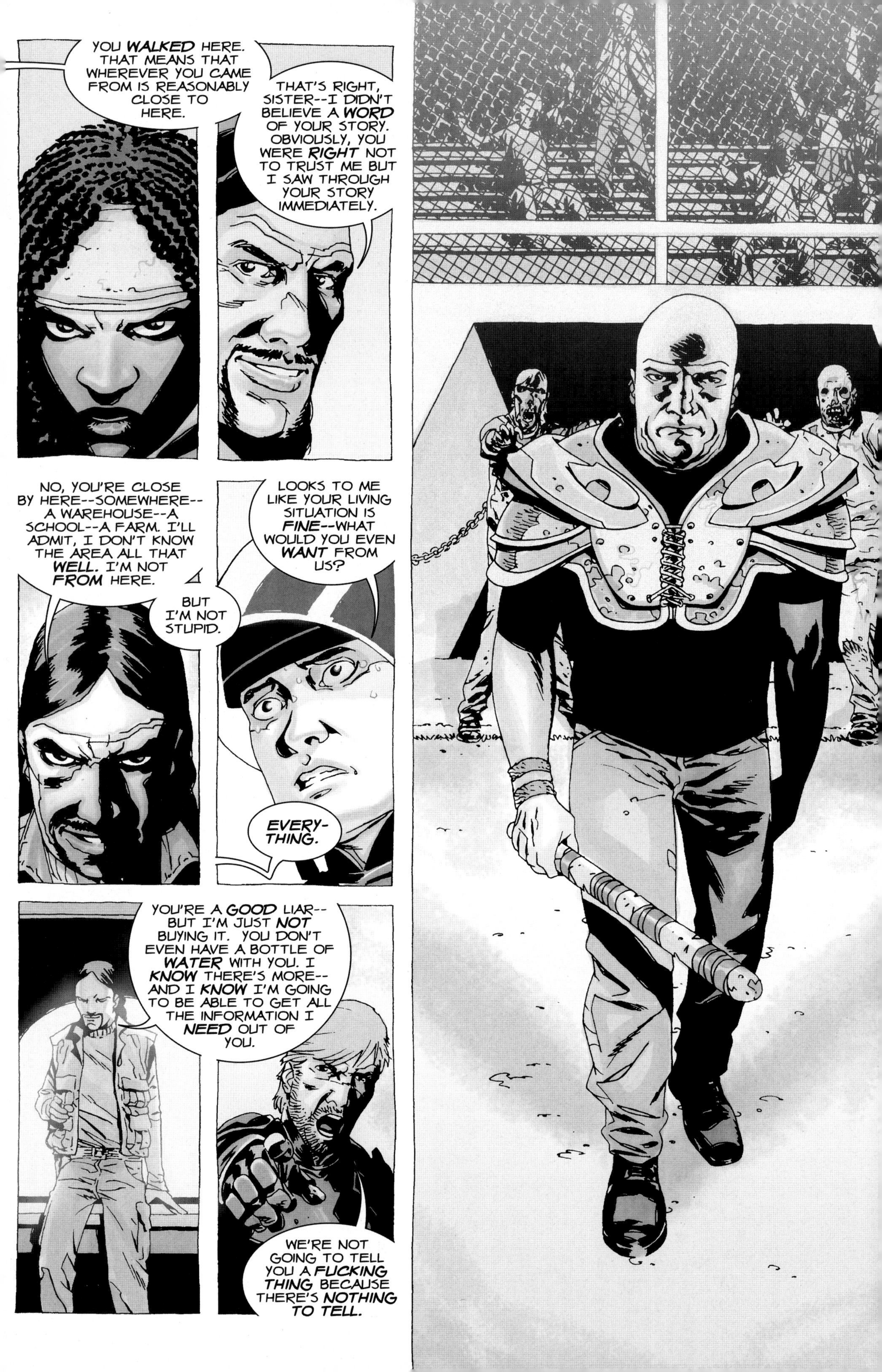
YOU WALKED HERE. THAT MEANS THAT WHEREVER YOU CAME FROM IS REASONABLY CLOSE TO HERE.
THAT'S RIGHT, SISTER--I DIDN'T BELIEVE A WORD OF YOUR STORY. OBVIOUSLY, YOU WERE RIGHT NOT TO TRUST ME BUT I SAW THROUGH YOUR STORY IMMEDIATELY.
NO, YOU'RE CLOSE BY HERE--SOMEWHERE--A WAREHOUSE--A SCHOOL--A FARM. I'LL ADMIT, I DON'T KNOW THE AREA ALL THAT WELL. I'M NOT FROM HERE.
BUT I'M NOT STUPID.
LOOKS TO ME LIKE YOUR LIVING SITUATION IS FINE--WHAT WOULD YOU EVEN WANT FROM US?
EVERY-THING.
YOU'RE A GOOD LIAR--BUT I'M JUST NOT BUYING IT. YOU DON'T EVEN HAVE A BOTTLE OF WATER WITH YOU. I KNOW THERE'S MORE--AND I KNOW I'M GOING TO BE ABLE TO GET ALL THE INFORMATION I NEED OUT OF YOU.
WE'RE NOT GOING TO TELL YOU A FUCKING THING BECAUSE THERE'S NOTHING TO TELL.

HOLD THEM! I DON'T THINK THIS MOTHER FUCKER REALIZES JUST HOW SERIOUS THIS SITUATION IS.

HEY!

BRUCE--HOLD THIS ONE DOWN FOR ME.

GABE, YOU KEEP AN EYE ON THE OTHER TWO.

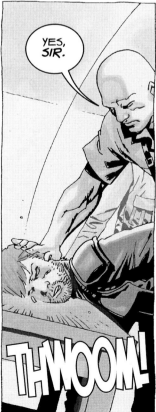

YES, SIR.

THWOOM!

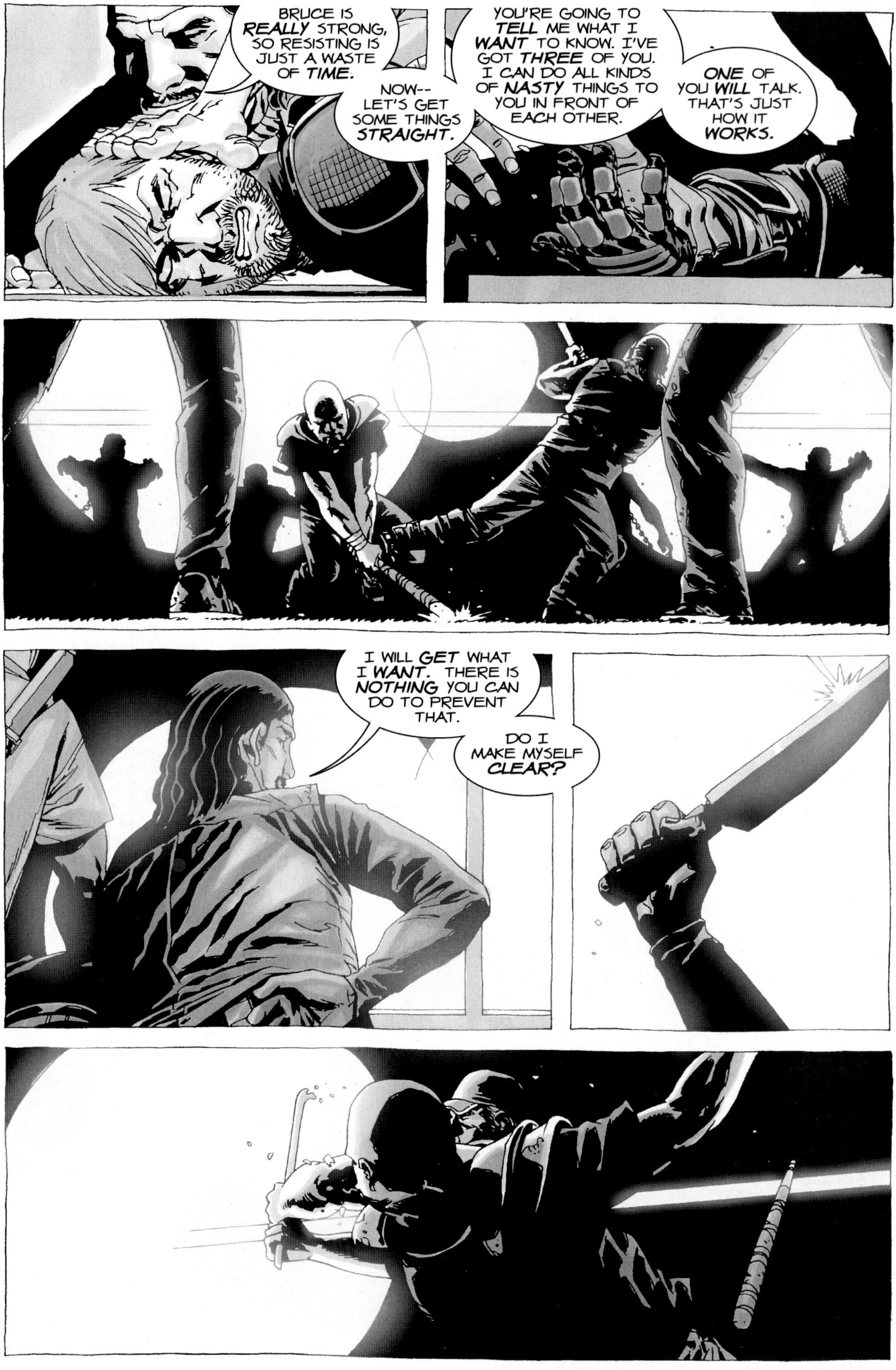
BRUCE IS REALLY STRONG, SO RESISTING IS JUST A WASTE OF TIME.
NOW-- LET'S GET SOME THINGS STRAIGHT.
YOU'RE GOING TO TELL ME WHAT I WANT TO KNOW. I'VE GOT THREE OF YOU. I CAN DO ALL KINDS OF NASTY THINGS TO YOU IN FRONT OF EACH OTHER.
ONE OF YOU WILL TALK. THAT'S JUST HOW IT WORKS.
I WILL GET WHAT I WANT. THERE IS NOTHING YOU CAN DO TO PREVENT THAT.
DO I MAKE MYSELF CLEAR?

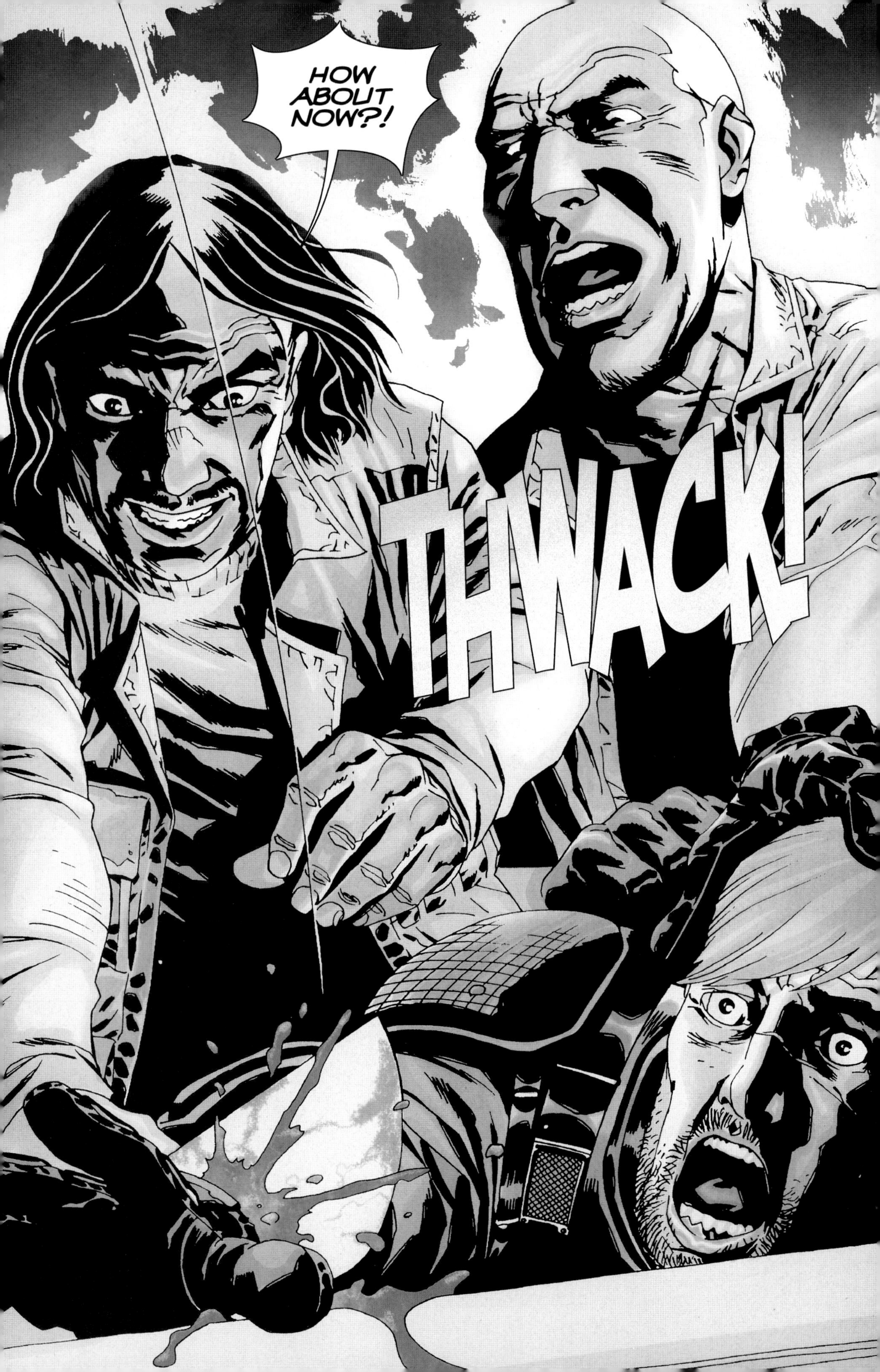
HOW ABOUT NOW?!
THWACK!

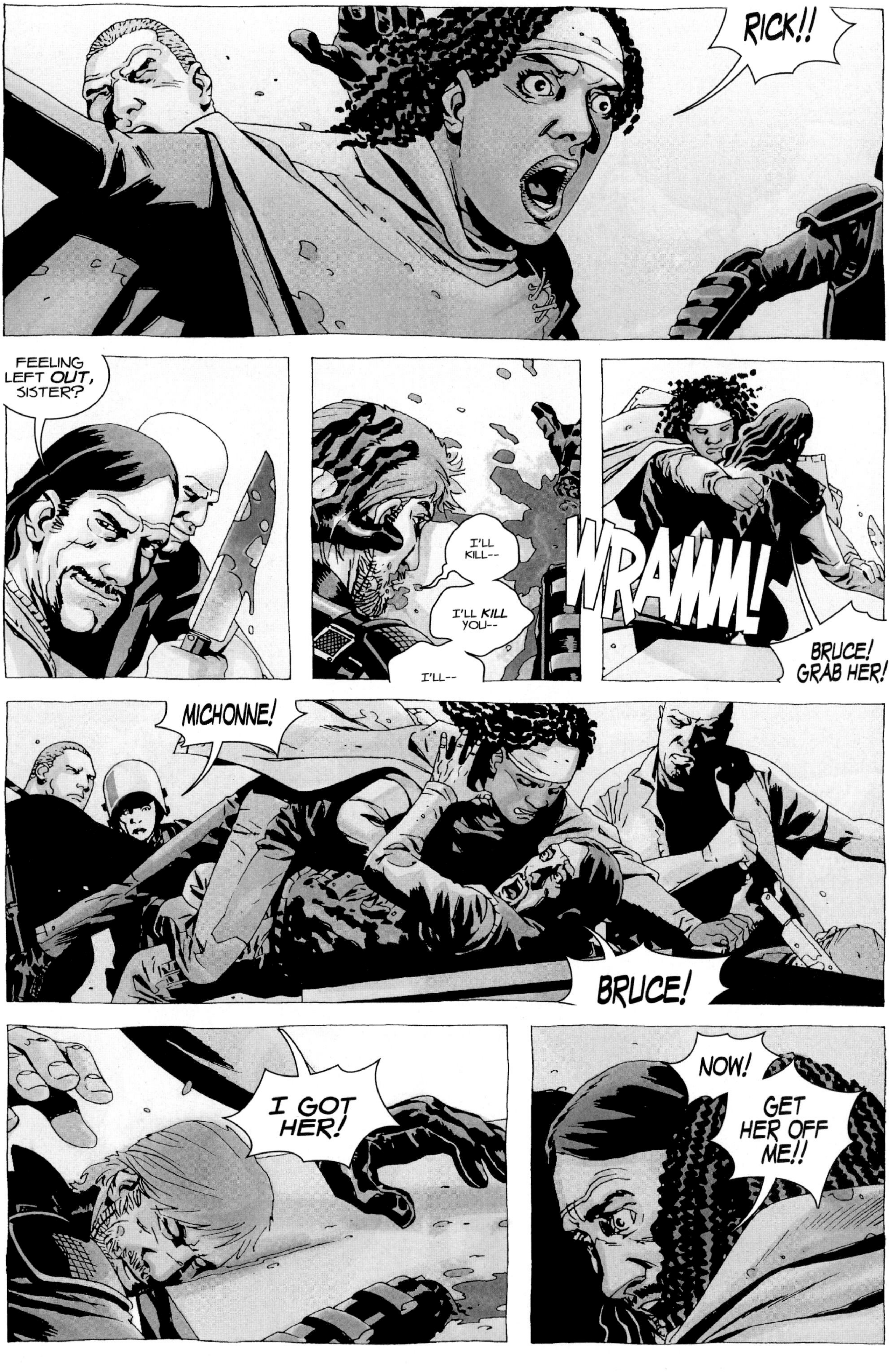
RICK!!
FEELING LEFT OUT, SISTER?
I'LL KILL--
I'LL KILL YOU--
I'LL--
WRAMM!
BRUCE! GRAB HER!
MICHONNE!
BRUCE!
I GOT HER!
NOW!
GET HER OFF ME!!

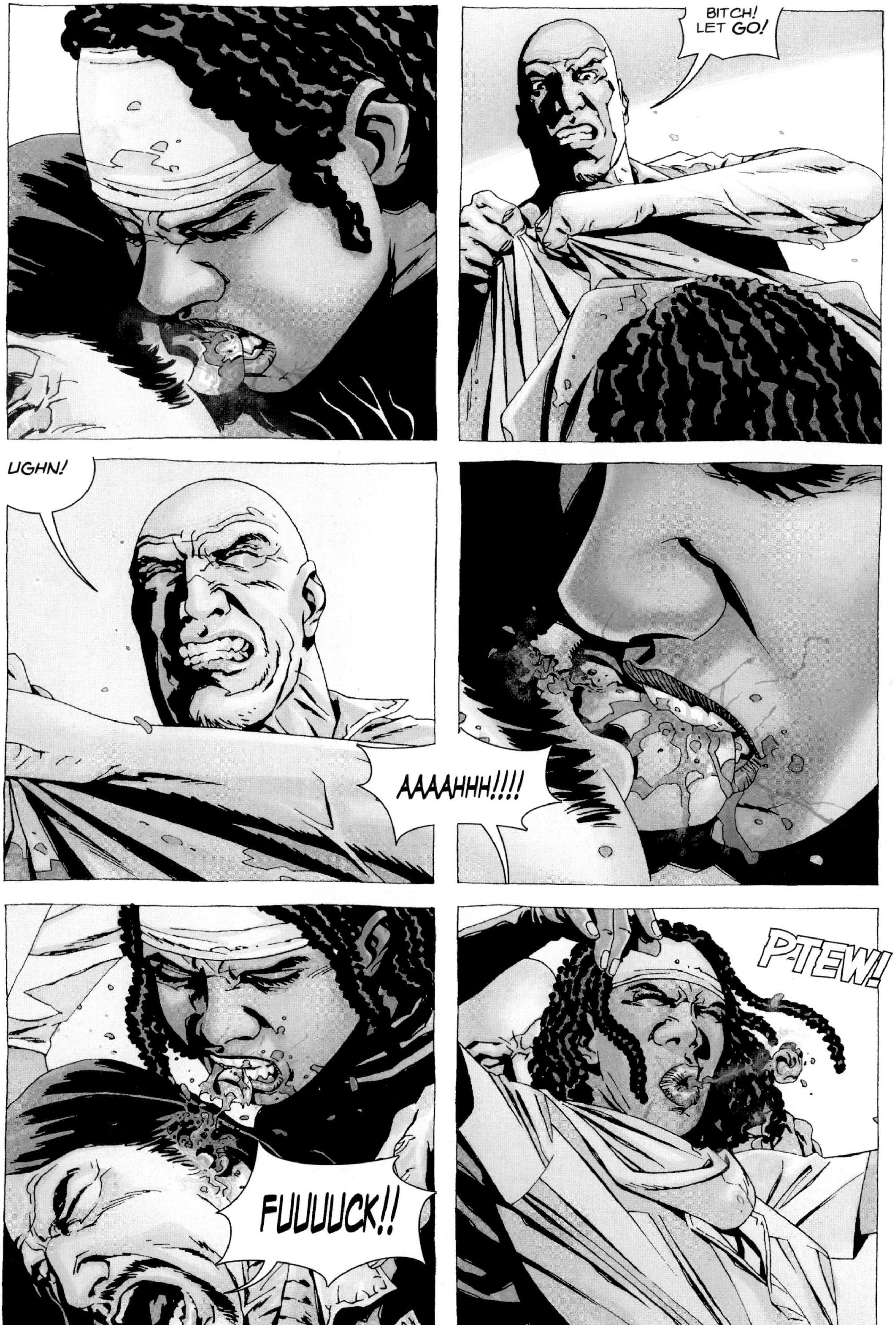
BITCH! LET GO!
UGHN!
AAAAHHH!!!!
FUUUUCK!!
P-TEW!

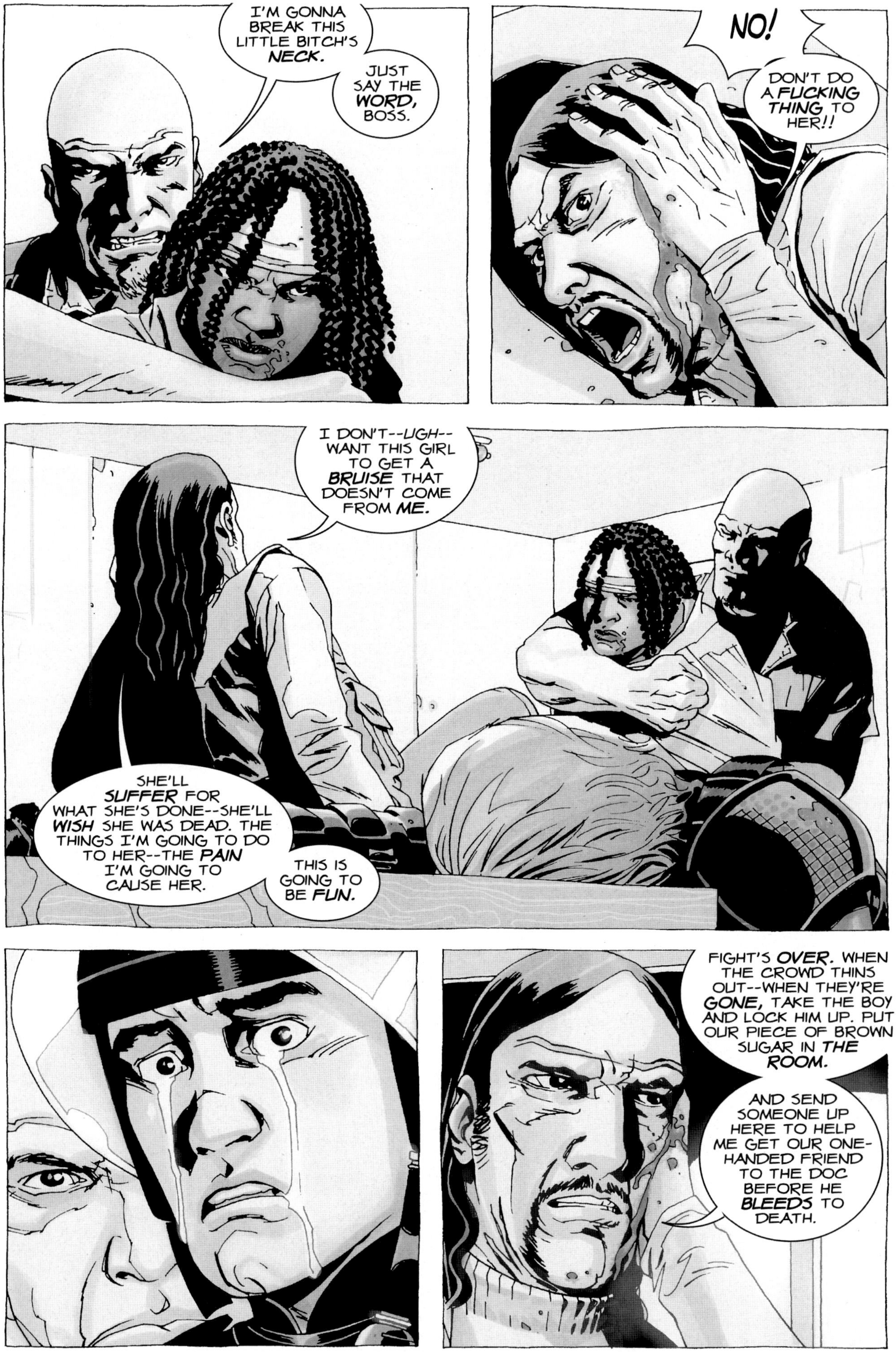
I'M GONNA BREAK THIS LITTLE BITCH'S NECK.
JUST SAY THE WORD, BOSS.
NO!
DON'T DO A FUCKING THING TO HER!!
I DON'T--UGH--WANT THIS GIRL TO GET A BRUISE THAT DOESN'T COME FROM ME.
SHE'LL SUFFER FOR WHAT SHE'S DONE--SHE'LL WISH SHE WAS DEAD. THE THINGS I'M GOING TO DO TO HER--THE PAIN I'M GOING TO CAUSE HER.
THIS IS GOING TO BE FUN.
FIGHT'S OVER. WHEN THE CROWD THINS OUT--WHEN THEY'RE GONE, TAKE THE BOY AND LOCK HIM UP. PUT OUR PIECE OF BROWN SUGAR IN THE ROOM.
AND SEND SOMEONE UP HERE TO HELP ME GET OUR ONE-HANDED FRIEND TO THE DOC BEFORE HE BLEEDS TO DEATH.

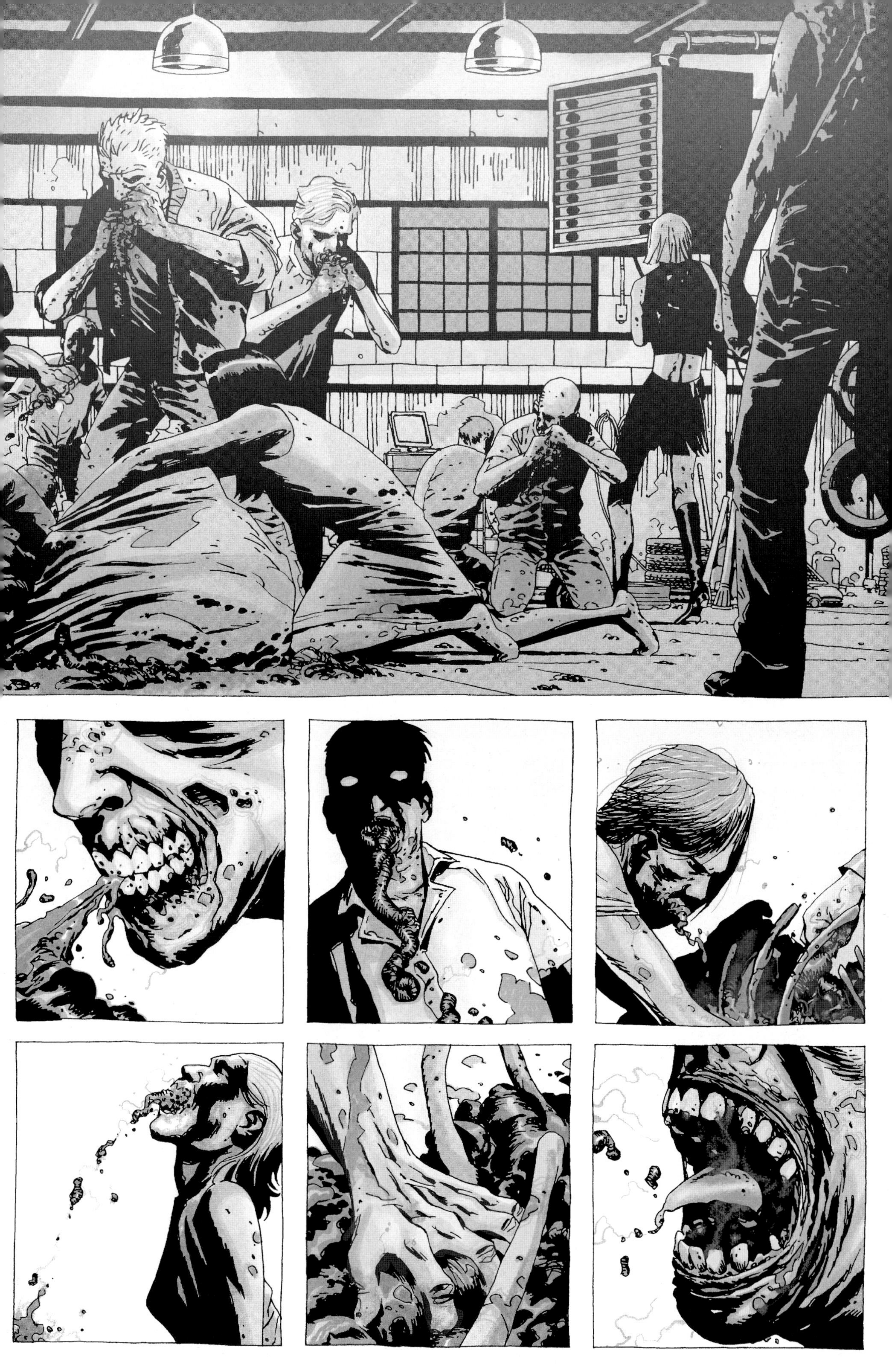

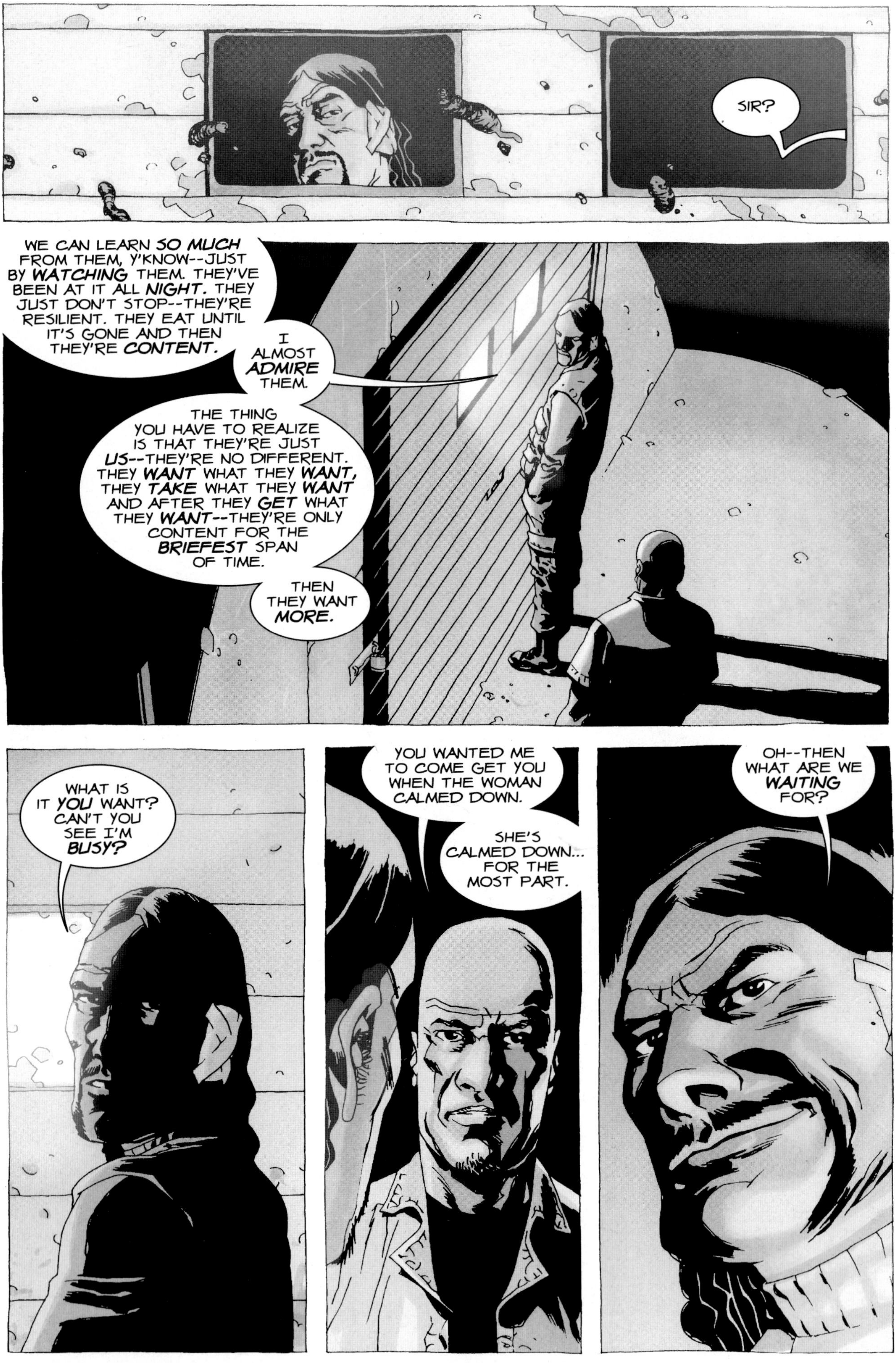
SIR?
WE CAN LEARN SO MUCH FROM THEM, Y'KNOW--JUST BY WATCHING THEM. THEY'VE BEEN AT IT ALL NIGHT. THEY JUST DON'T STOP--THEY'RE RESILIENT. THEY EAT UNTIL IT'S GONE AND THEN THEY'RE CONTENT.
I ALMOST ADMIRE THEM.
THE THING YOU HAVE TO REALIZE IS THAT THEY'RE JUST US--THEY'RE NO DIFFERENT. THEY WANT WHAT THEY WANT, THEY TAKE WHAT THEY WANT AND AFTER THEY GET WHAT THEY WANT--THEY'RE ONLY CONTENT FOR THE BRIEFEST SPAN OF TIME.
THEN THEY WANT MORE.
WHAT IS IT YOU WANT? CAN'T YOU SEE I'M BUSY?
YOU WANTED ME TO COME GET YOU WHEN THE WOMAN CALMED DOWN.
SHE'S CALMED DOWN... FOR THE MOST PART.
OH--THEN WHAT ARE WE WAITING FOR?

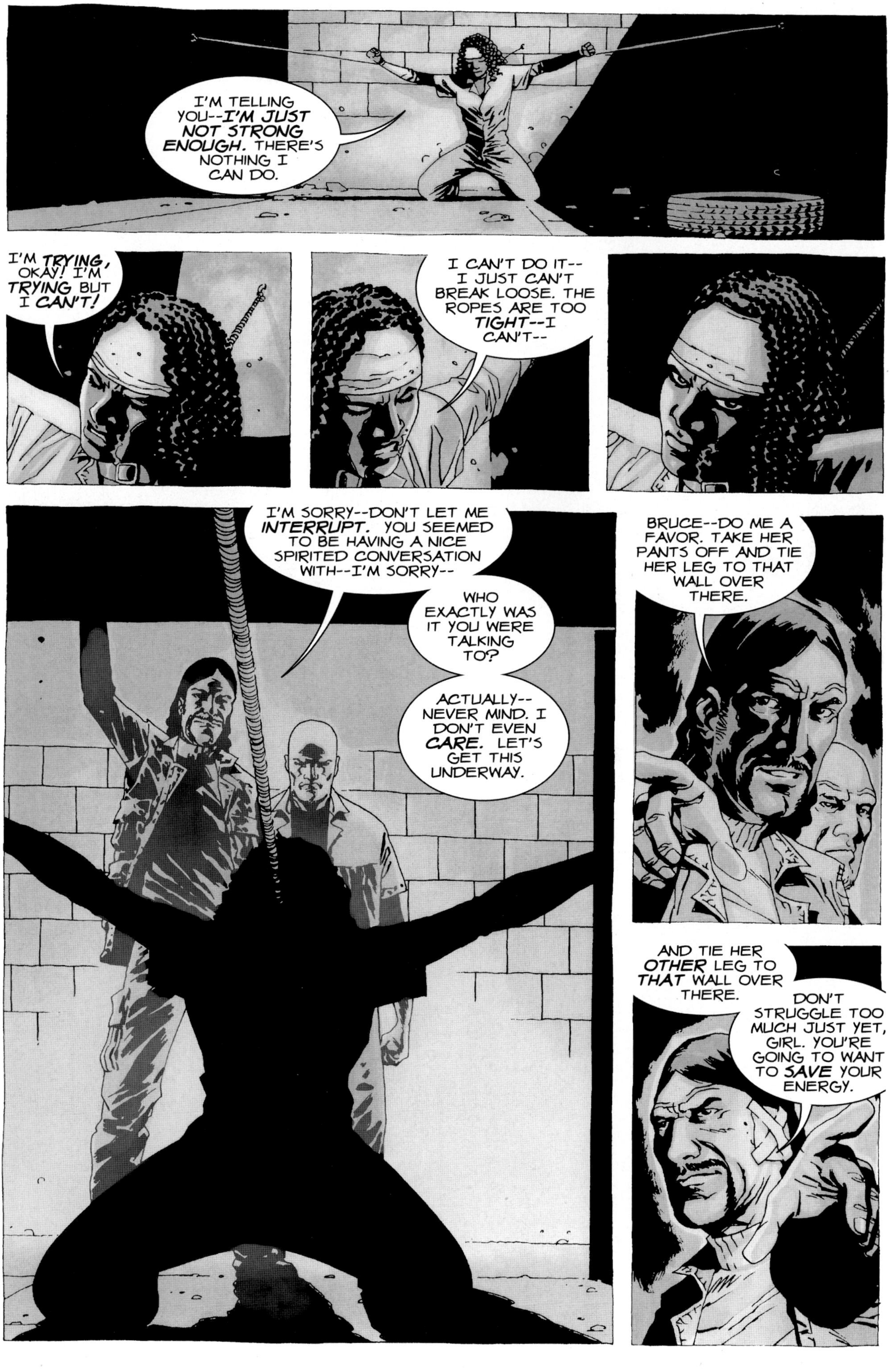
I'M TELLING YOU--I'M JUST NOT STRONG ENOUGH. THERE'S NOTHING I CAN DO.
I'M TRYING, OKAY! I'M TRYING BUT I CAN'T!
I CAN'T DO IT-- I JUST CAN'T BREAK LOOSE. THE ROPES ARE TOO TIGHT--I CAN'T--
I'M SORRY--DON'T LET ME INTERRUPT. YOU SEEMED TO BE HAVING A NICE SPIRITED CONVERSATION WITH--I'M SORRY--
WHO EXACTLY WAS IT YOU WERE TALKING TO?
ACTUALLY-- NEVER MIND. I DON'T EVEN CARE. LET'S GET THIS UNDERWAY.
BRUCE--DO ME A FAVOR. TAKE HER PANTS OFF AND TIE HER LEG TO THAT WALL OVER THERE.
AND TIE HER OTHER LEG TO THAT WALL OVER THERE.
DON'T STRUGGLE TOO MUCH JUST YET, GIRL. YOU'RE GOING TO WANT TO SAVE YOUR ENERGY.

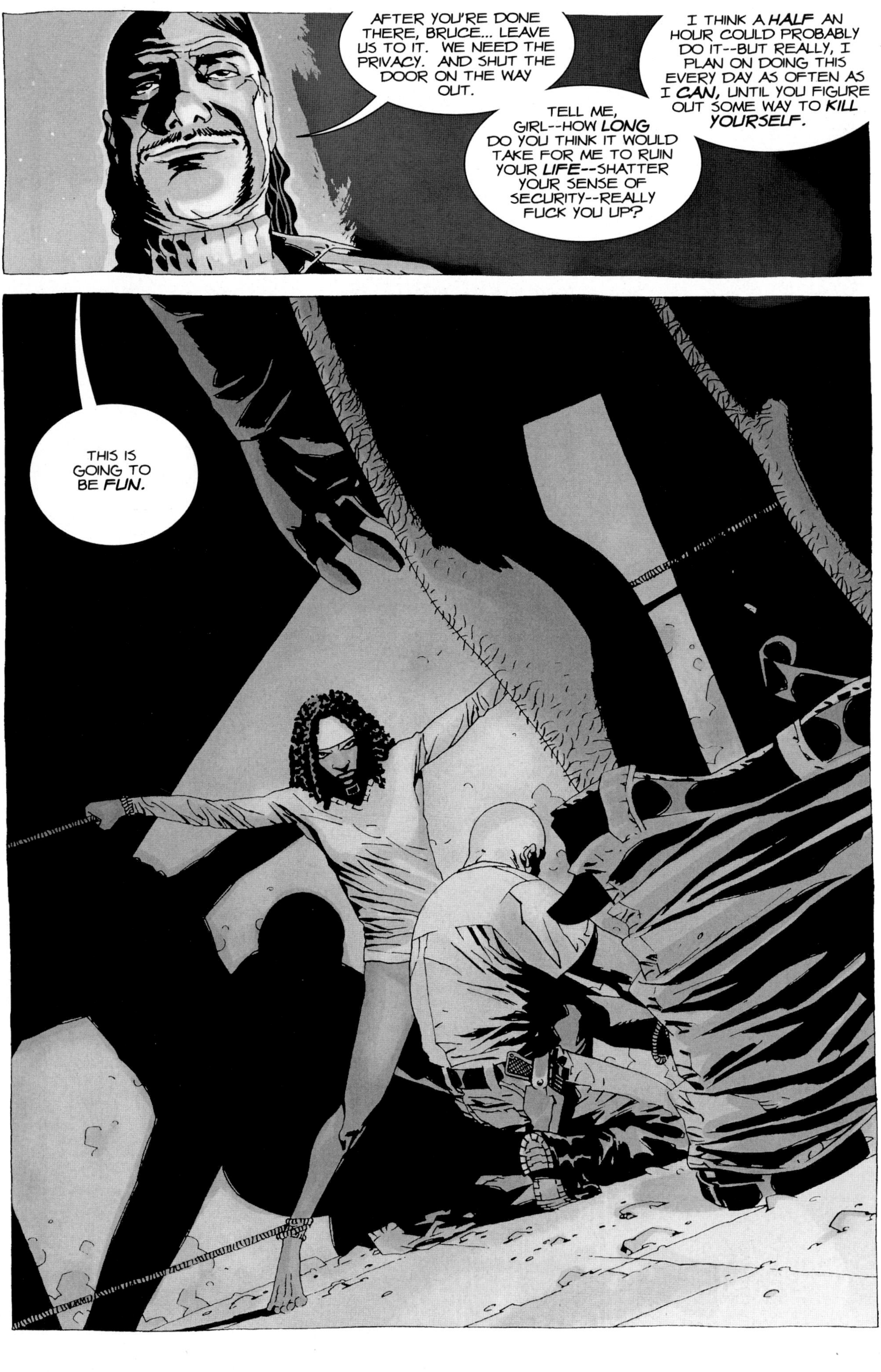

AFTER YOU'RE DONE THERE, BRUCE... LEAVE US TO IT. WE NEED THE PRIVACY. AND SHUT THE DOOR ON THE WAY OUT.
TELL ME, GIRL--HOW LONG DO YOU THINK IT WOULD TAKE FOR ME TO RUIN YOUR LIFE--SHATTER YOUR SENSE OF SECURITY--REALLY FUCK YOU UP?
I THINK A HALF AN HOUR COULD PROBABLY DO IT--BUT REALLY, I PLAN ON DOING THIS EVERY DAY AS OFTEN AS I CAN, UNTIL YOU FIGURE OUT SOME WAY TO KILL YOURSELF.
THIS IS GOING TO BE FUN.

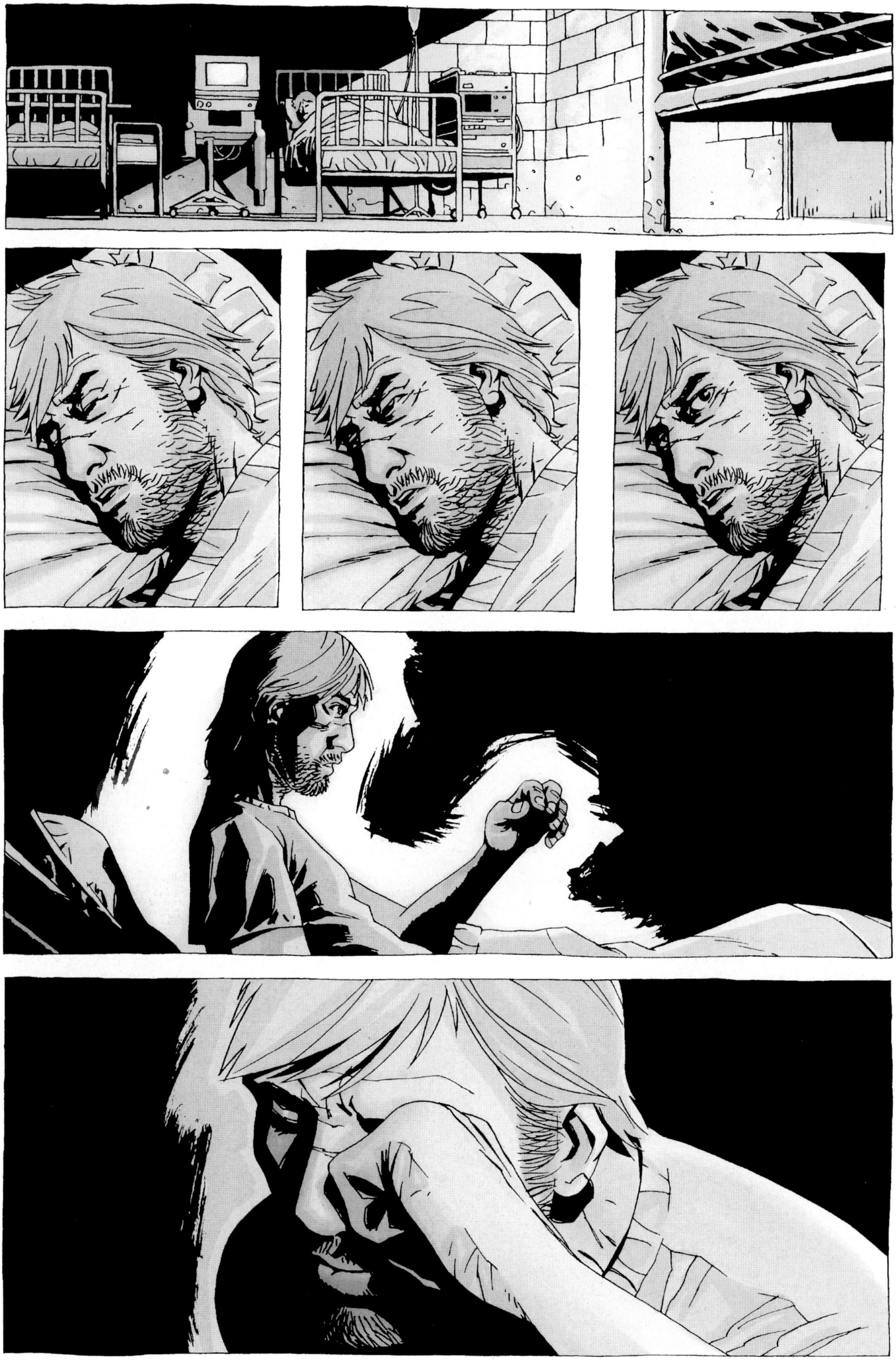

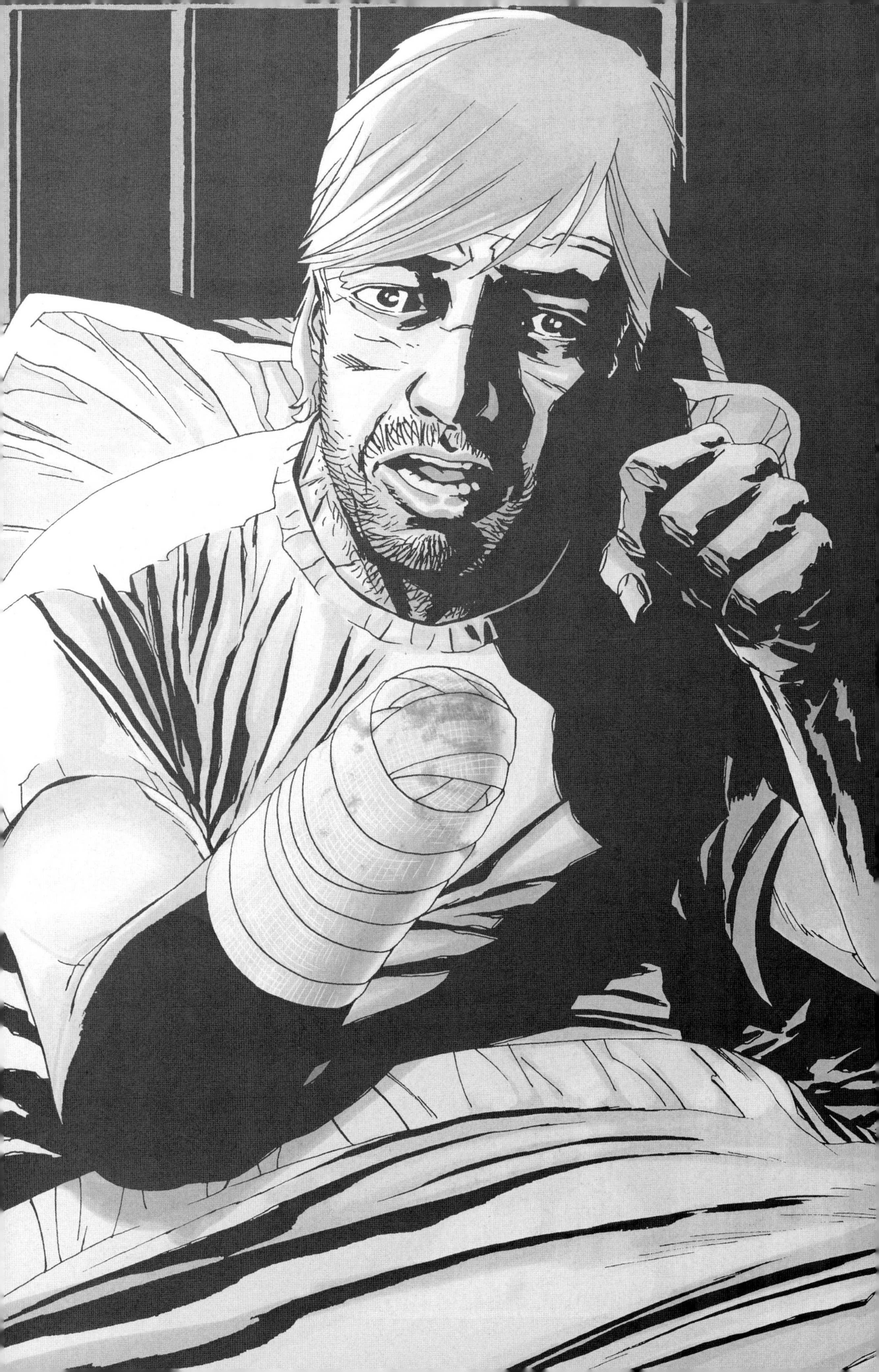

HU-- UNGH.

≥HUFF≥

≥HUFF≥

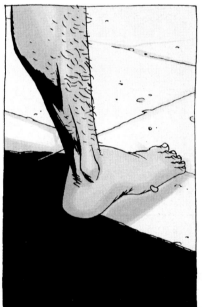

...

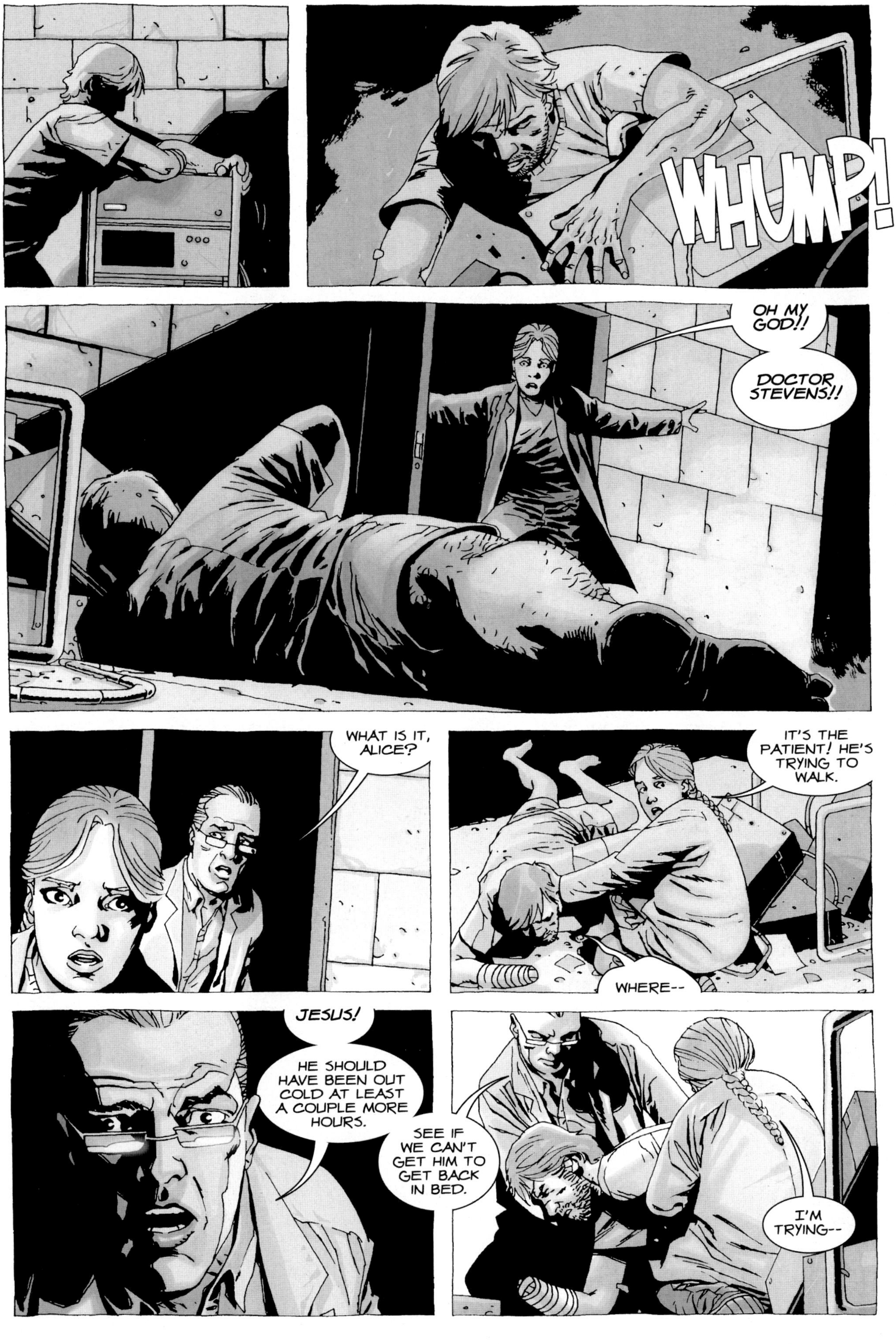
WHUMP!
OH MY GOD!!
DOCTOR STEVENS!!
WHAT IS IT, ALICE?
IT'S THE PATIENT! HE'S TRYING TO WALK.
WHERE--
JESUS!
HE SHOULD HAVE BEEN OUT COLD AT LEAST A COUPLE MORE HOURS.
SEE IF WE CAN'T GET HIM TO GET BACK IN BED.
I'M TRYING--

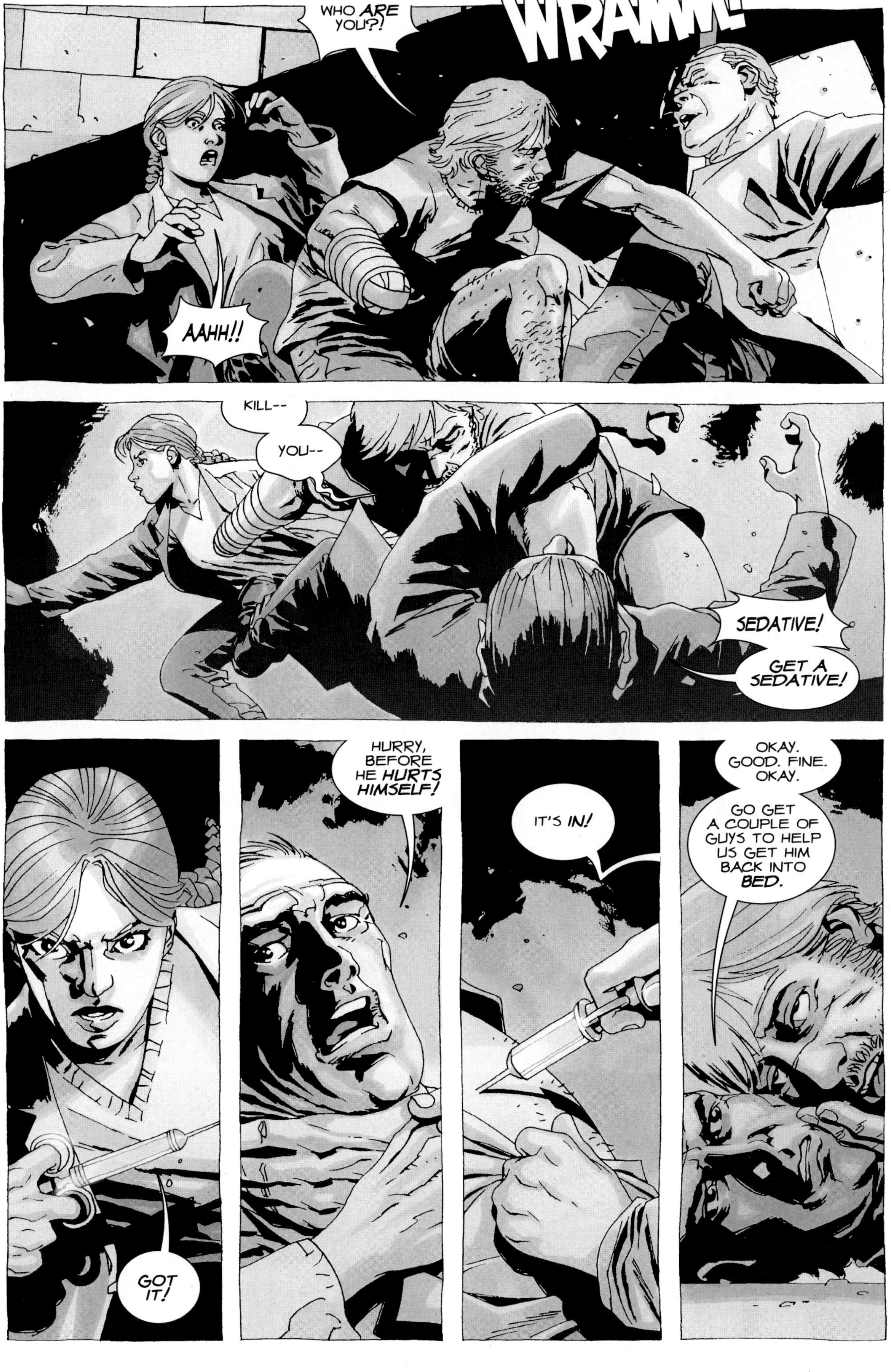
WHO ARE YOU?!
WRAMM!
AAHH!!
KILL--
YOU--
SEDATIVE!
GET A SEDATIVE!
GOT IT!
HURRY, BEFORE HE HURTS HIMSELF!
IT'S IN!
OKAY. GOOD. FINE. OKAY.
GO GET A COUPLE OF GUYS TO HELP US GET HIM BACK INTO BED.

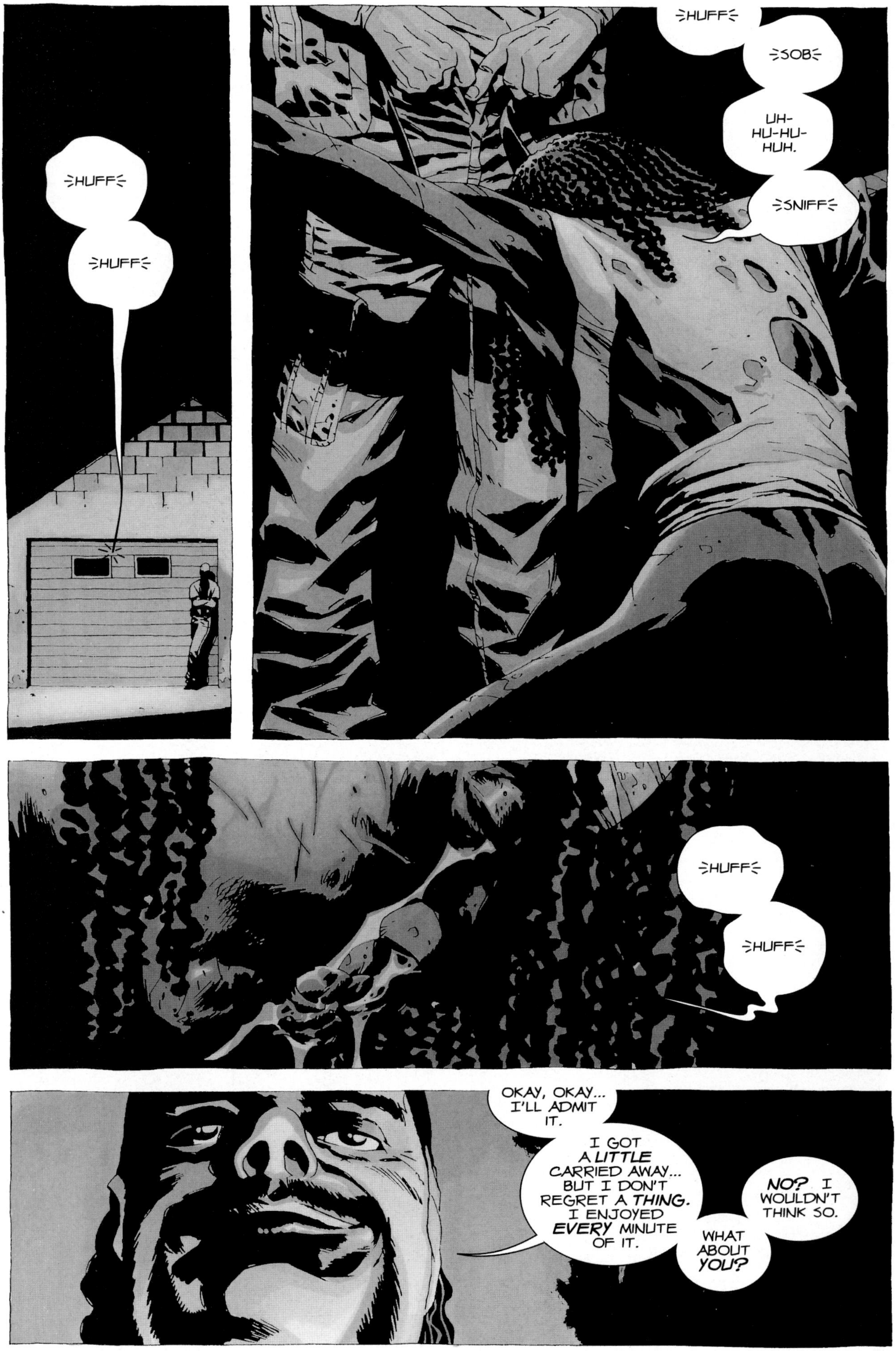

≥HUFF≤
≥HUFF≤
≥HUFF≤
≥SOB≤
UH-
HU-HU-
HUH.
≥SNIFF≤
≥HUFF≤
≥HUFF≤
OKAY, OKAY... I'LL ADMIT IT.
I GOT A LITTLE CARRIED AWAY... BUT I DON'T REGRET A THING. I ENJOYED EVERY MINUTE OF IT.
NO? I WOULDN'T THINK SO.
WHAT ABOUT YOU?

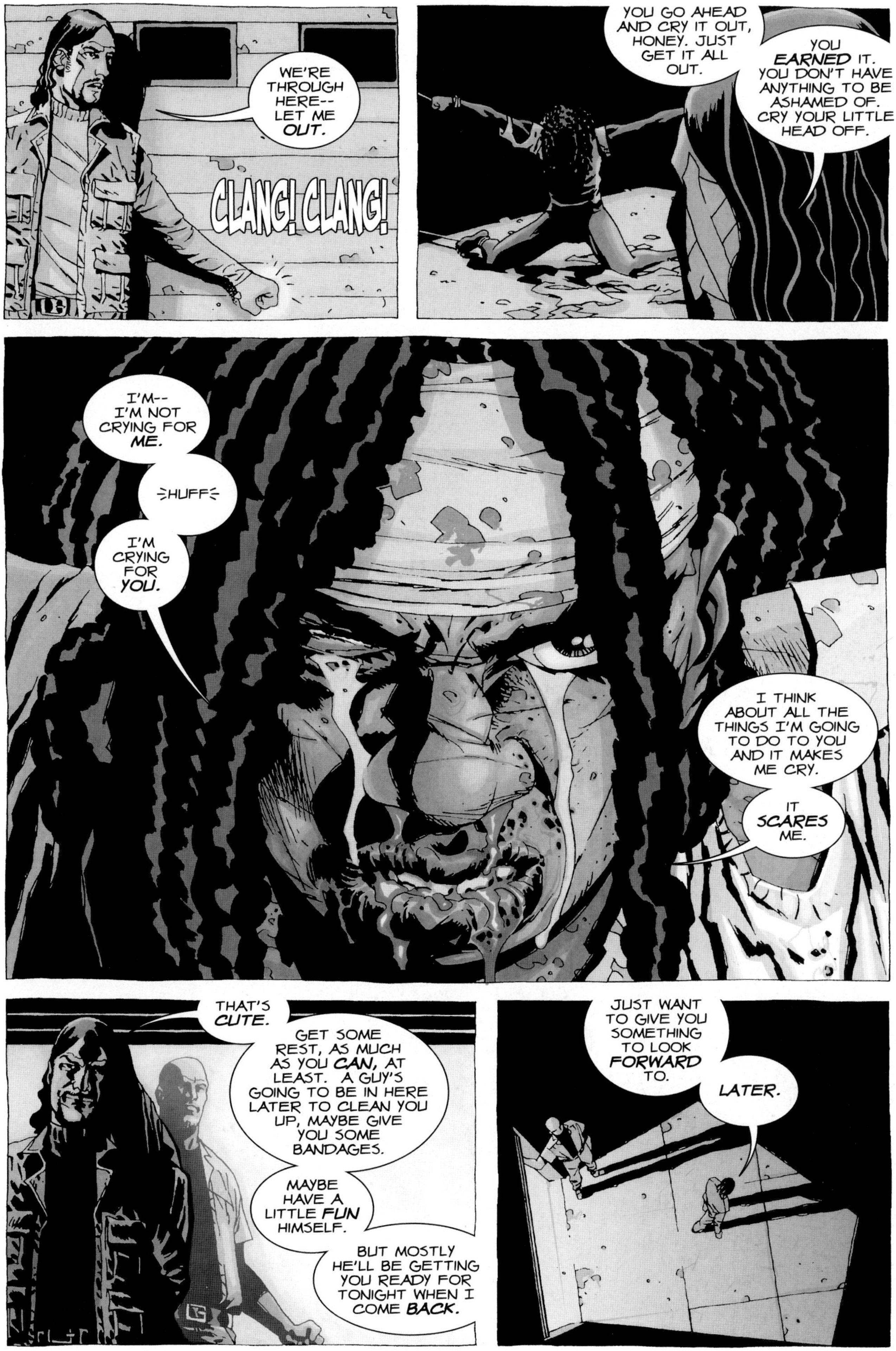
WE'RE THROUGH HERE-- LET ME OUT.
CLANG! CLANG!
YOU GO AHEAD AND CRY IT OUT, HONEY. JUST GET IT ALL OUT.
YOU EARNED IT. YOU DON'T HAVE ANYTHING TO BE ASHAMED OF. CRY YOUR LITTLE HEAD OFF.
I'M-- I'M NOT CRYING FOR ME.
HUFF
I'M CRYING FOR YOU.
I THINK ABOUT ALL THE THINGS I'M GOING TO DO TO YOU AND IT MAKES ME CRY.
IT SCARES ME.
THAT'S CUTE.
GET SOME REST, AS MUCH AS YOU CAN, AT LEAST. A GUY'S GOING TO BE IN HERE LATER TO CLEAN YOU UP, MAYBE GIVE YOU SOME BANDAGES.
MAYBE HAVE A LITTLE FUN HIMSELF.
BUT MOSTLY HE'LL BE GETTING YOU READY FOR TONIGHT WHEN I COME BACK.
JUST WANT TO GIVE YOU SOMETHING TO LOOK FORWARD TO.
LATER.

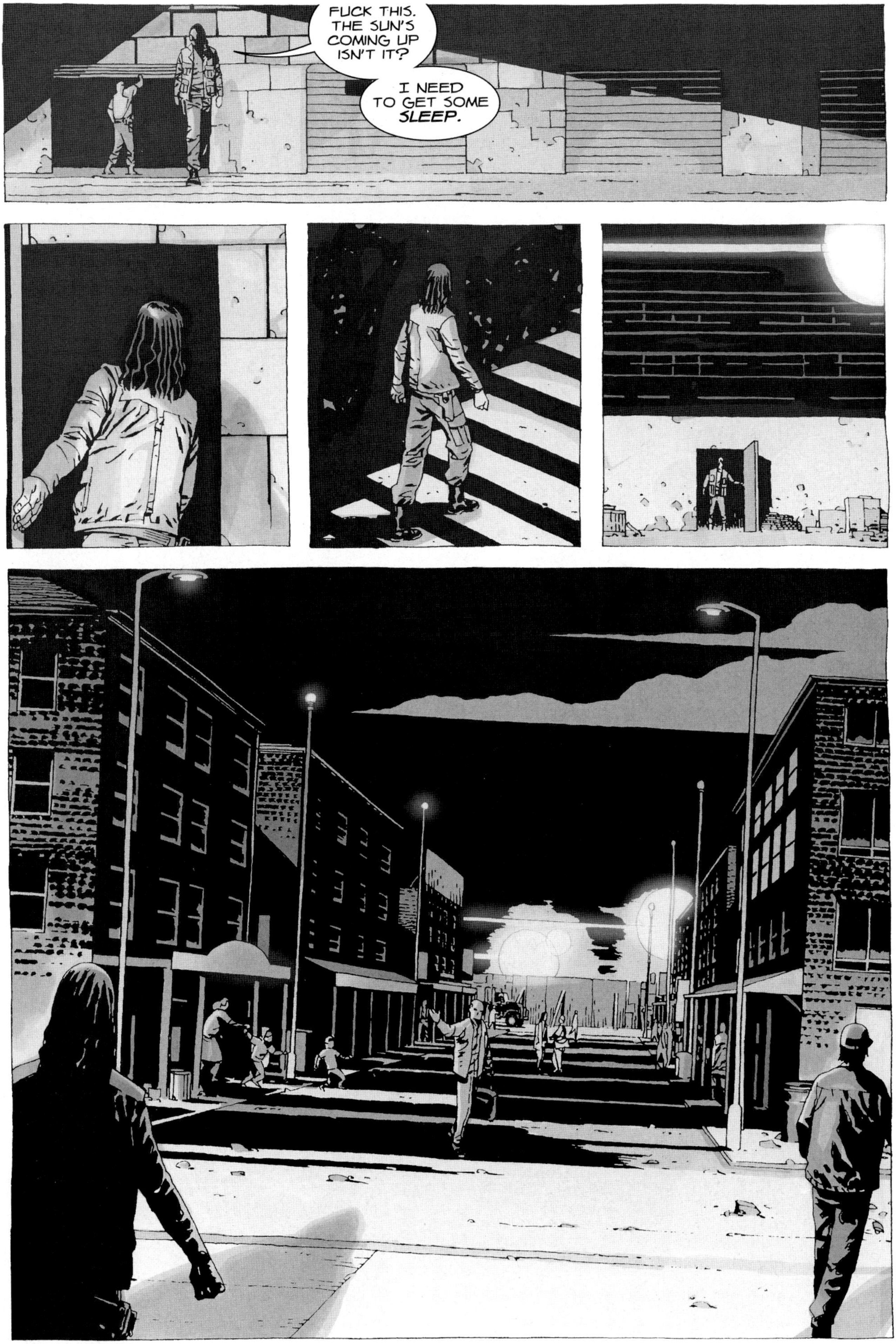

FUCK THIS. THE SUN'S COMING UP ISN'T IT?
I NEED TO GET SOME SLEEP.

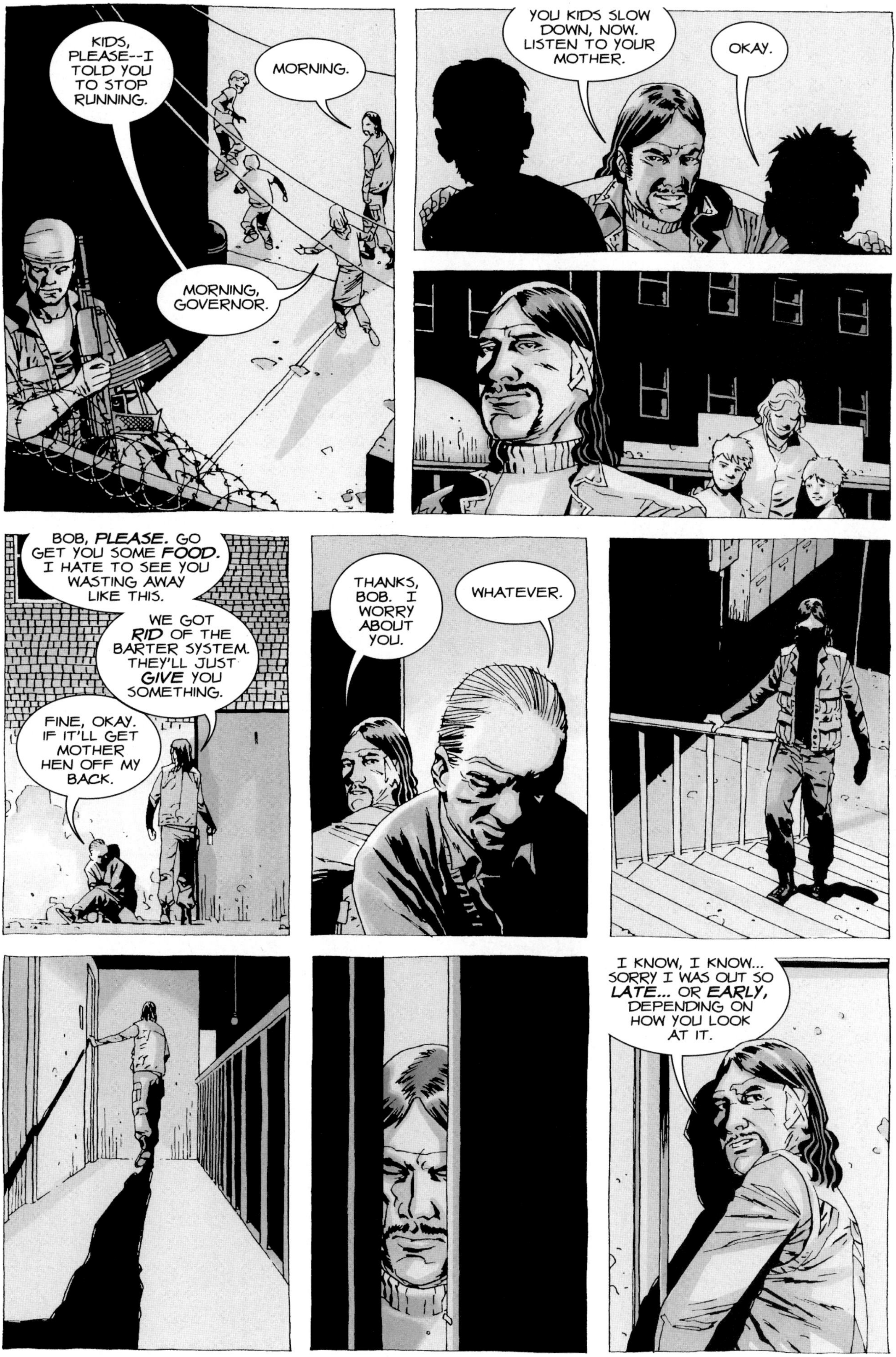
KIDS, PLEASE--I TOLD YOU TO STOP RUNNING.
MORNING.
MORNING, GOVERNOR.
YOU KIDS SLOW DOWN, NOW. LISTEN TO YOUR MOTHER.
OKAY.
BOB, PLEASE. GO GET YOU SOME FOOD. I HATE TO SEE YOU WASTING AWAY LIKE THIS.
WE GOT RID OF THE BARTER SYSTEM. THEY'LL JUST GIVE YOU SOMETHING.
FINE, OKAY. IF IT'LL GET MOTHER HEN OFF MY BACK.
THANKS, BOB. I WORRY ABOUT YOU.
WHATEVER.
I KNOW, I KNOW... SORRY I WAS OUT SO LATE... OR EARLY, DEPENDING ON HOW YOU LOOK AT IT.

ROAARGH!

WRAMM!!

BEHAVE YOURSELF, GODDAMN IT!

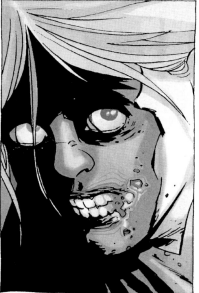

I'M SORRY, HONEY. WHAT'S GOT YOU SO UPSET?

YOU HAVEN'T TRIED TO ATTACK ME IN MONTHS.

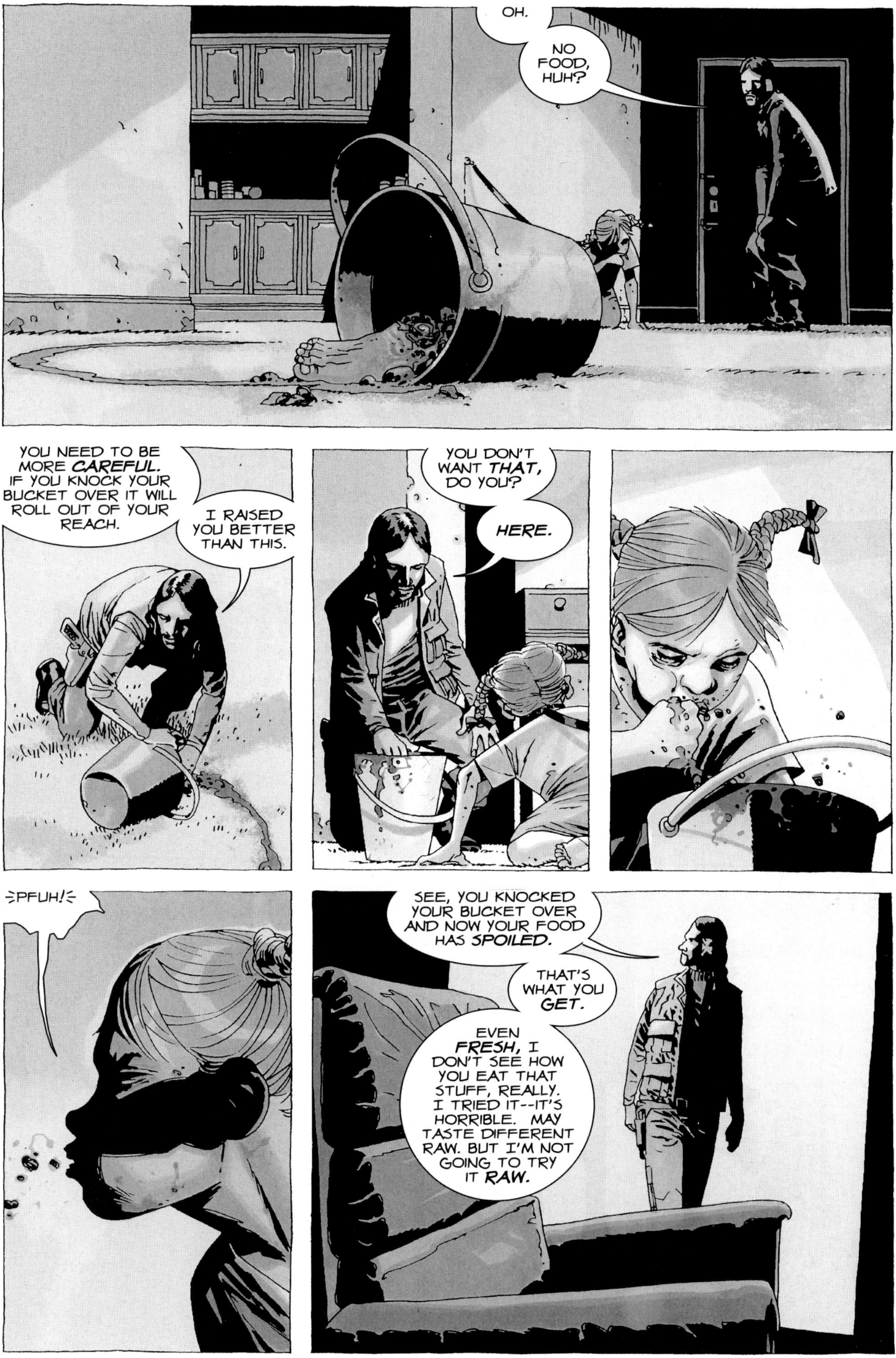
OH.
NO FOOD, HUH?
YOU NEED TO BE MORE CAREFUL. IF YOU KNOCK YOUR BUCKET OVER IT WILL ROLL OUT OF YOUR REACH.
I RAISED YOU BETTER THAN THIS.
YOU DON'T WANT THAT, DO YOU?
HERE.
PFUH!
SEE, YOU KNOCKED YOUR BUCKET OVER AND NOW YOUR FOOD HAS SPOILED.
THAT'S WHAT YOU GET.
EVEN FRESH, I DON'T SEE HOW YOU EAT THAT STUFF, REALLY. I TRIED IT--IT'S HORRIBLE. MAY TASTE DIFFERENT RAW. BUT I'M NOT GOING TO TRY IT RAW.

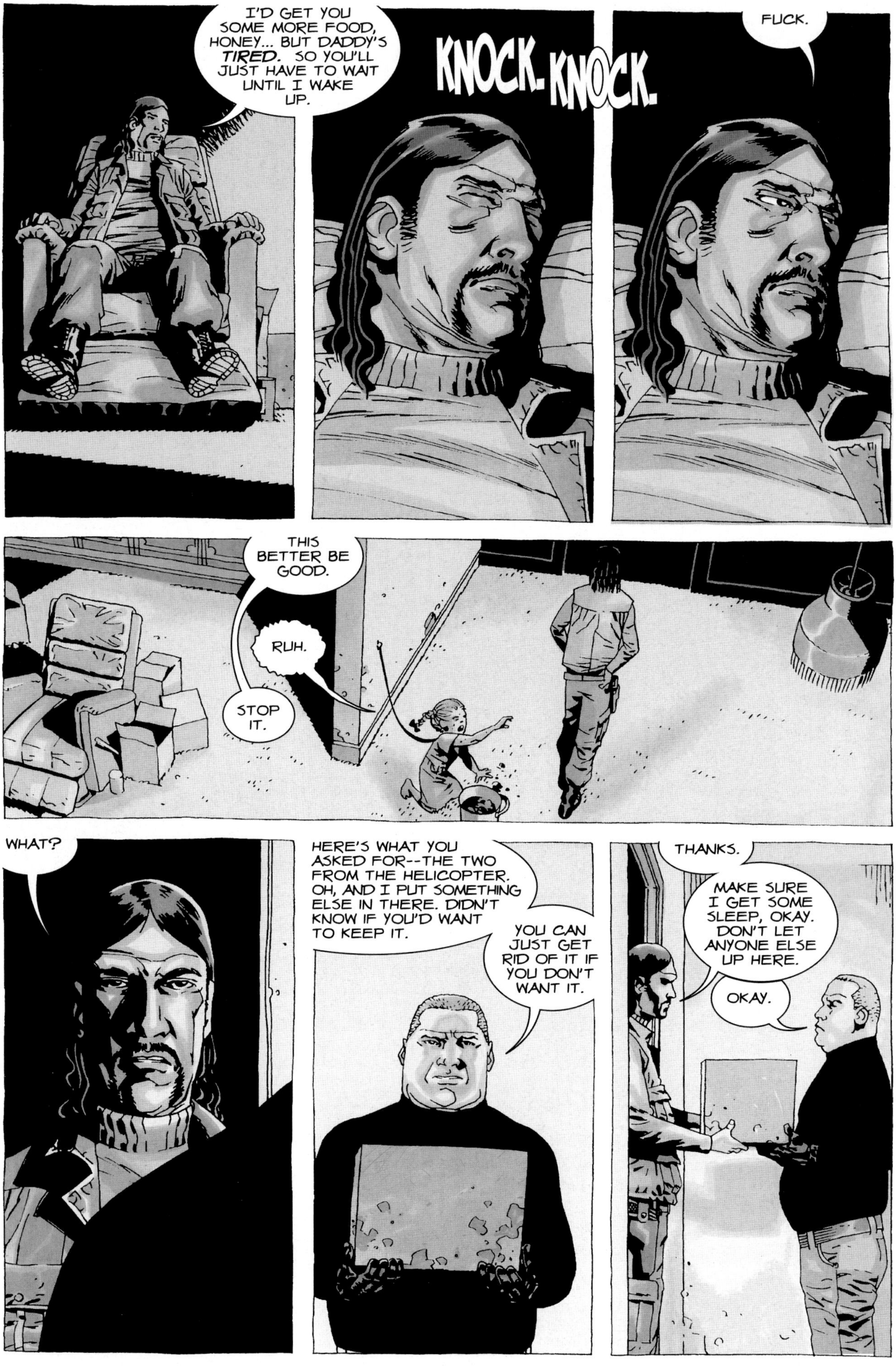

I'D GET YOU SOME MORE FOOD, HONEY... BUT DADDY'S TIRED. SO YOU'LL JUST HAVE TO WAIT UNTIL I WAKE UP.
KNOCK. KNOCK.
FUCK.
THIS BETTER BE GOOD.
RUH.
STOP IT.
WHAT?
HERE'S WHAT YOU ASKED FOR--THE TWO FROM THE HELICOPTER. OH, AND I PUT SOMETHING ELSE IN THERE. DIDN'T KNOW IF YOU'D WANT TO KEEP IT.
YOU CAN JUST GET RID OF IT IF YOU DON'T WANT IT.
THANKS.
MAKE SURE I GET SOME SLEEP, OKAY. DON'T LET ANYONE ELSE UP HERE.
OKAY.

NO. THIS ISN'T FOR YOU.

WELL...

...I SUPPOSE YOU CAN HAVE THIS.

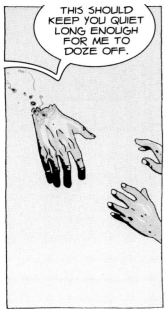

THIS SHOULD KEEP YOU QUIET LONG ENOUGH FOR ME TO DOZE OFF.

YOU GUYS HAVE GOT GUESTS-- NEW NEIGHBORS, ACTUALLY.

YOU TWO CAN KEEP EACH OTHER COMPANY.

GOTTA GET OFF MY FEET...

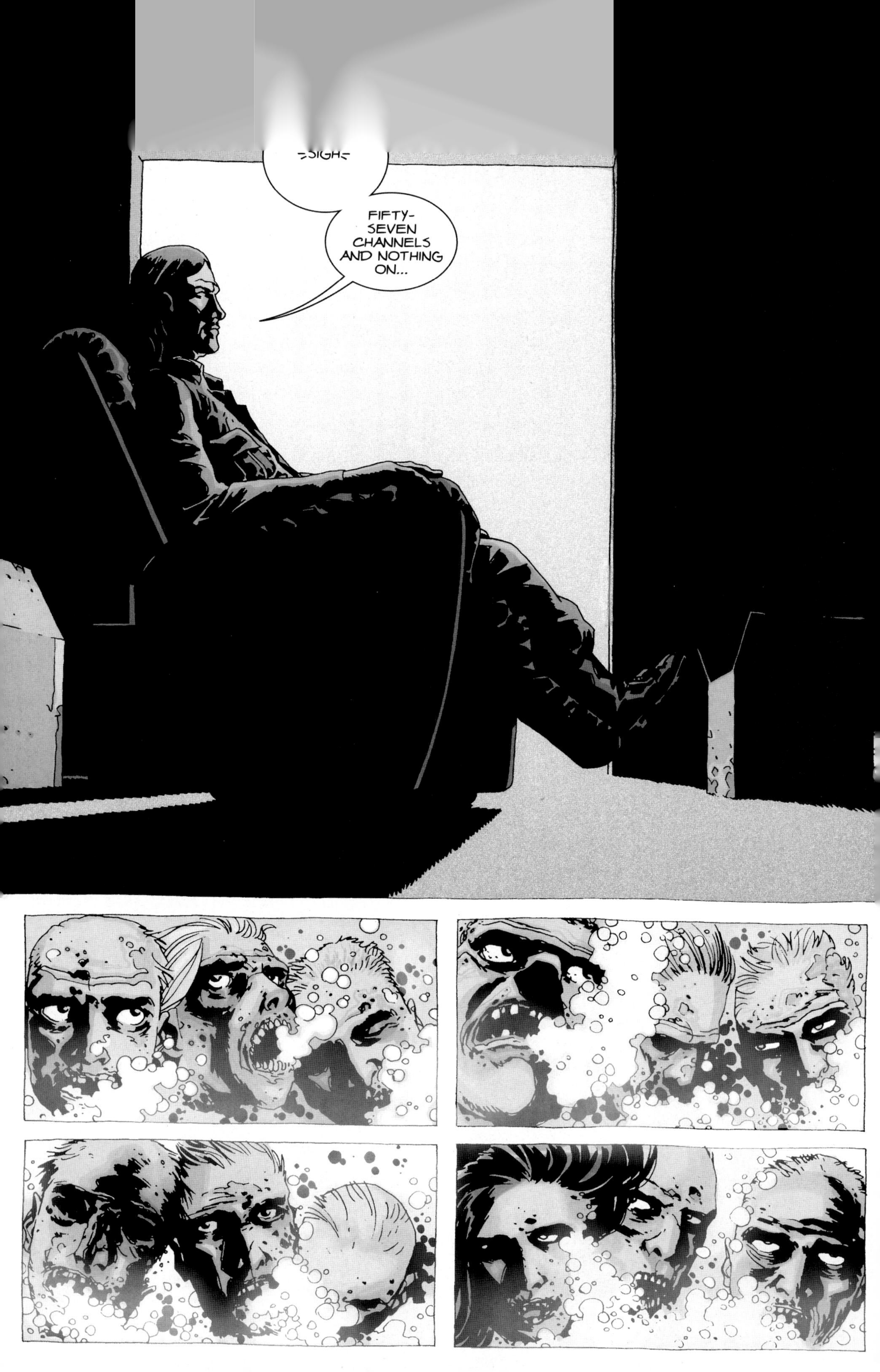

=SIGH=
FIFTY-SEVEN CHANNELS AND NOTHING ON...

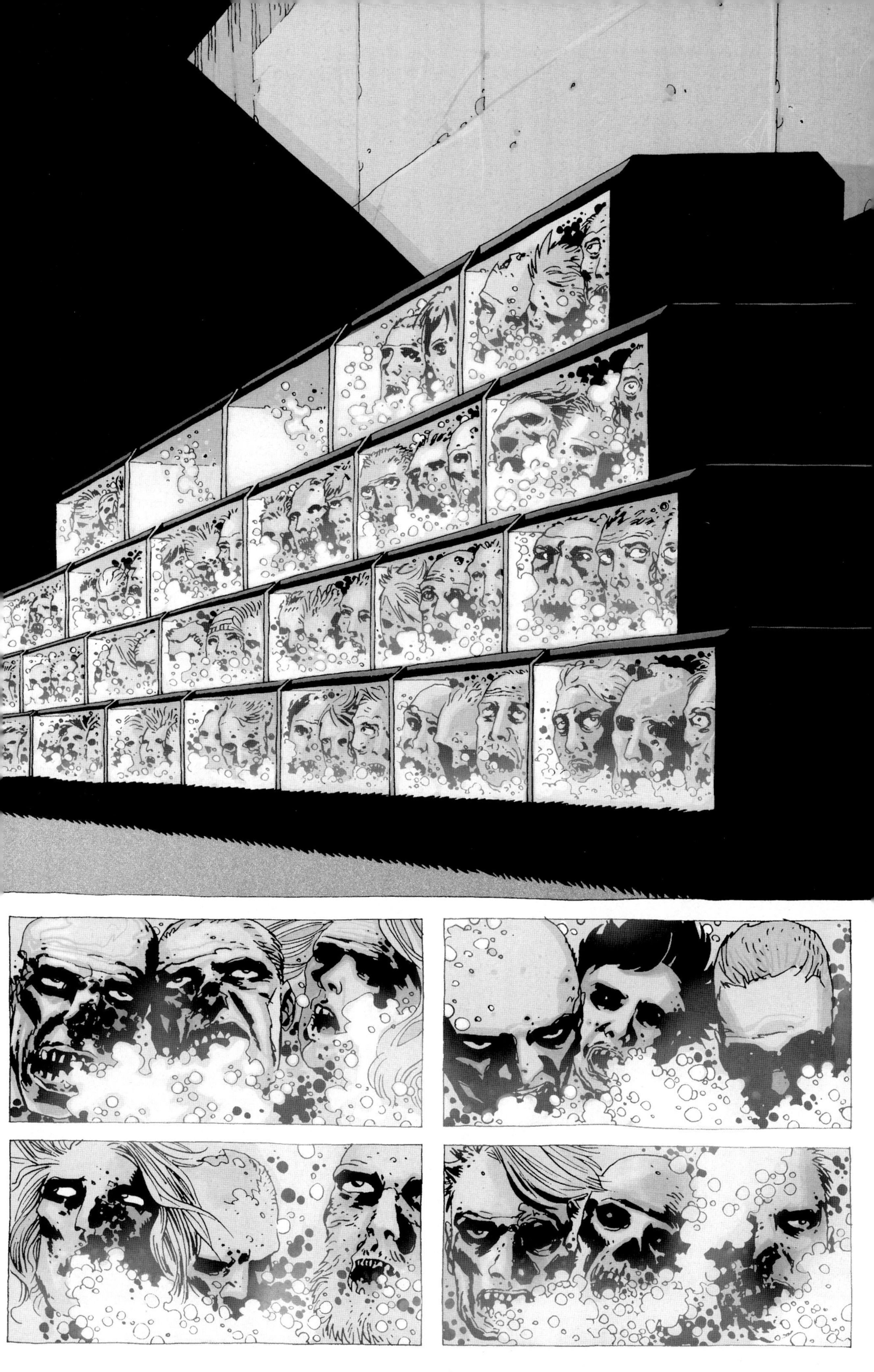

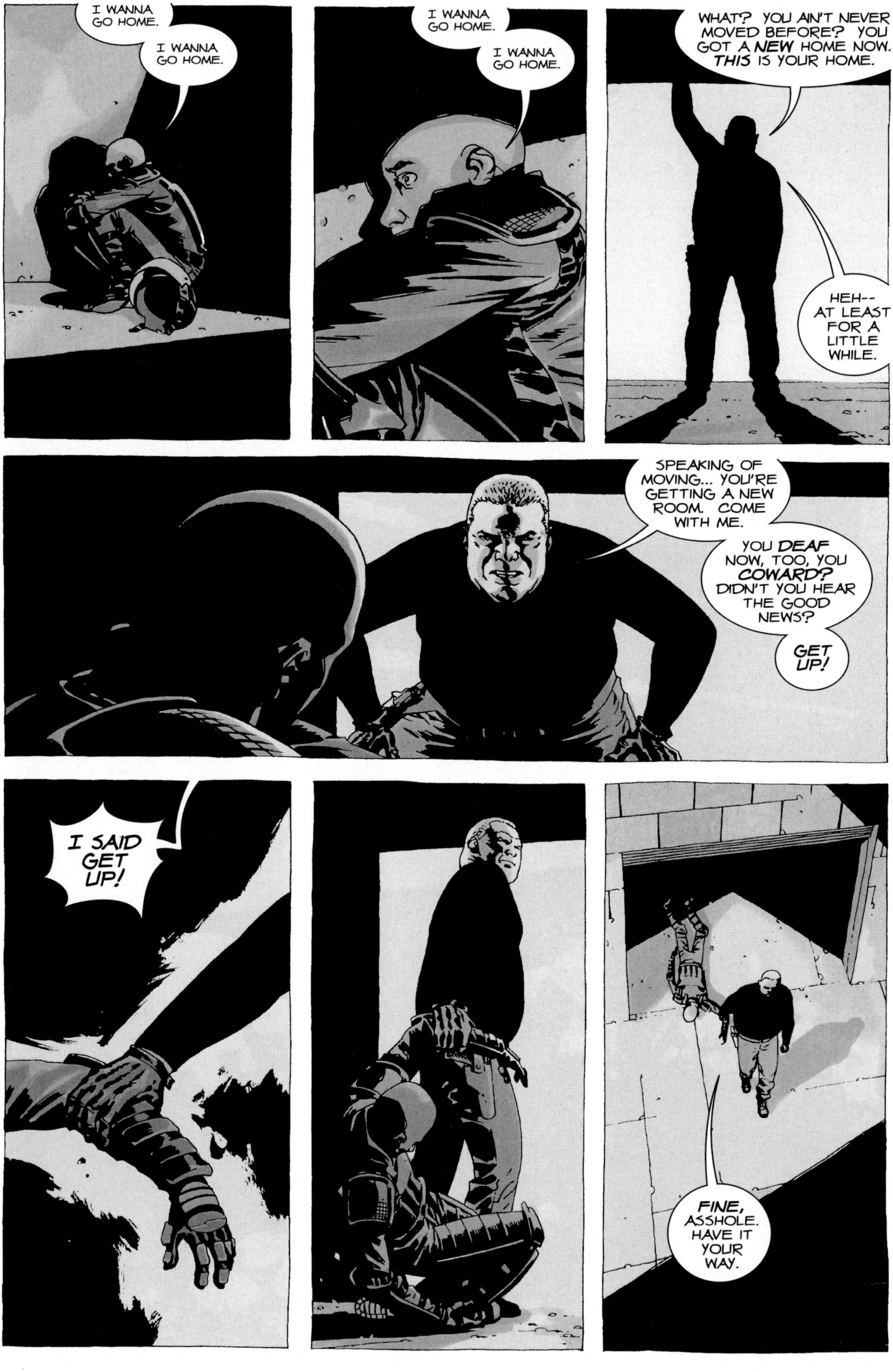
I WANNA GO HOME.
I WANNA GO HOME.
I WANNA GO HOME.
I WANNA GO HOME.
WHAT? YOU AIN'T NEVER MOVED BEFORE? YOU GOT A NEW HOME NOW. THIS IS YOUR HOME.
HEH-- AT LEAST FOR A LITTLE WHILE.
SPEAKING OF MOVING... YOU'RE GETTING A NEW ROOM. COME WITH ME.
YOU DEAF NOW, TOO, YOU COWARD? DIDN'T YOU HEAR THE GOOD NEWS?
GET UP!
I SAID GET UP!
FINE, ASSHOLE. HAVE IT YOUR WAY.

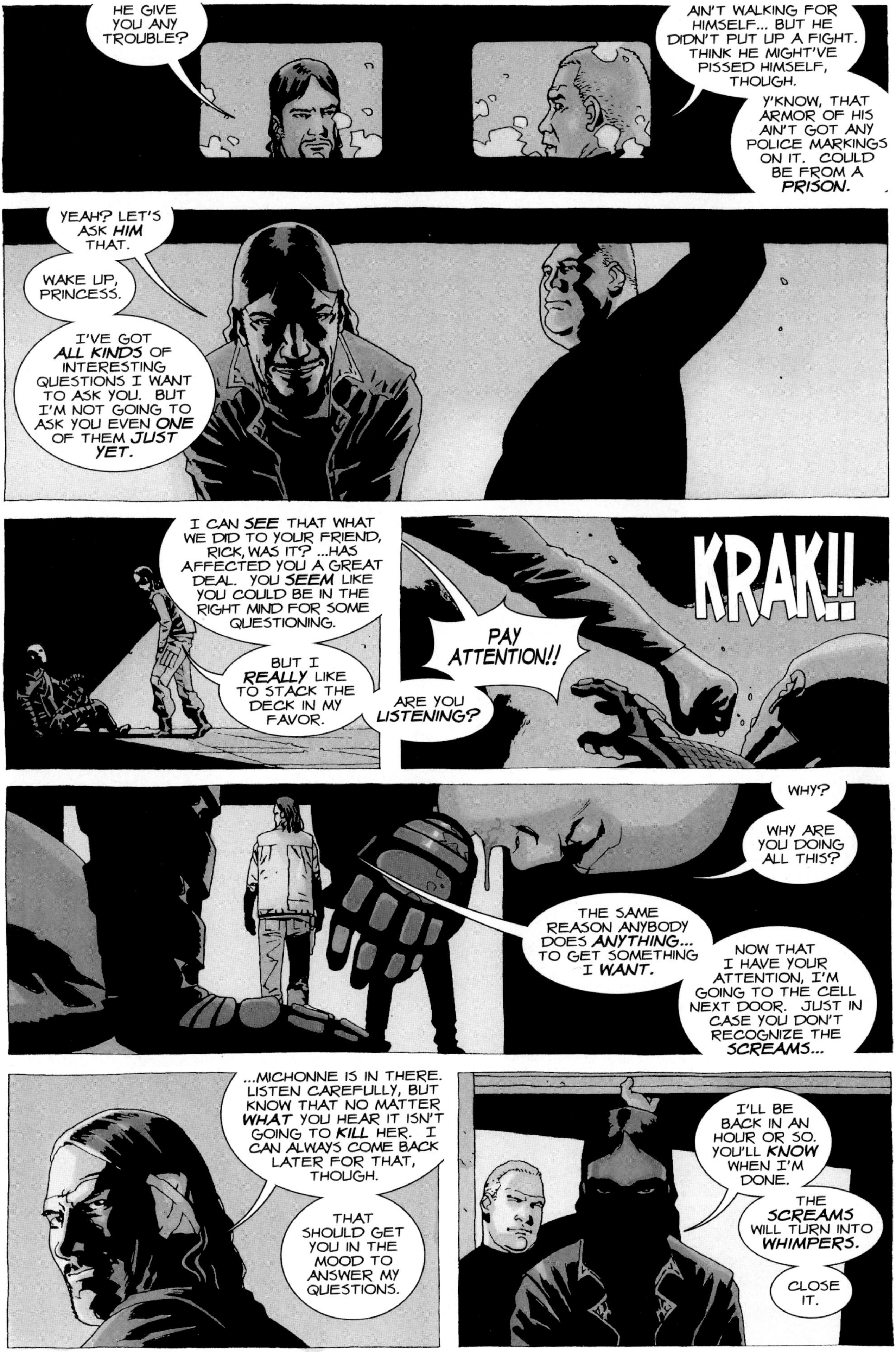
HE GIVE YOU ANY TROUBLE?
AIN'T WALKING FOR HIMSELF... BUT HE DIDN'T PUT UP A FIGHT. THINK HE MIGHT'VE PISSED HIMSELF, THOUGH.
Y'KNOW, THAT ARMOR OF HIS AIN'T GOT ANY POLICE MARKINGS ON IT. COULD BE FROM A PRISON.
YEAH? LET'S ASK HIM THAT.
WAKE UP, PRINCESS.
I'VE GOT ALL KINDS OF INTERESTING QUESTIONS I WANT TO ASK YOU. BUT I'M NOT GOING TO ASK YOU EVEN ONE OF THEM JUST YET.
I CAN SEE THAT WHAT WE DID TO YOUR FRIEND, RICK, WAS IT? ...HAS AFFECTED YOU A GREAT DEAL. YOU SEEM LIKE YOU COULD BE IN THE RIGHT MIND FOR SOME QUESTIONING.
BUT I REALLY LIKE TO STACK THE DECK IN MY FAVOR.
ARE YOU LISTENING?
PAY ATTENTION!!
KRAK!!
WHY?
WHY ARE YOU DOING ALL THIS?
THE SAME REASON ANYBODY DOES ANYTHING... TO GET SOMETHING I WANT.
NOW THAT I HAVE YOUR ATTENTION, I'M GOING TO THE CELL NEXT DOOR. JUST IN CASE YOU DON'T RECOGNIZE THE SCREAMS...
...MICHONNE IS IN THERE. LISTEN CAREFULLY, BUT KNOW THAT NO MATTER WHAT YOU HEAR IT ISN'T GOING TO KILL HER. I CAN ALWAYS COME BACK LATER FOR THAT, THOUGH.
THAT SHOULD GET YOU IN THE MOOD TO ANSWER MY QUESTIONS.
I'LL BE BACK IN AN HOUR OR SO. YOU'LL KNOW WHEN I'M DONE.
THE SCREAMS WILL TURN INTO WHIMPERS.
CLOSE IT.

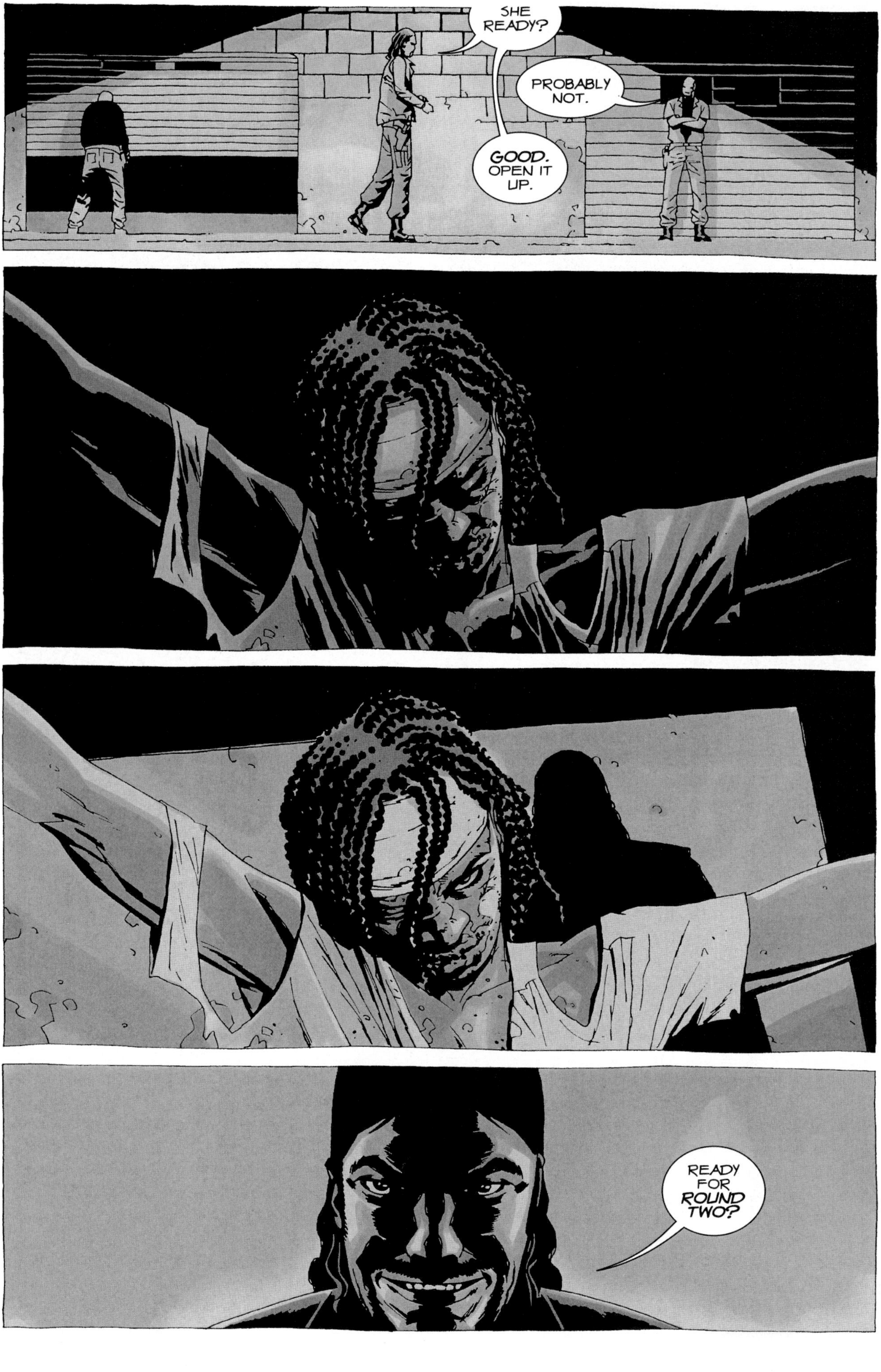
SHE READY?
PROBABLY NOT.
GOOD. OPEN IT UP.
READY FOR ROUND TWO?

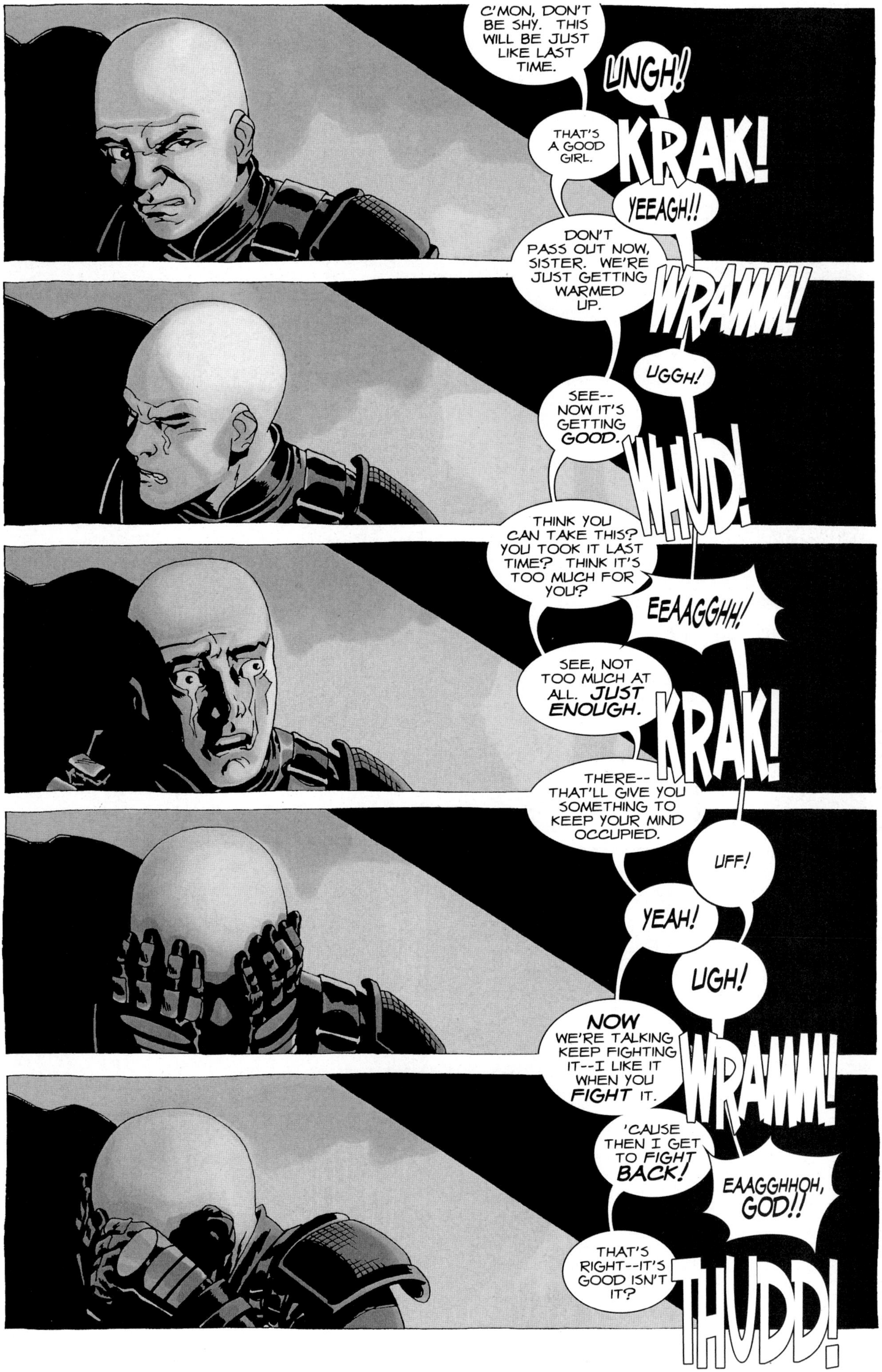
C'MON, DON'T BE SHY. THIS WILL BE JUST LIKE LAST TIME.
UNGH!
THAT'S A GOOD GIRL.
KRAK!
YEEAGH!!
DON'T PASS OUT NOW, SISTER. WE'RE JUST GETTING WARMED UP.
WRAMM!
UGGH!
SEE--NOW IT'S GETTING GOOD.
WHUD!
THINK YOU CAN TAKE THIS? YOU TOOK IT LAST TIME? THINK IT'S TOO MUCH FOR YOU?
EEAAGGHH!
SEE, NOT TOO MUCH AT ALL. JUST ENOUGH.
KRAK!
THERE--THAT'LL GIVE YOU SOMETHING TO KEEP YOUR MIND OCCUPIED.
UFF!
YEAH!
UGH!
NOW WE'RE TALKING KEEP FIGHTING IT--I LIKE IT WHEN YOU FIGHT IT.
WRAMM!
'CAUSE THEN I GET TO FIGHT BACK!
EAAGGHHOH, GOD!!
THAT'S RIGHT--IT'S GOOD ISN'T IT?
THUDD!

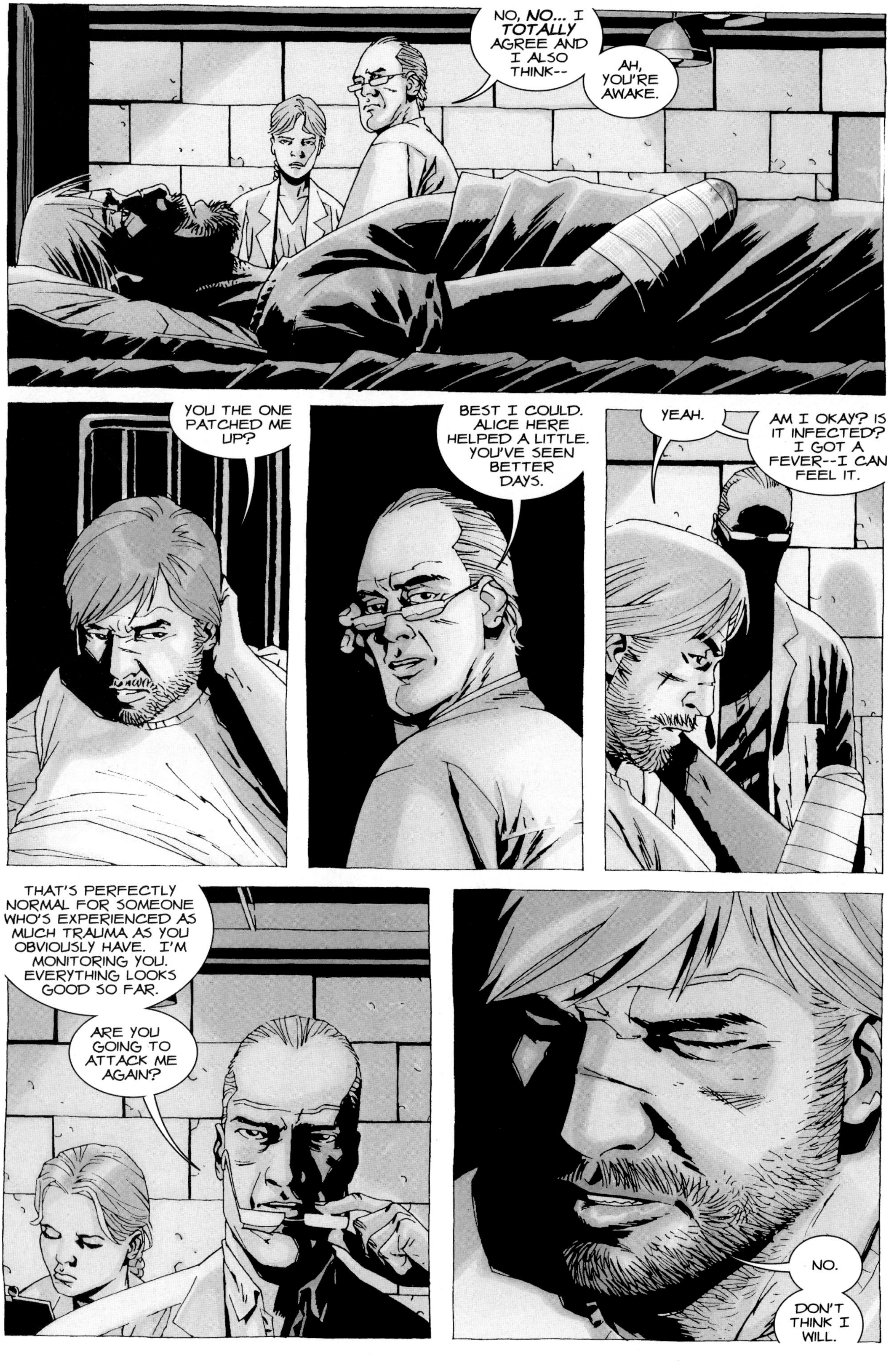
NO, NO... I TOTALLY AGREE AND I ALSO THINK--
AH, YOU'RE AWAKE.
YOU THE ONE PATCHED ME UP?
BEST I COULD. ALICE HERE HELPED A LITTLE. YOU'VE SEEN BETTER DAYS.
YEAH.
AM I OKAY? IS IT INFECTED? I GOT A FEVER--I CAN FEEL IT.
THAT'S PERFECTLY NORMAL FOR SOMEONE WHO'S EXPERIENCED AS MUCH TRAUMA AS YOU OBVIOUSLY HAVE. I'M MONITORING YOU. EVERYTHING LOOKS GOOD SO FAR.
ARE YOU GOING TO ATTACK ME AGAIN?
NO.
DON'T THINK I WILL.

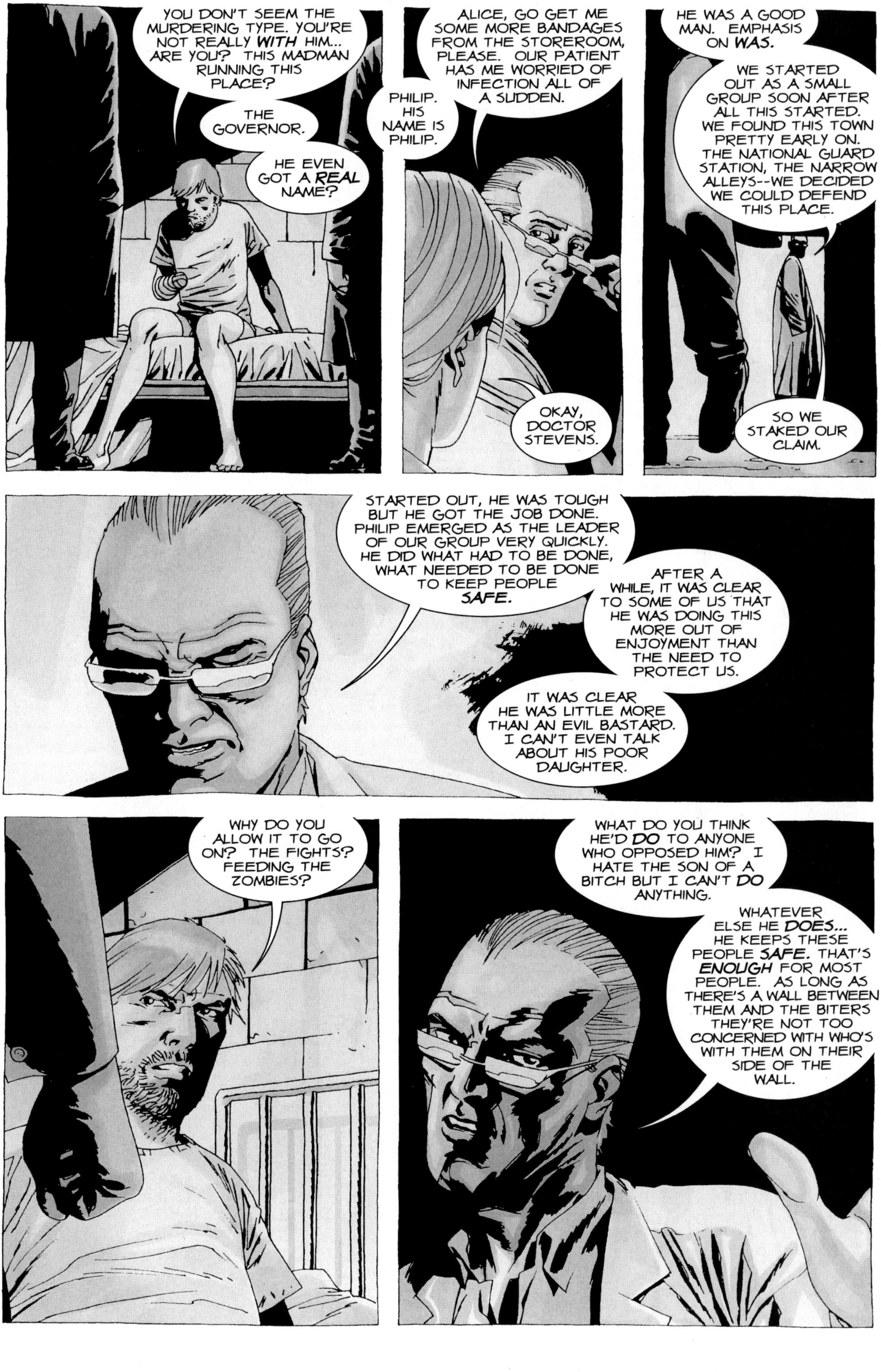

YOU DON'T SEEM THE MURDERING TYPE. YOU'RE NOT REALLY WITH HIM... ARE YOU? THIS MADMAN RUNNING THIS PLACE?
THE GOVERNOR.
HE EVEN GOT A REAL NAME?
PHILIP. HIS NAME IS PHILIP.
ALICE, GO GET ME SOME MORE BANDAGES FROM THE STOREROOM, PLEASE. OUR PATIENT HAS ME WORRIED OF INFECTION ALL OF A SUDDEN.
OKAY, DOCTOR STEVENS.
HE WAS A GOOD MAN. EMPHASIS ON WAS.
WE STARTED OUT AS A SMALL GROUP SOON AFTER ALL THIS STARTED. WE FOUND THIS TOWN PRETTY EARLY ON. THE NATIONAL GUARD STATION, THE NARROW ALLEYS--WE DECIDED WE COULD DEFEND THIS PLACE.
SO WE STAKED OUR CLAIM.
STARTED OUT, HE WAS TOUGH BUT HE GOT THE JOB DONE. PHILIP EMERGED AS THE LEADER OF OUR GROUP VERY QUICKLY. HE DID WHAT HAD TO BE DONE, WHAT NEEDED TO BE DONE TO KEEP PEOPLE SAFE.
AFTER A WHILE, IT WAS CLEAR TO SOME OF US THAT HE WAS DOING THIS MORE OUT OF ENJOYMENT THAN THE NEED TO PROTECT US.
IT WAS CLEAR HE WAS LITTLE MORE THAN AN EVIL BASTARD. I CAN'T EVEN TALK ABOUT HIS POOR DAUGHTER.
WHY DO YOU ALLOW IT TO GO ON? THE FIGHTS? FEEDING THE ZOMBIES?
WHAT DO YOU THINK HE'D DO TO ANYONE WHO OPPOSED HIM? I HATE THE SON OF A BITCH BUT I CAN'T DO ANYTHING.
WHATEVER ELSE HE DOES... HE KEEPS THESE PEOPLE SAFE. THAT'S ENOUGH FOR MOST PEOPLE. AS LONG AS THERE'S A WALL BETWEEN THEM AND THE BITERS THEY'RE NOT TOO CONCERNED WITH WHO'S WITH THEM ON THEIR SIDE OF THE WALL.

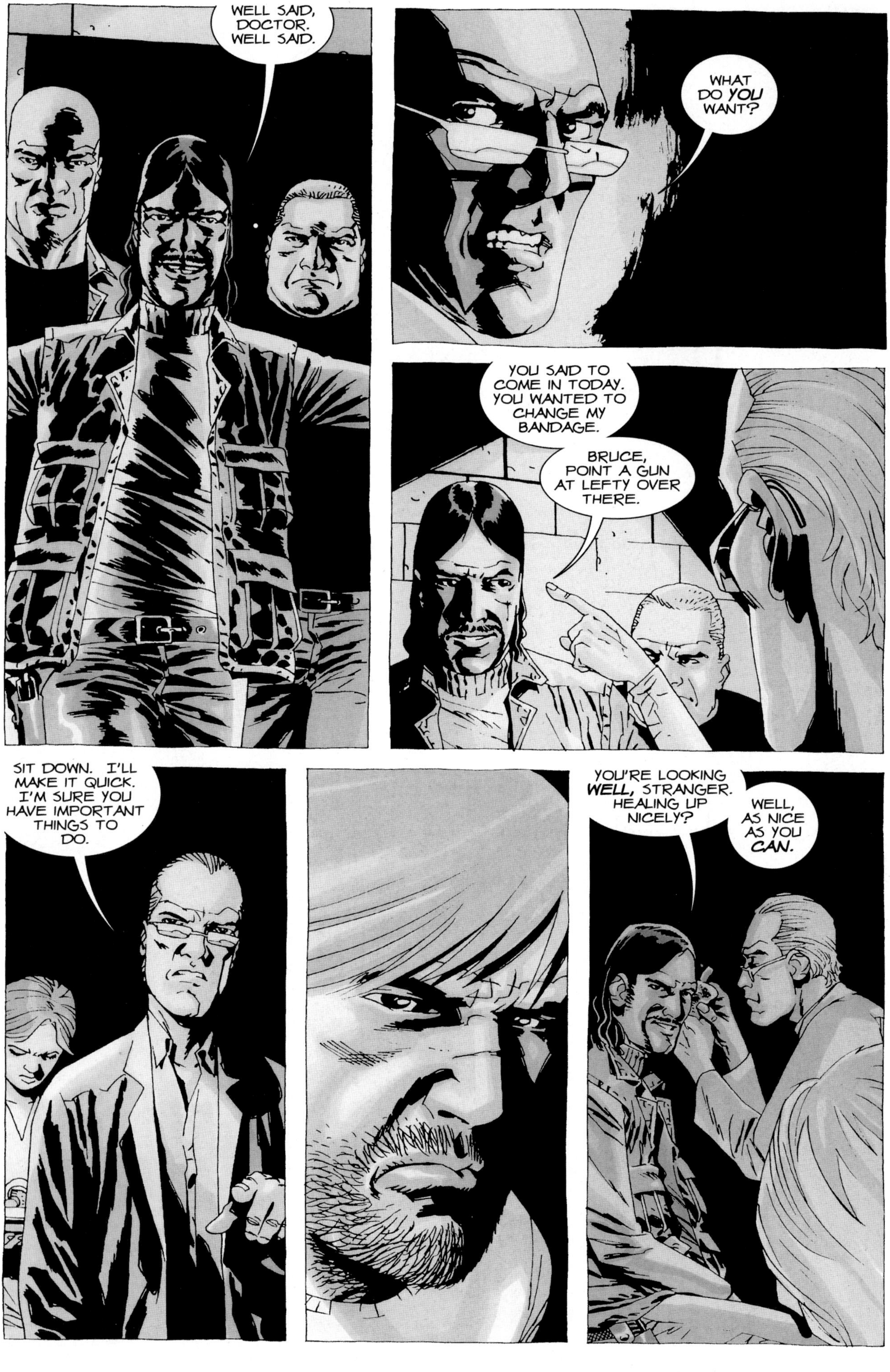
WELL SAID, DOCTOR. WELL SAID.
WHAT DO *YOU* WANT?
YOU SAID TO COME IN TODAY. YOU WANTED TO CHANGE MY BANDAGE.
BRUCE, POINT A GUN AT LEFTY OVER THERE.
SIT DOWN. I'LL MAKE IT QUICK. I'M SURE YOU HAVE IMPORTANT THINGS TO DO.
YOU'RE LOOKING *WELL,* STRANGER. HEALING UP NICELY?
WELL, AS NICE AS YOU *CAN.*

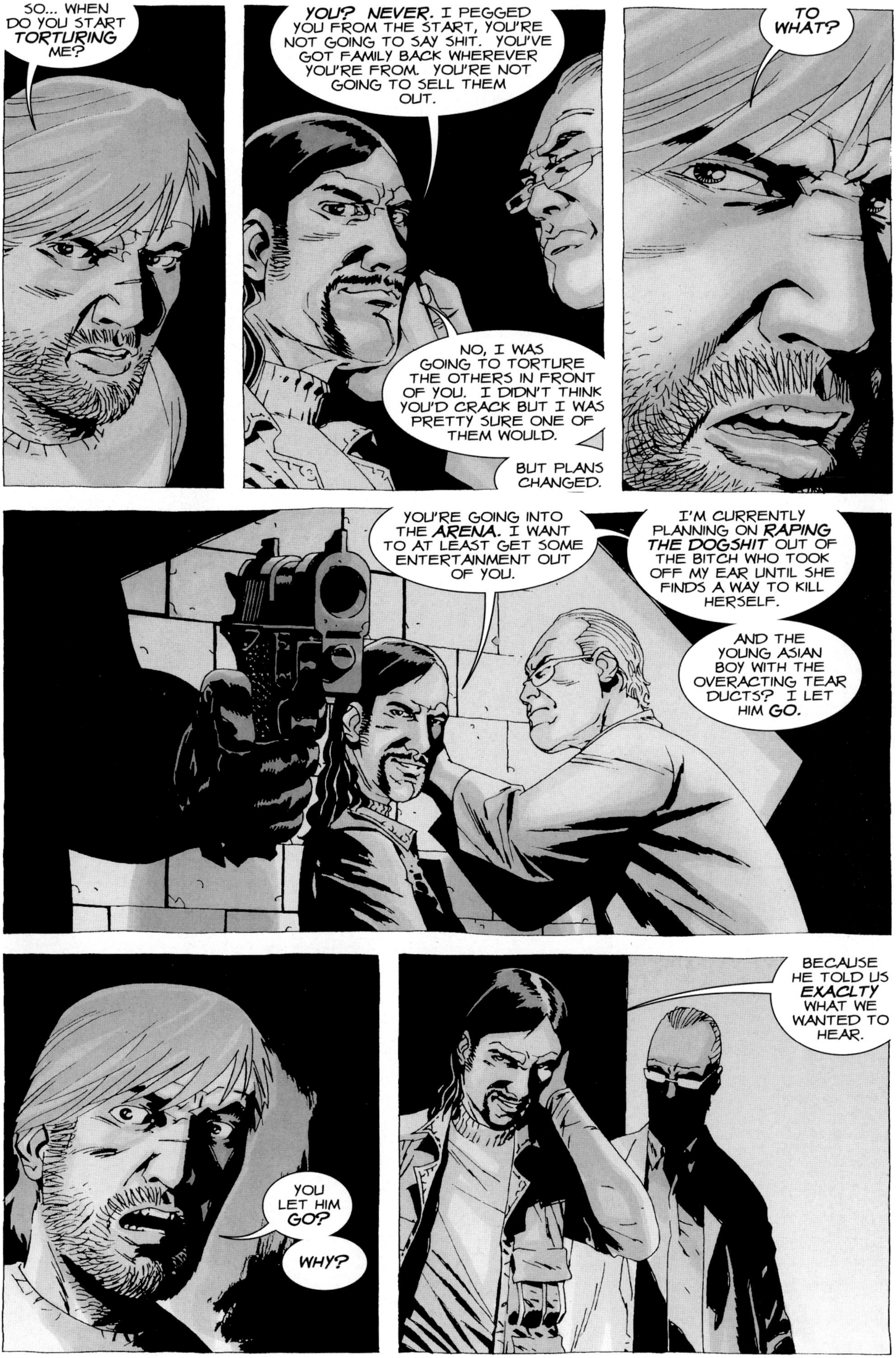
SO... WHEN DO YOU START TORTURING ME?
YOU? NEVER. I PEGGED YOU FROM THE START, YOU'RE NOT GOING TO SAY SHIT. YOU'VE GOT FAMILY BACK WHEREVER YOU'RE FROM. YOU'RE NOT GOING TO SELL THEM OUT.
NO, I WAS GOING TO TORTURE THE OTHERS IN FRONT OF YOU. I DIDN'T THINK YOU'D CRACK BUT I WAS PRETTY SURE ONE OF THEM WOULD.
BUT PLANS CHANGED.
TO WHAT?
YOU'RE GOING INTO THE ARENA. I WANT TO AT LEAST GET SOME ENTERTAINMENT OUT OF YOU.
I'M CURRENTLY PLANNING ON RAPING THE DOGSHIT OUT OF THE BITCH WHO TOOK OFF MY EAR UNTIL SHE FINDS A WAY TO KILL HERSELF.
AND THE YOUNG ASIAN BOY WITH THE OVERACTING TEAR DUCTS? I LET HIM GO.
YOU LET HIM GO?
WHY?
BECAUSE HE TOLD US EXACLTY WHAT WE WANTED TO HEAR.

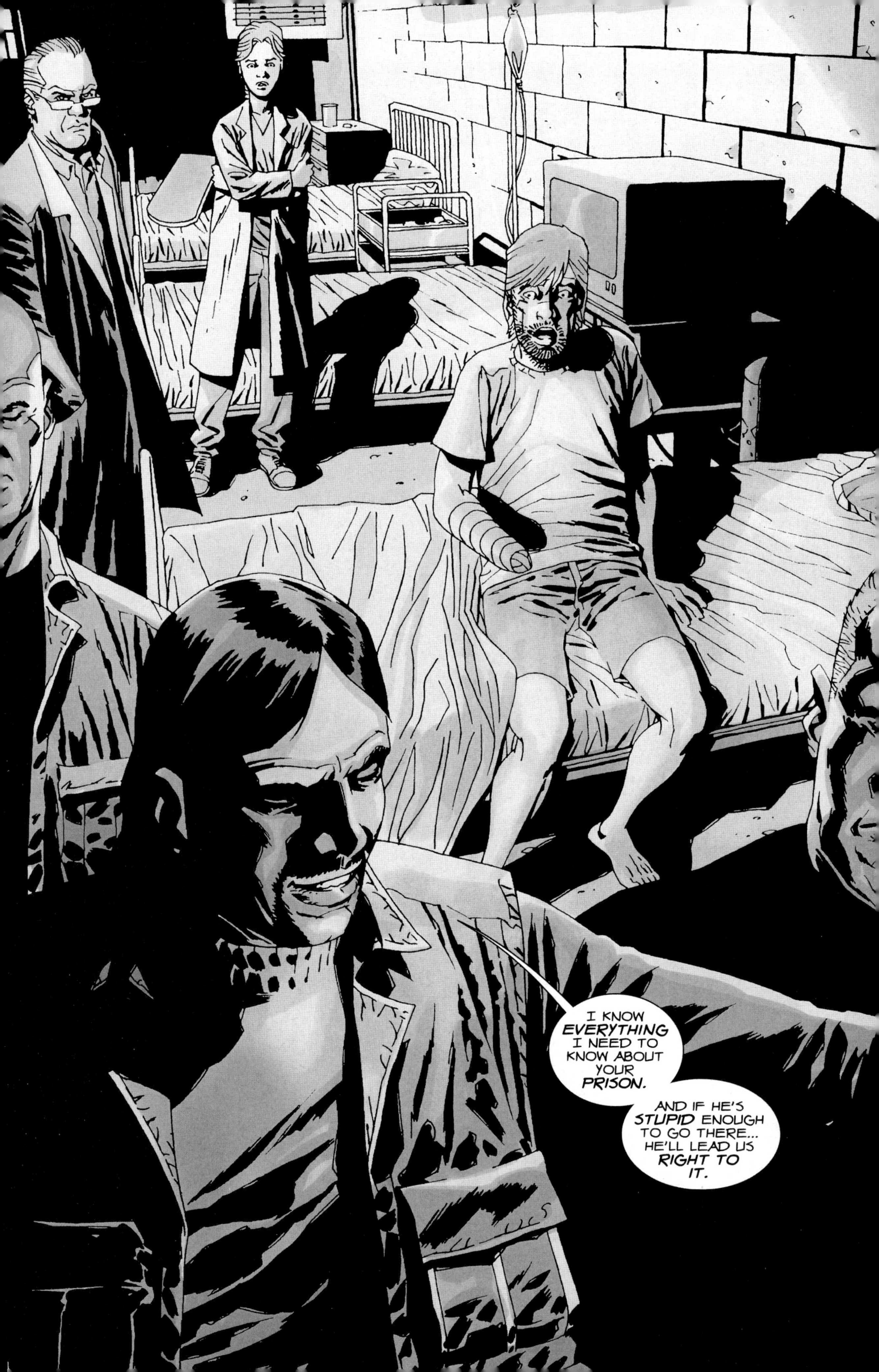
I KNOW EVERYTHING I NEED TO KNOW ABOUT YOUR PRISON.
AND IF HE'S STUPID ENOUGH TO GO THERE... HE'LL LEAD US RIGHT TO IT.

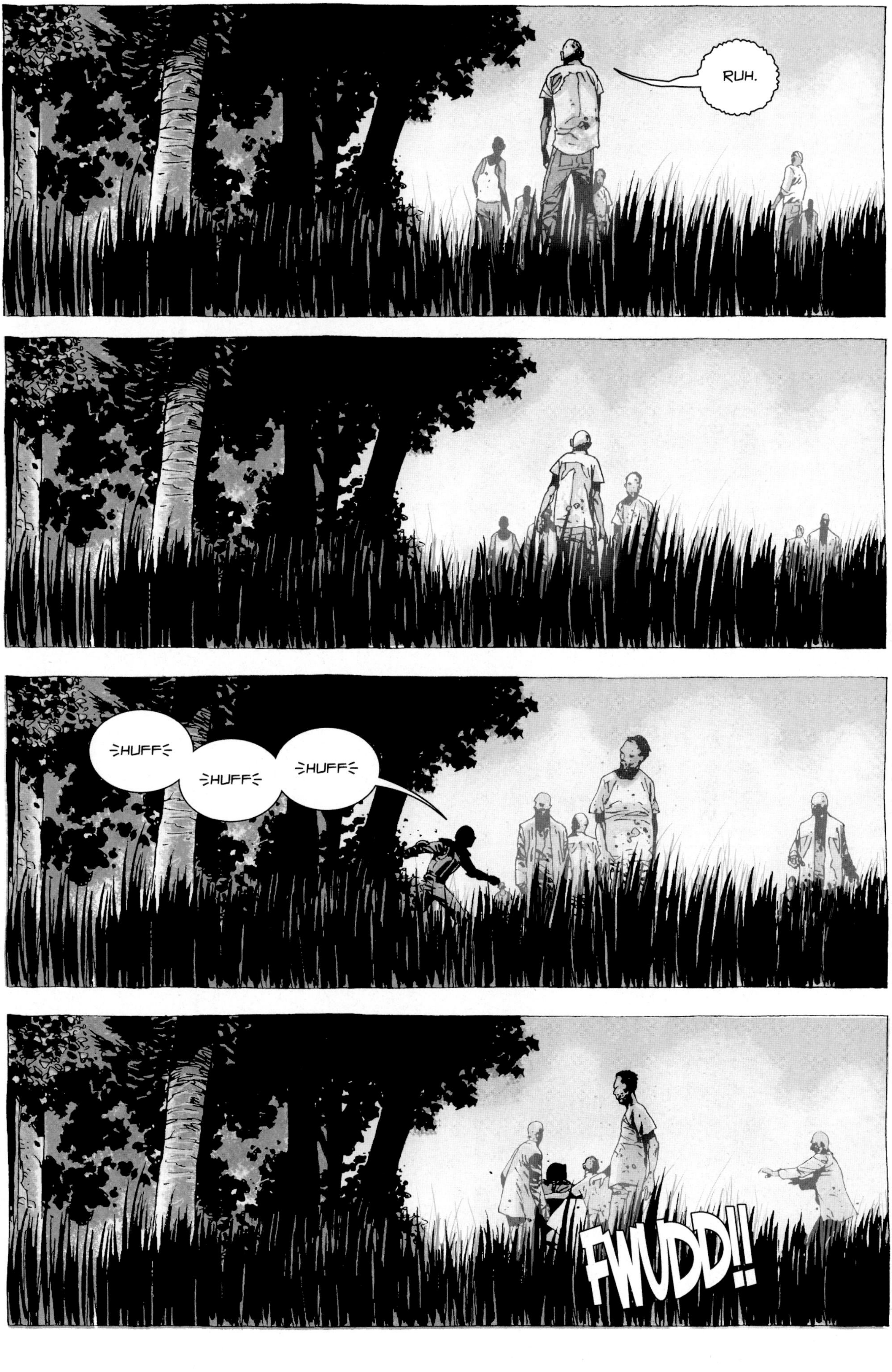
RUH.
HUFF
HUFF
HUFF
FWUDD!!

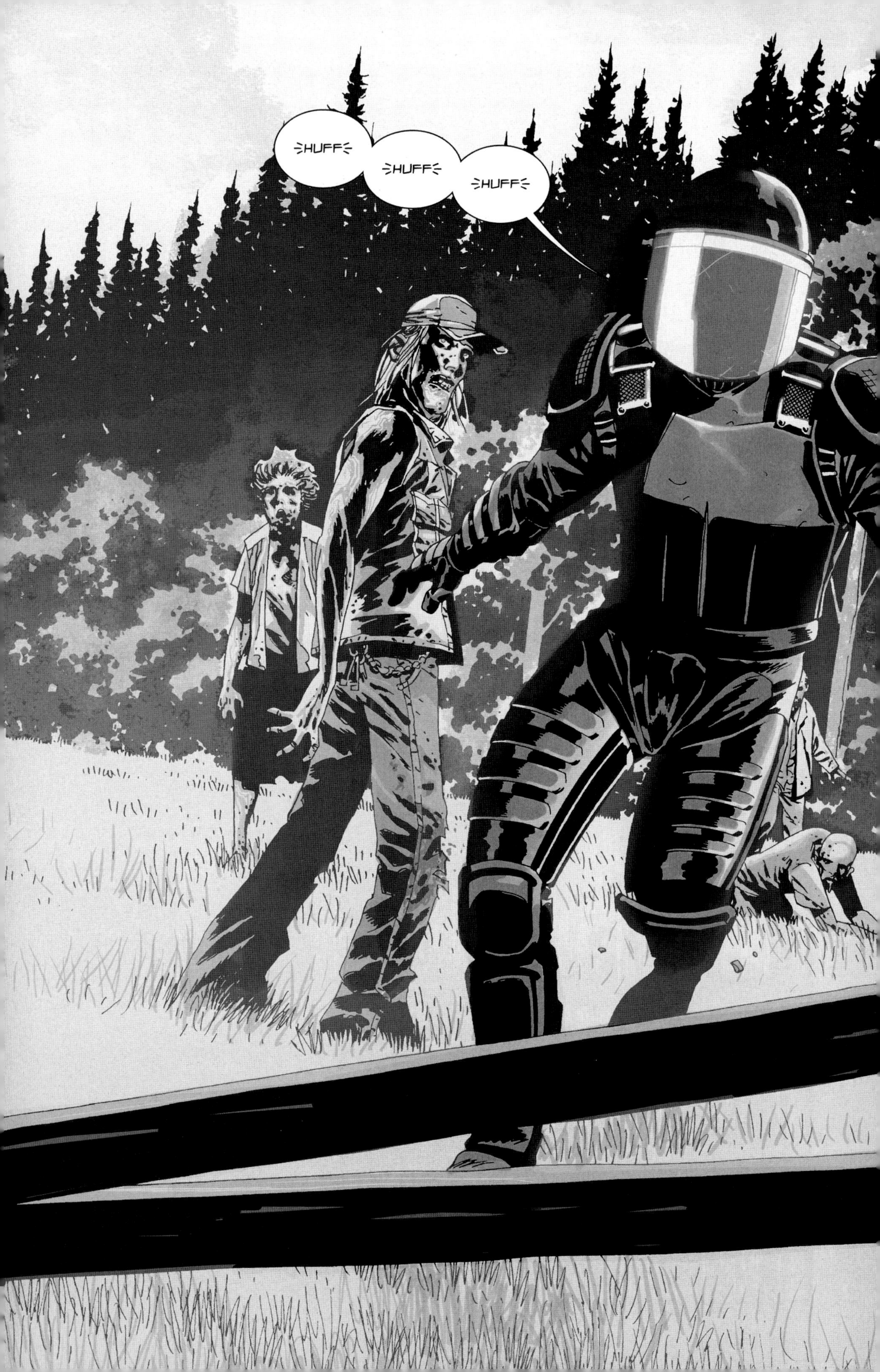
HUFF
HUFF
HUFF

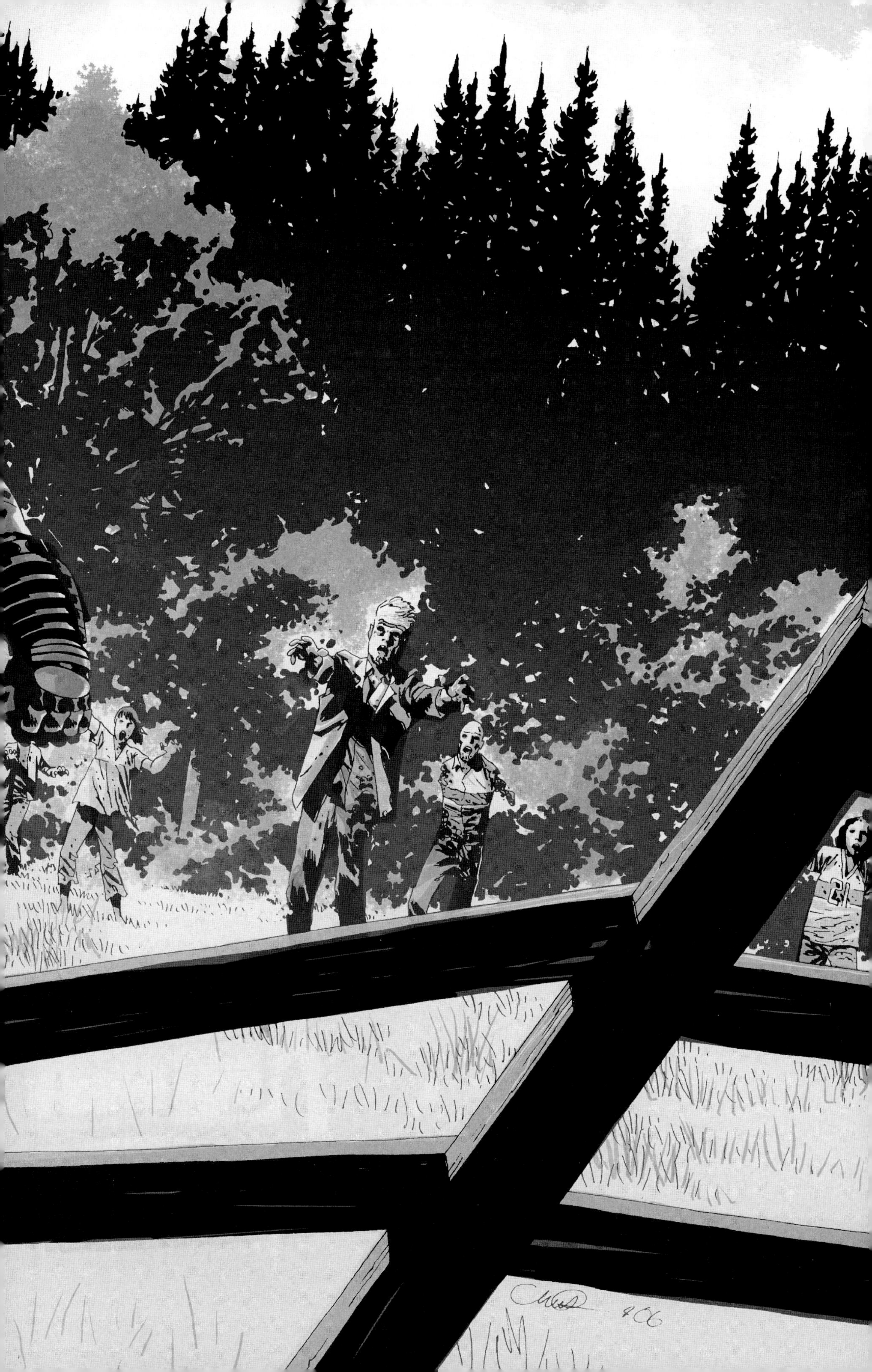

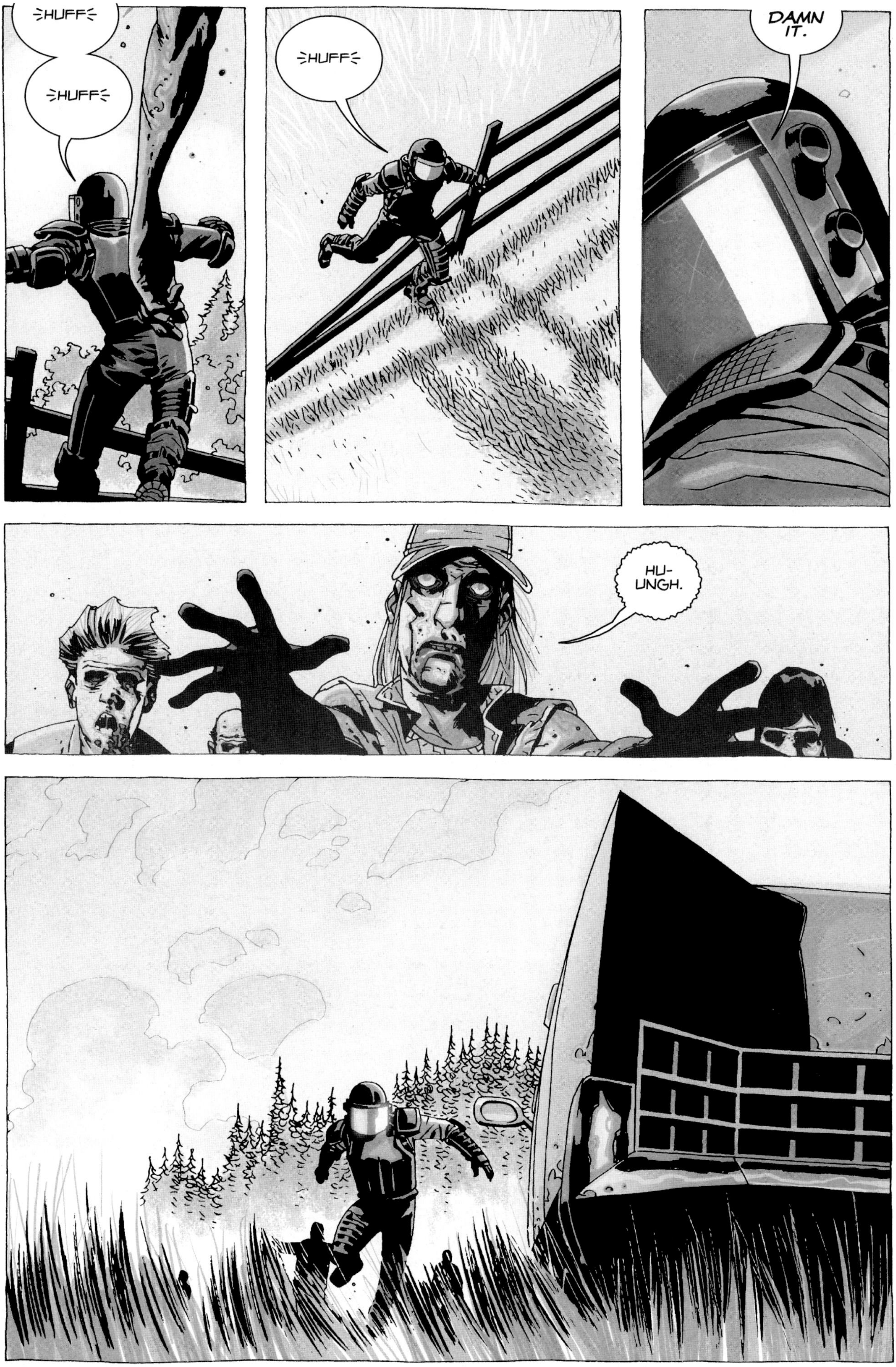

HUFF
HUFF
HUFF
DAMN IT.
HU-UNGH.

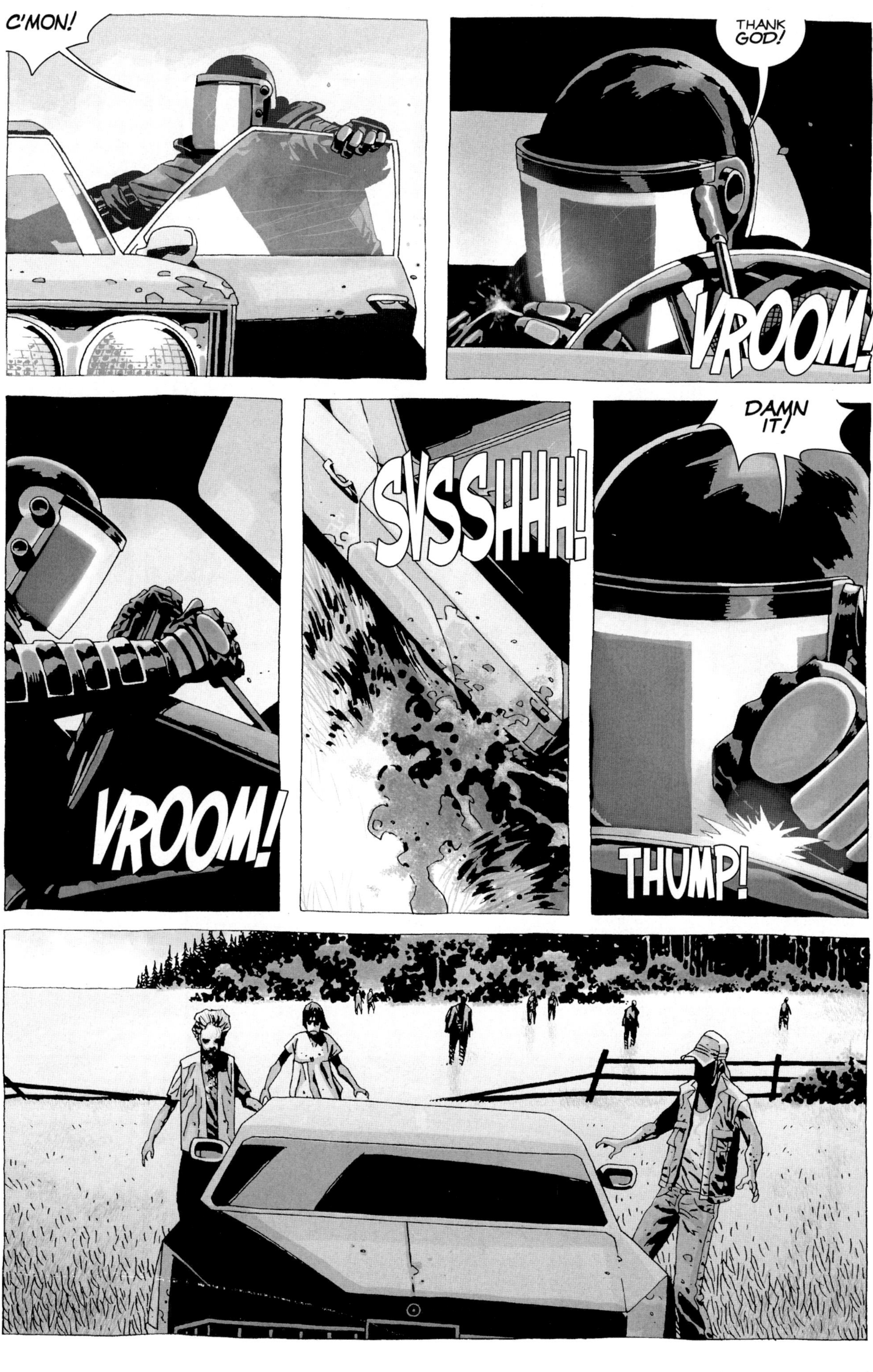
C'MON!
THANK GOD!
VROOM!
VROOM!
SVSSHHH!
DAMN IT!
THUMP!

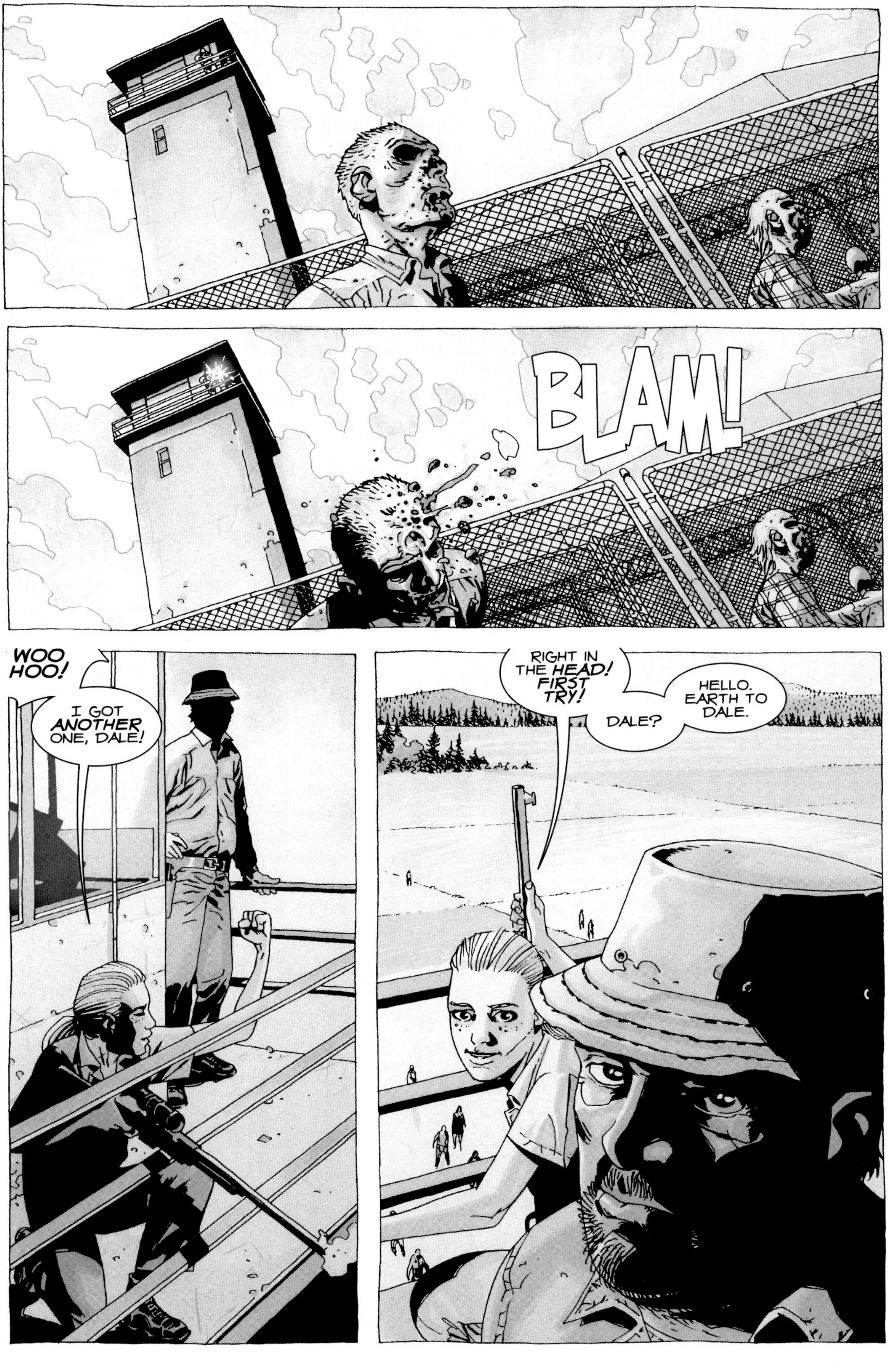
BLAM!
WOO HOO!
I GOT ANOTHER ONE, DALE!
RIGHT IN THE HEAD! FIRST TRY!
DALE?
HELLO. EARTH TO DALE.

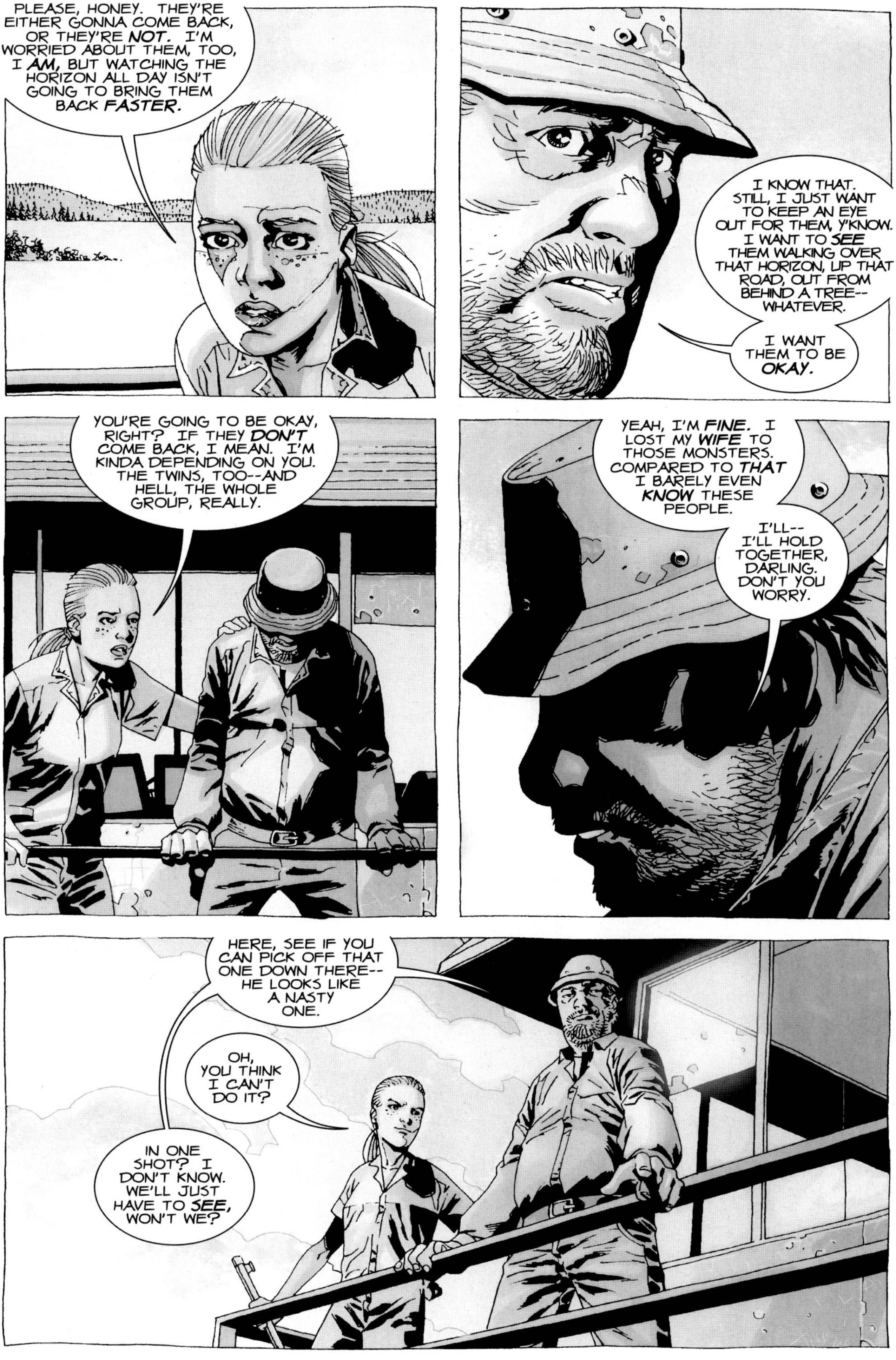
PLEASE, HONEY. THEY'RE EITHER GONNA COME BACK, OR THEY'RE NOT. I'M WORRIED ABOUT THEM, TOO, I AM, BUT WATCHING THE HORIZON ALL DAY ISN'T GOING TO BRING THEM BACK FASTER.
I KNOW THAT. STILL, I JUST WANT TO KEEP AN EYE OUT FOR THEM, Y'KNOW. I WANT TO SEE THEM WALKING OVER THAT HORIZON, UP THAT ROAD, OUT FROM BEHIND A TREE-- WHATEVER.
I WANT THEM TO BE OKAY.
YOU'RE GOING TO BE OKAY, RIGHT? IF THEY DON'T COME BACK, I MEAN. I'M KINDA DEPENDING ON YOU. THE TWINS, TOO--AND HELL, THE WHOLE GROUP, REALLY.
YEAH, I'M FINE. I LOST MY WIFE TO THOSE MONSTERS. COMPARED TO THAT I BARELY EVEN KNOW THESE PEOPLE.
I'LL-- I'LL HOLD TOGETHER, DARLING. DON'T YOU WORRY.
HERE, SEE IF YOU CAN PICK OFF THAT ONE DOWN THERE-- HE LOOKS LIKE A NASTY ONE.
OH, YOU THINK I CAN'T DO IT?
IN ONE SHOT? I DON'T KNOW. WE'LL JUST HAVE TO SEE, WON'T WE?

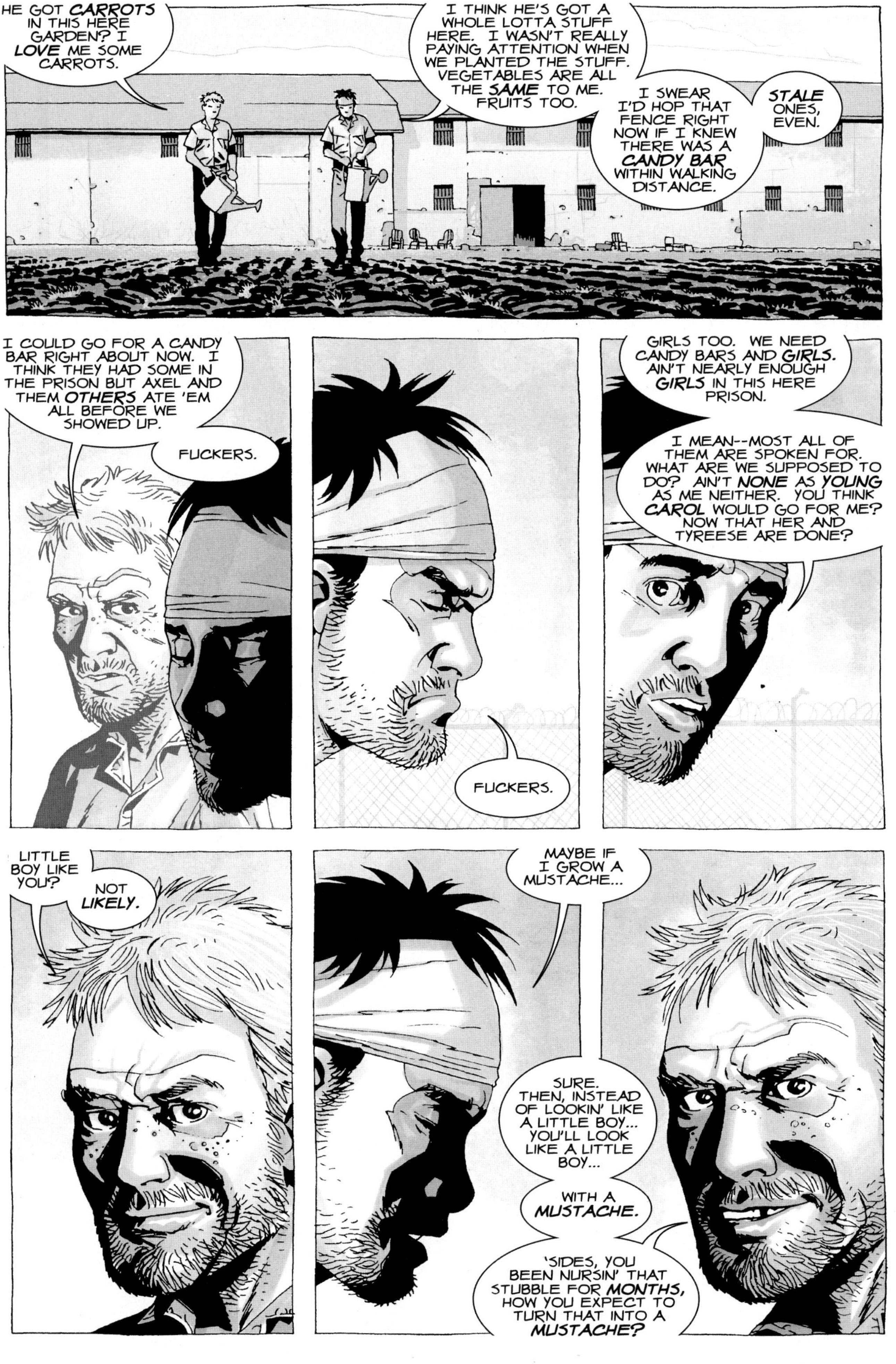
HE GOT CARROTS IN THIS HERE GARDEN? I LOVE ME SOME CARROTS.
I THINK HE'S GOT A WHOLE LOTTA STUFF HERE. I WASN'T REALLY PAYING ATTENTION WHEN WE PLANTED THE STUFF. VEGETABLES ARE ALL THE SAME TO ME. FRUITS TOO.
I SWEAR I'D HOP THAT FENCE RIGHT NOW IF I KNEW THERE WAS A CANDY BAR WITHIN WALKING DISTANCE.
STALE ONES, EVEN.
I COULD GO FOR A CANDY BAR RIGHT ABOUT NOW. I THINK THEY HAD SOME IN THE PRISON BUT AXEL AND THEM OTHERS ATE 'EM ALL BEFORE WE SHOWED UP.
FUCKERS.
FUCKERS.
GIRLS TOO. WE NEED CANDY BARS AND GIRLS. AIN'T NEARLY ENOUGH GIRLS IN THIS HERE PRISON.
I MEAN--MOST ALL OF THEM ARE SPOKEN FOR. WHAT ARE WE SUPPOSED TO DO? AIN'T NONE AS YOUNG AS ME NEITHER. YOU THINK CAROL WOULD GO FOR ME? NOW THAT HER AND TYREESE ARE DONE?
LITTLE BOY LIKE YOU?
NOT LIKELY.
MAYBE IF I GROW A MUSTACHE...
SURE. THEN, INSTEAD OF LOOKIN' LIKE A LITTLE BOY... YOU'LL LOOK LIKE A LITTLE BOY...
WITH A MUSTACHE.
'SIDES, YOU BEEN NURSIN' THAT STUBBLE FOR MONTHS, HOW YOU EXPECT TO TURN THAT INTO A MUSTACHE?

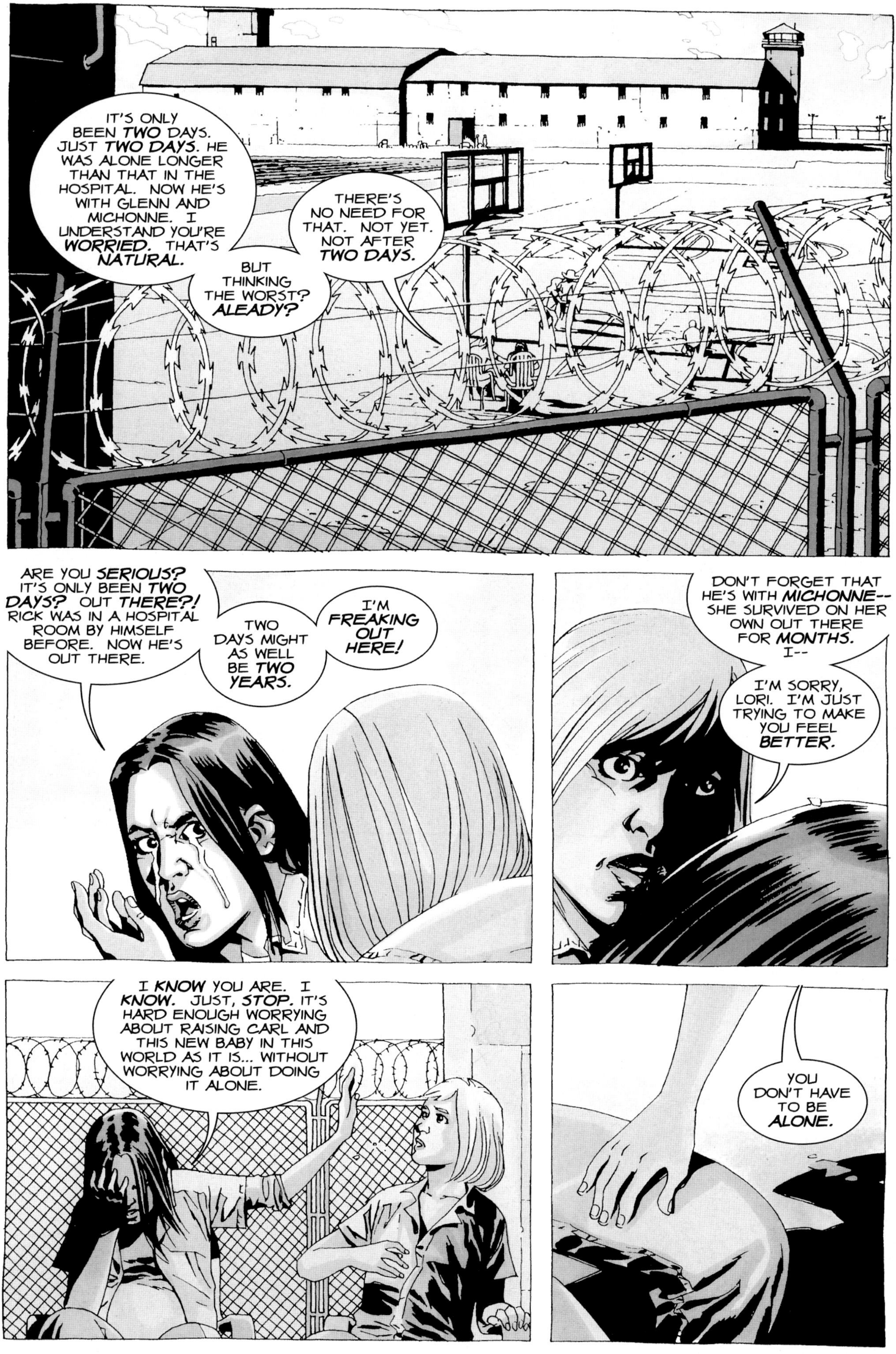
IT'S ONLY BEEN TWO DAYS. JUST TWO DAYS. HE WAS ALONE LONGER THAN THAT IN THE HOSPITAL. NOW HE'S WITH GLENN AND MICHONNE. I UNDERSTAND YOU'RE WORRIED. THAT'S NATURAL.
BUT THINKING THE WORST? ALEADY?
THERE'S NO NEED FOR THAT. NOT YET. NOT AFTER TWO DAYS.
ARE YOU SERIOUS? IT'S ONLY BEEN TWO DAYS? OUT THERE?! RICK WAS IN A HOSPITAL ROOM BY HIMSELF BEFORE. NOW HE'S OUT THERE.
TWO DAYS MIGHT AS WELL BE TWO YEARS.
I'M FREAKING OUT HERE!
DON'T FORGET THAT HE'S WITH MICHONNE-- SHE SURVIVED ON HER OWN OUT THERE FOR MONTHS. I--
I'M SORRY, LORI. I'M JUST TRYING TO MAKE YOU FEEL BETTER.
I KNOW YOU ARE. I KNOW. JUST, STOP. IT'S HARD ENOUGH WORRYING ABOUT RAISING CARL AND THIS NEW BABY IN THIS WORLD AS IT IS... WITHOUT WORRYING ABOUT DOING IT ALONE.
YOU DON'T HAVE TO BE ALONE.

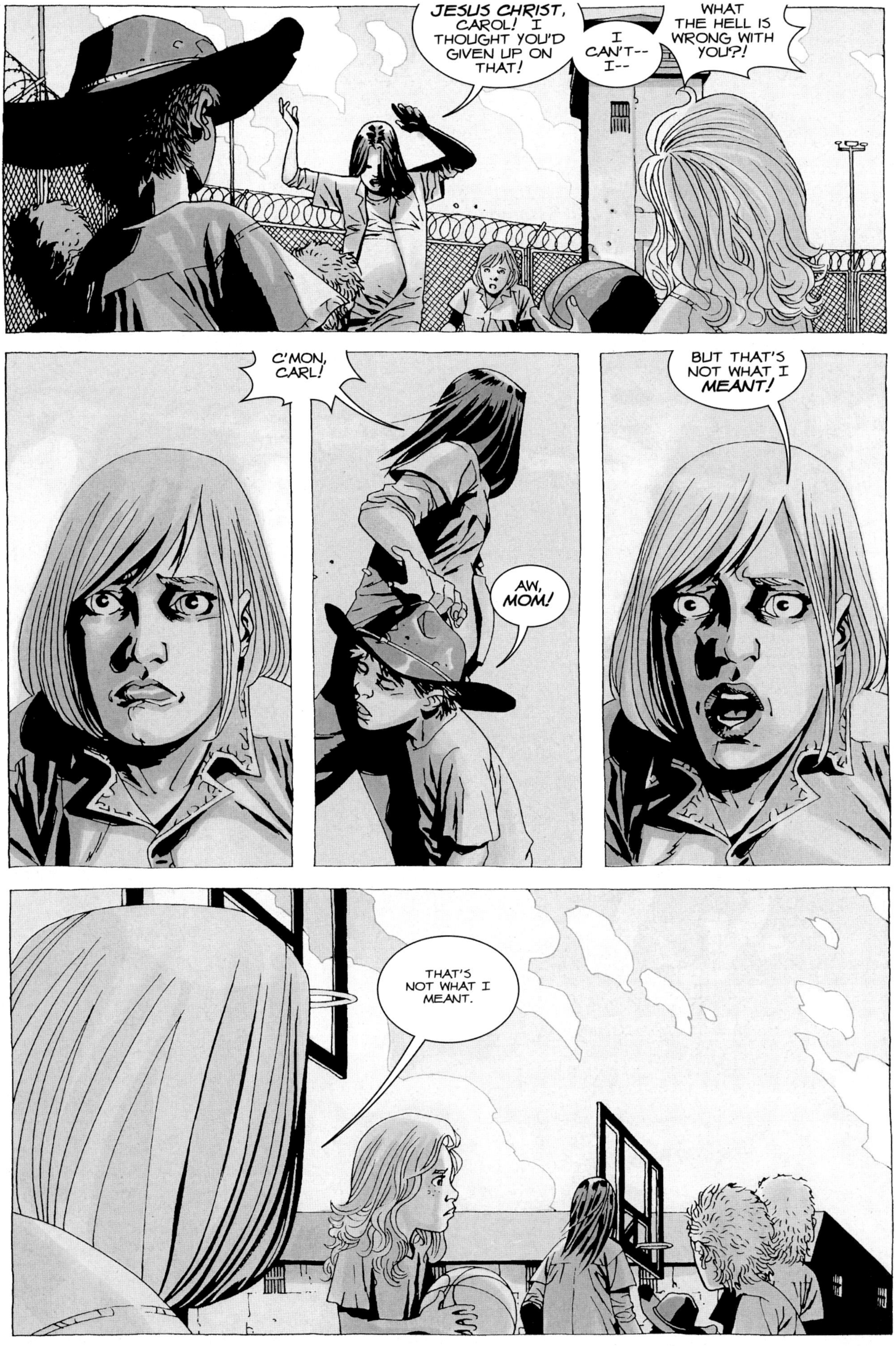
JESUS CHRIST, CAROL! I THOUGHT YOU'D GIVEN UP ON THAT!
I CAN'T-- I--
WHAT THE HELL IS WRONG WITH YOU?!
C'MON, CARL!
AW, MOM!
BUT THAT'S NOT WHAT I MEANT!
THAT'S NOT WHAT I MEANT.

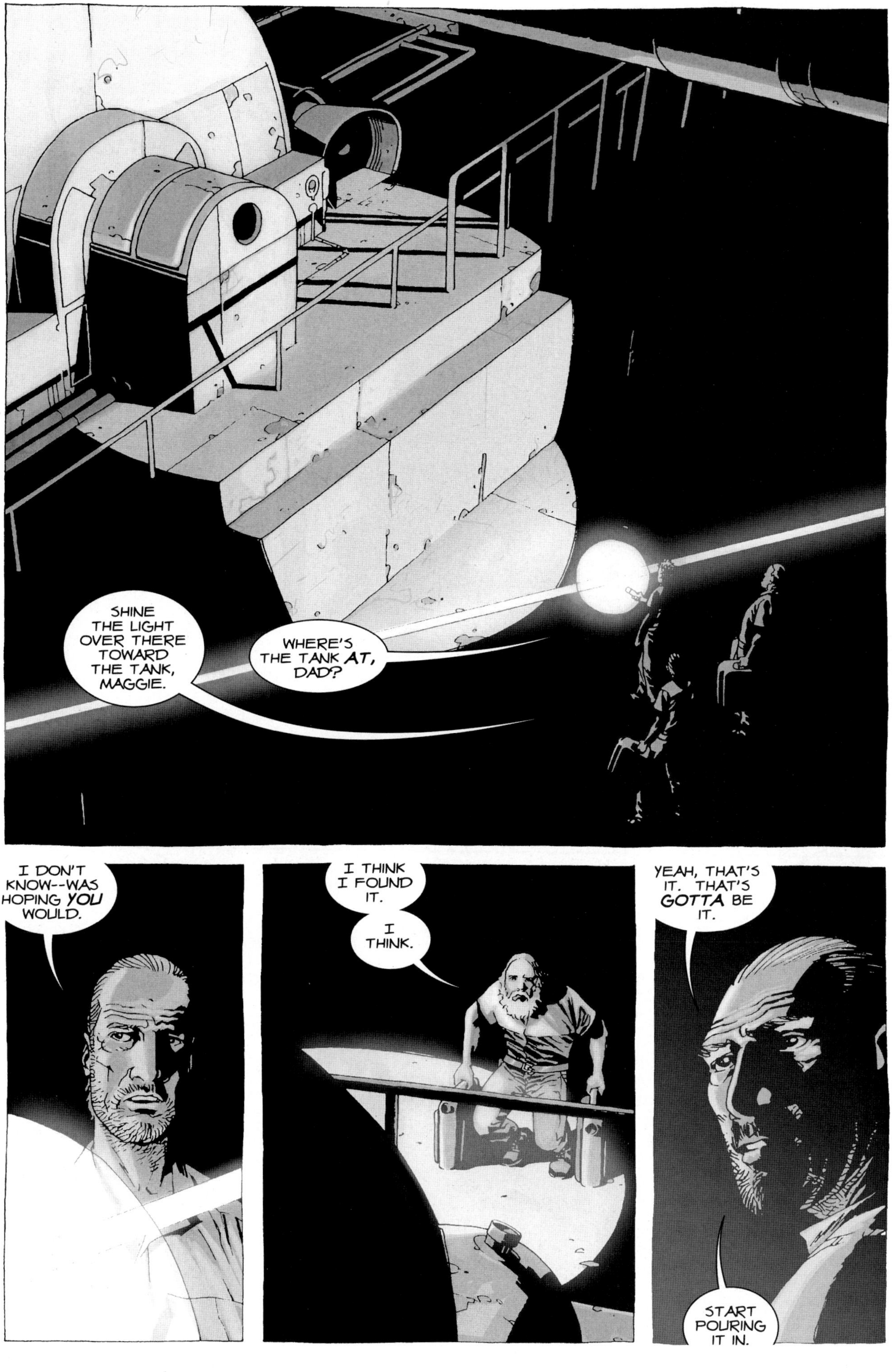
SHINE THE LIGHT OVER THERE TOWARD THE TANK, MAGGIE.
WHERE'S THE TANK AT, DAD?
I DON'T KNOW--WAS HOPING YOU WOULD.
I THINK I FOUND IT.
I THINK.
YEAH, THAT'S IT. THAT'S GOTTA BE IT.
START POURING IT IN.

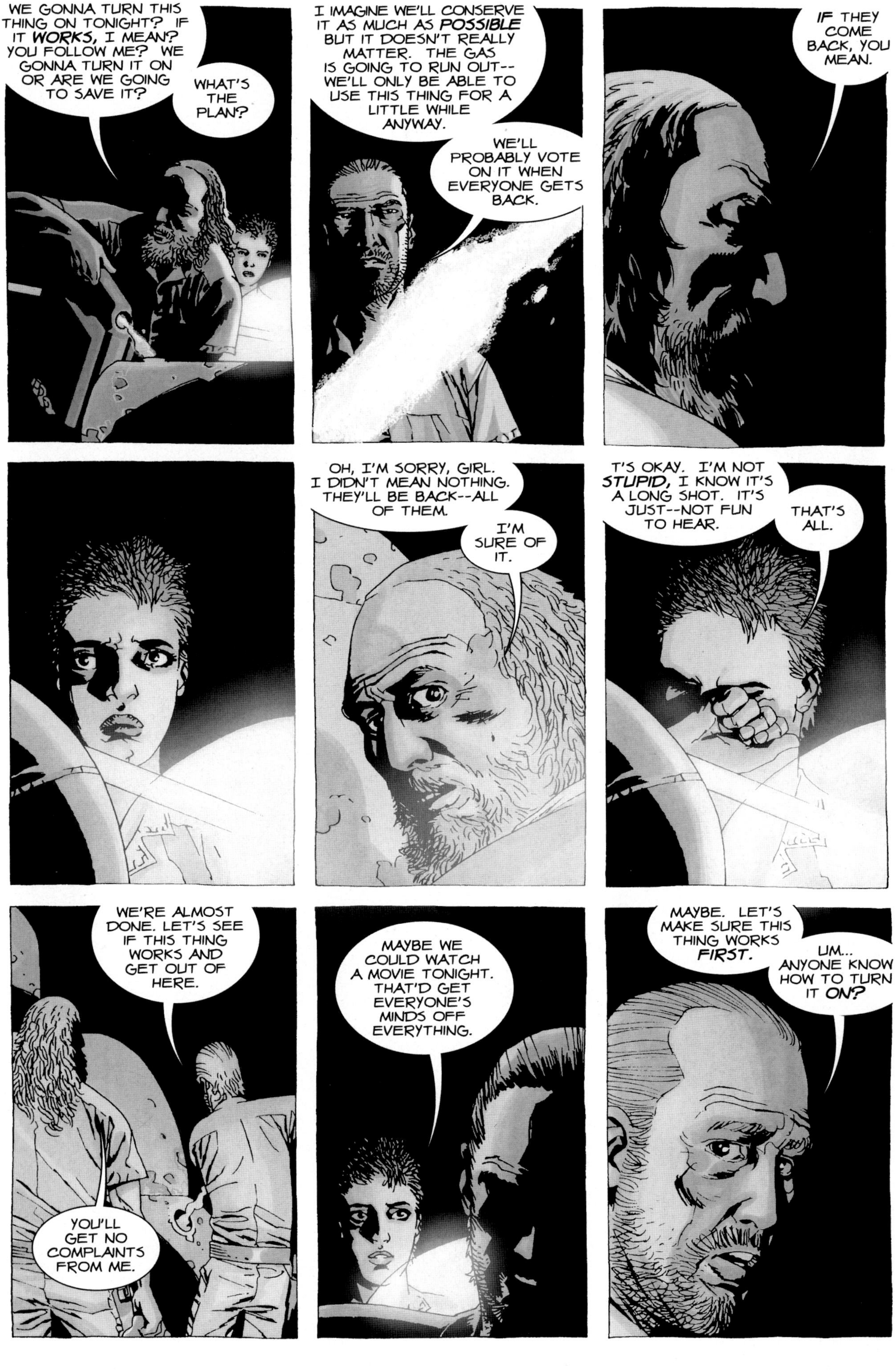
WE GONNA TURN THIS THING ON TONIGHT? IF IT WORKS, I MEAN? YOU FOLLOW ME? WE GONNA TURN IT ON OR ARE WE GOING TO SAVE IT?
WHAT'S THE PLAN?
I IMAGINE WE'LL CONSERVE IT AS MUCH AS POSSIBLE BUT IT DOESN'T REALLY MATTER. THE GAS IS GOING TO RUN OUT-- WE'LL ONLY BE ABLE TO USE THIS THING FOR A LITTLE WHILE ANYWAY.
WE'LL PROBABLY VOTE ON IT WHEN EVERYONE GETS BACK.
IF THEY COME BACK, YOU MEAN.
OH, I'M SORRY, GIRL. I DIDN'T MEAN NOTHING. THEY'LL BE BACK--ALL OF THEM.
I'M SURE OF IT.
T'S OKAY. I'M NOT STUPID, I KNOW IT'S A LONG SHOT. IT'S JUST--NOT FUN TO HEAR.
THAT'S ALL.
WE'RE ALMOST DONE. LET'S SEE IF THIS THING WORKS AND GET OUT OF HERE.
YOU'LL GET NO COMPLAINTS FROM ME.
MAYBE WE COULD WATCH A MOVIE TONIGHT. THAT'D GET EVERYONE'S MINDS OFF EVERYTHING.
MAYBE. LET'S MAKE SURE THIS THING WORKS FIRST.
UM... ANYONE KNOW HOW TO TURN IT ON?

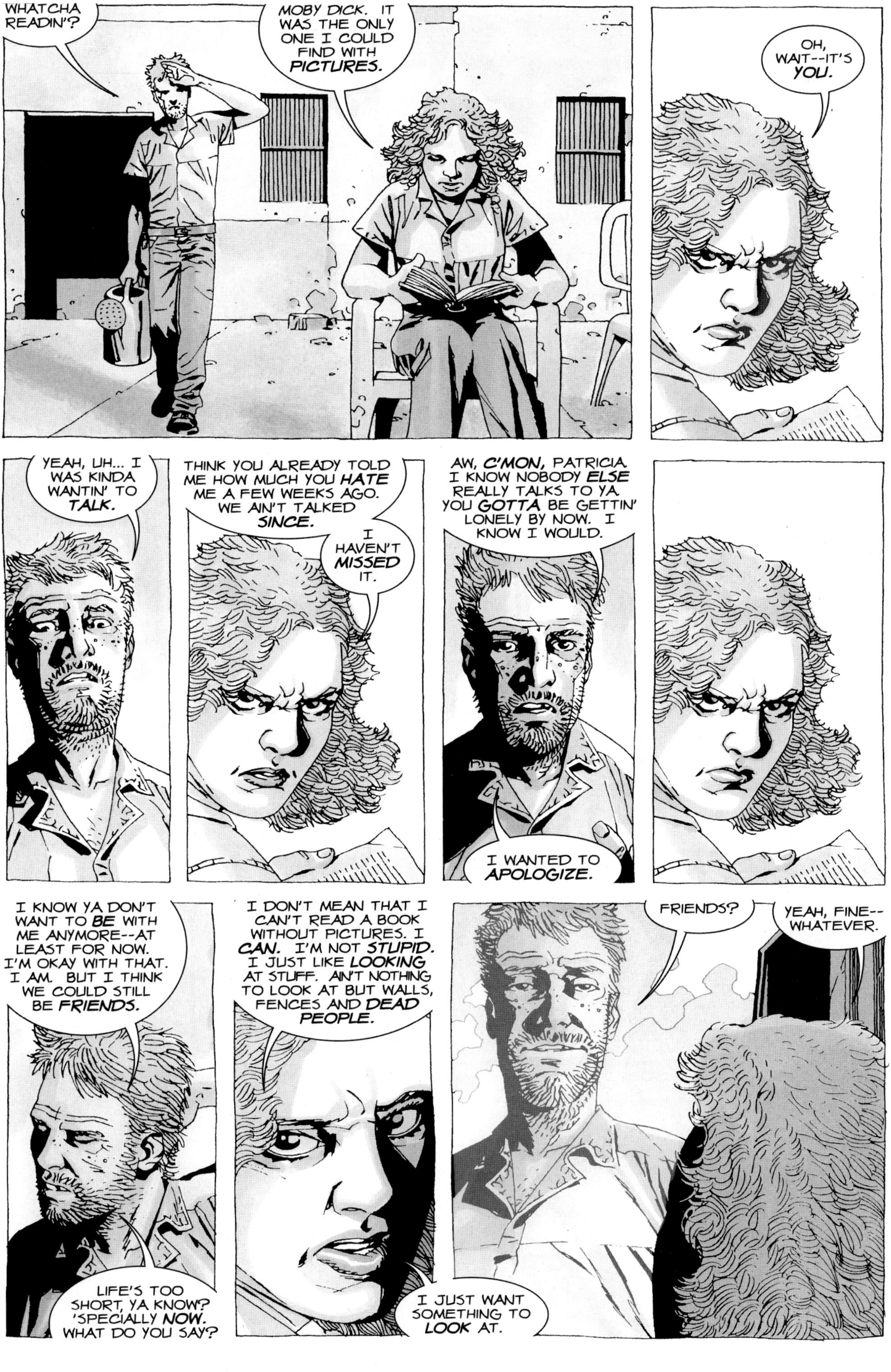
WHATCHA READIN'?
MOBY DICK. IT WAS THE ONLY ONE I COULD FIND WITH PICTURES.
OH, WAIT--IT'S YOU.
YEAH, UH... I WAS KINDA WANTIN' TO TALK.
THINK YOU ALREADY TOLD ME HOW MUCH YOU HATE ME A FEW WEEKS AGO. WE AIN'T TALKED SINCE.
I HAVEN'T MISSED IT.
AW, C'MON, PATRICIA. I KNOW NOBODY ELSE REALLY TALKS TO YA. YOU GOTTA BE GETTIN' LONELY BY NOW. I KNOW I WOULD.
I WANTED TO APOLOGIZE.
I KNOW YA DON'T WANT TO BE WITH ME ANYMORE--AT LEAST FOR NOW. I'M OKAY WITH THAT. I AM. BUT I THINK WE COULD STILL BE FRIENDS.
LIFE'S TOO SHORT, YA KNOW? 'SPECIALLY NOW. WHAT DO YOU SAY?
I DON'T MEAN THAT I CAN'T READ A BOOK WITHOUT PICTURES. I CAN. I'M NOT STUPID. I JUST LIKE LOOKING AT STUFF. AIN'T NOTHING TO LOOK AT BUT WALLS, FENCES AND DEAD PEOPLE.
I JUST WANT SOMETHING TO LOOK AT.
FRIENDS?
YEAH, FINE--WHATEVER.

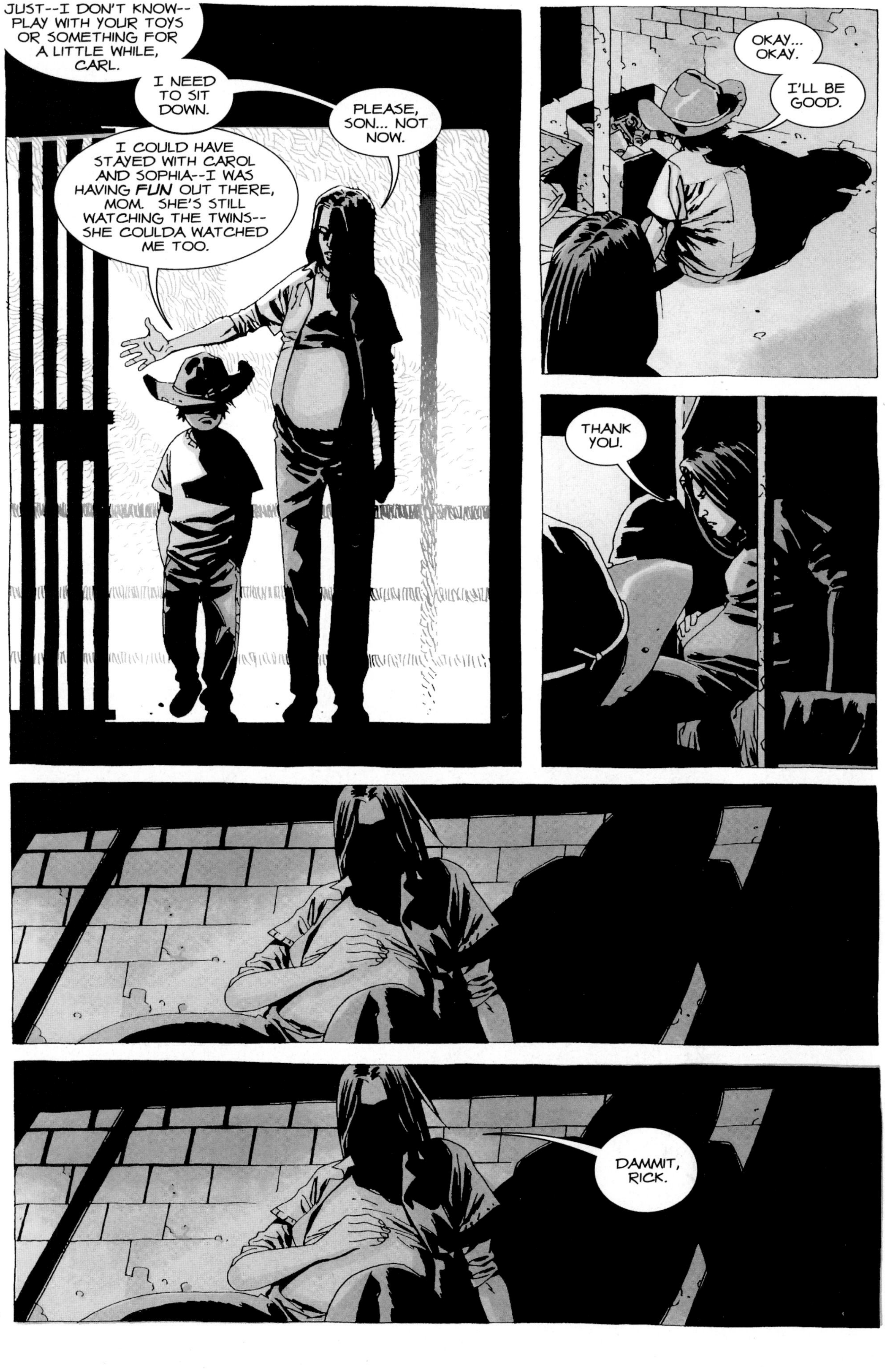
JUST--I DON'T KNOW--PLAY WITH YOUR TOYS OR SOMETHING FOR A LITTLE WHILE, CARL.
I NEED TO SIT DOWN.
I COULD HAVE STAYED WITH CAROL AND SOPHIA--I WAS HAVING FUN OUT THERE, MOM. SHE'S STILL WATCHING THE TWINS--SHE COULDA WATCHED ME TOO.
PLEASE, SON... NOT NOW.
OKAY... OKAY.
I'LL BE GOOD.
THANK YOU.
DAMMIT, RICK.

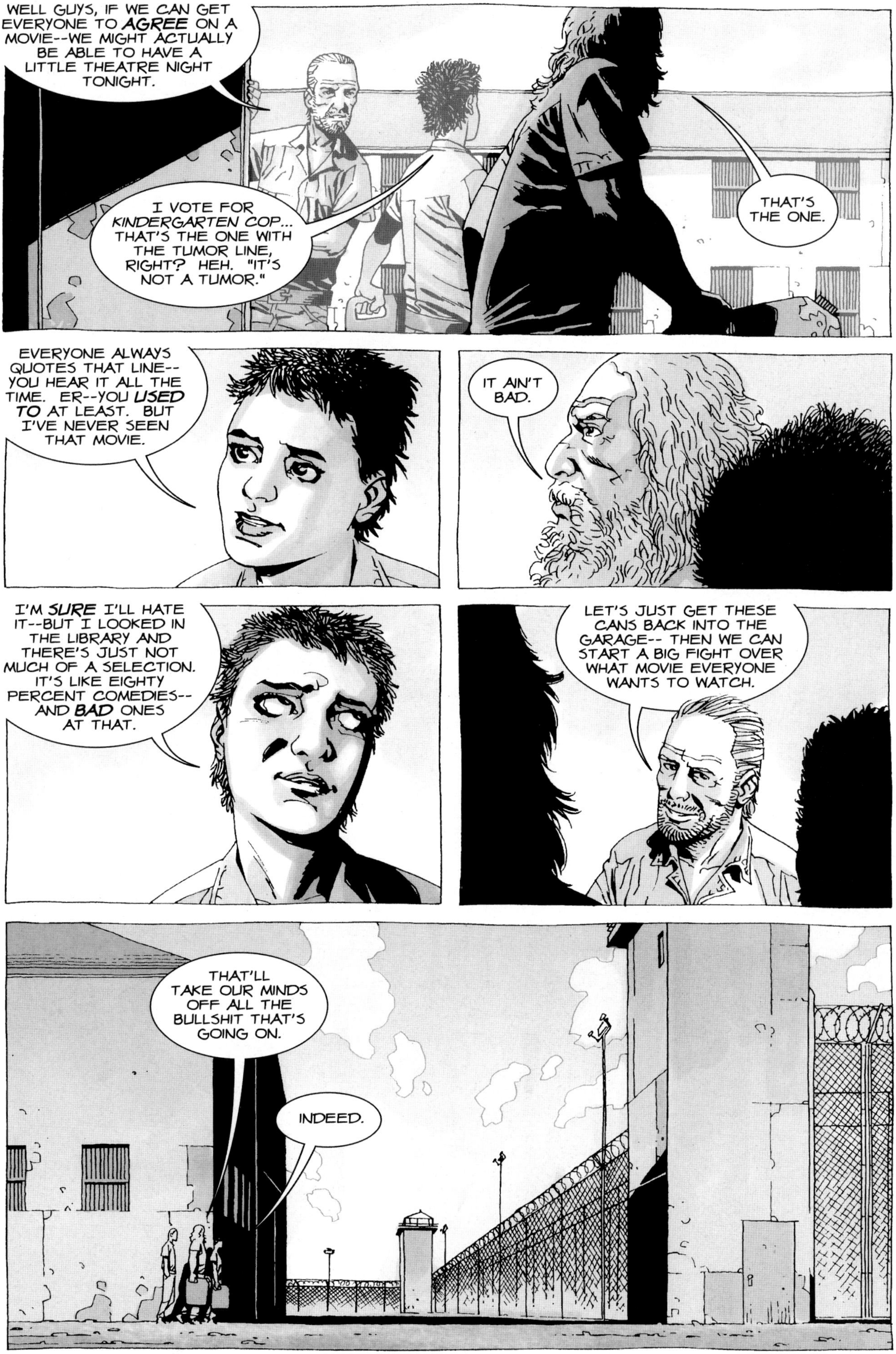
WELL GUYS, IF WE CAN GET EVERYONE TO AGREE ON A MOVIE--WE MIGHT ACTUALLY BE ABLE TO HAVE A LITTLE THEATRE NIGHT TONIGHT.
I VOTE FOR KINDERGARTEN COP... THAT'S THE ONE WITH THE TUMOR LINE, RIGHT? HEH. "IT'S NOT A TUMOR."
THAT'S THE ONE.
EVERYONE ALWAYS QUOTES THAT LINE-- YOU HEAR IT ALL THE TIME. ER--YOU USED TO AT LEAST. BUT I'VE NEVER SEEN THAT MOVIE.
IT AIN'T BAD.
I'M SURE I'LL HATE IT--BUT I LOOKED IN THE LIBRARY AND THERE'S JUST NOT MUCH OF A SELECTION. IT'S LIKE EIGHTY PERCENT COMEDIES-- AND BAD ONES AT THAT.
LET'S JUST GET THESE CANS BACK INTO THE GARAGE-- THEN WE CAN START A BIG FIGHT OVER WHAT MOVIE EVERYONE WANTS TO WATCH.
THAT'LL TAKE OUR MINDS OFF ALL THE BULLSHIT THAT'S GOING ON.
INDEED.

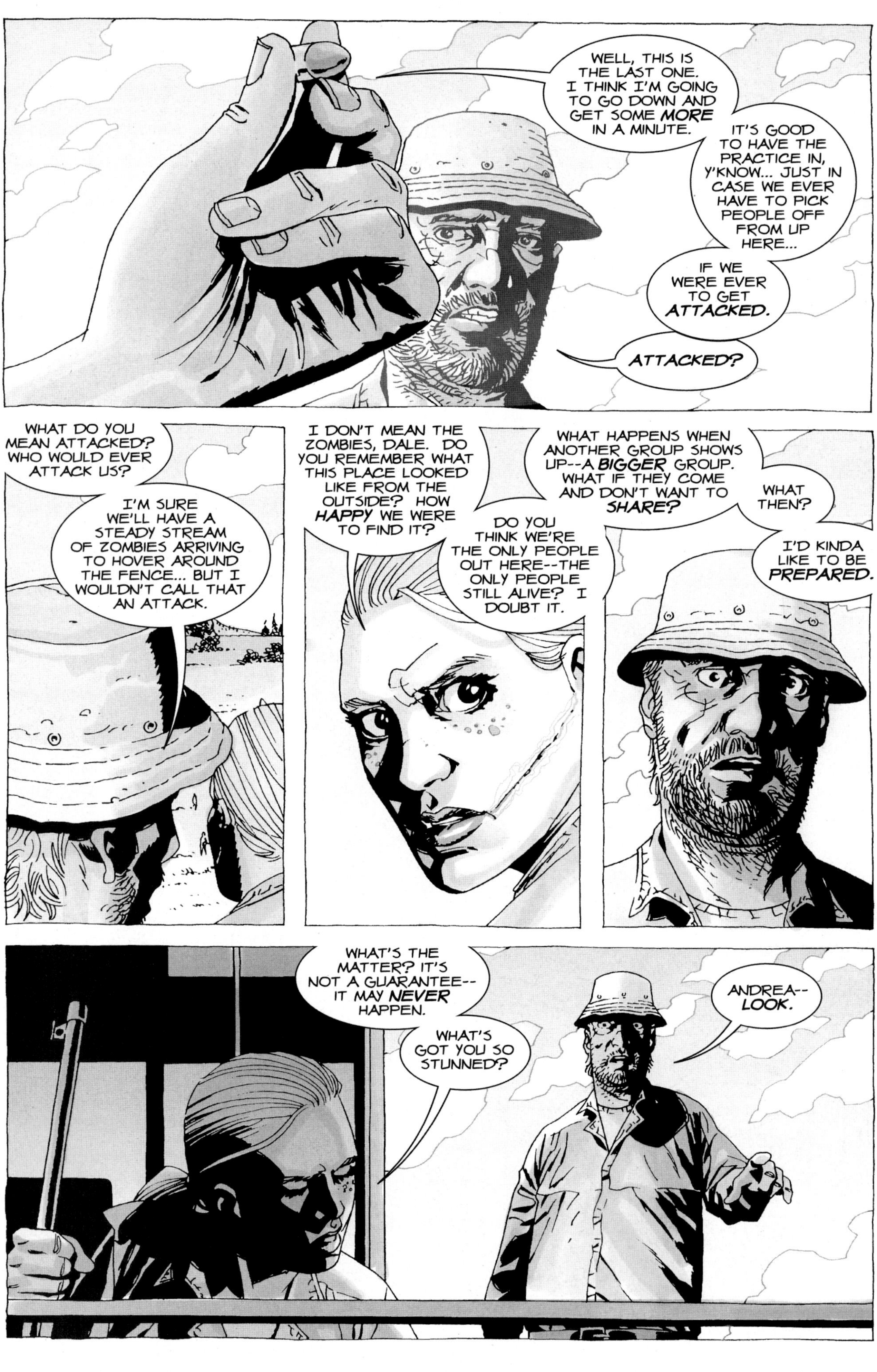
WELL, THIS IS THE LAST ONE. I THINK I'M GOING TO GO DOWN AND GET SOME MORE IN A MINUTE.
IT'S GOOD TO HAVE THE PRACTICE IN, Y'KNOW... JUST IN CASE WE EVER HAVE TO PICK PEOPLE OFF FROM UP HERE...
IF WE WERE EVER TO GET ATTACKED.
ATTACKED?
WHAT DO YOU MEAN ATTACKED? WHO WOULD EVER ATTACK US?
I'M SURE WE'LL HAVE A STEADY STREAM OF ZOMBIES ARRIVING TO HOVER AROUND THE FENCE... BUT I WOULDN'T CALL THAT AN ATTACK.
I DON'T MEAN THE ZOMBIES, DALE. DO YOU REMEMBER WHAT THIS PLACE LOOKED LIKE FROM THE OUTSIDE? HOW HAPPY WE WERE TO FIND IT?
DO YOU THINK WE'RE THE ONLY PEOPLE OUT HERE--THE ONLY PEOPLE STILL ALIVE? I DOUBT IT.
WHAT HAPPENS WHEN ANOTHER GROUP SHOWS UP--A BIGGER GROUP. WHAT IF THEY COME AND DON'T WANT TO SHARE?
WHAT THEN?
I'D KINDA LIKE TO BE PREPARED.
WHAT'S THE MATTER? IT'S NOT A GUARANTEE-- IT MAY NEVER HAPPEN.
WHAT'S GOT YOU SO STUNNED?
ANDREA-- LOOK.

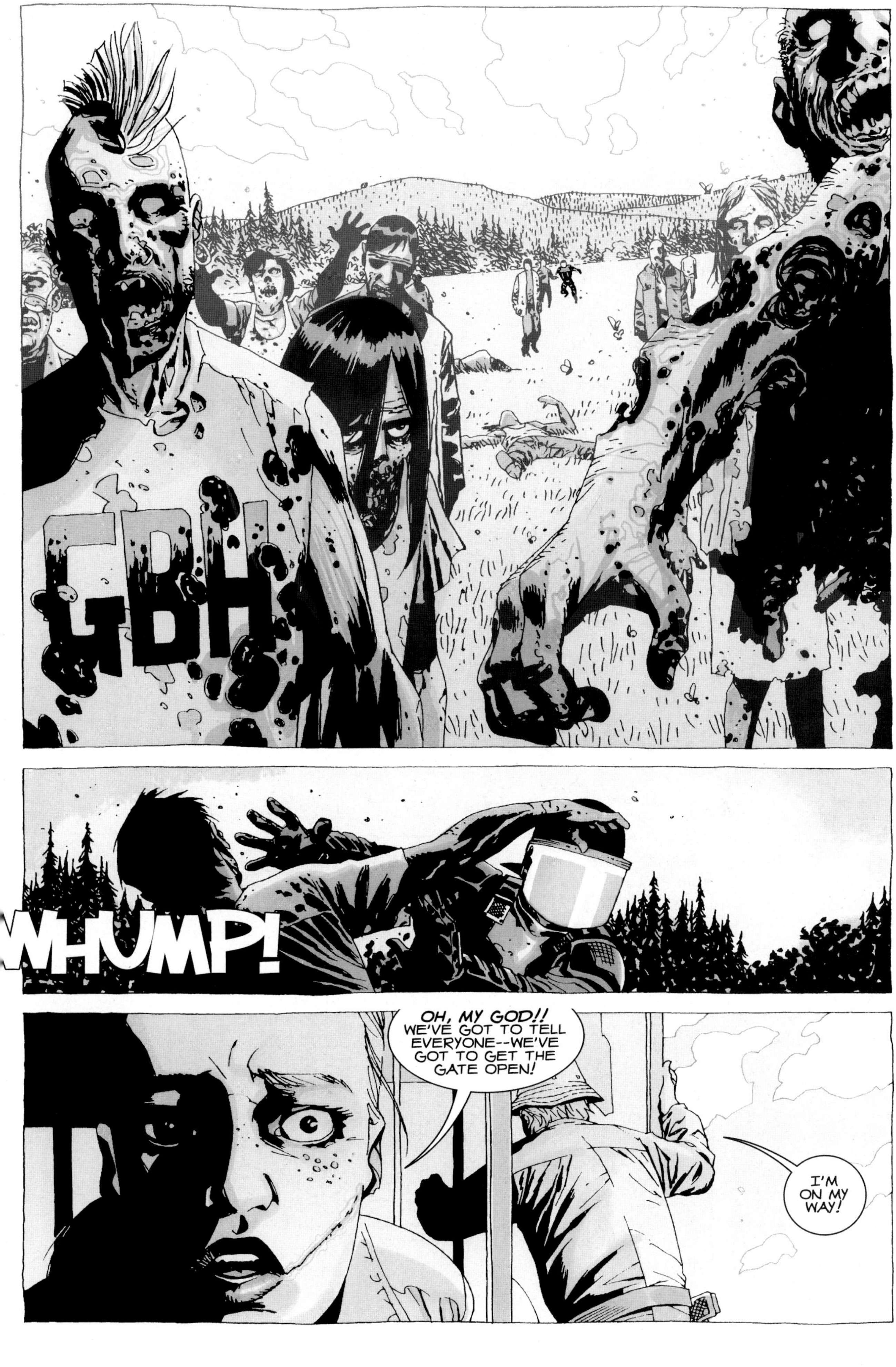
GBH
WHUMP!
OH, MY GOD!! WE'VE GOT TO TELL EVERYONE--WE'VE GOT TO GET THE GATE OPEN!
I'M ON MY WAY!

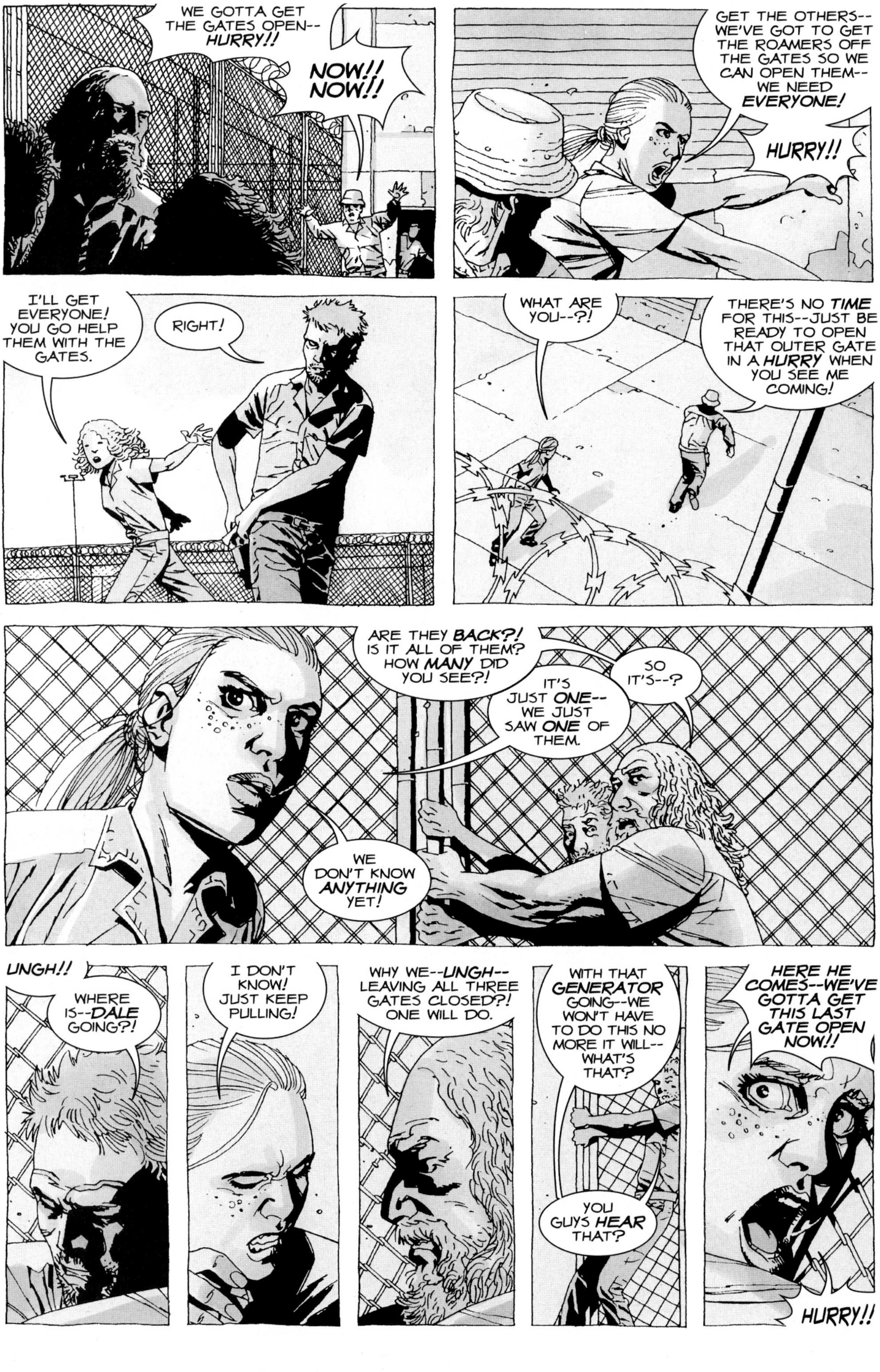
WE GOTTA GET THE GATES OPEN-- HURRY!!
NOW!! NOW!!
GET THE OTHERS-- WE'VE GOT TO GET THE ROAMERS OFF THE GATES SO WE CAN OPEN THEM-- WE NEED EVERYONE!
HURRY!!
I'LL GET EVERYONE! YOU GO HELP THEM WITH THE GATES.
RIGHT!
WHAT ARE YOU--?!
THERE'S NO TIME FOR THIS--JUST BE READY TO OPEN THAT OUTER GATE IN A HURRY WHEN YOU SEE ME COMING!
ARE THEY BACK?! IS IT ALL OF THEM? HOW MANY DID YOU SEE?!
SO IT'S--?
IT'S JUST ONE-- WE JUST SAW ONE OF THEM.
WE DON'T KNOW ANYTHING YET!
UNGH!!
WHERE IS--DALE GOING?!
I DON'T KNOW! JUST KEEP PULLING!
WHY WE--UNGH-- LEAVING ALL THREE GATES CLOSED?! ONE WILL DO.
WITH THAT GENERATOR GOING--WE WON'T HAVE TO DO THIS NO MORE IT WILL-- WHAT'S THAT?
YOU GUYS HEAR THAT?
HERE HE COMES--WE'VE GOTTA GET THIS LAST GATE OPEN NOW!!
HURRY!!

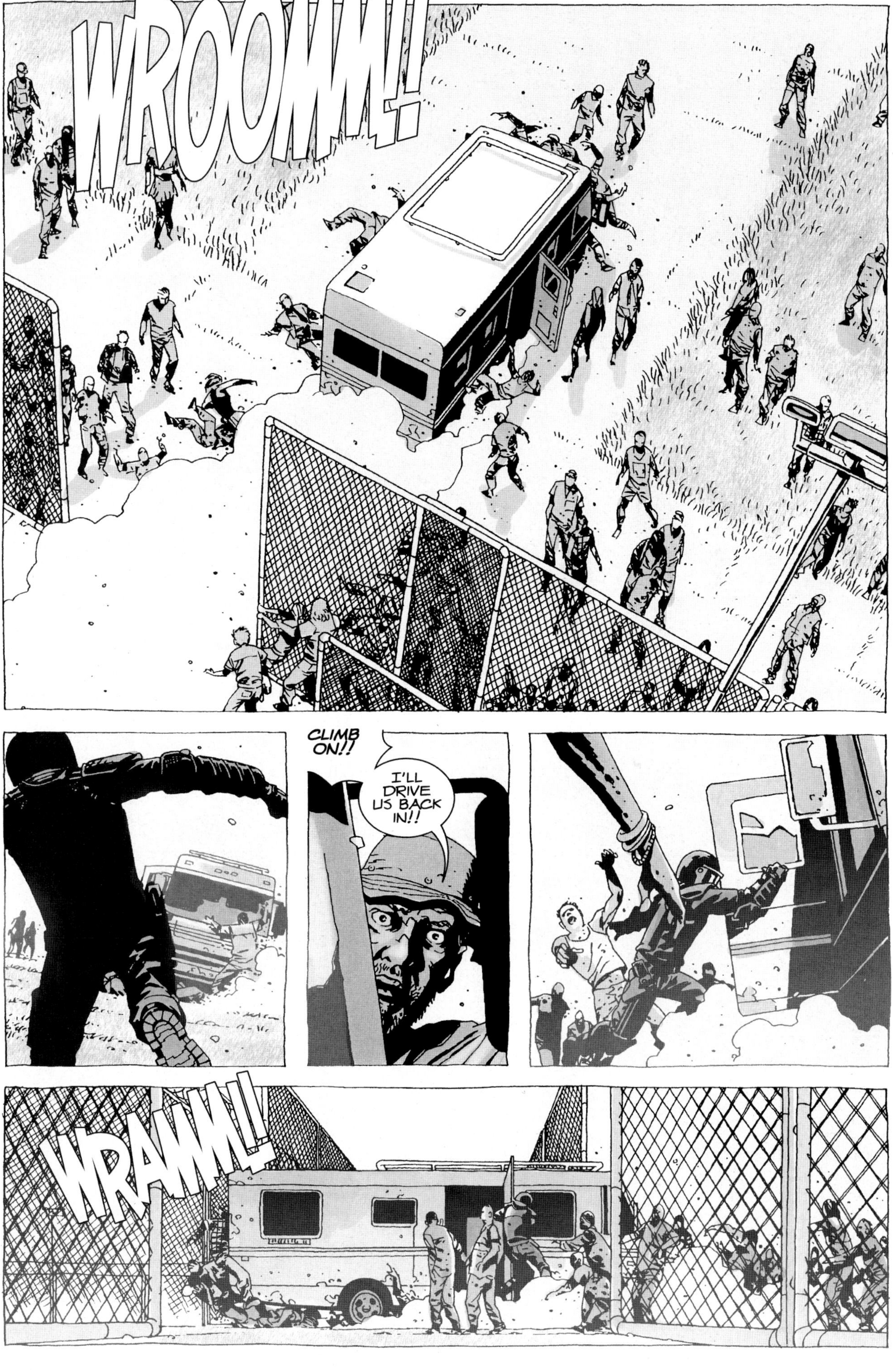
WROOMM!!
CLIMB ON!!
I'LL DRIVE US BACK IN!!
WRAMM!!

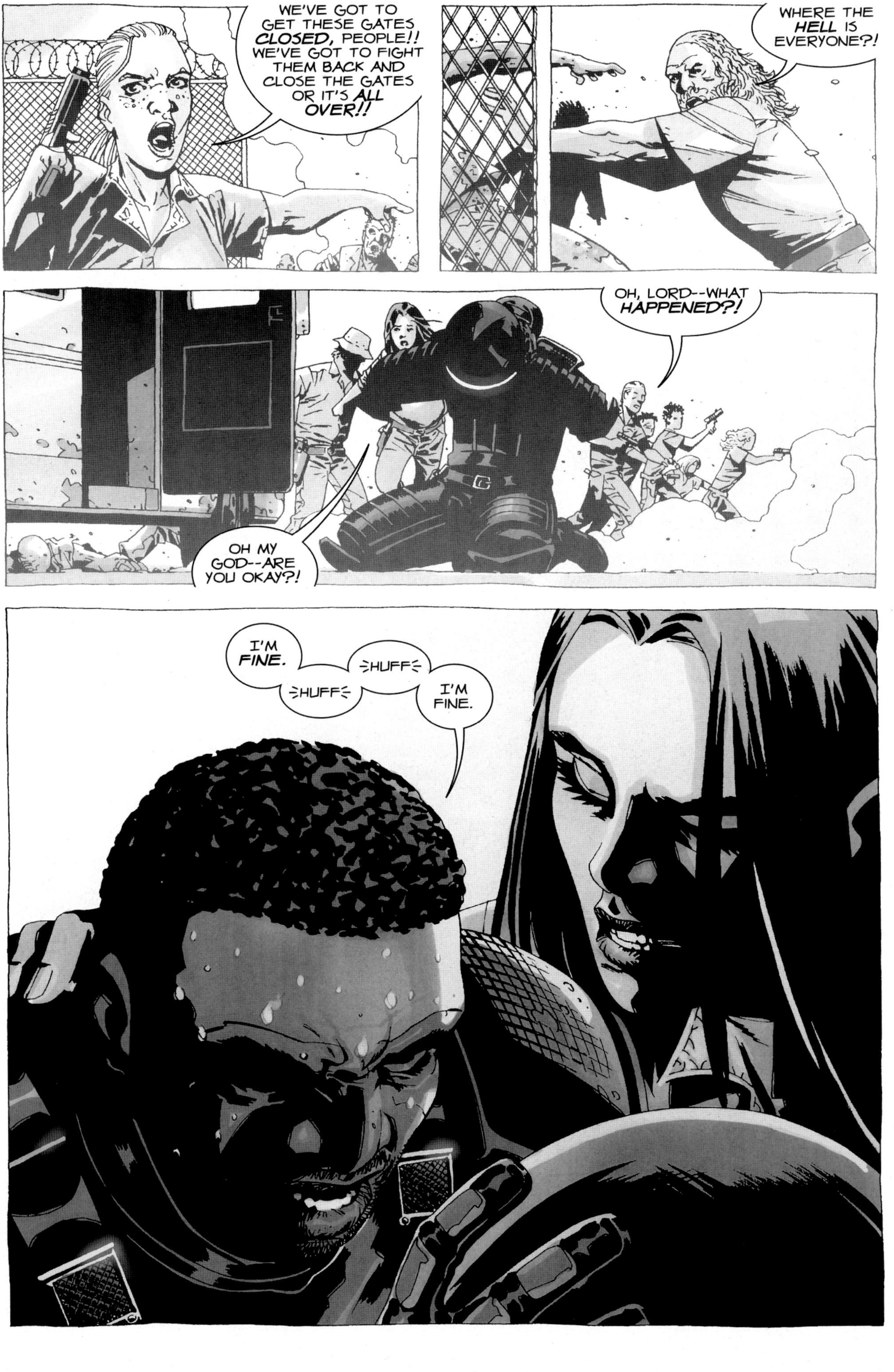
WE'VE GOT TO GET THESE GATES CLOSED, PEOPLE!! WE'VE GOT TO FIGHT THEM BACK AND CLOSE THE GATES OR IT'S ALL OVER!!
WHERE THE HELL IS EVERYONE?!
OH, LORD--WHAT HAPPENED?!
OH MY GOD--ARE YOU OKAY?!
I'M FINE.
HUFF
HUFF
I'M FINE.

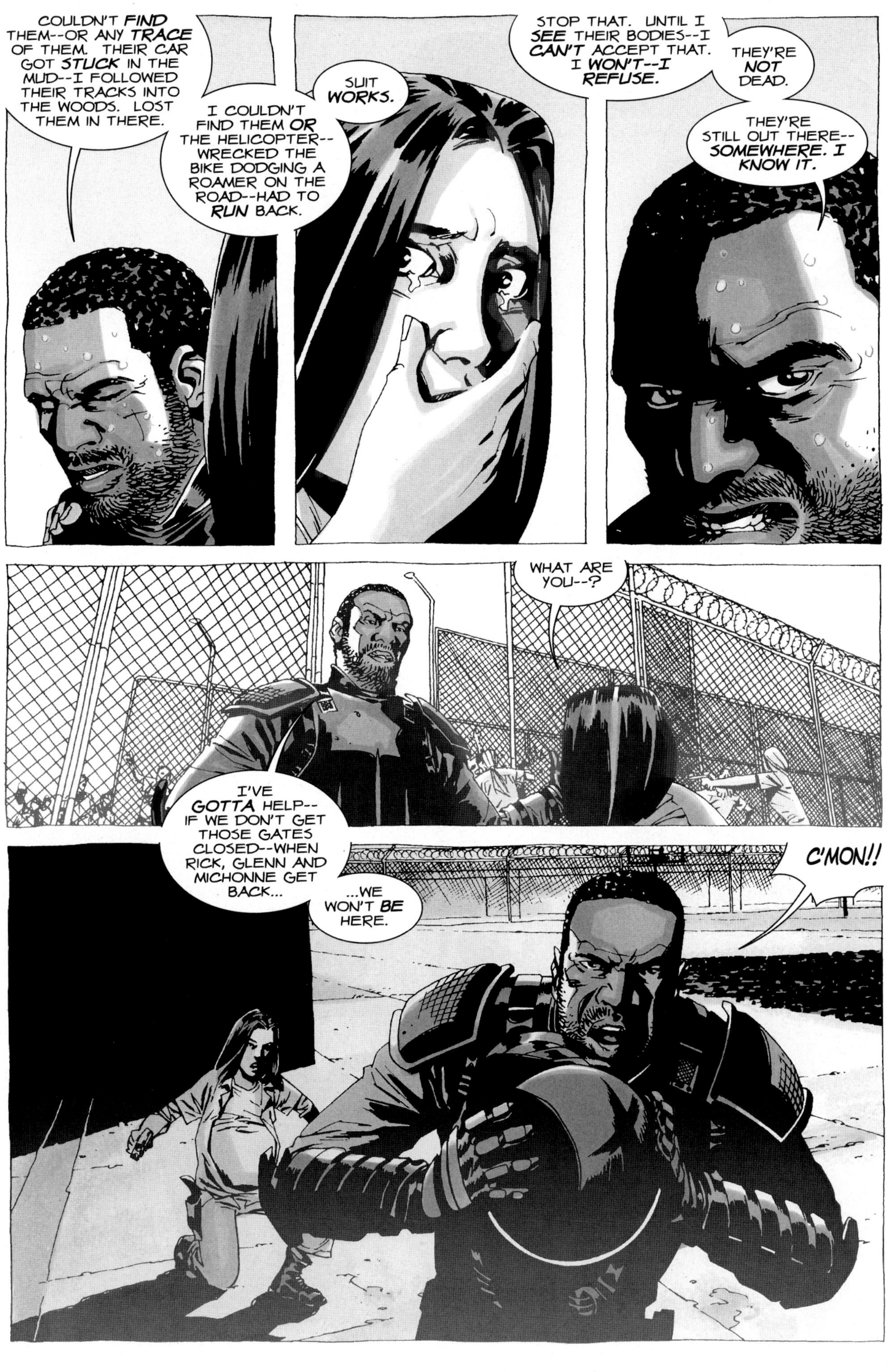
COULDN'T FIND THEM--OR ANY TRACE OF THEM. THEIR CAR GOT STUCK IN THE MUD--I FOLLOWED THEIR TRACKS INTO THE WOODS. LOST THEM IN THERE.
I COULDN'T FIND THEM OR THE HELICOPTER--WRECKED THE BIKE DODGING A ROAMER ON THE ROAD--HAD TO RUN BACK.
SUIT WORKS.
STOP THAT. UNTIL I SEE THEIR BODIES--I CAN'T ACCEPT THAT. I WON'T--I REFUSE.
THEY'RE NOT DEAD.
THEY'RE STILL OUT THERE--SOMEWHERE. I KNOW IT.
WHAT ARE YOU--?
I'VE GOTTA HELP--IF WE DON'T GET THOSE GATES CLOSED--WHEN RICK, GLENN AND MICHONNE GET BACK...
...WE WON'T BE HERE.
C'MON!!

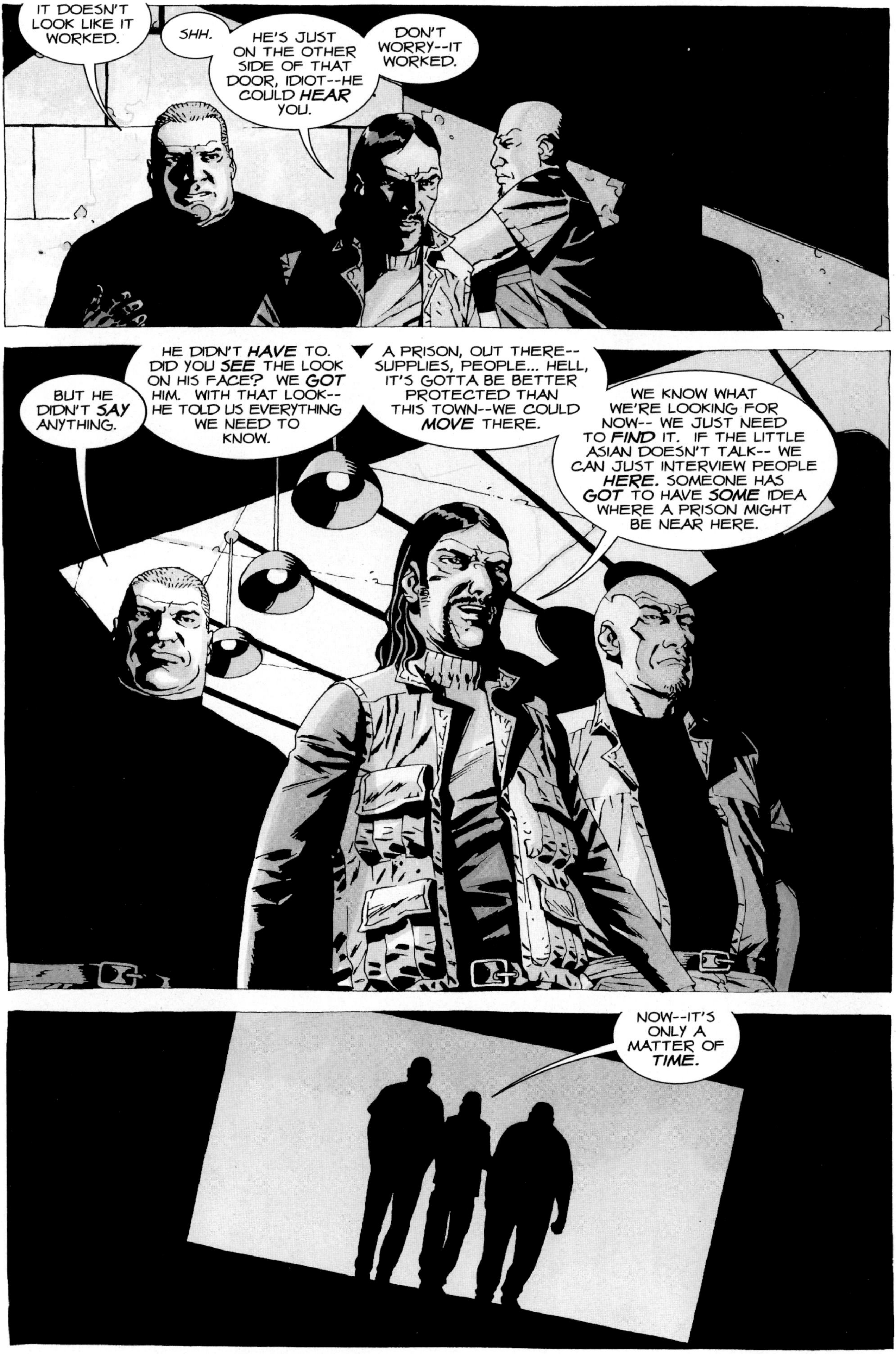
IT DOESN'T LOOK LIKE IT WORKED.
SHH.
HE'S JUST ON THE OTHER SIDE OF THAT DOOR, IDIOT--HE COULD HEAR YOU.
DON'T WORRY--IT WORKED.
BUT HE DIDN'T SAY ANYTHING.
HE DIDN'T HAVE TO. DID YOU SEE THE LOOK ON HIS FACE? WE GOT HIM. WITH THAT LOOK-- HE TOLD US EVERYTHING WE NEED TO KNOW.
A PRISON, OUT THERE-- SUPPLIES, PEOPLE... HELL, IT'S GOTTA BE BETTER PROTECTED THAN THIS TOWN--WE COULD MOVE THERE.
WE KNOW WHAT WE'RE LOOKING FOR NOW-- WE JUST NEED TO FIND IT. IF THE LITTLE ASIAN DOESN'T TALK-- WE CAN JUST INTERVIEW PEOPLE HERE. SOMEONE HAS GOT TO HAVE SOME IDEA WHERE A PRISON MIGHT BE NEAR HERE.
NOW--IT'S ONLY A MATTER OF TIME.

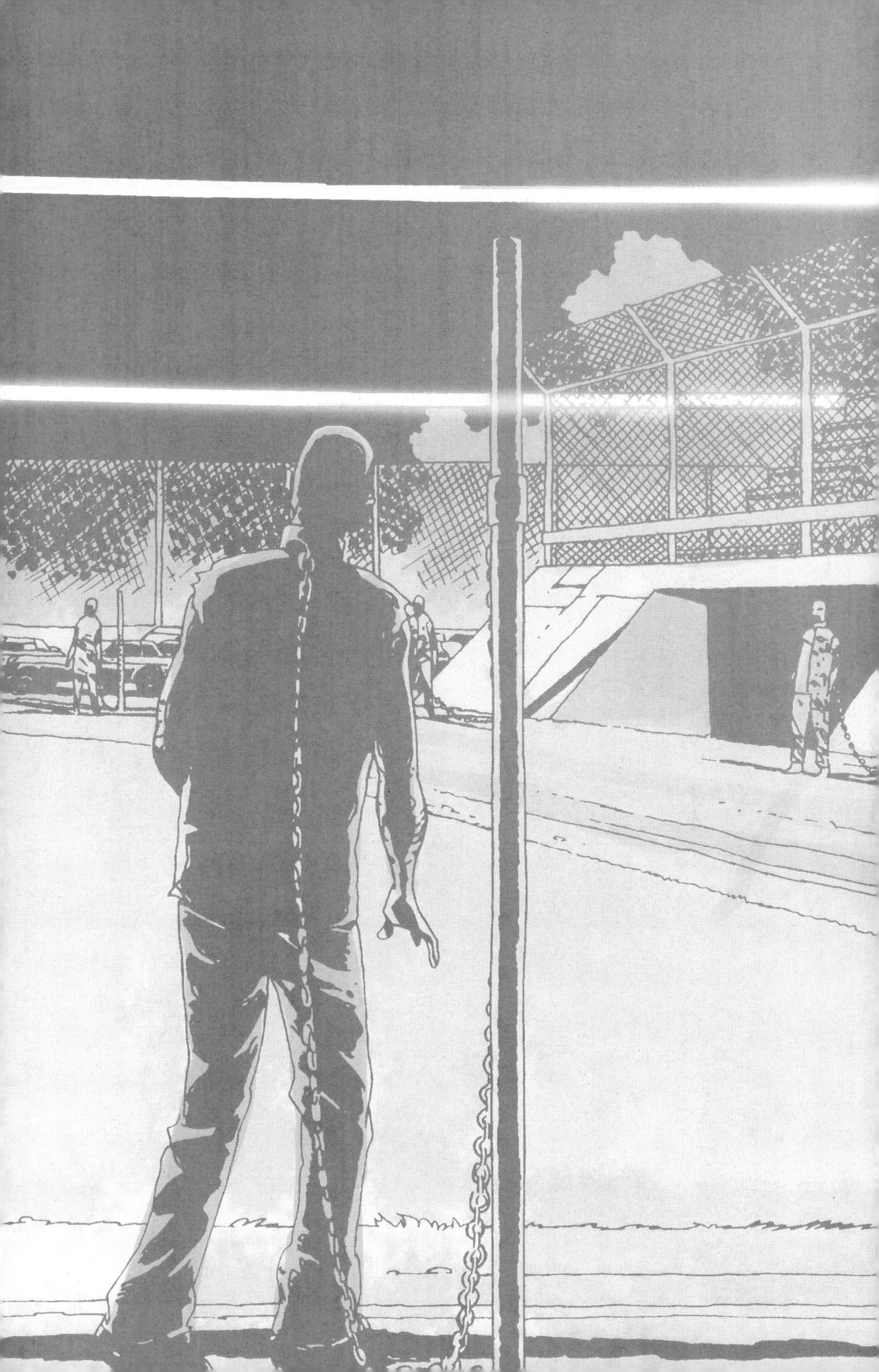

Chapter Six:
This Sorrowful Life

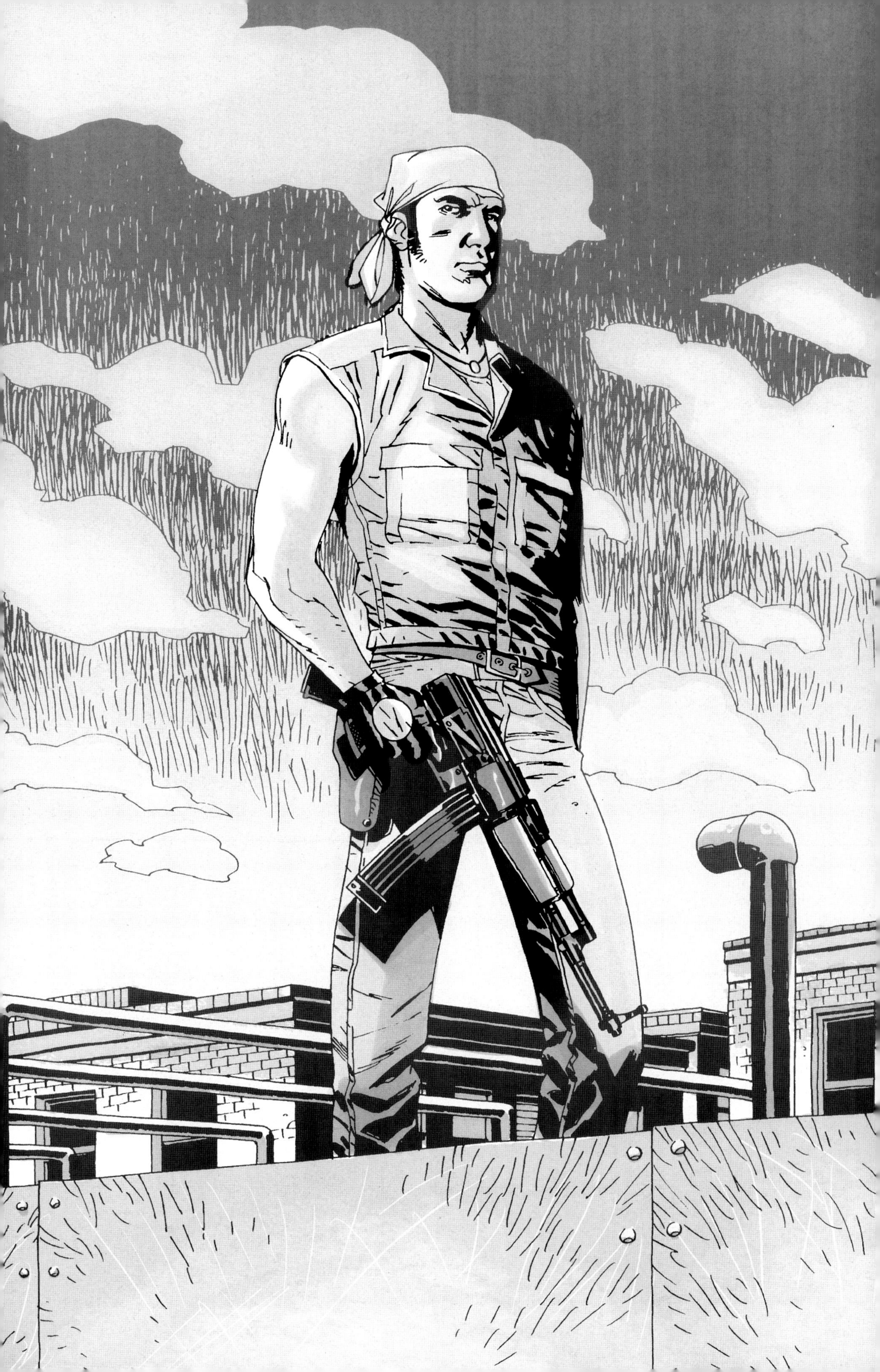

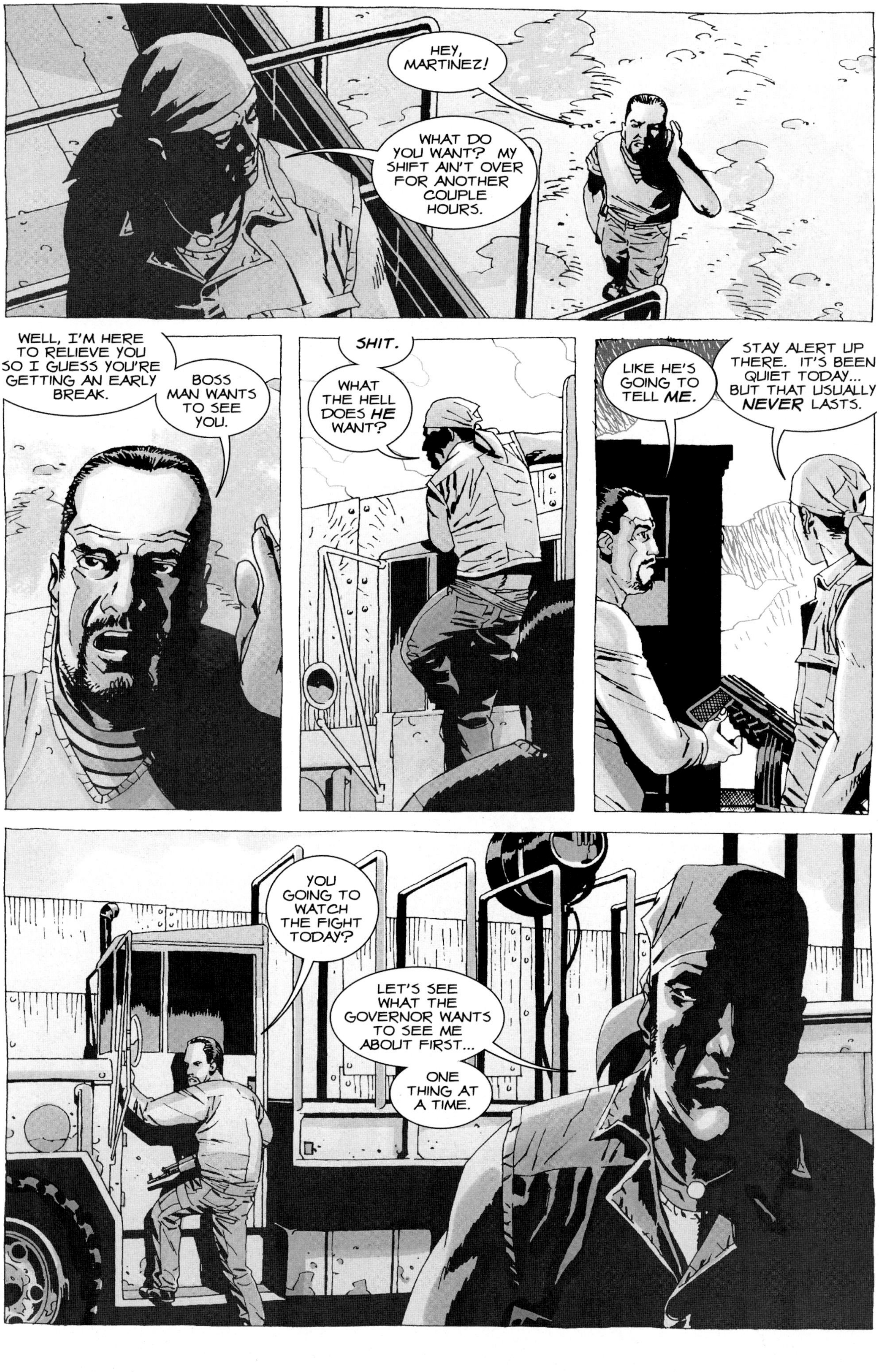
HEY, MARTINEZ!
WHAT DO YOU WANT? MY SHIFT AIN'T OVER FOR ANOTHER COUPLE HOURS.
WELL, I'M HERE TO RELIEVE YOU SO I GUESS YOU'RE GETTING AN EARLY BREAK.
BOSS MAN WANTS TO SEE YOU.
SHIT.
WHAT THE HELL DOES HE WANT?
LIKE HE'S GOING TO TELL ME.
STAY ALERT UP THERE. IT'S BEEN QUIET TODAY... BUT THAT USUALLY NEVER LASTS.
YOU GOING TO WATCH THE FIGHT TODAY?
LET'S SEE WHAT THE GOVERNOR WANTS TO SEE ME ABOUT FIRST...
ONE THING AT A TIME.

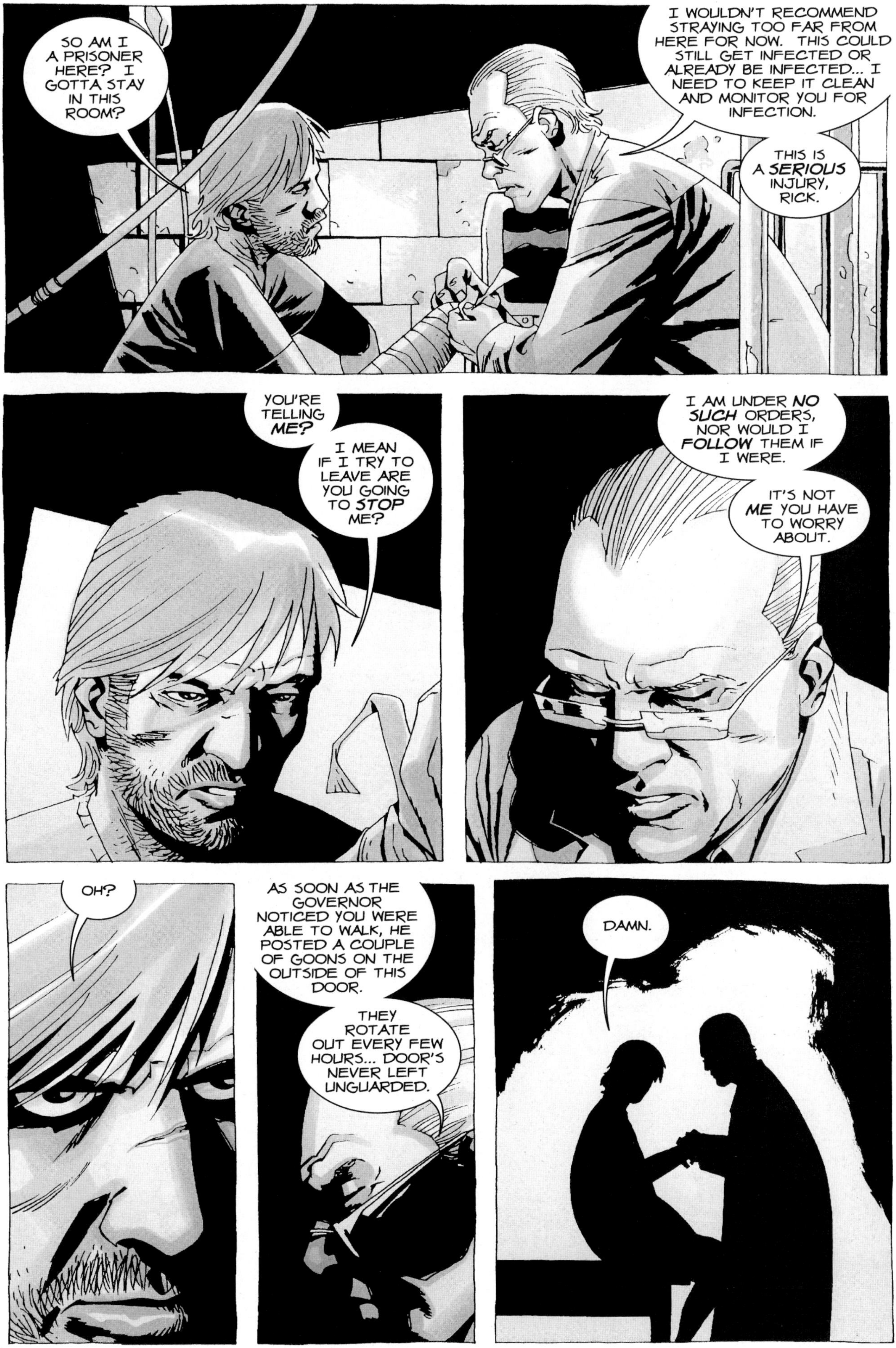
SO AM I A PRISONER HERE? I GOTTA STAY IN THIS ROOM?
I WOULDN'T RECOMMEND STRAYING TOO FAR FROM HERE FOR NOW. THIS COULD STILL GET INFECTED OR ALREADY BE INFECTED... I NEED TO KEEP IT CLEAN AND MONITOR YOU FOR INFECTION.
THIS IS A SERIOUS INJURY, RICK.
YOU'RE TELLING ME?
I MEAN IF I TRY TO LEAVE ARE YOU GOING TO STOP ME?
I AM UNDER NO SUCH ORDERS, NOR WOULD I FOLLOW THEM IF I WERE.
IT'S NOT ME YOU HAVE TO WORRY ABOUT.
OH?
AS SOON AS THE GOVERNOR NOTICED YOU WERE ABLE TO WALK, HE POSTED A COUPLE OF GOONS ON THE OUTSIDE OF THIS DOOR.
THEY ROTATE OUT EVERY FEW HOURS... DOOR'S NEVER LEFT UNGUARDED.
DAMN.

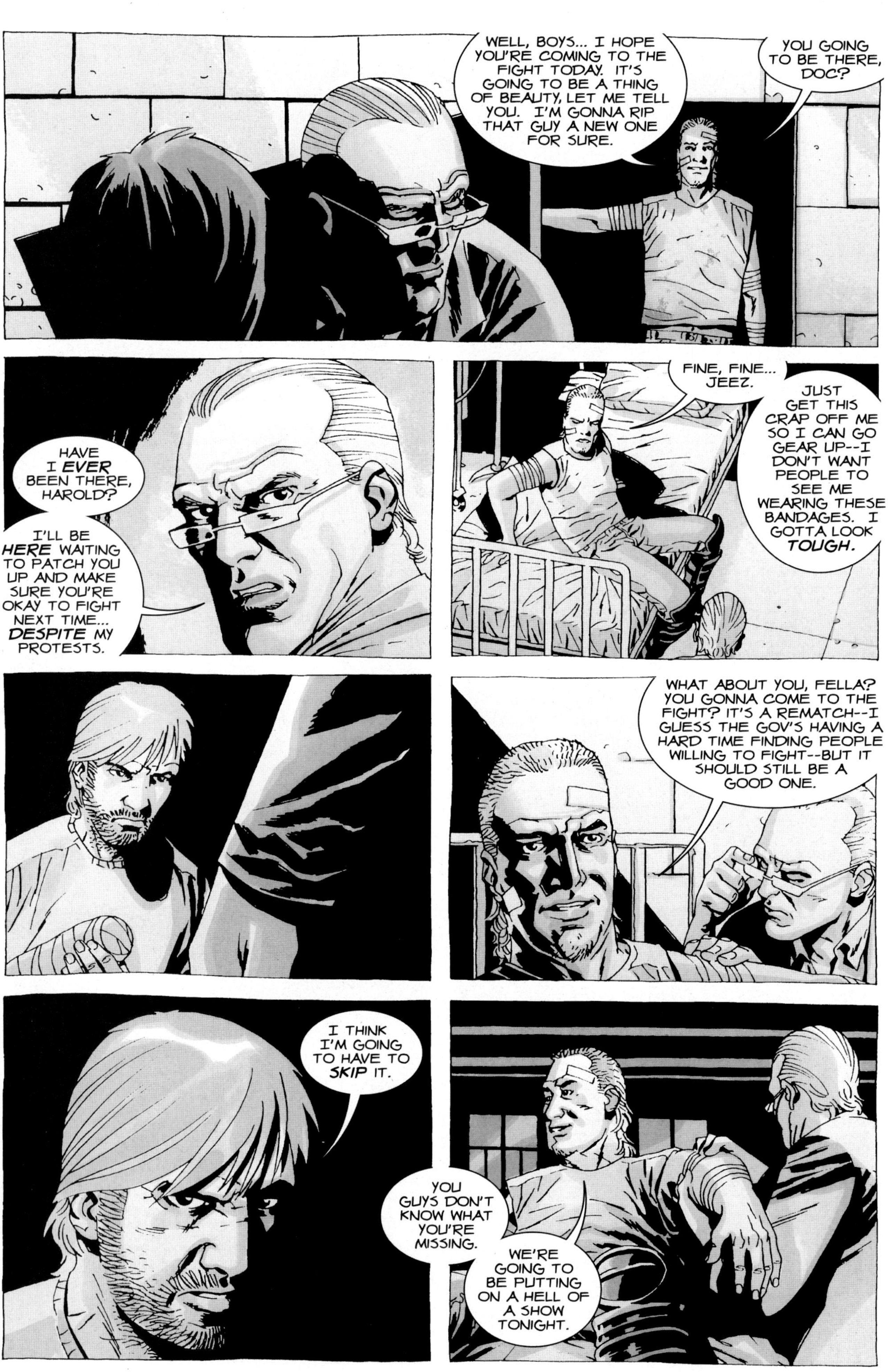
WELL, BOYS... I HOPE YOU'RE COMING TO THE FIGHT TODAY. IT'S GOING TO BE A THING OF BEAUTY, LET ME TELL YOU. I'M GONNA RIP THAT GUY A NEW ONE FOR SURE.
YOU GOING TO BE THERE, DOC?
HAVE I EVER BEEN THERE, HAROLD?
I'LL BE HERE WAITING TO PATCH YOU UP AND MAKE SURE YOU'RE OKAY TO FIGHT NEXT TIME... DESPITE MY PROTESTS.
FINE, FINE... JEEZ.
JUST GET THIS CRAP OFF ME SO I CAN GO GEAR UP--I DON'T WANT PEOPLE TO SEE ME WEARING THESE BANDAGES. I GOTTA LOOK TOUGH.
WHAT ABOUT YOU, FELLA? YOU GONNA COME TO THE FIGHT? IT'S A REMATCH--I GUESS THE GOV'S HAVING A HARD TIME FINDING PEOPLE WILLING TO FIGHT--BUT IT SHOULD STILL BE A GOOD ONE.
I THINK I'M GOING TO HAVE TO SKIP IT.
YOU GUYS DON'T KNOW WHAT YOU'RE MISSING.
WE'RE GOING TO BE PUTTING ON A HELL OF A SHOW TONIGHT.

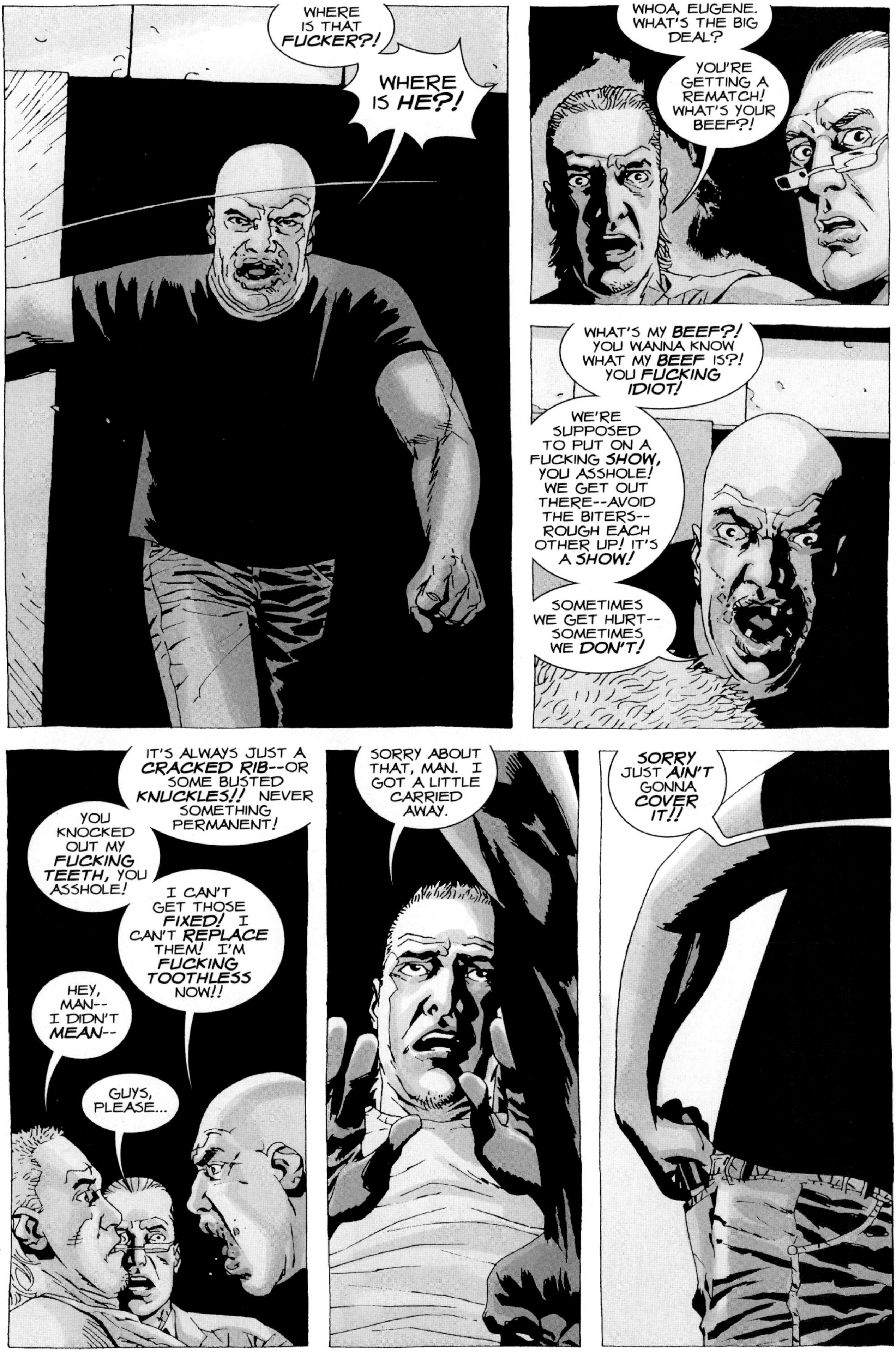
WHERE IS THAT FUCKER?!
WHERE IS HE?!
WHOA, EUGENE. WHAT'S THE BIG DEAL?
YOU'RE GETTING A REMATCH! WHAT'S YOUR BEEF?!
WHAT'S MY BEEF?! YOU WANNA KNOW WHAT MY BEEF IS?! YOU FUCKING IDIOT!
WE'RE SUPPOSED TO PUT ON A FUCKING SHOW, YOU ASSHOLE! WE GET OUT THERE--AVOID THE BITERS--ROUGH EACH OTHER UP! IT'S A SHOW!
SOMETIMES WE GET HURT--SOMETIMES WE DON'T!
IT'S ALWAYS JUST A CRACKED RIB--OR SOME BUSTED KNUCKLES!! NEVER SOMETHING PERMANENT!
YOU KNOCKED OUT MY FUCKING TEETH, YOU ASSHOLE!
I CAN'T GET THOSE FIXED! I CAN'T REPLACE THEM! I'M FUCKING TOOTHLESS NOW!!
HEY, MAN-- I DIDN'T MEAN--
GUYS, PLEASE...
SORRY ABOUT THAT, MAN. I GOT A LITTLE CARRIED AWAY.
SORRY JUST AIN'T GONNA COVER IT!!

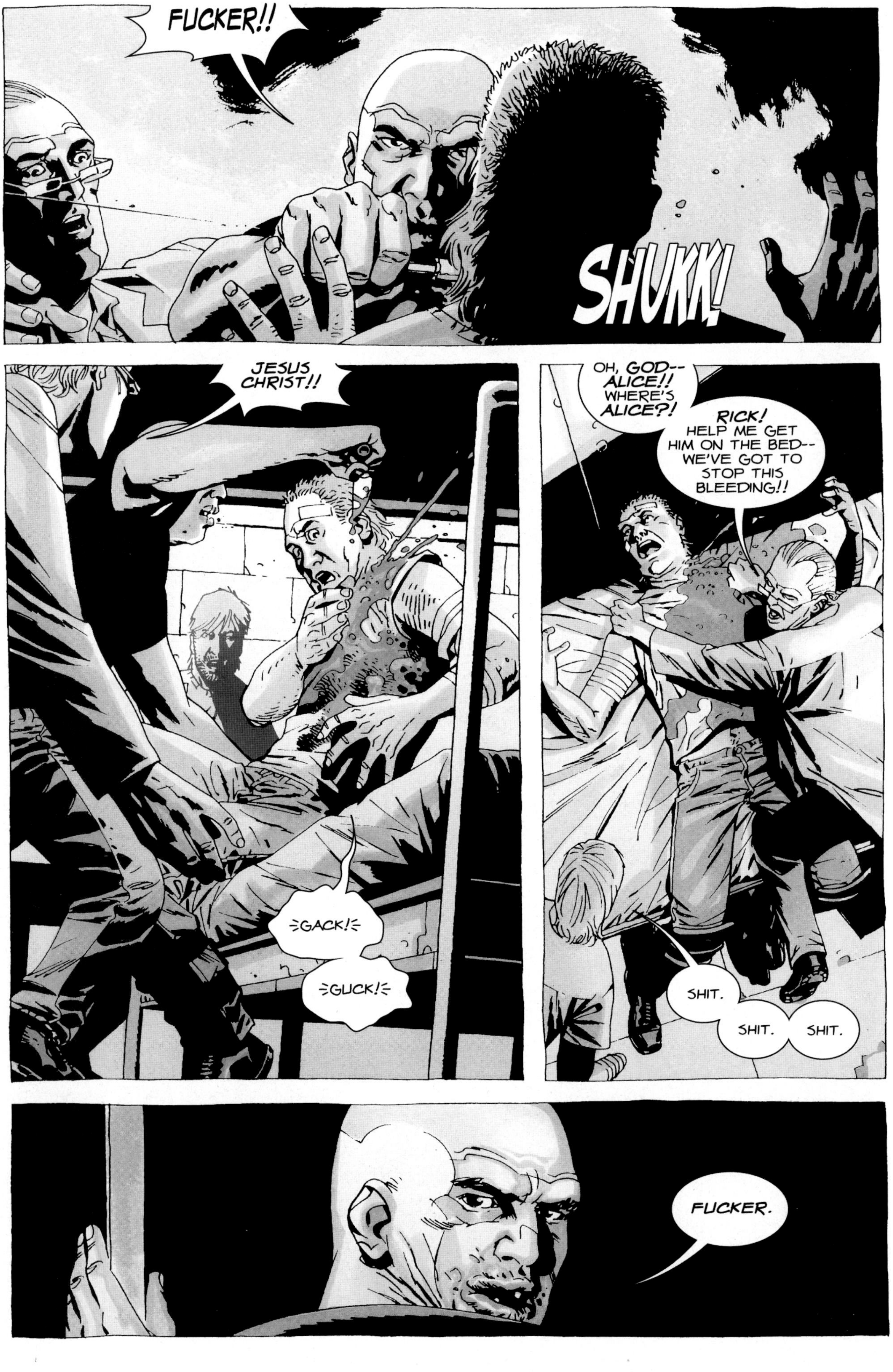
FUCKER!!
SHUKK!
JESUS CHRIST!!
GACK!
GUCK!
OH, GOD-- ALICE!! WHERE'S ALICE?!
RICK! HELP ME GET HIM ON THE BED-- WE'VE GOT TO STOP THIS BLEEDING!!
SHIT.
SHIT.
SHIT.
FUCKER.

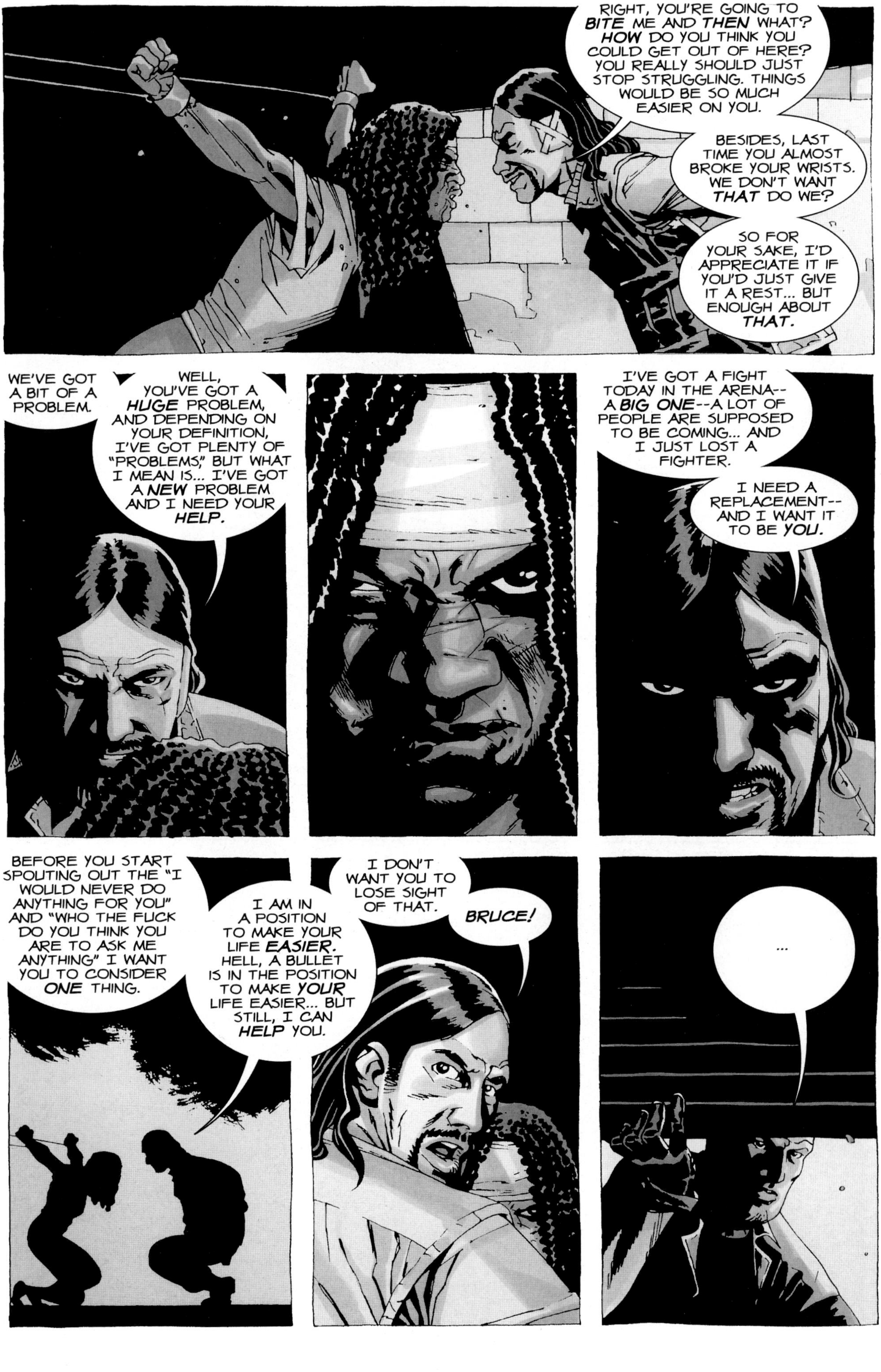
RIGHT, YOU'RE GOING TO BITE ME AND THEN WHAT? HOW DO YOU THINK YOU COULD GET OUT OF HERE? YOU REALLY SHOULD JUST STOP STRUGGLING. THINGS WOULD BE SO MUCH EASIER ON YOU.
BESIDES, LAST TIME YOU ALMOST BROKE YOUR WRISTS. WE DON'T WANT THAT DO WE?
SO FOR YOUR SAKE, I'D APPRECIATE IT IF YOU'D JUST GIVE IT A REST... BUT ENOUGH ABOUT THAT.
WE'VE GOT A BIT OF A PROBLEM.
WELL, YOU'VE GOT A HUGE PROBLEM, AND DEPENDING ON YOUR DEFINITION, I'VE GOT PLENTY OF "PROBLEMS," BUT WHAT I MEAN IS... I'VE GOT A NEW PROBLEM AND I NEED YOUR HELP.
I'VE GOT A FIGHT TODAY IN THE ARENA-- A BIG ONE--A LOT OF PEOPLE ARE SUPPOSED TO BE COMING... AND I JUST LOST A FIGHTER.
I NEED A REPLACEMENT-- AND I WANT IT TO BE YOU.
BEFORE YOU START SPOUTING OUT THE "I WOULD NEVER DO ANYTHING FOR YOU" AND "WHO THE FUCK DO YOU THINK YOU ARE TO ASK ME ANYTHING" I WANT YOU TO CONSIDER ONE THING.
I AM IN A POSITION TO MAKE YOUR LIFE EASIER. HELL, A BULLET IS IN THE POSITION TO MAKE YOUR LIFE EASIER... BUT STILL, I CAN HELP YOU.
I DON'T WANT YOU TO LOSE SIGHT OF THAT.
BRUCE!
...

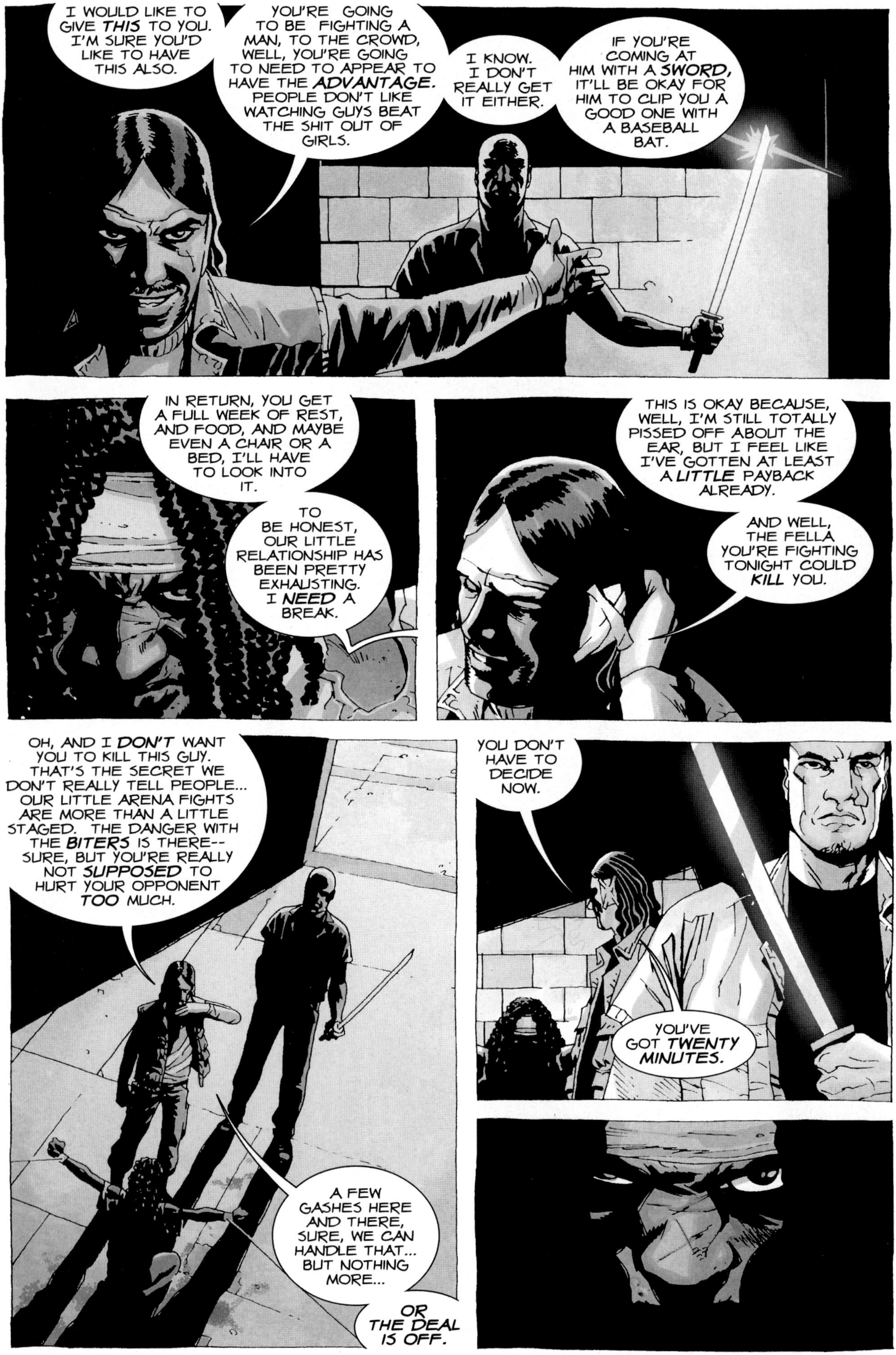
I WOULD LIKE TO GIVE THIS TO YOU. I'M SURE YOU'D LIKE TO HAVE THIS ALSO.
YOU'RE GOING TO BE FIGHTING A MAN, TO THE CROWD, WELL, YOU'RE GOING TO NEED TO APPEAR TO HAVE THE ADVANTAGE. PEOPLE DON'T LIKE WATCHING GUYS BEAT THE SHIT OUT OF GIRLS.
I KNOW. I DON'T REALLY GET IT EITHER.
IF YOU'RE COMING AT HIM WITH A SWORD, IT'LL BE OKAY FOR HIM TO CLIP YOU A GOOD ONE WITH A BASEBALL BAT.
IN RETURN, YOU GET A FULL WEEK OF REST, AND FOOD, AND MAYBE EVEN A CHAIR OR A BED, I'LL HAVE TO LOOK INTO IT.
TO BE HONEST, OUR LITTLE RELATIONSHIP HAS BEEN PRETTY EXHAUSTING. I NEED A BREAK.
THIS IS OKAY BECAUSE, WELL, I'M STILL TOTALLY PISSED OFF ABOUT THE EAR, BUT I FEEL LIKE I'VE GOTTEN AT LEAST A LITTLE PAYBACK ALREADY.
AND WELL, THE FELLA YOU'RE FIGHTING TONIGHT COULD KILL YOU.
OH, AND I DON'T WANT YOU TO KILL THIS GUY. THAT'S THE SECRET WE DON'T REALLY TELL PEOPLE... OUR LITTLE ARENA FIGHTS ARE MORE THAN A LITTLE STAGED. THE DANGER WITH THE BITERS IS THERE-- SURE, BUT YOU'RE REALLY NOT SUPPOSED TO HURT YOUR OPPONENT TOO MUCH.
A FEW GASHES HERE AND THERE, SURE, WE CAN HANDLE THAT... BUT NOTHING MORE...
OR THE DEAL IS OFF.
YOU DON'T HAVE TO DECIDE NOW.
YOU'VE GOT TWENTY MINUTES.

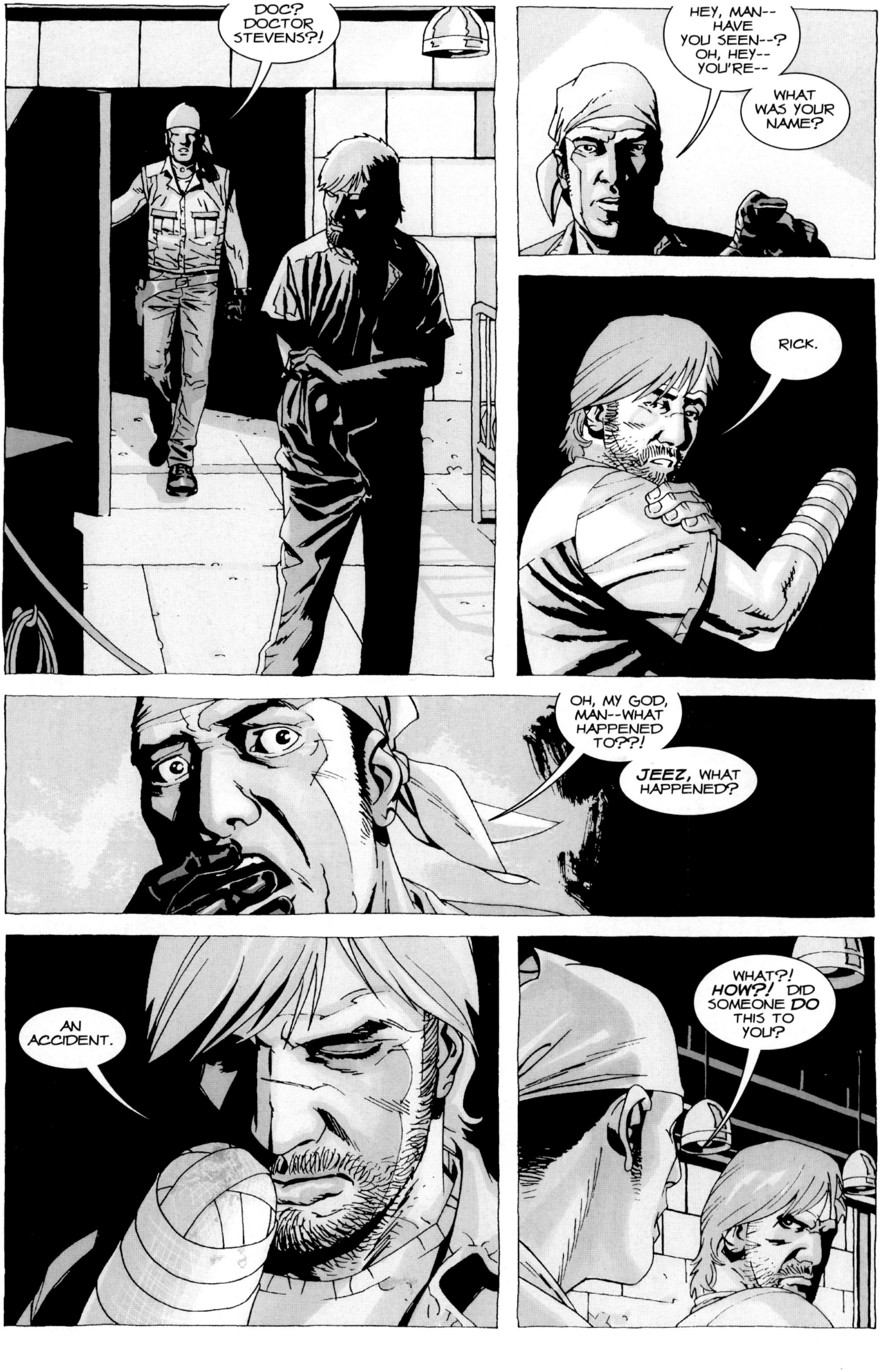
DOC? DOCTOR STEVENS?!
HEY, MAN-- HAVE YOU SEEN--? OH, HEY-- YOU'RE--
WHAT WAS YOUR NAME?
RICK.
OH, MY GOD, MAN--WHAT HAPPENED TO??!
JEEZ, WHAT HAPPENED?
AN ACCIDENT.
WHAT?! HOW?! DID SOMEONE DO THIS TO YOU?

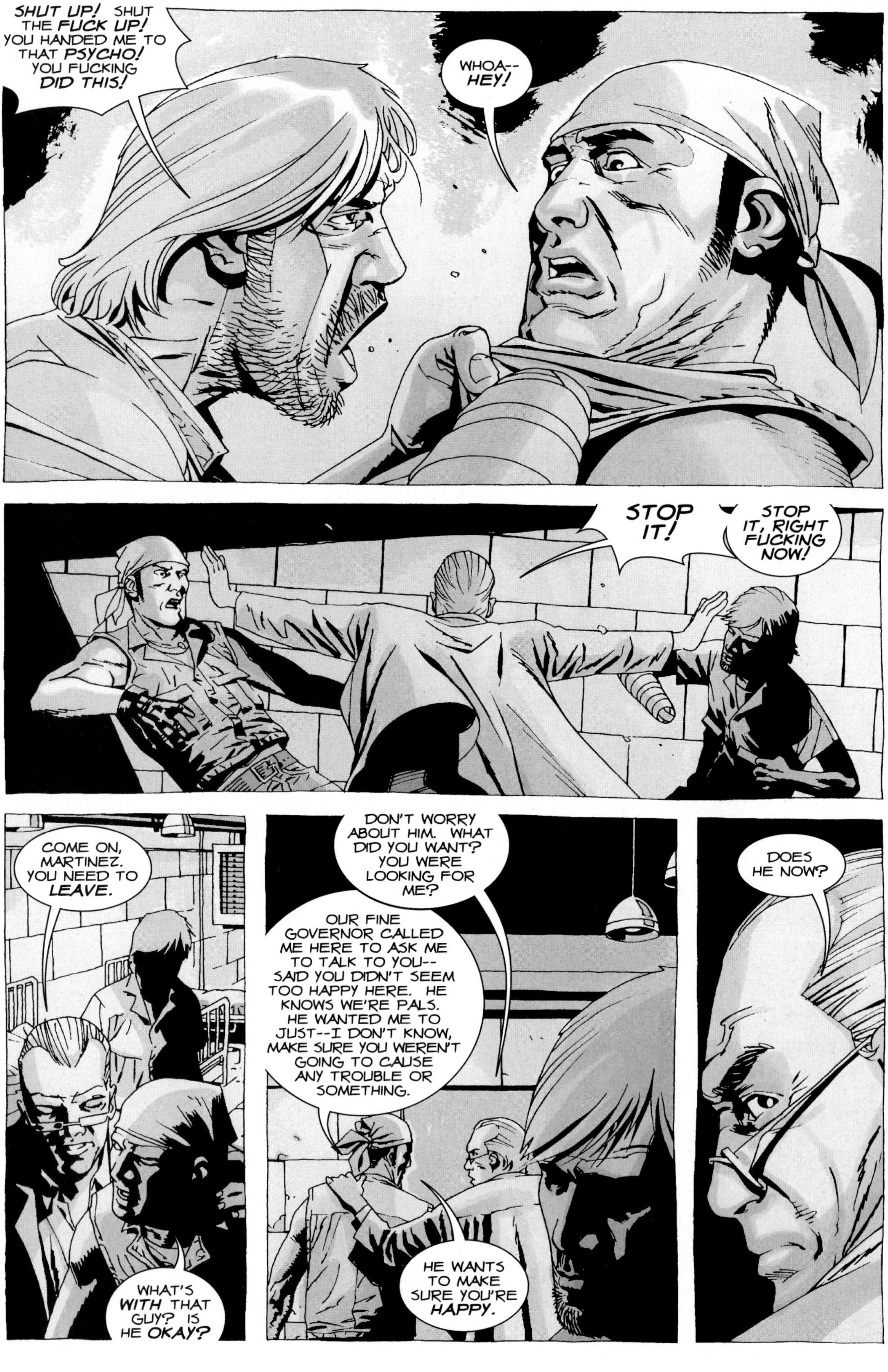
SHUT UP! SHUT THE FUCK UP! YOU HANDED ME TO THAT PSYCHO! YOU FUCKING DID THIS!
WHOA-- HEY!
STOP IT!
STOP IT, RIGHT FUCKING NOW!
COME ON, MARTINEZ. YOU NEED TO LEAVE.
WHAT'S WITH THAT GUY? IS HE OKAY?
DON'T WORRY ABOUT HIM. WHAT DID YOU WANT? YOU WERE LOOKING FOR ME?
OUR FINE GOVERNOR CALLED ME HERE TO ASK ME TO TALK TO YOU-- SAID YOU DIDN'T SEEM TOO HAPPY HERE. HE KNOWS WE'RE PALS. HE WANTED ME TO JUST--I DON'T KNOW, MAKE SURE YOU WEREN'T GOING TO CAUSE ANY TROUBLE OR SOMETHING.
HE WANTS TO MAKE SURE YOU'RE HAPPY.
DOES HE NOW?

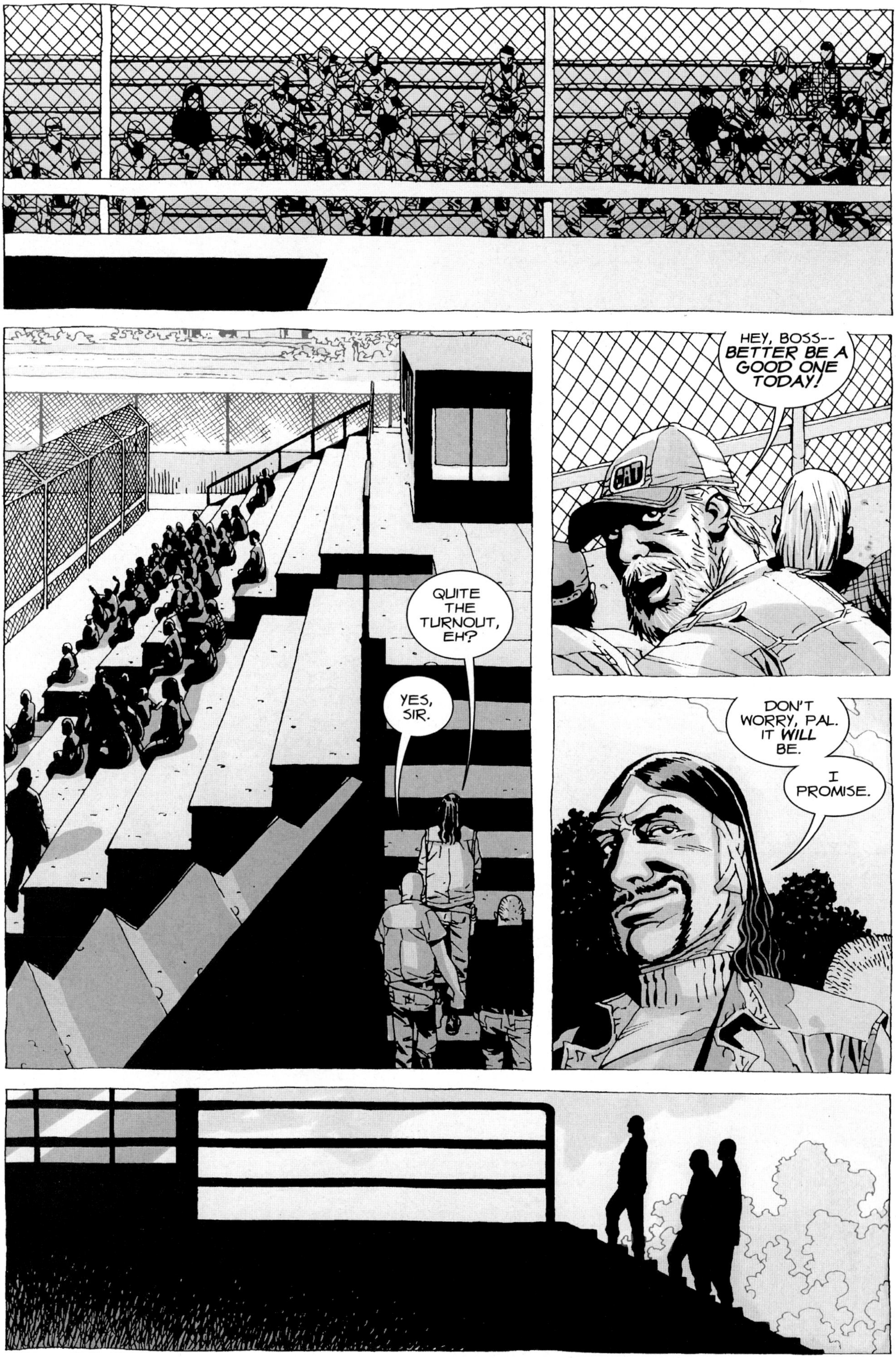
QUITE THE TURNOUT, EH?
YES, SIR.
HEY, BOSS-- BETTER BE A GOOD ONE TODAY!
DON'T WORRY, PAL. IT WILL BE.
I PROMISE.

YOU SURE ABOUT THIS, BOSS?

THIS IS GOING TO BE GOOD.

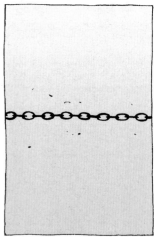

THE CHANCE TO SEE THIS BITCH TAKE A BEATING WITHOUT *ME* BREAKING A SWEAT?

YEAH-- I THINK IT'S A GOOD MOVE.

HERE WE GO.

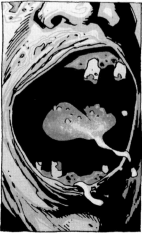

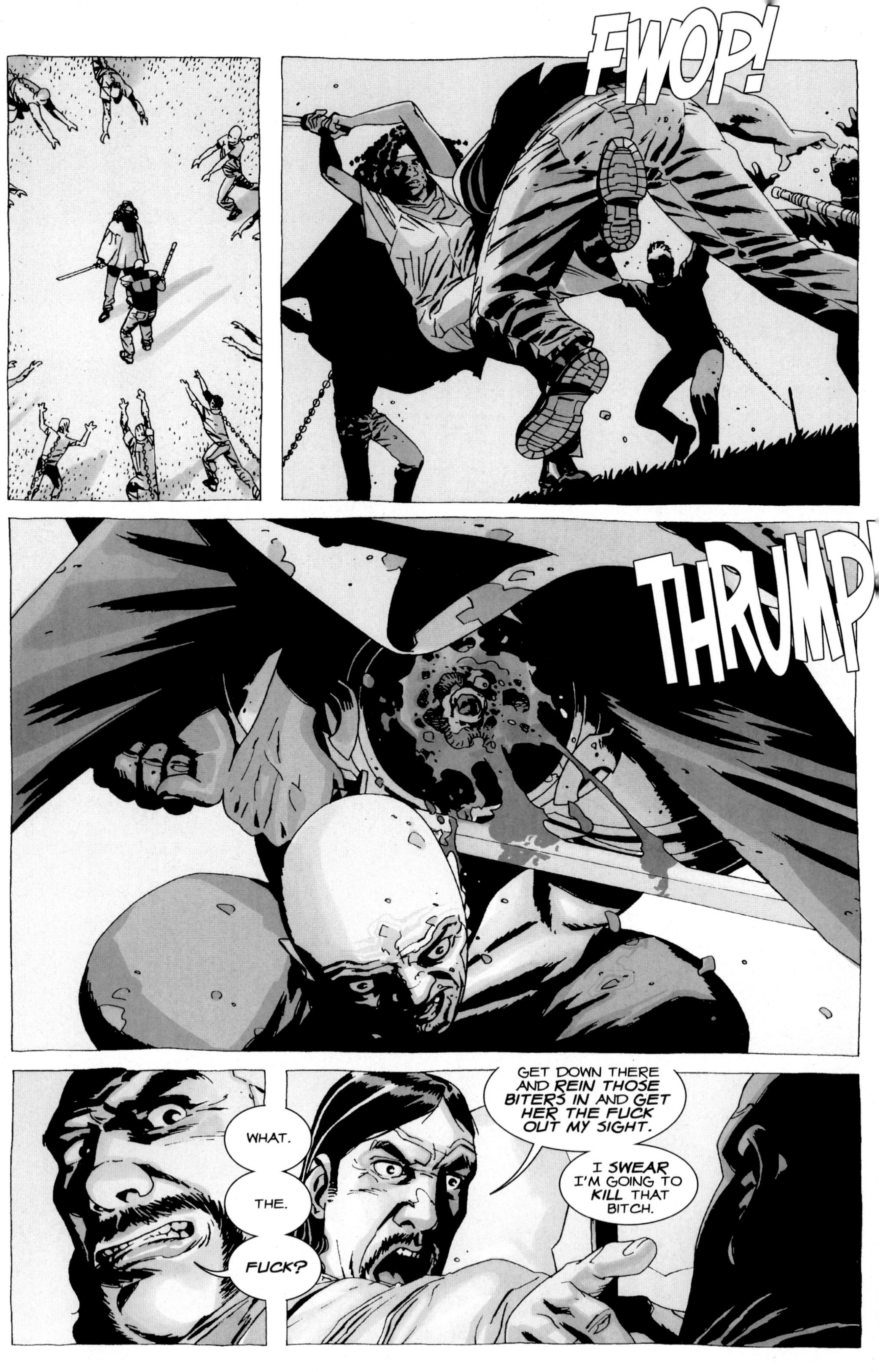
FWOP!
THRUMP!
WHAT.
THE.
FUCK?
GET DOWN THERE AND REIN THOSE BITERS IN AND GET HER THE FUCK OUT MY SIGHT.
I SWEAR I'M GOING TO KILL THAT BITCH.

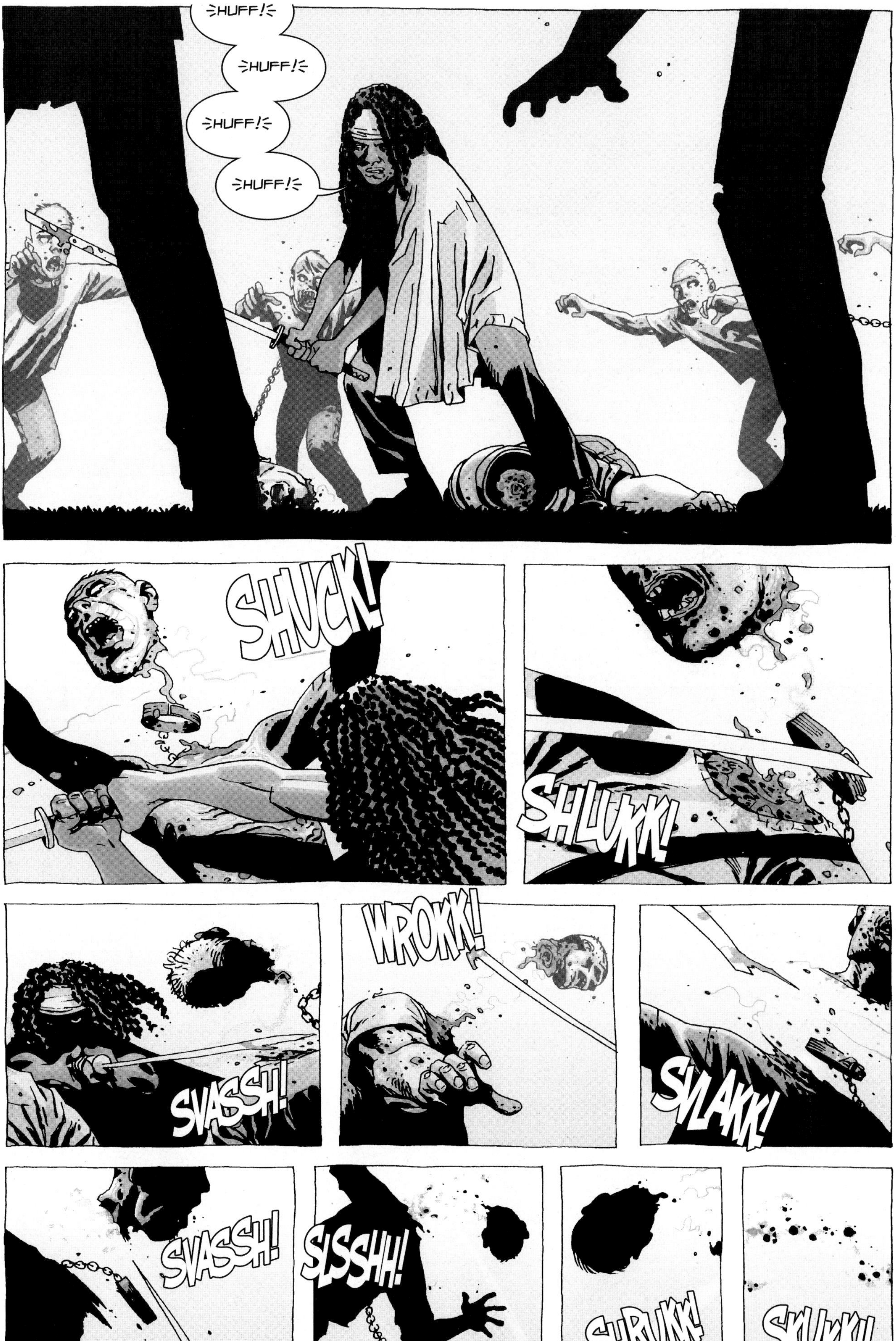
HUFF!
HUFF!
HUFF!
HUFF!
SHUCK!
SHLUKK!
SVASSH!
WROKK!
SVLAKK!
SVASSH!
SLSSHH!
SHRUKK!
SKUKK!!

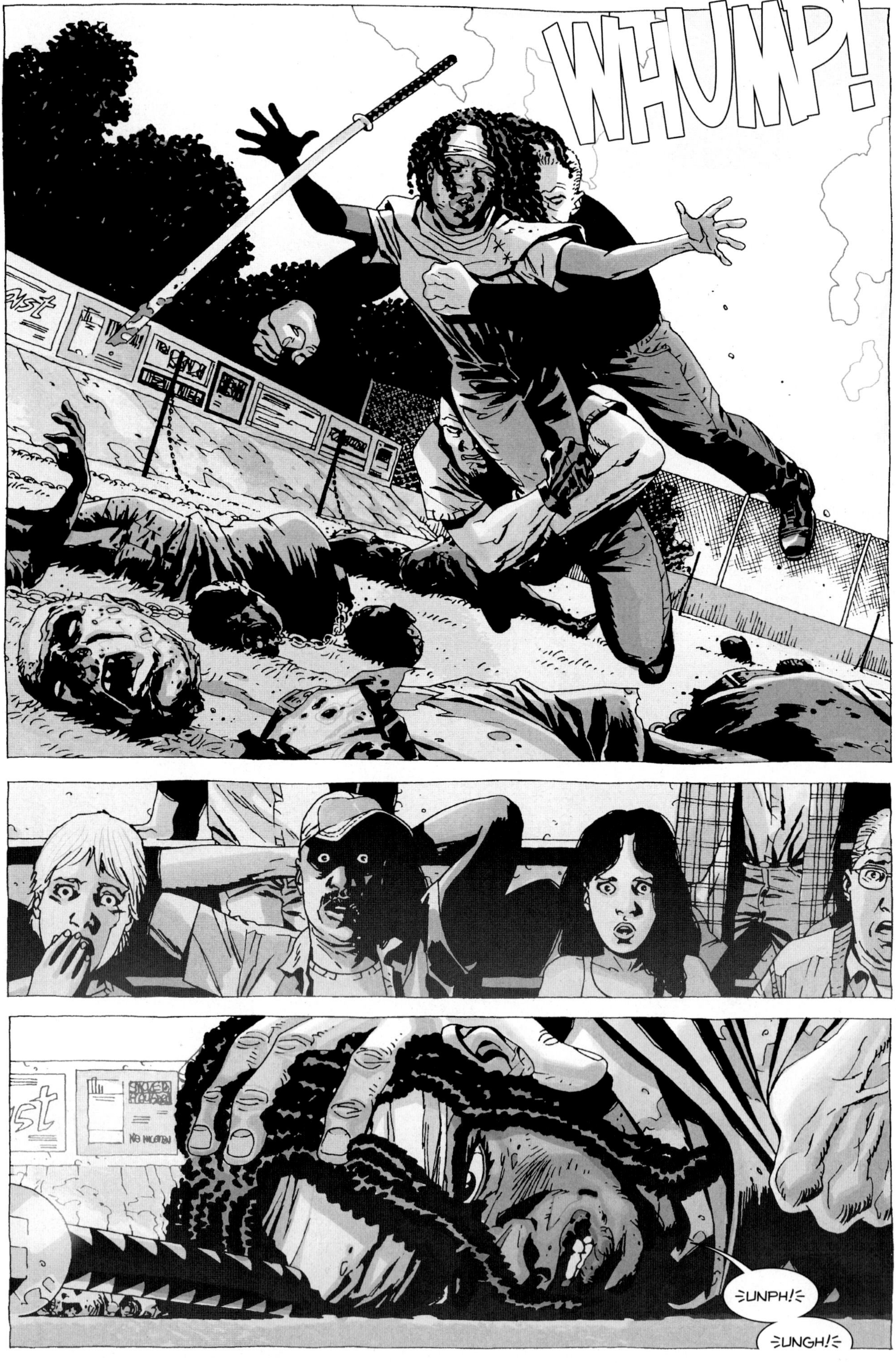
WHUMP!
UNPH!
UNGH!

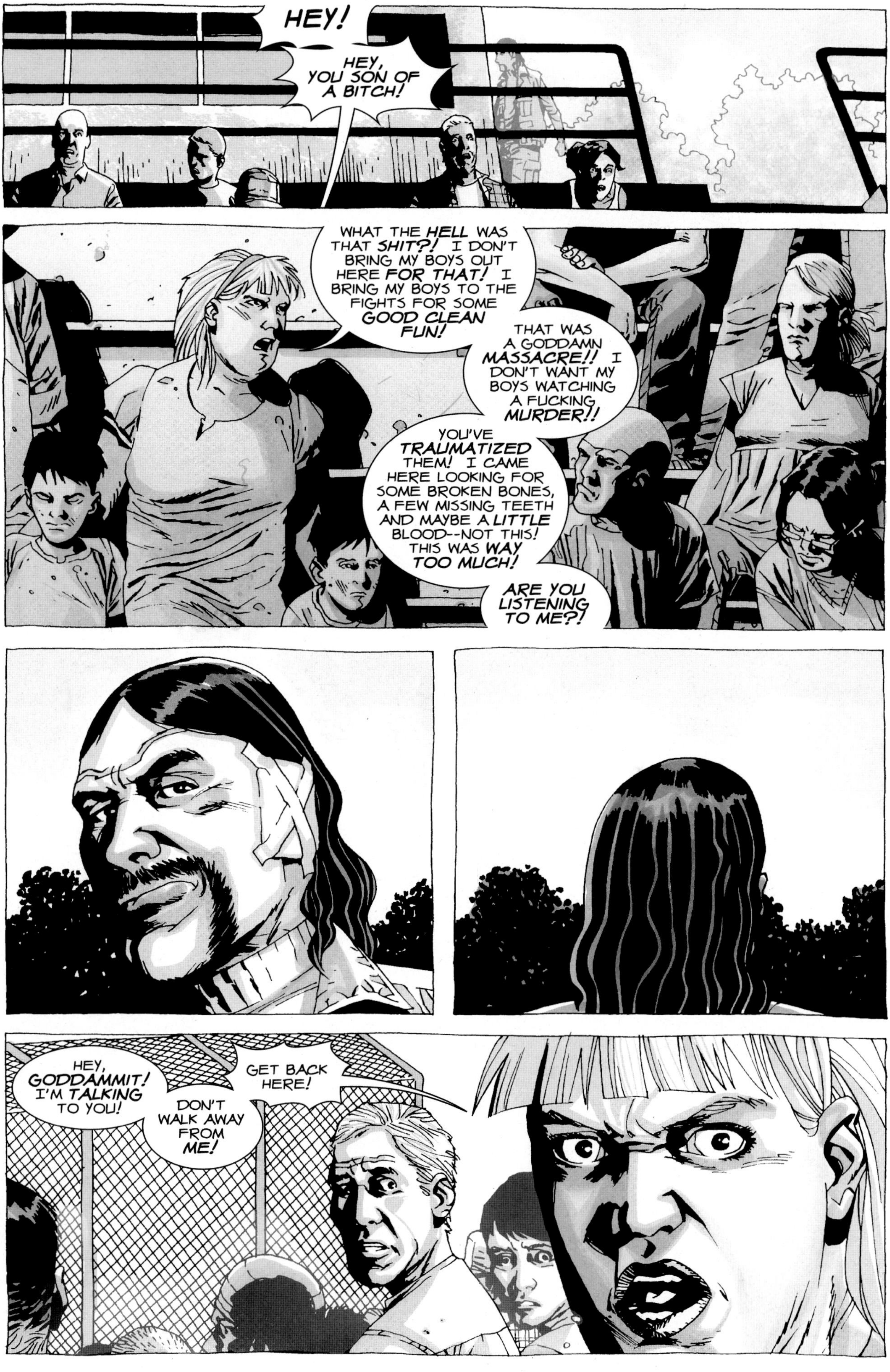
HEY!
HEY, YOU SON OF A BITCH!
WHAT THE HELL WAS THAT SHIT?! I DON'T BRING MY BOYS OUT HERE FOR THAT! I BRING MY BOYS TO THE FIGHTS FOR SOME GOOD CLEAN FUN!
THAT WAS A GODDAMN MASSACRE!! I DON'T WANT MY BOYS WATCHING A FUCKING MURDER!!
YOU'VE TRAUMATIZED THEM! I CAME HERE LOOKING FOR SOME BROKEN BONES, A FEW MISSING TEETH AND MAYBE A LITTLE BLOOD--NOT THIS! THIS WAS WAY TOO MUCH!
ARE YOU LISTENING TO ME?!
HEY, GODDAMMIT! I'M TALKING TO YOU!
DON'T WALK AWAY FROM ME!
GET BACK HERE!

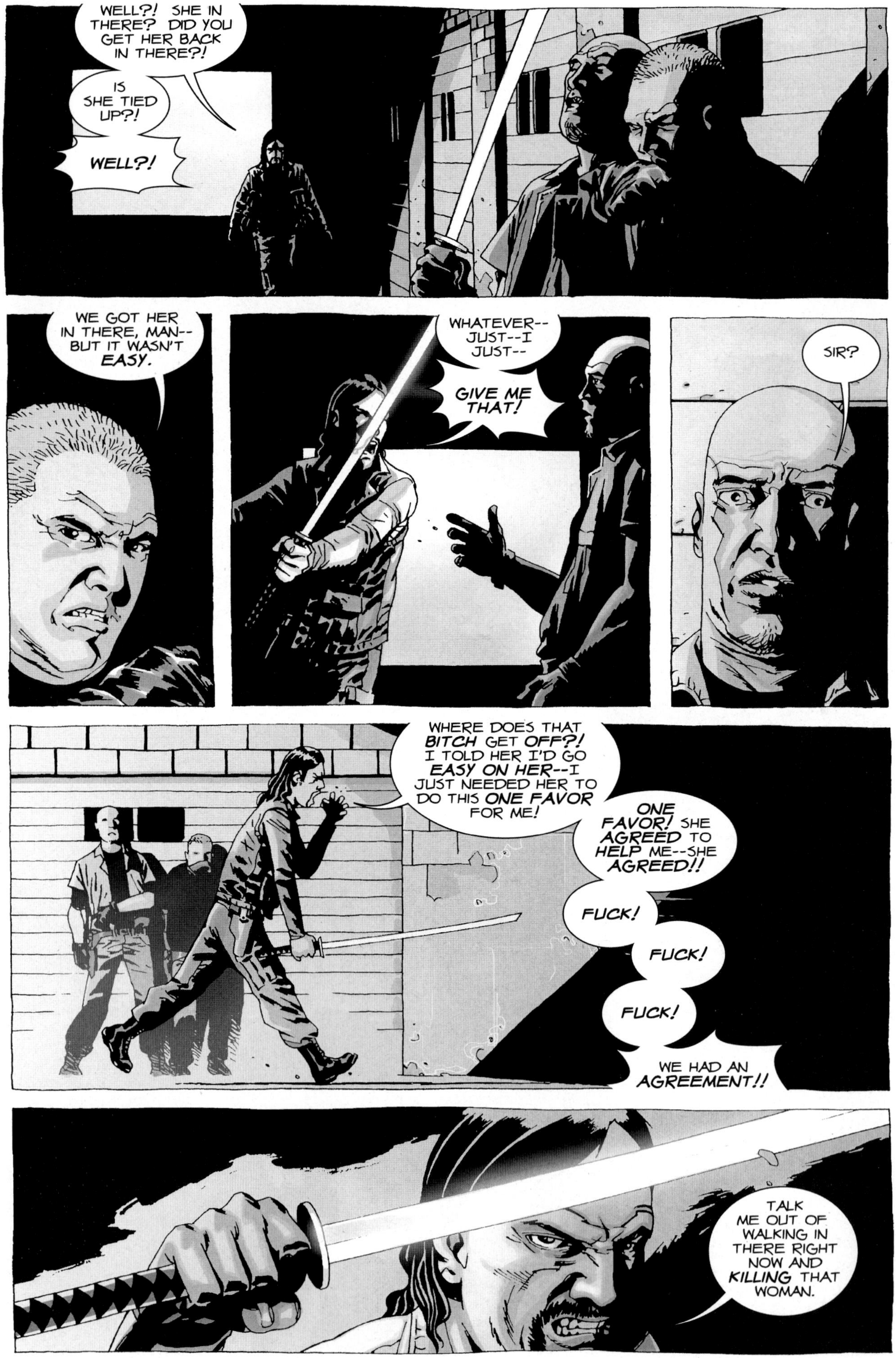
WELL?! SHE IN THERE? DID YOU GET HER BACK IN THERE?!
IS SHE TIED UP?!
WELL?!
WE GOT HER IN THERE, MAN-- BUT IT WASN'T EASY.
WHATEVER-- JUST--I JUST--
GIVE ME THAT!
SIR?
WHERE DOES THAT BITCH GET OFF?! I TOLD HER I'D GO EASY ON HER--I JUST NEEDED HER TO DO THIS ONE FAVOR FOR ME!
ONE FAVOR! SHE AGREED TO HELP ME--SHE AGREED!!
FUCK!
FUCK!
FUCK!
WE HAD AN AGREEMENT!!
TALK ME OUT OF WALKING IN THERE RIGHT NOW AND KILLING THAT WOMAN.

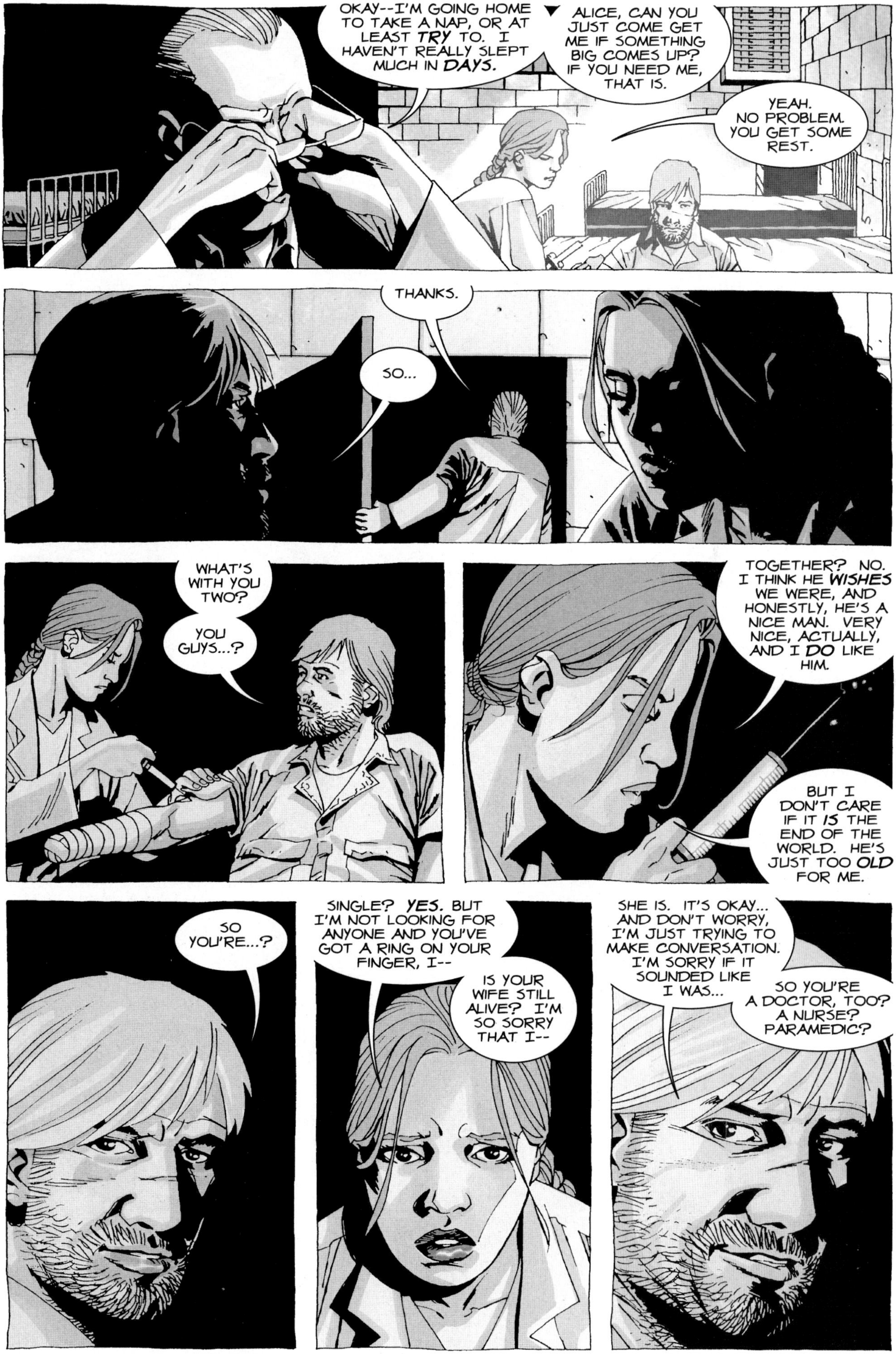
OKAY--I'M GOING HOME TO TAKE A NAP, OR AT LEAST TRY TO. I HAVEN'T REALLY SLEPT MUCH IN DAYS.
ALICE, CAN YOU JUST COME GET ME IF SOMETHING BIG COMES UP? IF YOU NEED ME, THAT IS.
YEAH. NO PROBLEM. YOU GET SOME REST.
THANKS.
SO...
WHAT'S WITH YOU TWO?
YOU GUYS...?
TOGETHER? NO. I THINK HE WISHES WE WERE, AND HONESTLY, HE'S A NICE MAN. VERY NICE, ACTUALLY, AND I DO LIKE HIM.
BUT I DON'T CARE IF IT IS THE END OF THE WORLD. HE'S JUST TOO OLD FOR ME.
SO YOU'RE...?
SINGLE? YES. BUT I'M NOT LOOKING FOR ANYONE AND YOU'VE GOT A RING ON YOUR FINGER, I--
IS YOUR WIFE STILL ALIVE? I'M SO SORRY THAT I--
SHE IS. IT'S OKAY... AND DON'T WORRY, I'M JUST TRYING TO MAKE CONVERSATION. I'M SORRY IF IT SOUNDED LIKE I WAS...
SO YOU'RE A DOCTOR, TOO? A NURSE? PARAMEDIC?

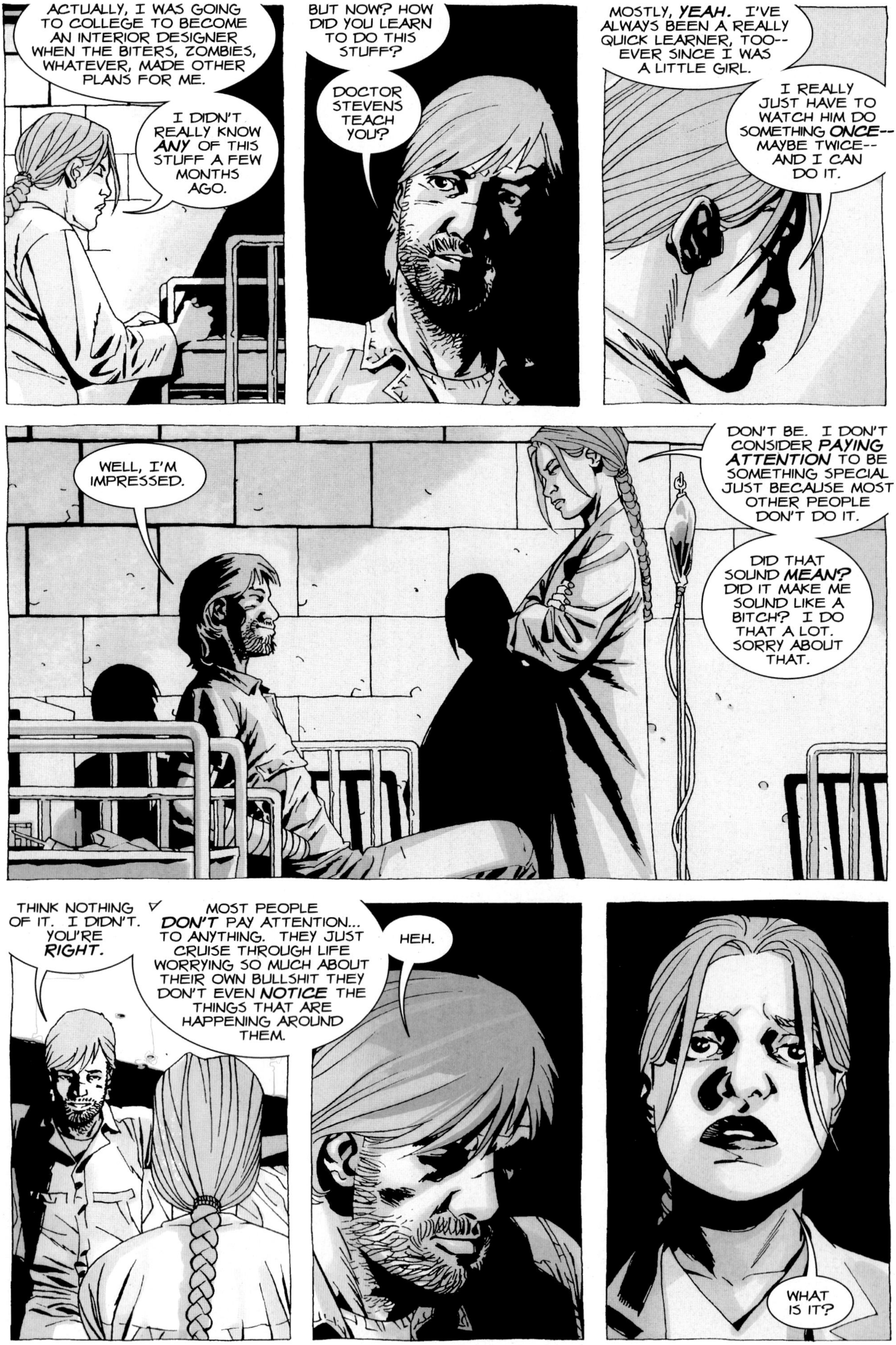
ACTUALLY, I WAS GOING TO COLLEGE TO BECOME AN INTERIOR DESIGNER WHEN THE BITERS, ZOMBIES, WHATEVER, MADE OTHER PLANS FOR ME.
I DIDN'T REALLY KNOW ANY OF THIS STUFF A FEW MONTHS AGO.
BUT NOW? HOW DID YOU LEARN TO DO THIS STUFF?
DOCTOR STEVENS TEACH YOU?
MOSTLY, YEAH. I'VE ALWAYS BEEN A REALLY QUICK LEARNER, TOO-- EVER SINCE I WAS A LITTLE GIRL.
I REALLY JUST HAVE TO WATCH HIM DO SOMETHING ONCE-- MAYBE TWICE-- AND I CAN DO IT.
WELL, I'M IMPRESSED.
DON'T BE. I DON'T CONSIDER PAYING ATTENTION TO BE SOMETHING SPECIAL JUST BECAUSE MOST OTHER PEOPLE DON'T DO IT.
DID THAT SOUND MEAN? DID IT MAKE ME SOUND LIKE A BITCH? I DO THAT A LOT. SORRY ABOUT THAT.
THINK NOTHING OF IT. I DIDN'T. YOU'RE RIGHT.
MOST PEOPLE DON'T PAY ATTENTION... TO ANYTHING. THEY JUST CRUISE THROUGH LIFE WORRYING SO MUCH ABOUT THEIR OWN BULLSHIT THEY DON'T EVEN NOTICE THE THINGS THAT ARE HAPPENING AROUND THEM.
HEH.
WHAT IS IT?

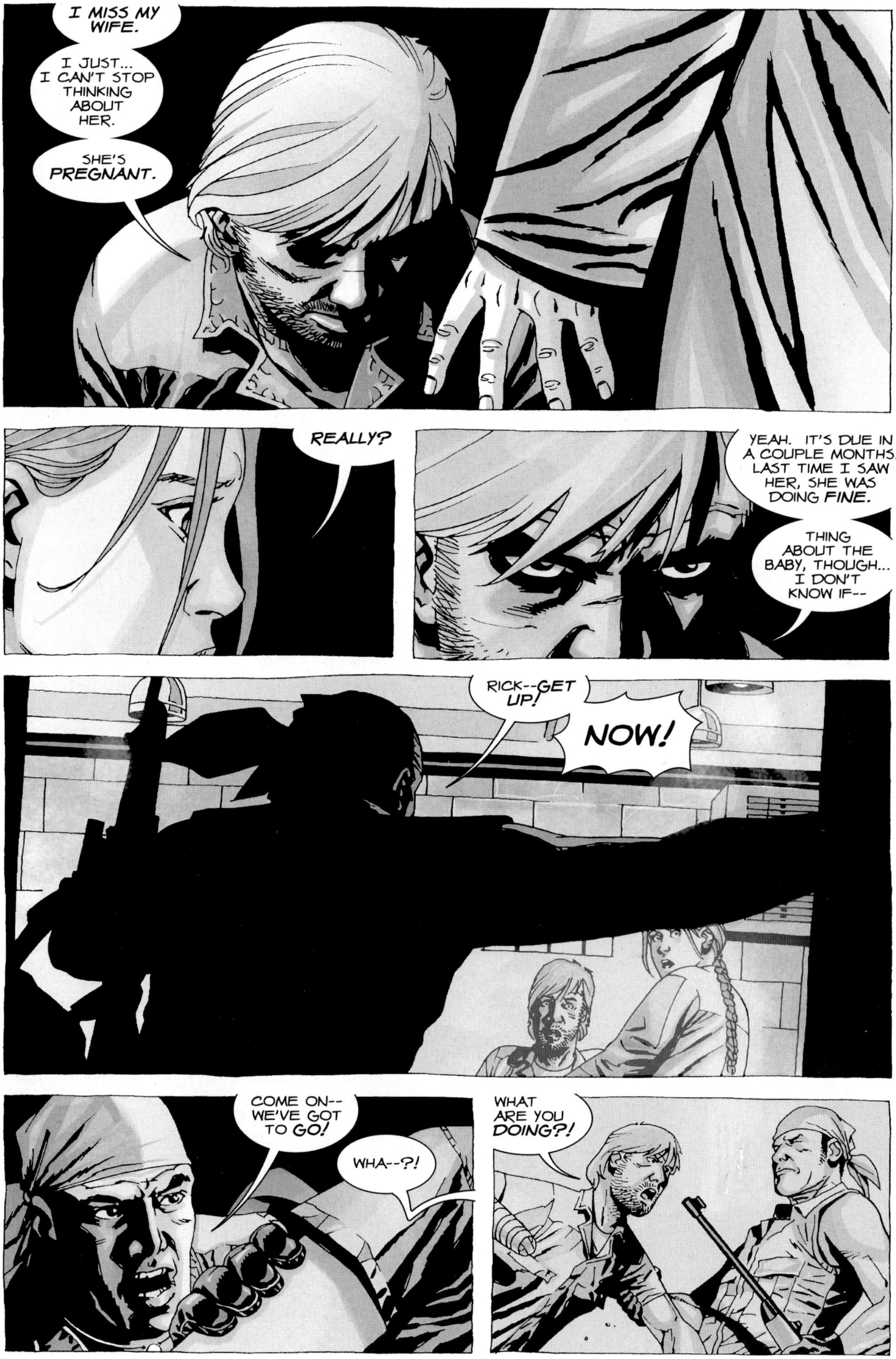
I MISS MY WIFE.
I JUST... I CAN'T STOP THINKING ABOUT HER.
SHE'S PREGNANT.
REALLY?
YEAH. IT'S DUE IN A COUPLE MONTHS. LAST TIME I SAW HER, SHE WAS DOING FINE.
THING ABOUT THE BABY, THOUGH... I DON'T KNOW IF--
RICK--GET UP!
NOW!
COME ON-- WE'VE GOT TO GO!
WHA--?!
WHAT ARE YOU DOING?!

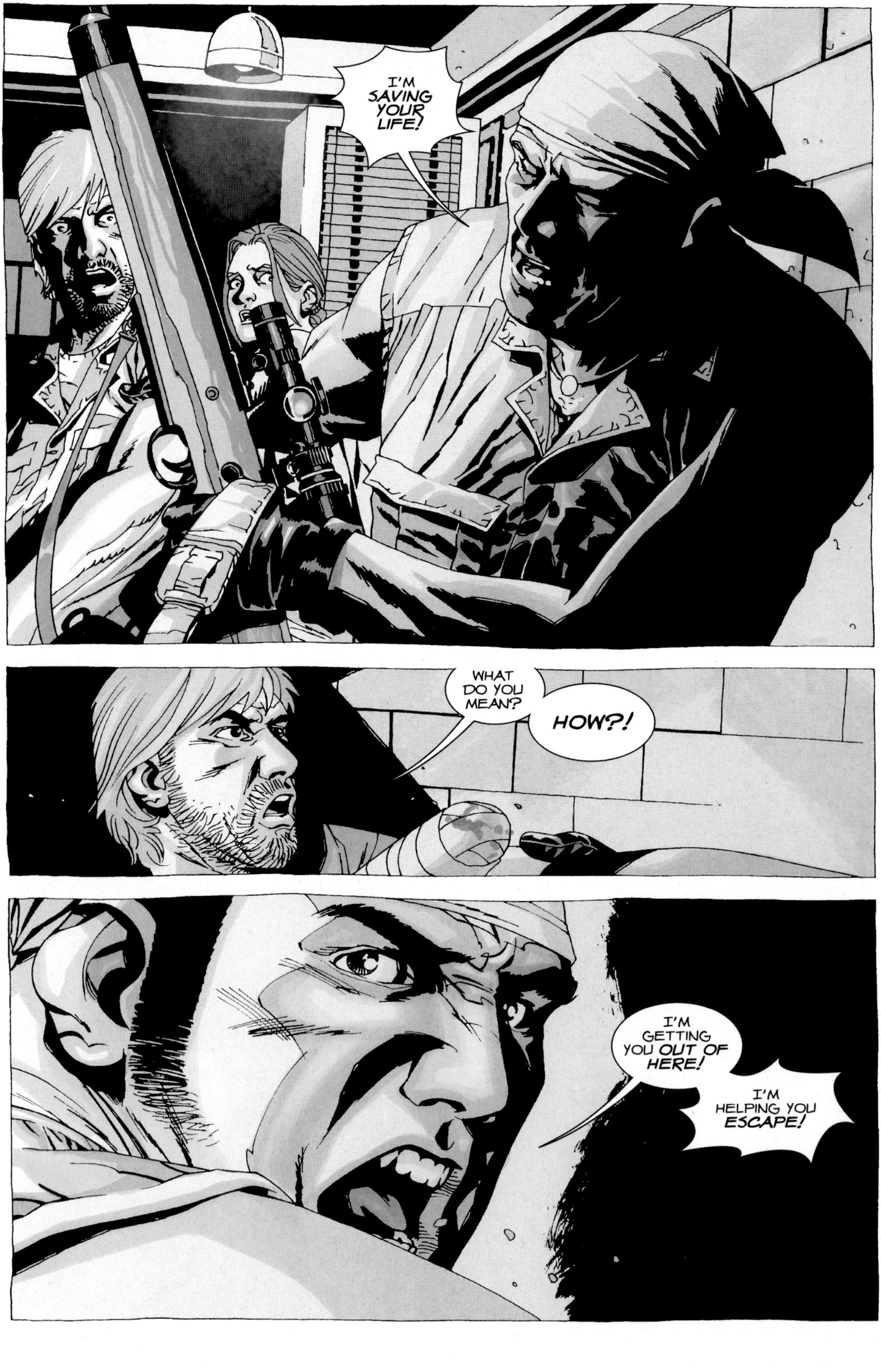
I'M SAVING YOUR LIFE!
WHAT DO YOU MEAN?
HOW?!
I'M GETTING YOU OUT OF HERE!
I'M HELPING YOU ESCAPE!

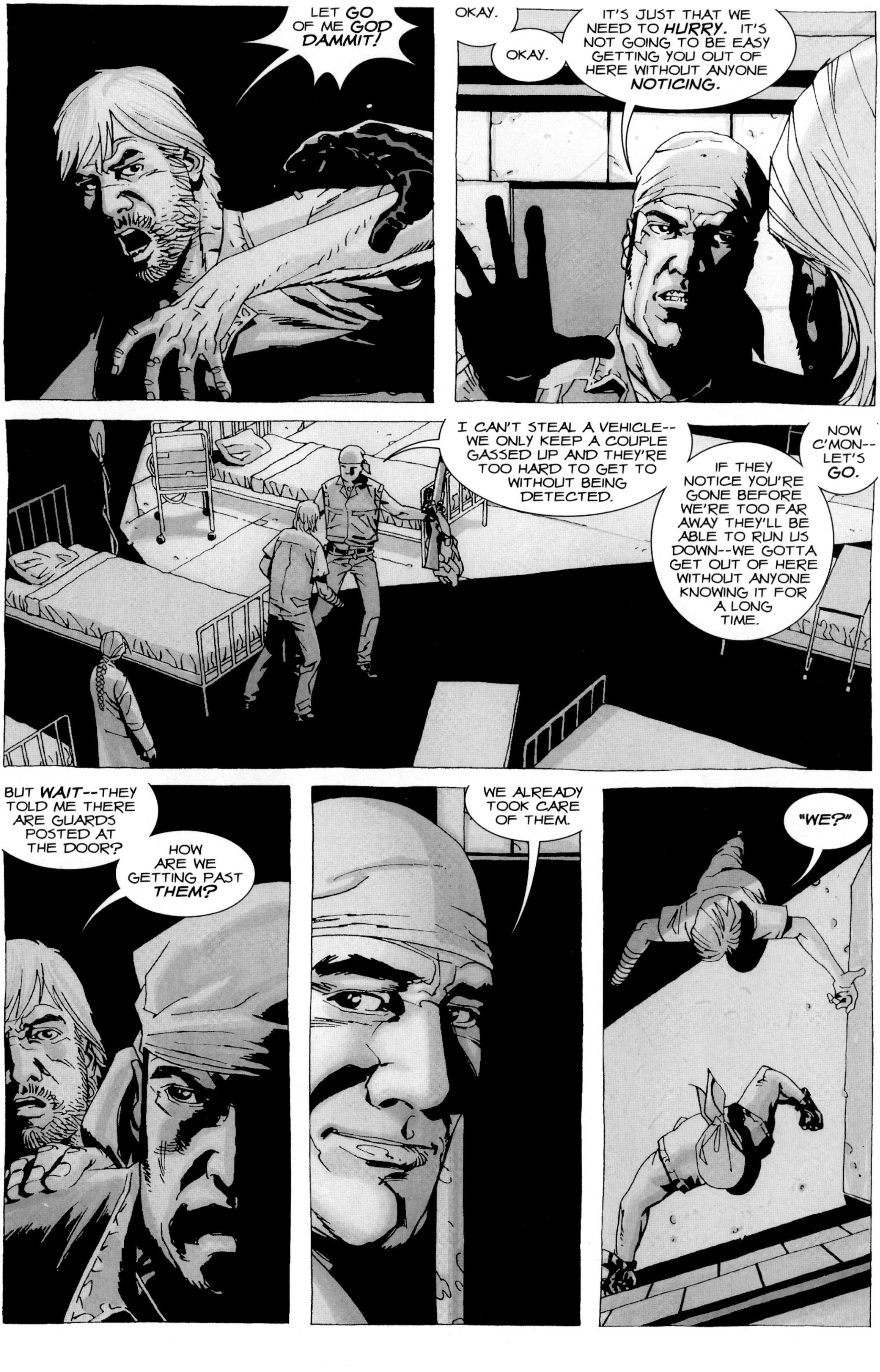
LET GO OF ME GOD DAMMIT!
OKAY.
OKAY.
IT'S JUST THAT WE NEED TO HURRY. IT'S NOT GOING TO BE EASY GETTING YOU OUT OF HERE WITHOUT ANYONE NOTICING.
I CAN'T STEAL A VEHICLE-- WE ONLY KEEP A COUPLE GASSED UP AND THEY'RE TOO HARD TO GET TO WITHOUT BEING DETECTED.
IF THEY NOTICE YOU'RE GONE BEFORE WE'RE TOO FAR AWAY THEY'LL BE ABLE TO RUN US DOWN--WE GOTTA GET OUT OF HERE WITHOUT ANYONE KNOWING IT FOR A LONG TIME.
NOW C'MON-- LET'S GO.
BUT WAIT--THEY TOLD ME THERE ARE GUARDS POSTED AT THE DOOR?
HOW ARE WE GETTING PAST THEM?
WE ALREADY TOOK CARE OF THEM.
"WE?"

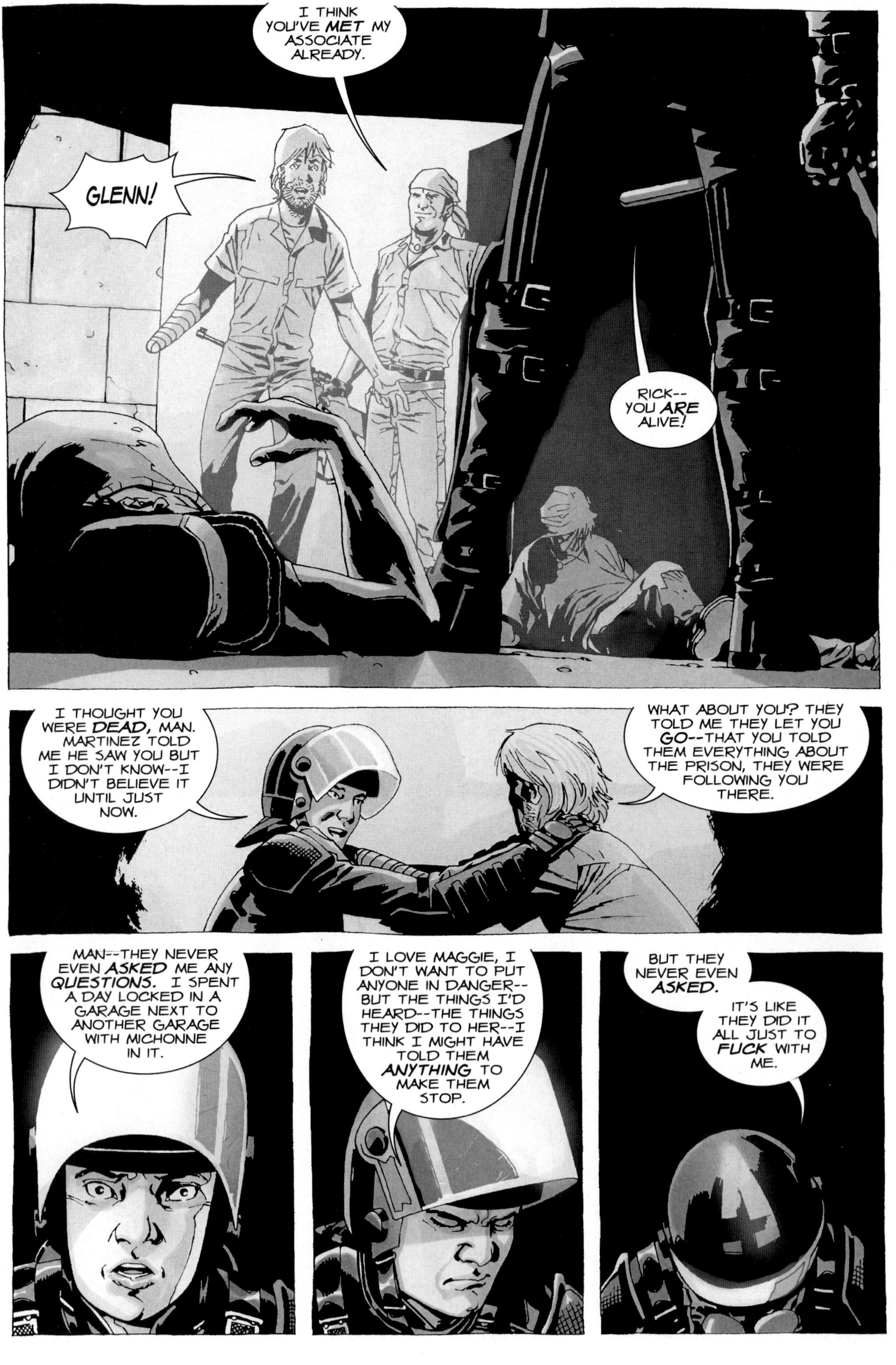
I THINK YOU'VE MET MY ASSOCIATE ALREADY.
GLENN!
RICK-- YOU ARE ALIVE!
I THOUGHT YOU WERE DEAD, MAN. MARTINEZ TOLD ME HE SAW YOU BUT I DON'T KNOW--I DIDN'T BELIEVE IT UNTIL JUST NOW.
WHAT ABOUT YOU? THEY TOLD ME THEY LET YOU GO--THAT YOU TOLD THEM EVERYTHING ABOUT THE PRISON, THEY WERE FOLLOWING YOU THERE.
MAN--THEY NEVER EVEN ASKED ME ANY QUESTIONS. I SPENT A DAY LOCKED IN A GARAGE NEXT TO ANOTHER GARAGE WITH MICHONNE IN IT.
I LOVE MAGGIE, I DON'T WANT TO PUT ANYONE IN DANGER--BUT THE THINGS I'D HEARD--THE THINGS THEY DID TO HER--I THINK I MIGHT HAVE TOLD THEM ANYTHING TO MAKE THEM STOP.
BUT THEY NEVER EVEN ASKED.
IT'S LIKE THEY DID IT ALL JUST TO FUCK WITH ME.

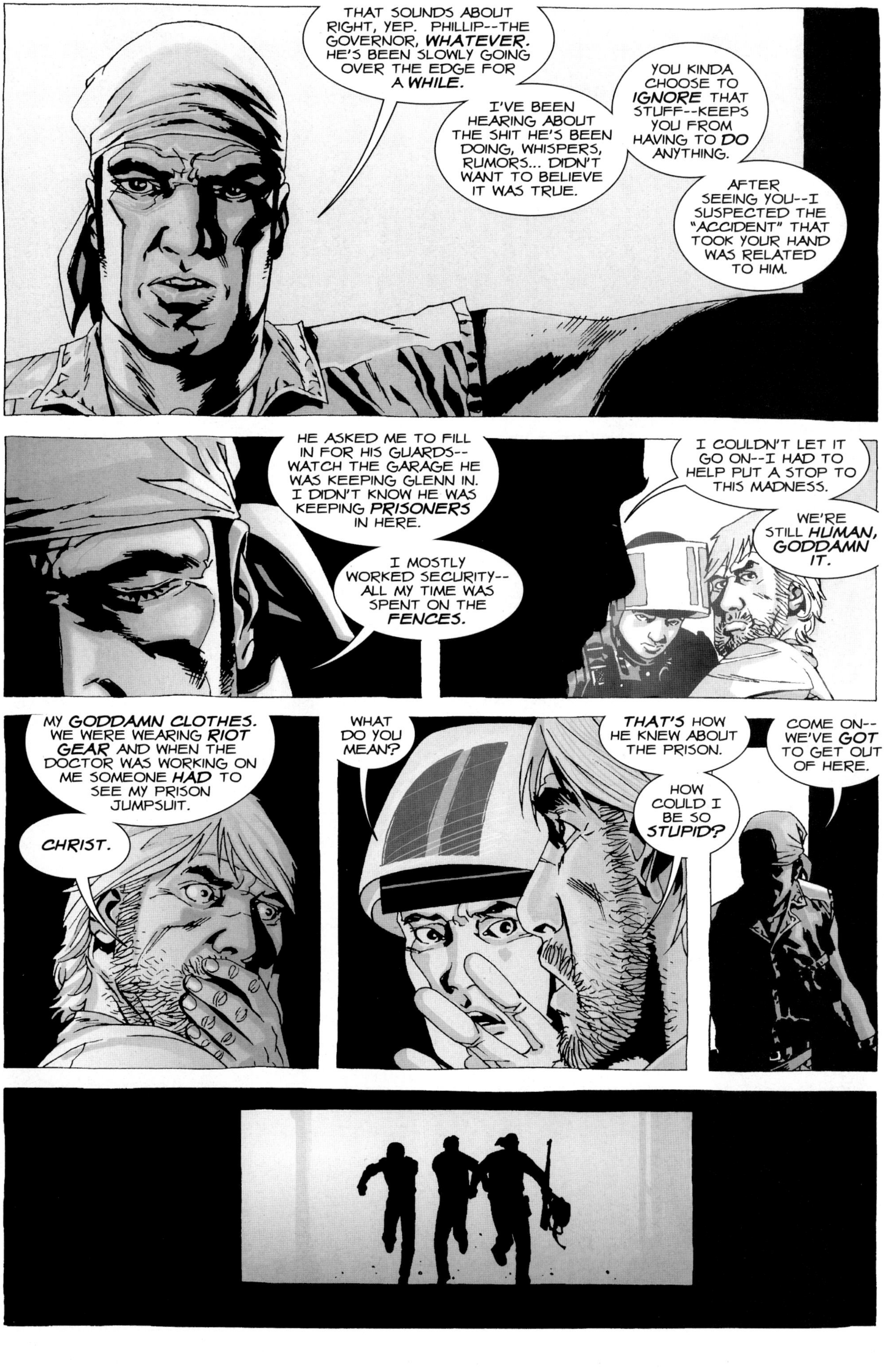
THAT SOUNDS ABOUT RIGHT, YEP. PHILLIP--THE GOVERNOR, WHATEVER. HE'S BEEN SLOWLY GOING OVER THE EDGE FOR A WHILE.
I'VE BEEN HEARING ABOUT THE SHIT HE'S BEEN DOING, WHISPERS, RUMORS... DIDN'T WANT TO BELIEVE IT WAS TRUE.
YOU KINDA CHOOSE TO IGNORE THAT STUFF--KEEPS YOU FROM HAVING TO DO ANYTHING.
AFTER SEEING YOU--I SUSPECTED THE "ACCIDENT" THAT TOOK YOUR HAND WAS RELATED TO HIM.
HE ASKED ME TO FILL IN FOR HIS GUARDS-- WATCH THE GARAGE HE WAS KEEPING GLENN IN. I DIDN'T KNOW HE WAS KEEPING PRISONERS IN HERE.
I MOSTLY WORKED SECURITY-- ALL MY TIME WAS SPENT ON THE FENCES.
I COULDN'T LET IT GO ON--I HAD TO HELP PUT A STOP TO THIS MADNESS.
WE'RE STILL HUMAN, GODDAMN IT.
MY GODDAMN CLOTHES. WE WERE WEARING RIOT GEAR AND WHEN THE DOCTOR WAS WORKING ON ME SOMEONE HAD TO SEE MY PRISON JUMPSUIT.
CHRIST.
WHAT DO YOU MEAN?
THAT'S HOW HE KNEW ABOUT THE PRISON.
HOW COULD I BE SO STUPID?
COME ON-- WE'VE GOT TO GET OUT OF HERE.

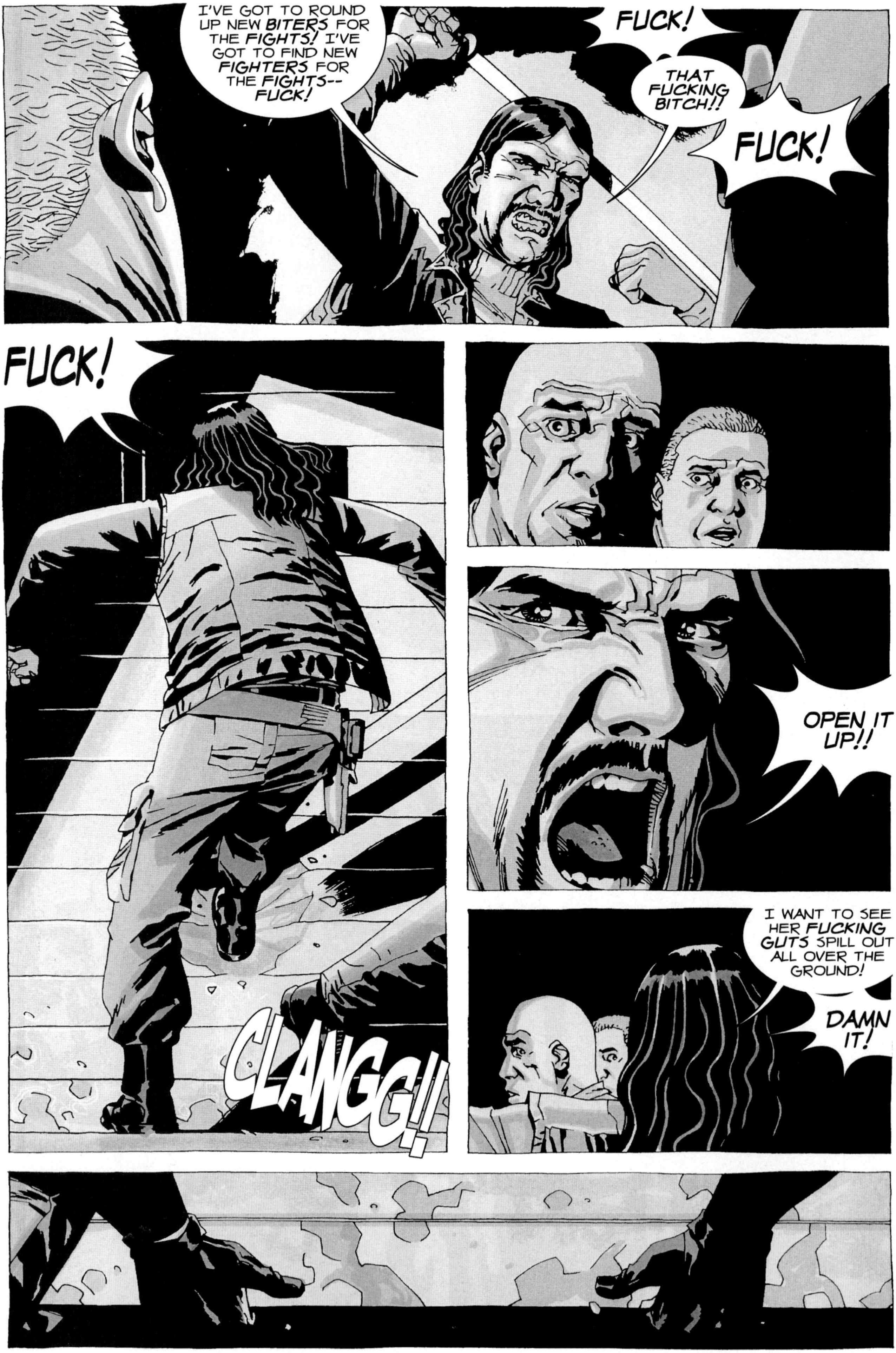
I'VE GOT TO ROUND UP NEW BITERS FOR THE FIGHTS! I'VE GOT TO FIND NEW FIGHTERS FOR THE FIGHTS-- FUCK!
FUCK!
THAT FUCKING BITCH!!
FUCK!
FUCK!
CLANGG!!
OPEN IT UP!!
I WANT TO SEE HER FUCKING GUTS SPILL OUT ALL OVER THE GROUND!
DAMN IT!

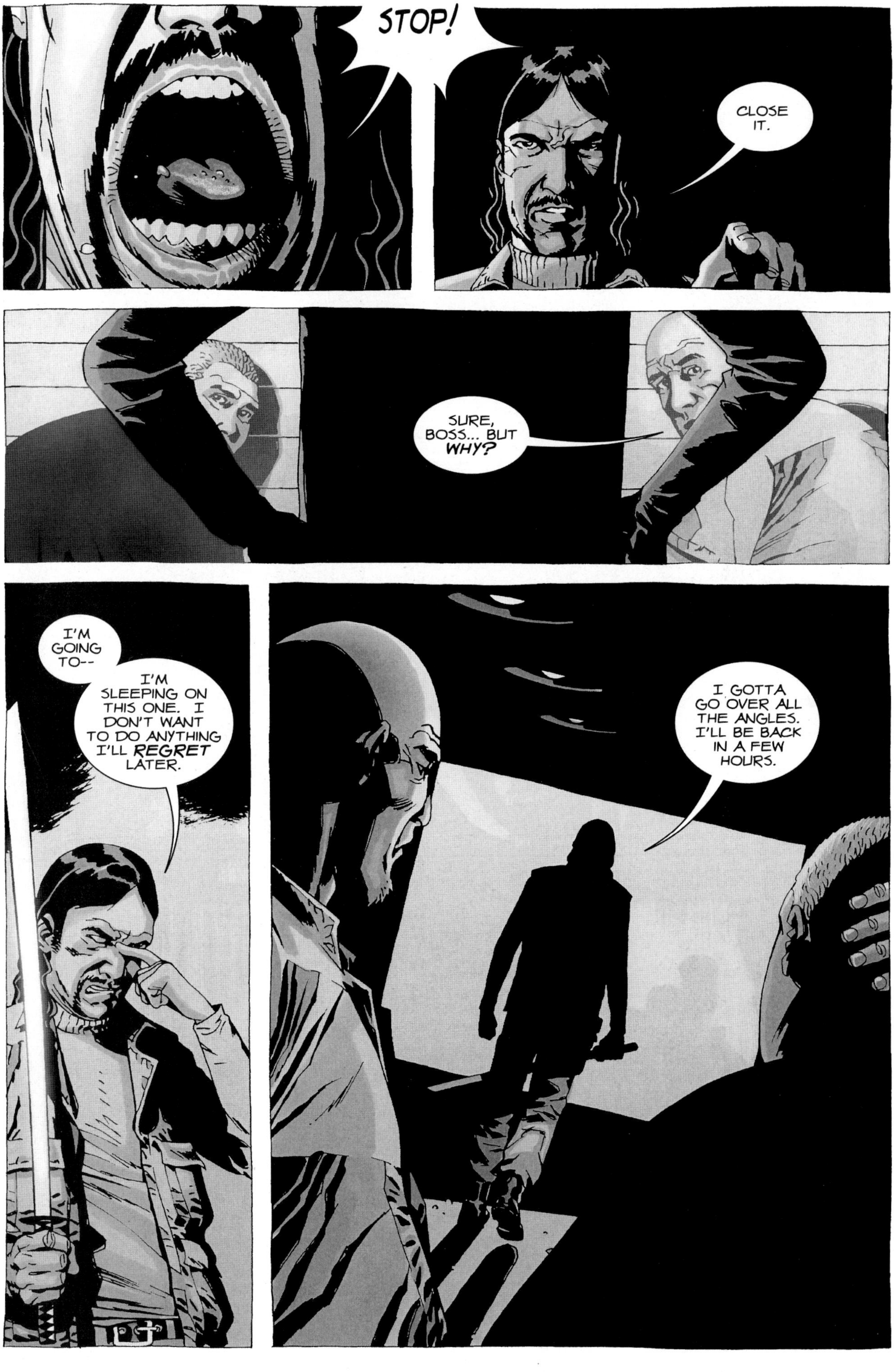
STOP!
CLOSE IT.
SURE, BOSS... BUT WHY?
I'M GOING TO--
I'M SLEEPING ON THIS ONE. I DON'T WANT TO DO ANYTHING I'LL REGRET LATER.
I GOTTA GO OVER ALL THE ANGLES. I'LL BE BACK IN A FEW HOURS.

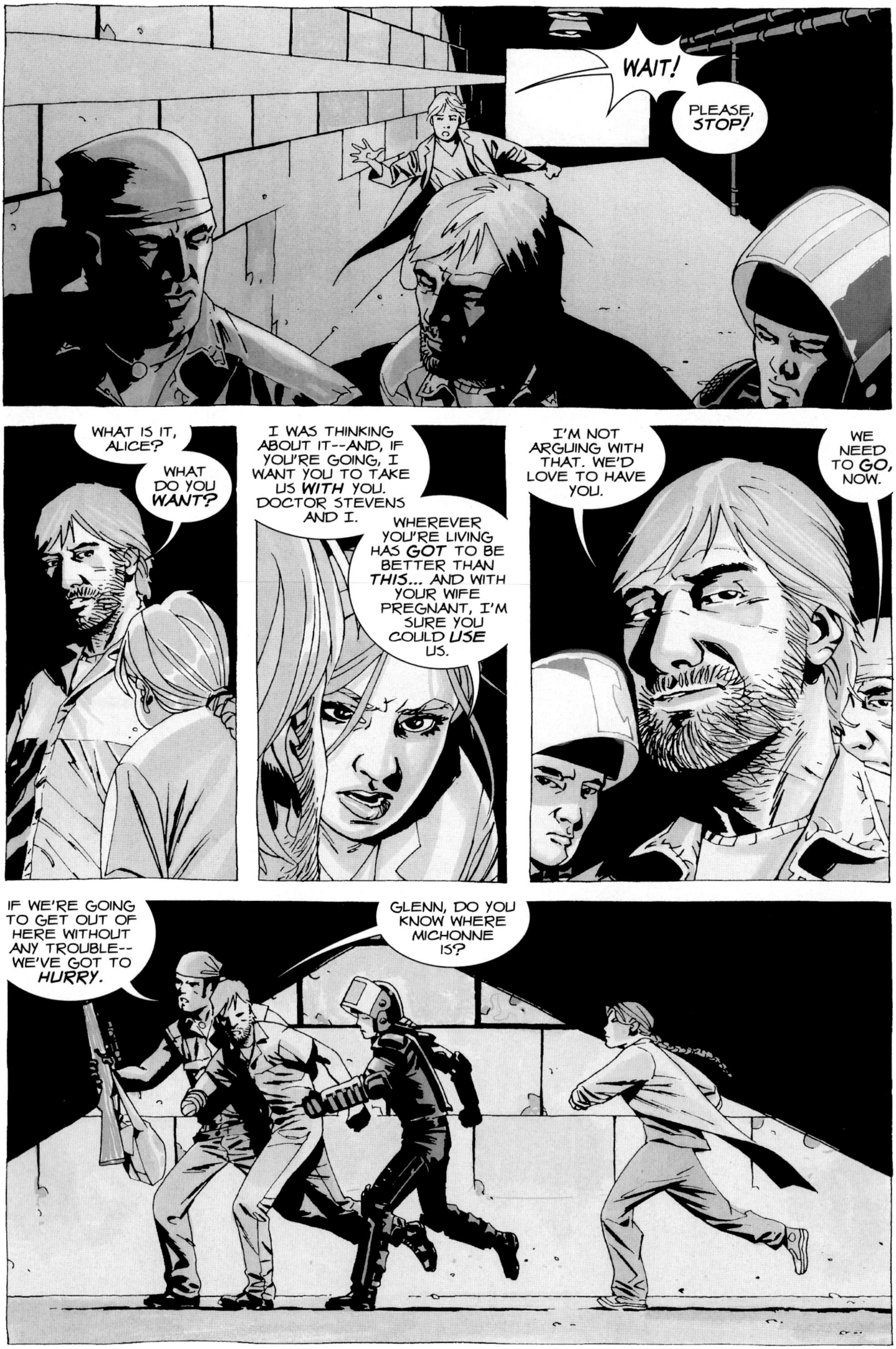
WAIT!
PLEASE, STOP!
WHAT IS IT, ALICE?
WHAT DO YOU WANT?
I WAS THINKING ABOUT IT--AND, IF YOU'RE GOING, I WANT YOU TO TAKE US WITH YOU. DOCTOR STEVENS AND I.
WHEREVER YOU'RE LIVING HAS GOT TO BE BETTER THAN THIS... AND WITH YOUR WIFE PREGNANT, I'M SURE YOU COULD USE US.
I'M NOT ARGUING WITH THAT. WE'D LOVE TO HAVE YOU.
WE NEED TO GO, NOW.
IF WE'RE GOING TO GET OUT OF HERE WITHOUT ANY TROUBLE-- WE'VE GOT TO HURRY.
GLENN, DO YOU KNOW WHERE MICHONNE IS?

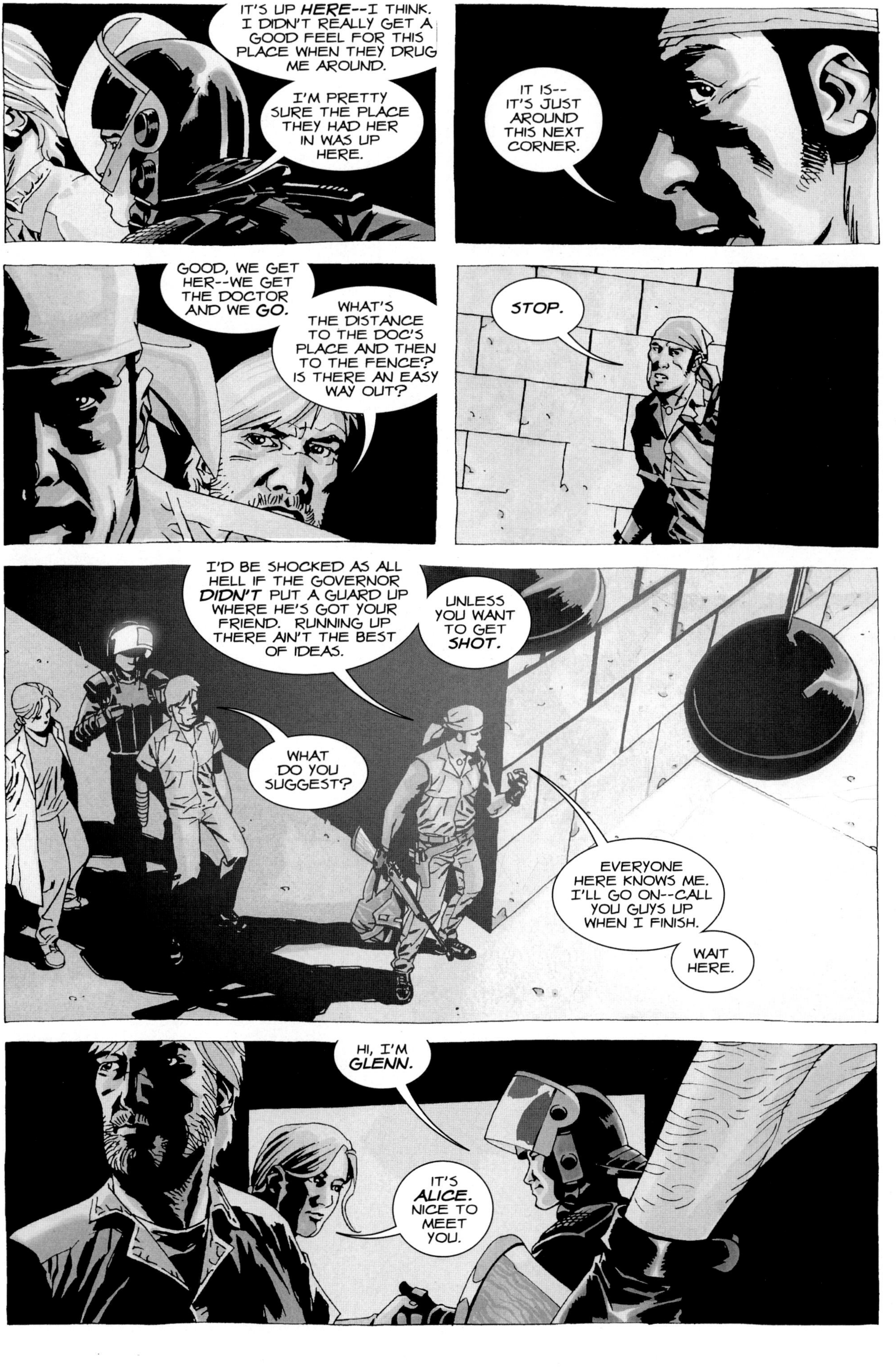
IT'S UP HERE--I THINK. I DIDN'T REALLY GET A GOOD FEEL FOR THIS PLACE WHEN THEY DRUG ME AROUND.
I'M PRETTY SURE THE PLACE THEY HAD HER IN WAS UP HERE.
IT IS-- IT'S JUST AROUND THIS NEXT CORNER.
GOOD, WE GET HER--WE GET THE DOCTOR AND WE GO.
WHAT'S THE DISTANCE TO THE DOC'S PLACE AND THEN TO THE FENCE? IS THERE AN EASY WAY OUT?
STOP.
I'D BE SHOCKED AS ALL HELL IF THE GOVERNOR DIDN'T PUT A GUARD UP WHERE HE'S GOT YOUR FRIEND. RUNNING UP THERE AIN'T THE BEST OF IDEAS.
UNLESS YOU WANT TO GET SHOT.
WHAT DO YOU SUGGEST?
EVERYONE HERE KNOWS ME. I'LL GO ON--CALL YOU GUYS UP WHEN I FINISH.
WAIT HERE.
HI, I'M GLENN.
IT'S ALICE. NICE TO MEET YOU.

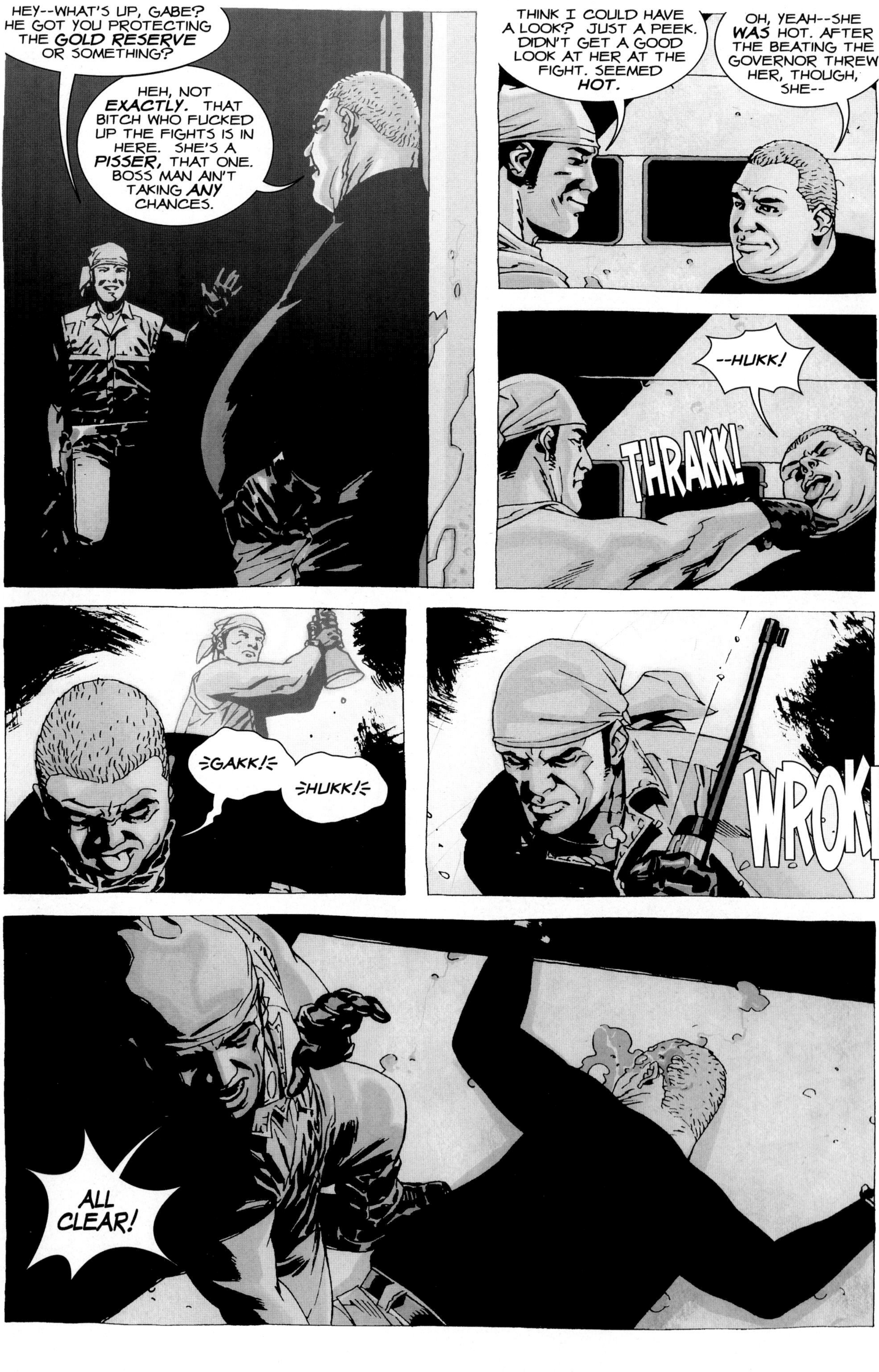
HEY--WHAT'S UP, GABE? HE GOT YOU PROTECTING THE GOLD RESERVE OR SOMETHING?
HEH, NOT EXACTLY. THAT BITCH WHO FUCKED UP THE FIGHTS IS IN HERE. SHE'S A PISSER, THAT ONE. BOSS MAN AIN'T TAKING ANY CHANCES.
THINK I COULD HAVE A LOOK? JUST A PEEK. DIDN'T GET A GOOD LOOK AT HER AT THE FIGHT. SEEMED HOT.
OH, YEAH--SHE WAS HOT. AFTER THE BEATING THE GOVERNOR THREW HER, THOUGH, SHE--
--HUKK!
THRAKK!
GAKK!
HUKK!
WROKK!
ALL CLEAR!

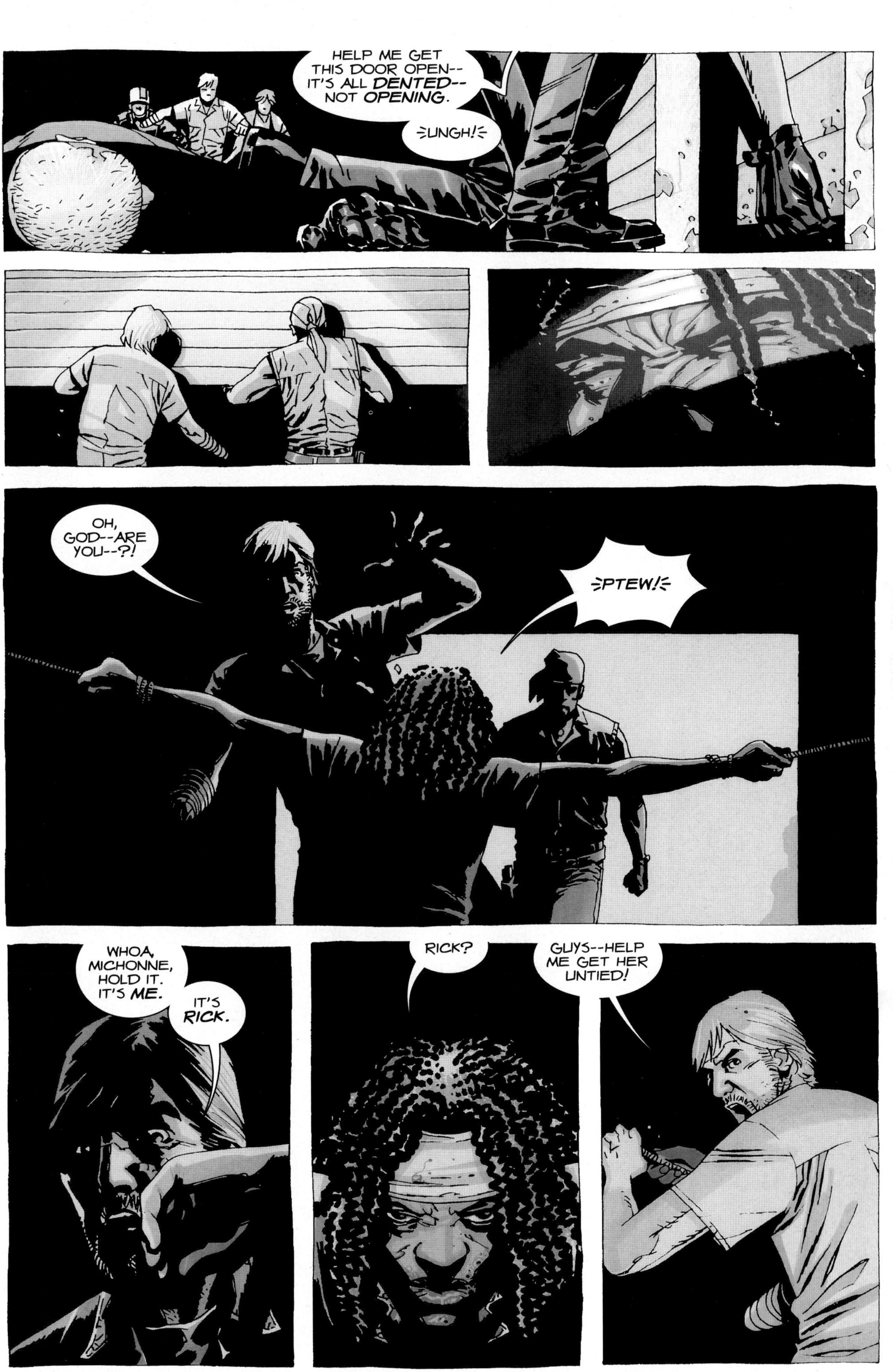
HELP ME GET THIS DOOR OPEN-- IT'S ALL DENTED-- NOT OPENING.
UNGH!
OH, GOD--ARE YOU--?!
PTEW!
WHOA, MICHONNE, HOLD IT. IT'S ME.
IT'S RICK.
RICK?
GUYS--HELP ME GET HER UNTIED!

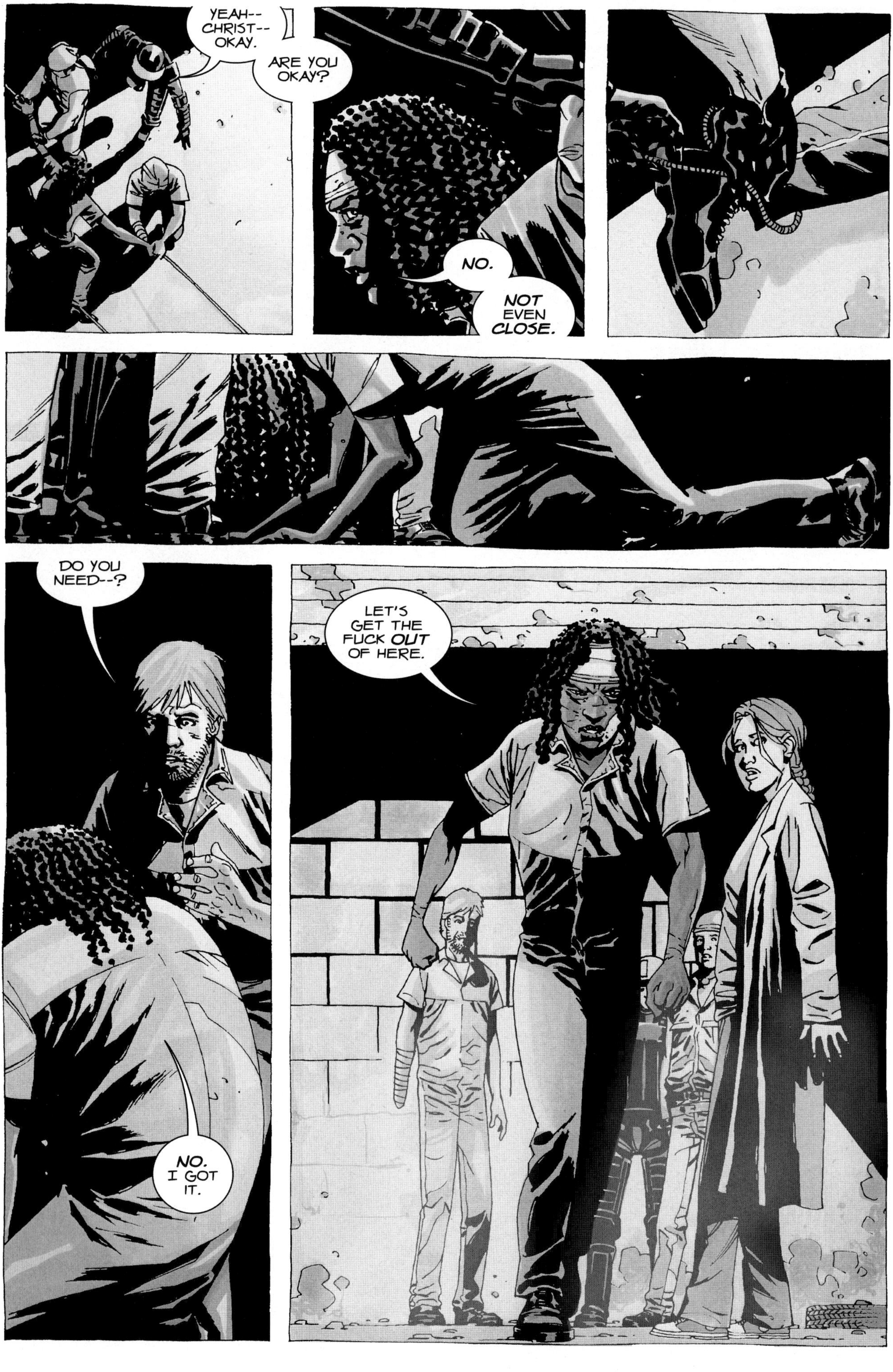
YEAH-- CHRIST-- OKAY.
ARE YOU OKAY?
NO.
NOT EVEN CLOSE.
DO YOU NEED--?
NO. I GOT IT.
LET'S GET THE FUCK OUT OF HERE.

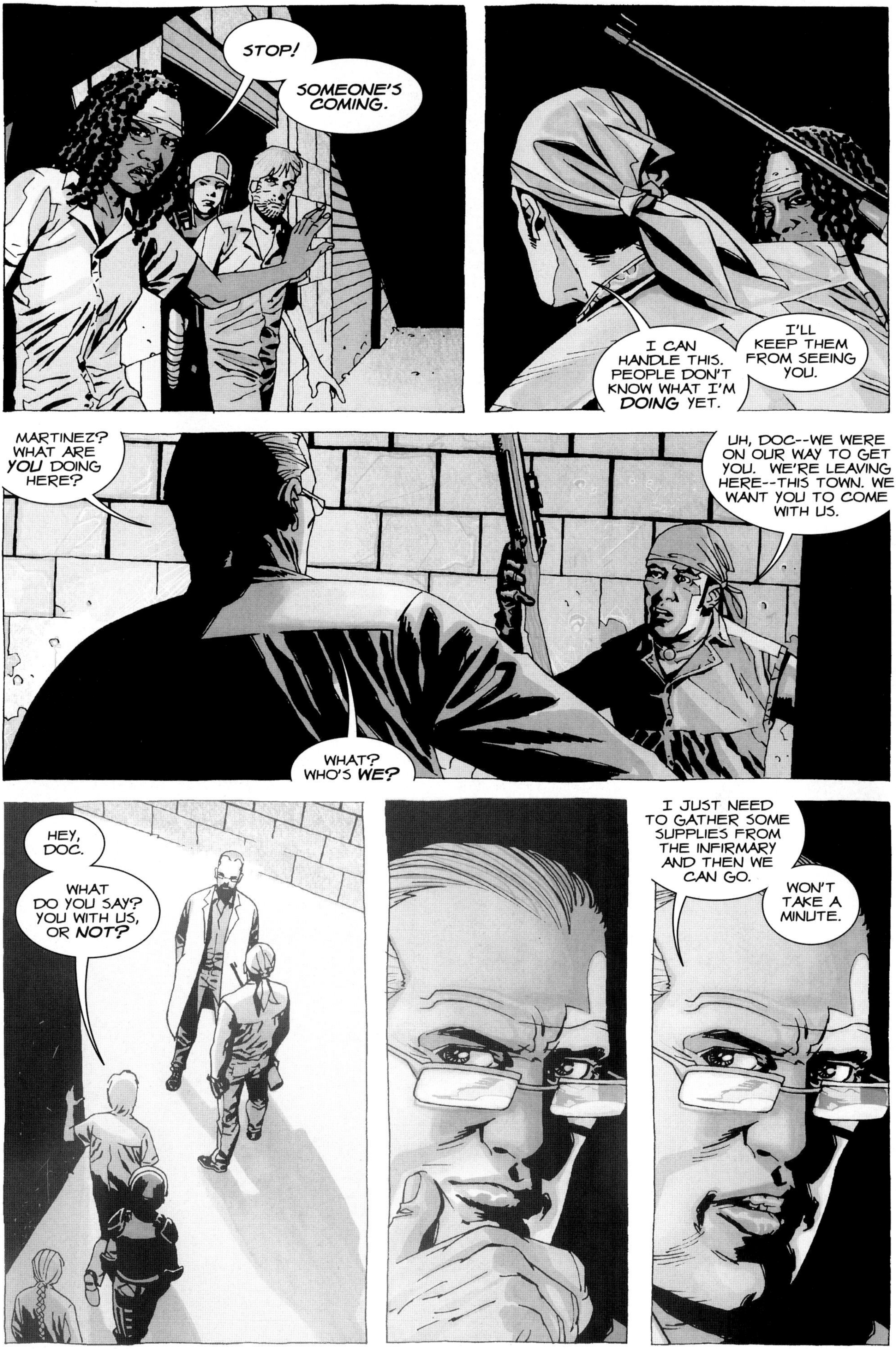
STOP!
SOMEONE'S COMING.
I CAN HANDLE THIS. PEOPLE DON'T KNOW WHAT I'M DOING YET.
I'LL KEEP THEM FROM SEEING YOU.
MARTINEZ? WHAT ARE YOU DOING HERE?
UH, DOC--WE WERE ON OUR WAY TO GET YOU. WE'RE LEAVING HERE--THIS TOWN. WE WANT YOU TO COME WITH US.
WHAT? WHO'S WE?
HEY, DOC.
WHAT DO YOU SAY? YOU WITH US, OR NOT?
I JUST NEED TO GATHER SOME SUPPLIES FROM THE INFIRMARY AND THEN WE CAN GO.
WON'T TAKE A MINUTE.

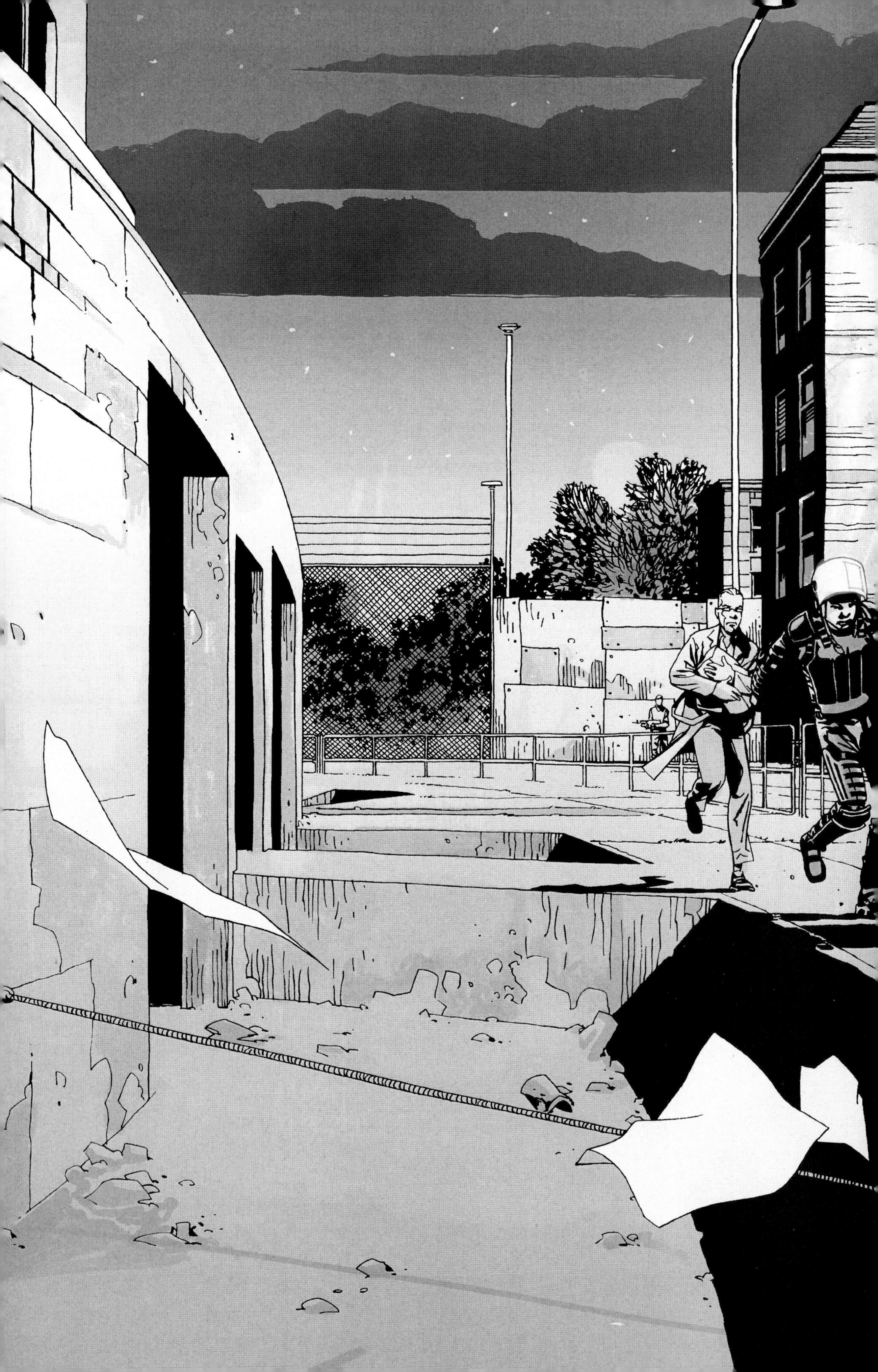

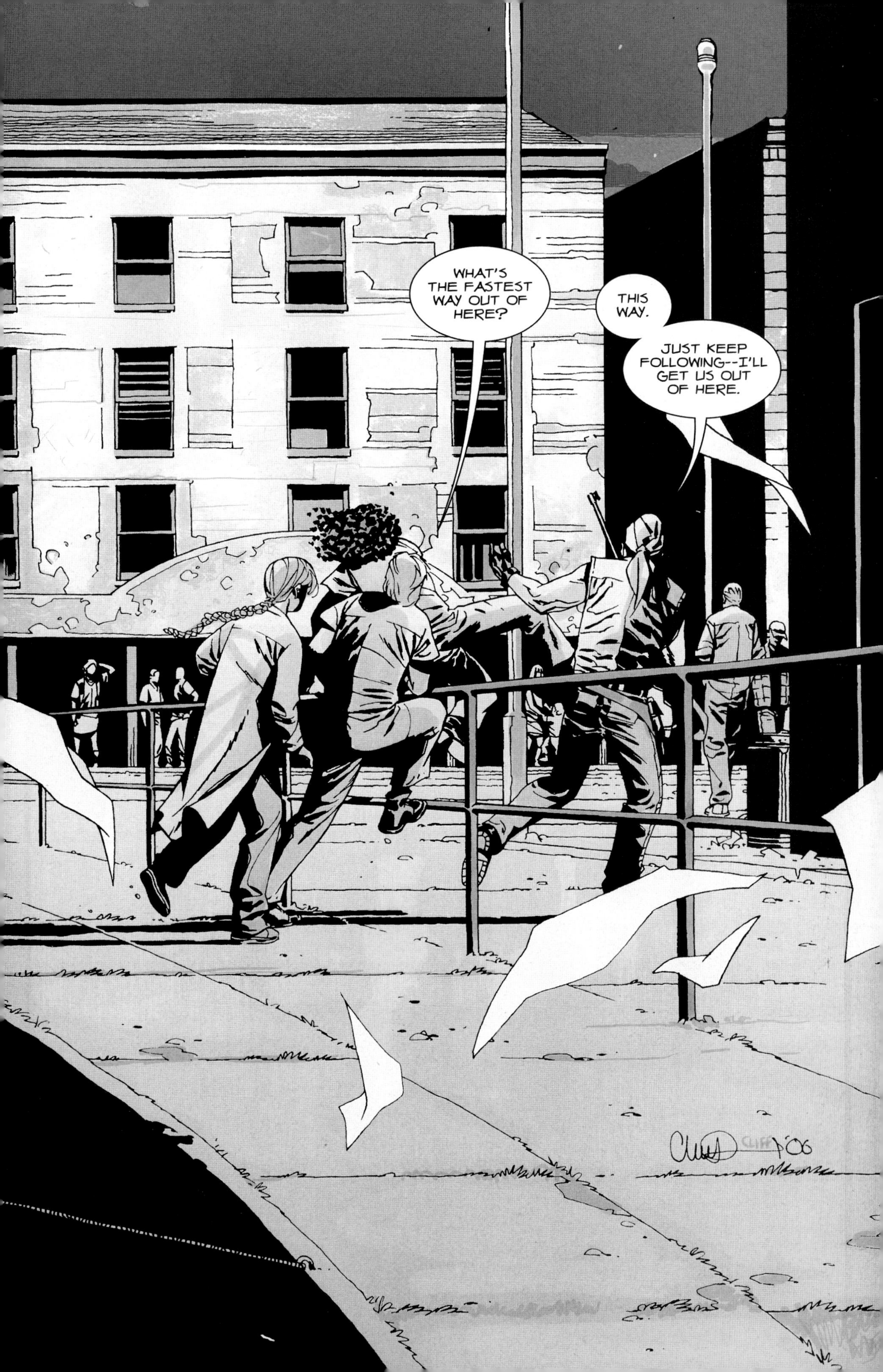
WHAT'S THE FASTEST WAY OUT OF HERE?
THIS WAY.
JUST KEEP FOLLOWING--I'LL GET US OUT OF HERE.
CLIFF '06

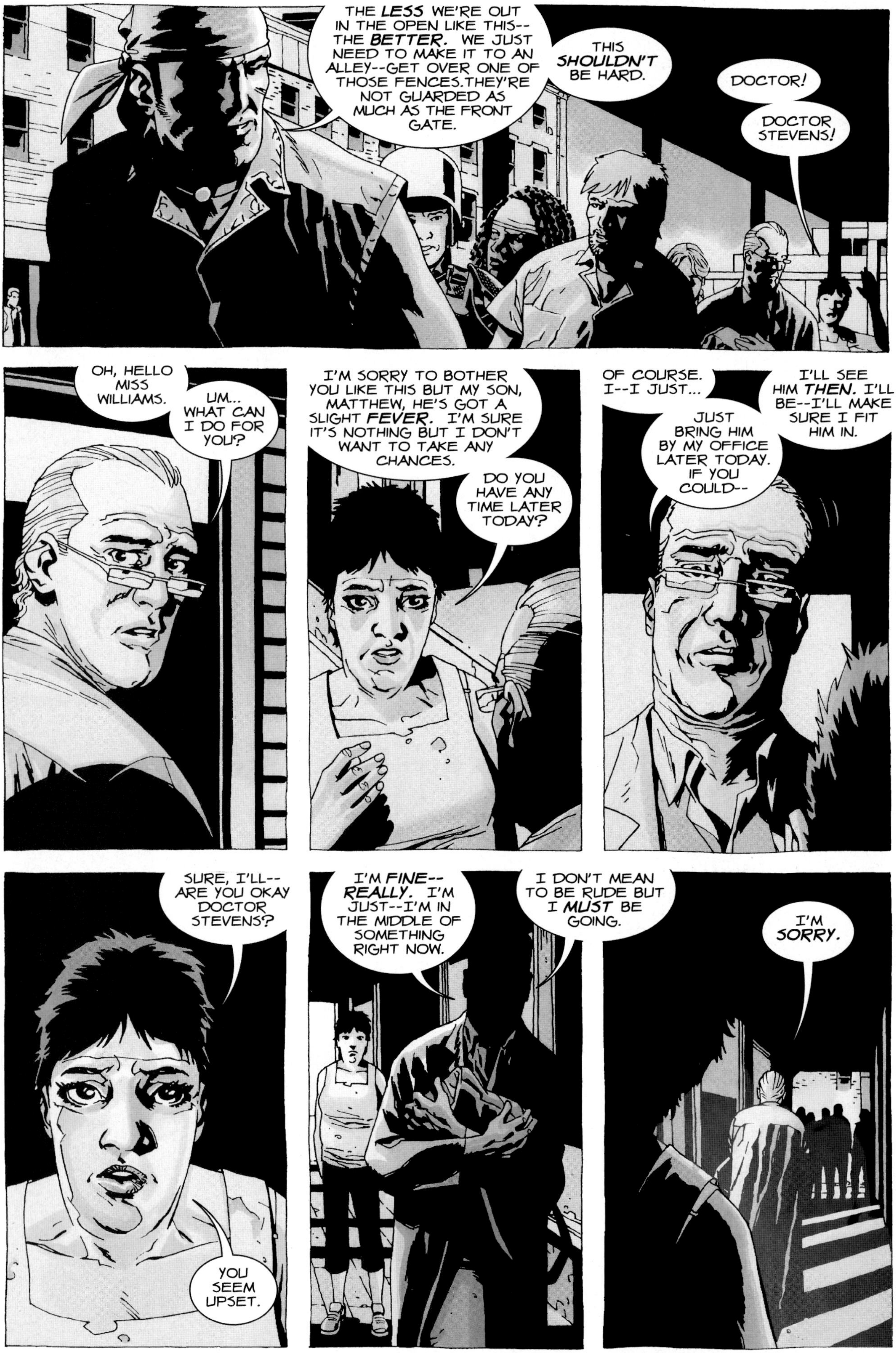
THE LESS WE'RE OUT IN THE OPEN LIKE THIS-- THE BETTER. WE JUST NEED TO MAKE IT TO AN ALLEY--GET OVER ONE OF THOSE FENCES. THEY'RE NOT GUARDED AS MUCH AS THE FRONT GATE.
THIS SHOULDN'T BE HARD.
DOCTOR!
DOCTOR STEVENS!
OH, HELLO MISS WILLIAMS.
UM... WHAT CAN I DO FOR YOU?
I'M SORRY TO BOTHER YOU LIKE THIS BUT MY SON, MATTHEW, HE'S GOT A SLIGHT FEVER. I'M SURE IT'S NOTHING BUT I DON'T WANT TO TAKE ANY CHANCES.
DO YOU HAVE ANY TIME LATER TODAY?
OF COURSE. I--I JUST...
JUST BRING HIM BY MY OFFICE LATER TODAY. IF YOU COULD--
I'LL SEE HIM THEN. I'LL BE--I'LL MAKE SURE I FIT HIM IN.
SURE, I'LL-- ARE YOU OKAY DOCTOR STEVENS?
YOU SEEM UPSET.
I'M FINE-- REALLY. I'M JUST--I'M IN THE MIDDLE OF SOMETHING RIGHT NOW.
I DON'T MEAN TO BE RUDE BUT I MUST BE GOING.
I'M SORRY.

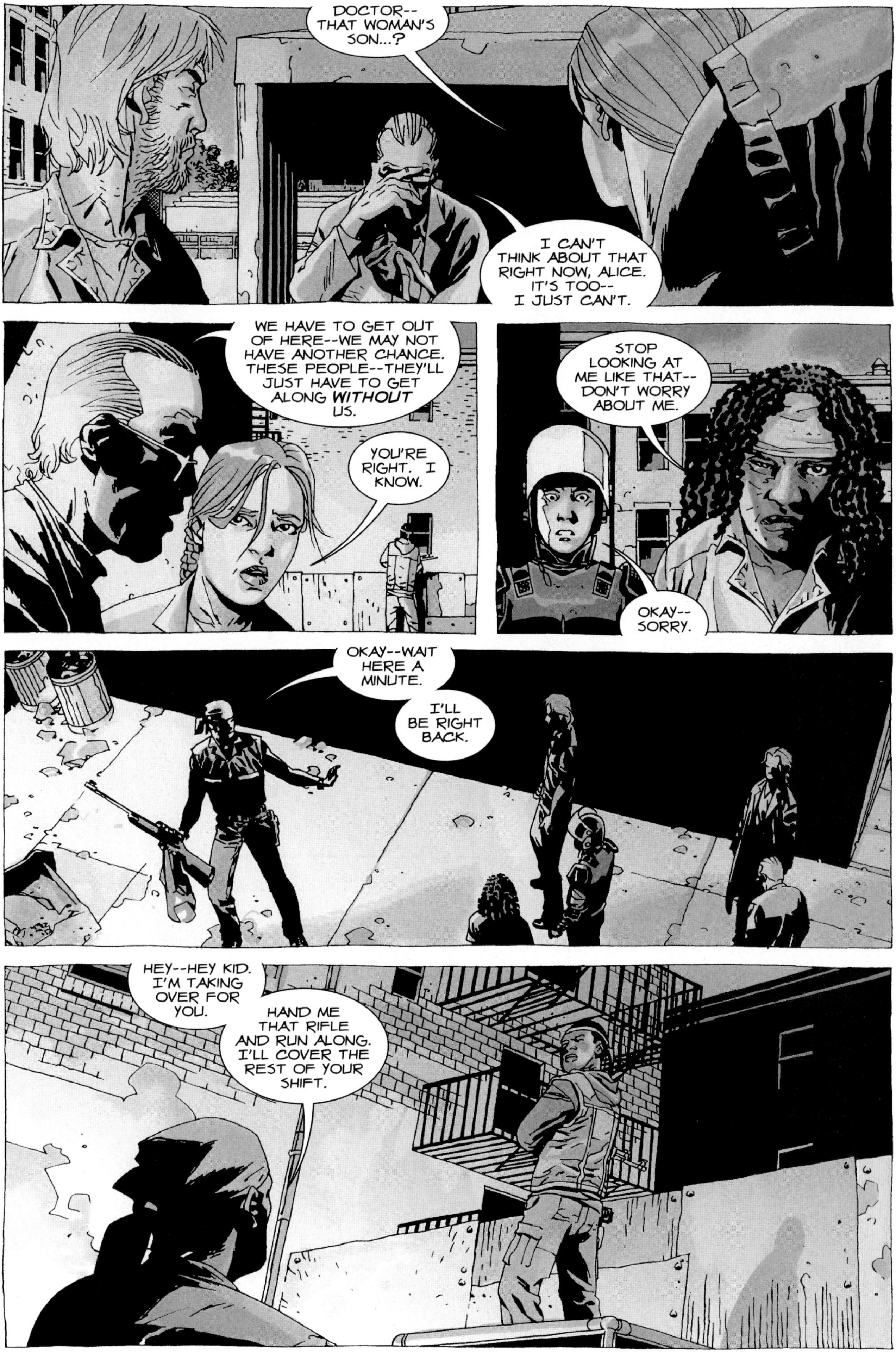
DOCTOR-- THAT WOMAN'S SON...?
I CAN'T THINK ABOUT THAT RIGHT NOW, ALICE. IT'S TOO-- I JUST CAN'T.
WE HAVE TO GET OUT OF HERE--WE MAY NOT HAVE ANOTHER CHANCE. THESE PEOPLE--THEY'LL JUST HAVE TO GET ALONG *WITHOUT* US.
YOU'RE RIGHT. I KNOW.
STOP LOOKING AT ME LIKE THAT-- DON'T WORRY ABOUT ME.
OKAY-- SORRY.
OKAY--WAIT HERE A MINUTE.
I'LL BE RIGHT BACK.
HEY--HEY KID. I'M TAKING OVER FOR YOU.
HAND ME THAT RIFLE AND RUN ALONG. I'LL COVER THE REST OF YOUR SHIFT.

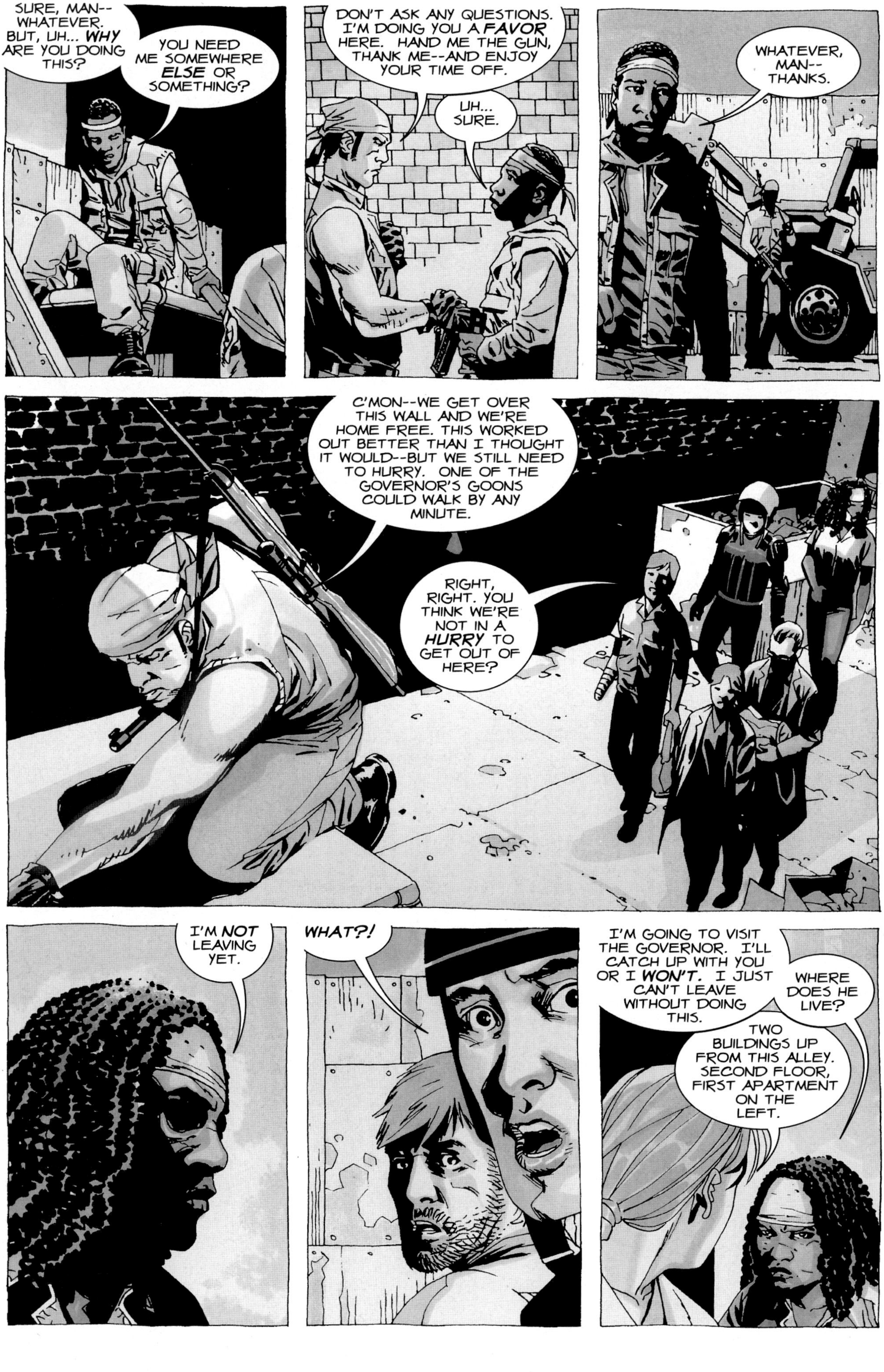
SURE, MAN--WHATEVER. BUT, UH... WHY ARE YOU DOING THIS?
YOU NEED ME SOMEWHERE ELSE OR SOMETHING?
DON'T ASK ANY QUESTIONS. I'M DOING YOU A FAVOR HERE. HAND ME THE GUN, THANK ME--AND ENJOY YOUR TIME OFF.
UH... SURE.
WHATEVER, MAN--THANKS.
C'MON--WE GET OVER THIS WALL AND WE'RE HOME FREE. THIS WORKED OUT BETTER THAN I THOUGHT IT WOULD--BUT WE STILL NEED TO HURRY. ONE OF THE GOVERNOR'S GOONS COULD WALK BY ANY MINUTE.
RIGHT, RIGHT. YOU THINK WE'RE NOT IN A HURRY TO GET OUT OF HERE?
I'M NOT LEAVING YET.
WHAT?!
I'M GOING TO VISIT THE GOVERNOR. I'LL CATCH UP WITH YOU OR I WON'T. I JUST CAN'T LEAVE WITHOUT DOING THIS.
WHERE DOES HE LIVE?
TWO BUILDINGS UP FROM THIS ALLEY. SECOND FLOOR, FIRST APARTMENT ON THE LEFT.

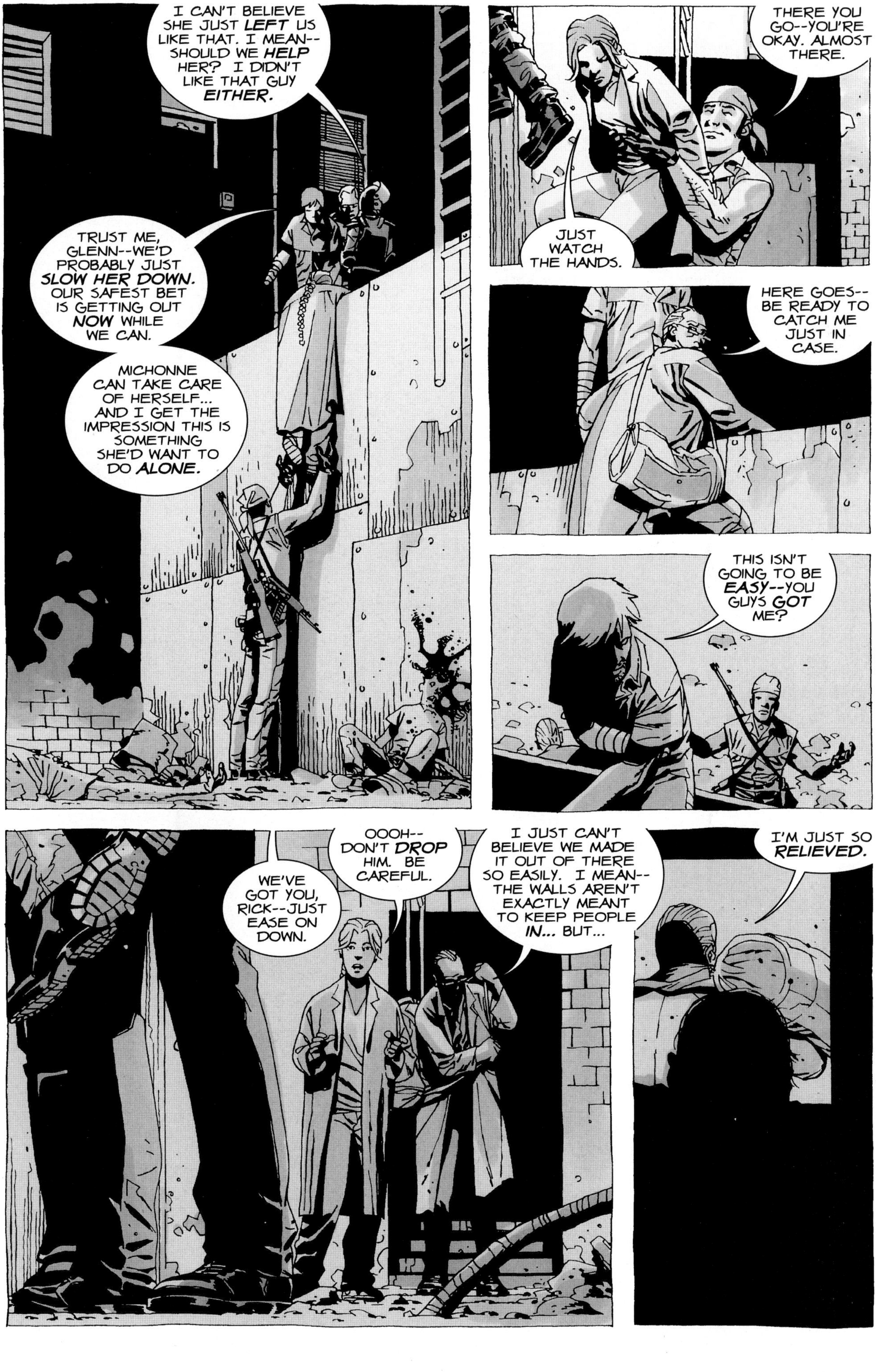
I CAN'T BELIEVE SHE JUST LEFT US LIKE THAT. I MEAN-- SHOULD WE HELP HER? I DIDN'T LIKE THAT GUY EITHER.
TRUST ME, GLENN--WE'D PROBABLY JUST SLOW HER DOWN. OUR SAFEST BET IS GETTING OUT NOW WHILE WE CAN.
MICHONNE CAN TAKE CARE OF HERSELF... AND I GET THE IMPRESSION THIS IS SOMETHING SHE'D WANT TO DO ALONE.
THERE YOU GO--YOU'RE OKAY. ALMOST THERE.
JUST WATCH THE HANDS.
HERE GOES-- BE READY TO CATCH ME JUST IN CASE.
THIS ISN'T GOING TO BE EASY--YOU GUYS GOT ME?
WE'VE GOT YOU, RICK--JUST EASE ON DOWN.
OOOH-- DON'T DROP HIM. BE CAREFUL.
I JUST CAN'T BELIEVE WE MADE IT OUT OF THERE SO EASILY. I MEAN-- THE WALLS AREN'T EXACTLY MEANT TO KEEP PEOPLE IN... BUT...
I'M JUST SO RELIEVED.

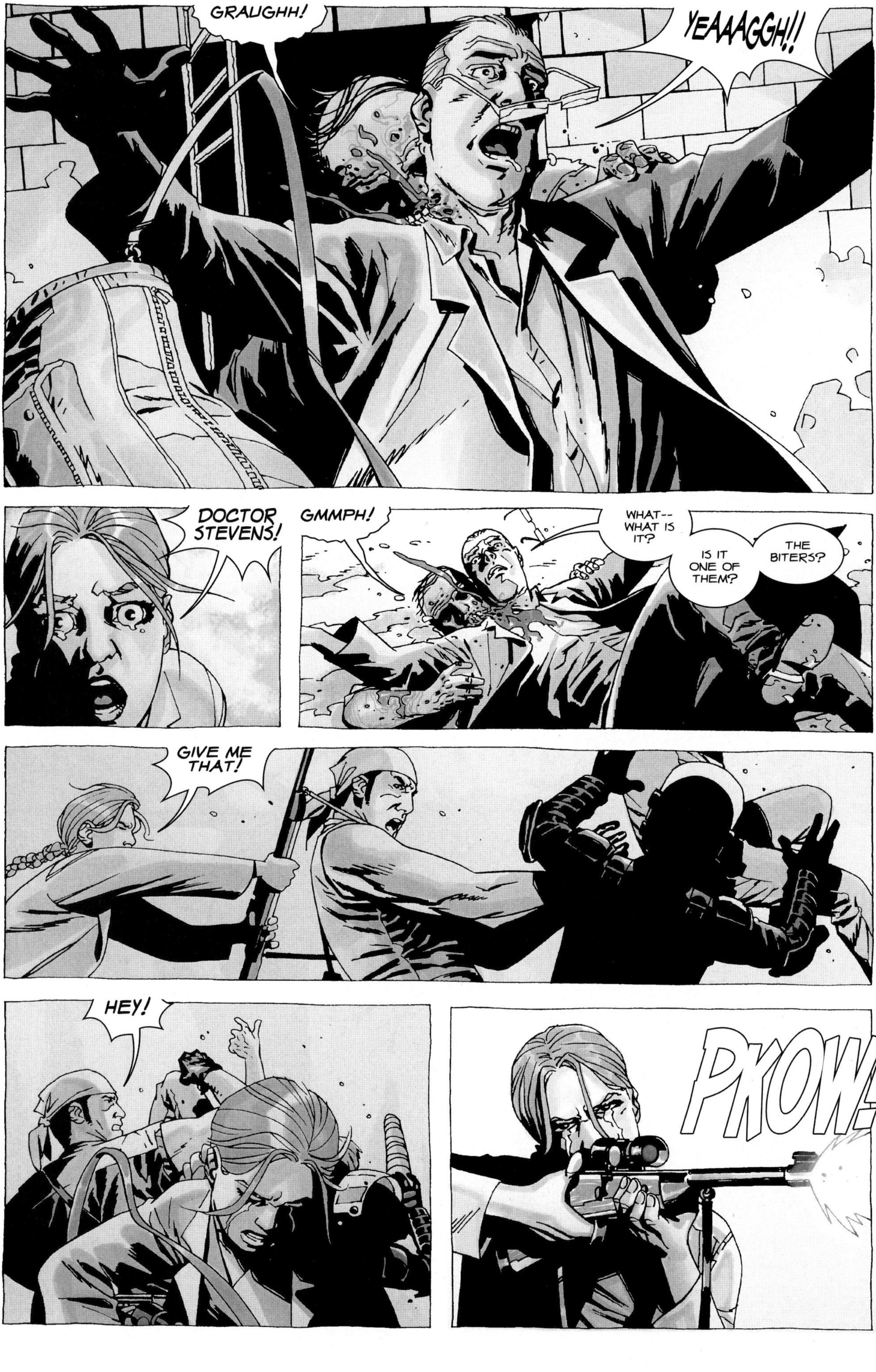
GRAUGHH!
YEAAAGGH!!
DOCTOR STEVENS!
GMMPH!
WHAT-- WHAT IS IT?
IS IT ONE OF THEM?
THE BITERS?
GIVE ME THAT!
HEY!
PKOW!

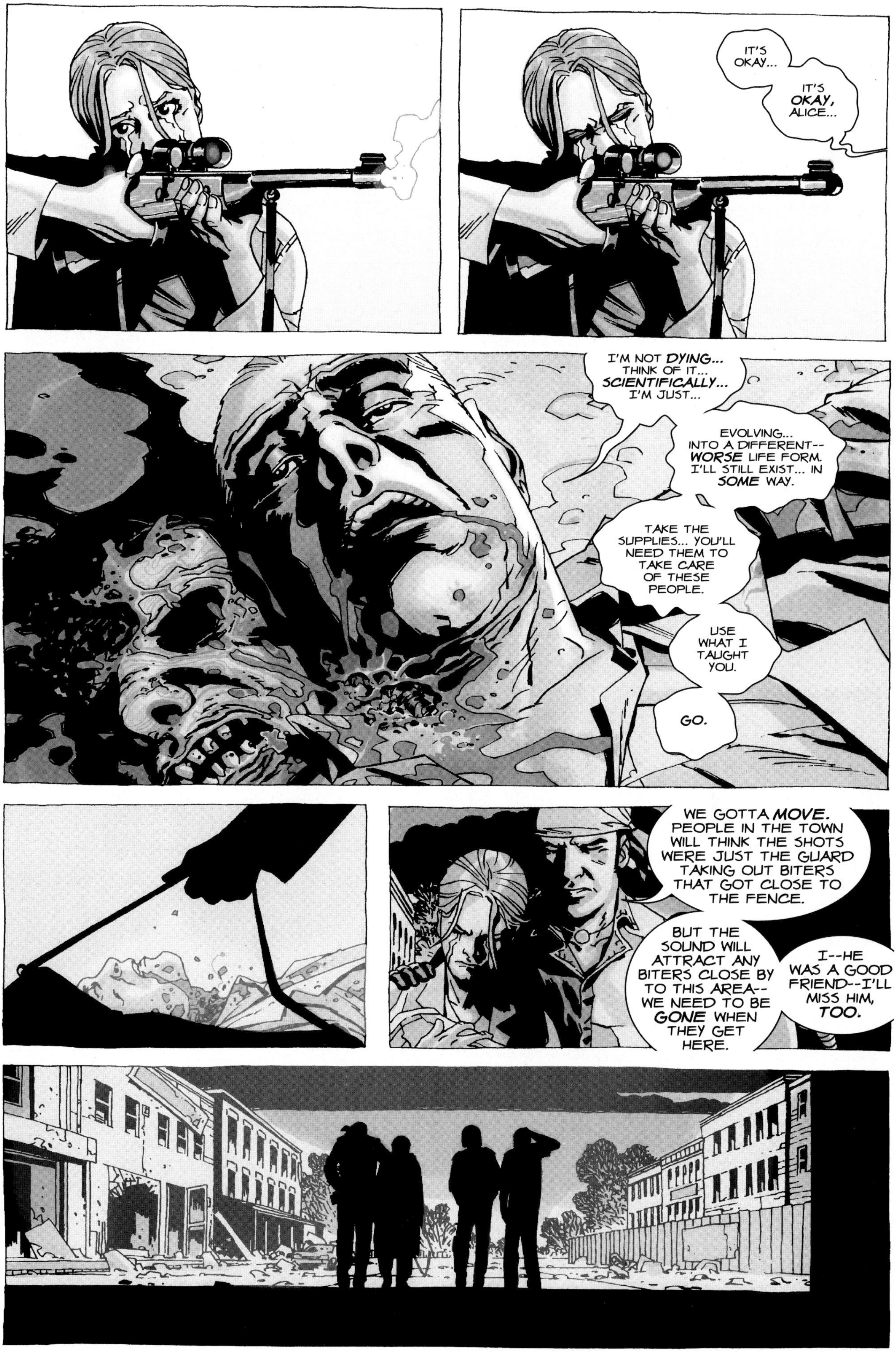
IT'S OKAY...
IT'S OKAY, ALICE...
I'M NOT DYING... THINK OF IT... SCIENTIFICALLY... I'M JUST...
EVOLVING... INTO A DIFFERENT-- WORSE LIFE FORM. I'LL STILL EXIST... IN SOME WAY.
TAKE THE SUPPLIES... YOU'LL NEED THEM TO TAKE CARE OF THESE PEOPLE.
USE WHAT I TAUGHT YOU.
GO.
WE GOTTA MOVE. PEOPLE IN THE TOWN WILL THINK THE SHOTS WERE JUST THE GUARD TAKING OUT BITERS THAT GOT CLOSE TO THE FENCE.
BUT THE SOUND WILL ATTRACT ANY BITERS CLOSE BY TO THIS AREA-- WE NEED TO BE GONE WHEN THEY GET HERE.
I--HE WAS A GOOD FRIEND--I'LL MISS HIM, TOO.

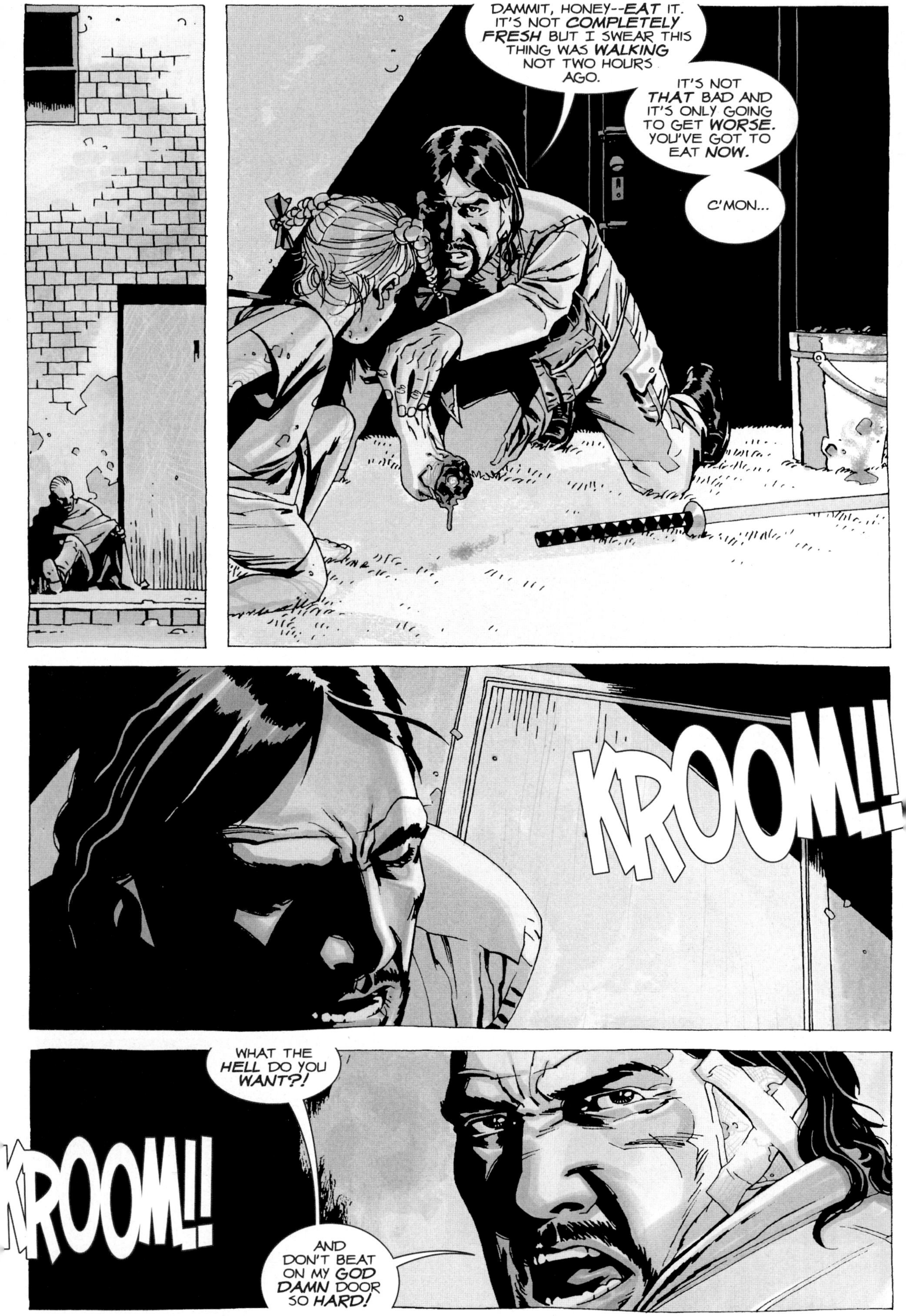
DAMMIT, HONEY--EAT IT. IT'S NOT COMPLETELY FRESH BUT I SWEAR THIS THING WAS WALKING NOT TWO HOURS AGO.
IT'S NOT THAT BAD AND IT'S ONLY GOING TO GET WORSE. YOU'VE GOT TO EAT NOW.
C'MON...
KROOM!!
KROOM!!
WHAT THE HELL DO YOU WANT?!
AND DON'T BEAT ON MY GOD DAMN DOOR SO HARD!

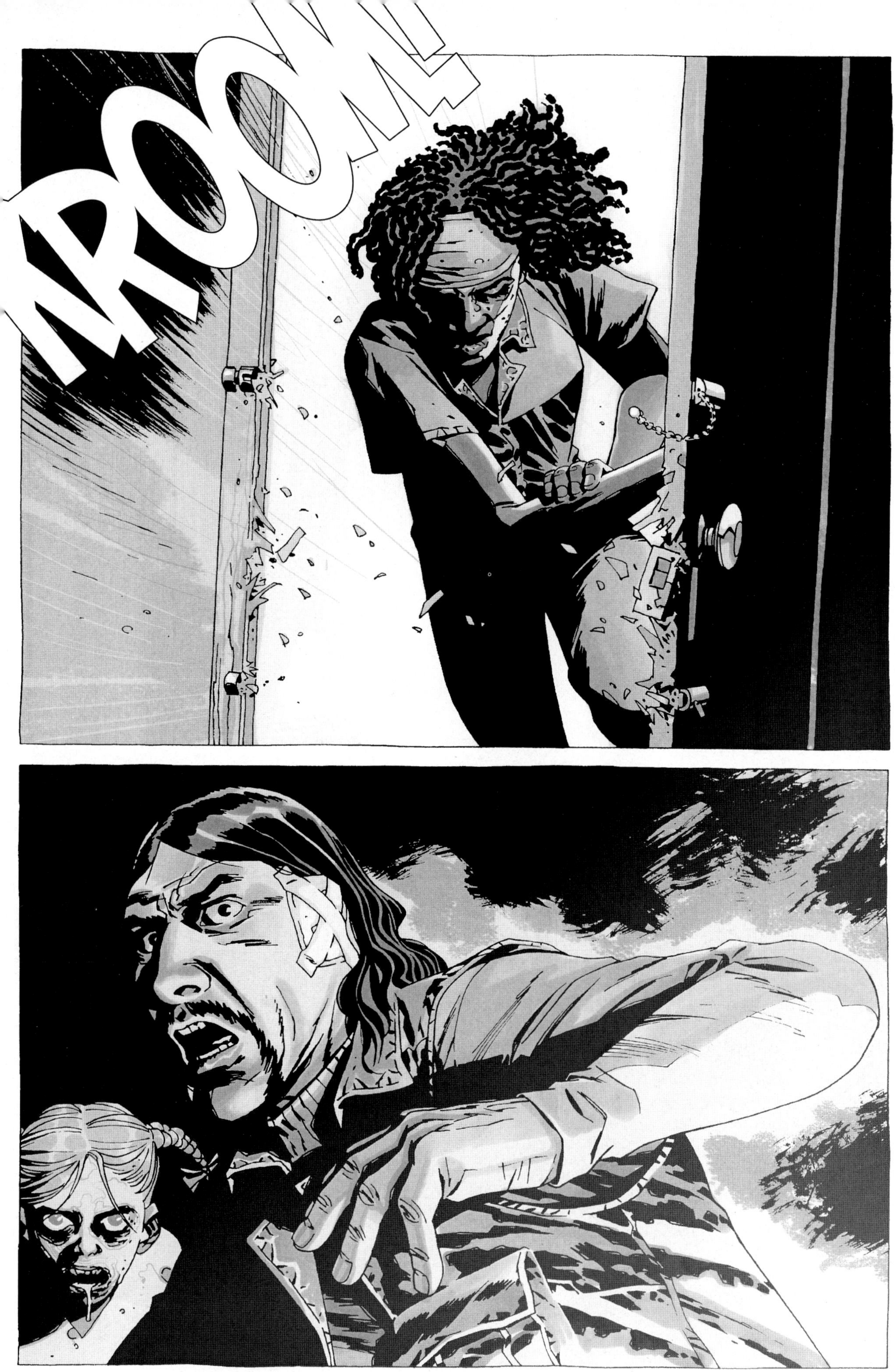
KROOM!

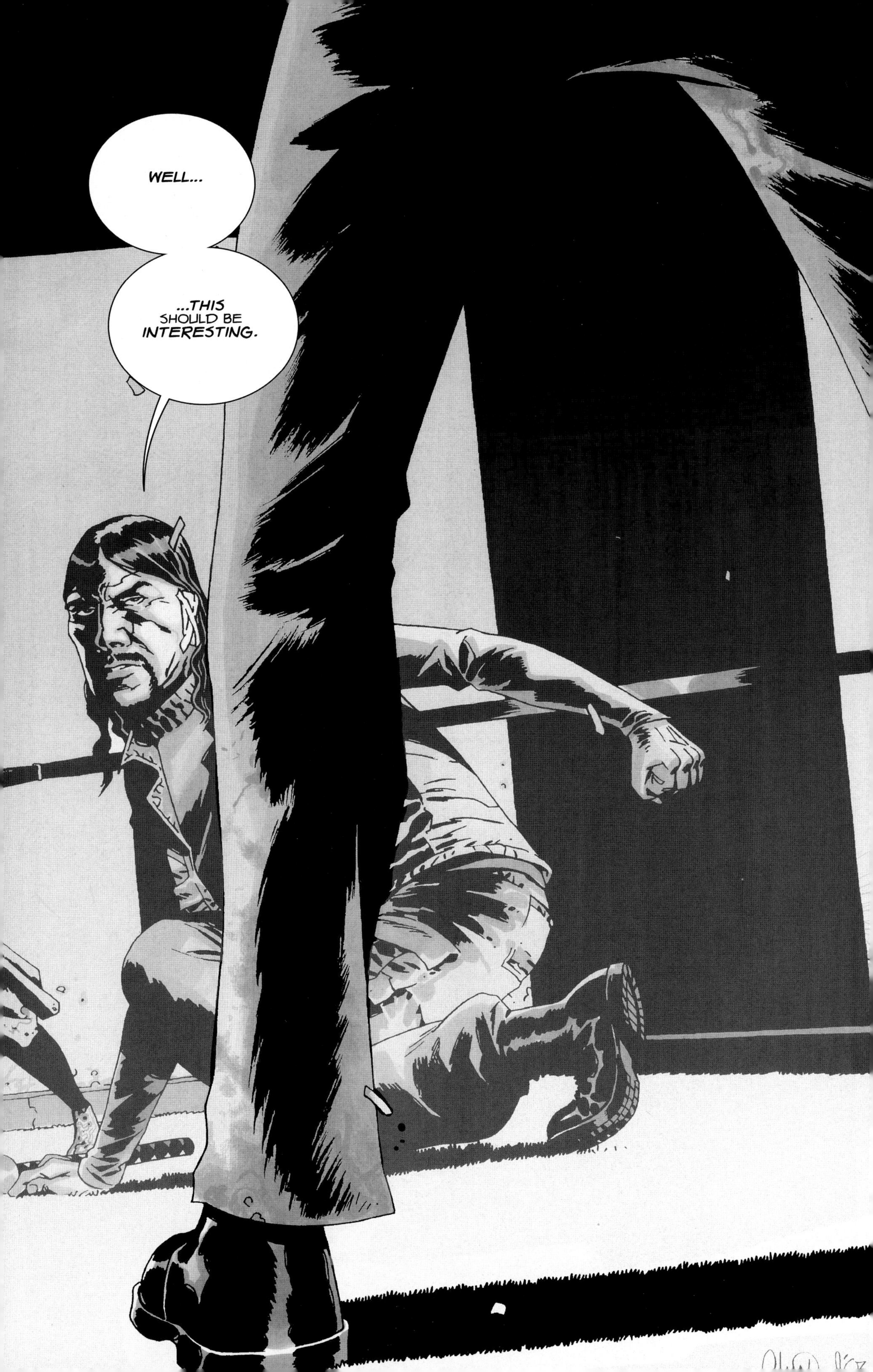
WELL...
...THIS SHOULD BE INTERESTING.

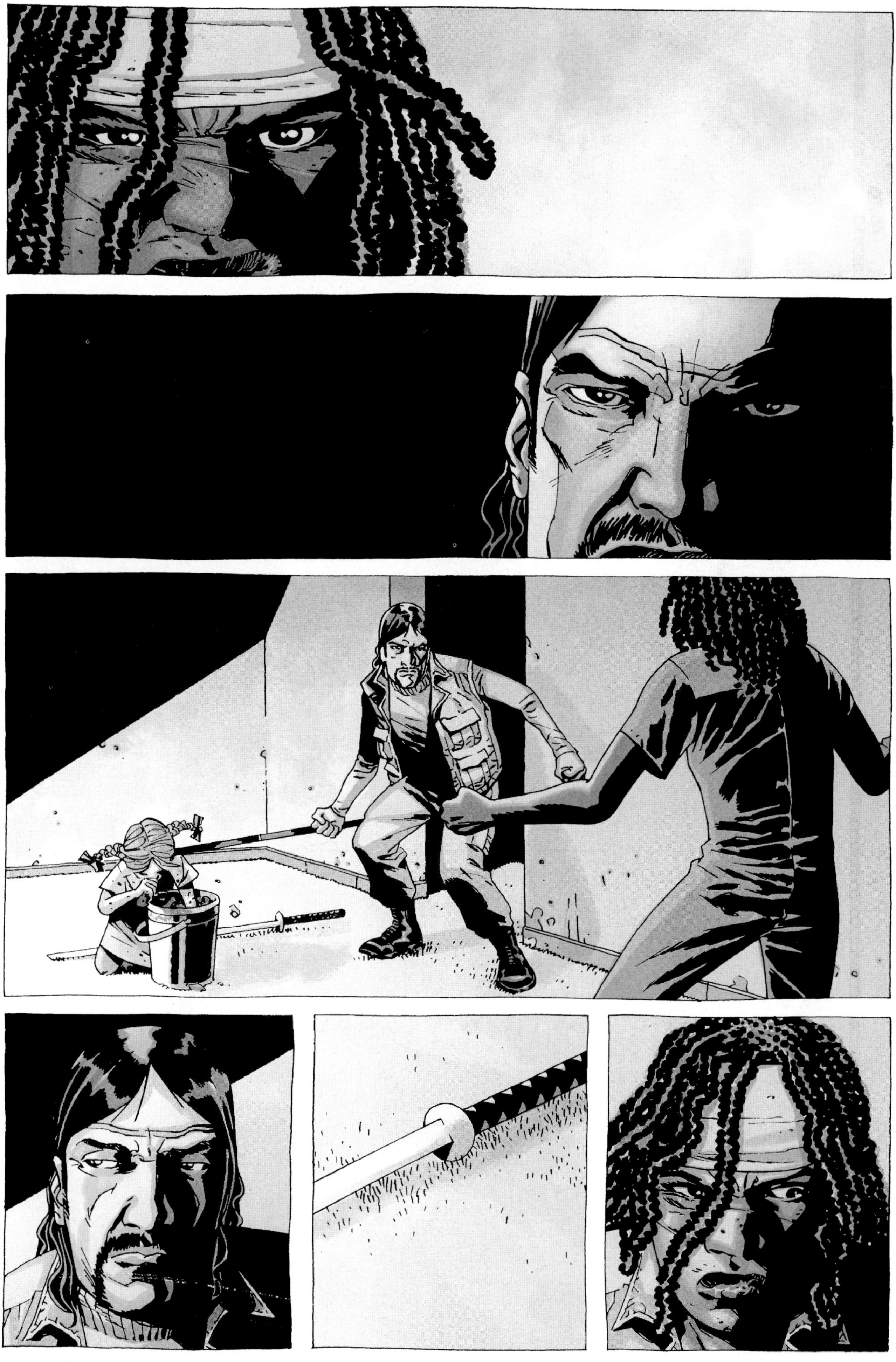

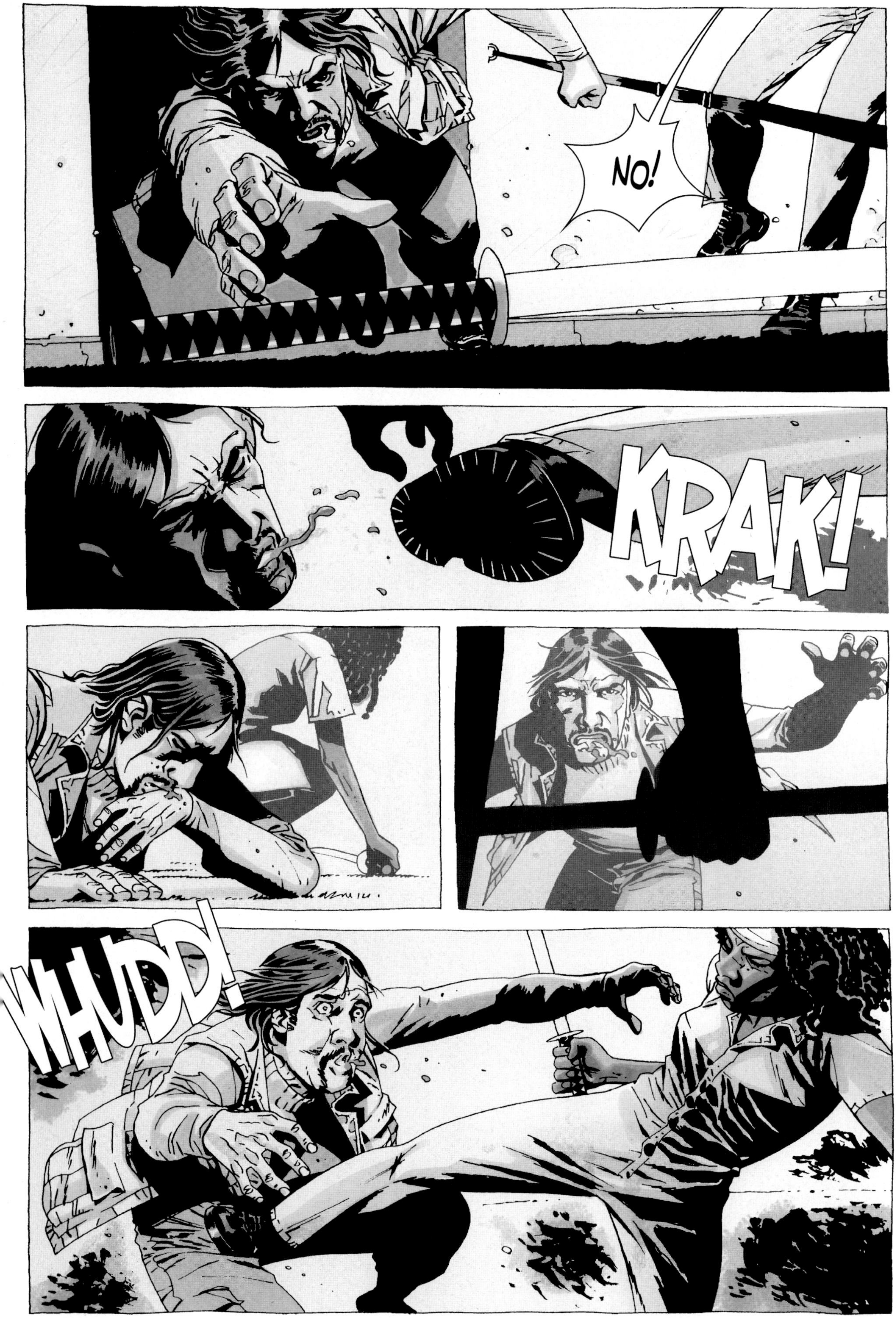
NO!
KRAK!
WHUDD!

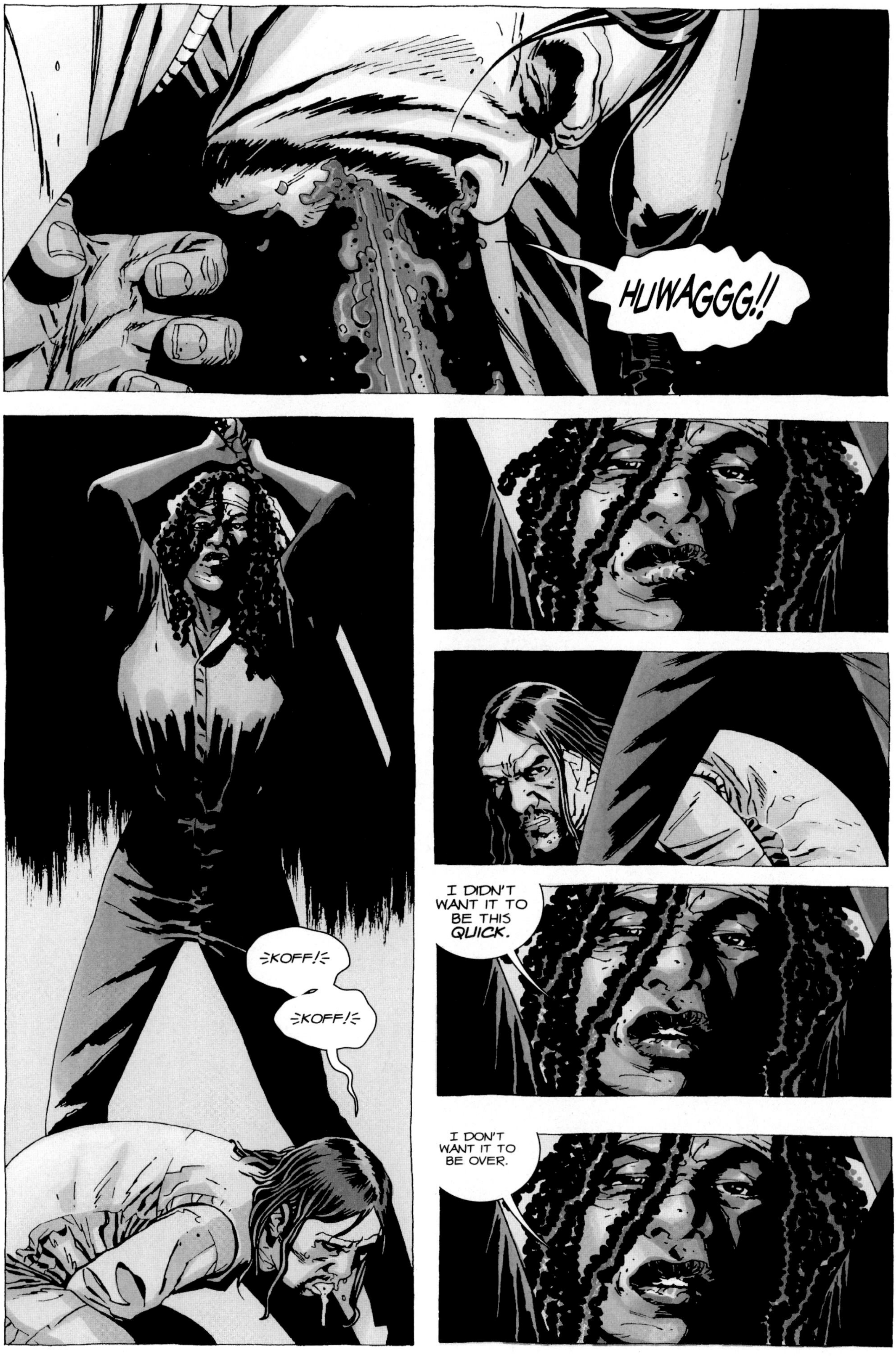
HUWAGGG!!
KOFF!
KOFF!
I DIDN'T WANT IT TO BE THIS QUICK.
I DON'T WANT IT TO BE OVER.

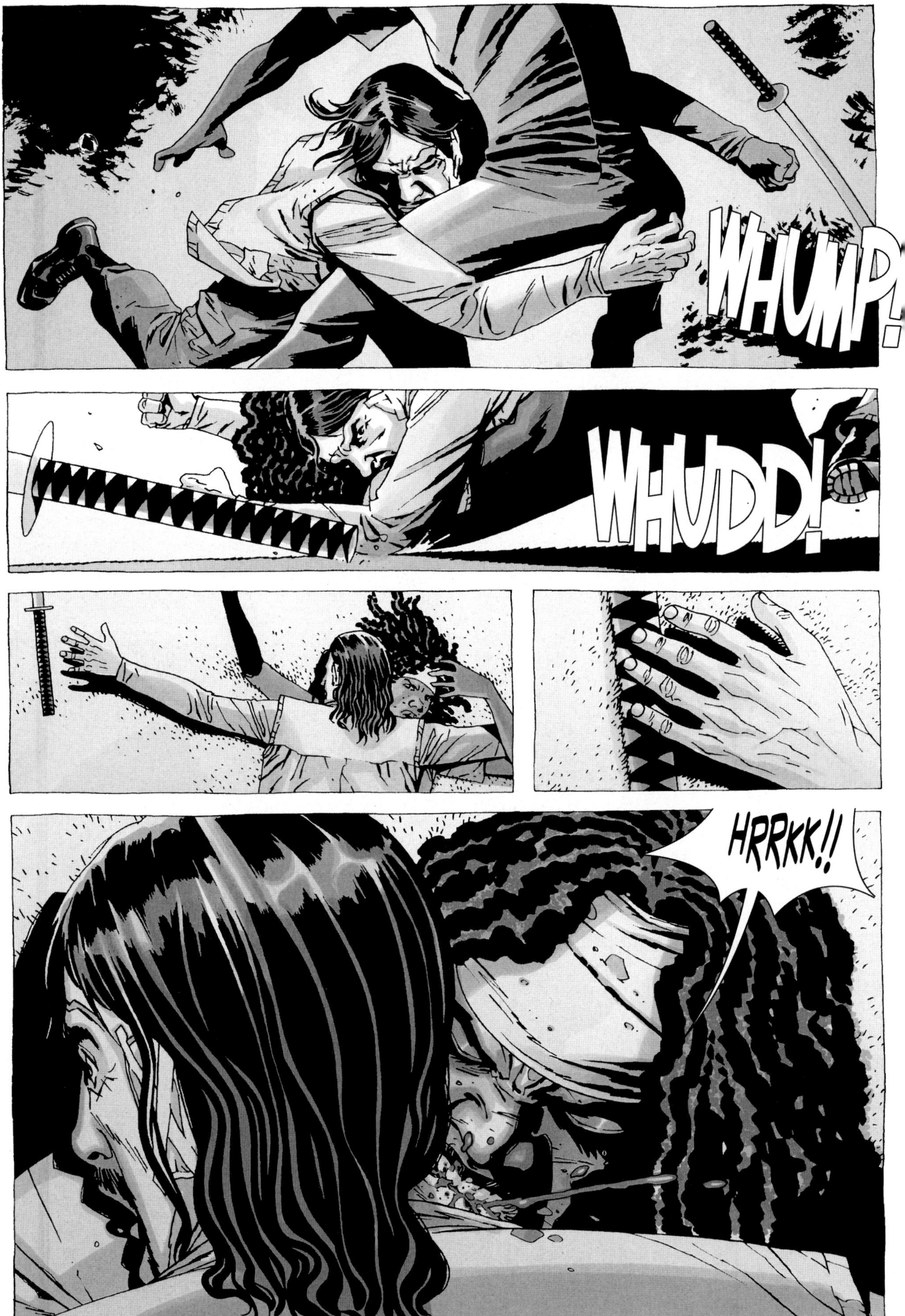
WHUMP!
WHUDD!
HRRKK!!

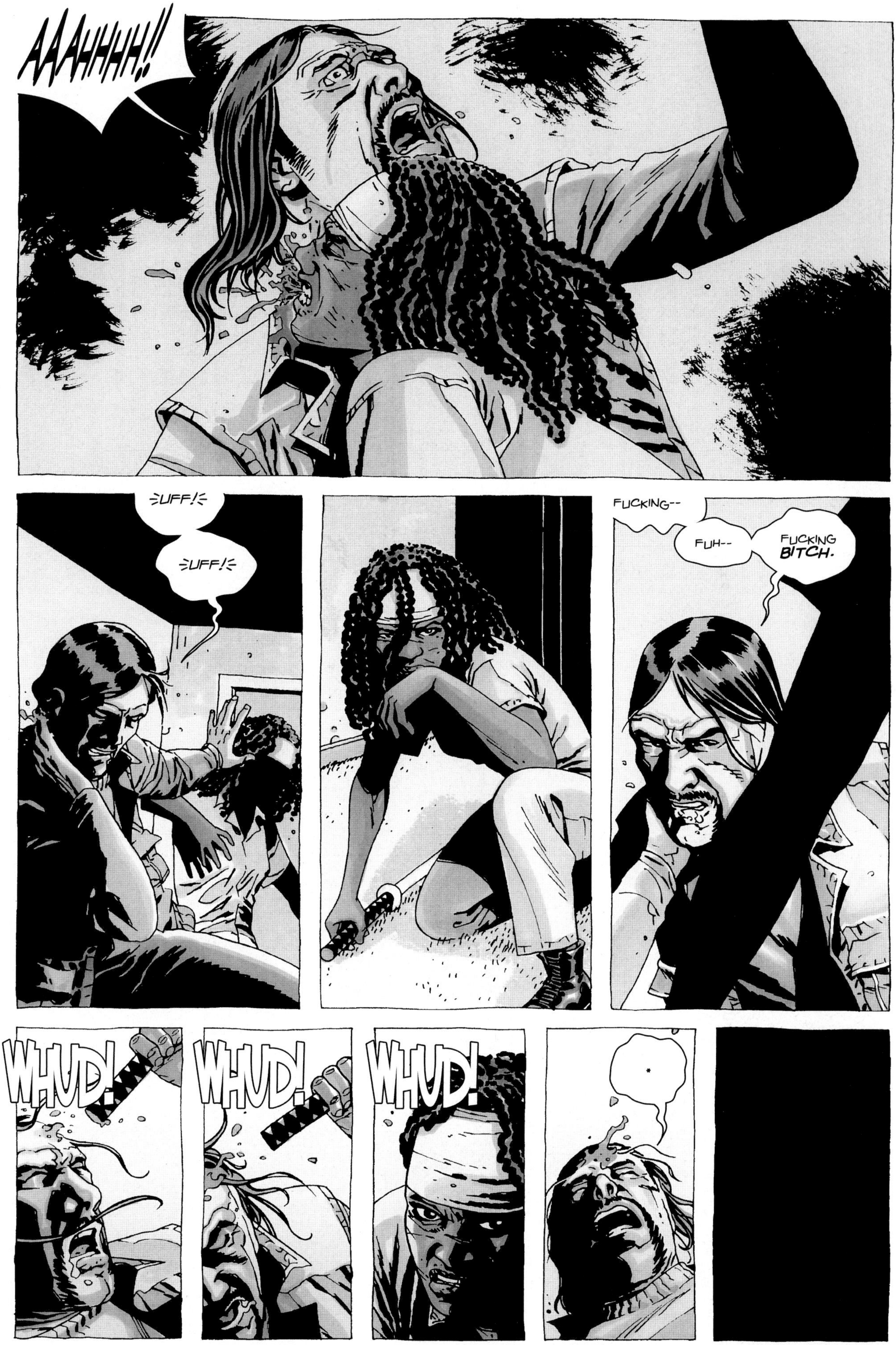
AAAHHHH!!
UFF!
UFF!
FUCKING--
FUH--
FUCKING BITCH.
WHUD!
WHUD!
WHUD!
*

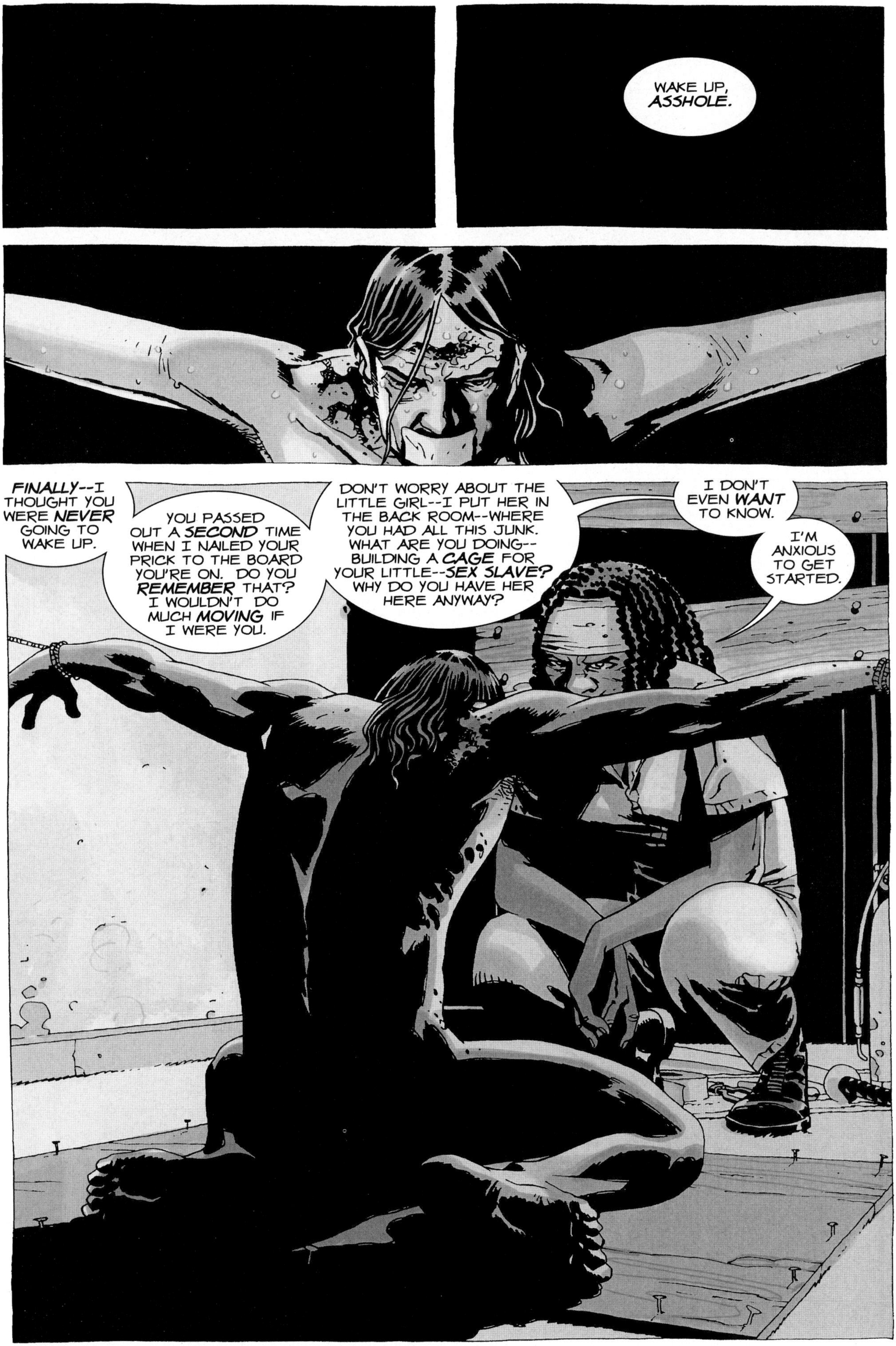
WAKE UP, ASSHOLE.
FINALLY--I THOUGHT YOU WERE NEVER GOING TO WAKE UP.
YOU PASSED OUT A SECOND TIME WHEN I NAILED YOUR PRICK TO THE BOARD YOU'RE ON. DO YOU REMEMBER THAT? I WOULDN'T DO MUCH MOVING IF I WERE YOU.
DON'T WORRY ABOUT THE LITTLE GIRL--I PUT HER IN THE BACK ROOM--WHERE YOU HAD ALL THIS JUNK. WHAT ARE YOU DOING--BUILDING A CAGE FOR YOUR LITTLE--SEX SLAVE? WHY DO YOU HAVE HER HERE ANYWAY?
I DON'T EVEN WANT TO KNOW.
I'M ANXIOUS TO GET STARTED.

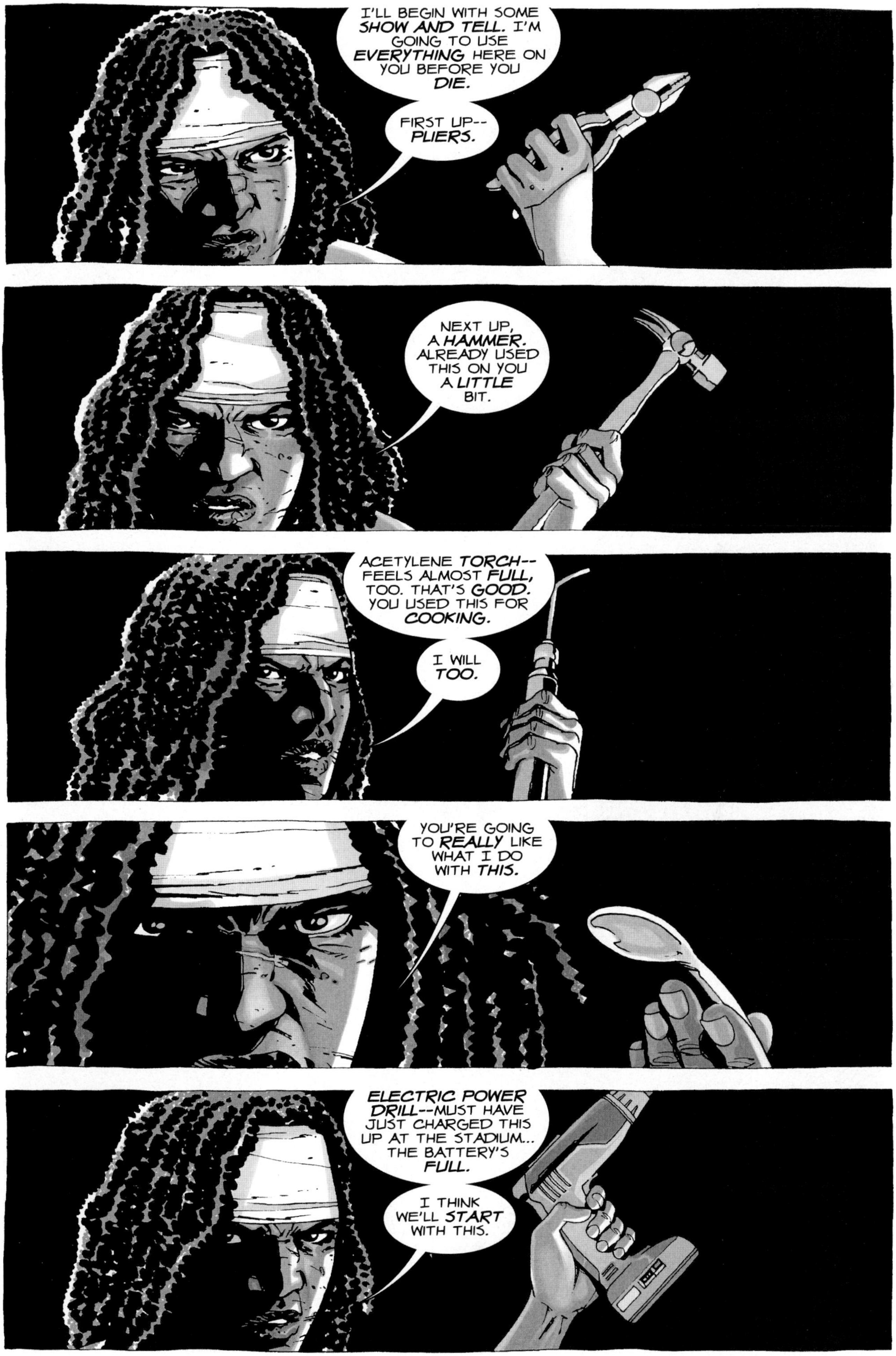
I'LL BEGIN WITH SOME SHOW AND TELL. I'M GOING TO USE EVERYTHING HERE ON YOU BEFORE YOU DIE.
FIRST UP-- PLIERS.
NEXT UP, A HAMMER. ALREADY USED THIS ON YOU A LITTLE BIT.
ACETYLENE TORCH-- FEELS ALMOST FULL, TOO. THAT'S GOOD. YOU USED THIS FOR COOKING.
I WILL TOO.
YOU'RE GOING TO REALLY LIKE WHAT I DO WITH THIS.
ELECTRIC POWER DRILL--MUST HAVE JUST CHARGED THIS UP AT THE STADIUM... THE BATTERY'S FULL.
I THINK WE'LL START WITH THIS.

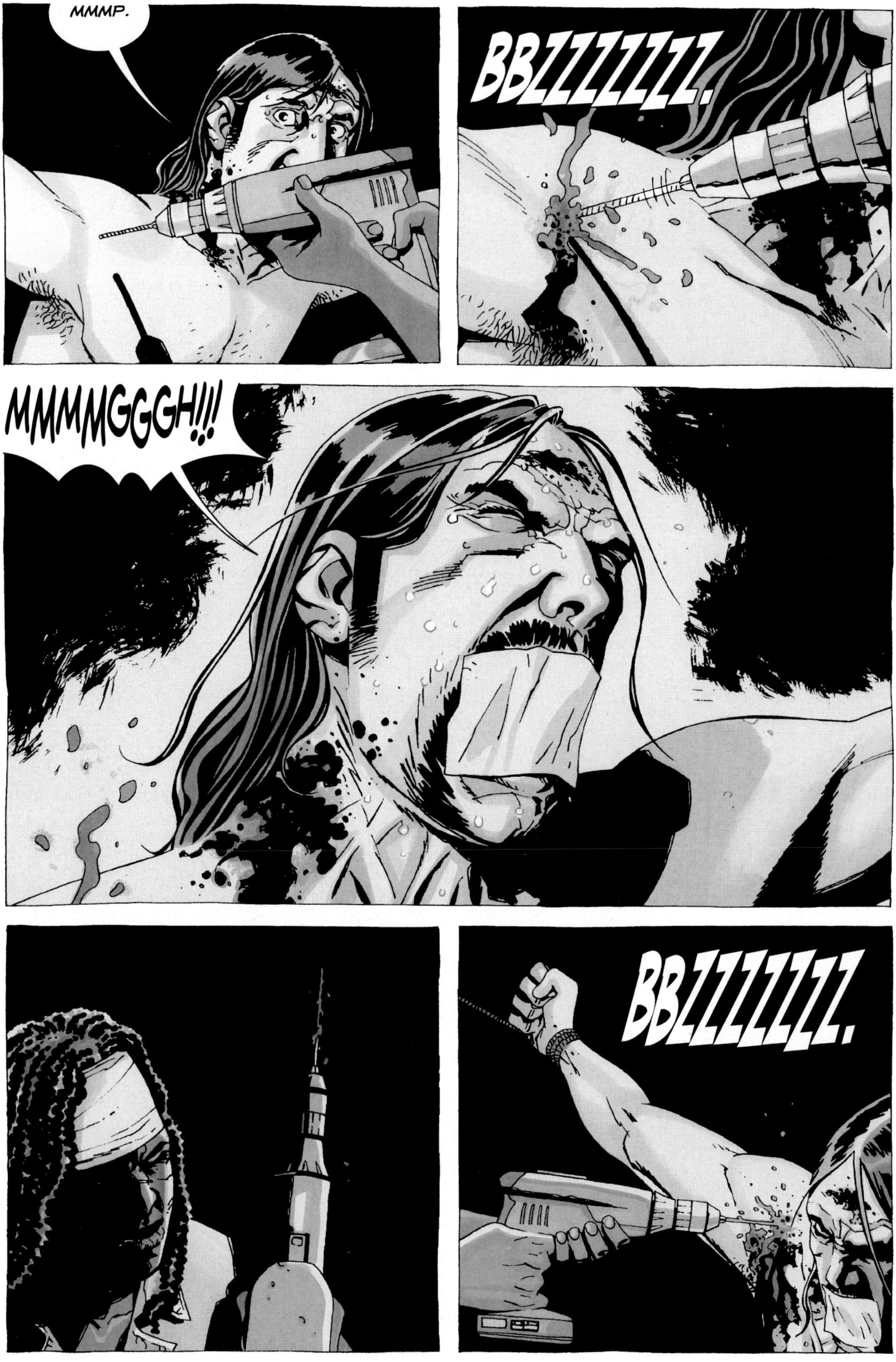
MMMP.
BBZZZZZZZ.
MMMMGGGH!!!
BBZZZZZZ.

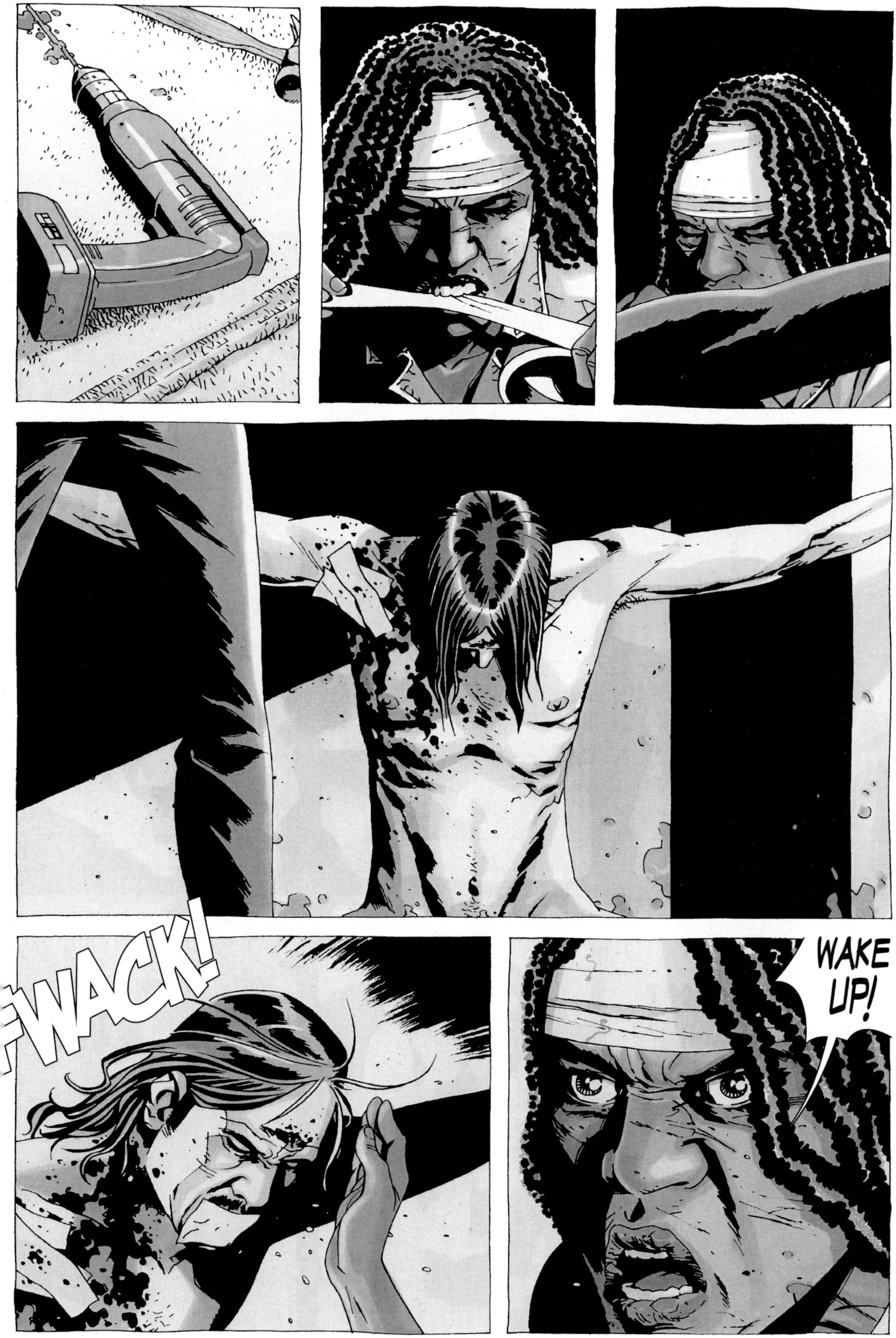
FWACK!
WAKE UP!

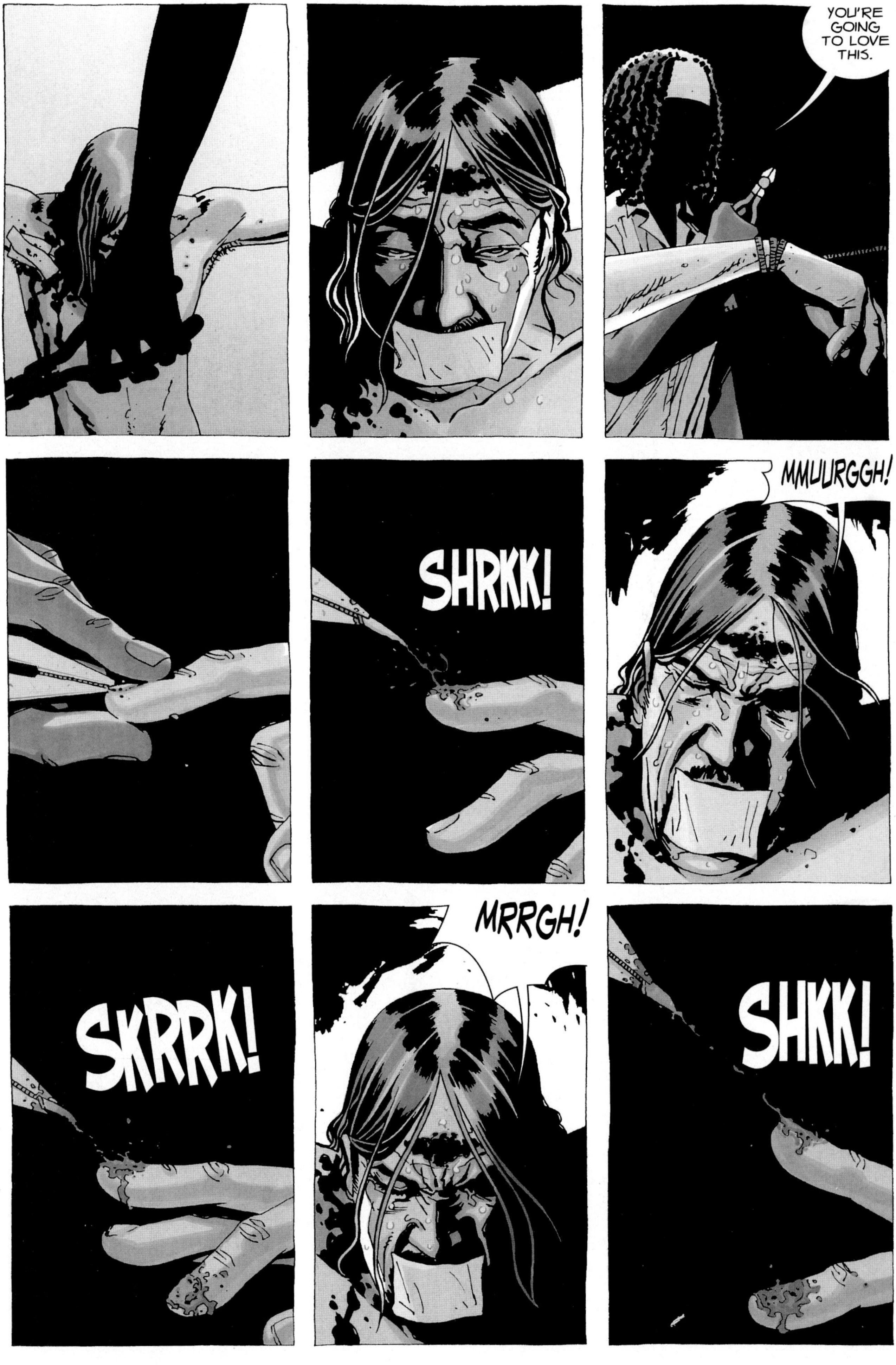
YOU'RE GOING TO LOVE THIS.
SHRKK!
MMUURGGH!
SKRRK!
MRRGH!
SHKK!

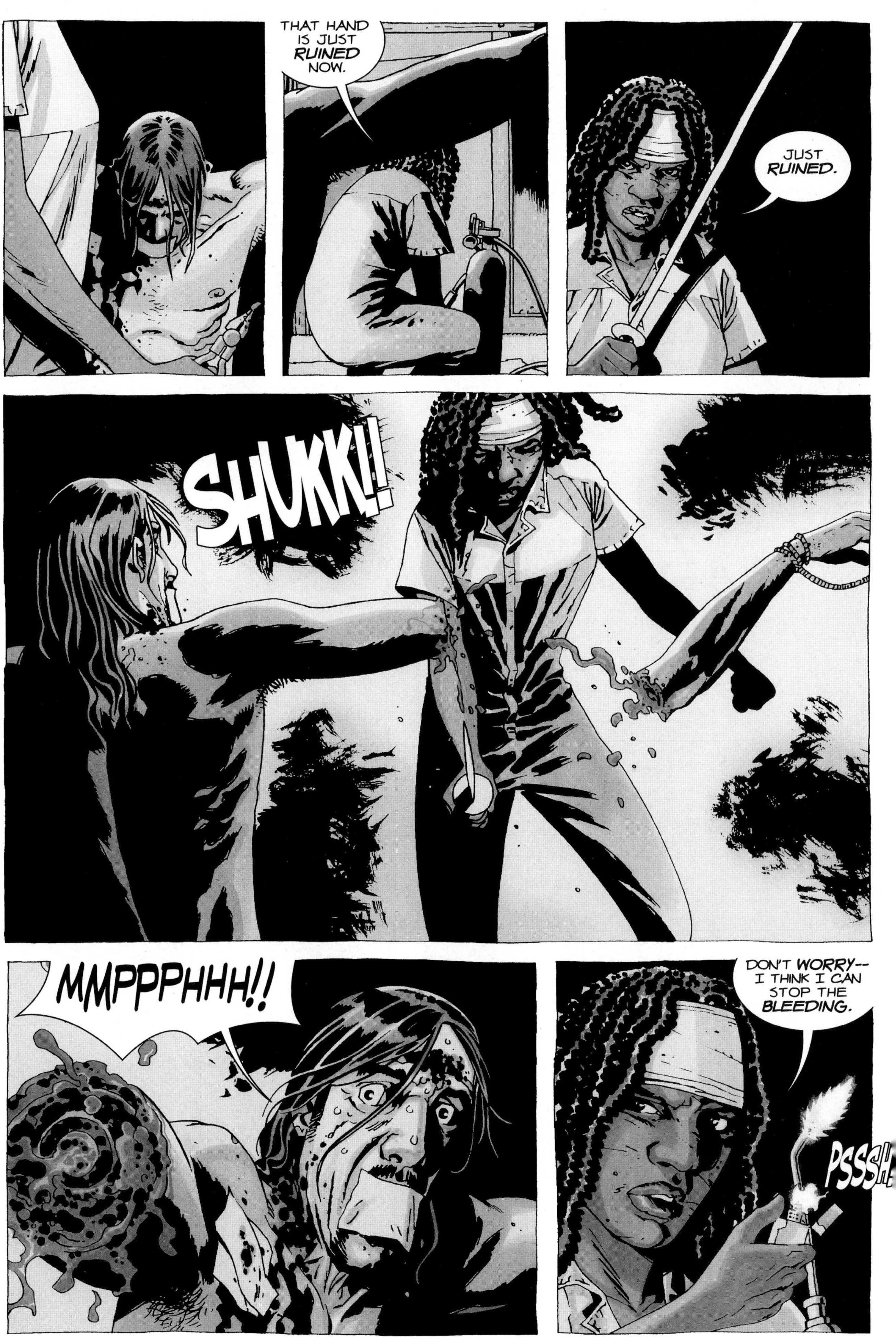
THAT HAND IS JUST RUINED NOW.
JUST RUINED.
SHUKK!!
MMPPPHHH!!
DON'T WORRY-- I THINK I CAN STOP THE BLEEDING.
PSSSH!

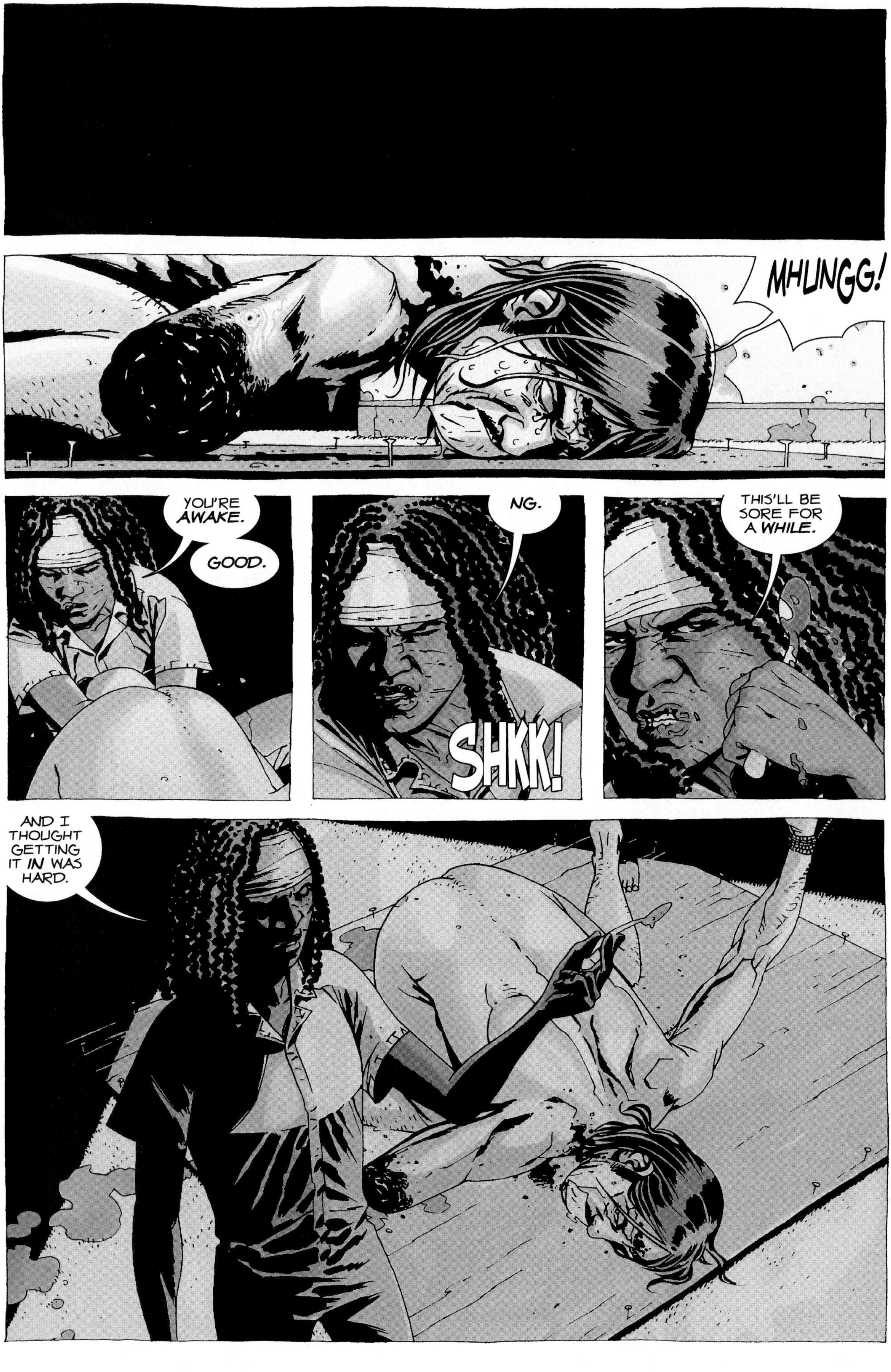
MHUNGG!
YOU'RE AWAKE.
GOOD.
NG.
SHKK!
THIS'LL BE SORE FOR A WHILE.
AND I THOUGHT GETTING IT IN WAS HARD.

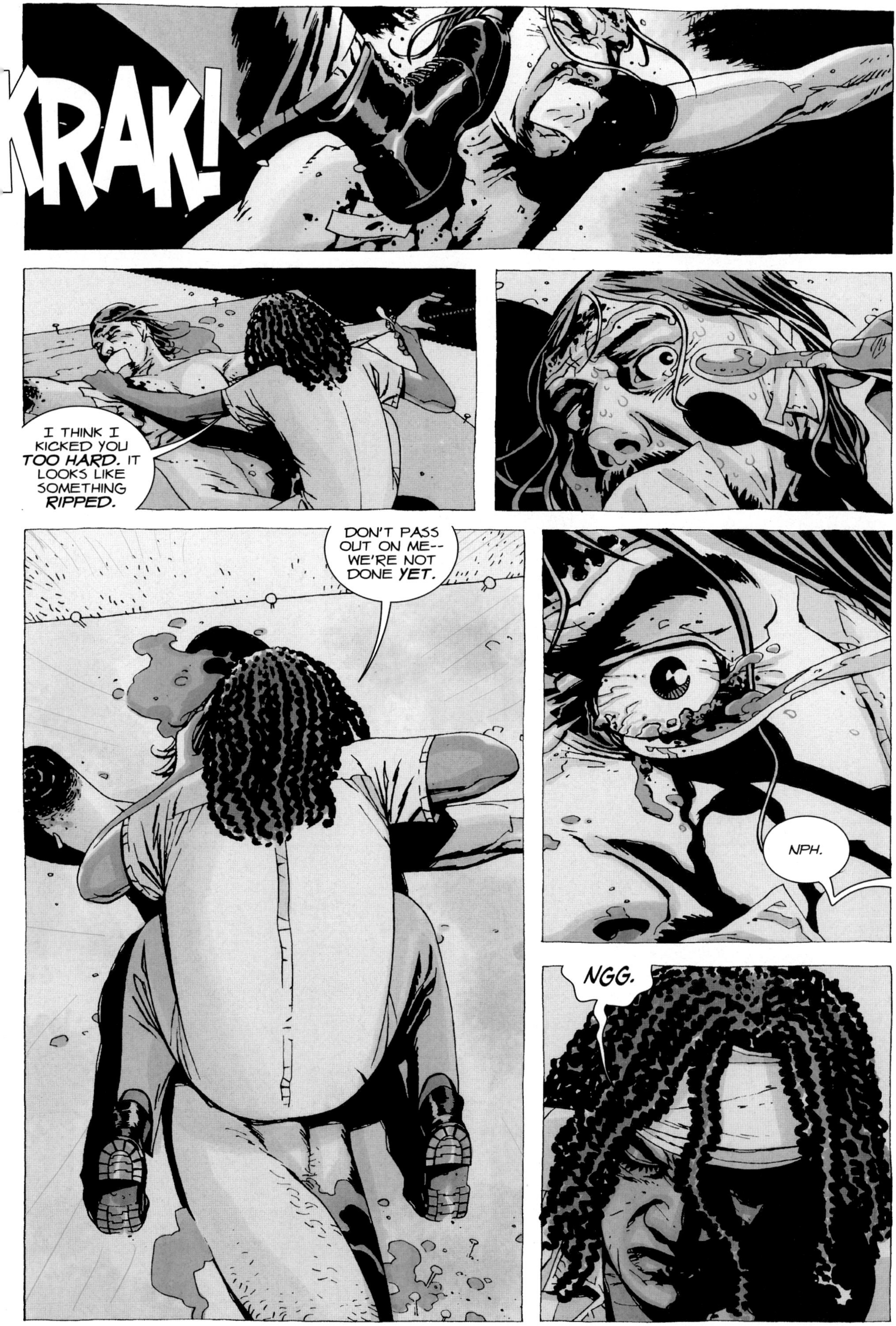
KRAK!
I THINK I KICKED YOU TOO HARD. IT LOOKS LIKE SOMETHING RIPPED.
DON'T PASS OUT ON ME-- WE'RE NOT DONE YET.
NPH.
NGG.

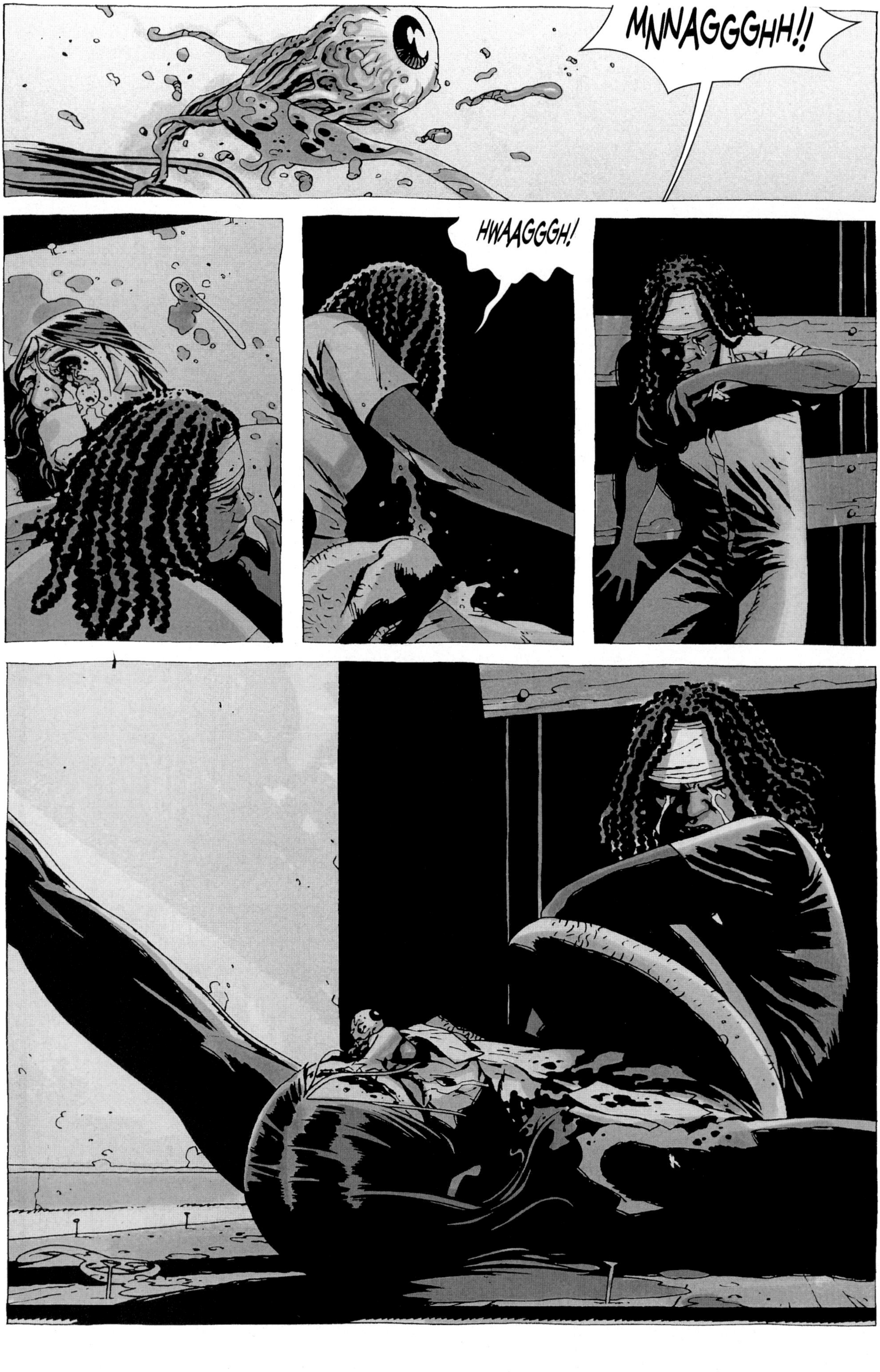
MNNAGGGHH!!
HWAAGGGH!

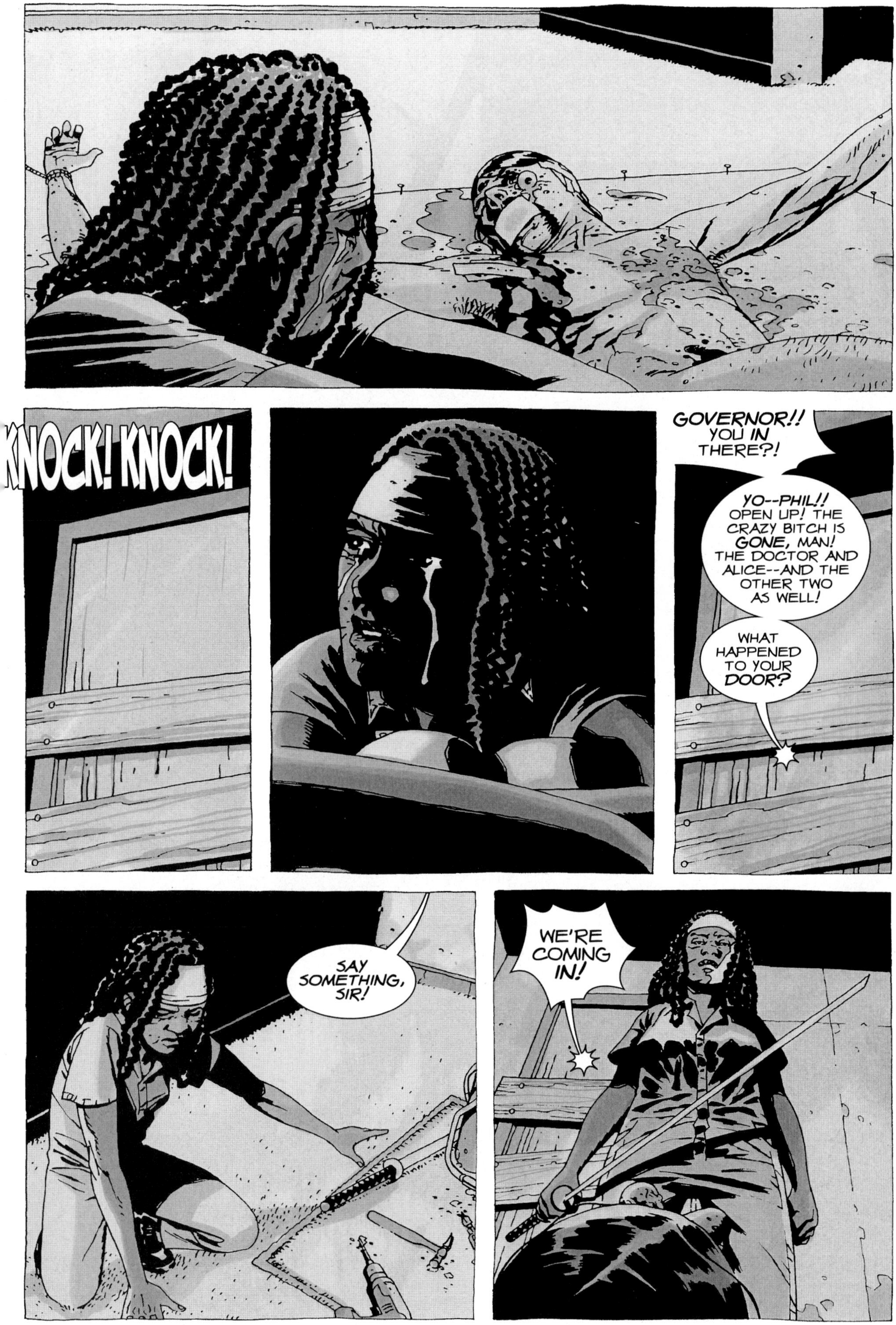
KNOCK! KNOCK!
GOVERNOR!! YOU IN THERE?!
YO--PHIL!! OPEN UP! THE CRAZY BITCH IS GONE, MAN! THE DOCTOR AND ALICE--AND THE OTHER TWO AS WELL!
WHAT HAPPENED TO YOUR DOOR?
SAY SOMETHING, SIR!
WE'RE COMING IN!

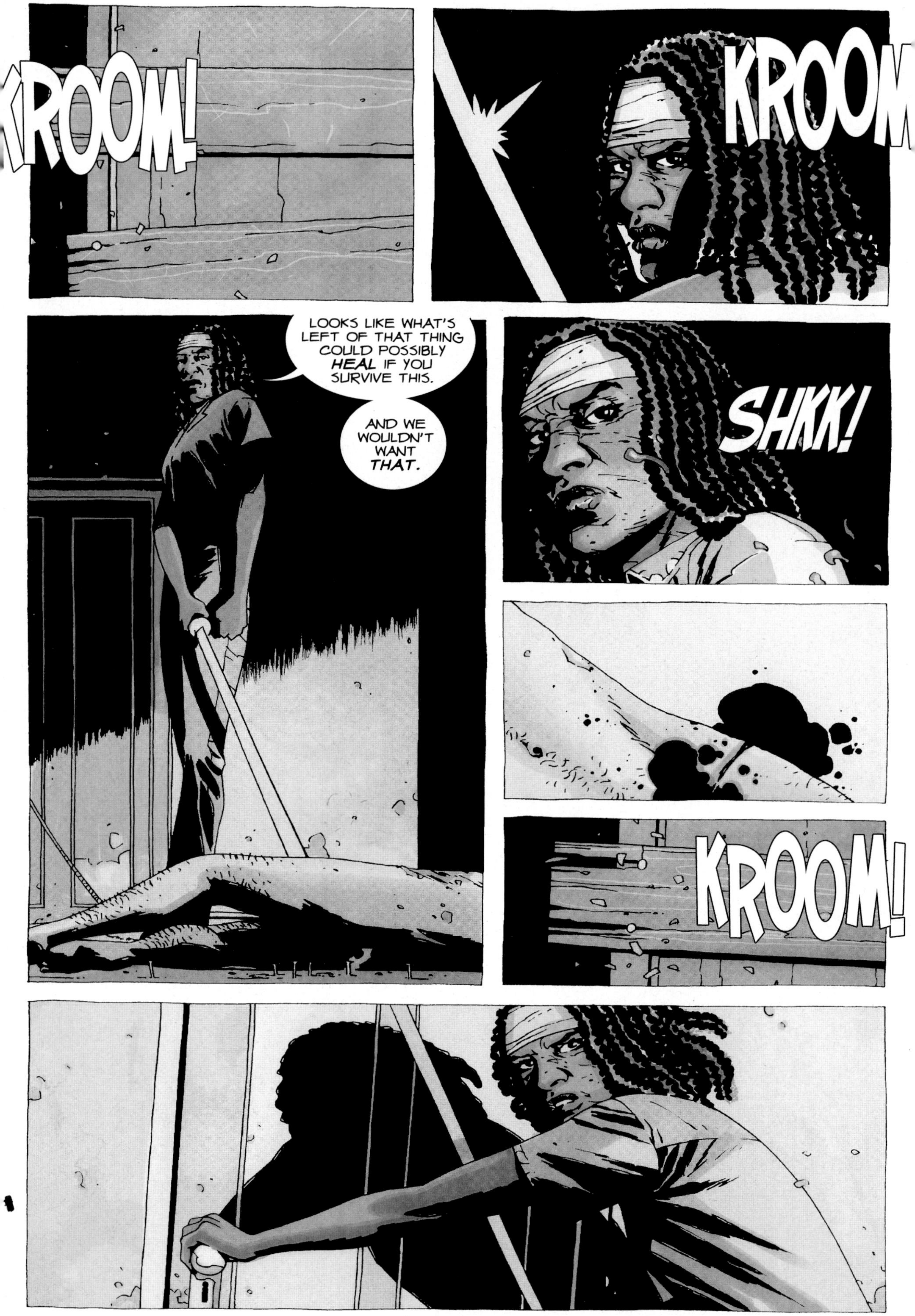
KROOM!
KROOM
LOOKS LIKE WHAT'S LEFT OF THAT THING COULD POSSIBLY HEAL IF YOU SURVIVE THIS.
AND WE WOULDN'T WANT THAT.
SHKK!
KROOM!

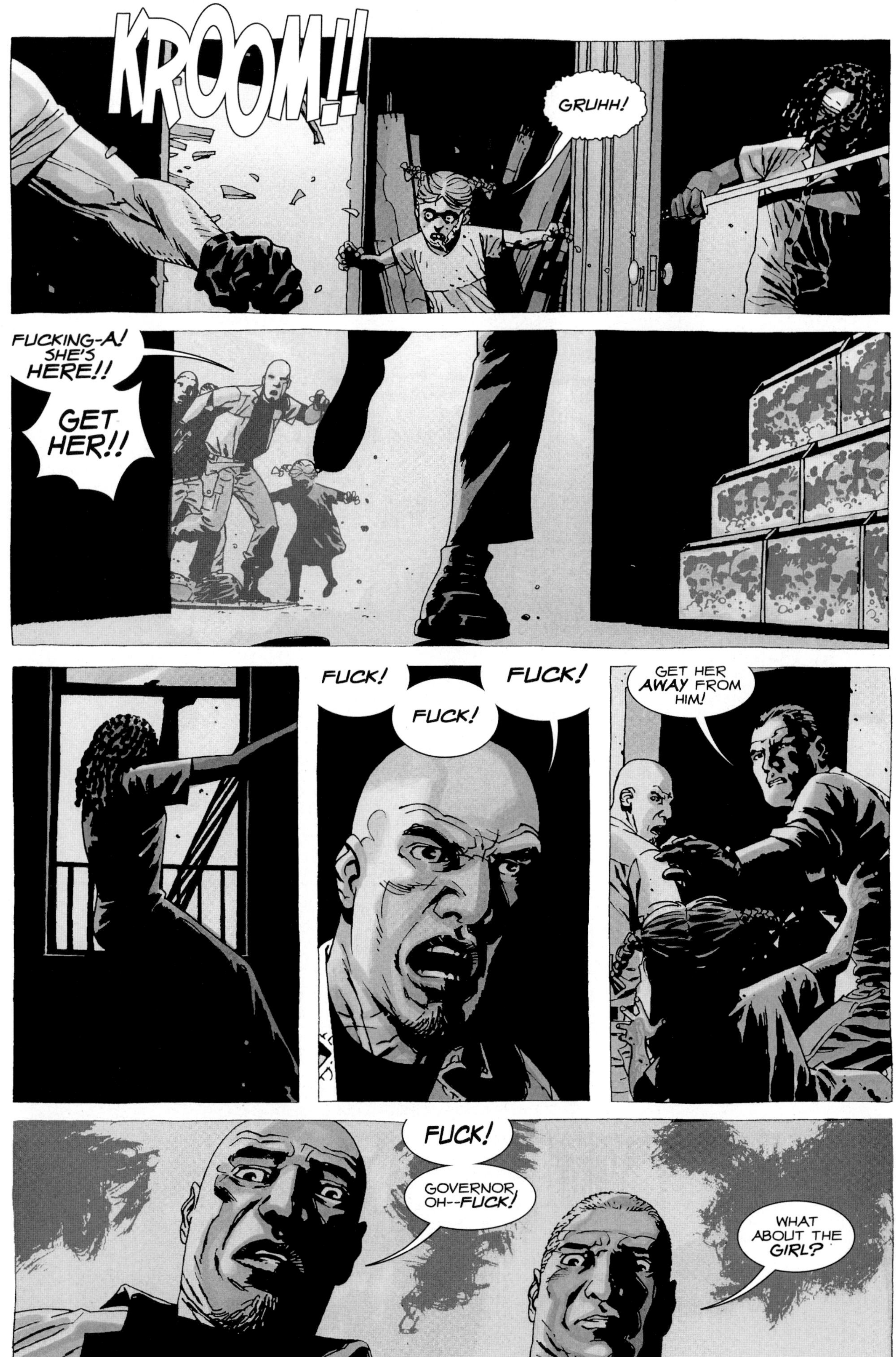
KROOM!!
GRUHH!
FUCKING-A! SHE'S HERE!!
GET HER!!
FUCK!
FUCK!
FUCK!
GET HER AWAY FROM HIM!
FUCK!
GOVERNOR OH--FUCK!
WHAT ABOUT THE GIRL?

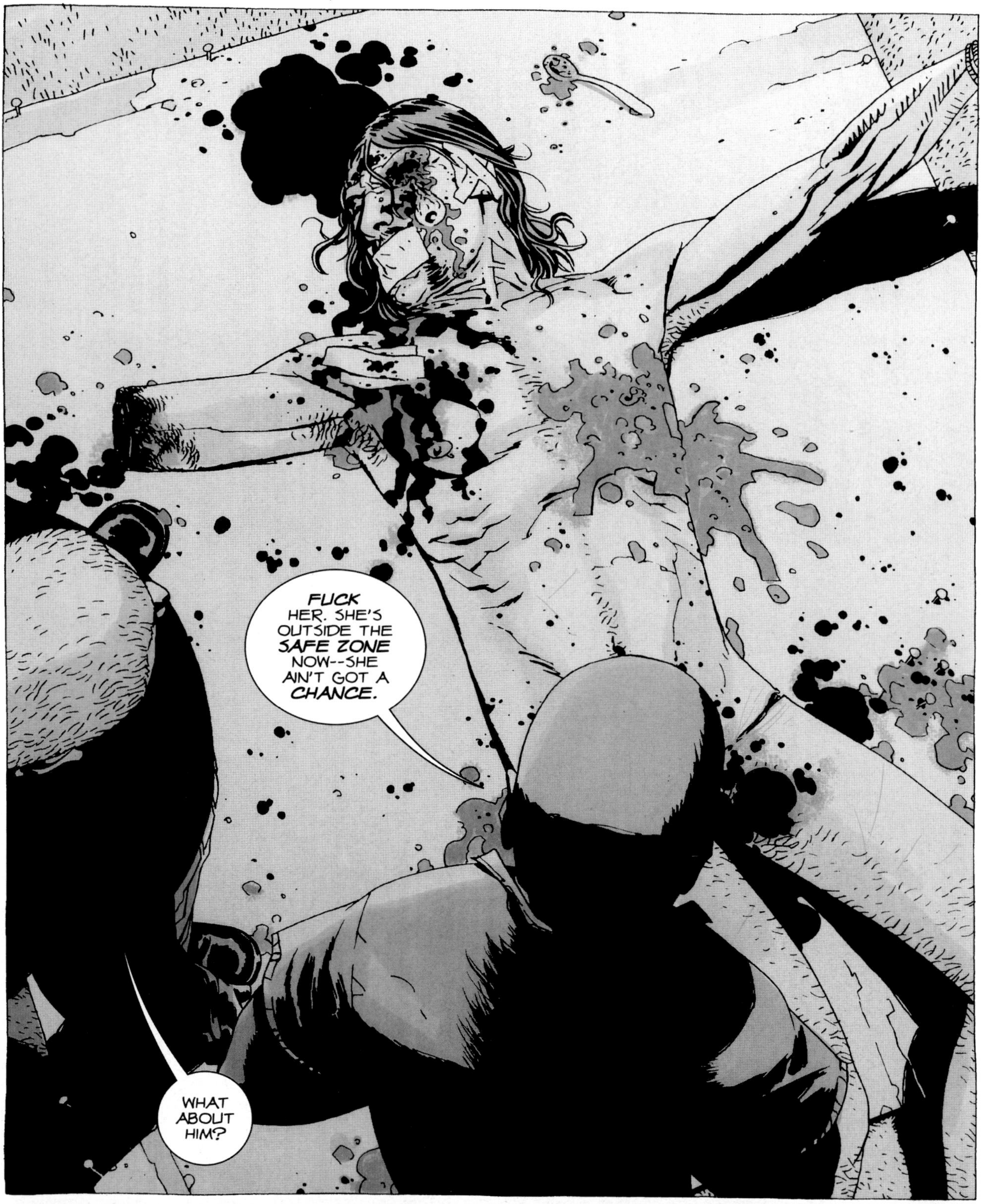
FUCK HER. SHE'S OUTSIDE THE SAFE ZONE NOW--SHE AIN'T GOT A CHANCE.
WHAT ABOUT HIM?

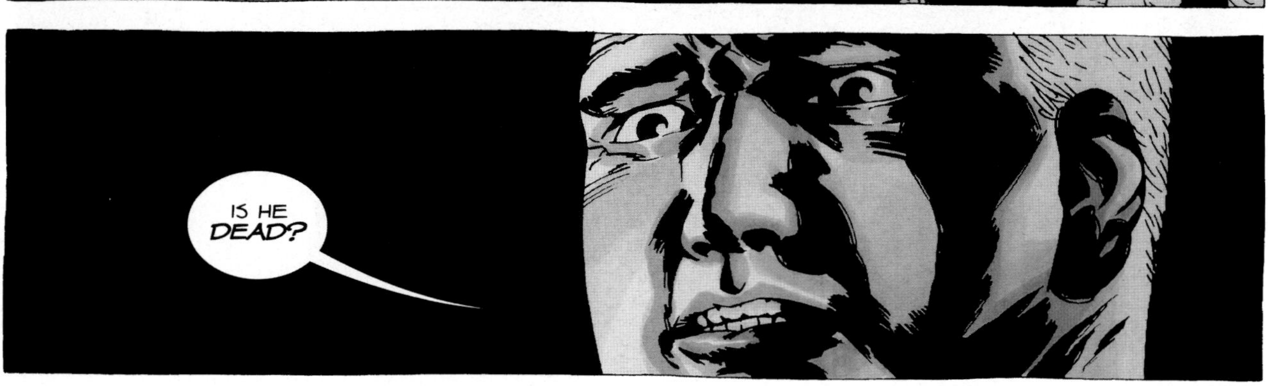
IS HE DEAD?

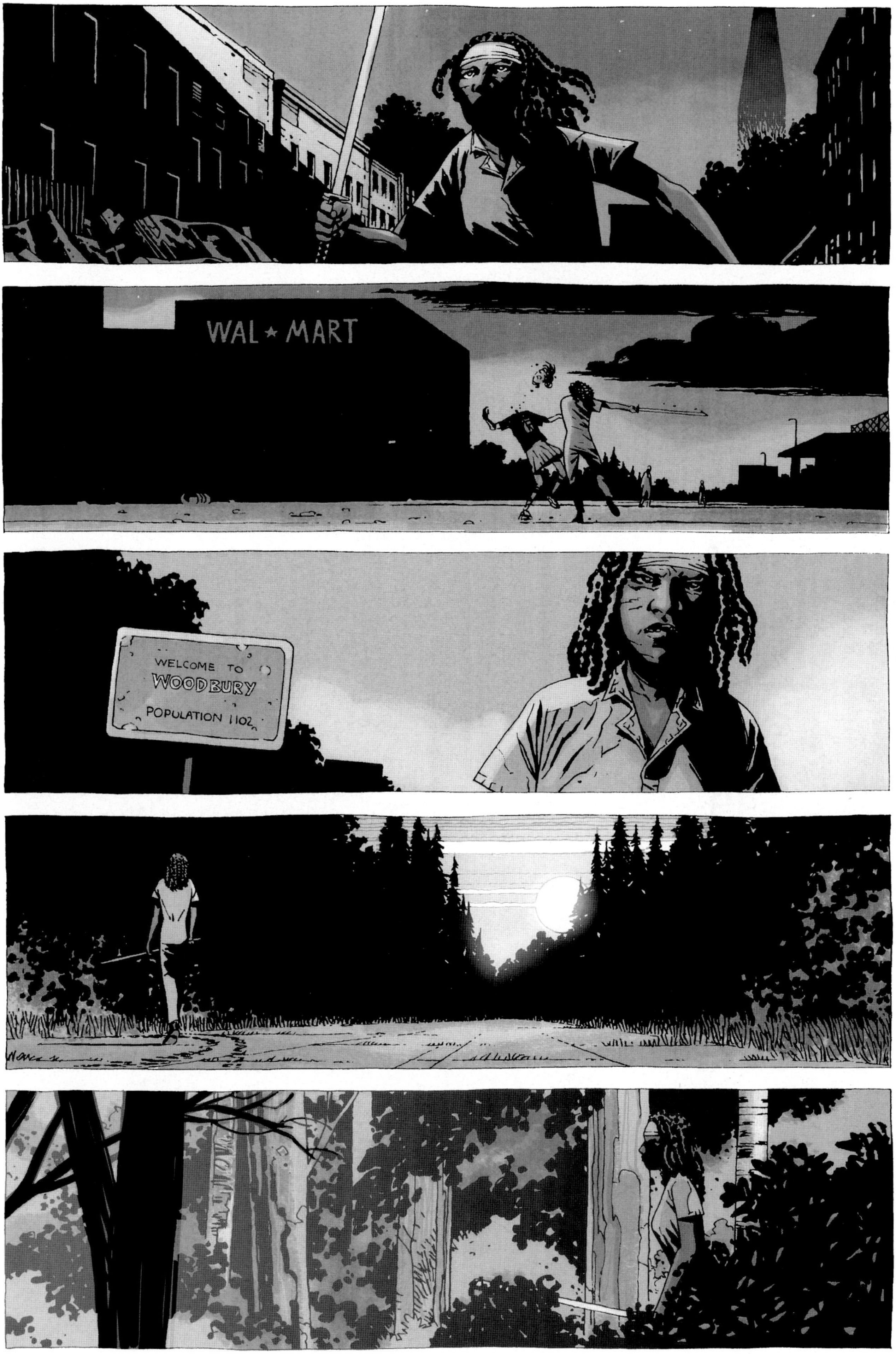
WAL★MART
WELCOME TO
WOODBURY
POPULATION 1102

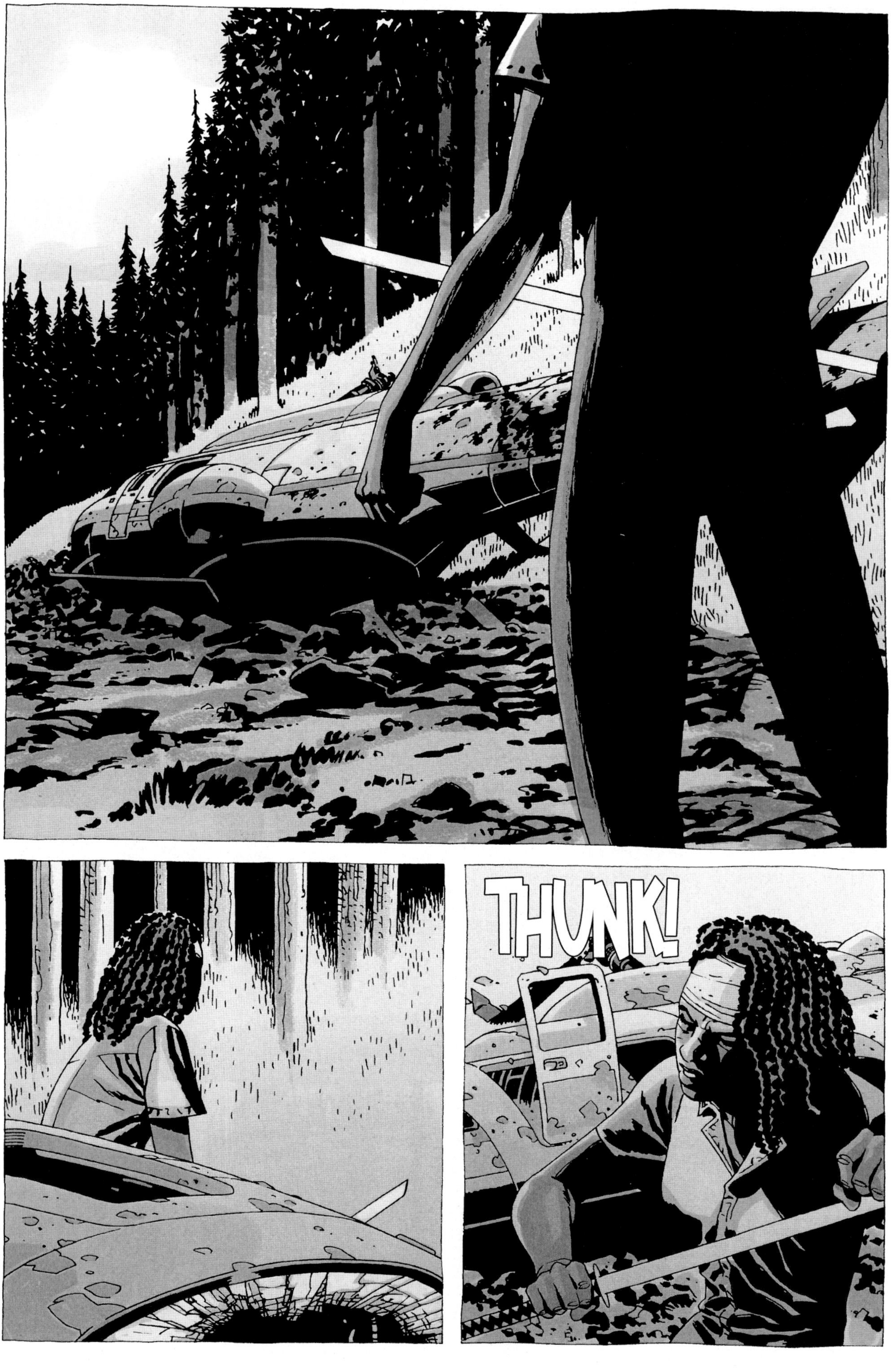
THUNK!

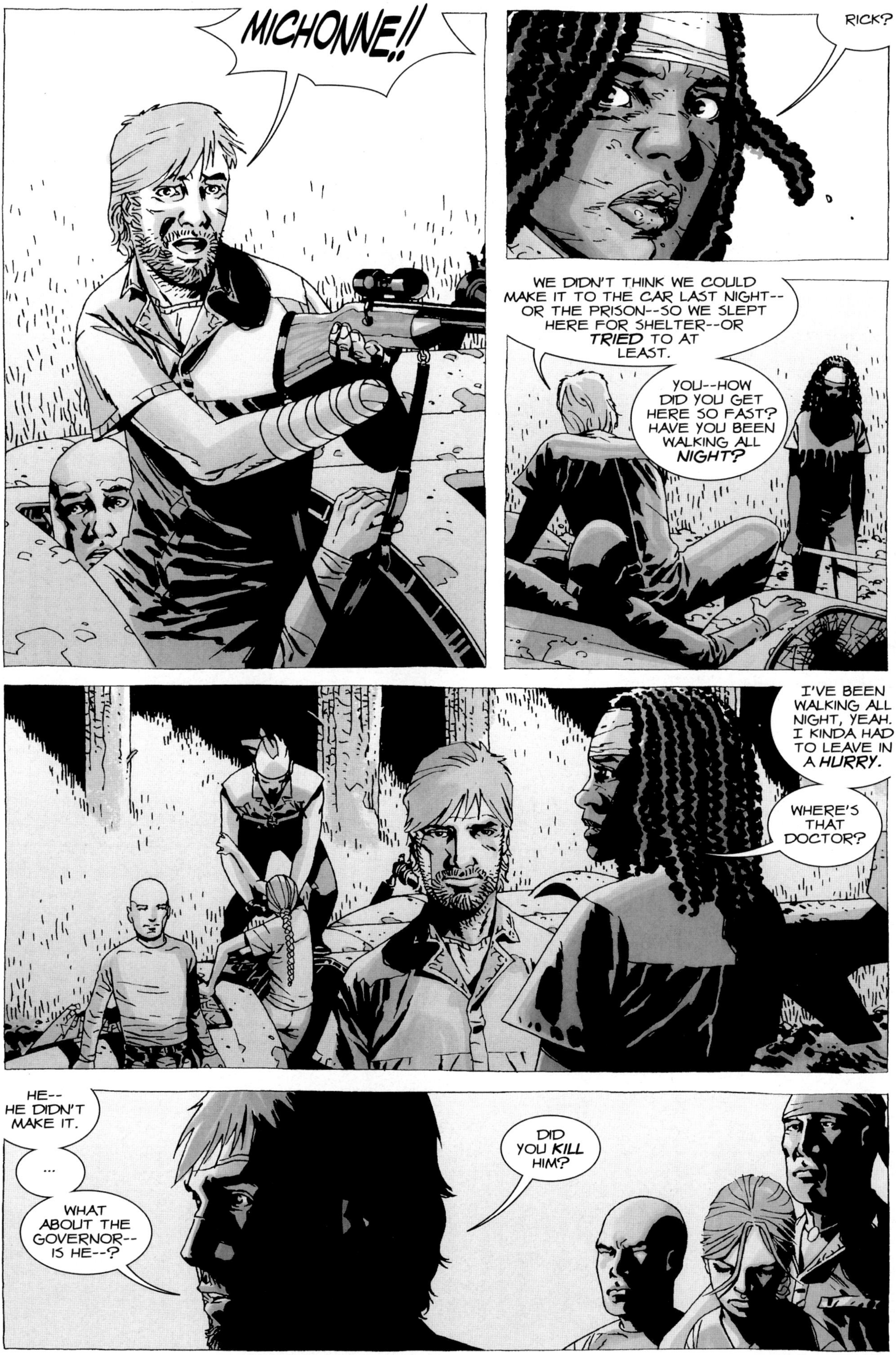
MICHONNE!!
RICK?
WE DIDN'T THINK WE COULD MAKE IT TO THE CAR LAST NIGHT-- OR THE PRISON--SO WE SLEPT HERE FOR SHELTER--OR TRIED TO AT LEAST.
YOU--HOW DID YOU GET HERE SO FAST? HAVE YOU BEEN WALKING ALL NIGHT?
I'VE BEEN WALKING ALL NIGHT, YEAH. I KINDA HAD TO LEAVE IN A HURRY.
WHERE'S THAT DOCTOR?
HE-- HE DIDN'T MAKE IT.
...
WHAT ABOUT THE GOVERNOR-- IS HE--?
DID YOU KILL HIM?

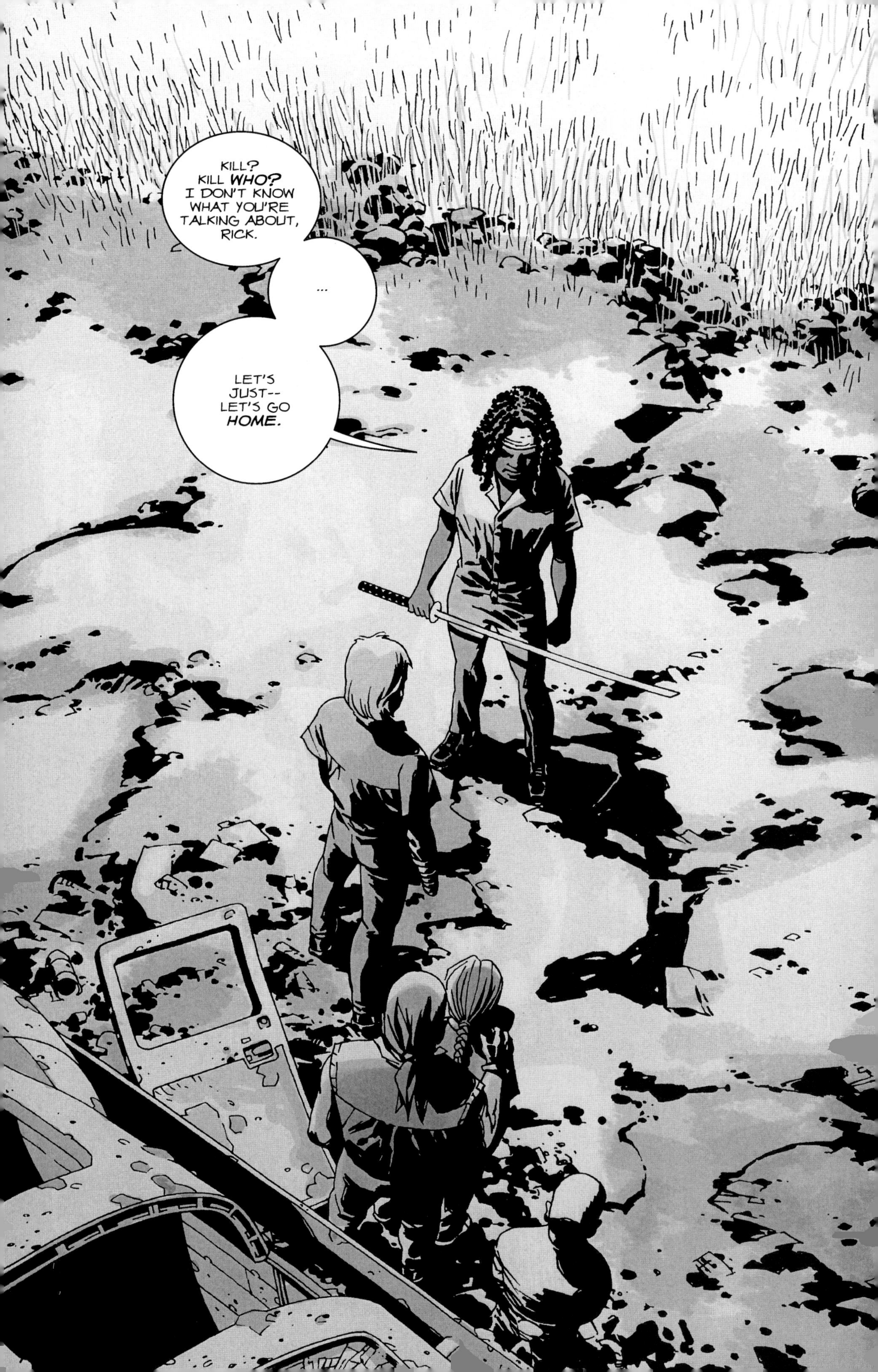
KILL? KILL WHO? I DON'T KNOW WHAT YOU'RE TALKING ABOUT, RICK.
...
LET'S JUST-- LET'S GO HOME.

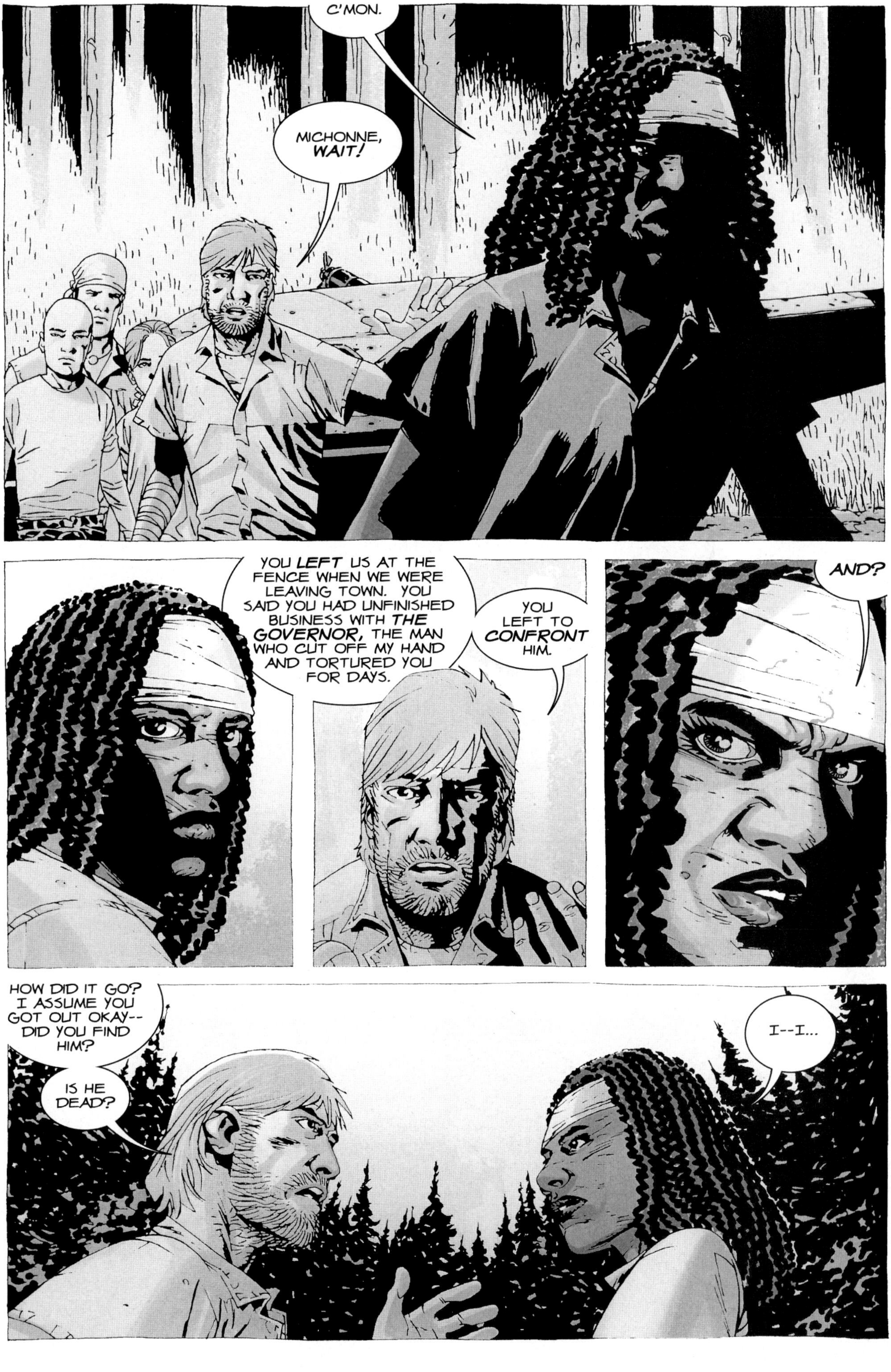
C'MON.
MICHONNE, WAIT!
YOU LEFT US AT THE FENCE WHEN WE WERE LEAVING TOWN. YOU SAID YOU HAD UNFINISHED BUSINESS WITH THE GOVERNOR, THE MAN WHO CUT OFF MY HAND AND TORTURED YOU FOR DAYS.
YOU LEFT TO CONFRONT HIM.
AND?
HOW DID IT GO? I ASSUME YOU GOT OUT OKAY-- DID YOU FIND HIM?
IS HE DEAD?
I--I...

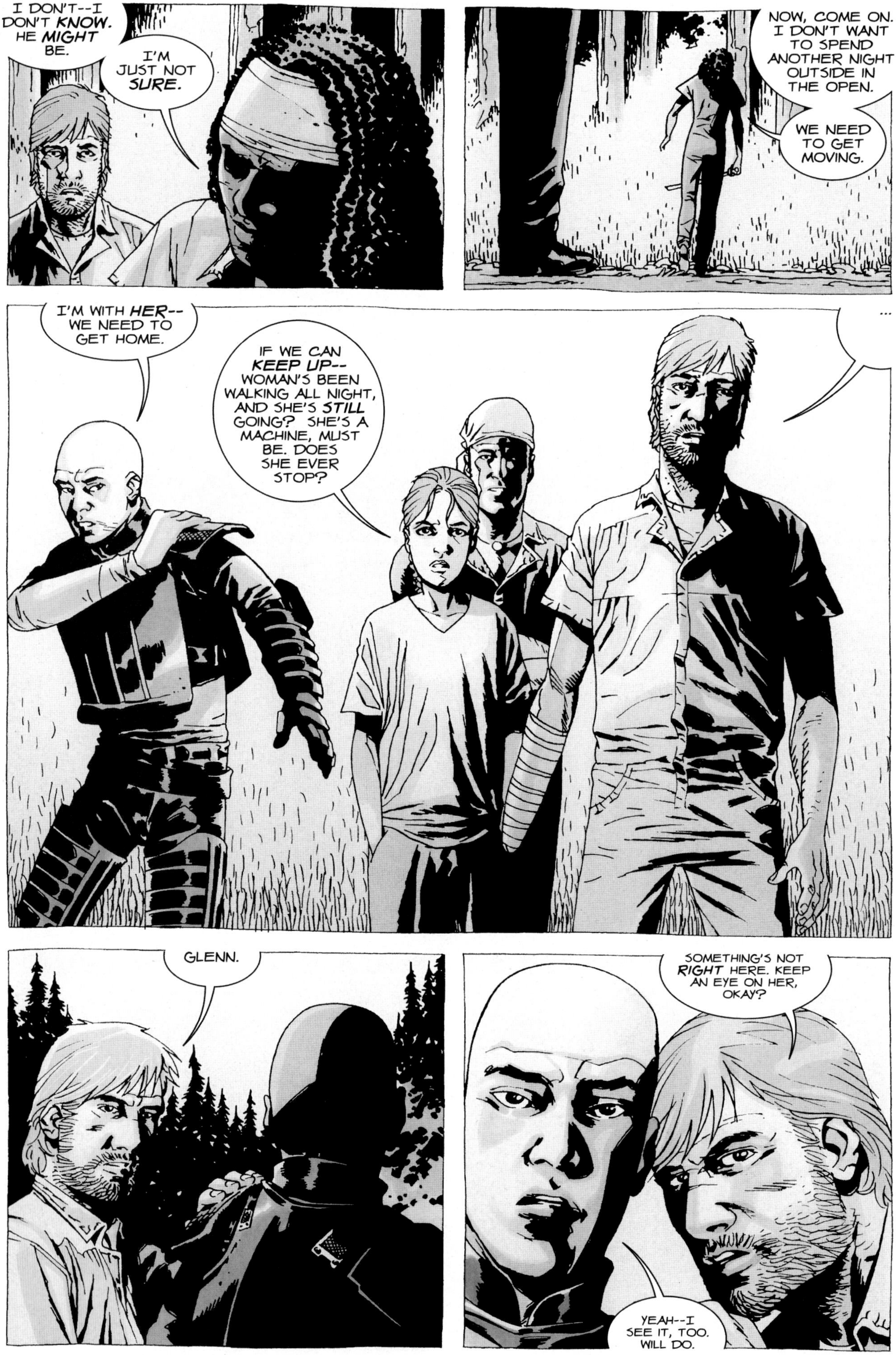
I DON'T--I DON'T KNOW. HE MIGHT BE.
I'M JUST NOT SURE.
NOW, COME ON. I DON'T WANT TO SPEND ANOTHER NIGHT OUTSIDE IN THE OPEN.
WE NEED TO GET MOVING.
I'M WITH HER-- WE NEED TO GET HOME.
IF WE CAN KEEP UP-- WOMAN'S BEEN WALKING ALL NIGHT, AND SHE'S STILL GOING? SHE'S A MACHINE, MUST BE. DOES SHE EVER STOP?
...
GLENN.
SOMETHING'S NOT RIGHT HERE. KEEP AN EYE ON HER, OKAY?
YEAH--I SEE IT, TOO. WILL DO.

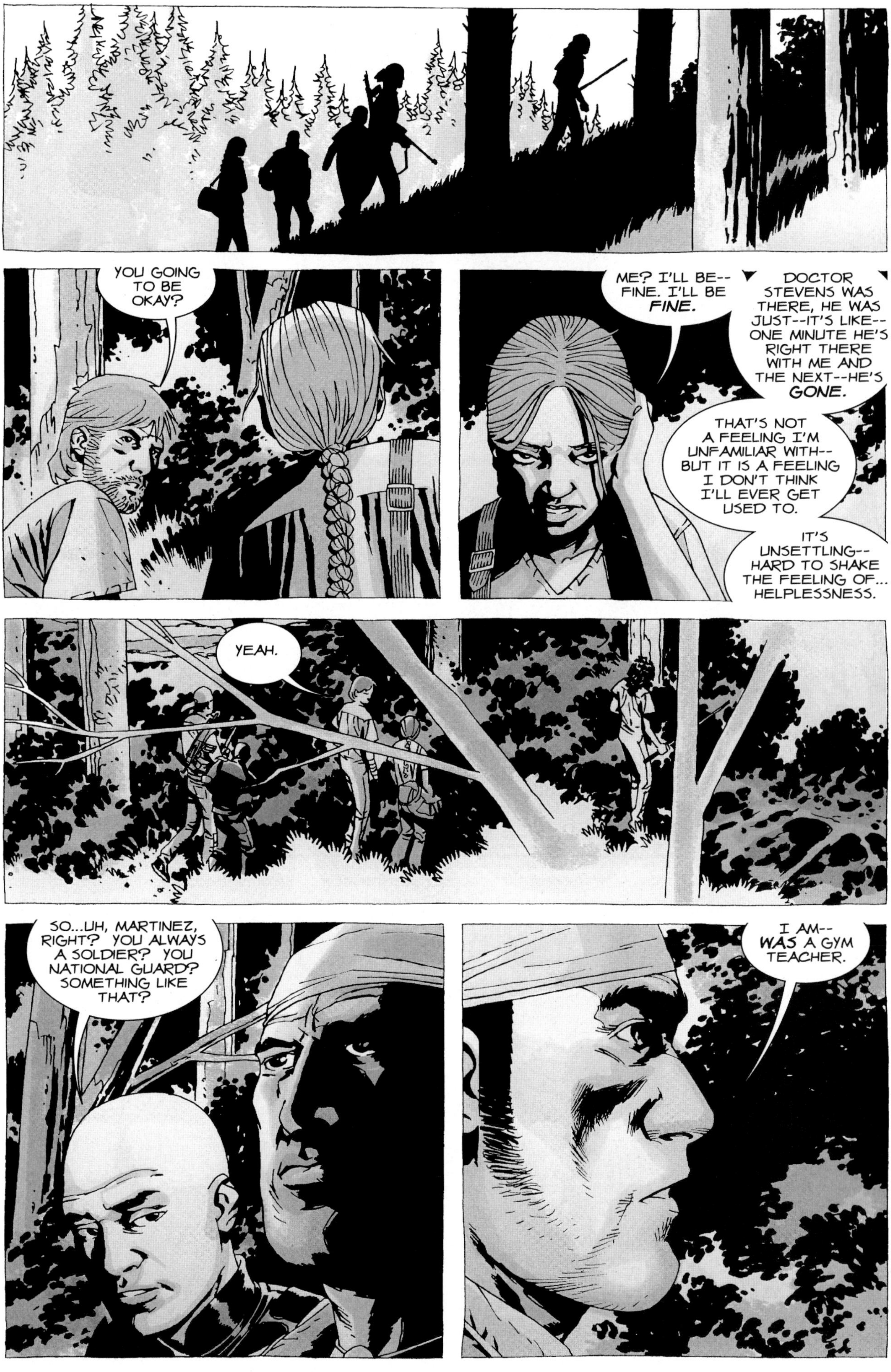
YOU GOING TO BE OKAY?
ME? I'LL BE-- FINE. I'LL BE FINE.
DOCTOR STEVENS WAS THERE, HE WAS JUST--IT'S LIKE-- ONE MINUTE HE'S RIGHT THERE WITH ME AND THE NEXT--HE'S GONE.
THAT'S NOT A FEELING I'M UNFAMILIAR WITH-- BUT IT IS A FEELING I DON'T THINK I'LL EVER GET USED TO.
IT'S UNSETTLING-- HARD TO SHAKE THE FEELING OF... HELPLESSNESS.
YEAH.
SO...UH, MARTINEZ, RIGHT? YOU ALWAYS A SOLDIER? YOU NATIONAL GUARD? SOMETHING LIKE THAT?
I AM-- WAS A GYM TEACHER.

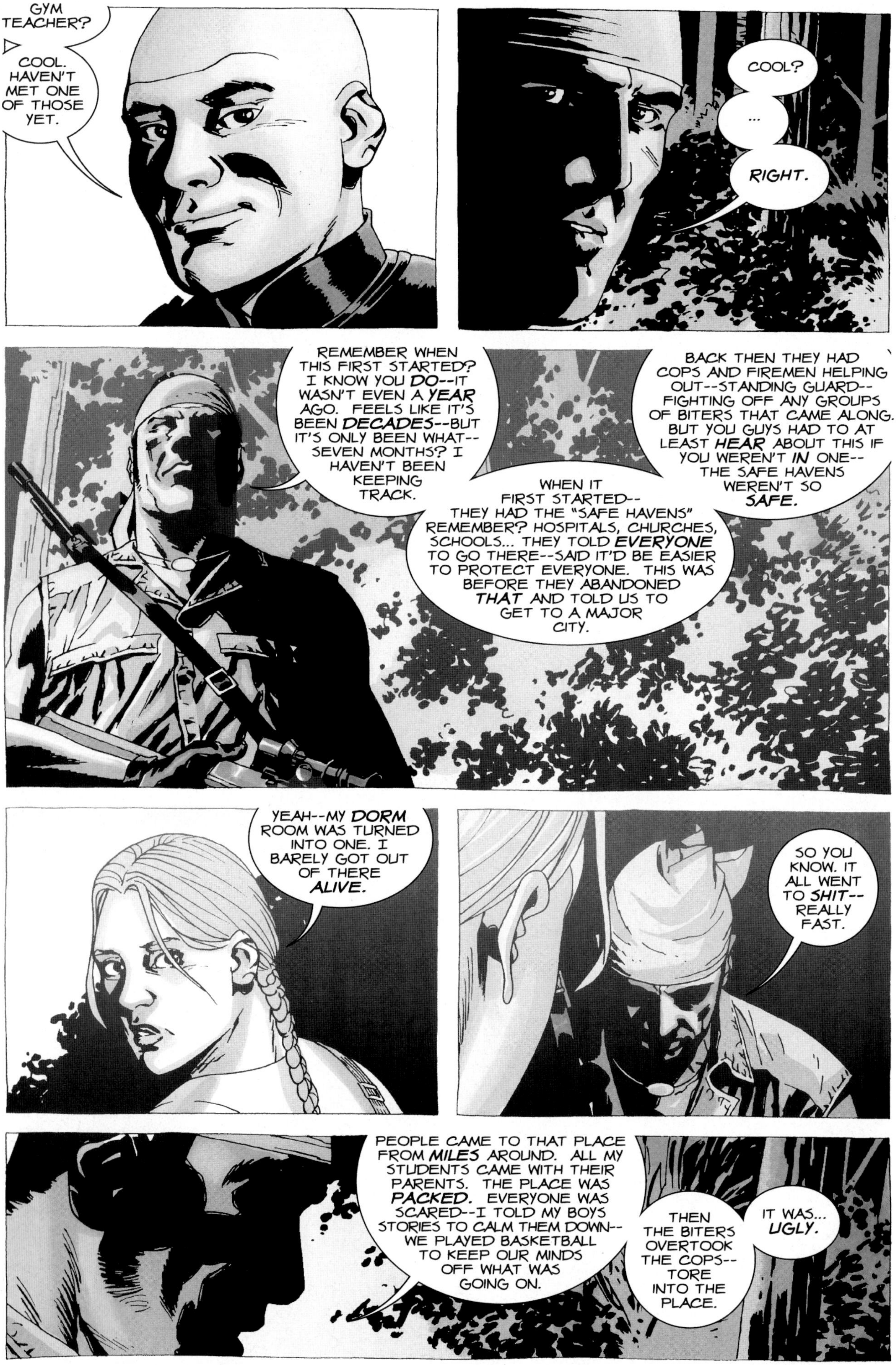
GYM TEACHER?
COOL. HAVEN'T MET ONE OF THOSE YET.
COOL?
...
RIGHT.
REMEMBER WHEN THIS FIRST STARTED? I KNOW YOU DO--IT WASN'T EVEN A YEAR AGO. FEELS LIKE IT'S BEEN DECADES--BUT IT'S ONLY BEEN WHAT--SEVEN MONTHS? I HAVEN'T BEEN KEEPING TRACK.
WHEN IT FIRST STARTED--THEY HAD THE "SAFE HAVENS" REMEMBER? HOSPITALS, CHURCHES, SCHOOLS... THEY TOLD EVERYONE TO GO THERE--SAID IT'D BE EASIER TO PROTECT EVERYONE. THIS WAS BEFORE THEY ABANDONED THAT AND TOLD US TO GET TO A MAJOR CITY.
BACK THEN THEY HAD COPS AND FIREMEN HELPING OUT--STANDING GUARD--FIGHTING OFF ANY GROUPS OF BITERS THAT CAME ALONG. BUT YOU GUYS HAD TO AT LEAST HEAR ABOUT THIS IF YOU WEREN'T IN ONE--THE SAFE HAVENS WEREN'T SO SAFE.
YEAH--MY DORM ROOM WAS TURNED INTO ONE. I BARELY GOT OUT OF THERE ALIVE.
SO YOU KNOW. IT ALL WENT TO SHIT--REALLY FAST.
PEOPLE CAME TO THAT PLACE FROM MILES AROUND. ALL MY STUDENTS CAME WITH THEIR PARENTS. THE PLACE WAS PACKED. EVERYONE WAS SCARED--I TOLD MY BOYS STORIES TO CALM THEM DOWN--WE PLAYED BASKETBALL TO KEEP OUR MINDS OFF WHAT WAS GOING ON.
THEN THE BITERS OVERTOOK THE COPS--TORE INTO THE PLACE.
IT WAS... UGLY.

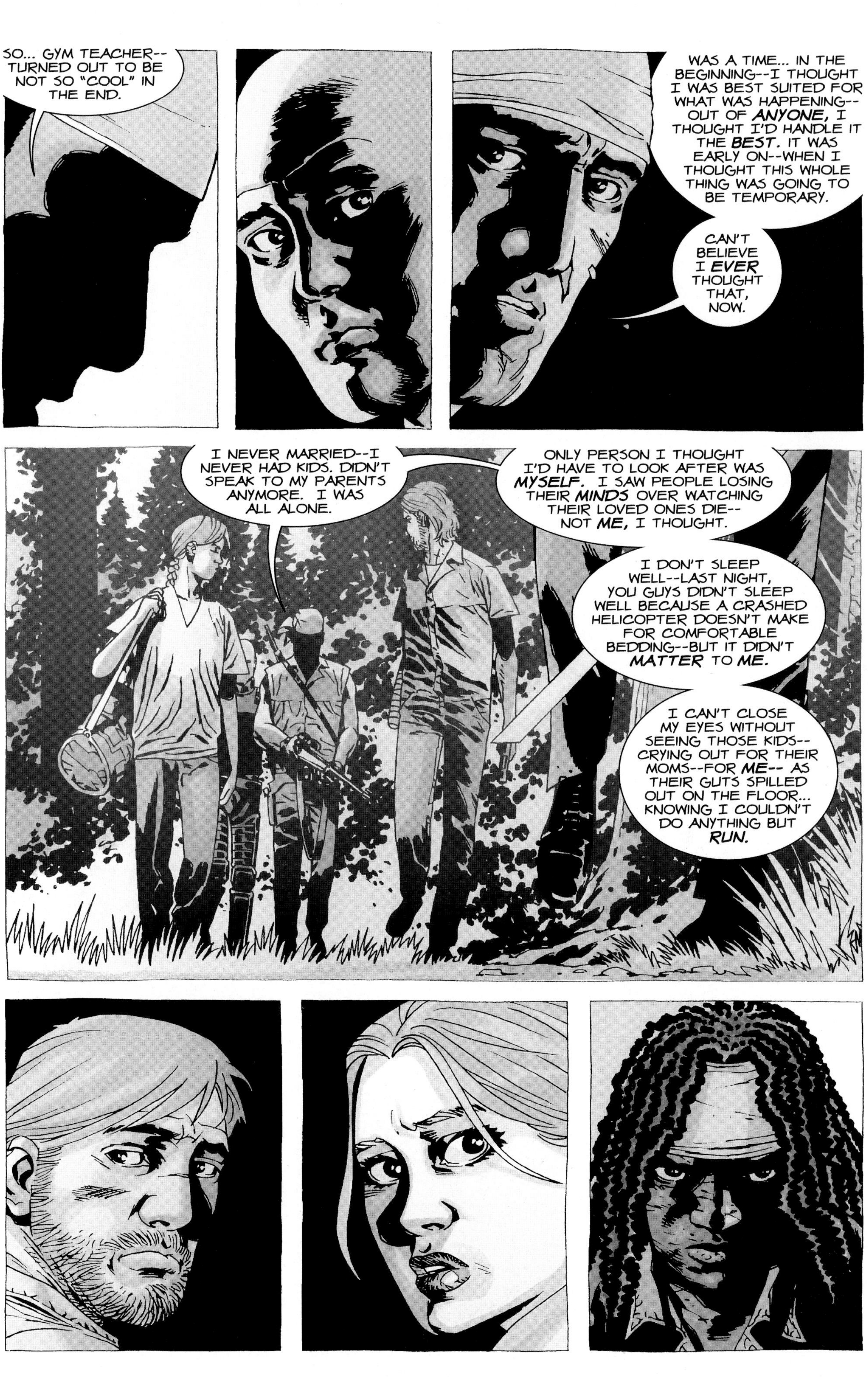
SO... GYM TEACHER-- TURNED OUT TO BE NOT SO "COOL" IN THE END.
WAS A TIME... IN THE BEGINNING--I THOUGHT I WAS BEST SUITED FOR WHAT WAS HAPPENING-- OUT OF ANYONE, I THOUGHT I'D HANDLE IT THE BEST. IT WAS EARLY ON--WHEN I THOUGHT THIS WHOLE THING WAS GOING TO BE TEMPORARY.
CAN'T BELIEVE I EVER THOUGHT THAT, NOW.
I NEVER MARRIED--I NEVER HAD KIDS. DIDN'T SPEAK TO MY PARENTS ANYMORE. I WAS ALL ALONE.
ONLY PERSON I THOUGHT I'D HAVE TO LOOK AFTER WAS MYSELF. I SAW PEOPLE LOSING THEIR MINDS OVER WATCHING THEIR LOVED ONES DIE-- NOT ME, I THOUGHT.
I DON'T SLEEP WELL--LAST NIGHT, YOU GUYS DIDN'T SLEEP WELL BECAUSE A CRASHED HELICOPTER DOESN'T MAKE FOR COMFORTABLE BEDDING--BUT IT DIDN'T MATTER TO ME.
I CAN'T CLOSE MY EYES WITHOUT SEEING THOSE KIDS-- CRYING OUT FOR THEIR MOMS--FOR ME-- AS THEIR GUTS SPILLED OUT ON THE FLOOR... KNOWING I COULDN'T DO ANYTHING BUT RUN.

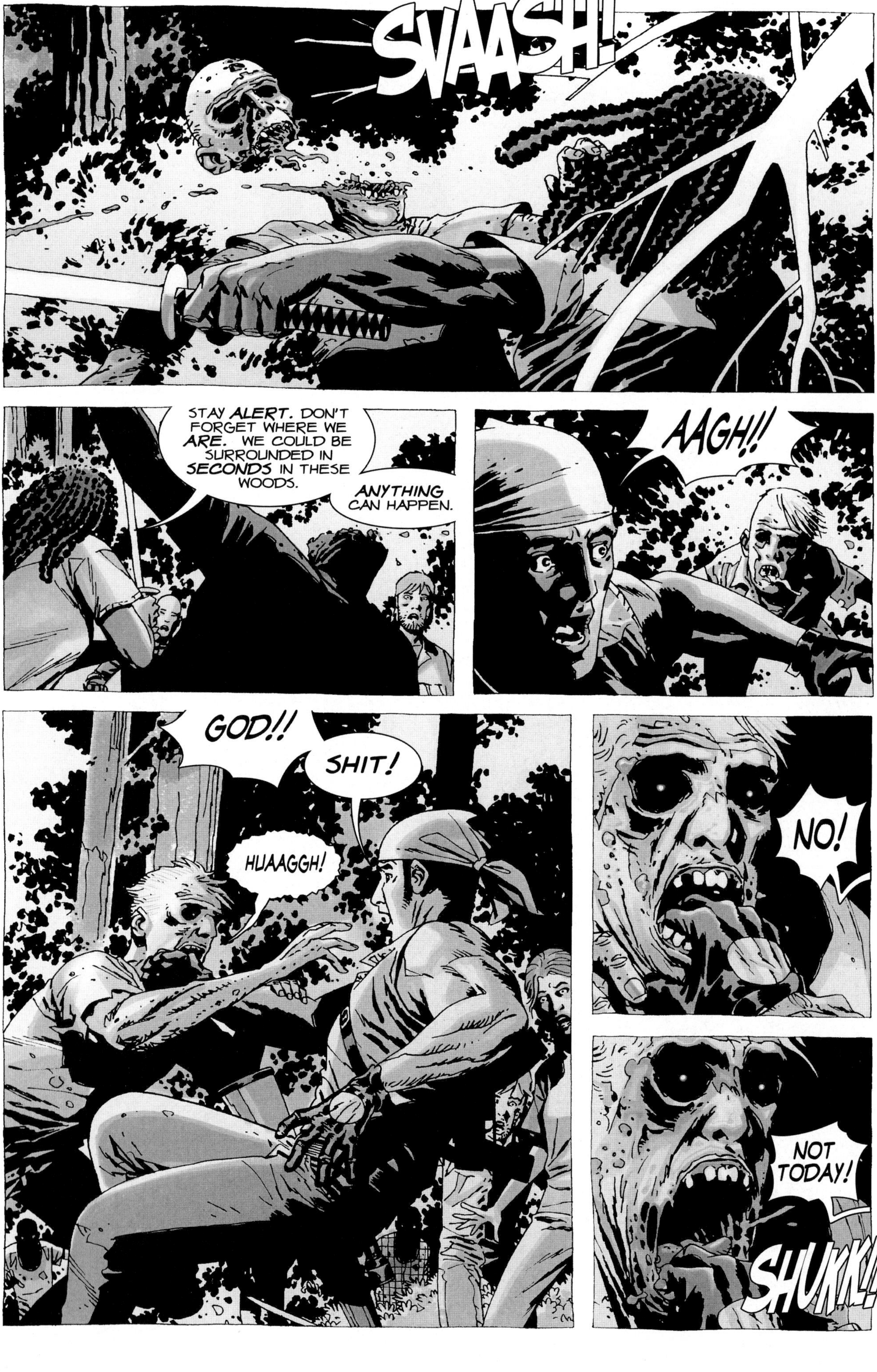
SVAASH!
STAY ALERT. DON'T FORGET WHERE WE ARE. WE COULD BE SURROUNDED IN SECONDS IN THESE WOODS.
ANYTHING CAN HAPPEN.
AAGH!!
GOD!!
SHIT!
HUAAGGH!
NO!
NOT TODAY!
SHUKK!!

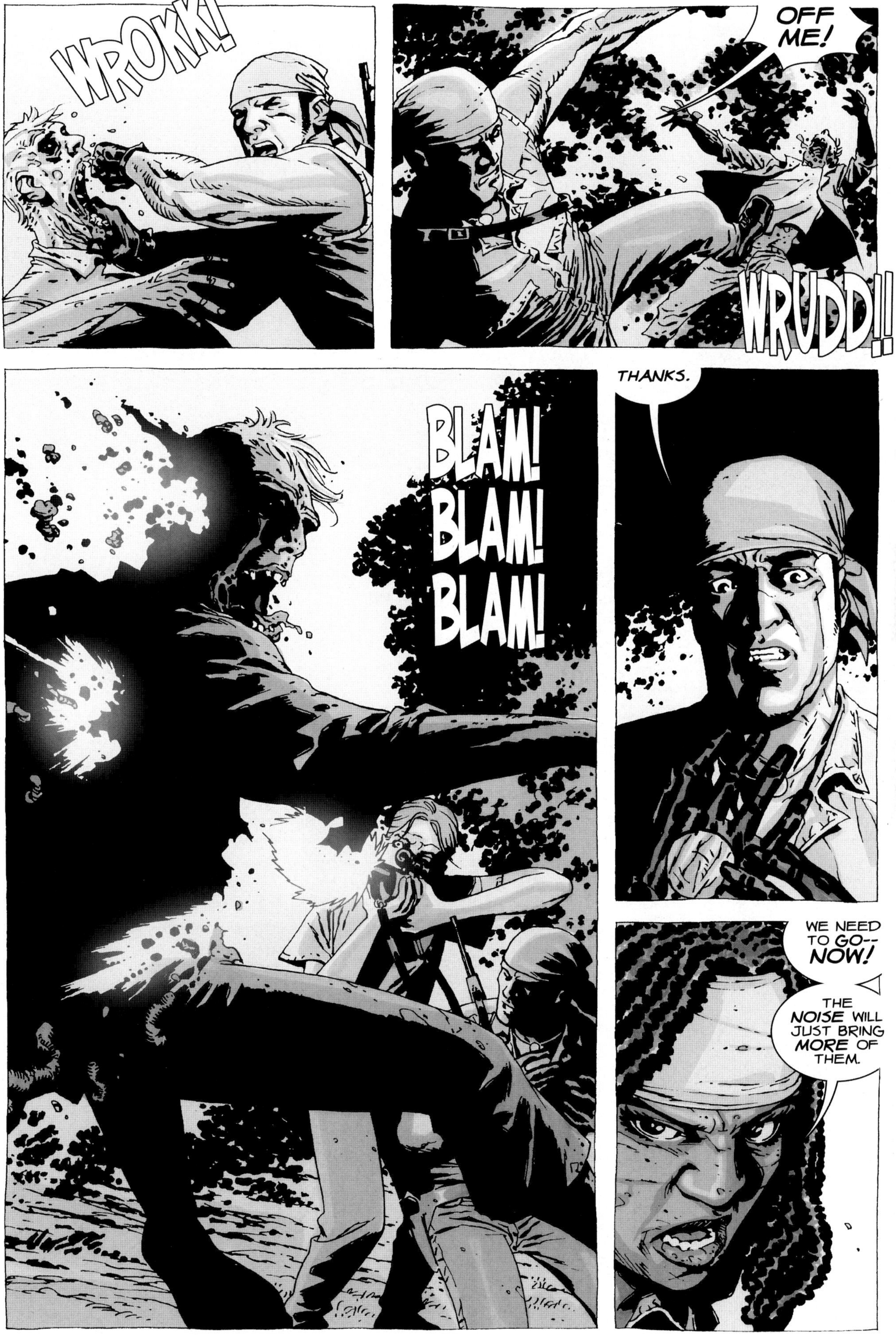
WROKK!
OFF ME!
WRUDD!!
BLAM! BLAM! BLAM!
THANKS.
WE NEED TO GO-- NOW!
THE NOISE WILL JUST BRING MORE OF THEM.

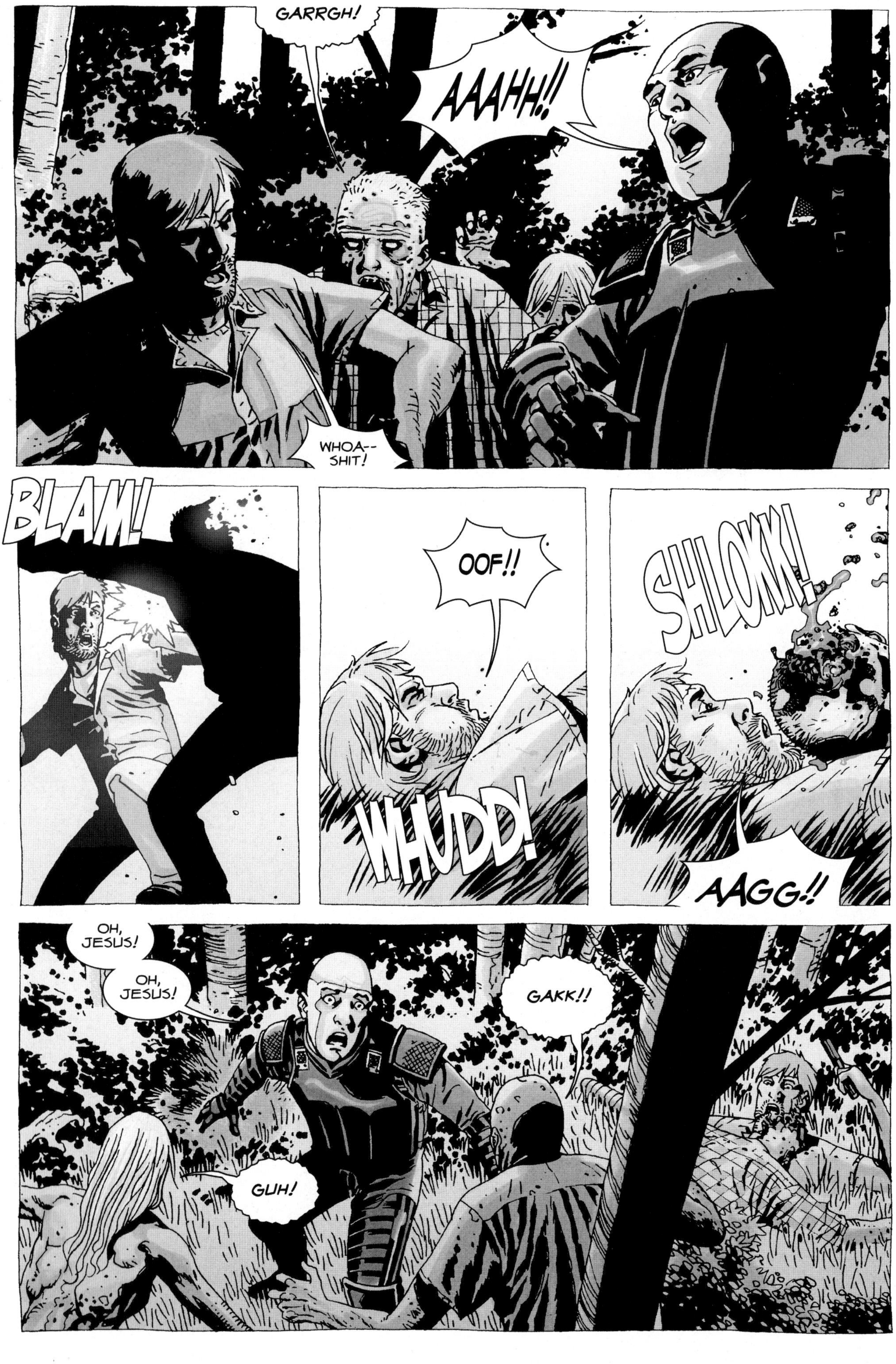

GARRGH!
AAAHH!!
WHOA-- SHIT!
BLAM!
OOF!!
WHUDD!
SHLOKK!
AAGG!!
OH, JESUS!
OH, JESUS!
GAKK!!
GUH!

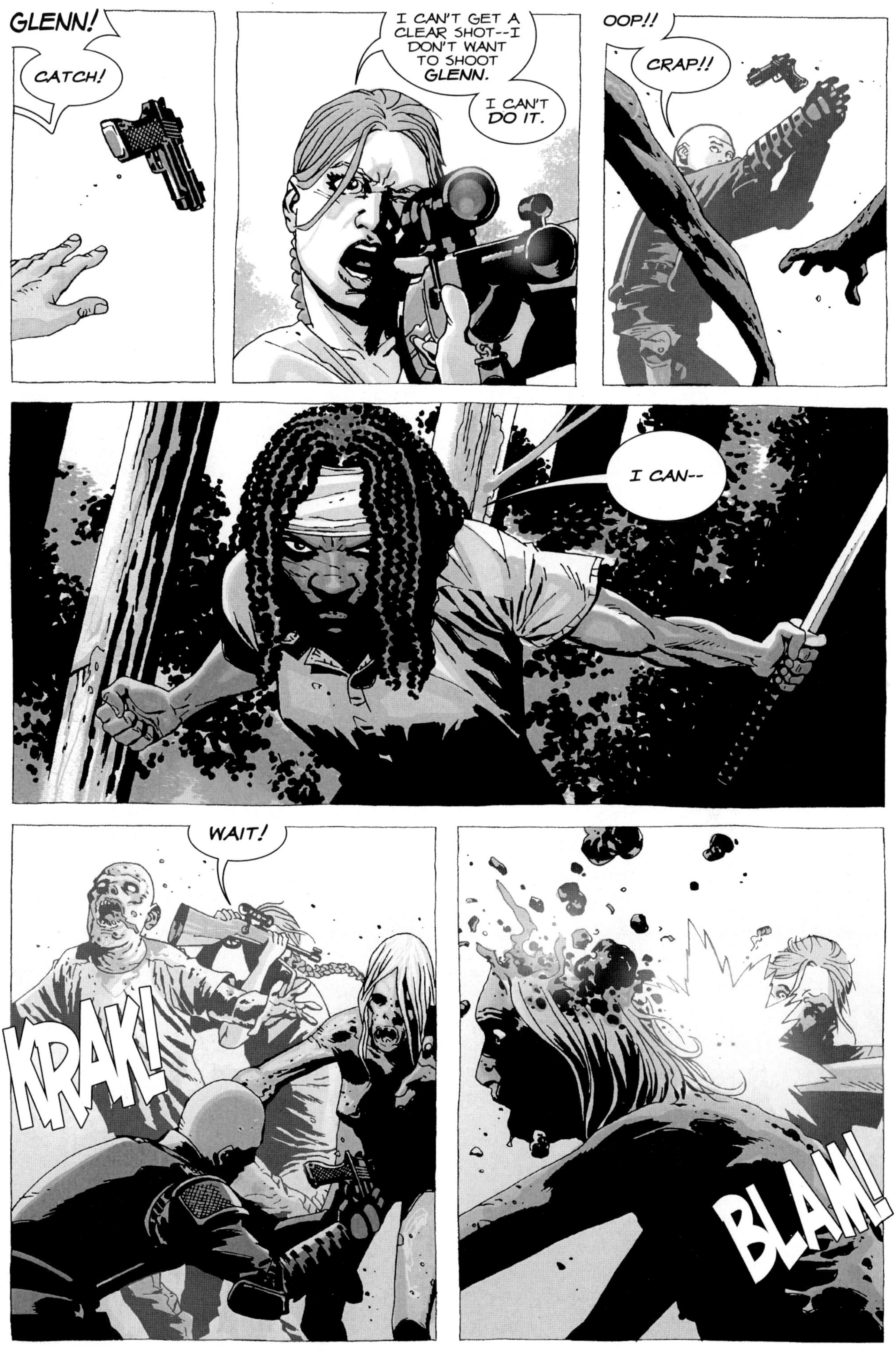
GLENN!
CATCH!
I CAN'T GET A CLEAR SHOT--I DON'T WANT TO SHOOT GLENN.
I CAN'T DO IT.
OOP!!
CRAP!!
I CAN--
WAIT!
KRAK!
BLAM!

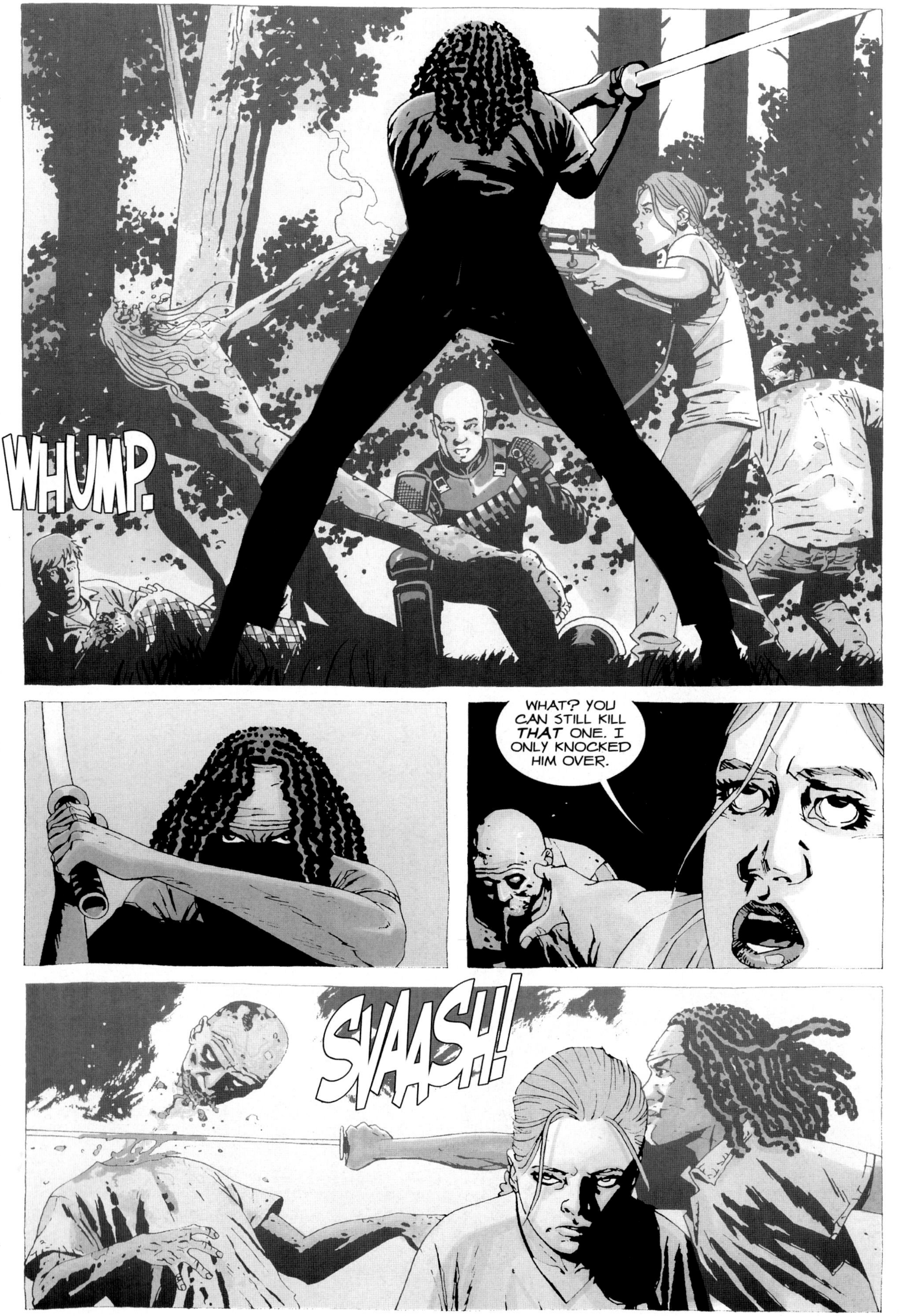
WHUMP.
WHAT? YOU CAN STILL KILL THAT ONE. I ONLY KNOCKED HIM OVER.
SVAASH!

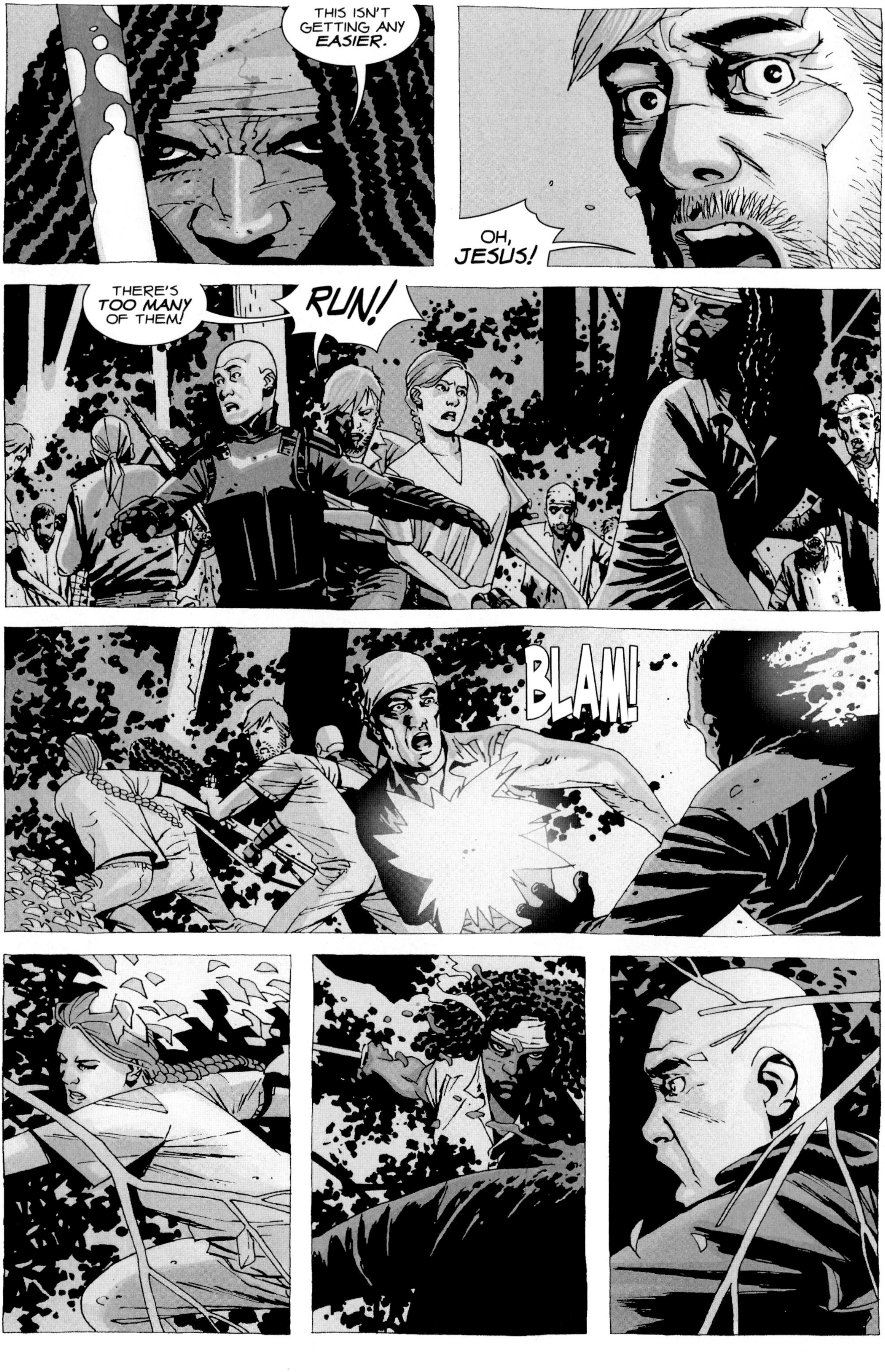
THIS ISN'T GETTING ANY EASIER.
OH, JESUS!
THERE'S TOO MANY OF THEM!
RUN!
BLAM!

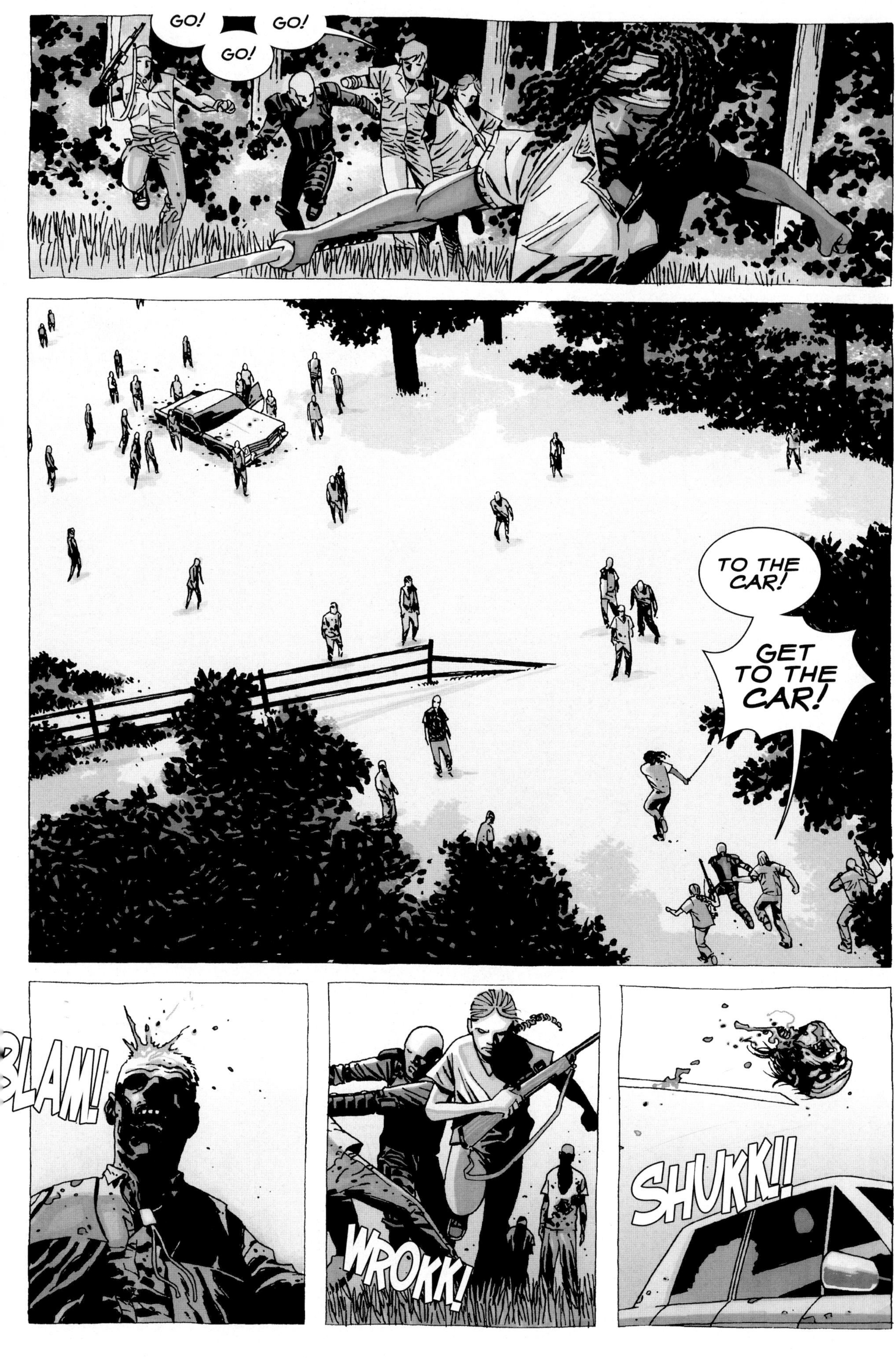
GO!
GO!
GO!
TO THE CAR!
GET TO THE CAR!
BLAM!
WROKK!
SHUKK!!

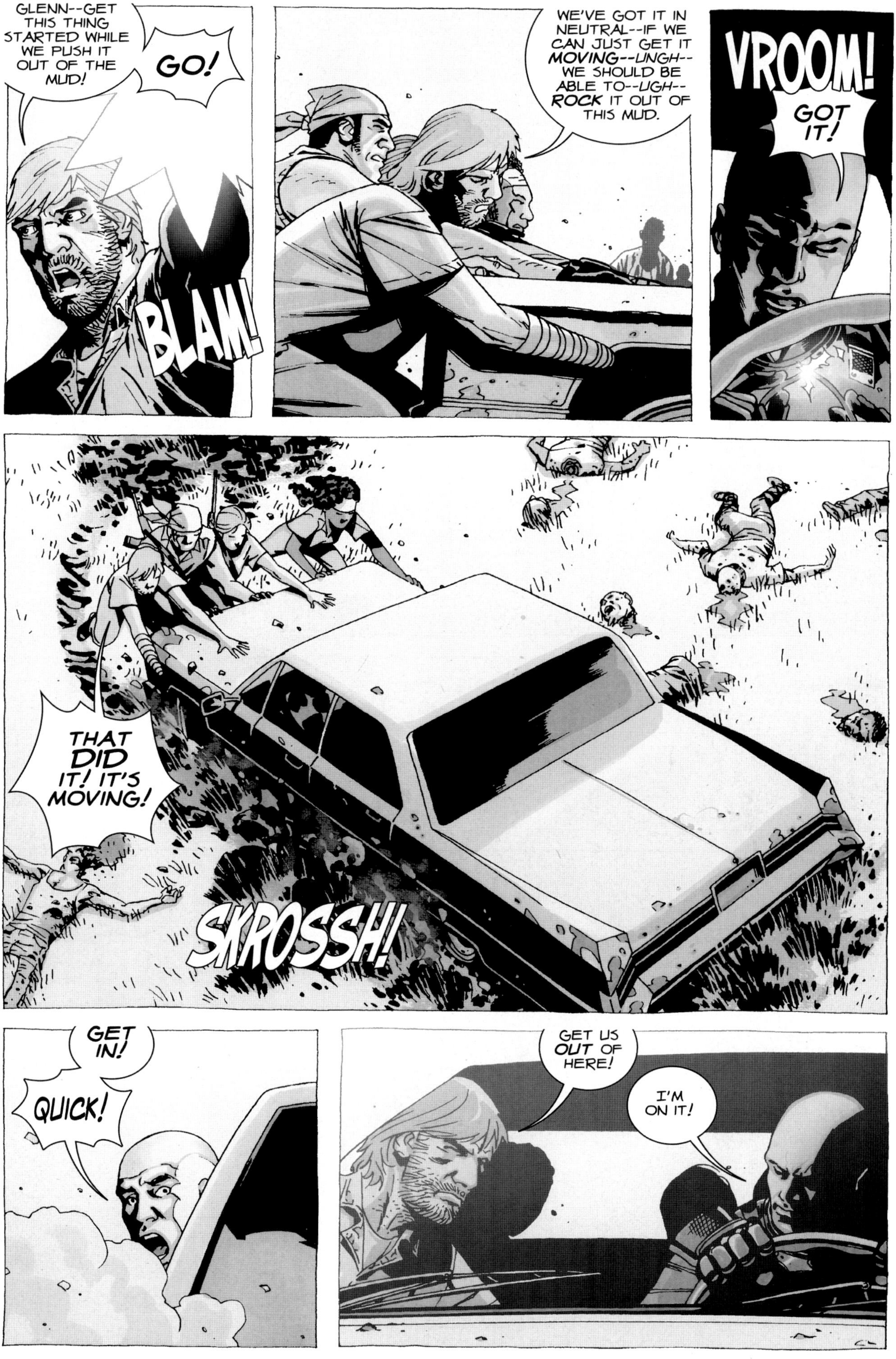
GLENN--GET THIS THING STARTED WHILE WE PUSH IT OUT OF THE MUD!
GO!
BLAM!
WE'VE GOT IT IN NEUTRAL--IF WE CAN JUST GET IT MOVING--UNGH-- WE SHOULD BE ABLE TO--UGH-- ROCK IT OUT OF THIS MUD.
VROOM!
GOT IT!
THAT DID IT! IT'S MOVING!
SKROSSH!
GET IN!
QUICK!
GET US OUT OF HERE!
I'M ON IT!

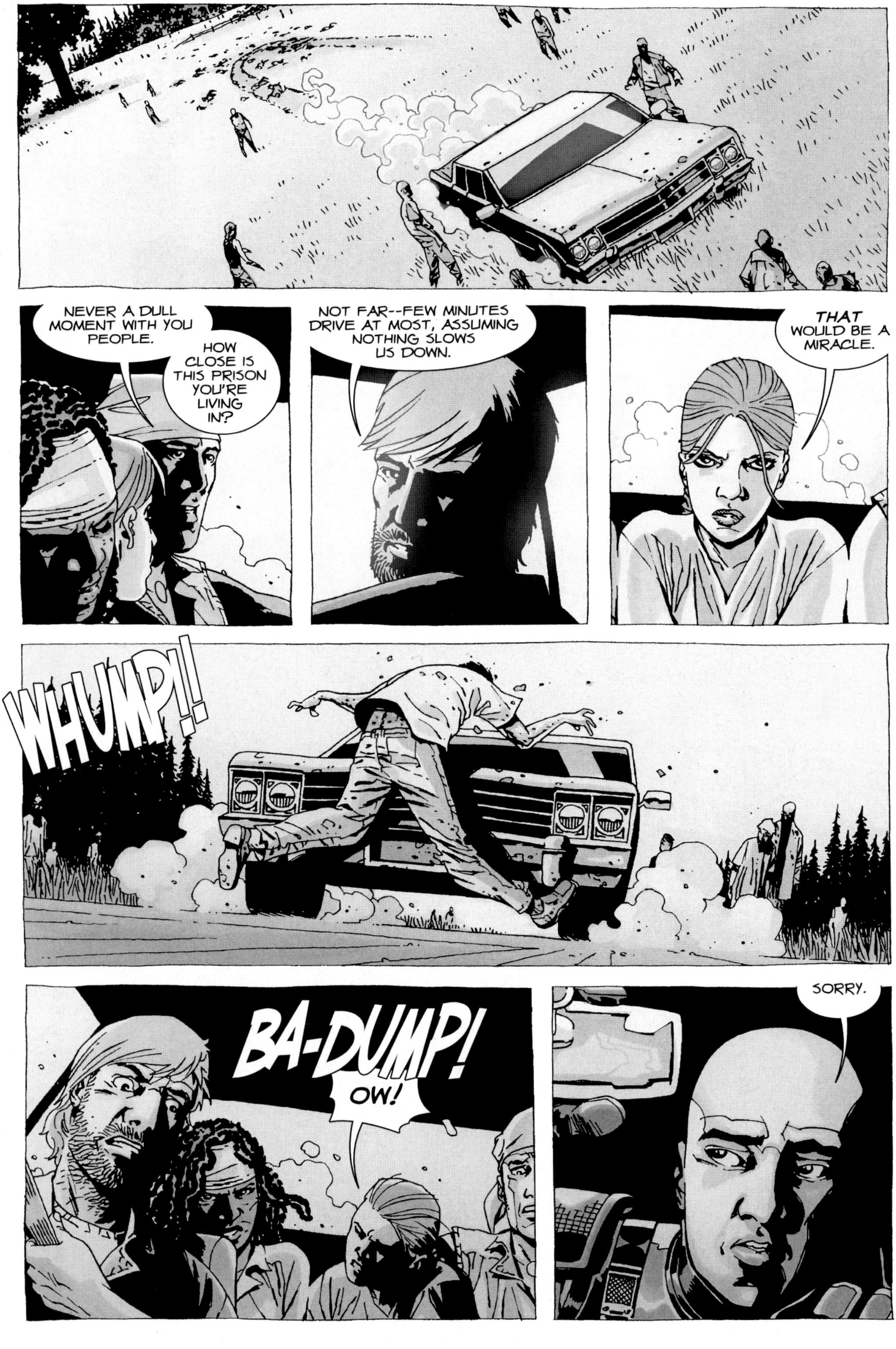
NEVER A DULL MOMENT WITH YOU PEOPLE.
HOW CLOSE IS THIS PRISON YOU'RE LIVING IN?
NOT FAR--FEW MINUTES DRIVE AT MOST, ASSUMING NOTHING SLOWS US DOWN.
THAT WOULD BE A MIRACLE.
WHUMP!!
BA-DUMP!
OW!
SORRY.

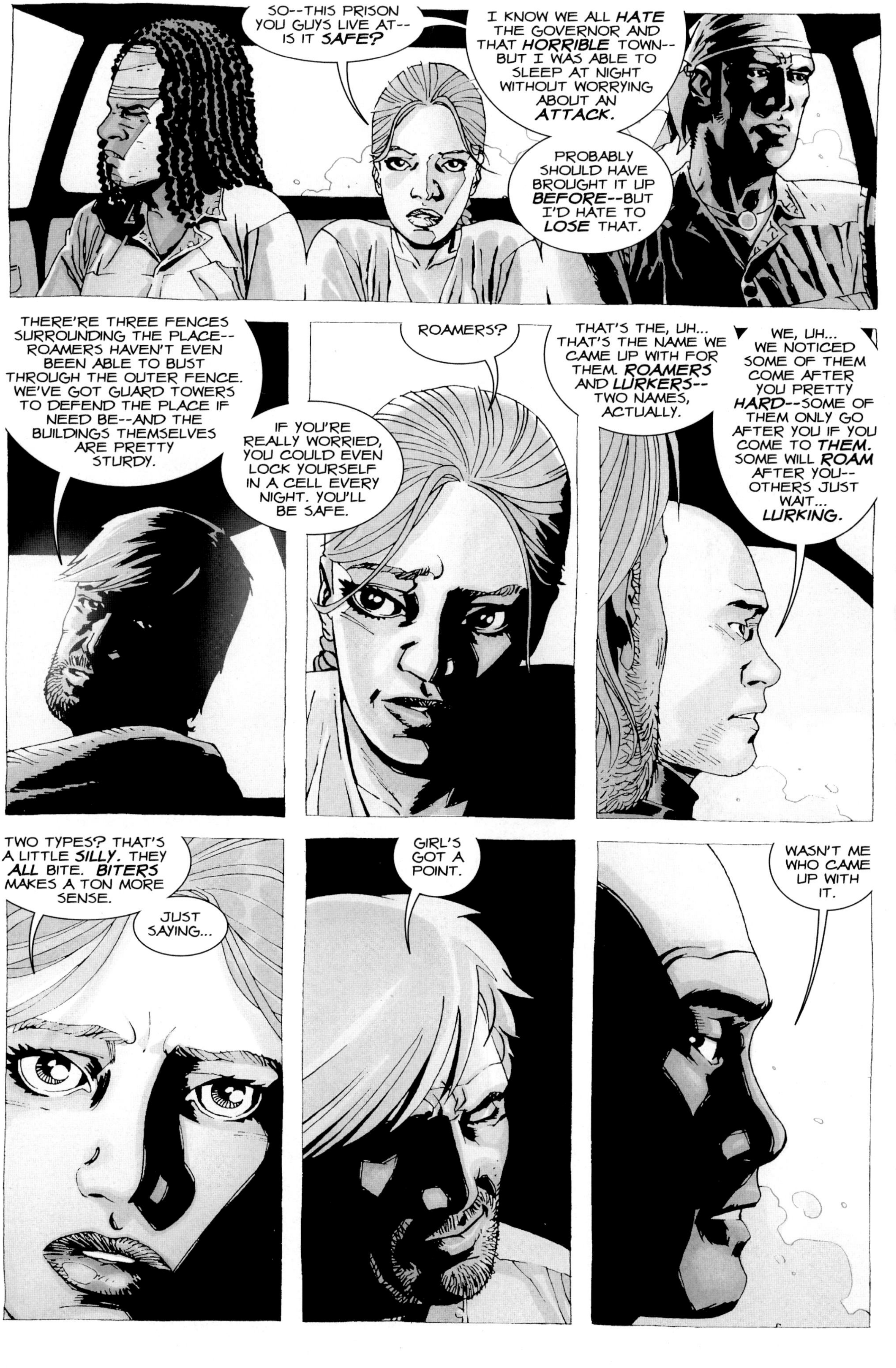
SO--THIS PRISON YOU GUYS LIVE AT-- IS IT SAFE?
I KNOW WE ALL HATE THE GOVERNOR AND THAT HORRIBLE TOWN-- BUT I WAS ABLE TO SLEEP AT NIGHT WITHOUT WORRYING ABOUT AN ATTACK.
PROBABLY SHOULD HAVE BROUGHT IT UP BEFORE--BUT I'D HATE TO LOSE THAT.
THERE'RE THREE FENCES SURROUNDING THE PLACE-- ROAMERS HAVEN'T EVEN BEEN ABLE TO BUST THROUGH THE OUTER FENCE. WE'VE GOT GUARD TOWERS TO DEFEND THE PLACE IF NEED BE--AND THE BUILDINGS THEMSELVES ARE PRETTY STURDY.
IF YOU'RE REALLY WORRIED, YOU COULD EVEN LOCK YOURSELF IN A CELL EVERY NIGHT. YOU'LL BE SAFE.
ROAMERS?
THAT'S THE, UH... THAT'S THE NAME WE CAME UP WITH FOR THEM. ROAMERS AND LURKERS-- TWO NAMES, ACTUALLY.
WE, UH... WE NOTICED SOME OF THEM COME AFTER YOU PRETTY HARD--SOME OF THEM ONLY GO AFTER YOU IF YOU COME TO THEM. SOME WILL ROAM AFTER YOU-- OTHERS JUST WAIT... LURKING.
TWO TYPES? THAT'S A LITTLE SILLY. THEY ALL BITE. BITERS MAKES A TON MORE SENSE.
JUST SAYING...
GIRL'S GOT A POINT.
WASN'T ME WHO CAME UP WITH IT.

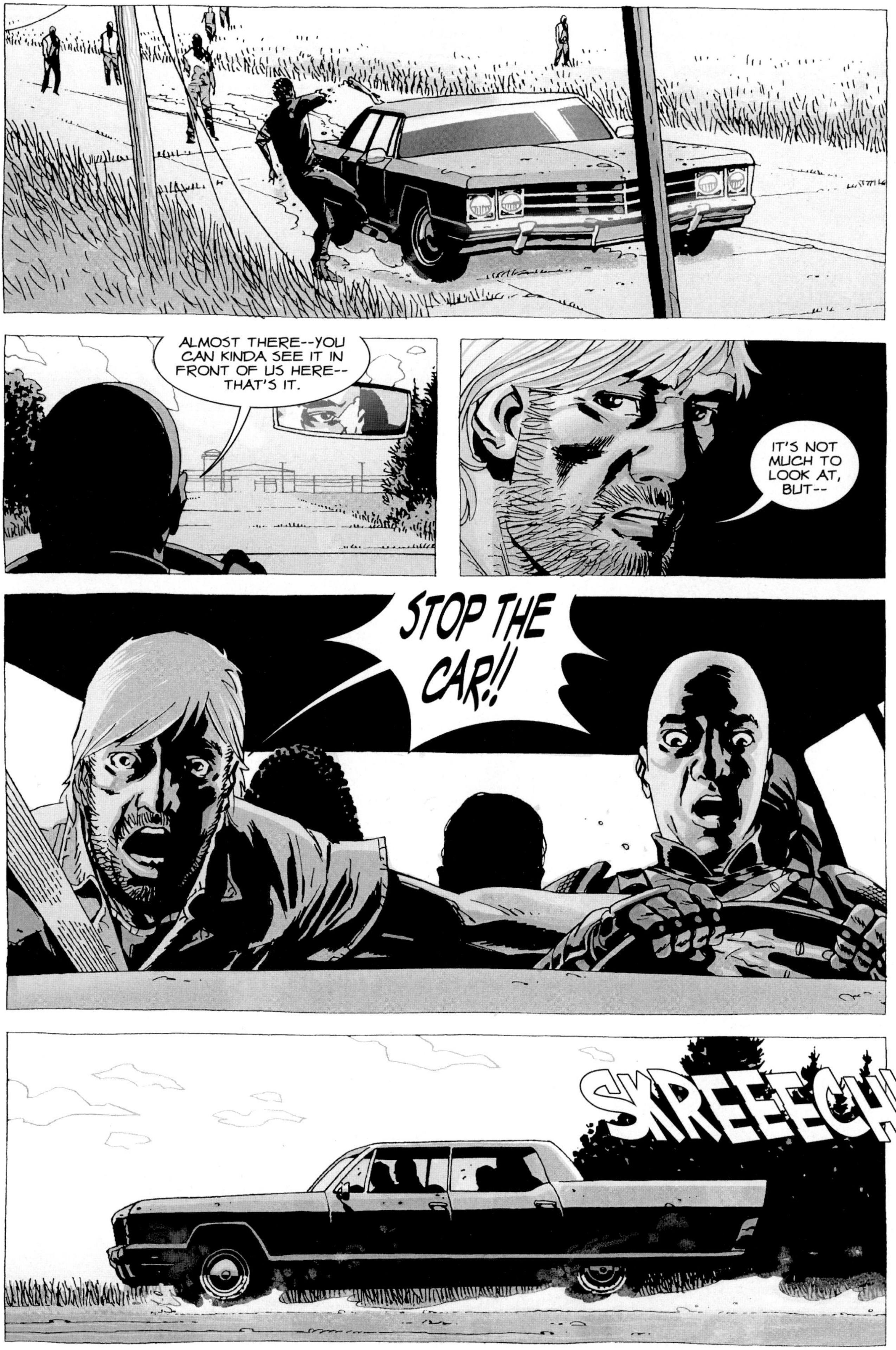
ALMOST THERE--YOU CAN KINDA SEE IT IN FRONT OF US HERE--THAT'S IT.
IT'S NOT MUCH TO LOOK AT, BUT--
STOP THE CAR!!
SKREEEECH!

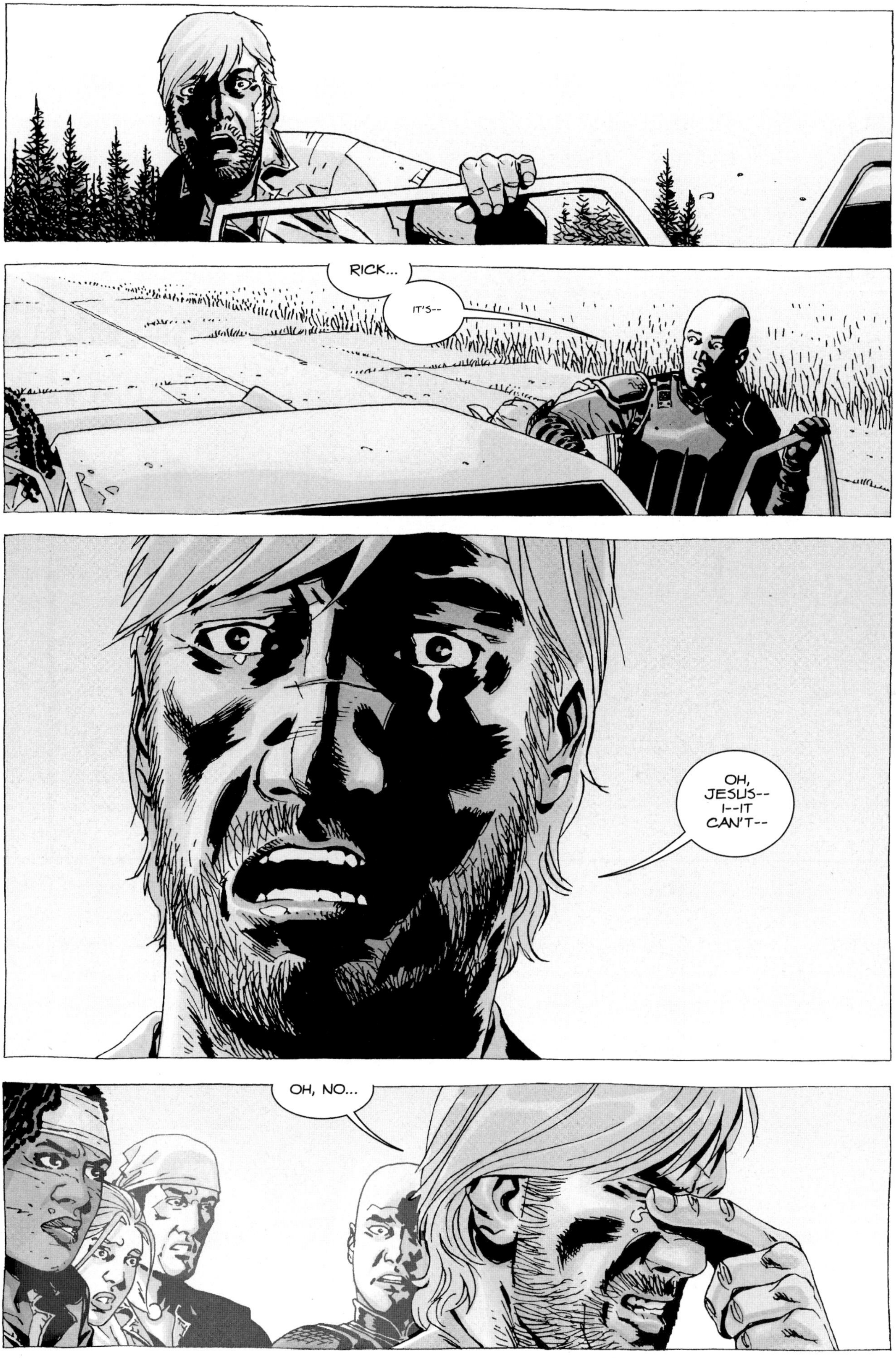
RICK...
IT'S--
OH, JESUS-- I--IT CAN'T--
OH, NO...

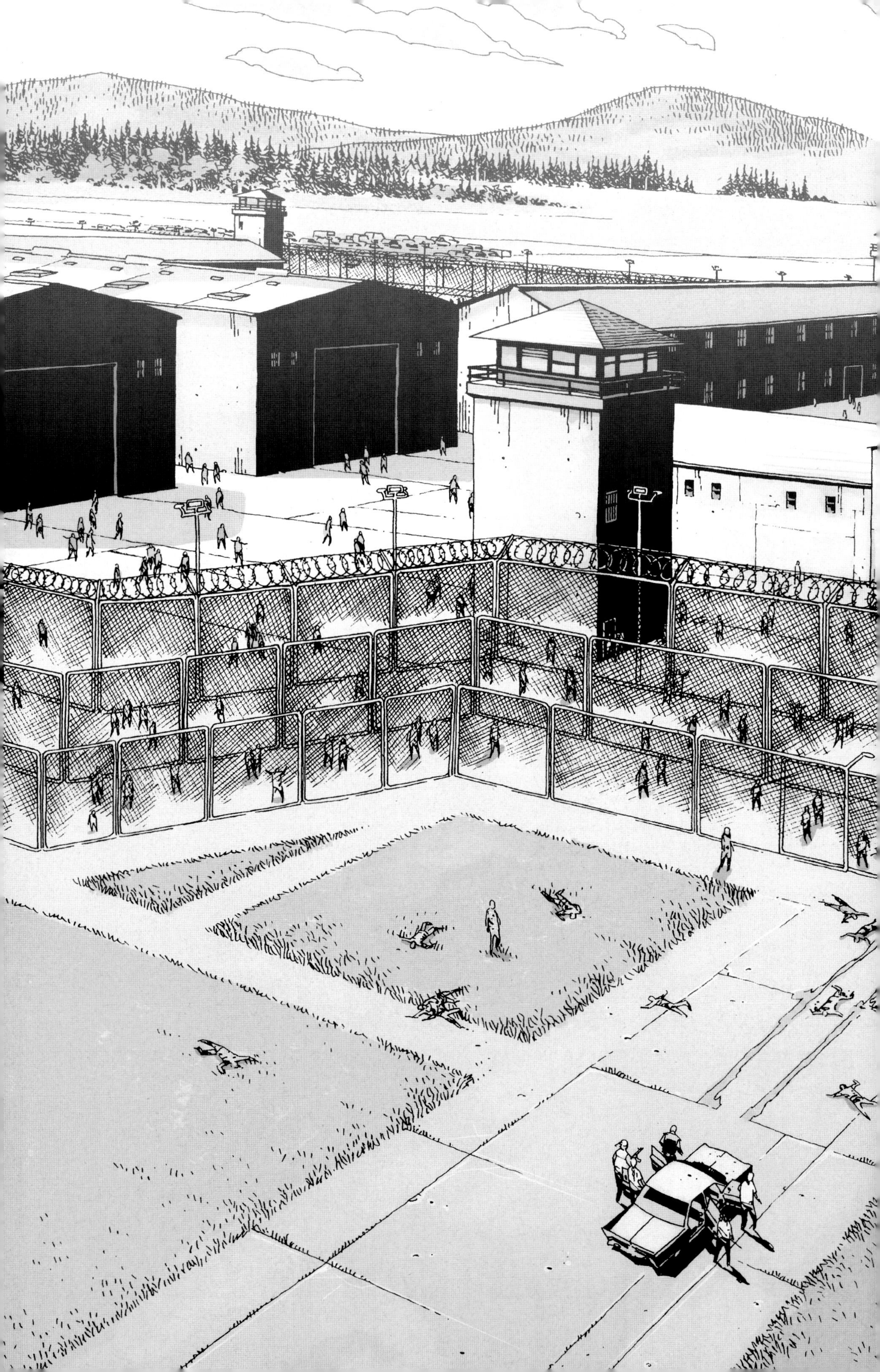

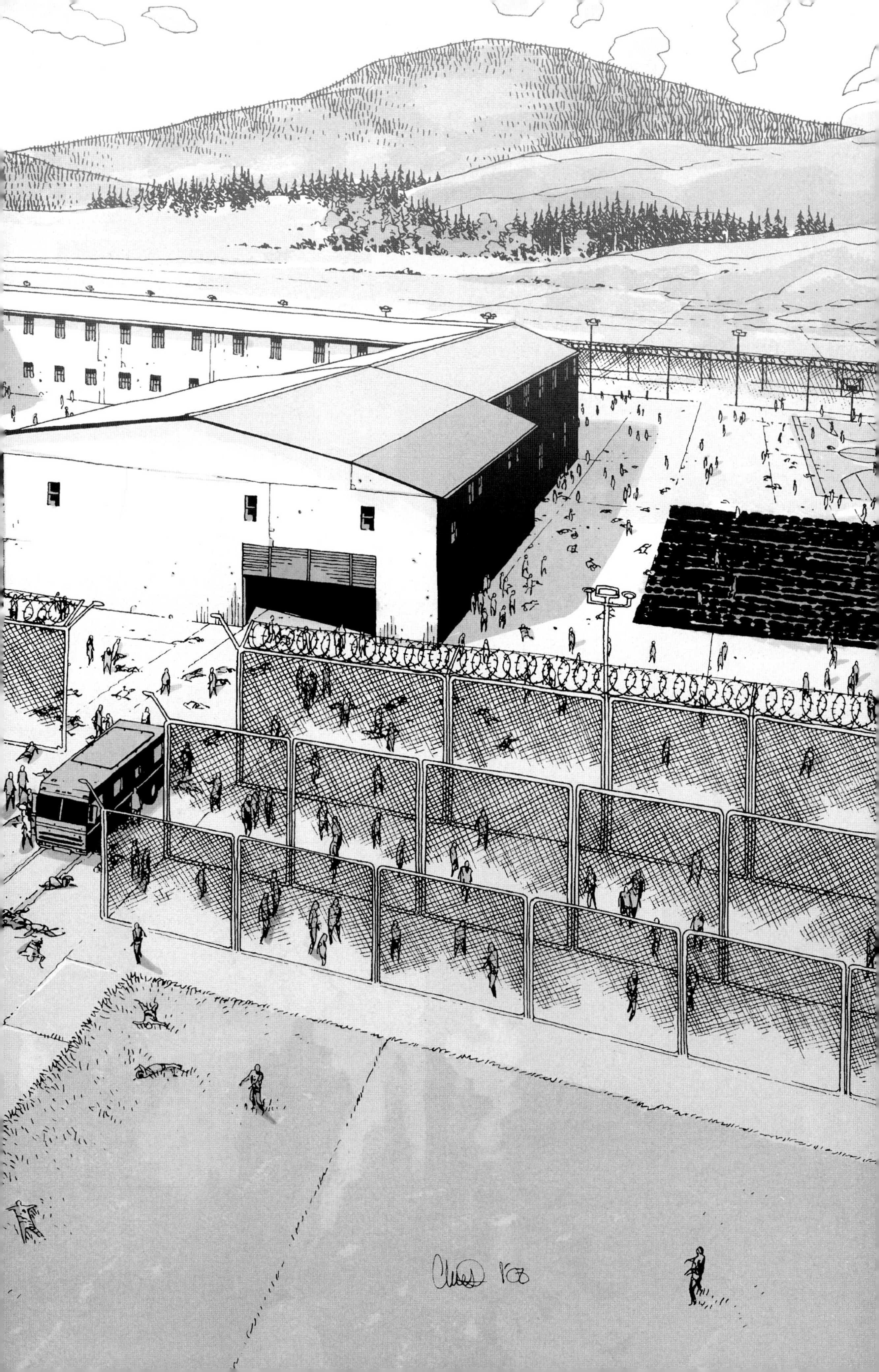

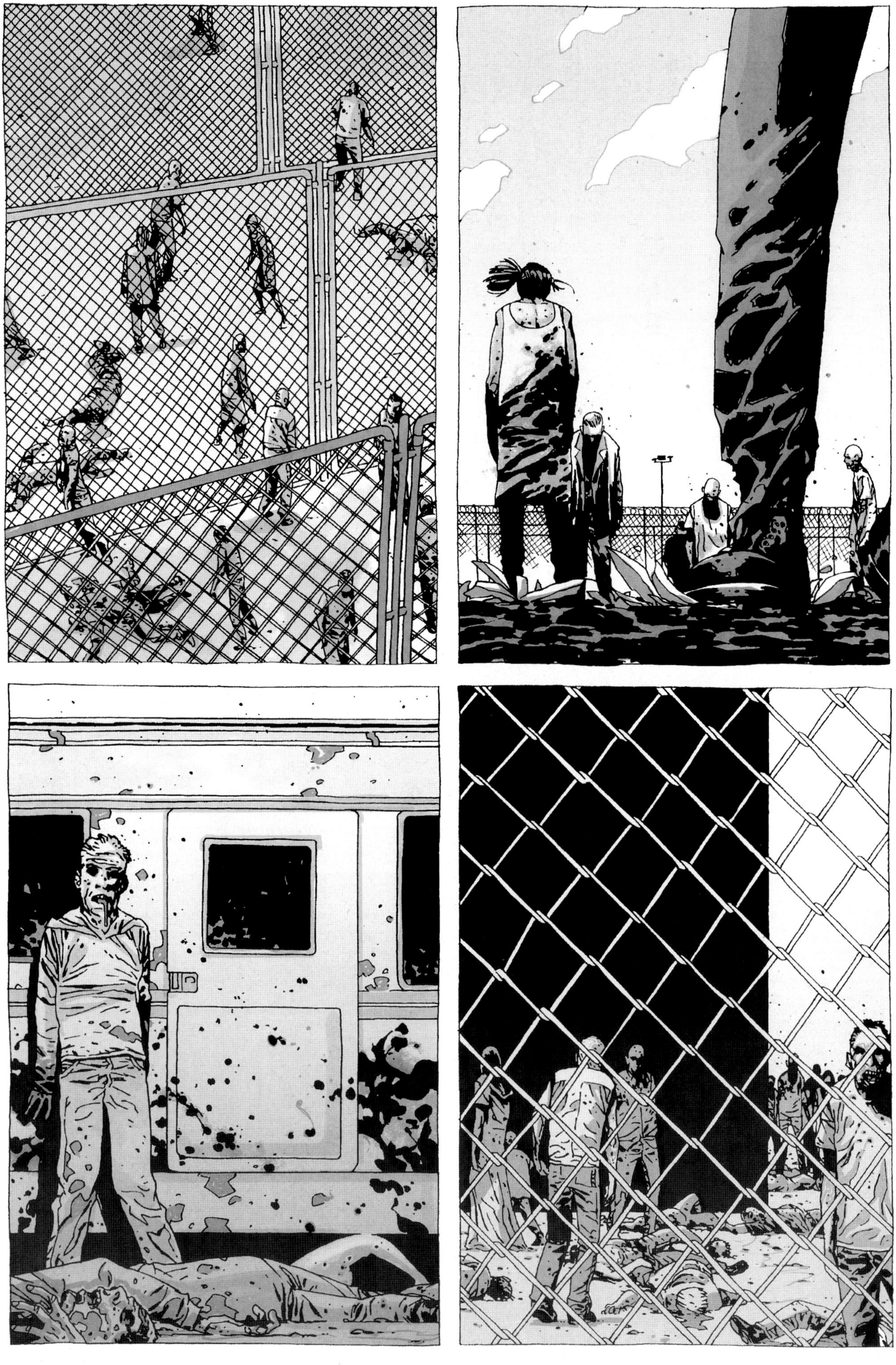

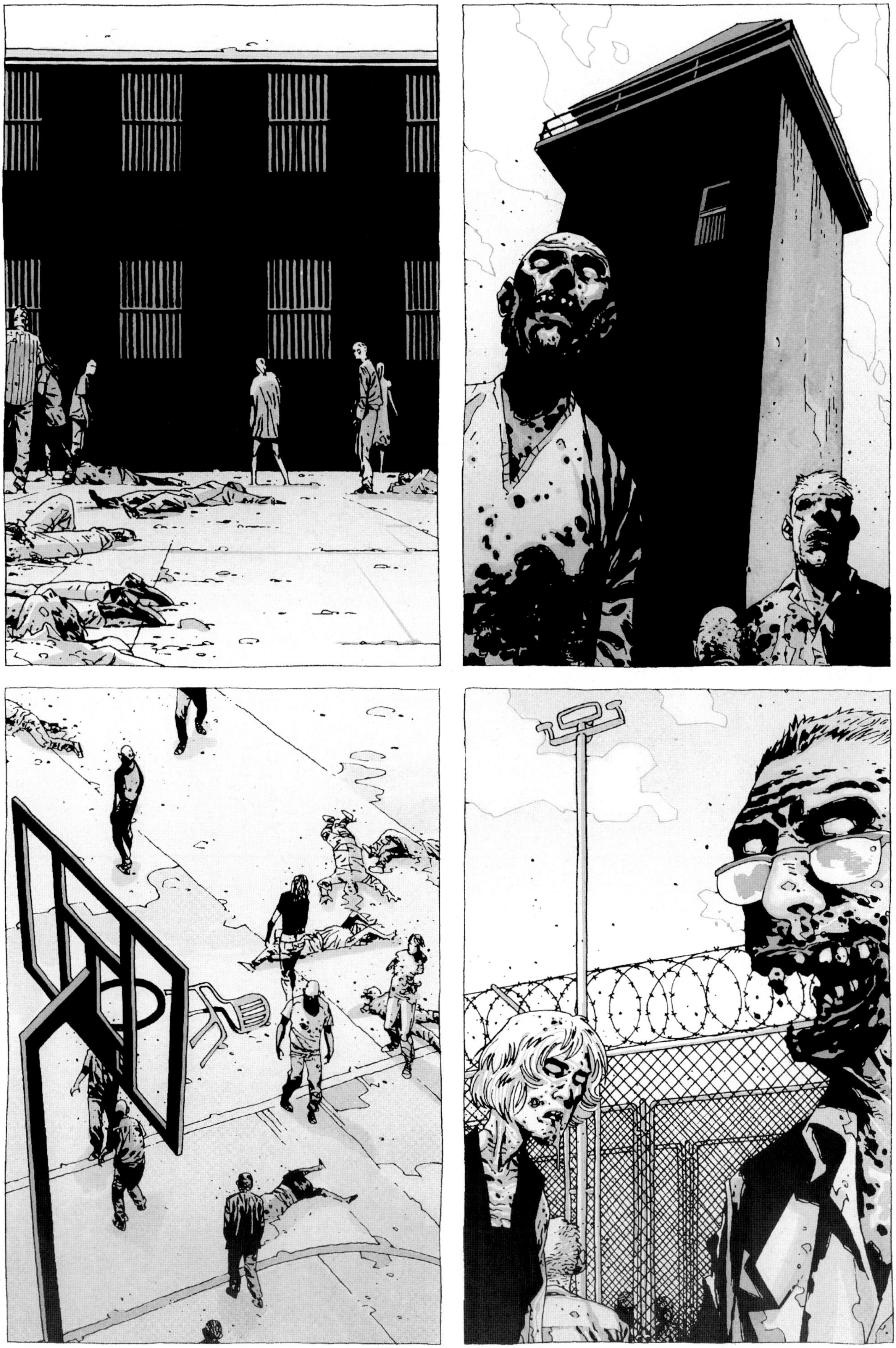

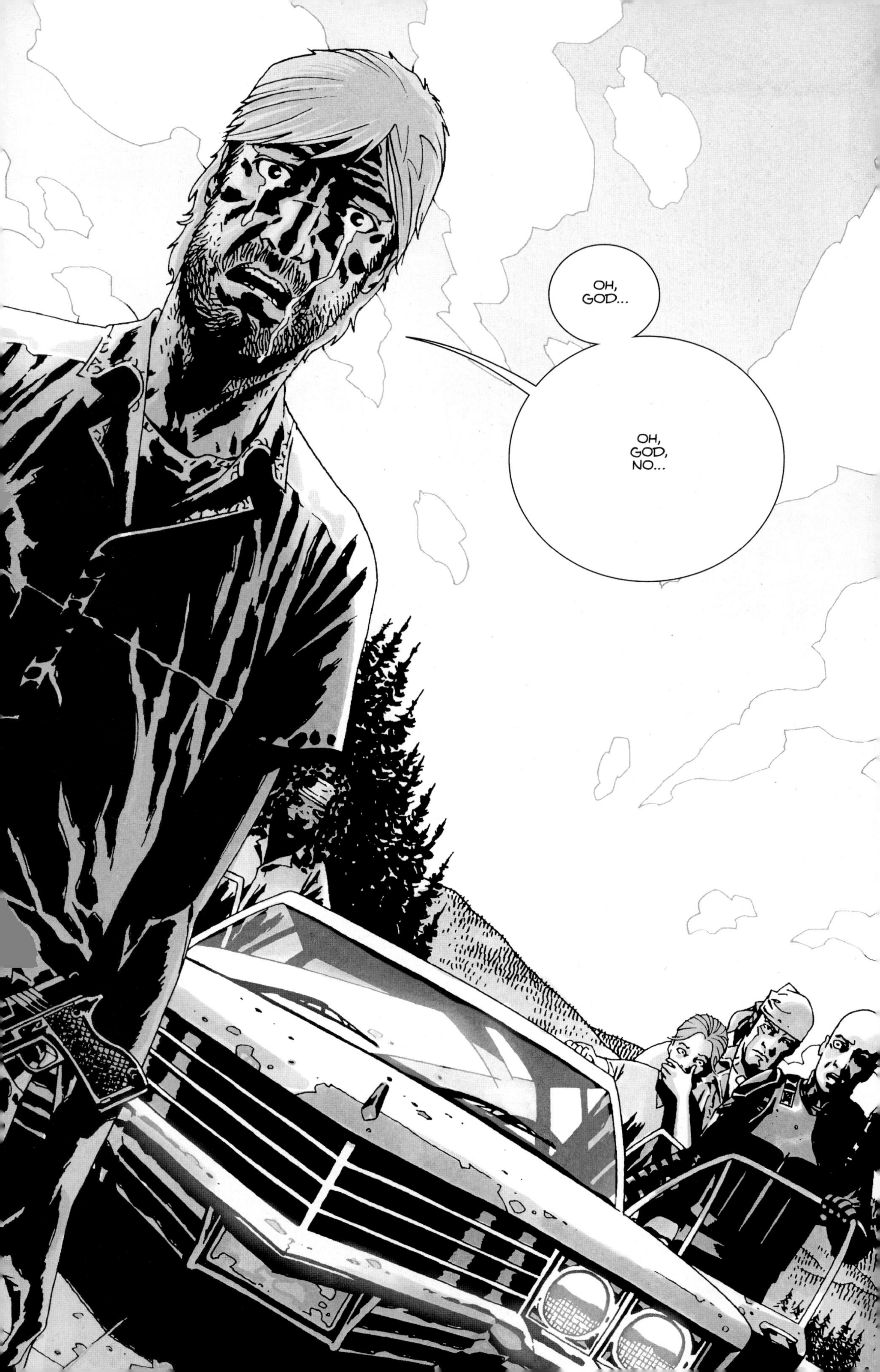
OH, GOD...
OH, GOD, NO...

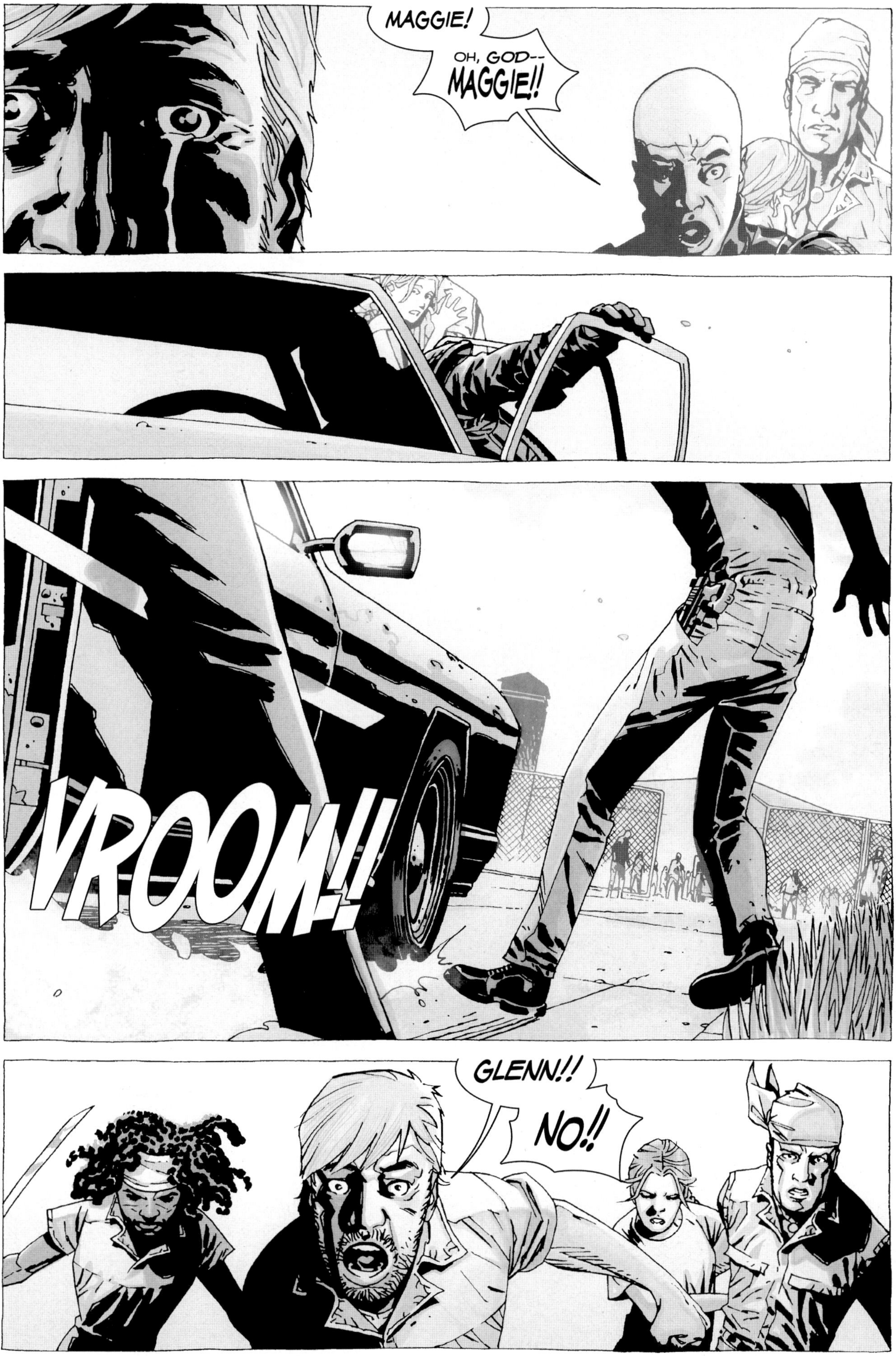
MAGGIE!
OH, GOD--
MAGGIE!!
VROOM!!
GLENN!!
NO!!

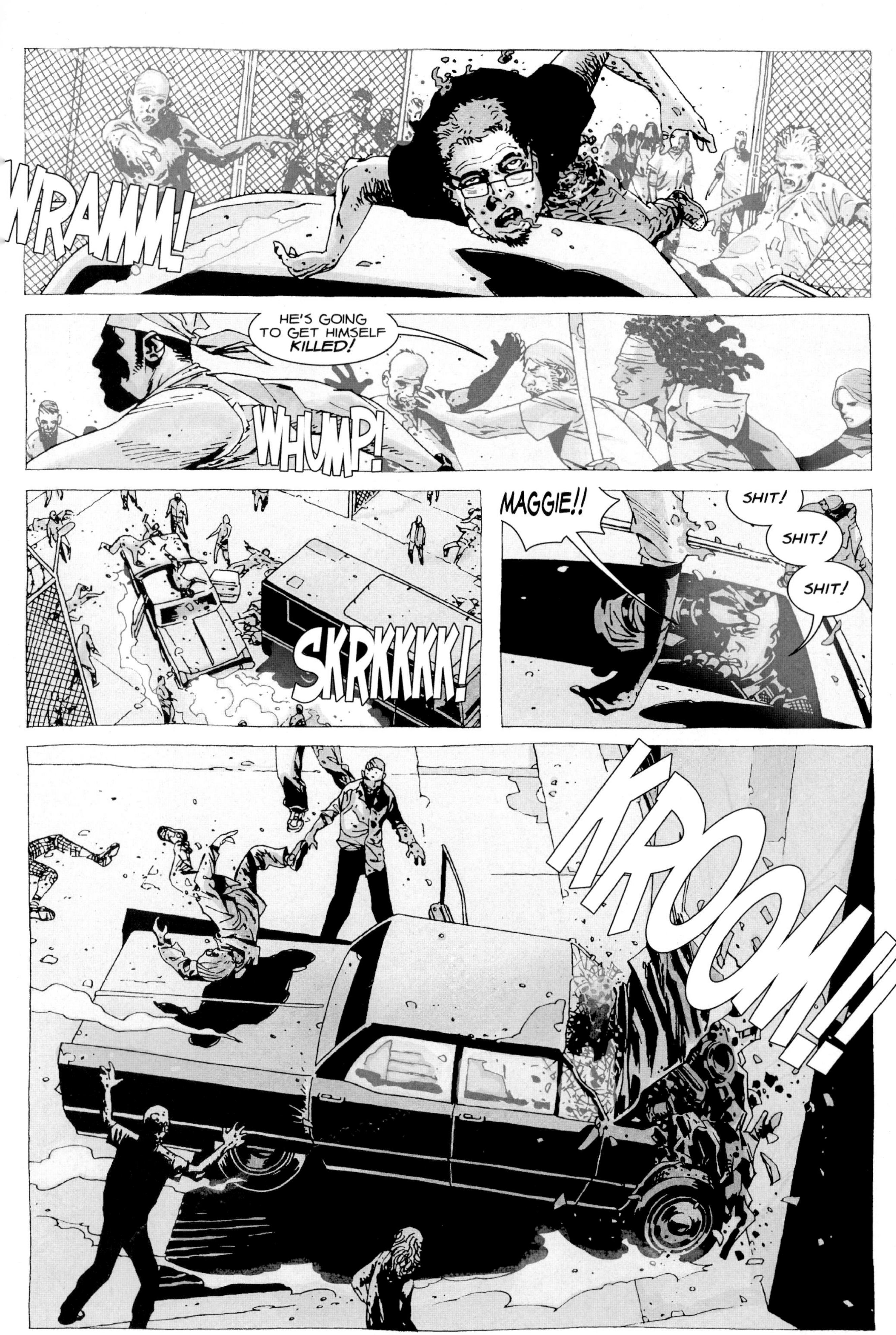
WRAMM!
HE'S GOING TO GET HIMSELF KILLED!
WHUMP!
SKRKKKK!
MAGGIE!!
SHIT!
SHIT!
SHIT!
KROOM!!

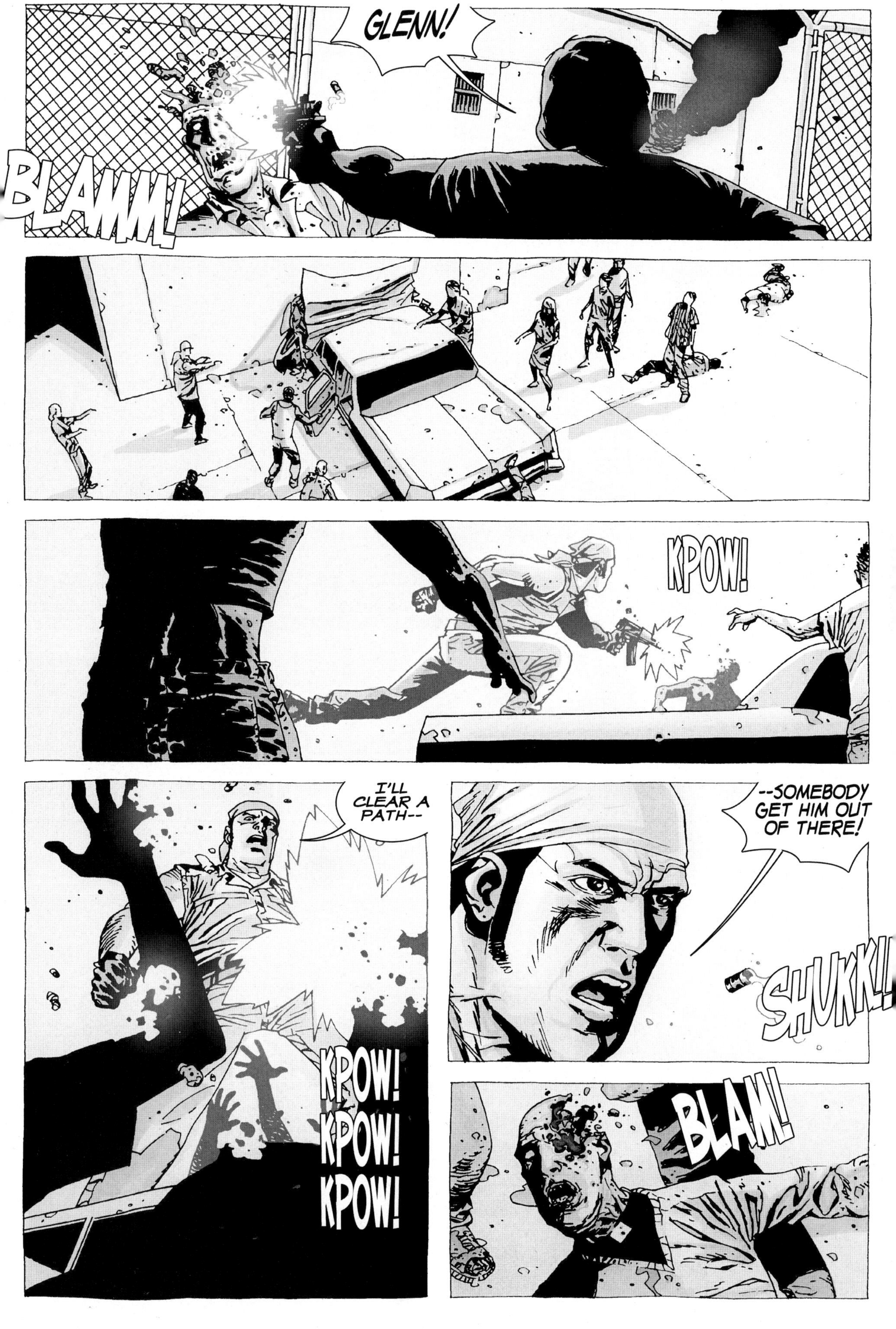
GLENN!
BLAMM!
KPOW!
I'LL CLEAR A PATH--
KPOW! KPOW! KPOW!
--SOMEBODY GET HIM OUT OF THERE!
SHUKK!!
BLAM!

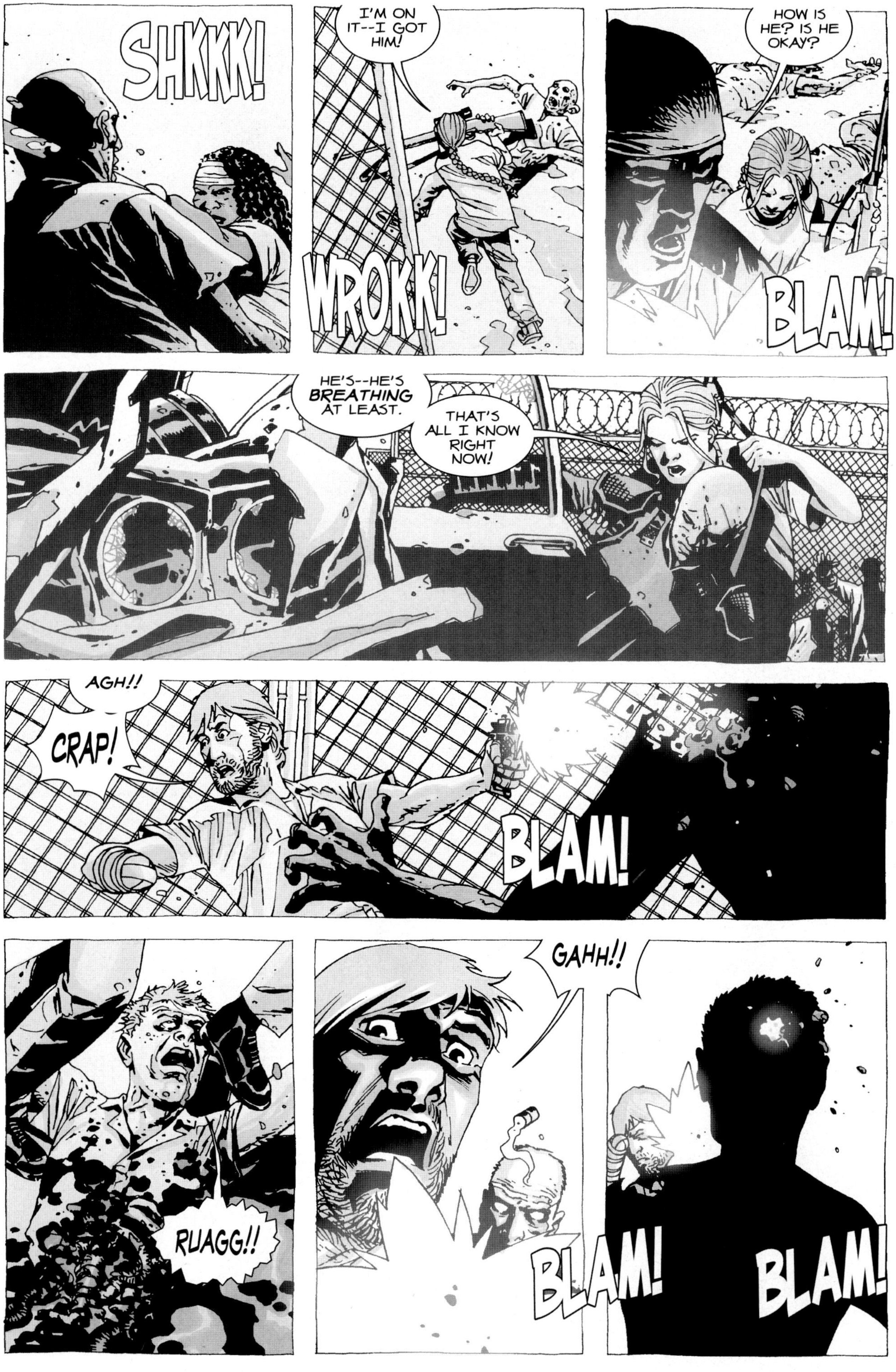
SHKKK!
I'M ON IT--I GOT HIM!
WROKK!
HOW IS HE? IS HE OKAY?
BLAM!
HE'S--HE'S BREATHING AT LEAST.
THAT'S ALL I KNOW RIGHT NOW!
AGH!!
CRAP!
BLAM!
RUAGG!!
GAHH!!
BLAM!
BLAM!

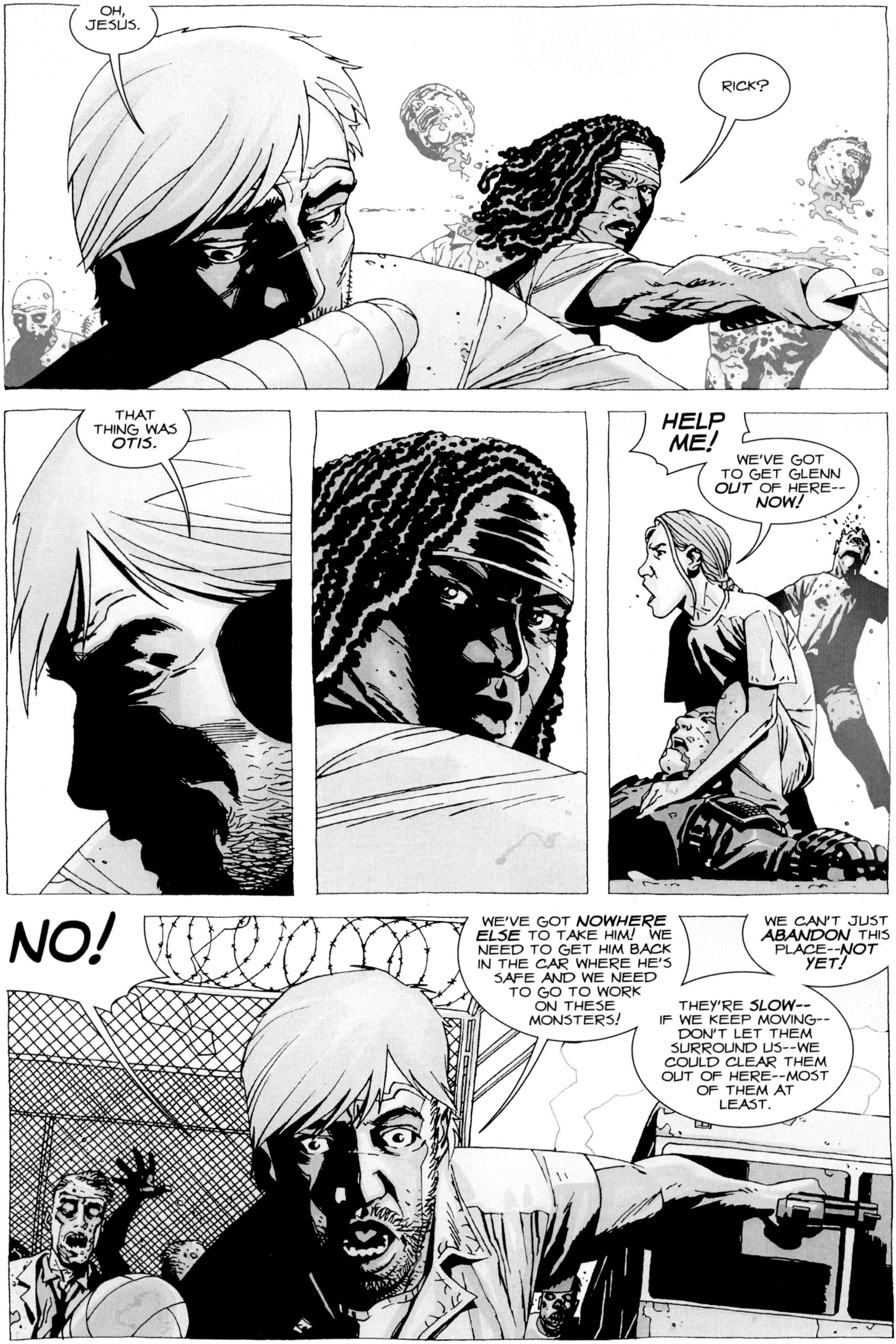
OH, JESUS.
RICK?
THAT THING WAS OTIS.
HELP ME!
WE'VE GOT TO GET GLENN OUT OF HERE-- NOW!
NO!
WE'VE GOT NOWHERE ELSE TO TAKE HIM! WE NEED TO GET HIM BACK IN THE CAR WHERE HE'S SAFE AND WE NEED TO GO TO WORK ON THESE MONSTERS!
WE CAN'T JUST ABANDON THIS PLACE--NOT YET!
THEY'RE SLOW-- IF WE KEEP MOVING-- DON'T LET THEM SURROUND US--WE COULD CLEAR THEM OUT OF HERE--MOST OF THEM AT LEAST.

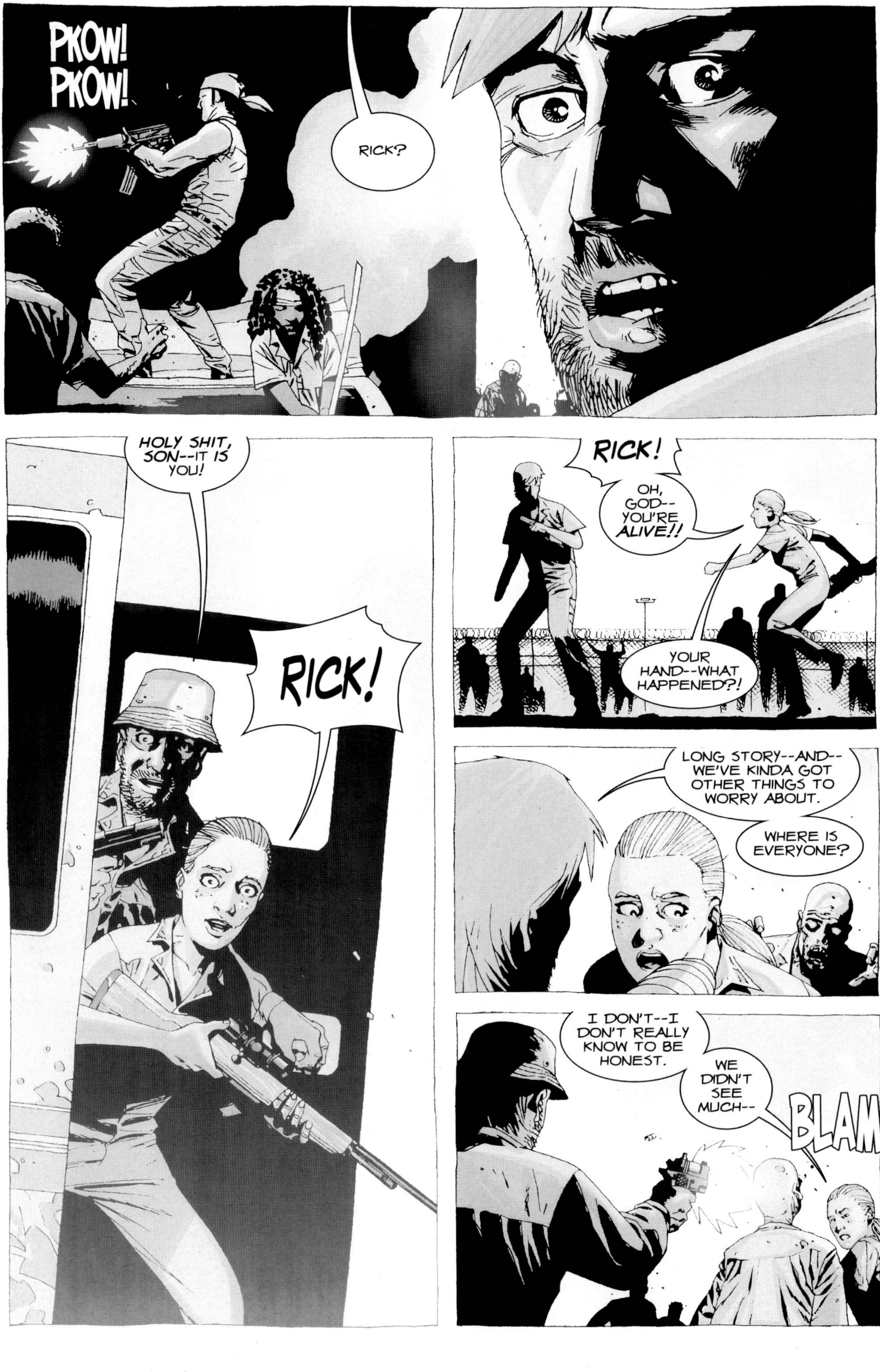
PKOW! PKOW!
RICK?
HOLY SHIT, SON--IT IS YOU!
RICK!
RICK!
OH, GOD--YOU'RE ALIVE!!
YOUR HAND--WHAT HAPPENED?!
LONG STORY--AND--WE'VE KINDA GOT OTHER THINGS TO WORRY ABOUT.
WHERE IS EVERYONE?
I DON'T--I DON'T REALLY KNOW TO BE HONEST.
WE DIDN'T SEE MUCH--
BLAM!

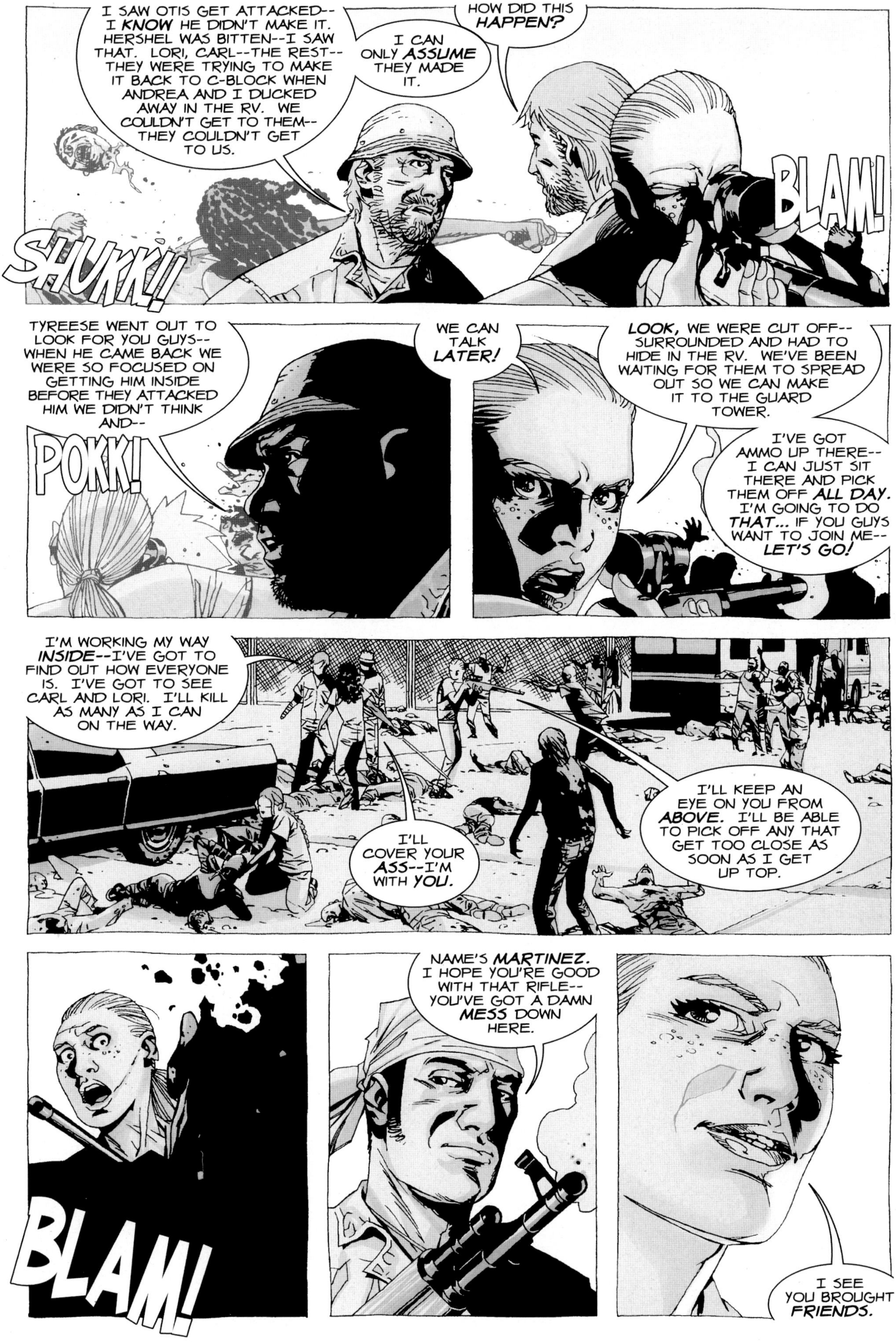
I SAW OTIS GET ATTACKED-- I KNOW HE DIDN'T MAKE IT. HERSHEL WAS BITTEN--I SAW THAT. LORI, CARL--THE REST-- THEY WERE TRYING TO MAKE IT BACK TO C-BLOCK WHEN ANDREA AND I DUCKED AWAY IN THE RV. WE COULDN'T GET TO THEM-- THEY COULDN'T GET TO US.
I CAN ONLY ASSUME THEY MADE IT.
HOW DID THIS HAPPEN?
SHUKK!!
BLAM!
TYREESE WENT OUT TO LOOK FOR YOU GUYS-- WHEN HE CAME BACK WE WERE SO FOCUSED ON GETTING HIM INSIDE BEFORE THEY ATTACKED HIM WE DIDN'T THINK AND--
POKK!
WE CAN TALK LATER!
LOOK, WE WERE CUT OFF-- SURROUNDED AND HAD TO HIDE IN THE RV. WE'VE BEEN WAITING FOR THEM TO SPREAD OUT SO WE CAN MAKE IT TO THE GUARD TOWER.
I'VE GOT AMMO UP THERE-- I CAN JUST SIT THERE AND PICK THEM OFF ALL DAY. I'M GOING TO DO THAT... IF YOU GUYS WANT TO JOIN ME-- LET'S GO!
I'M WORKING MY WAY INSIDE--I'VE GOT TO FIND OUT HOW EVERYONE IS. I'VE GOT TO SEE CARL AND LORI. I'LL KILL AS MANY AS I CAN ON THE WAY.
I'LL COVER YOUR ASS--I'M WITH YOU.
I'LL KEEP AN EYE ON YOU FROM ABOVE. I'LL BE ABLE TO PICK OFF ANY THAT GET TOO CLOSE AS SOON AS I GET UP TOP.
BLAM!
NAME'S MARTINEZ. I HOPE YOU'RE GOOD WITH THAT RIFLE-- YOU'VE GOT A DAMN MESS DOWN HERE.
I SEE YOU BROUGHT FRIENDS.

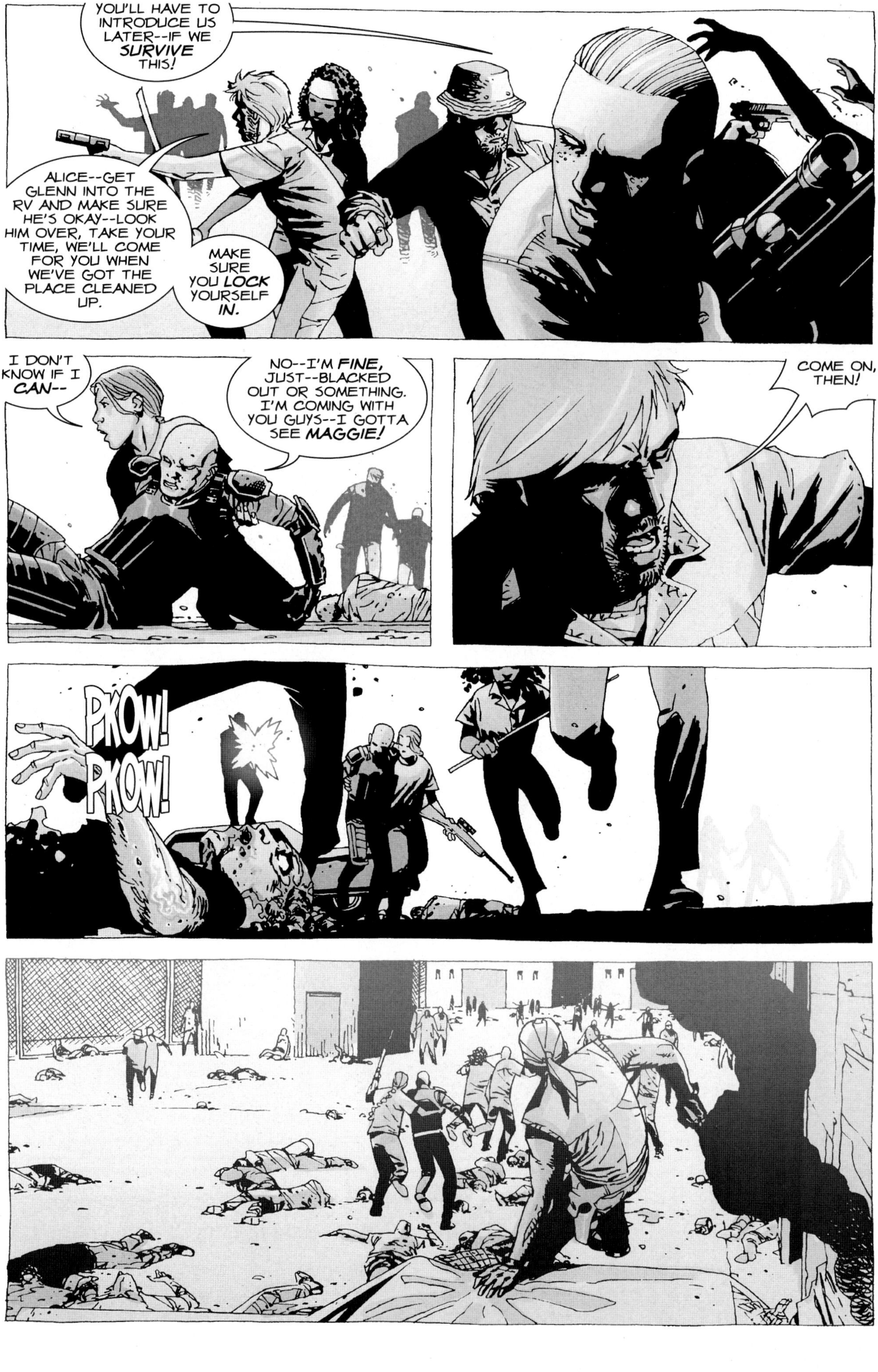
YOU'LL HAVE TO INTRODUCE US LATER--IF WE SURVIVE THIS!
ALICE--GET GLENN INTO THE RV AND MAKE SURE HE'S OKAY--LOOK HIM OVER, TAKE YOUR TIME, WE'LL COME FOR YOU WHEN WE'VE GOT THE PLACE CLEANED UP.
MAKE SURE YOU LOCK YOURSELF IN.
I DON'T KNOW IF I CAN--
NO--I'M FINE, JUST--BLACKED OUT OR SOMETHING. I'M COMING WITH YOU GUYS--I GOTTA SEE MAGGIE!
COME ON, THEN!
PKOW! PKOW!

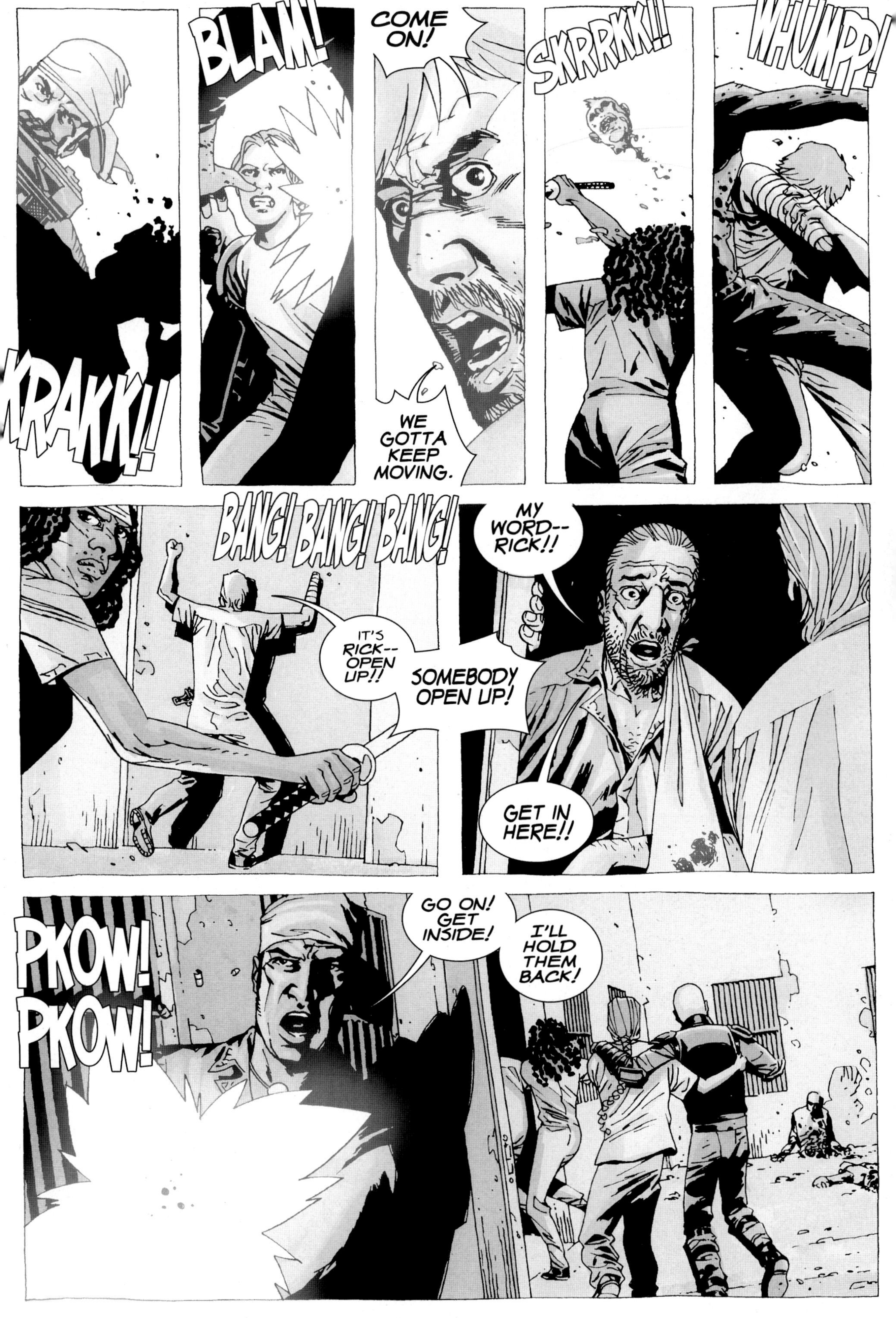
KRAKK!!
BLAM!
COME ON!
WE GOTTA KEEP MOVING.
SKRRKK!!
WHUMPP!
BANG! BANG! BANG!
IT'S RICK-- OPEN UP!!
SOMEBODY OPEN UP!
MY WORD-- RICK!!
GET IN HERE!!
PKOW! PKOW!
GO ON! GET INSIDE!
I'LL HOLD THEM BACK!

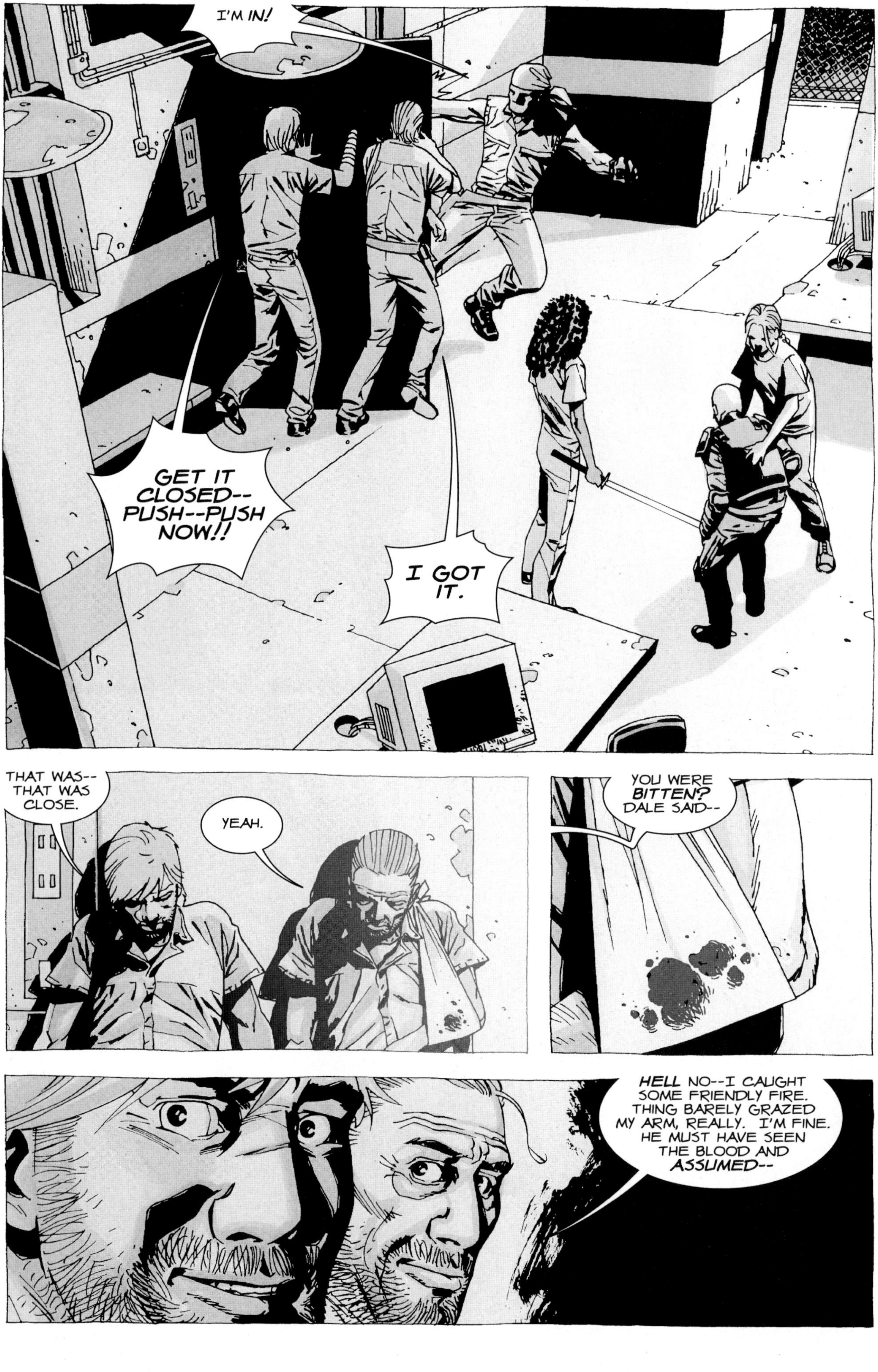
I'M IN!
GET IT CLOSED--PUSH--PUSH NOW!!
I GOT IT.
THAT WAS--THAT WAS CLOSE.
YEAH.
YOU WERE BITTEN? DALE SAID--
HELL NO--I CAUGHT SOME FRIENDLY FIRE. THING BARELY GRAZED MY ARM, REALLY. I'M FINE. HE MUST HAVE SEEN THE BLOOD AND ASSUMED--

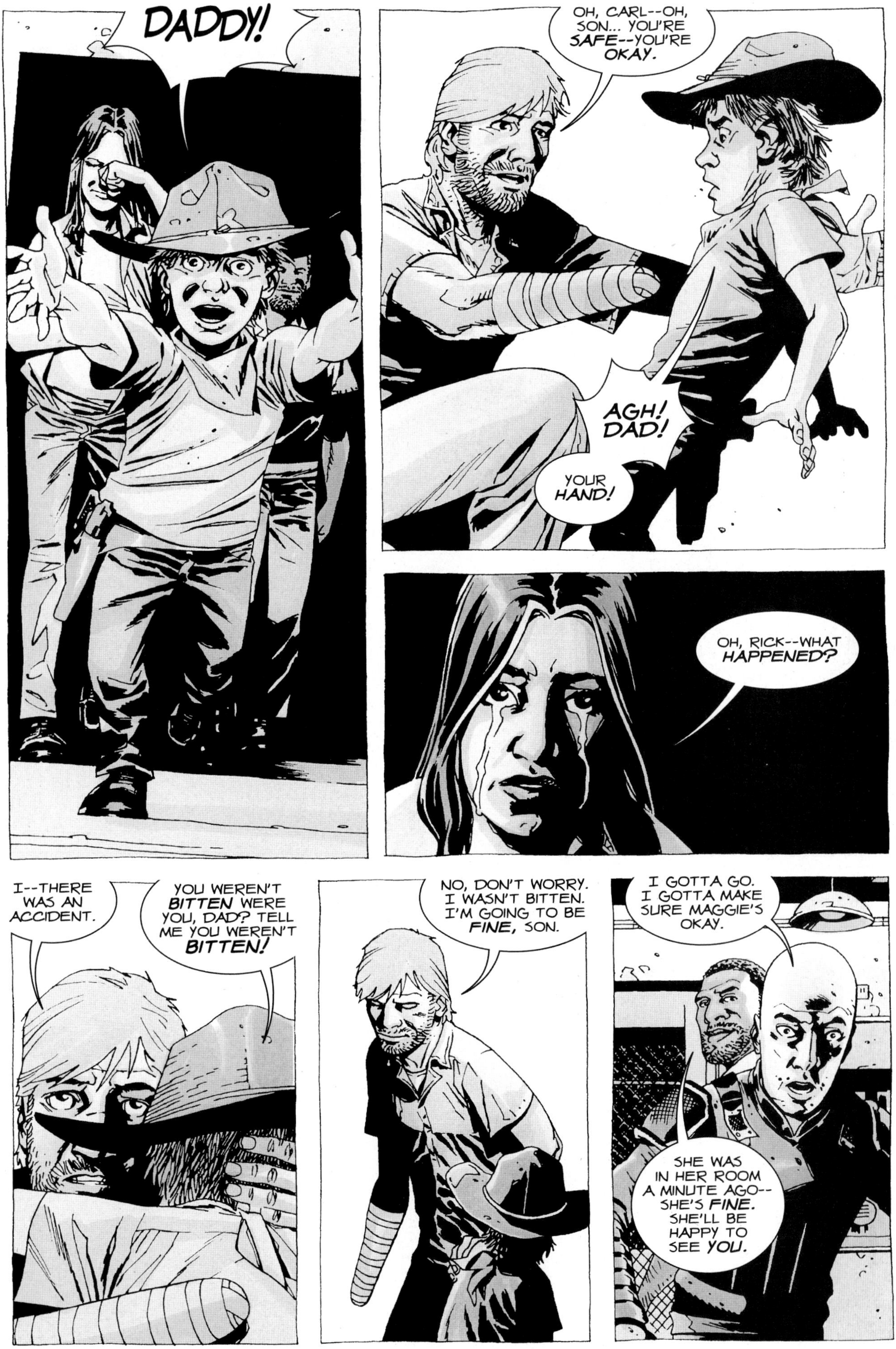
DADDY!
OH, CARL--OH, SON... YOU'RE SAFE--YOU'RE OKAY.
AGH! DAD!
YOUR HAND!
OH, RICK--WHAT HAPPENED?
I--THERE WAS AN ACCIDENT.
YOU WEREN'T BITTEN WERE YOU, DAD? TELL ME YOU WEREN'T BITTEN!
NO, DON'T WORRY. I WASN'T BITTEN. I'M GOING TO BE FINE, SON.
I GOTTA GO. I GOTTA MAKE SURE MAGGIE'S OKAY.
SHE WAS IN HER ROOM A MINUTE AGO--SHE'S FINE. SHE'LL BE HAPPY TO SEE YOU.

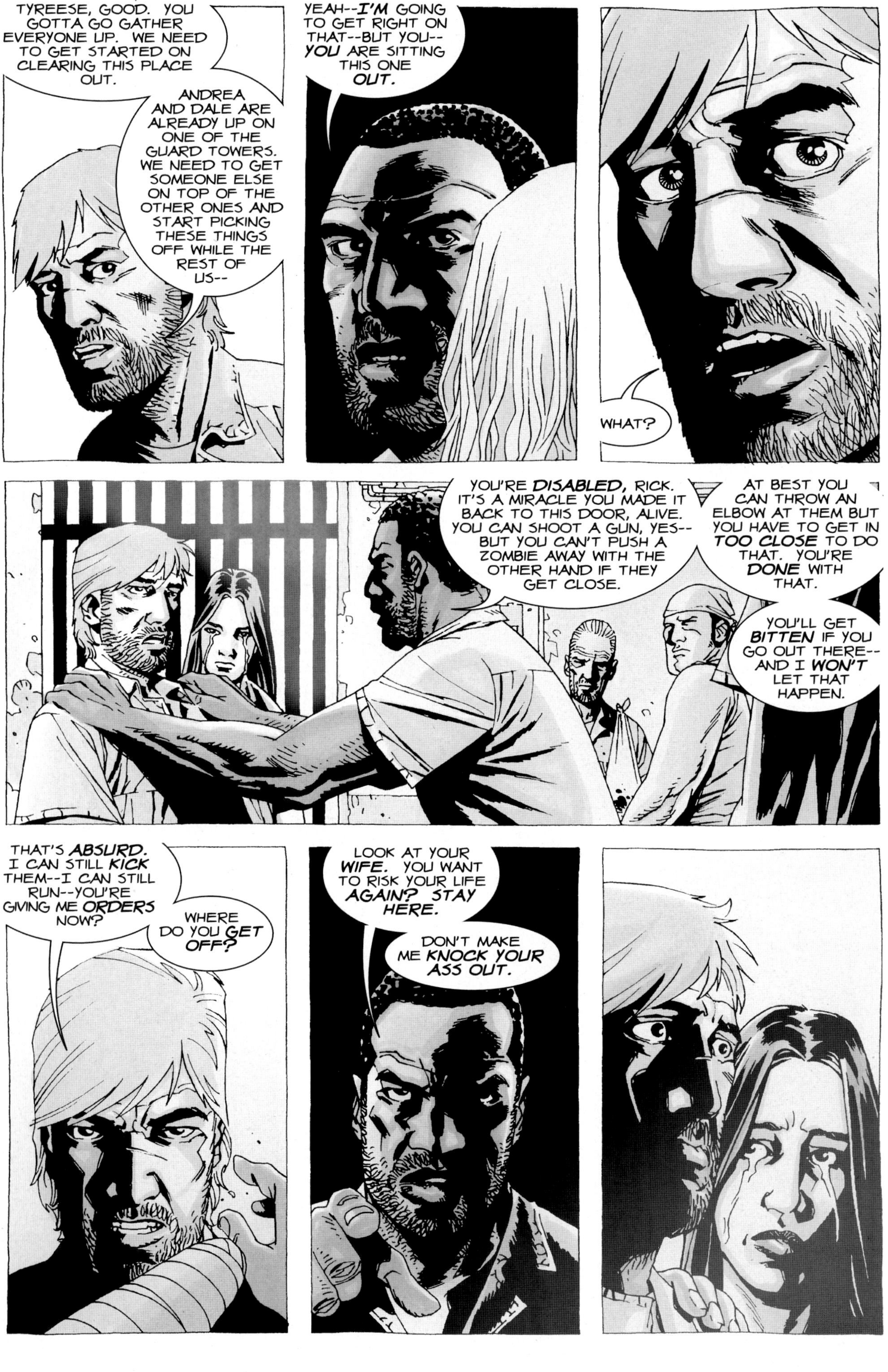
TYREESE, GOOD. YOU GOTTA GO GATHER EVERYONE UP. WE NEED TO GET STARTED ON CLEARING THIS PLACE OUT.
ANDREA AND DALE ARE ALREADY UP ON ONE OF THE GUARD TOWERS. WE NEED TO GET SOMEONE ELSE ON TOP OF THE OTHER ONES AND START PICKING THESE THINGS OFF WHILE THE REST OF US--
YEAH--I'M GOING TO GET RIGHT ON THAT--BUT YOU--YOU ARE SITTING THIS ONE OUT.
WHAT?
YOU'RE DISABLED, RICK. IT'S A MIRACLE YOU MADE IT BACK TO THIS DOOR, ALIVE. YOU CAN SHOOT A GUN, YES--BUT YOU CAN'T PUSH A ZOMBIE AWAY WITH THE OTHER HAND IF THEY GET CLOSE.
AT BEST YOU CAN THROW AN ELBOW AT THEM BUT YOU HAVE TO GET IN TOO CLOSE TO DO THAT. YOU'RE DONE WITH THAT.
YOU'LL GET BITTEN IF YOU GO OUT THERE--AND I WON'T LET THAT HAPPEN.
THAT'S ABSURD. I CAN STILL KICK THEM--I CAN STILL RUN--YOU'RE GIVING ME ORDERS NOW?
WHERE DO YOU GET OFF?
LOOK AT YOUR WIFE. YOU WANT TO RISK YOUR LIFE AGAIN? STAY HERE.
DON'T MAKE ME KNOCK YOUR ASS OUT.

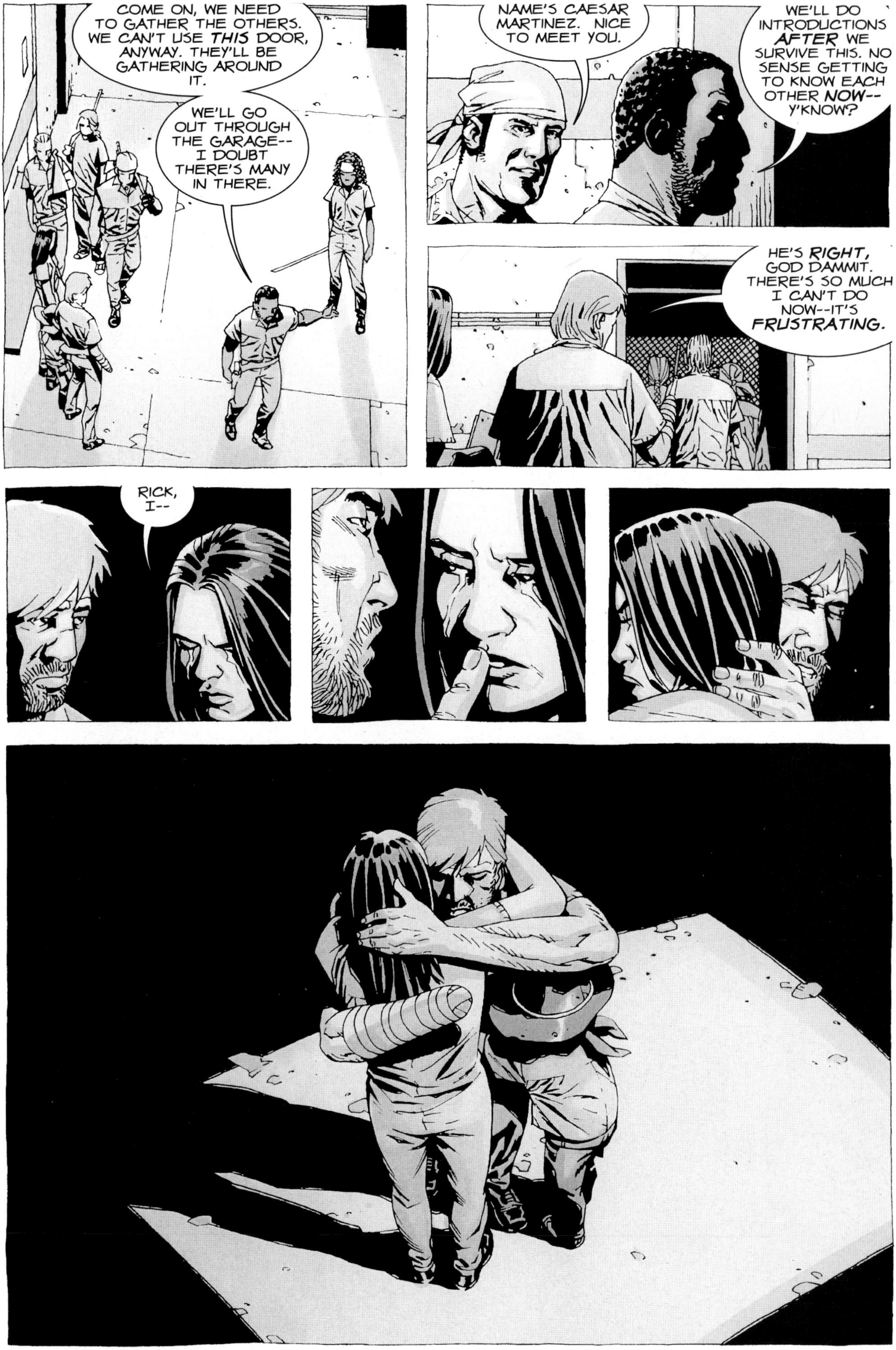
COME ON, WE NEED TO GATHER THE OTHERS. WE CAN'T USE THIS DOOR, ANYWAY. THEY'LL BE GATHERING AROUND IT.
WE'LL GO OUT THROUGH THE GARAGE-- I DOUBT THERE'S MANY IN THERE.
NAME'S CAESAR MARTINEZ. NICE TO MEET YOU.
WE'LL DO INTRODUCTIONS AFTER WE SURVIVE THIS. NO SENSE GETTING TO KNOW EACH OTHER NOW-- Y'KNOW?
HE'S RIGHT, GOD DAMMIT. THERE'S SO MUCH I CAN'T DO NOW--IT'S FRUSTRATING.
RICK, I--

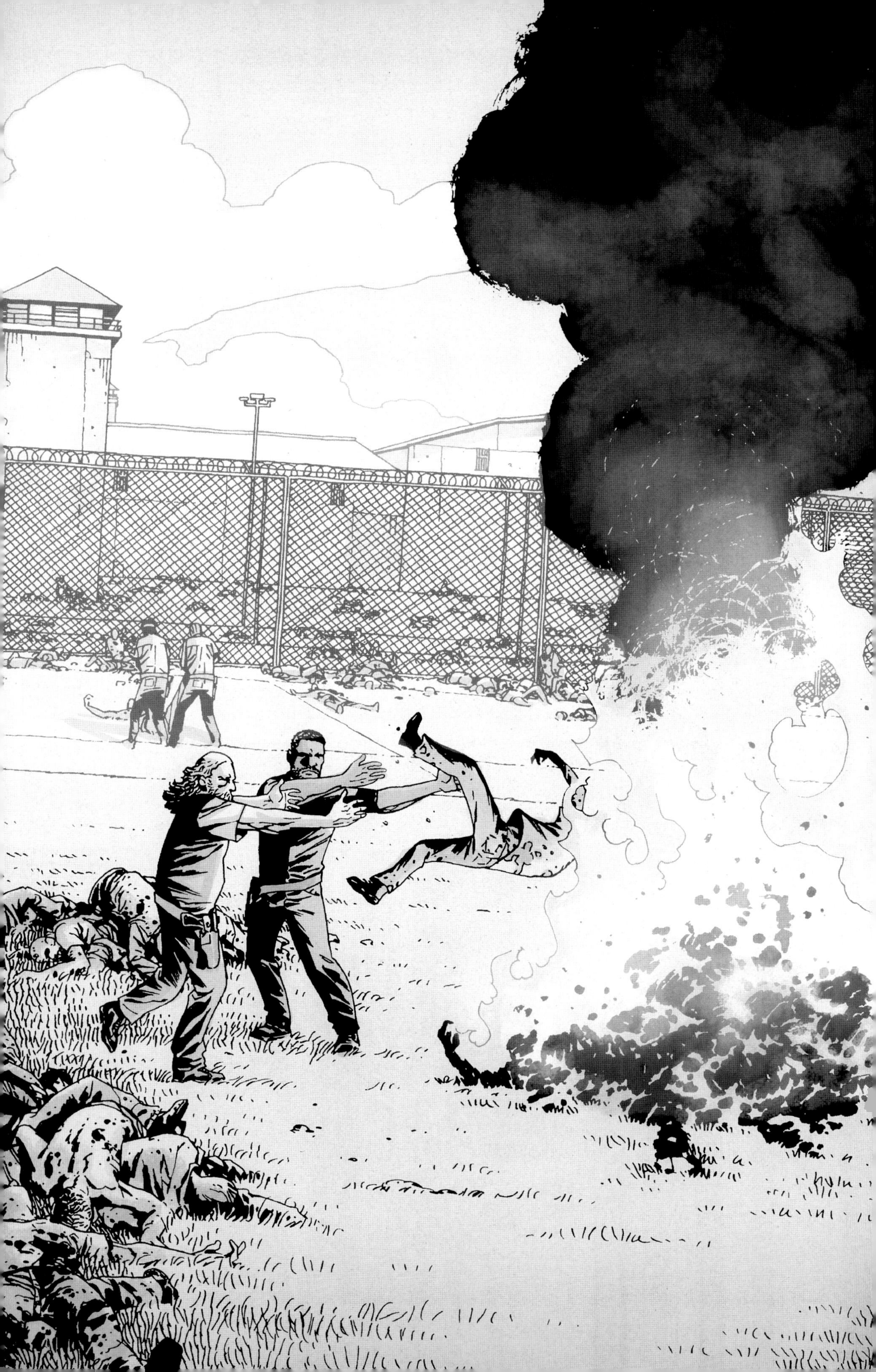

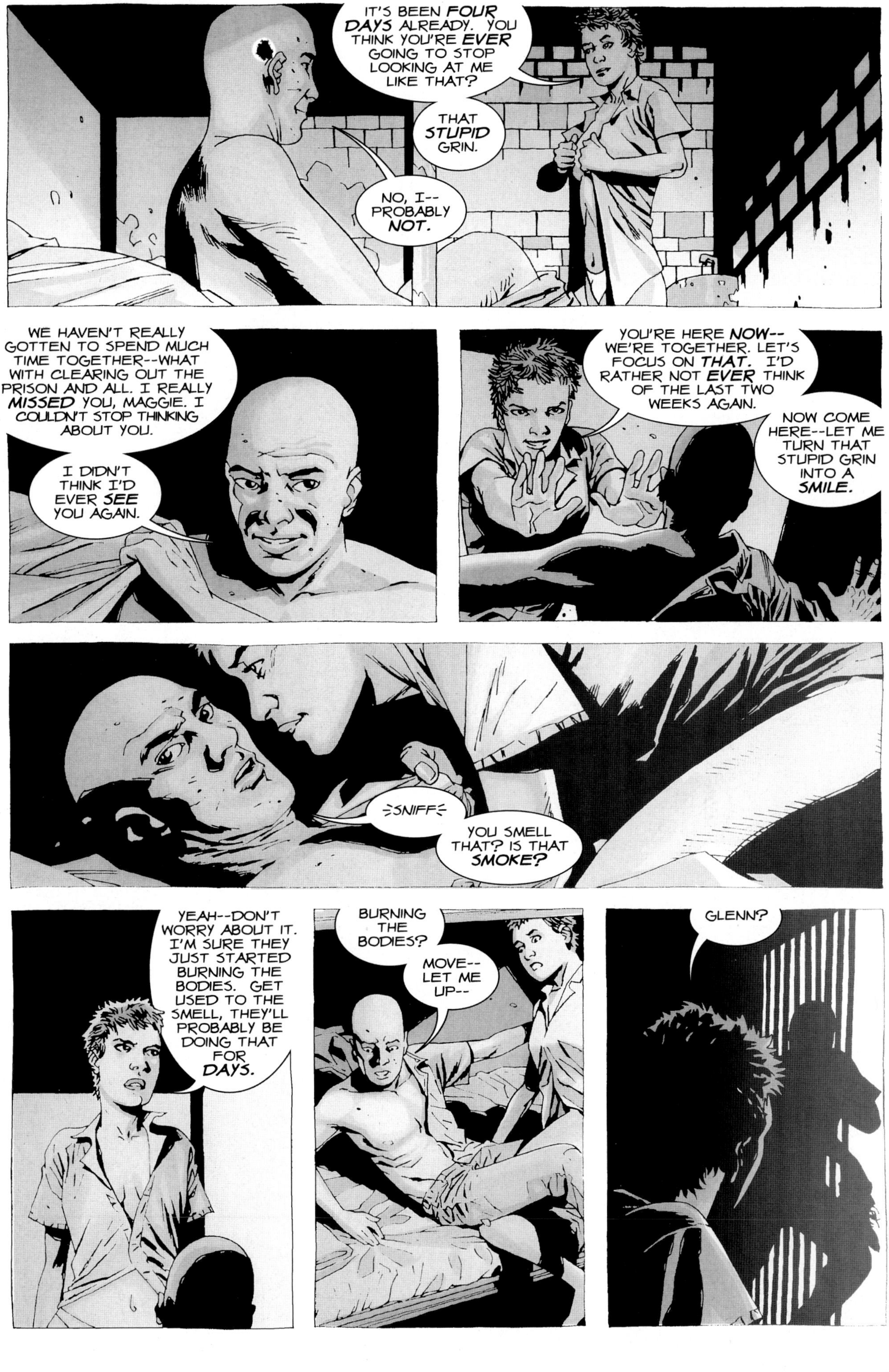
IT'S BEEN FOUR DAYS ALREADY. YOU THINK YOU'RE EVER GOING TO STOP LOOKING AT ME LIKE THAT?
THAT STUPID GRIN.
NO, I-- PROBABLY NOT.
WE HAVEN'T REALLY GOTTEN TO SPEND MUCH TIME TOGETHER--WHAT WITH CLEARING OUT THE PRISON AND ALL. I REALLY MISSED YOU, MAGGIE. I COULDN'T STOP THINKING ABOUT YOU.
I DIDN'T THINK I'D EVER SEE YOU AGAIN.
YOU'RE HERE NOW-- WE'RE TOGETHER. LET'S FOCUS ON THAT. I'D RATHER NOT EVER THINK OF THE LAST TWO WEEKS AGAIN.
NOW COME HERE--LET ME TURN THAT STUPID GRIN INTO A SMILE.
SNIFF
YOU SMELL THAT? IS THAT SMOKE?
YEAH--DON'T WORRY ABOUT IT. I'M SURE THEY JUST STARTED BURNING THE BODIES. GET USED TO THE SMELL, THEY'LL PROBABLY BE DOING THAT FOR DAYS.
BURNING THE BODIES?
MOVE-- LET ME UP--
GLENN?

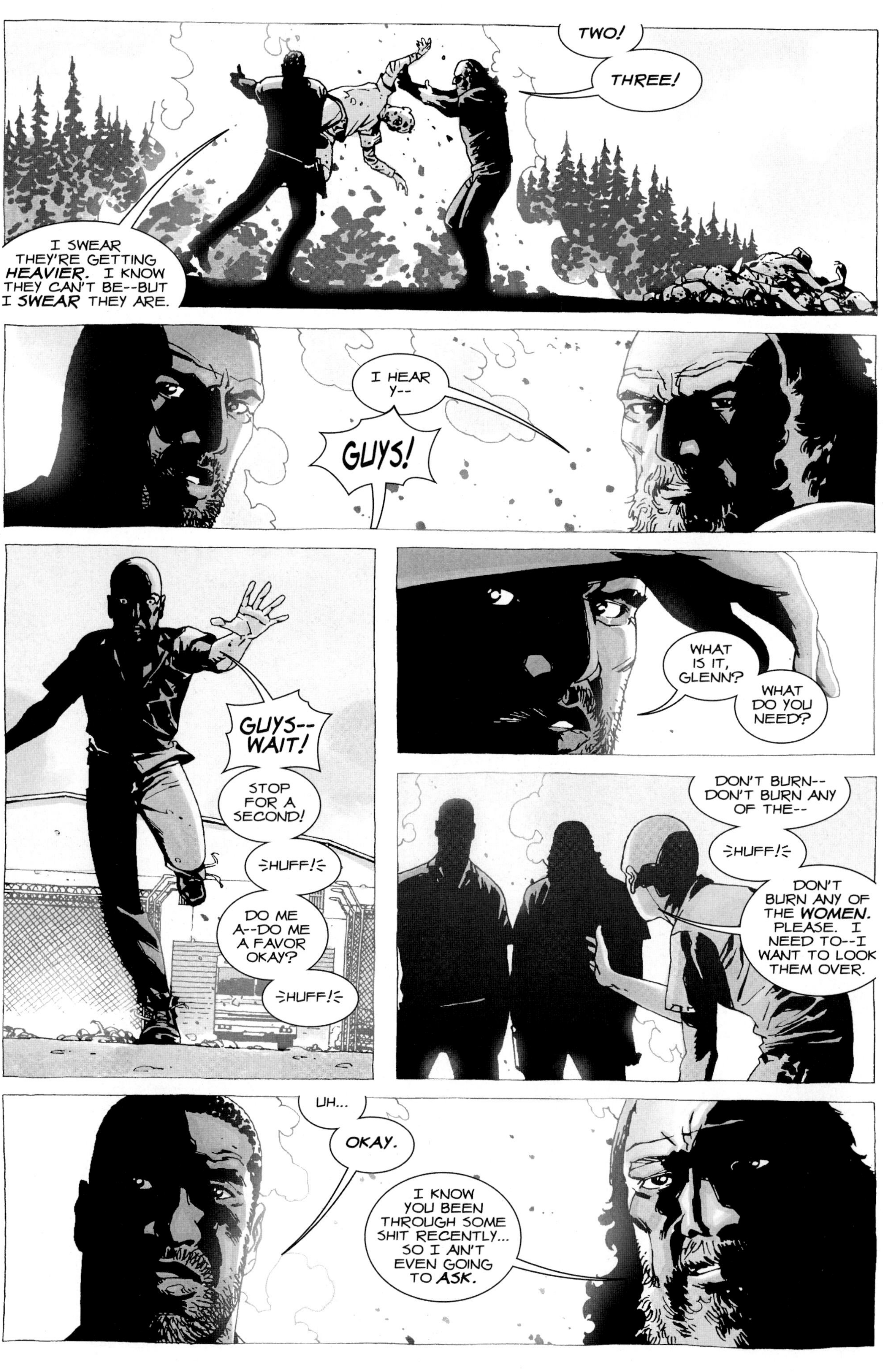
TWO!
THREE!
I SWEAR THEY'RE GETTING HEAVIER. I KNOW THEY CAN'T BE--BUT I SWEAR THEY ARE.
I HEAR Y--
GUYS!
GUYS--WAIT!
STOP FOR A SECOND!
HUFF!
DO ME A--DO ME A FAVOR OKAY?
HUFF!
WHAT IS IT, GLENN?
WHAT DO YOU NEED?
DON'T BURN--DON'T BURN ANY OF THE--
HUFF!
DON'T BURN ANY OF THE WOMEN. PLEASE. I NEED TO--I WANT TO LOOK THEM OVER.
UH...
OKAY.
I KNOW YOU BEEN THROUGH SOME SHIT RECENTLY... SO I AIN'T EVEN GOING TO ASK.

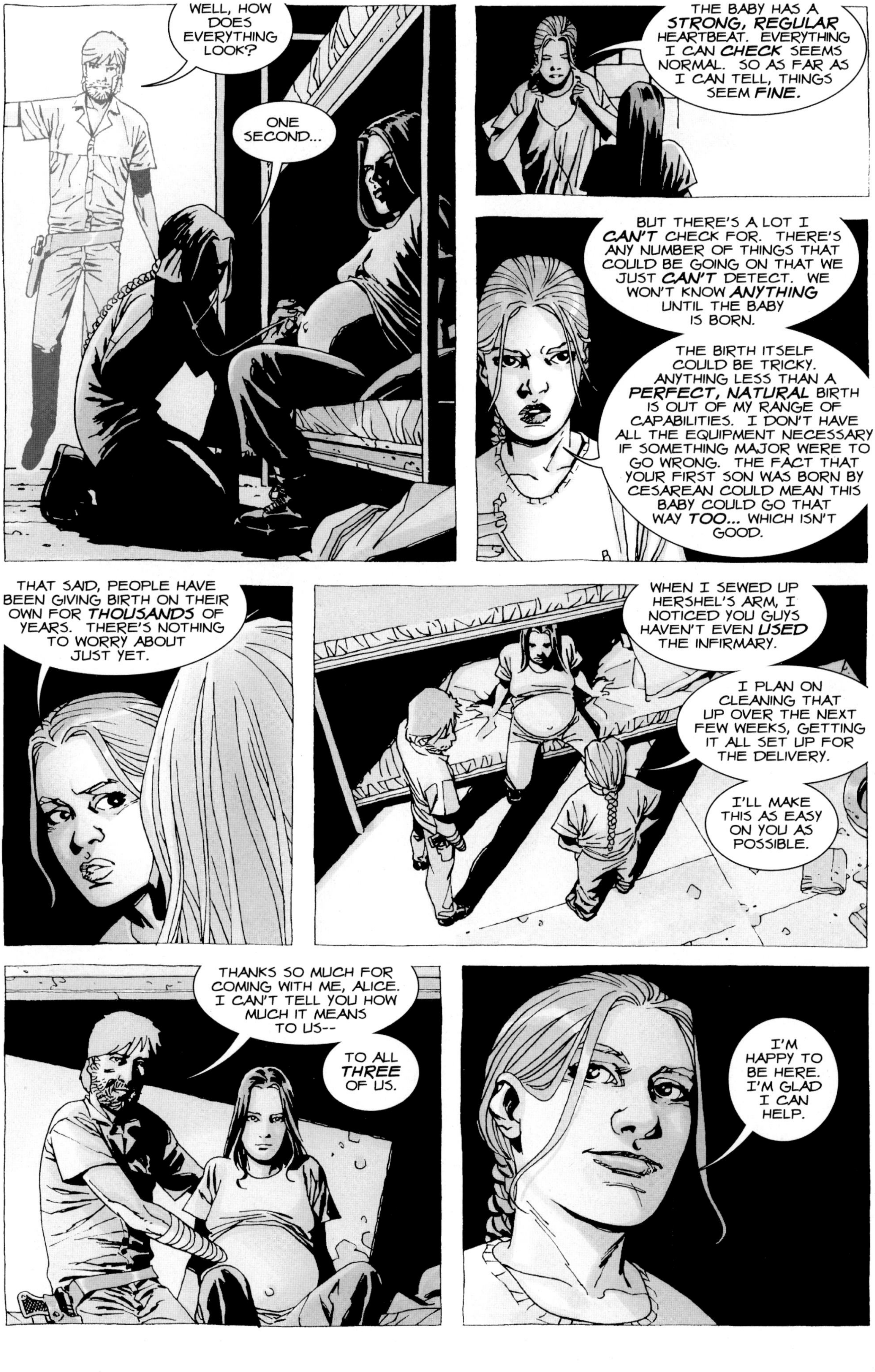
WELL, HOW DOES EVERYTHING LOOK?
ONE SECOND...
THE BABY HAS A STRONG, REGULAR HEARTBEAT. EVERYTHING I CAN CHECK SEEMS NORMAL. SO AS FAR AS I CAN TELL, THINGS SEEM FINE.
BUT THERE'S A LOT I CAN'T CHECK FOR. THERE'S ANY NUMBER OF THINGS THAT COULD BE GOING ON THAT WE JUST CAN'T DETECT. WE WON'T KNOW ANYTHING UNTIL THE BABY IS BORN.
THE BIRTH ITSELF COULD BE TRICKY. ANYTHING LESS THAN A PERFECT, NATURAL BIRTH IS OUT OF MY RANGE OF CAPABILITIES. I DON'T HAVE ALL THE EQUIPMENT NECESSARY IF SOMETHING MAJOR WERE TO GO WRONG. THE FACT THAT YOUR FIRST SON WAS BORN BY CESAREAN COULD MEAN THIS BABY COULD GO THAT WAY TOO... WHICH ISN'T GOOD.
THAT SAID, PEOPLE HAVE BEEN GIVING BIRTH ON THEIR OWN FOR THOUSANDS OF YEARS. THERE'S NOTHING TO WORRY ABOUT JUST YET.
WHEN I SEWED UP HERSHEL'S ARM, I NOTICED YOU GUYS HAVEN'T EVEN USED THE INFIRMARY.
I PLAN ON CLEANING THAT UP OVER THE NEXT FEW WEEKS, GETTING IT ALL SET UP FOR THE DELIVERY.
I'LL MAKE THIS AS EASY ON YOU AS POSSIBLE.
THANKS SO MUCH FOR COMING WITH ME, ALICE. I CAN'T TELL YOU HOW MUCH IT MEANS TO US--
TO ALL THREE OF US.
I'M HAPPY TO BE HERE. I'M GLAD I CAN HELP.

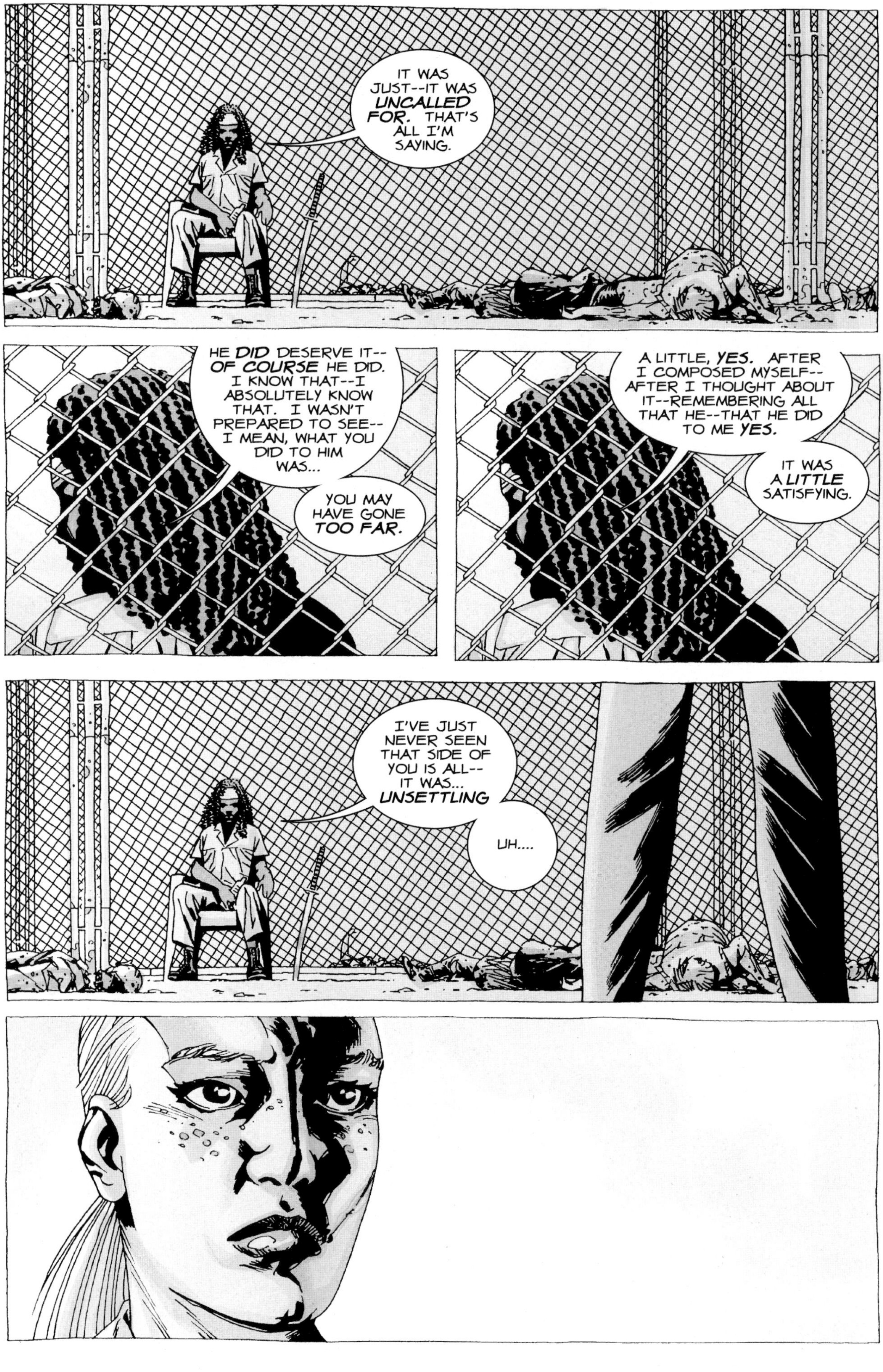
IT WAS JUST--IT WAS UNCALLED FOR. THAT'S ALL I'M SAYING.
HE DID DESERVE IT-- OF COURSE HE DID. I KNOW THAT--I ABSOLUTELY KNOW THAT. I WASN'T PREPARED TO SEE-- I MEAN, WHAT YOU DID TO HIM WAS...
YOU MAY HAVE GONE TOO FAR.
A LITTLE, YES. AFTER I COMPOSED MYSELF-- AFTER I THOUGHT ABOUT IT--REMEMBERING ALL THAT HE--THAT HE DID TO ME YES.
IT WAS A LITTLE SATISFYING.
I'VE JUST NEVER SEEN THAT SIDE OF YOU IS ALL-- IT WAS... UNSETTLING
UH....

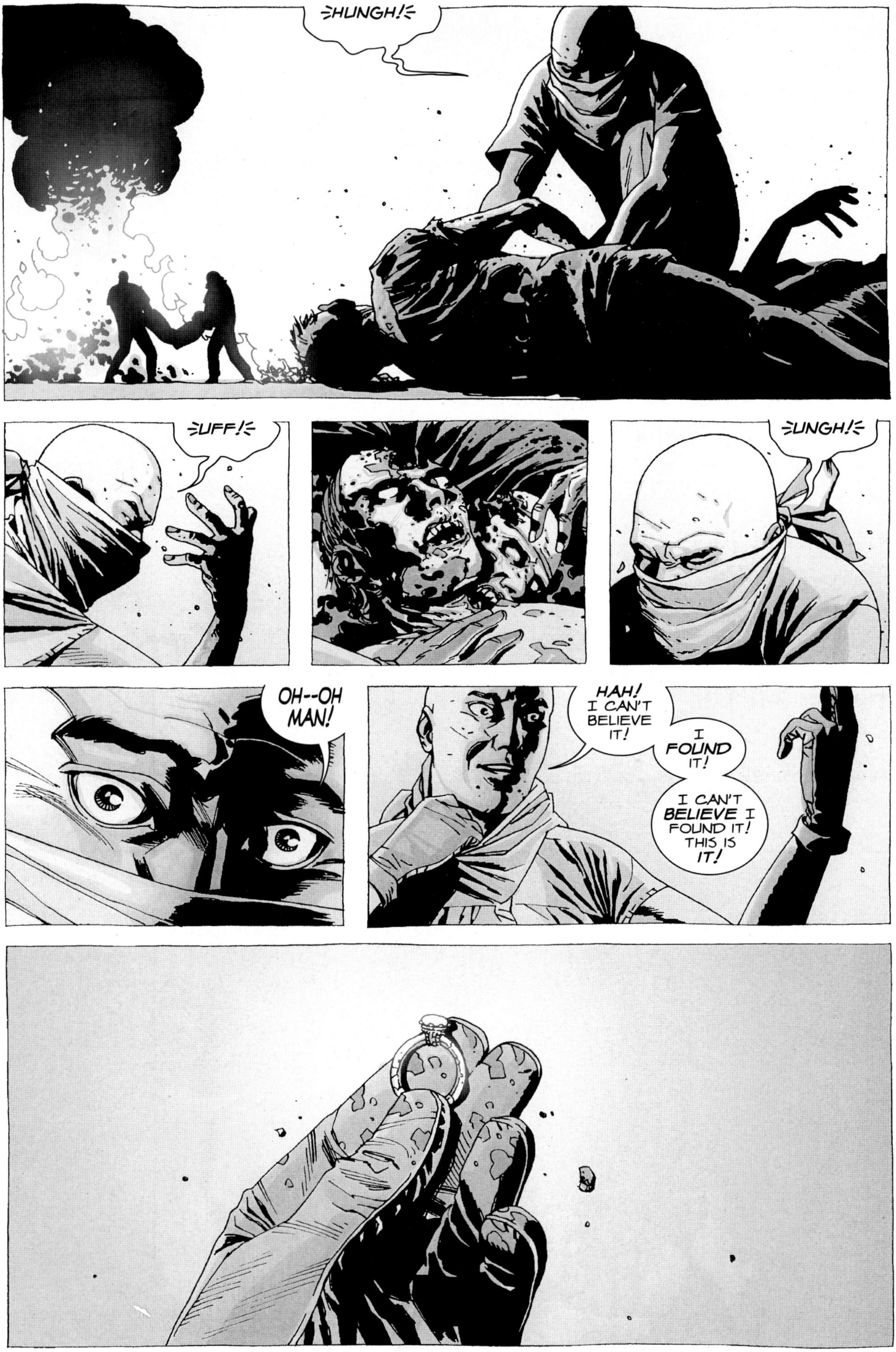

HUNGH!
UFF!
UNGH!
OH--OH MAN!
HAH! I CAN'T BELIEVE IT!
I FOUND IT!
I CAN'T BELIEVE I FOUND IT! THIS IS IT!

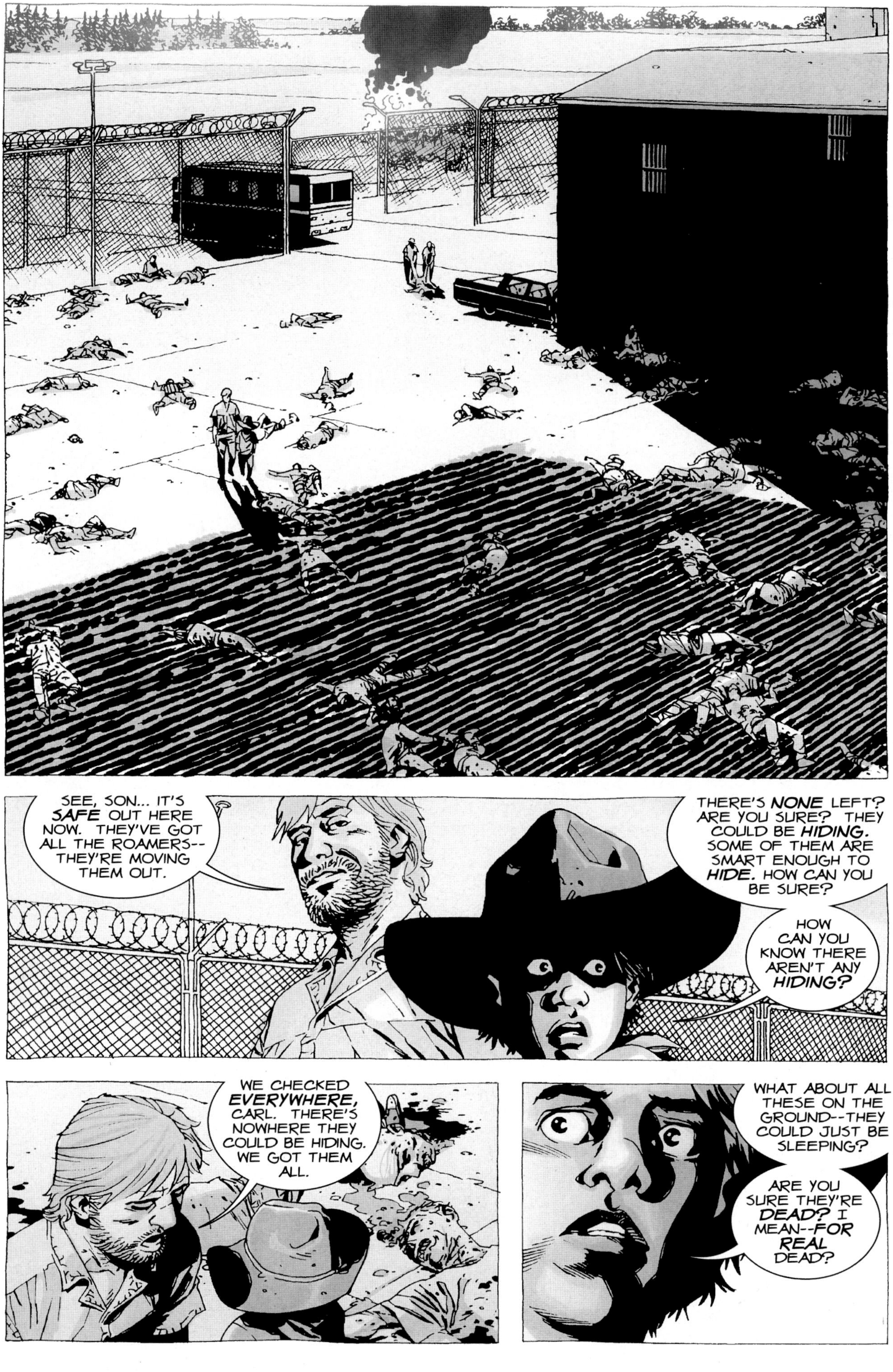
SEE, SON... IT'S SAFE OUT HERE NOW. THEY'VE GOT ALL THE ROAMERS-- THEY'RE MOVING THEM OUT.
THERE'S NONE LEFT? ARE YOU SURE? THEY COULD BE HIDING. SOME OF THEM ARE SMART ENOUGH TO HIDE. HOW CAN YOU BE SURE?
HOW CAN YOU KNOW THERE AREN'T ANY HIDING?
WE CHECKED EVERYWHERE, CARL. THERE'S NOWHERE THEY COULD BE HIDING. WE GOT THEM ALL.
WHAT ABOUT ALL THESE ON THE GROUND--THEY COULD JUST BE SLEEPING?
ARE YOU SURE THEY'RE DEAD? I MEAN--FOR REAL DEAD?

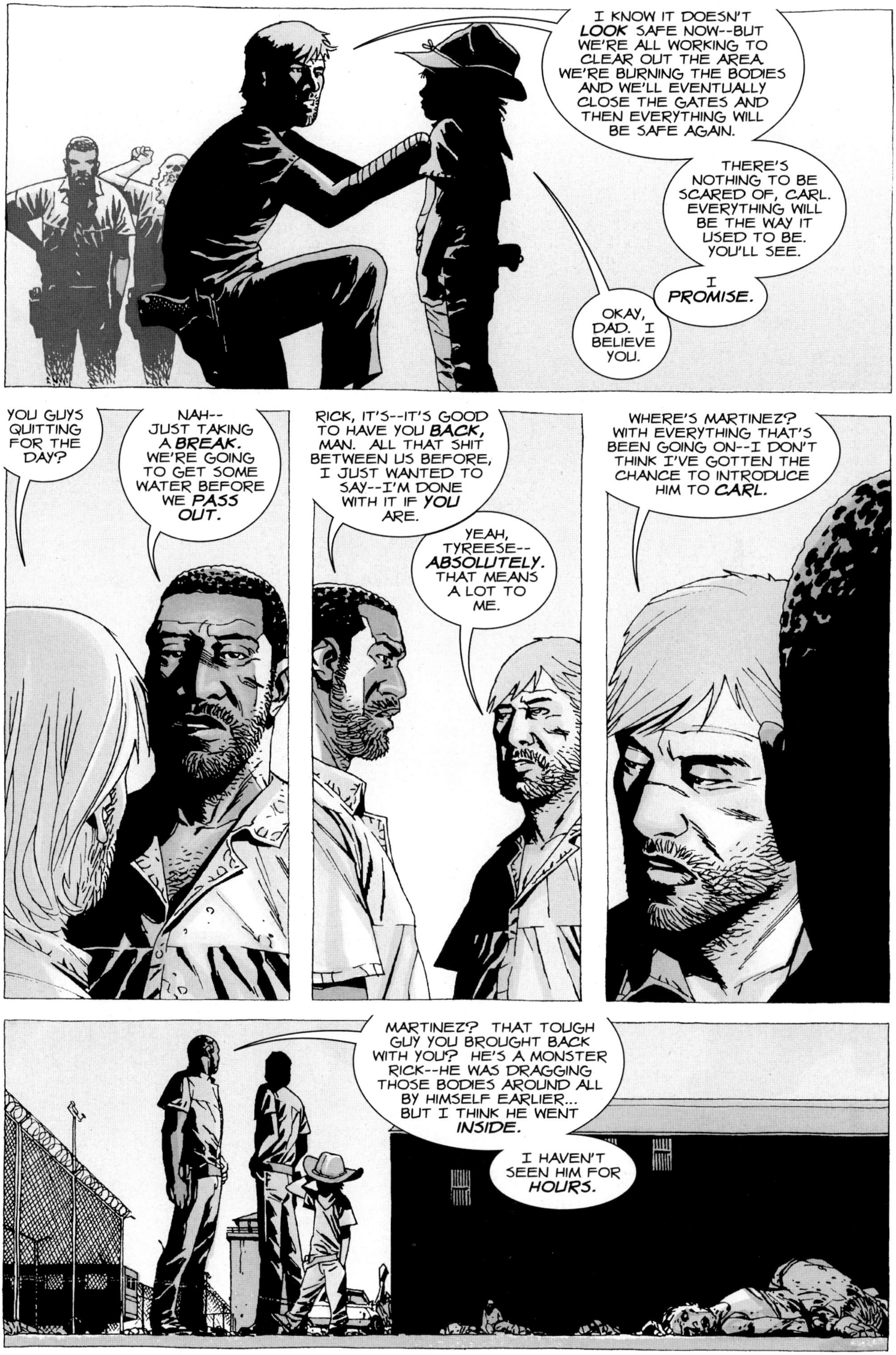
I KNOW IT DOESN'T LOOK SAFE NOW--BUT WE'RE ALL WORKING TO CLEAR OUT THE AREA. WE'RE BURNING THE BODIES AND WE'LL EVENTUALLY CLOSE THE GATES AND THEN EVERYTHING WILL BE SAFE AGAIN.
THERE'S NOTHING TO BE SCARED OF, CARL. EVERYTHING WILL BE THE WAY IT USED TO BE. YOU'LL SEE.
I PROMISE.
OKAY, DAD. I BELIEVE YOU.
YOU GUYS QUITTING FOR THE DAY?
NAH--JUST TAKING A BREAK. WE'RE GOING TO GET SOME WATER BEFORE WE PASS OUT.
RICK, IT'S--IT'S GOOD TO HAVE YOU BACK, MAN. ALL THAT SHIT BETWEEN US BEFORE, I JUST WANTED TO SAY--I'M DONE WITH IT IF YOU ARE.
YEAH, TYREESE--ABSOLUTELY. THAT MEANS A LOT TO ME.
WHERE'S MARTINEZ? WITH EVERYTHING THAT'S BEEN GOING ON--I DON'T THINK I'VE GOTTEN THE CHANCE TO INTRODUCE HIM TO CARL.
MARTINEZ? THAT TOUGH GUY YOU BROUGHT BACK WITH YOU? HE'S A MONSTER RICK--HE WAS DRAGGING THOSE BODIES AROUND ALL BY HIMSELF EARLIER... BUT I THINK HE WENT INSIDE.
I HAVEN'T SEEN HIM FOR HOURS.

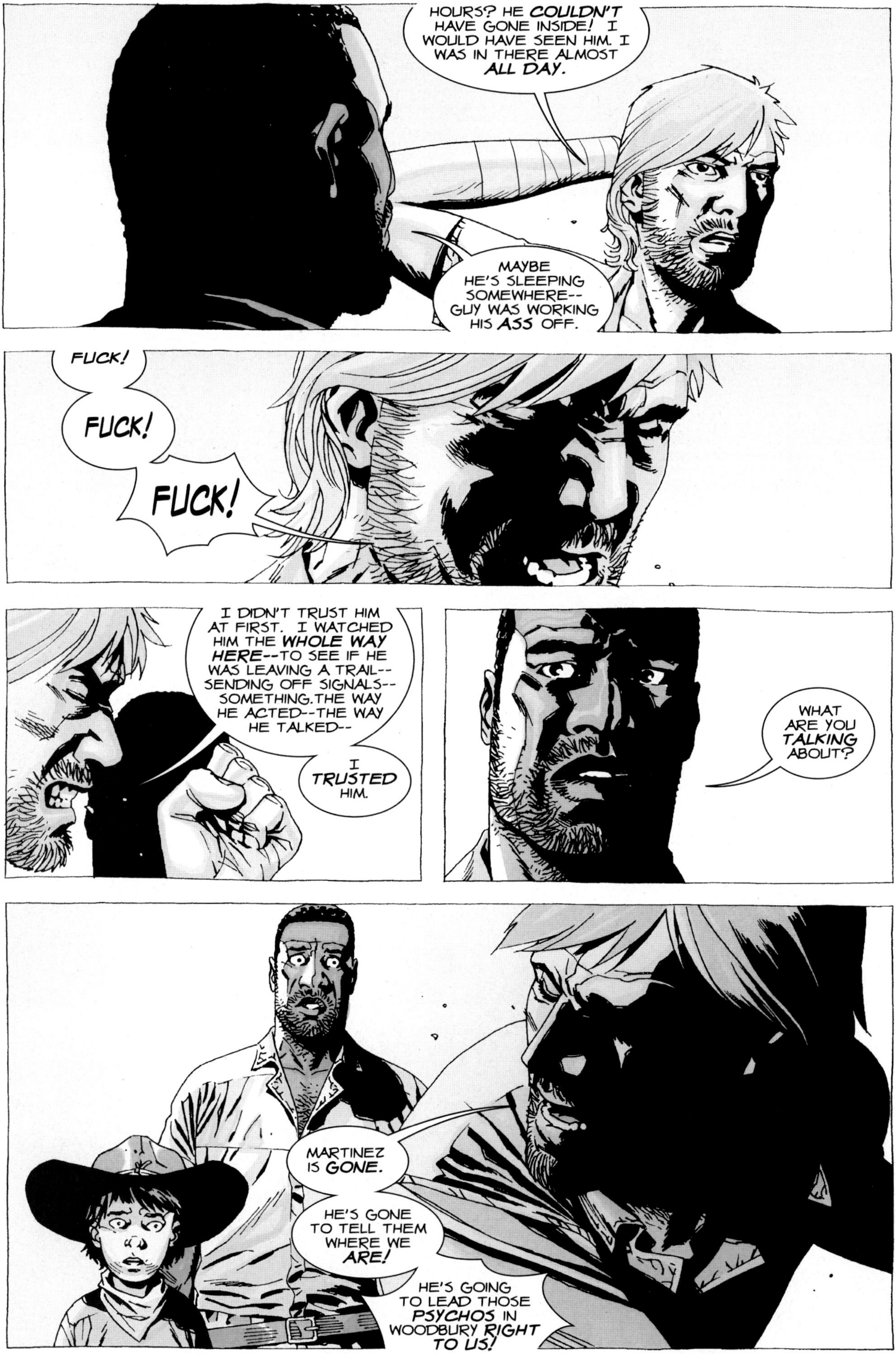
HOURS? HE COULDN'T HAVE GONE INSIDE! I WOULD HAVE SEEN HIM. I WAS IN THERE ALMOST ALL DAY.
MAYBE HE'S SLEEPING SOMEWHERE-- GUY WAS WORKING HIS ASS OFF.
FUCK!
FUCK!
FUCK!
I DIDN'T TRUST HIM AT FIRST. I WATCHED HIM THE WHOLE WAY HERE--TO SEE IF HE WAS LEAVING A TRAIL-- SENDING OFF SIGNALS-- SOMETHING. THE WAY HE ACTED--THE WAY HE TALKED--
I TRUSTED HIM.
WHAT ARE YOU TALKING ABOUT?
MARTINEZ IS GONE.
HE'S GONE TO TELL THEM WHERE WE ARE!
HE'S GOING TO LEAD THOSE PSYCHOS IN WOODBURY RIGHT TO US!

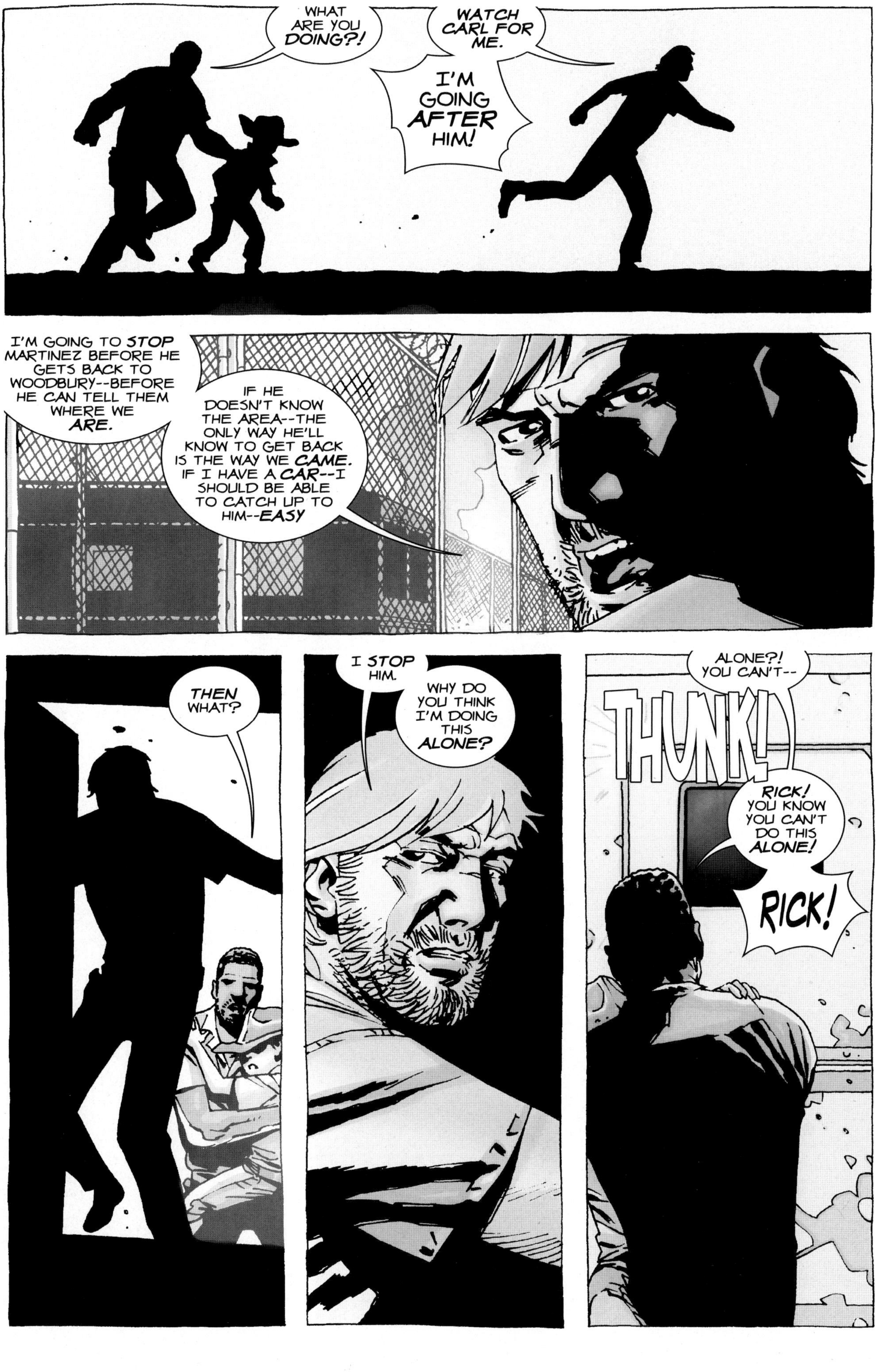
WHAT ARE YOU DOING?!
WATCH CARL FOR ME.
I'M GOING AFTER HIM!
I'M GOING TO STOP MARTINEZ BEFORE HE GETS BACK TO WOODBURY--BEFORE HE CAN TELL THEM WHERE WE ARE.
IF HE DOESN'T KNOW THE AREA--THE ONLY WAY HE'LL KNOW TO GET BACK IS THE WAY WE CAME. IF I HAVE A CAR--I SHOULD BE ABLE TO CATCH UP TO HIM--EASY
THEN WHAT?
I STOP HIM.
WHY DO YOU THINK I'M DOING THIS ALONE?
ALONE?! YOU CAN'T--
THUNK!
RICK! YOU KNOW YOU CAN'T DO THIS ALONE!
RICK!

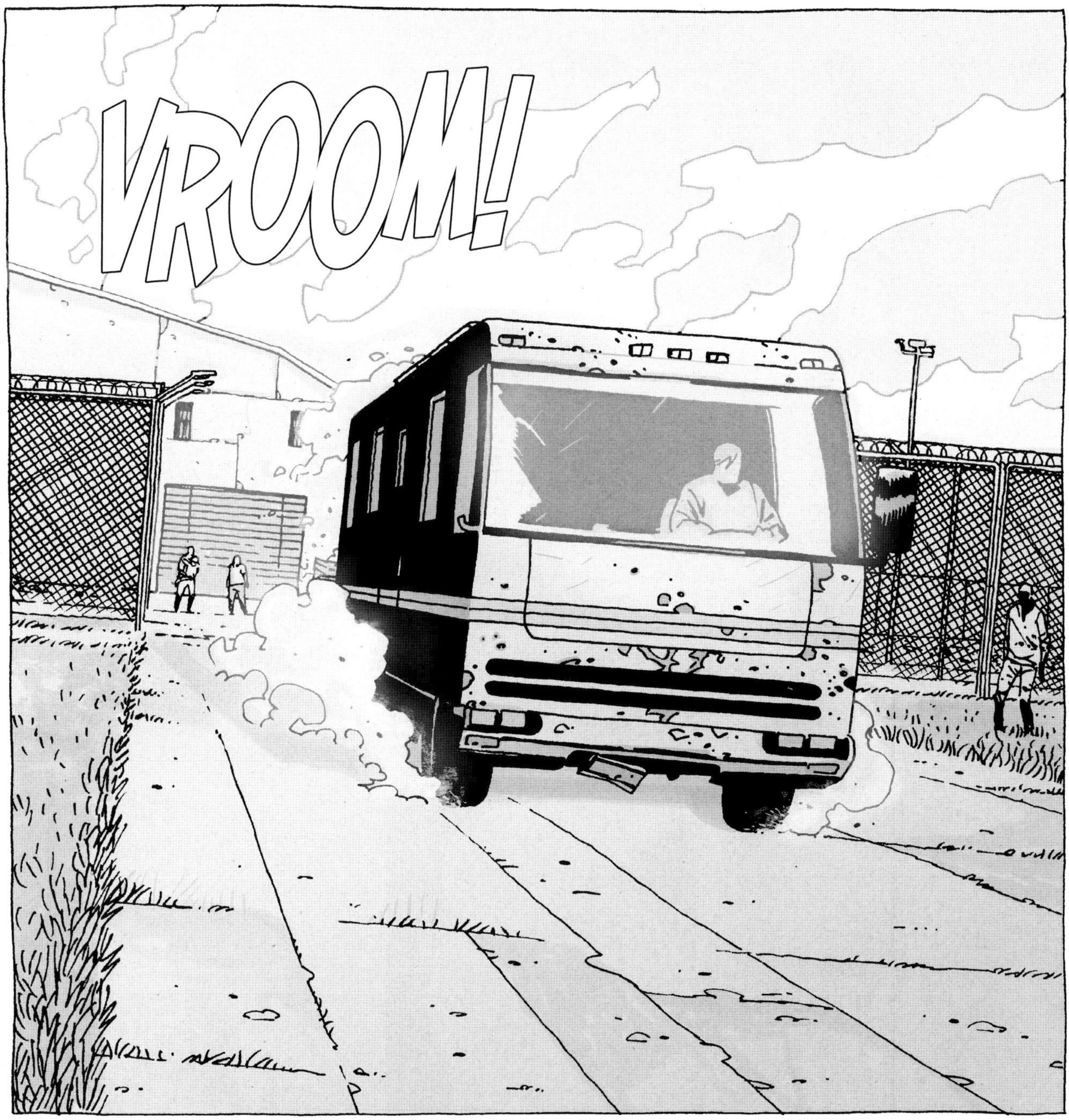
VROOM!

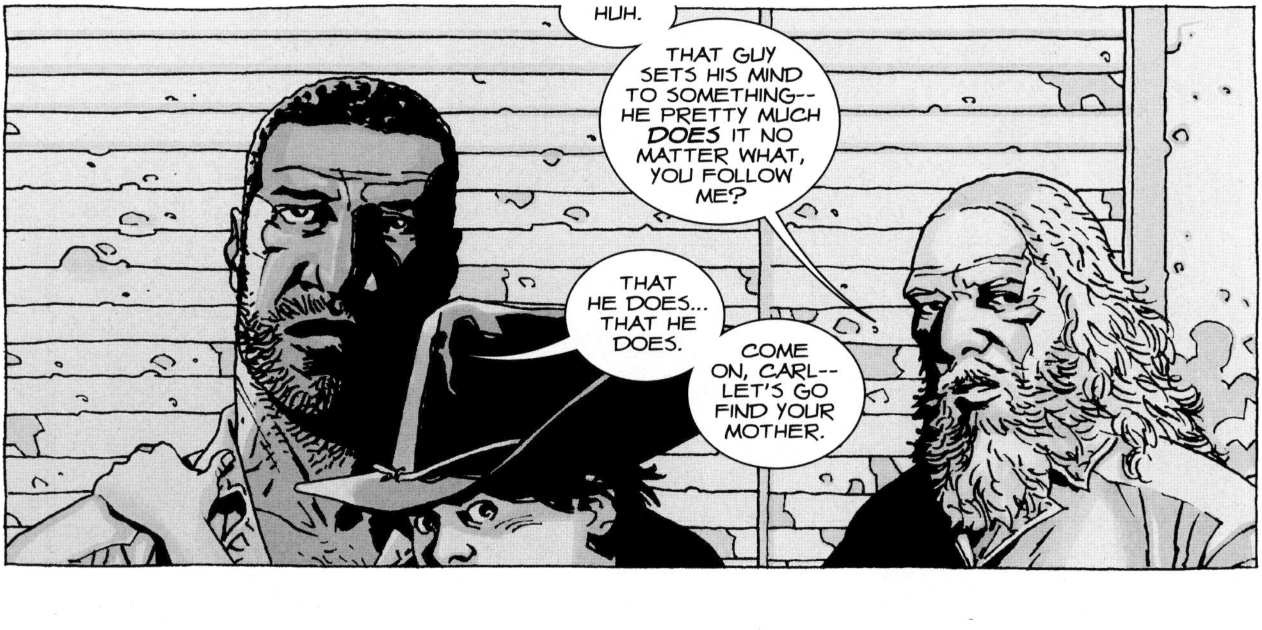
HUH.
THAT GUY SETS HIS MIND TO SOMETHING-- HE PRETTY MUCH DOES IT NO MATTER WHAT, YOU FOLLOW ME?
THAT HE DOES... THAT HE DOES.
COME ON, CARL-- LET'S GO FIND YOUR MOTHER.

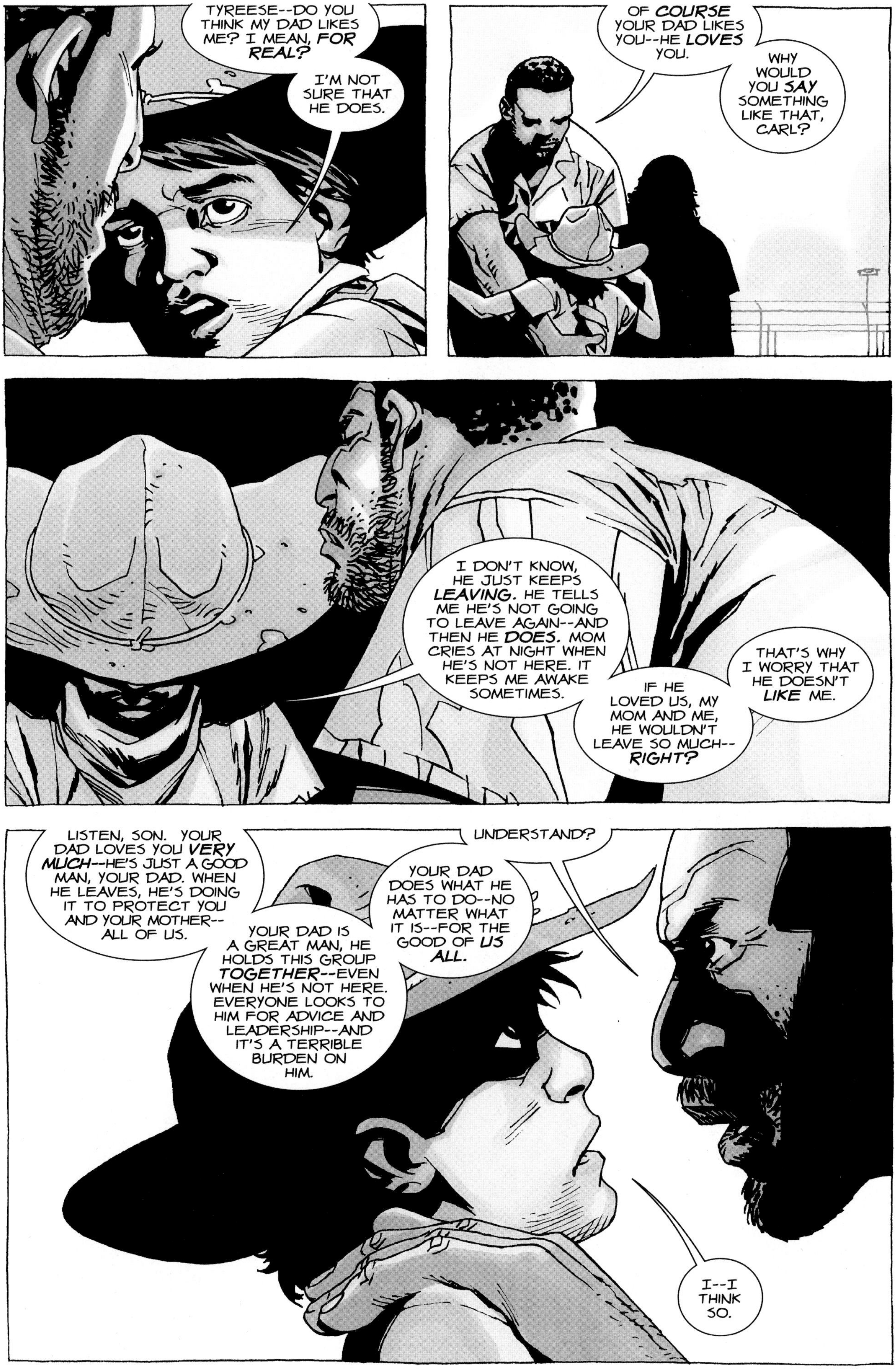
TYREESE--DO YOU THINK MY DAD LIKES ME? I MEAN, FOR REAL?
I'M NOT SURE THAT HE DOES.
OF COURSE YOUR DAD LIKES YOU--HE LOVES YOU.
WHY WOULD YOU SAY SOMETHING LIKE THAT, CARL?
I DON'T KNOW, HE JUST KEEPS LEAVING. HE TELLS ME HE'S NOT GOING TO LEAVE AGAIN--AND THEN HE DOES. MOM CRIES AT NIGHT WHEN HE'S NOT HERE. IT KEEPS ME AWAKE SOMETIMES.
IF HE LOVED US, MY MOM AND ME, HE WOULDN'T LEAVE SO MUCH--RIGHT?
THAT'S WHY I WORRY THAT HE DOESN'T LIKE ME.
LISTEN, SON. YOUR DAD LOVES YOU VERY MUCH--HE'S JUST A GOOD MAN, YOUR DAD. WHEN HE LEAVES, HE'S DOING IT TO PROTECT YOU AND YOUR MOTHER--ALL OF US.
YOUR DAD IS A GREAT MAN, HE HOLDS THIS GROUP TOGETHER--EVEN WHEN HE'S NOT HERE. EVERYONE LOOKS TO HIM FOR ADVICE AND LEADERSHIP--AND IT'S A TERRIBLE BURDEN ON HIM.
YOUR DAD DOES WHAT HE HAS TO DO--NO MATTER WHAT IT IS--FOR THE GOOD OF US ALL.
UNDERSTAND?
I--I THINK SO.

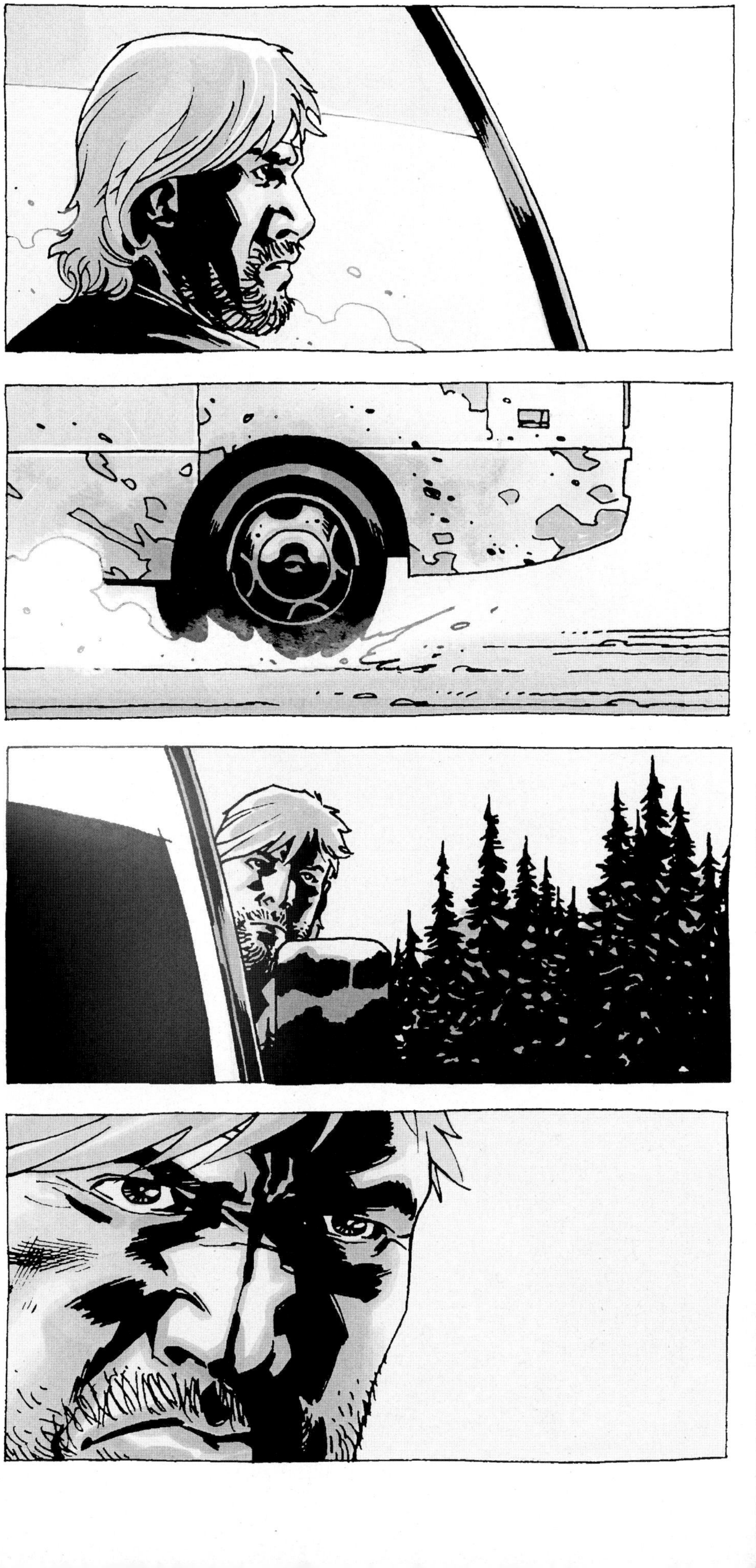
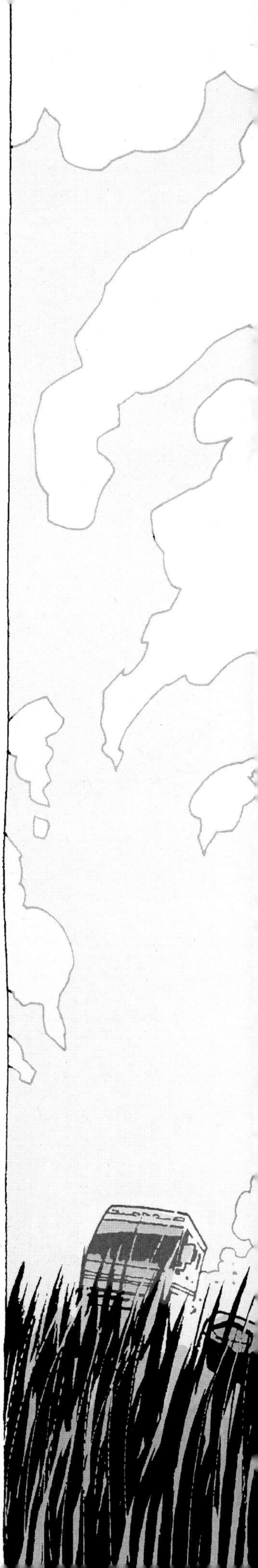

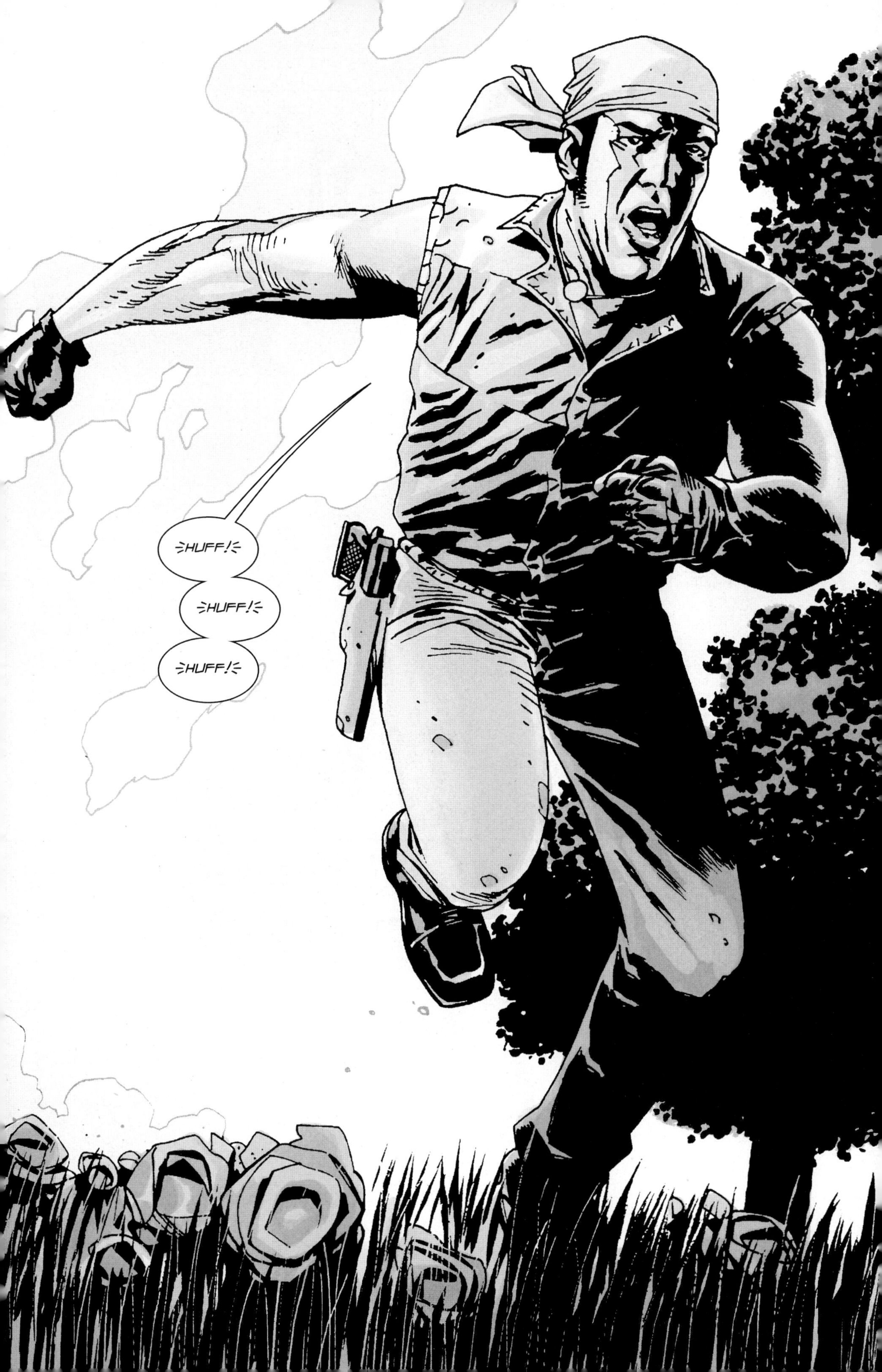
HUFF!
HUFF!
HUFF!

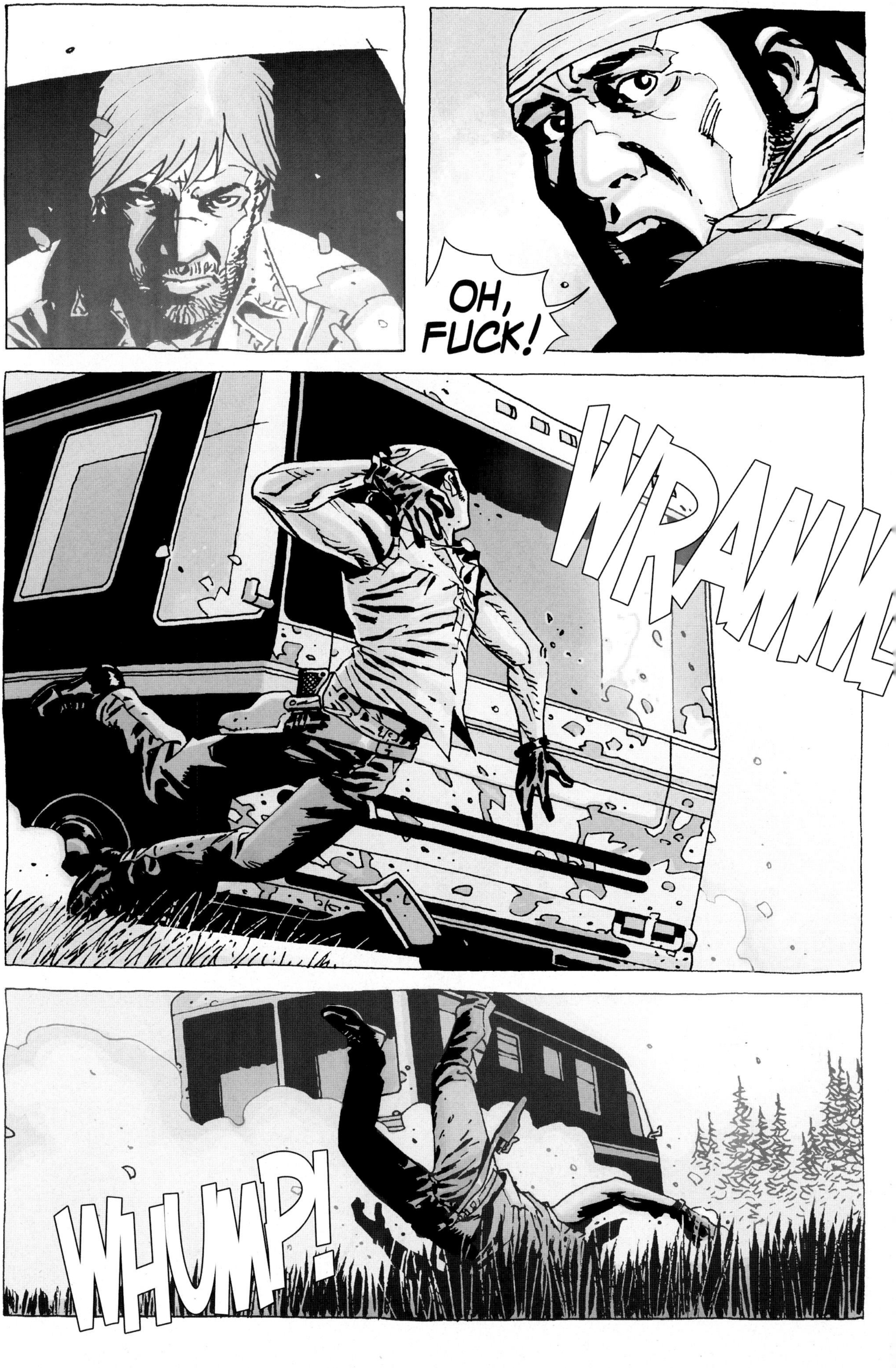
OH, FUCK!
WRAMM
WHUMP!

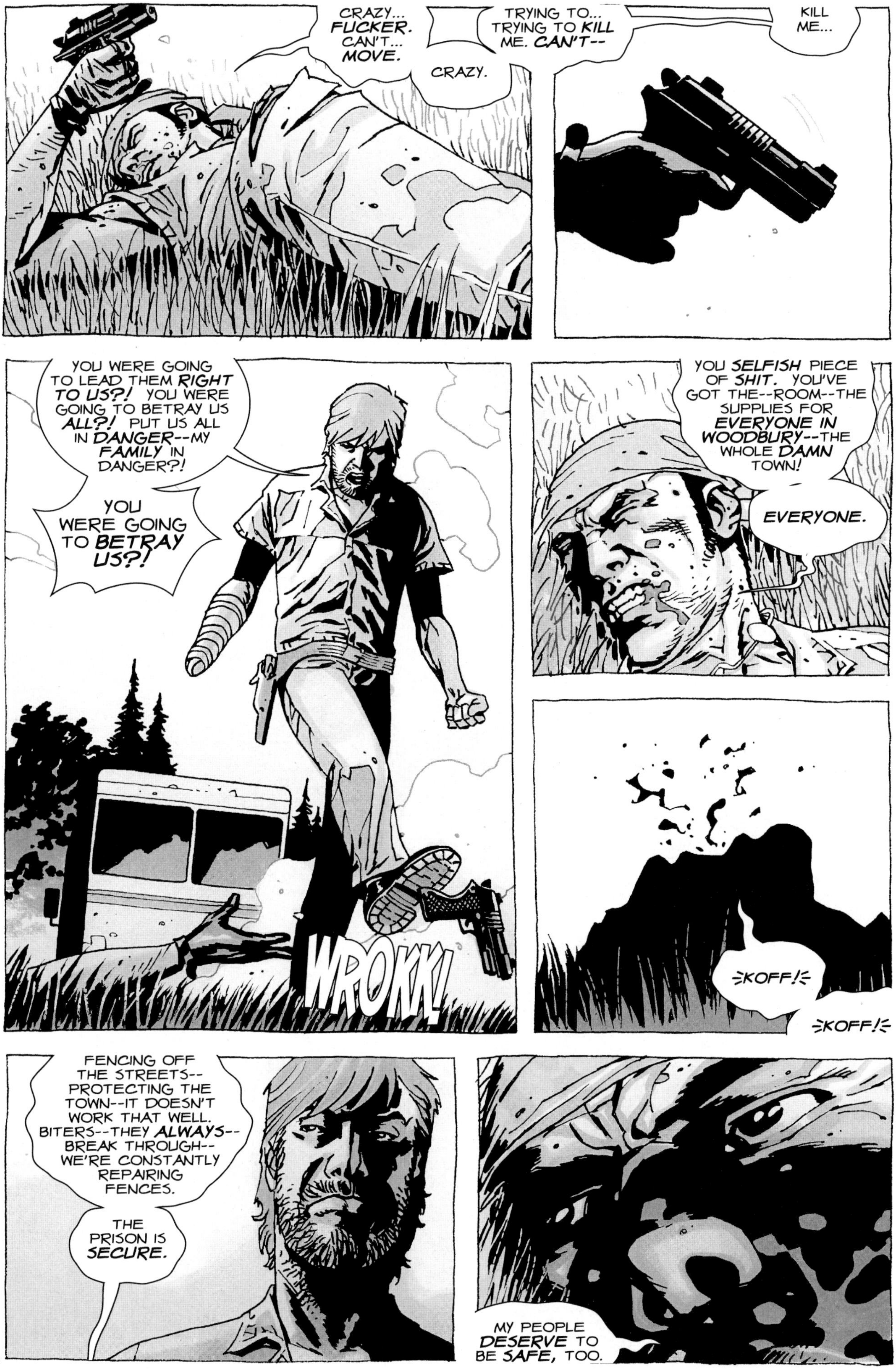
CRAZY... FUCKER. CAN'T... MOVE.
CRAZY.
TRYING TO... TRYING TO KILL ME. CAN'T--
KILL ME...
YOU WERE GOING TO LEAD THEM RIGHT TO US?! YOU WERE GOING TO BETRAY US ALL?! PUT US ALL IN DANGER--MY FAMILY IN DANGER?!
YOU WERE GOING TO BETRAY US?!
WROKK!
YOU SELFISH PIECE OF SHIT. YOU'VE GOT THE--ROOM--THE SUPPLIES FOR EVERYONE IN WOODBURY--THE WHOLE DAMN TOWN!
EVERYONE.
KOFF!
KOFF!
FENCING OFF THE STREETS--PROTECTING THE TOWN--IT DOESN'T WORK THAT WELL. BITERS--THEY ALWAYS--BREAK THROUGH--WE'RE CONSTANTLY REPAIRING FENCES.
THE PRISON IS SECURE.
MY PEOPLE DESERVE TO BE SAFE, TOO.

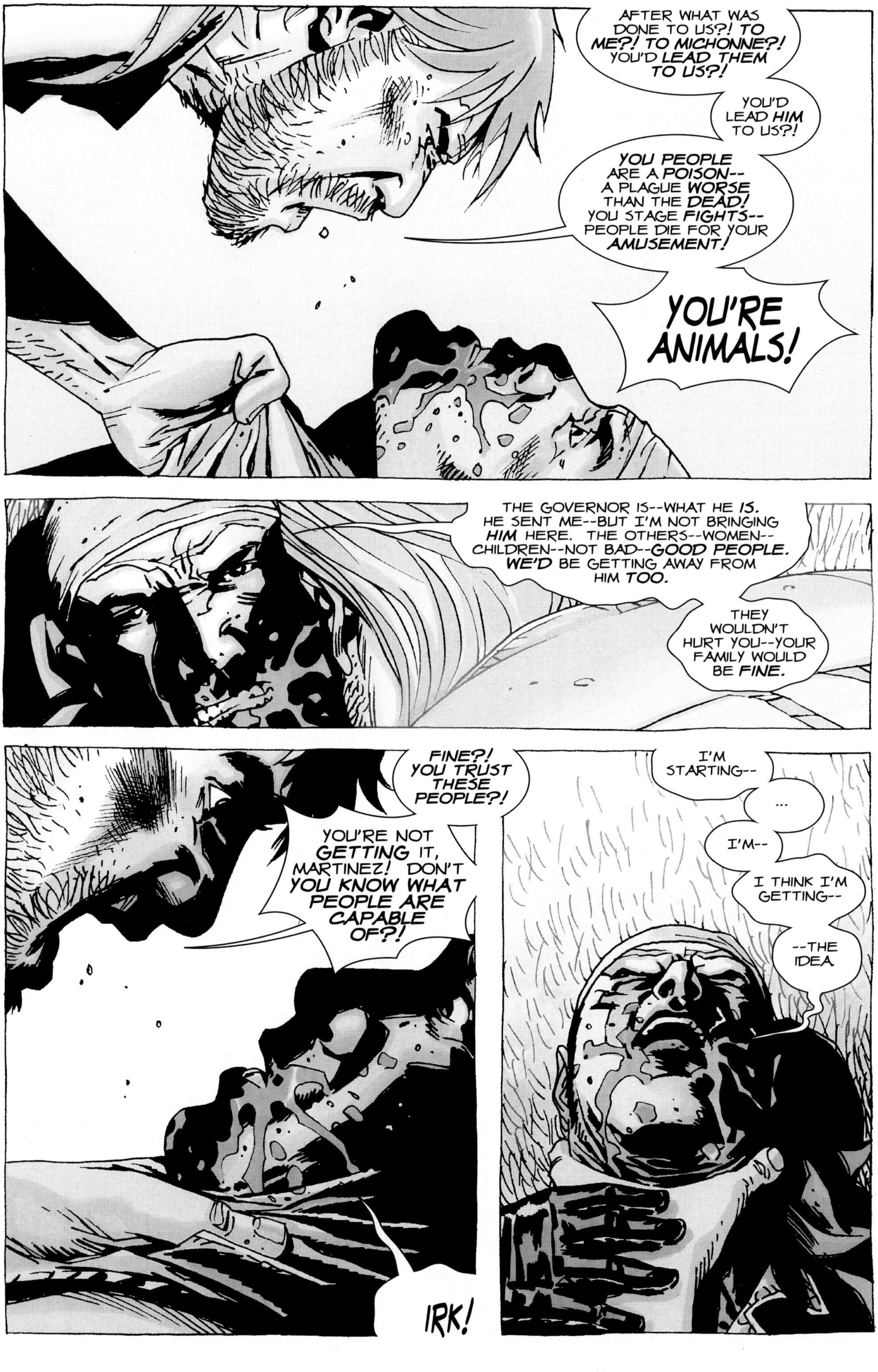
AFTER WHAT WAS DONE TO US?! TO ME?! TO MICHONNE?! YOU'D LEAD THEM TO US?!
YOU'D LEAD HIM TO US?!
YOU PEOPLE ARE A POISON-- A PLAGUE WORSE THAN THE DEAD! YOU STAGE FIGHTS-- PEOPLE DIE FOR YOUR AMUSEMENT!
YOU'RE ANIMALS!
THE GOVERNOR IS--WHAT HE IS. HE SENT ME--BUT I'M NOT BRINGING HIM HERE. THE OTHERS--WOMEN--CHILDREN--NOT BAD--GOOD PEOPLE. WE'D BE GETTING AWAY FROM HIM TOO.
THEY WOULDN'T HURT YOU--YOUR FAMILY WOULD BE FINE.
FINE?! YOU TRUST THESE PEOPLE?!
YOU'RE NOT GETTING IT, MARTINEZ! DON'T YOU KNOW WHAT PEOPLE ARE CAPABLE OF?!
IRK!
I'M STARTING--
...
I'M--
I THINK I'M GETTING--
--THE IDEA

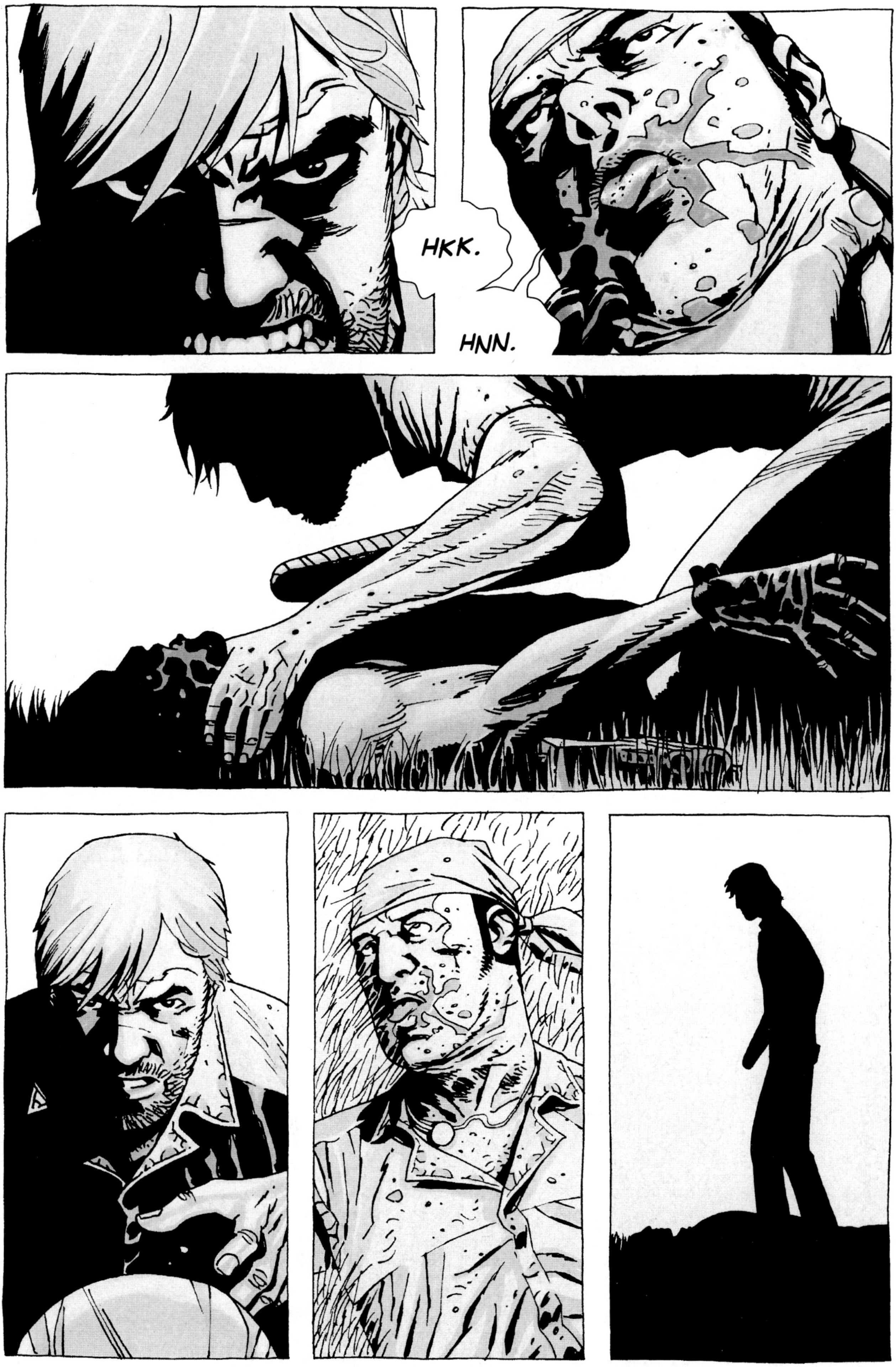
HKK.
HNN.

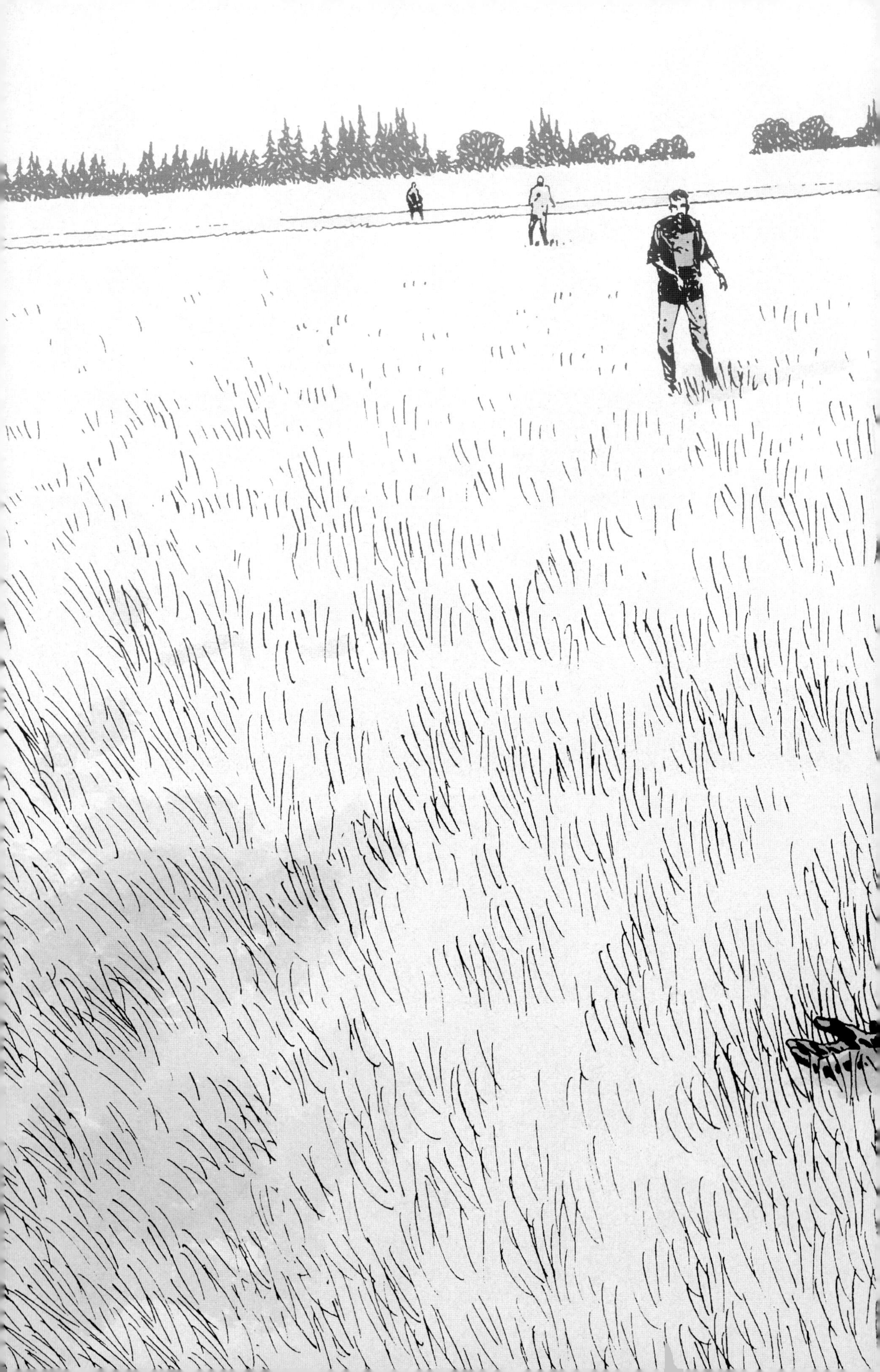

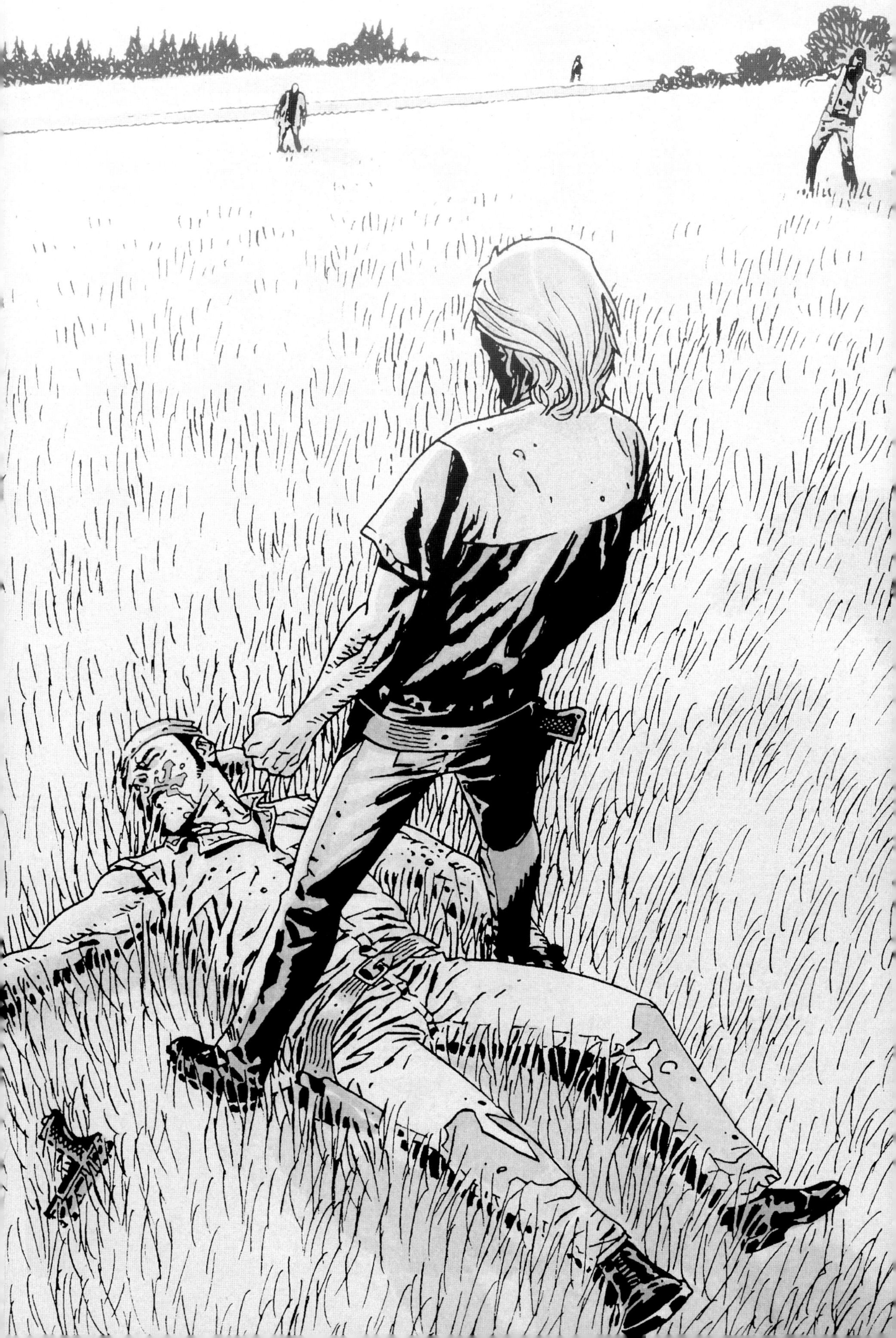

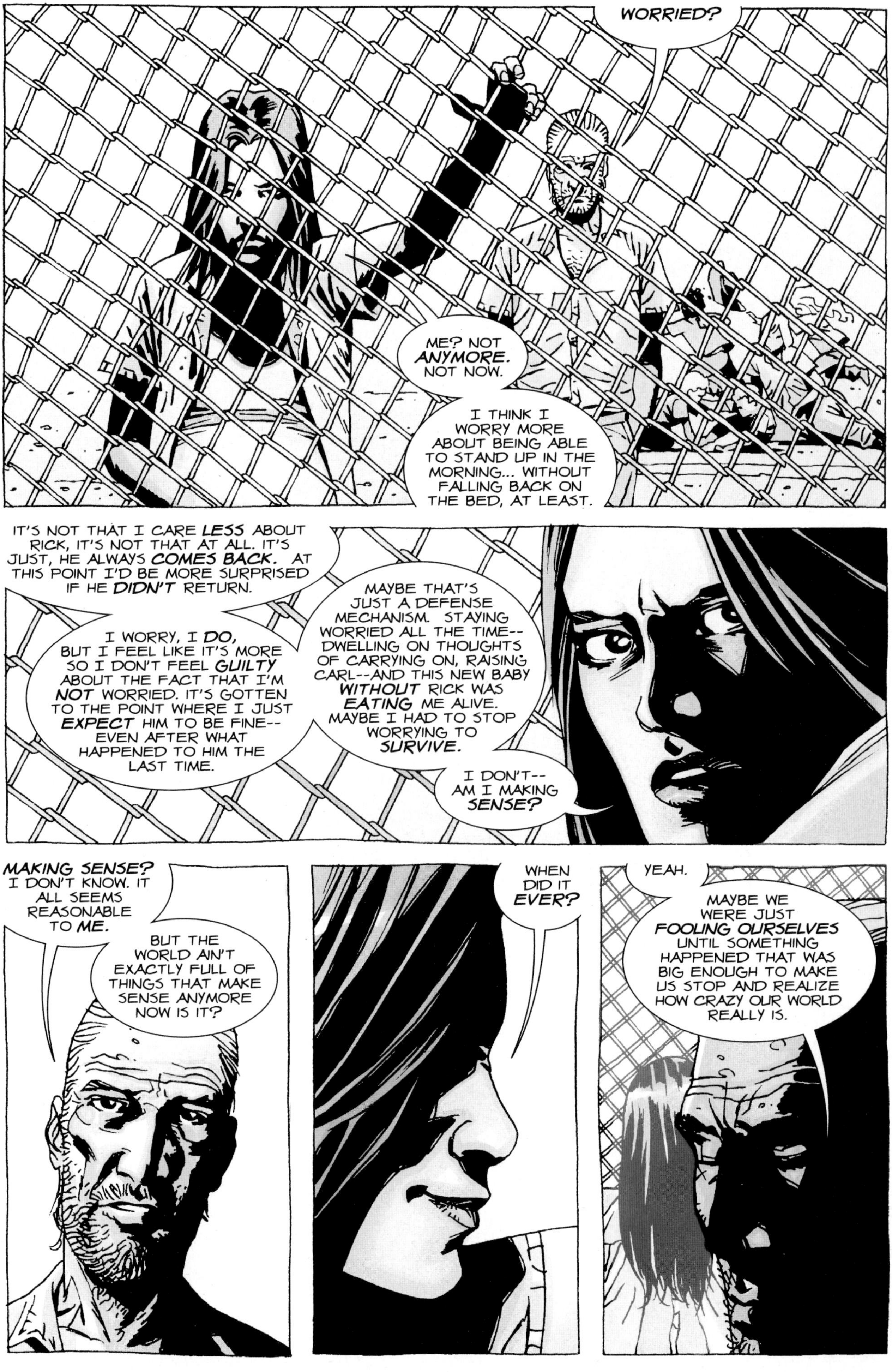
WORRIED?
ME? NOT ANYMORE. NOT NOW.
I THINK I WORRY MORE ABOUT BEING ABLE TO STAND UP IN THE MORNING... WITHOUT FALLING BACK ON THE BED, AT LEAST.
IT'S NOT THAT I CARE LESS ABOUT RICK, IT'S NOT THAT AT ALL. IT'S JUST, HE ALWAYS COMES BACK. AT THIS POINT I'D BE MORE SURPRISED IF HE DIDN'T RETURN.
I WORRY, I DO, BUT I FEEL LIKE IT'S MORE SO I DON'T FEEL GUILTY ABOUT THE FACT THAT I'M NOT WORRIED. IT'S GOTTEN TO THE POINT WHERE I JUST EXPECT HIM TO BE FINE-- EVEN AFTER WHAT HAPPENED TO HIM THE LAST TIME.
MAYBE THAT'S JUST A DEFENSE MECHANISM. STAYING WORRIED ALL THE TIME-- DWELLING ON THOUGHTS OF CARRYING ON, RAISING CARL--AND THIS NEW BABY WITHOUT RICK WAS EATING ME ALIVE. MAYBE I HAD TO STOP WORRYING TO SURVIVE.
I DON'T-- AM I MAKING SENSE?
MAKING SENSE? I DON'T KNOW. IT ALL SEEMS REASONABLE TO ME.
BUT THE WORLD AIN'T EXACTLY FULL OF THINGS THAT MAKE SENSE ANYMORE NOW IS IT?
WHEN DID IT EVER?
YEAH.
MAYBE WE WERE JUST FOOLING OURSELVES UNTIL SOMETHING HAPPENED THAT WAS BIG ENOUGH TO MAKE US STOP AND REALIZE HOW CRAZY OUR WORLD REALLY IS.

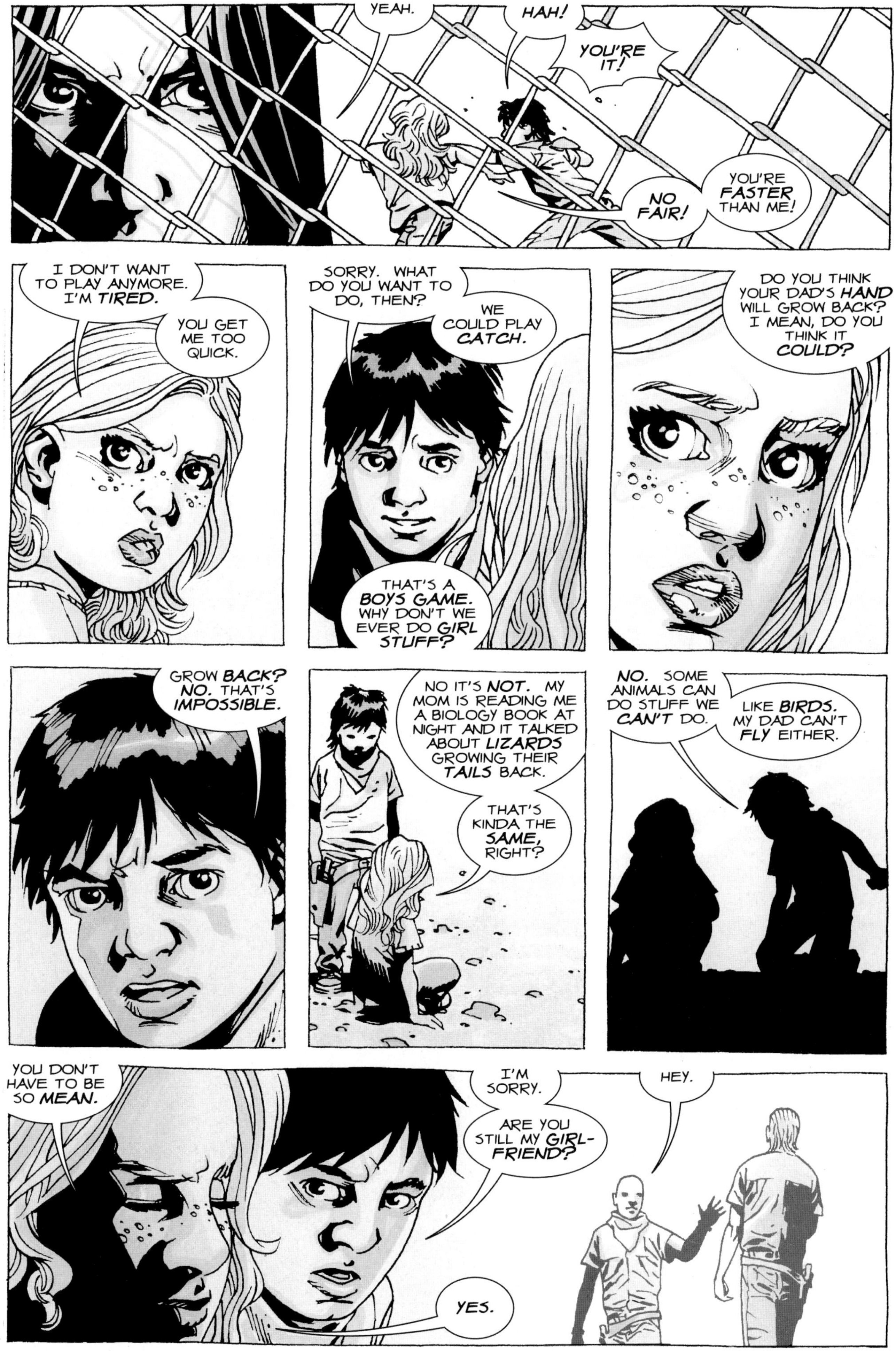

YEAH.
HAH!
YOU'RE IT!
YOU'RE FASTER THAN ME!
NO FAIR!
I DON'T WANT TO PLAY ANYMORE. I'M TIRED.
YOU GET ME TOO QUICK.
SORRY. WHAT DO YOU WANT TO DO, THEN?
WE COULD PLAY CATCH.
THAT'S A BOYS GAME. WHY DON'T WE EVER DO GIRL STUFF?
DO YOU THINK YOUR DAD'S HAND WILL GROW BACK? I MEAN, DO YOU THINK IT COULD?
GROW BACK? NO. THAT'S IMPOSSIBLE.
NO IT'S NOT. MY MOM IS READING ME A BIOLOGY BOOK AT NIGHT AND IT TALKED ABOUT LIZARDS GROWING THEIR TAILS BACK.
THAT'S KINDA THE SAME, RIGHT?
NO. SOME ANIMALS CAN DO STUFF WE CAN'T DO.
LIKE BIRDS. MY DAD CAN'T FLY EITHER.
YOU DON'T HAVE TO BE SO MEAN.
I'M SORRY.
ARE YOU STILL MY GIRL-FRIEND?
YES.
HEY.

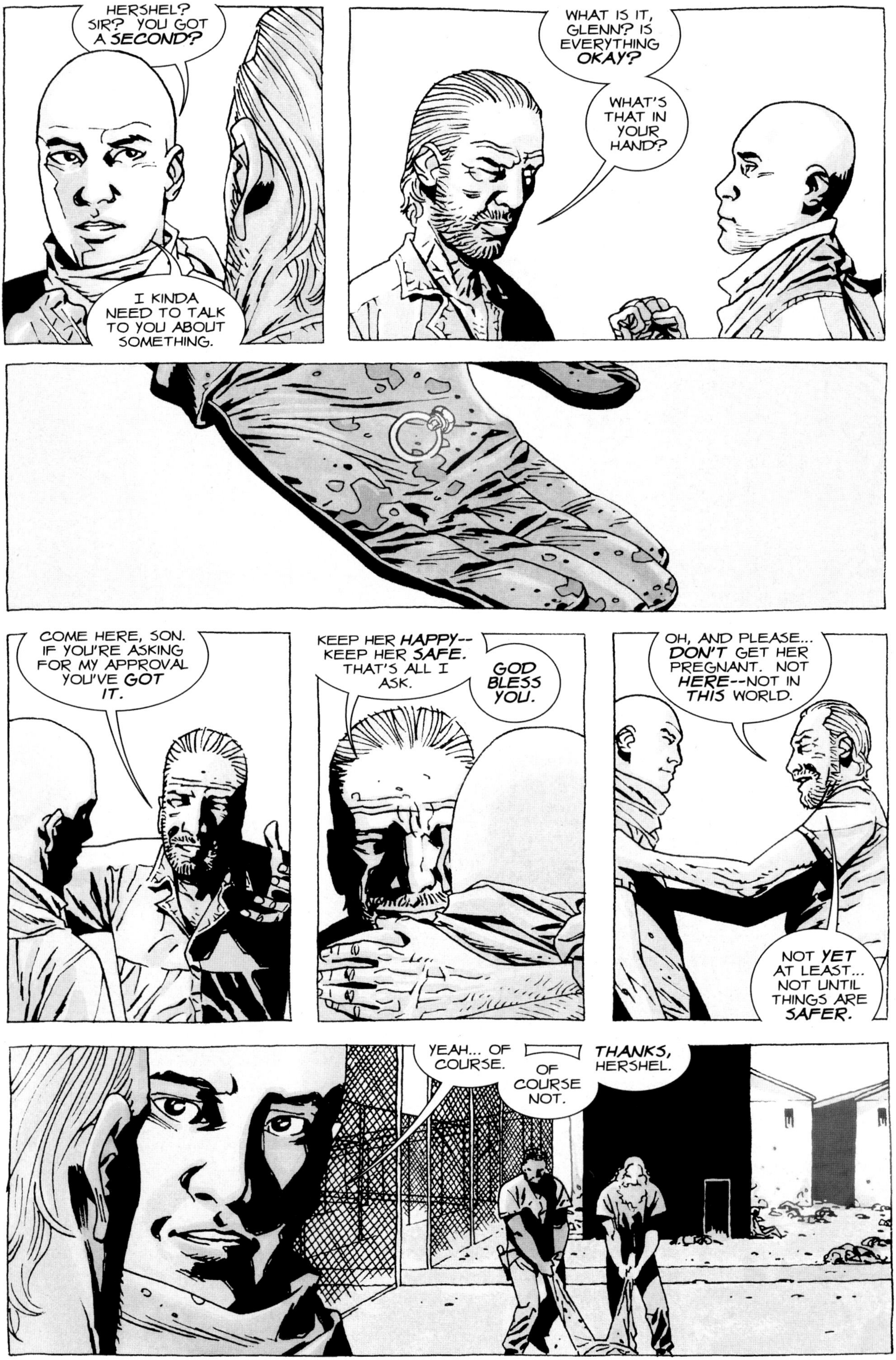
HERSHEL? SIR? YOU GOT A *SECOND?*
I KINDA NEED TO TALK TO YOU ABOUT SOMETHING.
WHAT IS IT, GLENN? IS EVERYTHING *OKAY?*
WHAT'S THAT IN YOUR HAND?
COME HERE, SON. IF YOU'RE ASKING FOR MY APPROVAL YOU'VE *GOT IT.*
KEEP HER *HAPPY*-- KEEP HER *SAFE.* THAT'S ALL I ASK.
GOD BLESS YOU.
OH, AND PLEASE... *DON'T* GET HER PREGNANT. NOT *HERE*--NOT IN *THIS* WORLD.
NOT *YET* AT LEAST... NOT UNTIL THINGS ARE *SAFER.*
YEAH... OF COURSE.
OF COURSE NOT.
THANKS, HERSHEL.

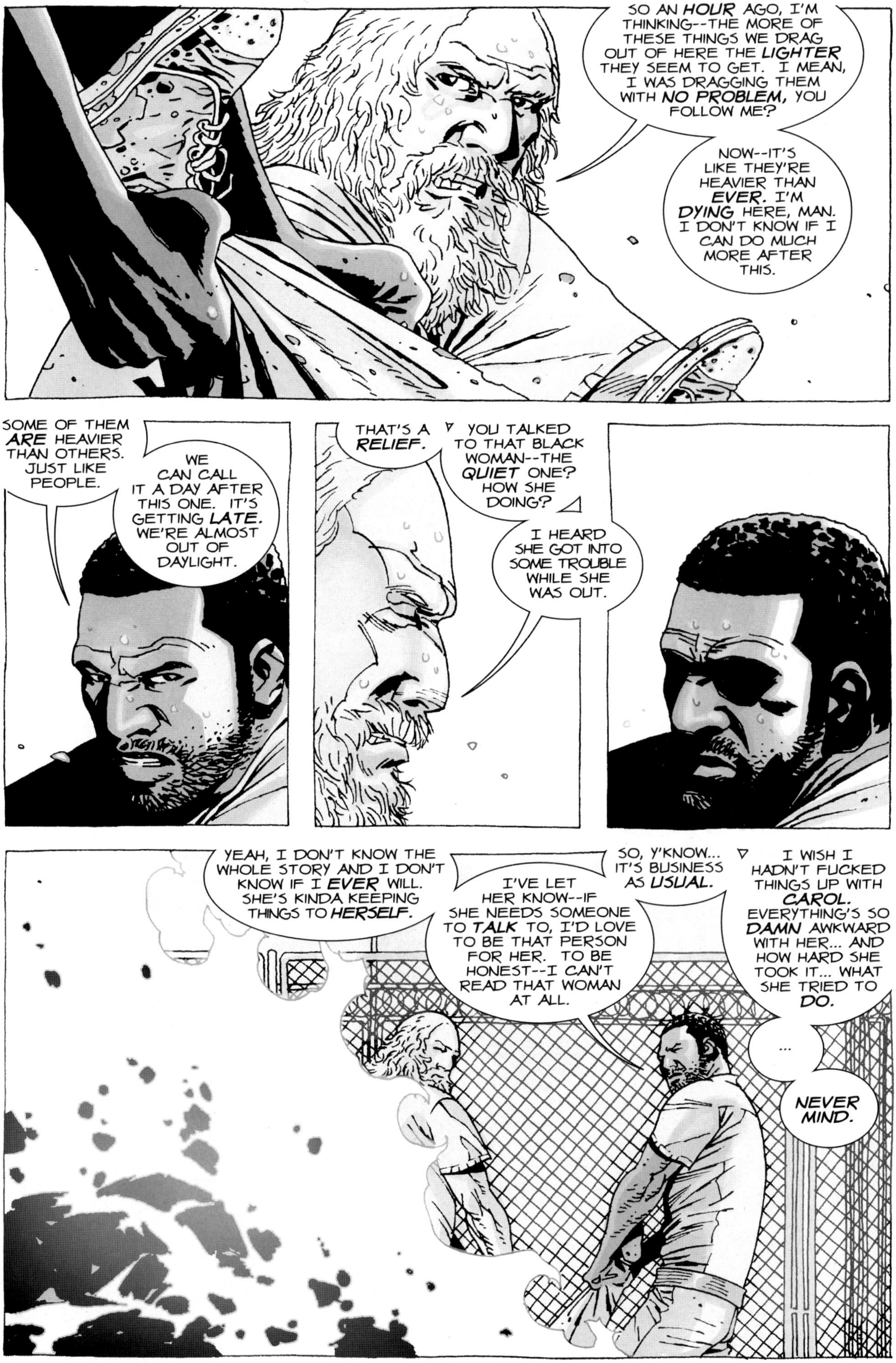
SO AN HOUR AGO, I'M THINKING--THE MORE OF THESE THINGS WE DRAG OUT OF HERE THE LIGHTER THEY SEEM TO GET. I MEAN, I WAS DRAGGING THEM WITH NO PROBLEM, YOU FOLLOW ME?
NOW--IT'S LIKE THEY'RE HEAVIER THAN EVER. I'M DYING HERE, MAN. I DON'T KNOW IF I CAN DO MUCH MORE AFTER THIS.
SOME OF THEM ARE HEAVIER THAN OTHERS. JUST LIKE PEOPLE.
WE CAN CALL IT A DAY AFTER THIS ONE. IT'S GETTING LATE. WE'RE ALMOST OUT OF DAYLIGHT.
THAT'S A RELIEF.
YOU TALKED TO THAT BLACK WOMAN--THE QUIET ONE? HOW SHE DOING?
I HEARD SHE GOT INTO SOME TROUBLE WHILE SHE WAS OUT.
YEAH, I DON'T KNOW THE WHOLE STORY AND I DON'T KNOW IF I EVER WILL. SHE'S KINDA KEEPING THINGS TO HERSELF.
I'VE LET HER KNOW--IF SHE NEEDS SOMEONE TO TALK TO, I'D LOVE TO BE THAT PERSON FOR HER. TO BE HONEST--I CAN'T READ THAT WOMAN AT ALL.
SO, Y'KNOW... IT'S BUSINESS AS USUAL.
I WISH I HADN'T FUCKED THINGS UP WITH CAROL. EVERYTHING'S SO DAMN AWKWARD WITH HER... AND HOW HARD SHE TOOK IT... WHAT SHE TRIED TO DO.
...
NEVER MIND.

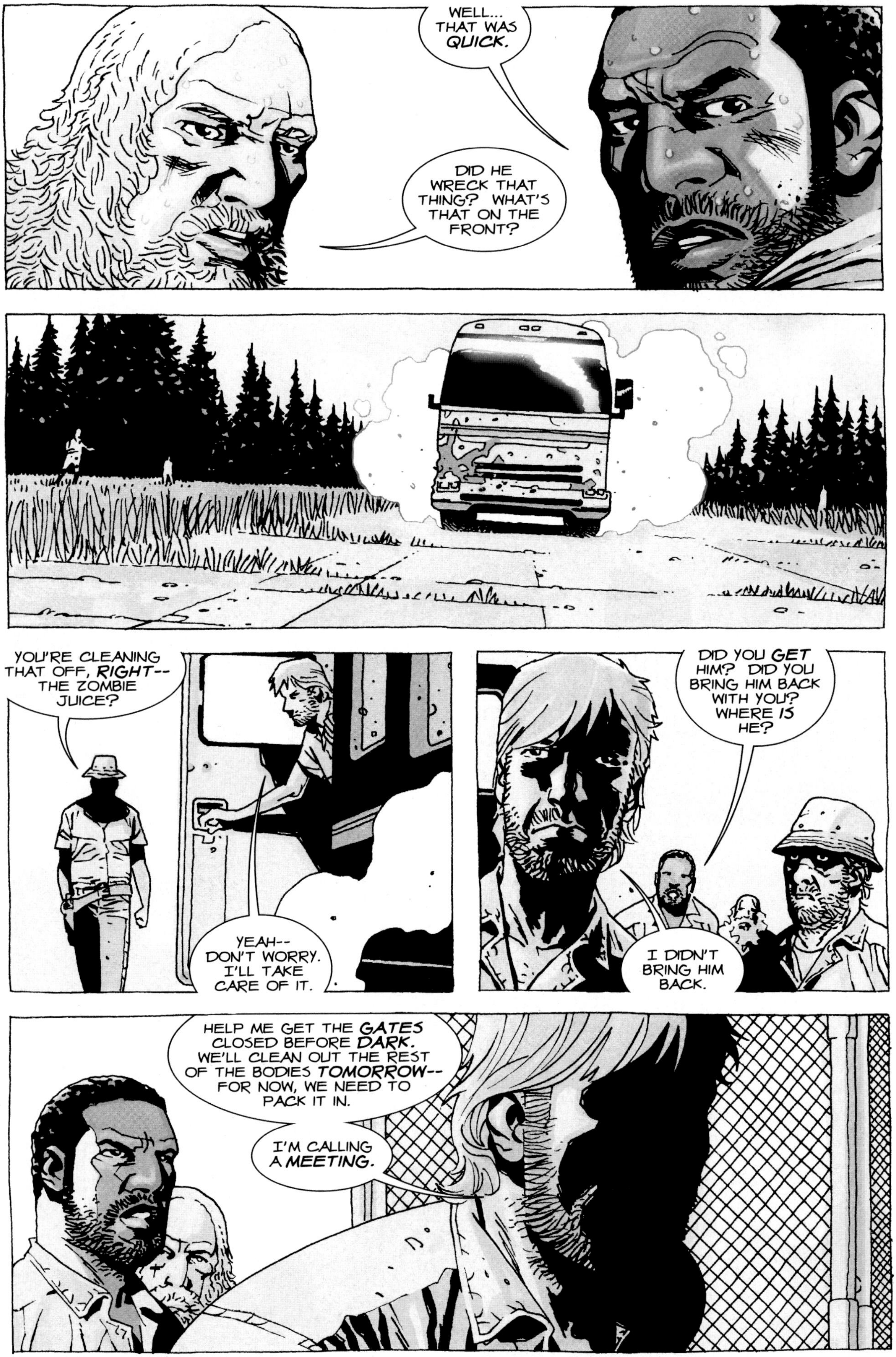
WELL... THAT WAS QUICK.
DID HE WRECK THAT THING? WHAT'S THAT ON THE FRONT?
YOU'RE CLEANING THAT OFF, RIGHT-- THE ZOMBIE JUICE?
YEAH-- DON'T WORRY. I'LL TAKE CARE OF IT.
DID YOU GET HIM? DID YOU BRING HIM BACK WITH YOU? WHERE IS HE?
I DIDN'T BRING HIM BACK.
HELP ME GET THE GATES CLOSED BEFORE DARK. WE'LL CLEAN OUT THE REST OF THE BODIES TOMORROW-- FOR NOW, WE NEED TO PACK IT IN.
I'M CALLING A MEETING.

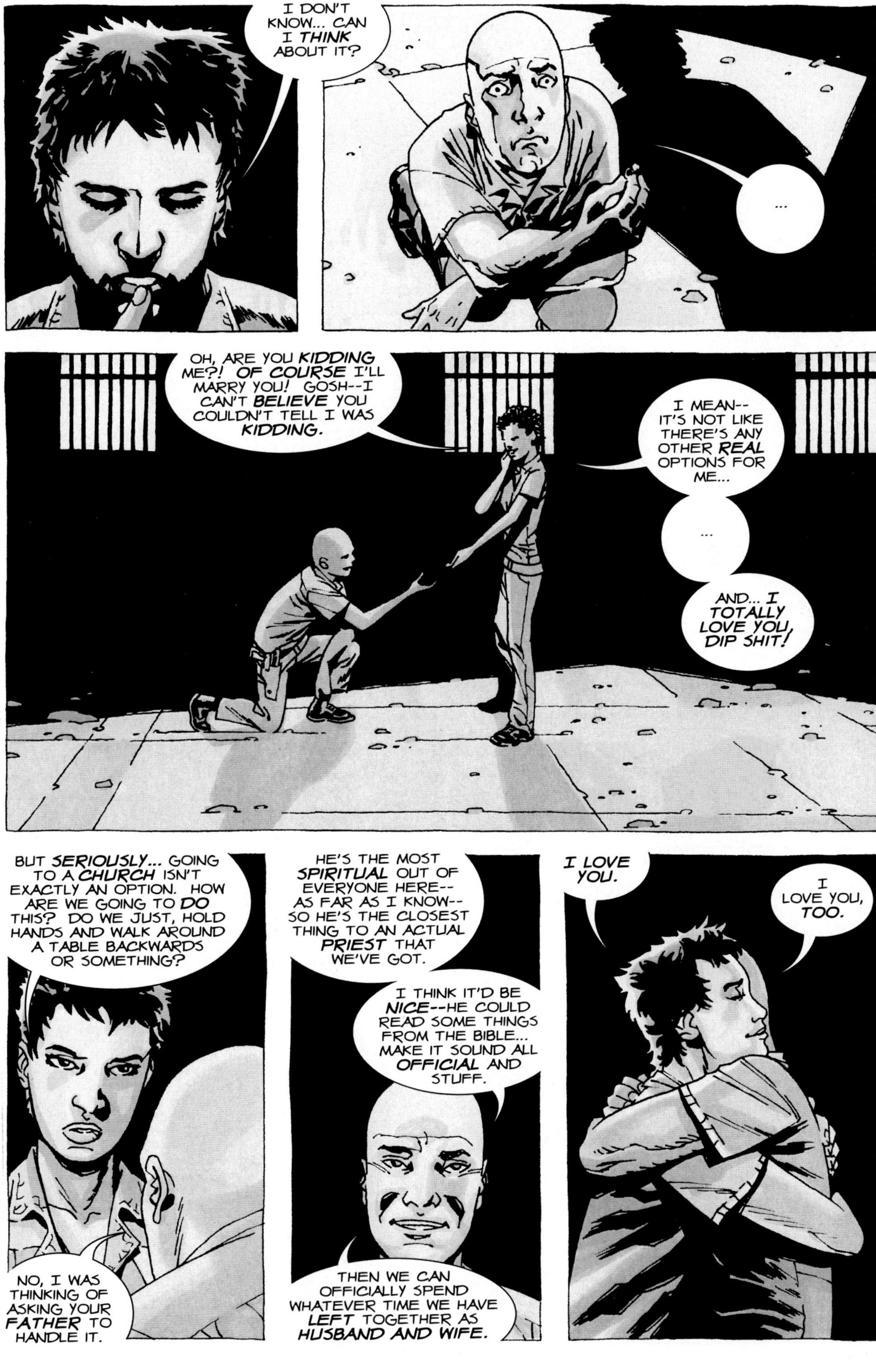
I DON'T KNOW... CAN I THINK ABOUT IT?
...
OH, ARE YOU KIDDING ME?! OF COURSE I'LL MARRY YOU! GOSH--I CAN'T BELIEVE YOU COULDN'T TELL I WAS KIDDING.
I MEAN-- IT'S NOT LIKE THERE'S ANY OTHER REAL OPTIONS FOR ME...
...
AND... I TOTALLY LOVE YOU, DIP SHIT!
BUT SERIOUSLY... GOING TO A CHURCH ISN'T EXACTLY AN OPTION. HOW ARE WE GOING TO DO THIS? DO WE JUST, HOLD HANDS AND WALK AROUND A TABLE BACKWARDS OR SOMETHING?
NO, I WAS THINKING OF ASKING YOUR FATHER TO HANDLE IT.
HE'S THE MOST SPIRITUAL OUT OF EVERYONE HERE-- AS FAR AS I KNOW-- SO HE'S THE CLOSEST THING TO AN ACTUAL PRIEST THAT WE'VE GOT.
I THINK IT'D BE NICE--HE COULD READ SOME THINGS FROM THE BIBLE... MAKE IT SOUND ALL OFFICIAL AND STUFF.
THEN WE CAN OFFICIALLY SPEND WHATEVER TIME WE HAVE LEFT TOGETHER AS HUSBAND AND WIFE.
I LOVE YOU.
I LOVE YOU, TOO.

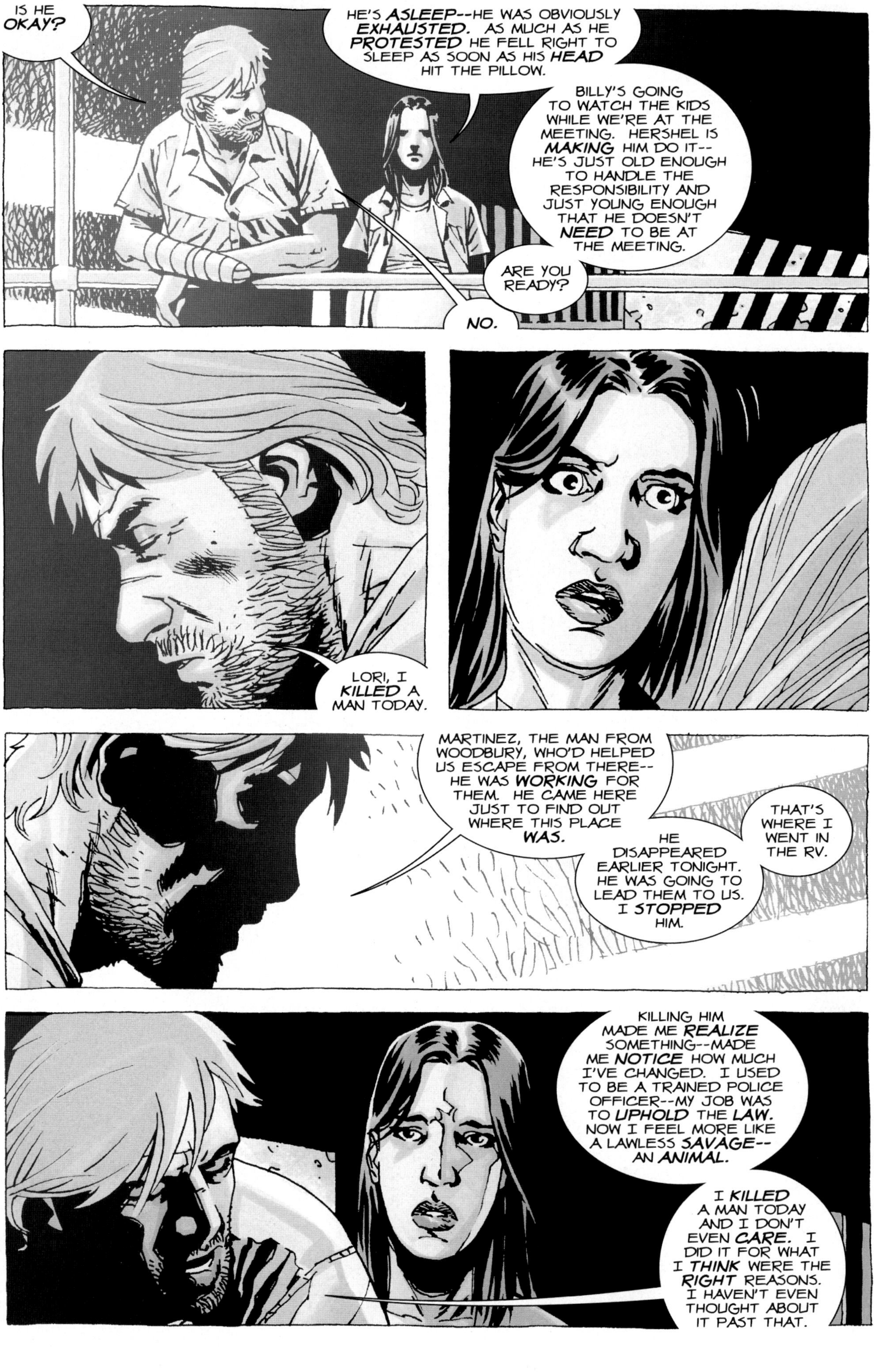
IS HE OKAY?
HE'S ASLEEP--HE WAS OBVIOUSLY EXHAUSTED. AS MUCH AS HE PROTESTED HE FELL RIGHT TO SLEEP AS SOON AS HIS HEAD HIT THE PILLOW.
BILLY'S GOING TO WATCH THE KIDS WHILE WE'RE AT THE MEETING. HERSHEL IS MAKING HIM DO IT-- HE'S JUST OLD ENOUGH TO HANDLE THE RESPONSIBILITY AND JUST YOUNG ENOUGH THAT HE DOESN'T NEED TO BE AT THE MEETING.
ARE YOU READY?
NO.
LORI, I KILLED A MAN TODAY.
MARTINEZ, THE MAN FROM WOODBURY, WHO'D HELPED US ESCAPE FROM THERE-- HE WAS WORKING FOR THEM. HE CAME HERE JUST TO FIND OUT WHERE THIS PLACE WAS.
HE DISAPPEARED EARLIER TONIGHT. HE WAS GOING TO LEAD THEM TO US. I STOPPED HIM.
THAT'S WHERE I WENT IN THE RV.
KILLING HIM MADE ME REALIZE SOMETHING--MADE ME NOTICE HOW MUCH I'VE CHANGED. I USED TO BE A TRAINED POLICE OFFICER--MY JOB WAS TO UPHOLD THE LAW. NOW I FEEL MORE LIKE A LAWLESS SAVAGE-- AN ANIMAL.
I KILLED A MAN TODAY AND I DON'T EVEN CARE. I DID IT FOR WHAT I THINK WERE THE RIGHT REASONS. I HAVEN'T EVEN THOUGHT ABOUT IT PAST THAT.

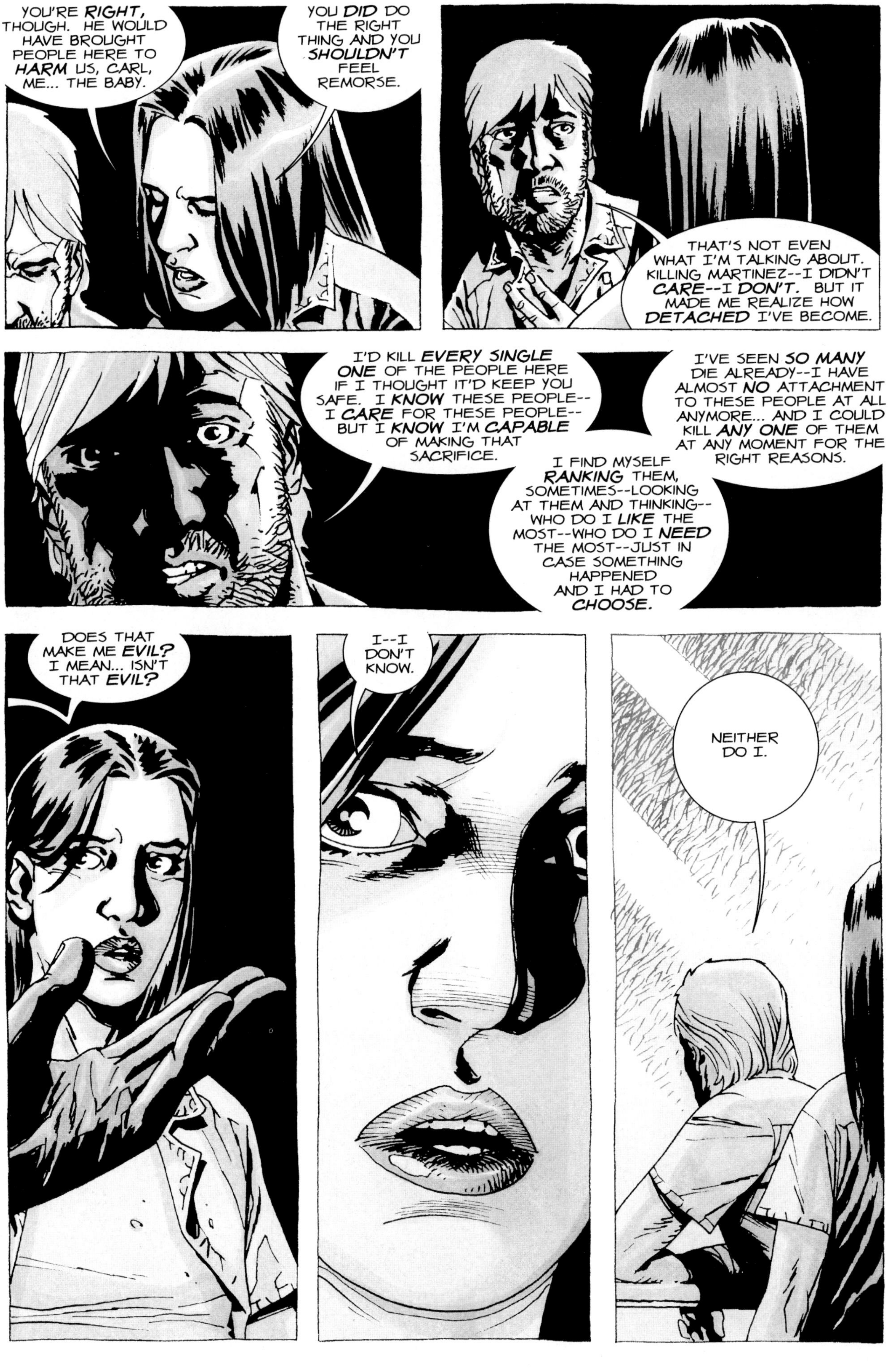
YOU'RE RIGHT, THOUGH. HE WOULD HAVE BROUGHT PEOPLE HERE TO HARM US, CARL, ME... THE BABY.
YOU DID DO THE RIGHT THING AND YOU SHOULDN'T FEEL REMORSE.
THAT'S NOT EVEN WHAT I'M TALKING ABOUT. KILLING MARTINEZ--I DIDN'T CARE--I DON'T. BUT IT MADE ME REALIZE HOW DETACHED I'VE BECOME.
I'D KILL EVERY SINGLE ONE OF THE PEOPLE HERE IF I THOUGHT IT'D KEEP YOU SAFE. I KNOW THESE PEOPLE-- I CARE FOR THESE PEOPLE-- BUT I KNOW I'M CAPABLE OF MAKING THAT SACRIFICE.
I'VE SEEN SO MANY DIE ALREADY--I HAVE ALMOST NO ATTACHMENT TO THESE PEOPLE AT ALL ANYMORE... AND I COULD KILL ANY ONE OF THEM AT ANY MOMENT FOR THE RIGHT REASONS.
I FIND MYSELF RANKING THEM, SOMETIMES--LOOKING AT THEM AND THINKING-- WHO DO I LIKE THE MOST--WHO DO I NEED THE MOST--JUST IN CASE SOMETHING HAPPENED AND I HAD TO CHOOSE.
DOES THAT MAKE ME EVIL? I MEAN... ISN'T THAT EVIL?
I--I DON'T KNOW.
NEITHER DO I.

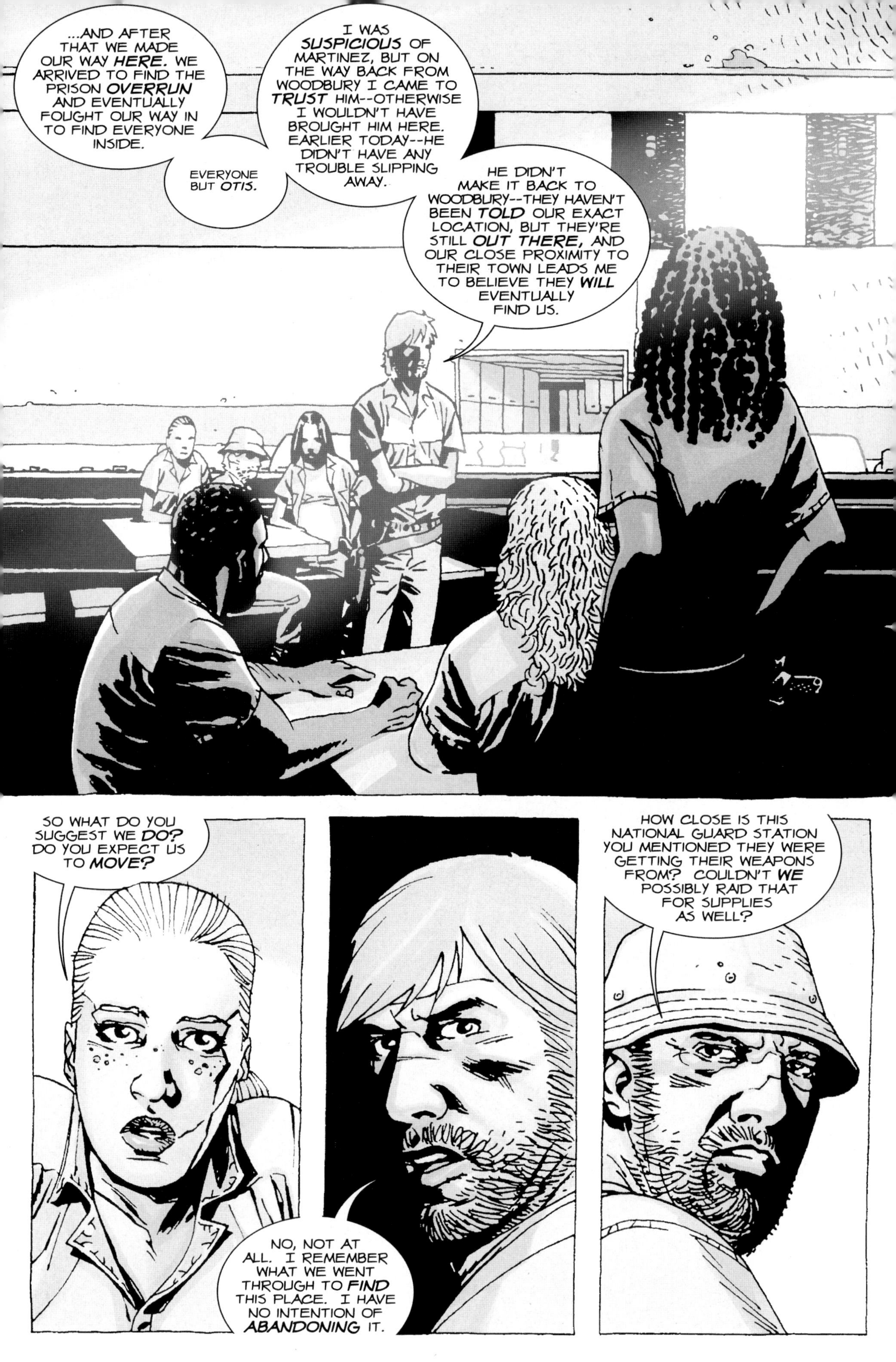
...AND AFTER THAT WE MADE OUR WAY HERE. WE ARRIVED TO FIND THE PRISON OVERRUN AND EVENTUALLY FOUGHT OUR WAY IN TO FIND EVERYONE INSIDE.
EVERYONE BUT OTIS.
I WAS SUSPICIOUS OF MARTINEZ, BUT ON THE WAY BACK FROM WOODBURY I CAME TO TRUST HIM--OTHERWISE I WOULDN'T HAVE BROUGHT HIM HERE. EARLIER TODAY--HE DIDN'T HAVE ANY TROUBLE SLIPPING AWAY.
HE DIDN'T MAKE IT BACK TO WOODBURY--THEY HAVEN'T BEEN TOLD OUR EXACT LOCATION, BUT THEY'RE STILL OUT THERE, AND OUR CLOSE PROXIMITY TO THEIR TOWN LEADS ME TO BELIEVE THEY WILL EVENTUALLY FIND US.
SO WHAT DO YOU SUGGEST WE DO? DO YOU EXPECT US TO MOVE?
NO, NOT AT ALL. I REMEMBER WHAT WE WENT THROUGH TO FIND THIS PLACE. I HAVE NO INTENTION OF ABANDONING IT.
HOW CLOSE IS THIS NATIONAL GUARD STATION YOU MENTIONED THEY WERE GETTING THEIR WEAPONS FROM? COULDN'T WE POSSIBLY RAID THAT FOR SUPPLIES AS WELL?

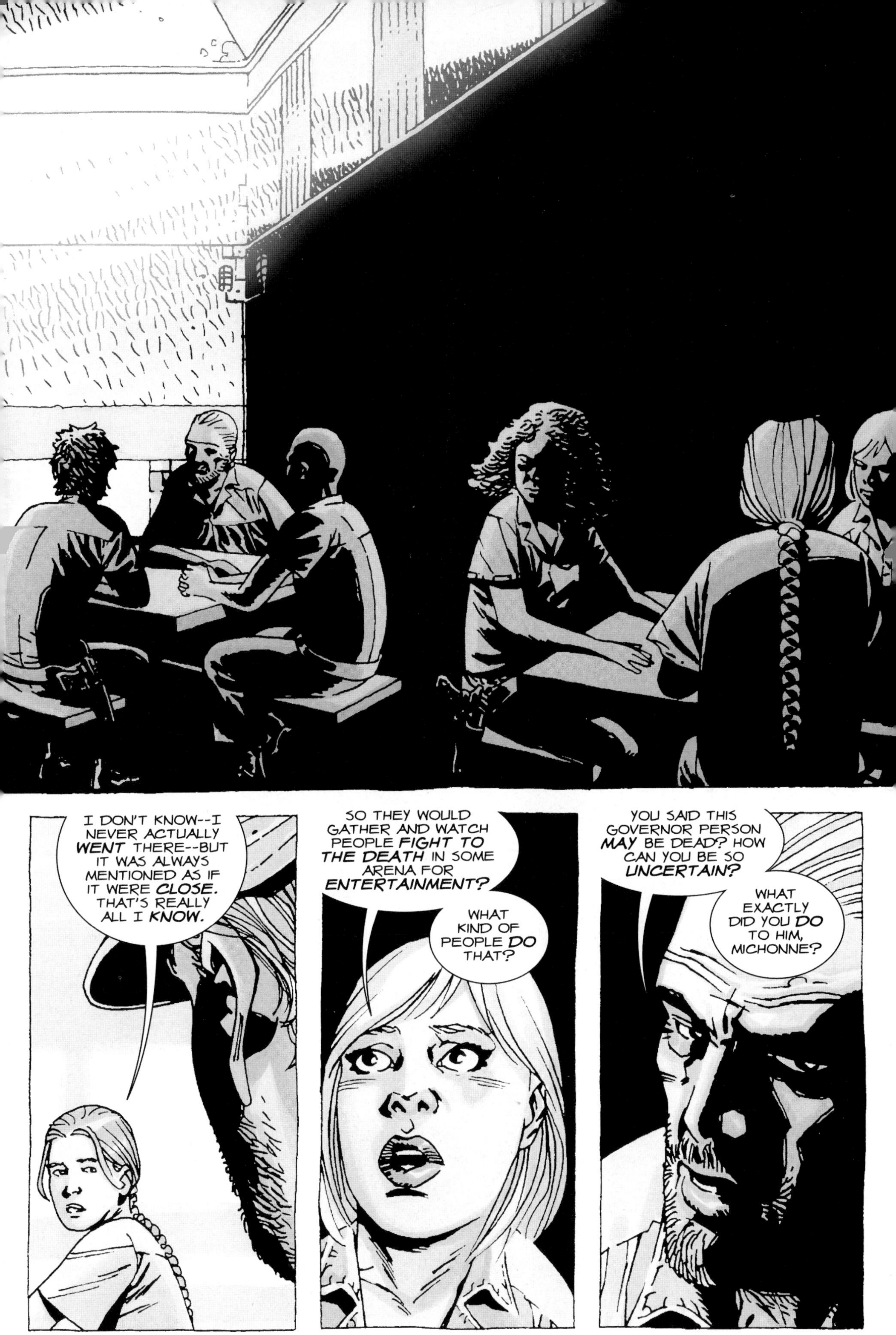
I DON'T KNOW--I NEVER ACTUALLY WENT THERE--BUT IT WAS ALWAYS MENTIONED AS IF IT WERE CLOSE. THAT'S REALLY ALL I KNOW.
SO THEY WOULD GATHER AND WATCH PEOPLE FIGHT TO THE DEATH IN SOME ARENA FOR ENTERTAINMENT?
WHAT KIND OF PEOPLE DO THAT?
YOU SAID THIS GOVERNOR PERSON MAY BE DEAD? HOW CAN YOU BE SO UNCERTAIN?
WHAT EXACTLY DID YOU DO TO HIM, MICHONNE?

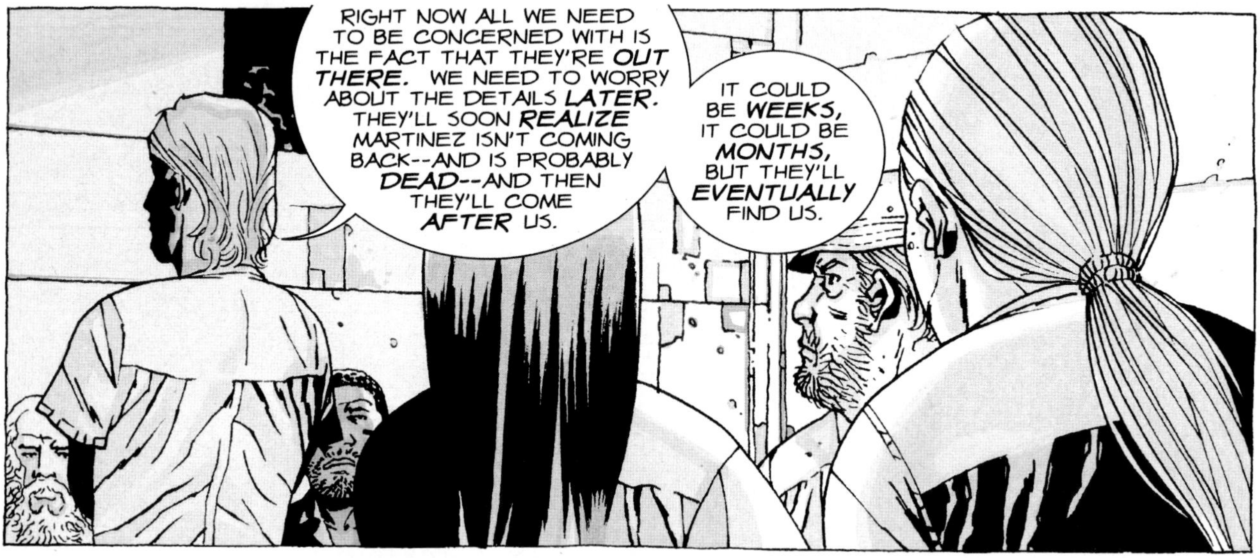
RIGHT NOW ALL WE NEED TO BE CONCERNED WITH IS THE FACT THAT THEY'RE OUT THERE. WE NEED TO WORRY ABOUT THE DETAILS LATER. THEY'LL SOON REALIZE MARTINEZ ISN'T COMING BACK--AND IS PROBABLY DEAD--AND THEN THEY'LL COME AFTER US.
IT COULD BE WEEKS, IT COULD BE MONTHS, BUT THEY'LL EVENTUALLY FIND US.

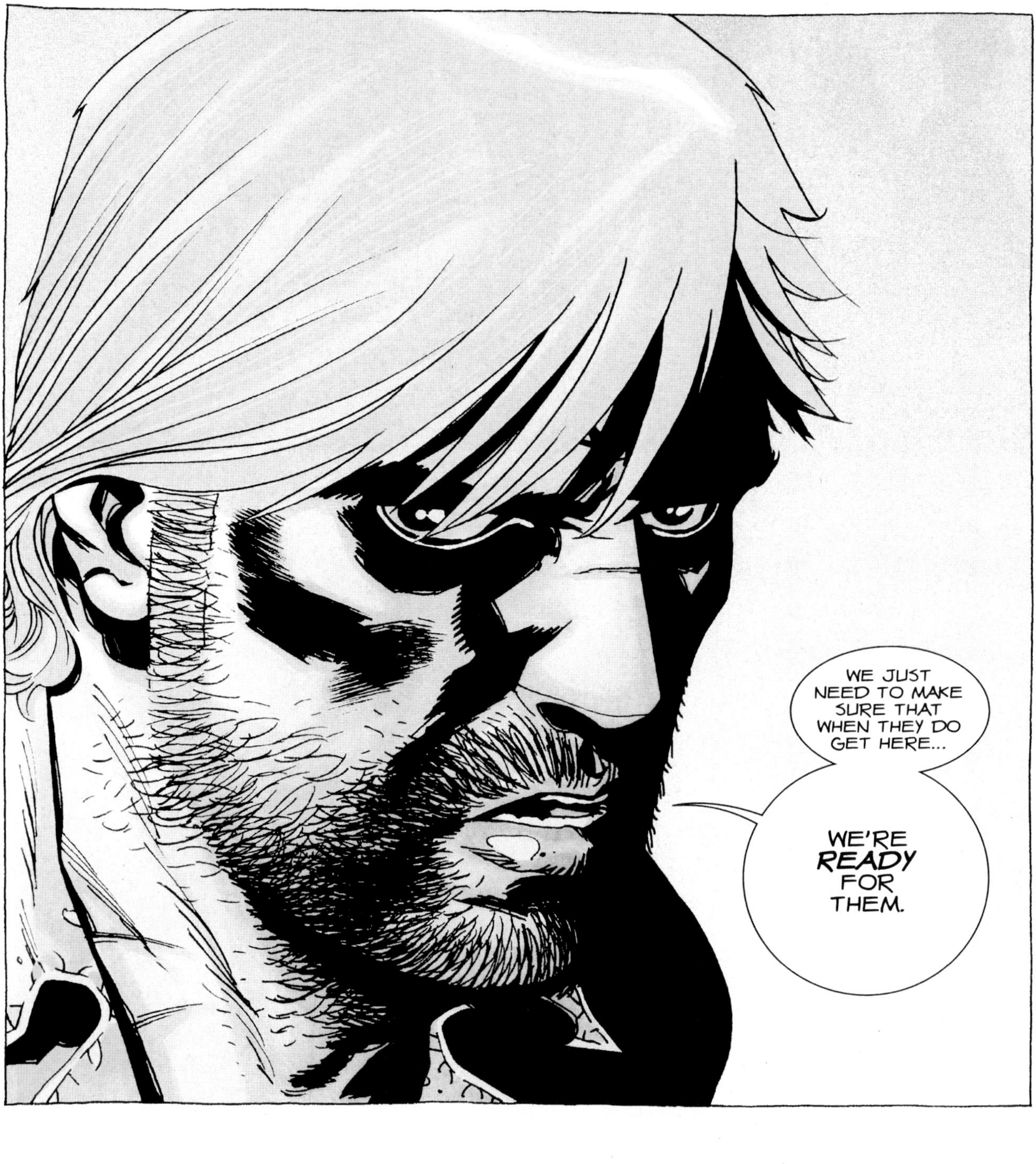
WE JUST NEED TO MAKE SURE THAT WHEN THEY DO GET HERE...
WE'RE READY FOR THEM.

to be continued...

Sketchbook

There's really not a lot of sketching that gets done in the course of making this book, which I think I've mentioned before—so here on the following two pages, you'll see the sum total of additional work done on this series past what you see in the single issues. It ain't a lot.

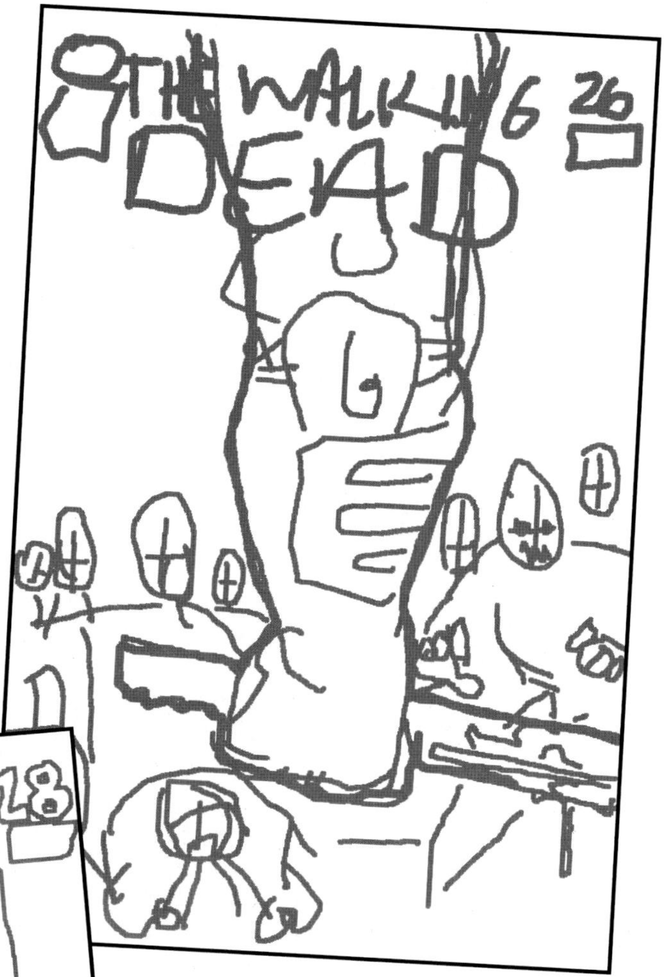
THE WALKING
26
DEAD

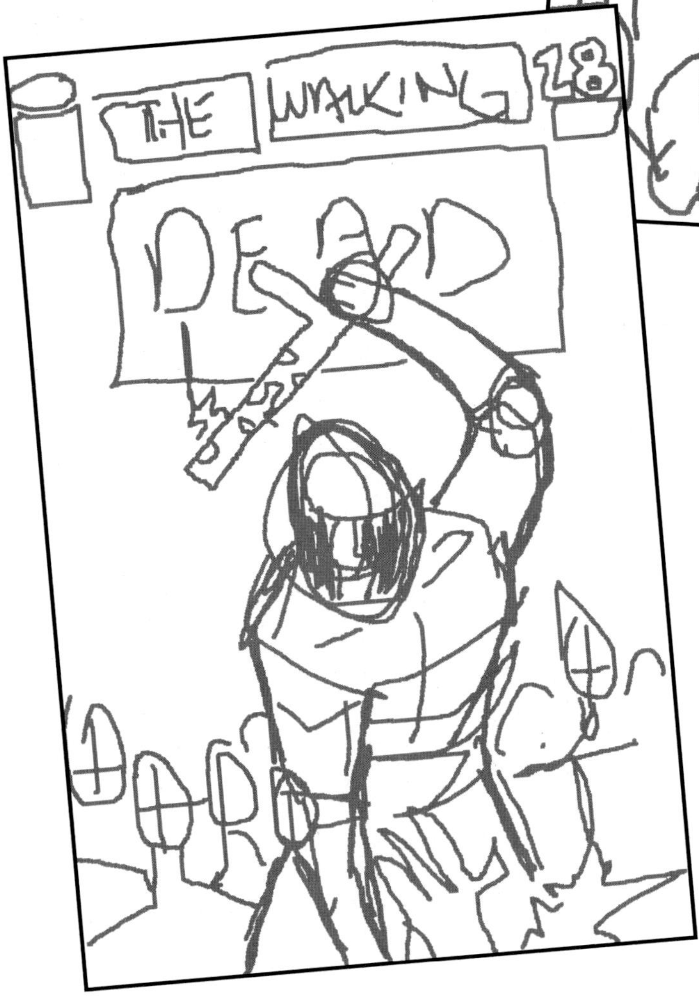
THE
WALKING
28
DEAD

On this page you'll see my layouts for the covers to issue 26 and 28. I did this on the computer—drawn with a mouse, so be kind... I can do much better work when I draw with a real pencil.

See how much better the layouts for 30 and 32 look on this page? These were done on actual paper—so much better, right? Right?! Most of the time I just send Charlie a few sentences telling him what I'm thinking for the cover—but every now and then I'll be after something specific... so I do a pretty little sketch.

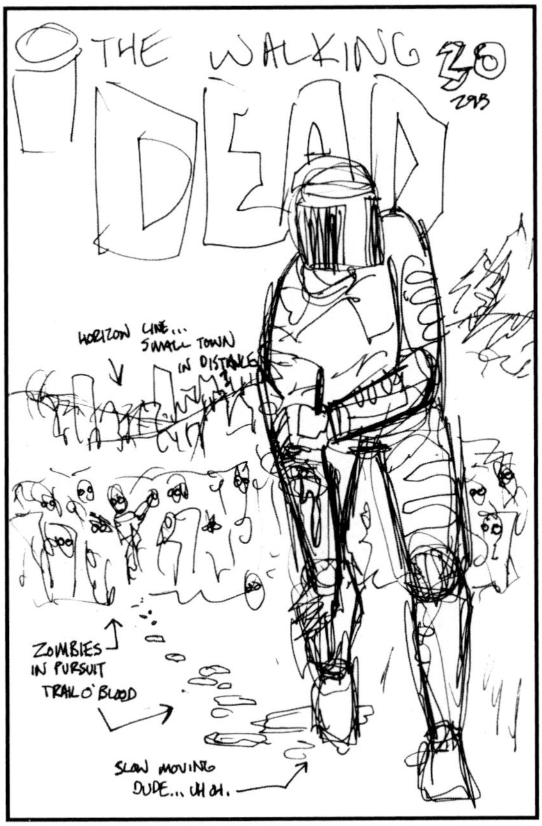
THE WALKING DEAD 30
HORIZON LINE... SMALL TOWN IN DISTANCE
ZOMBIES IN PURSUIT
TRAIL O' BLOOD
SLOW MOVING DUDE... UH OH.

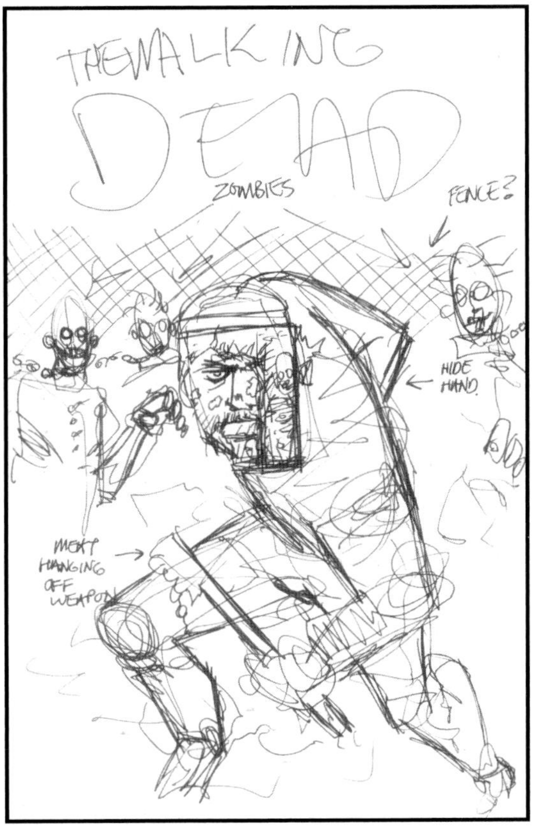
THE WALKING DEAD
ZOMBIES
FENCE?
HIDE HAND
MEAT HANGING OFF WEAPON

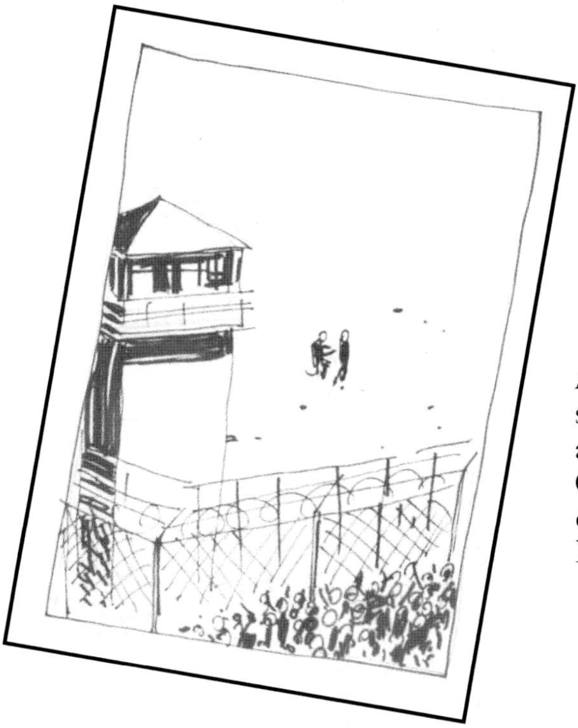

Also on this page, you'll find Charlie's cover sketch for the cover to issue 36. I had asked for a close-up of Glenn proposing to Maggie—but Charlie thought it'd be cooler to do it from a distance, and he sent along a sketch to prove it. Nice job, huh? I thought so.

—Robert Kirkman

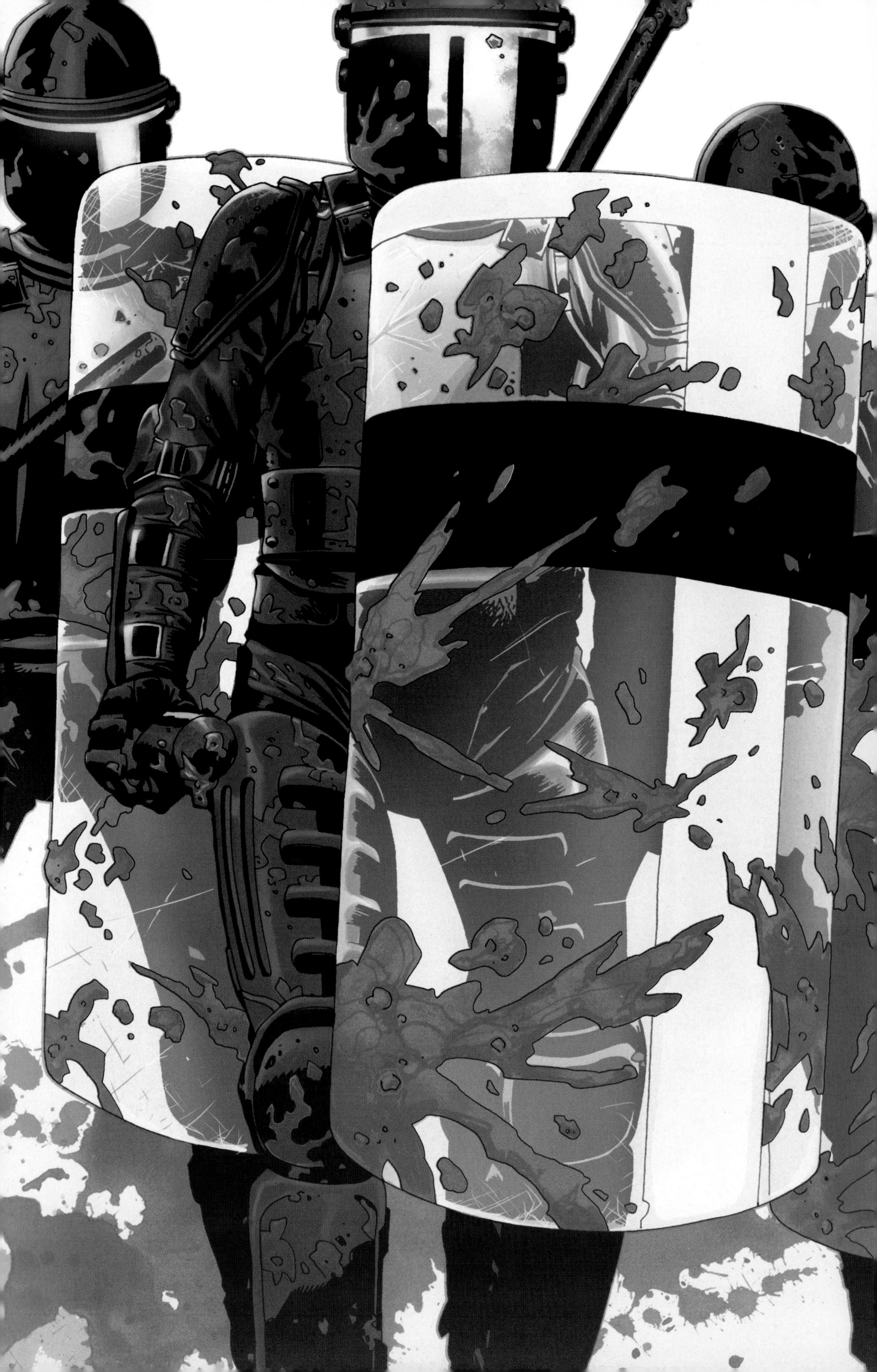

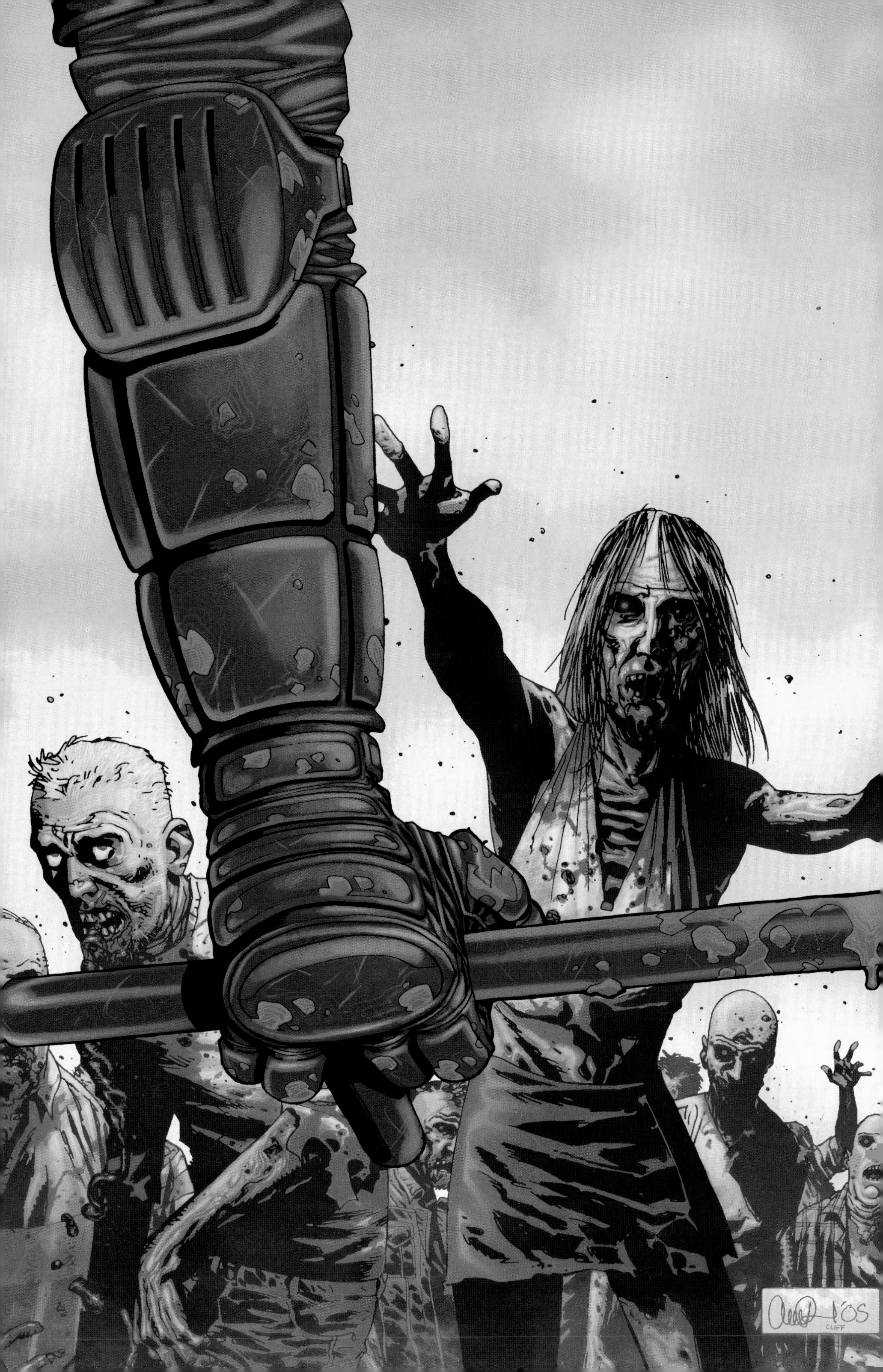

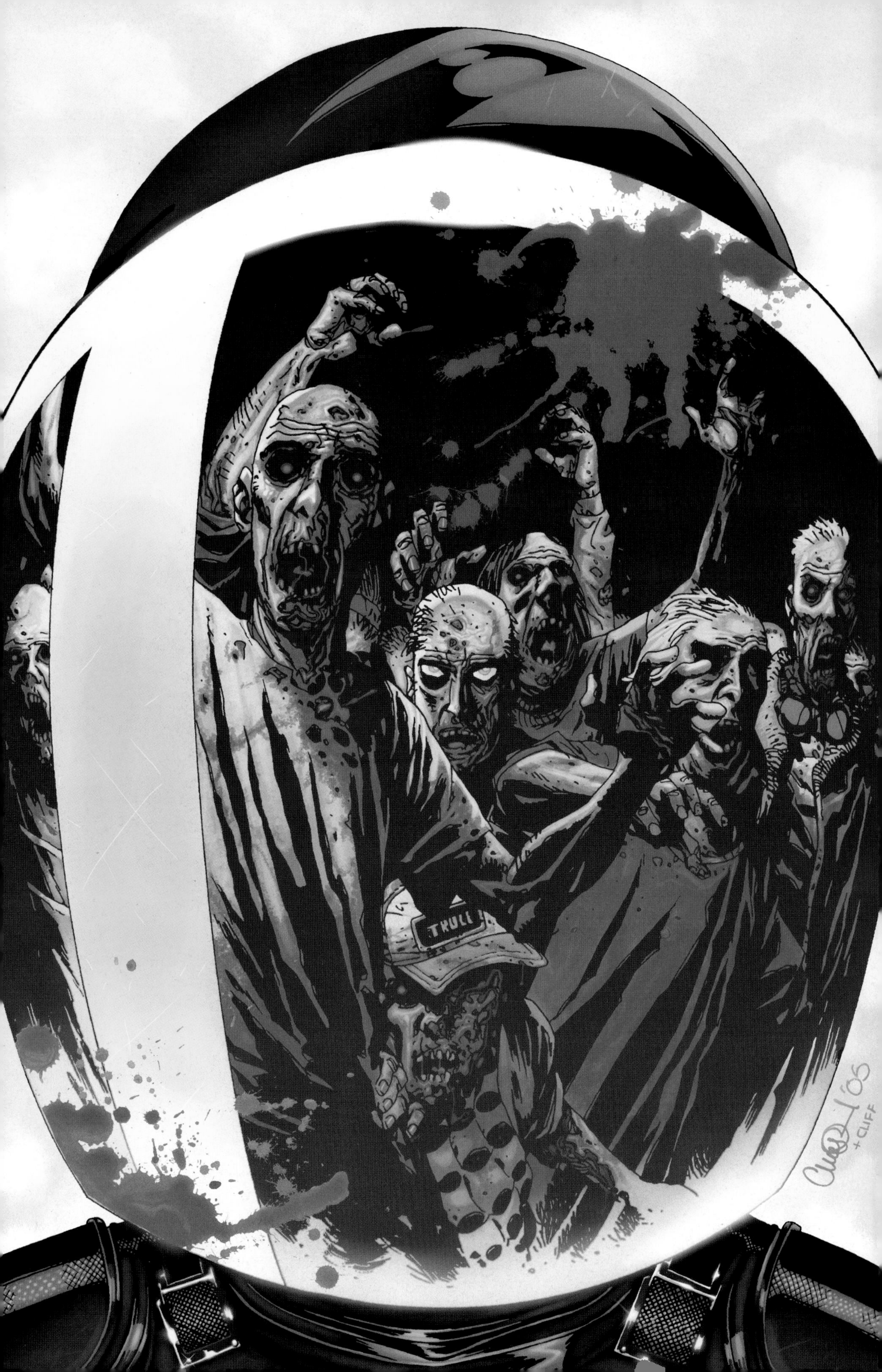

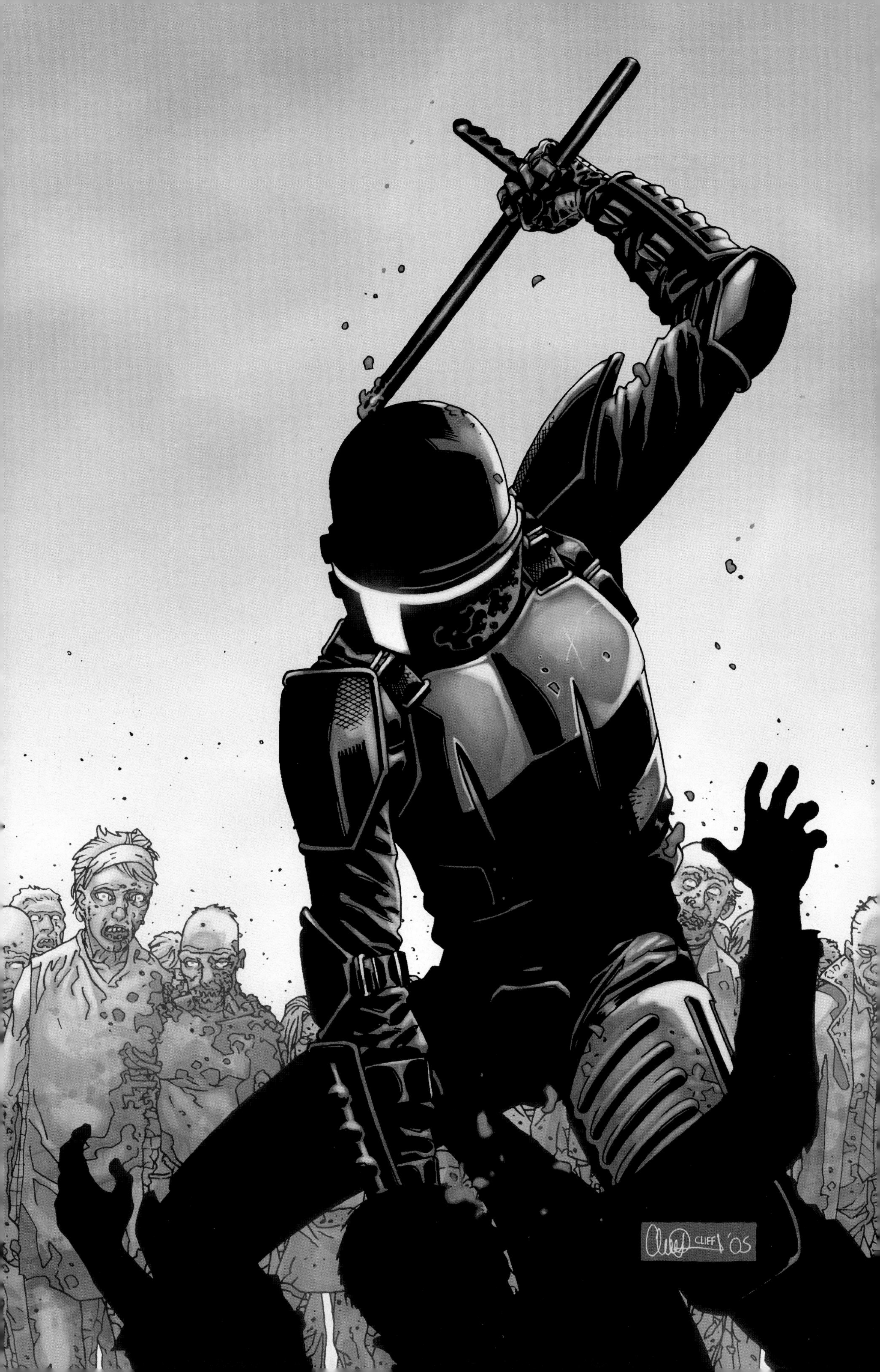
CLIFF '05

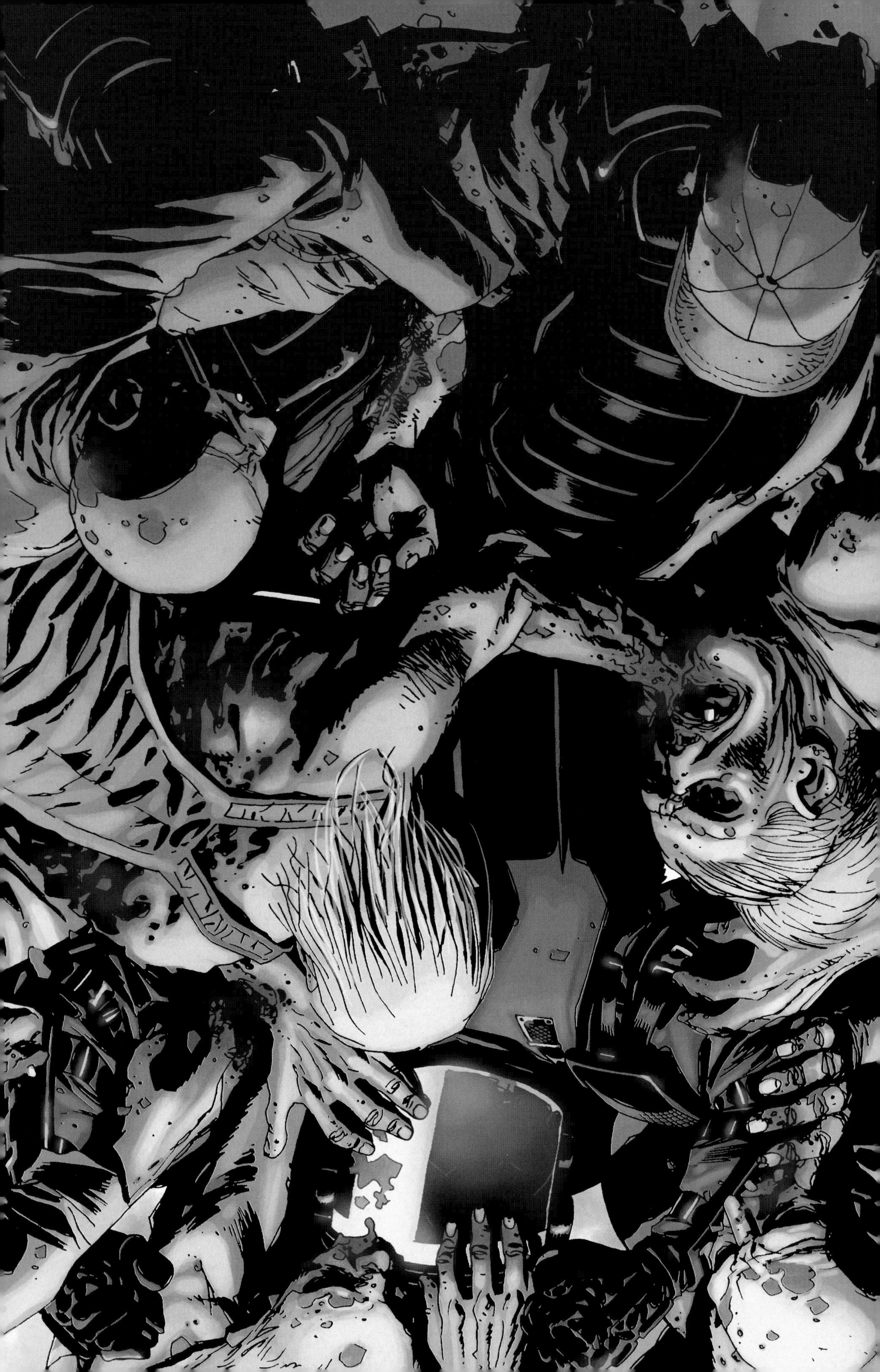

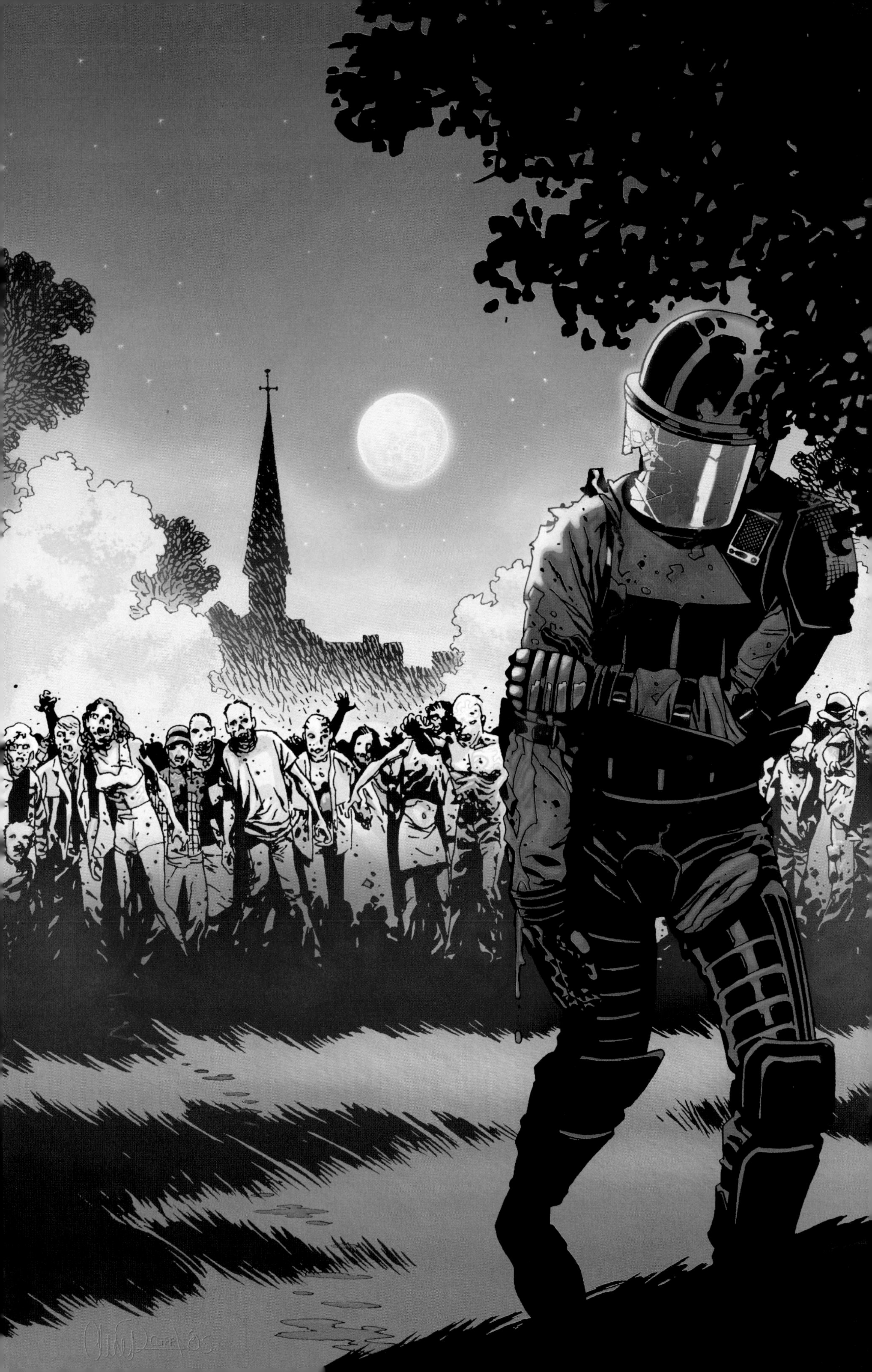

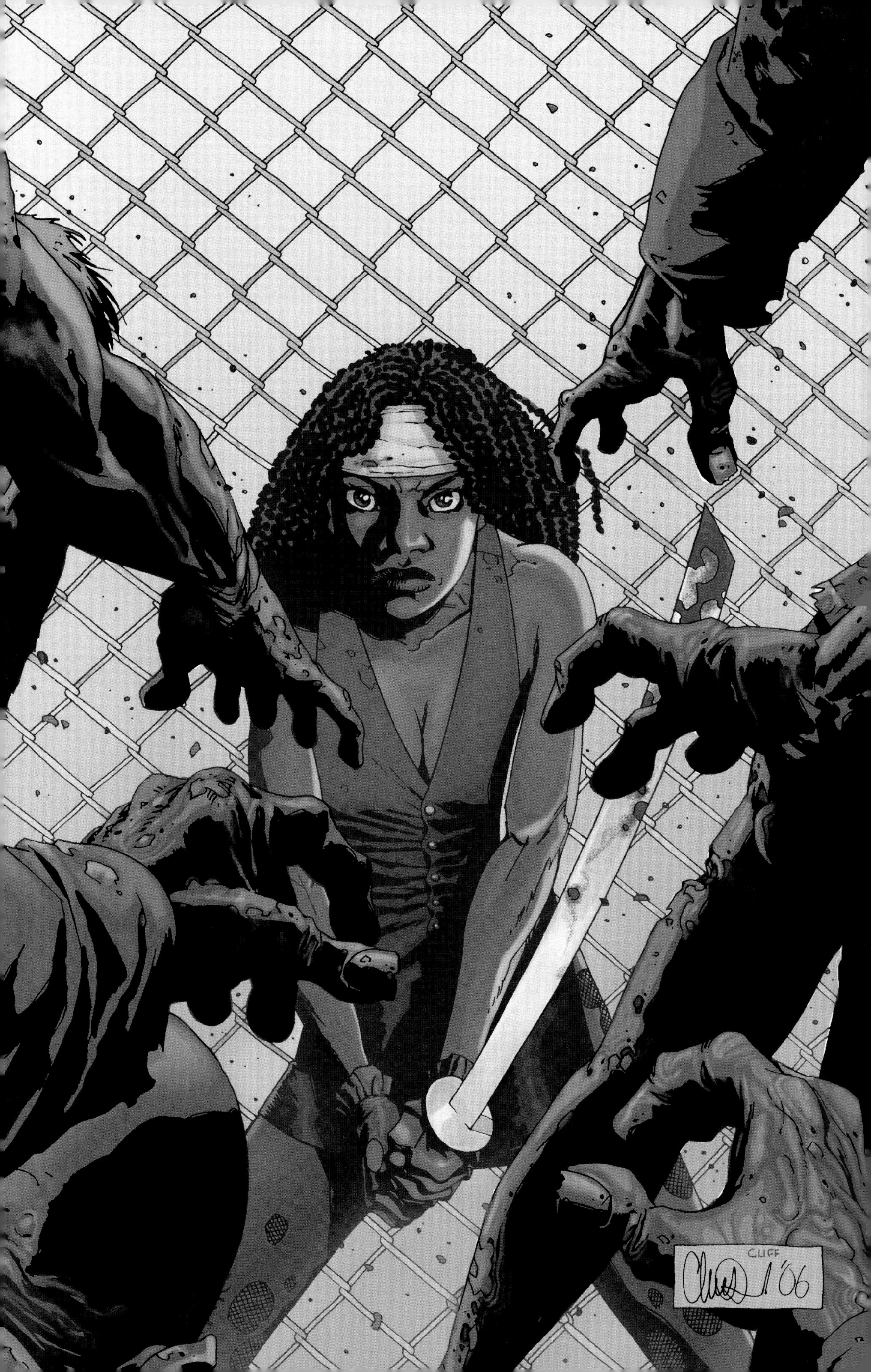
CLIFF
'06

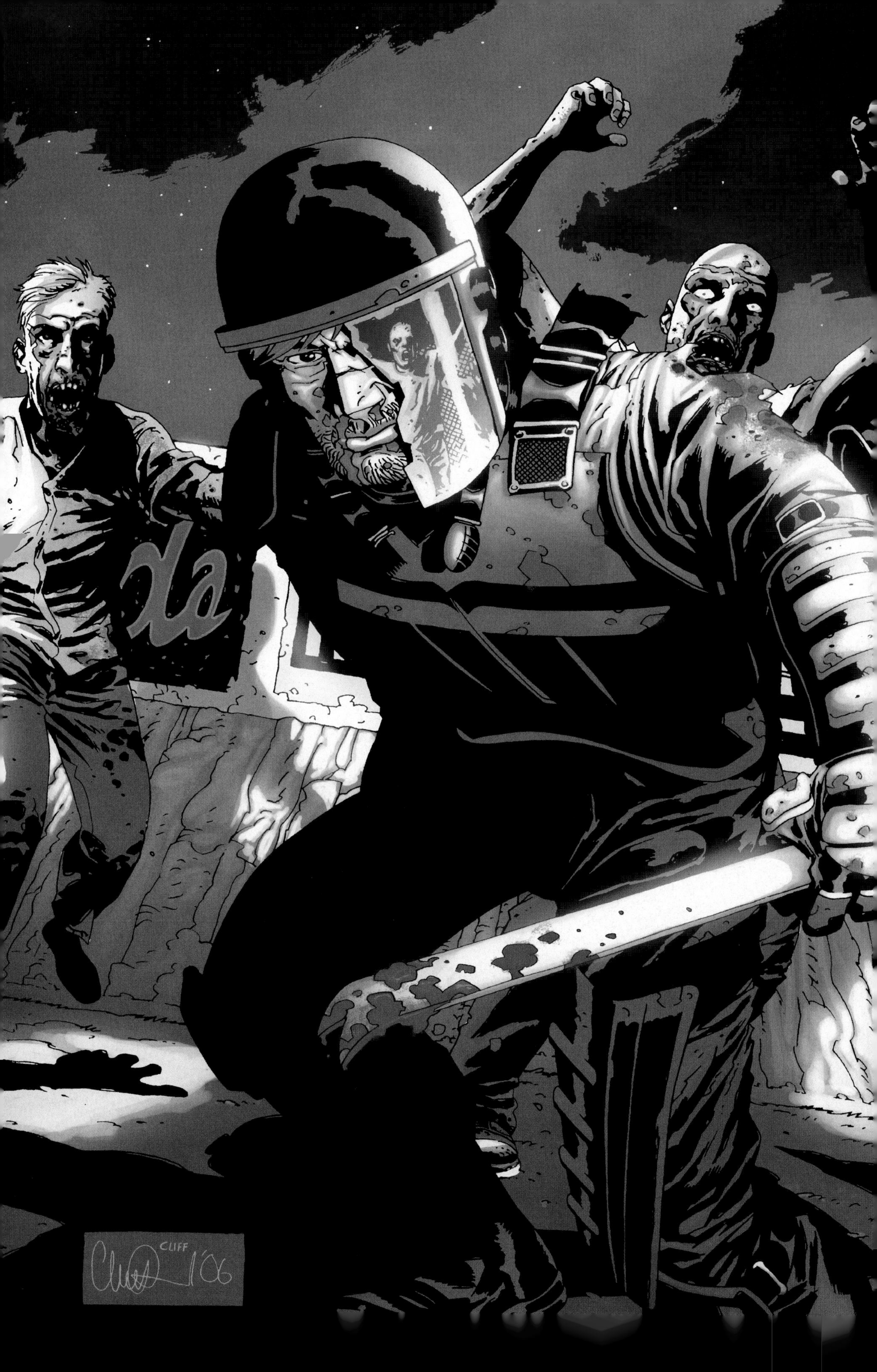
CLIFF
'06

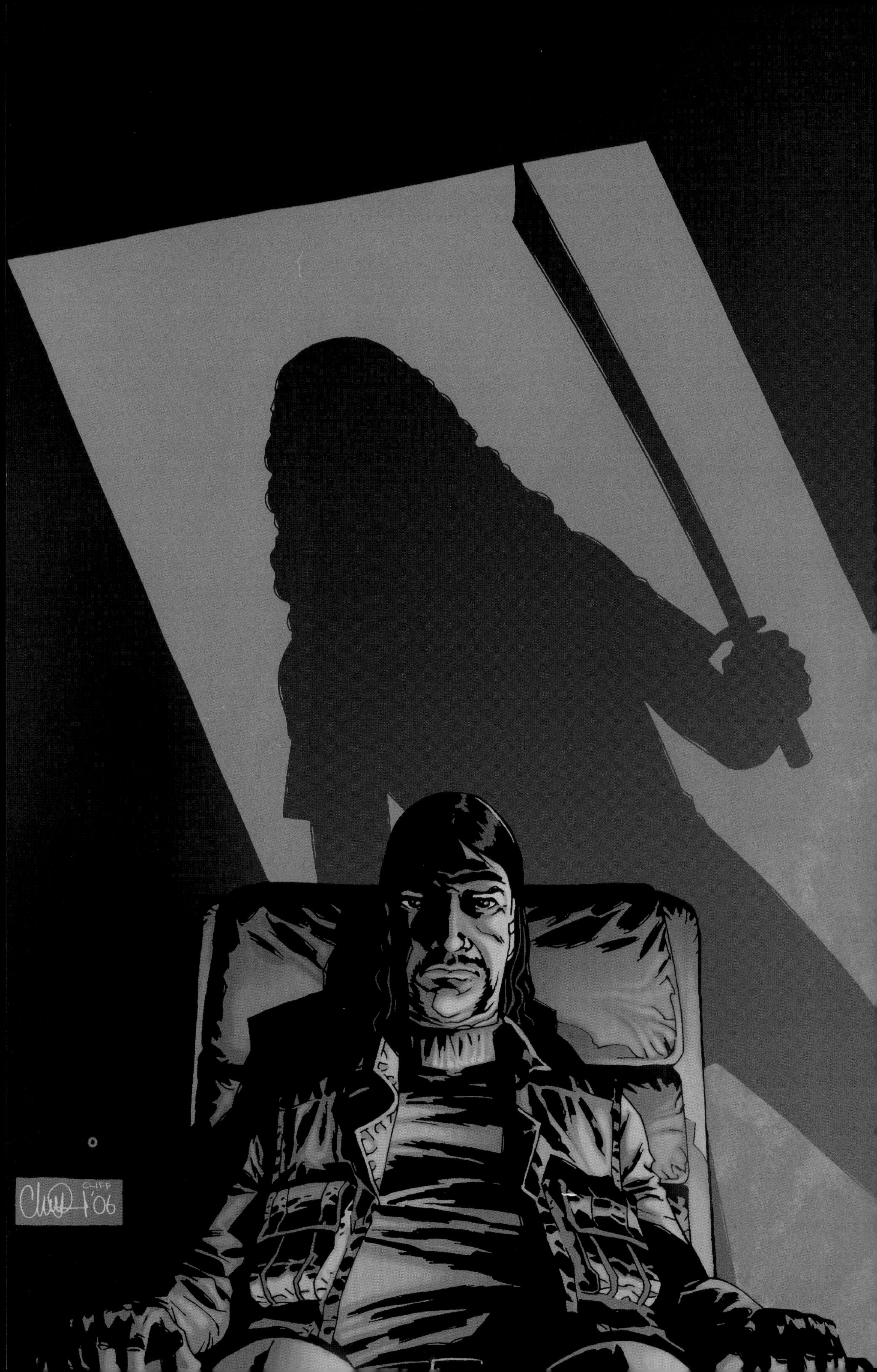

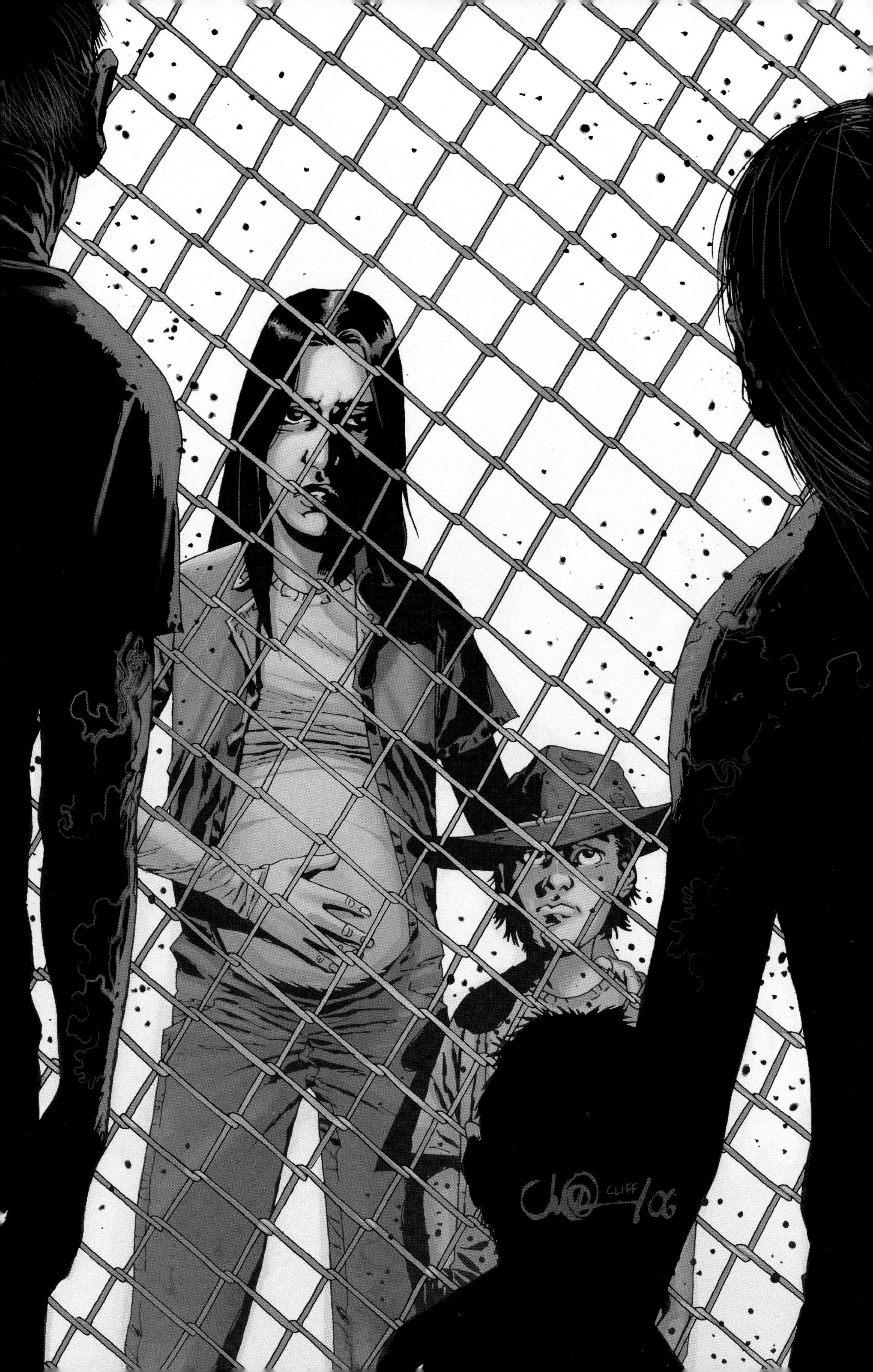
CLIFF

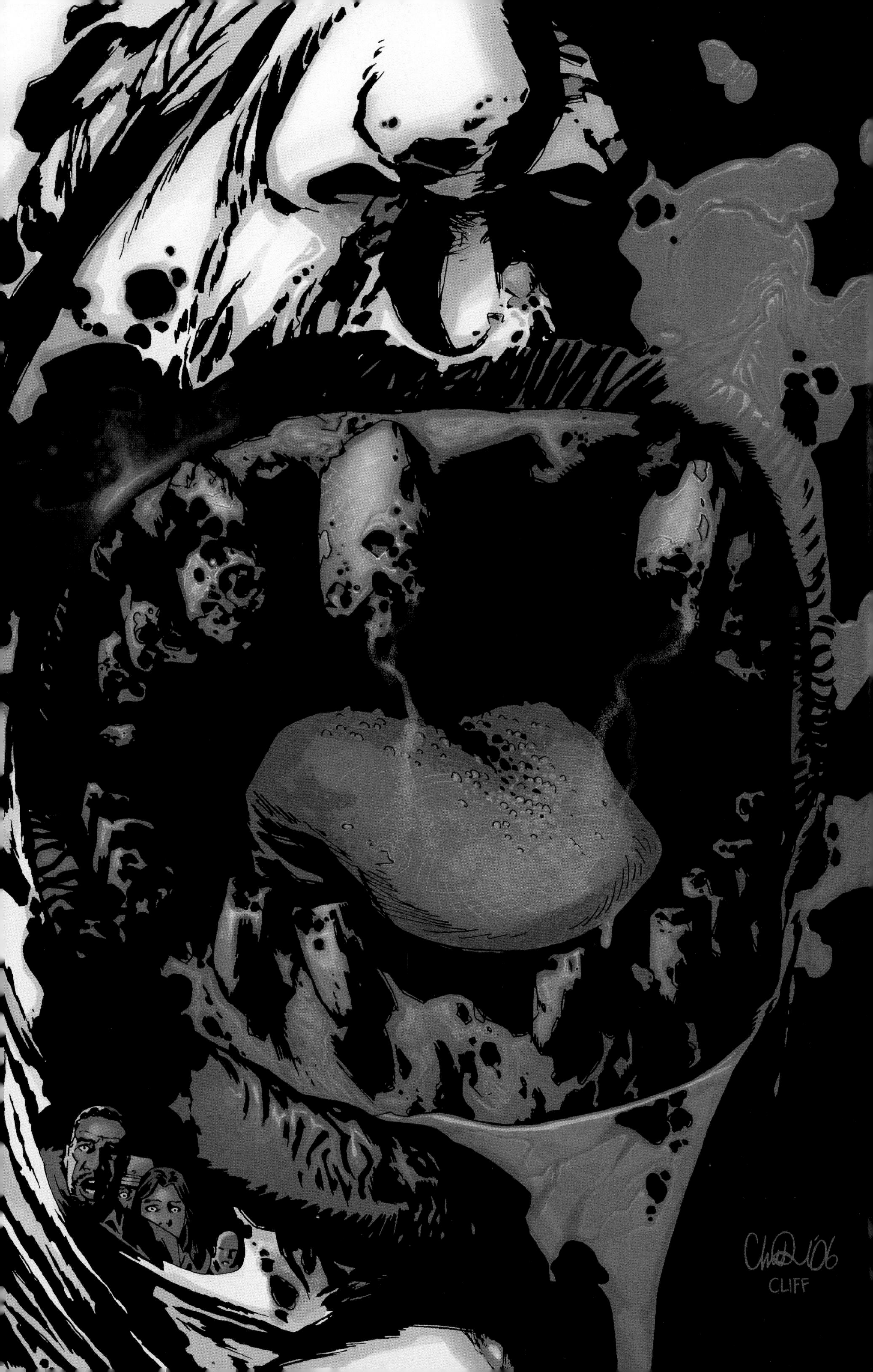
CLIFF

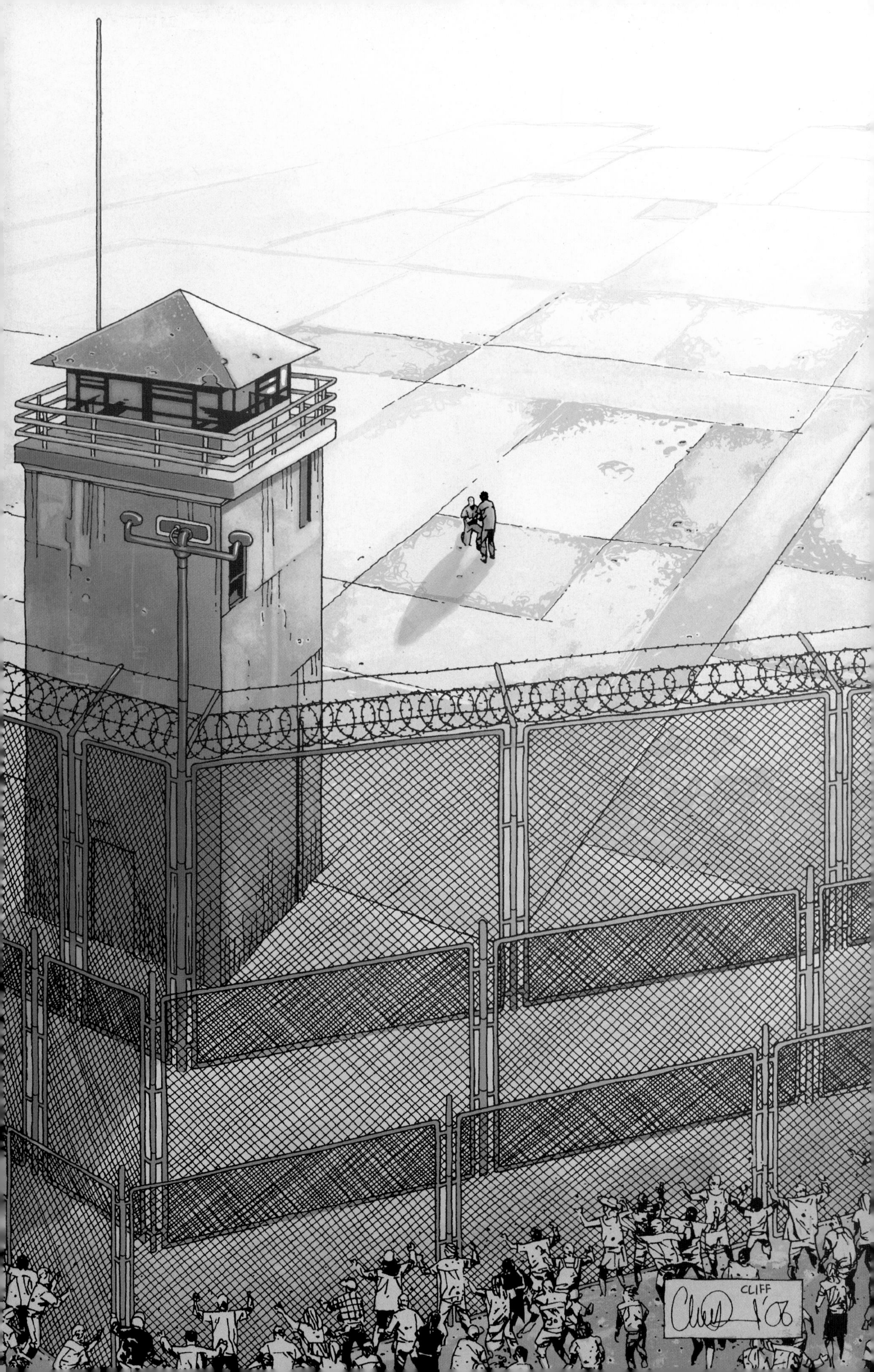
CLIFF

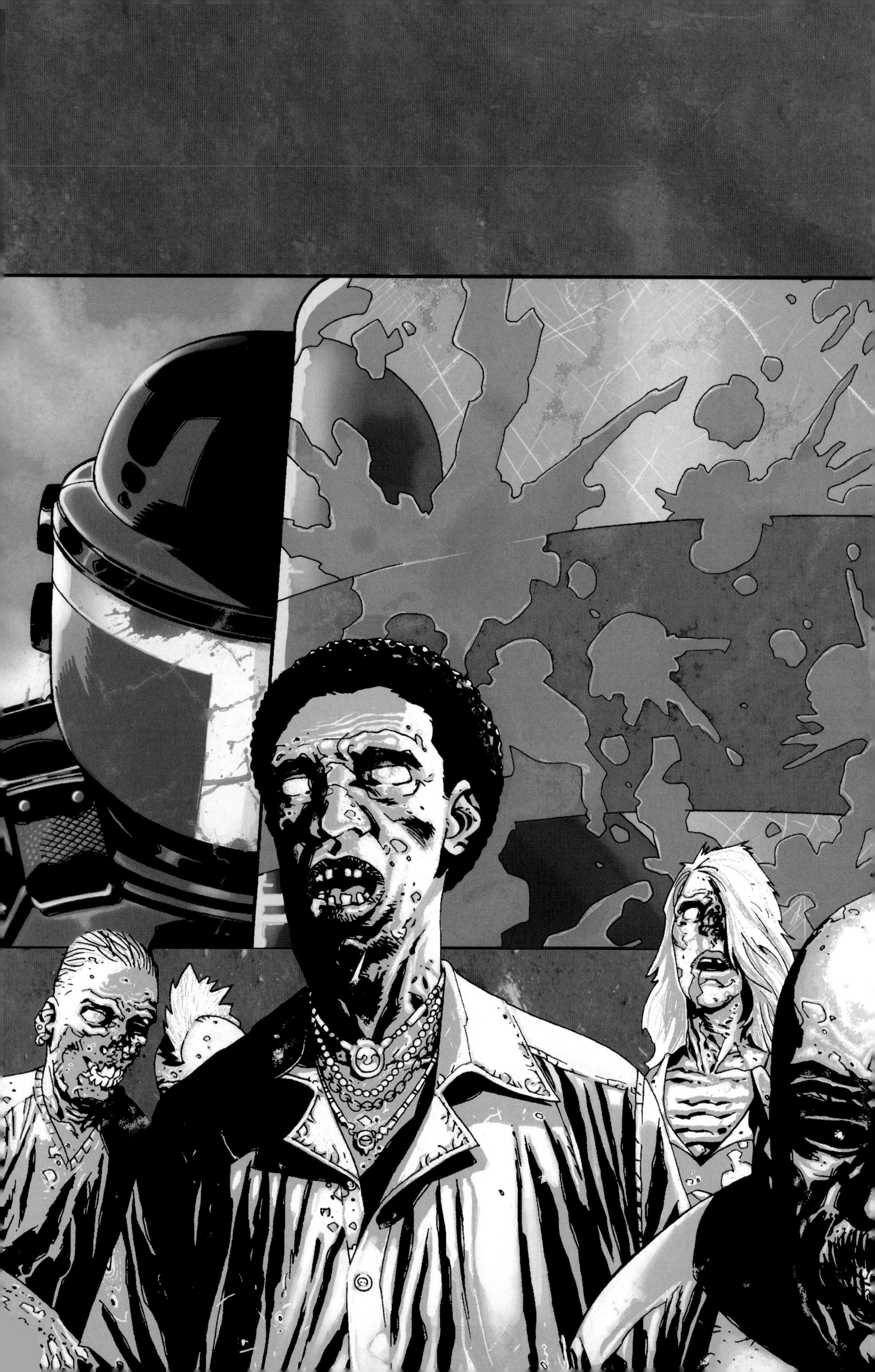

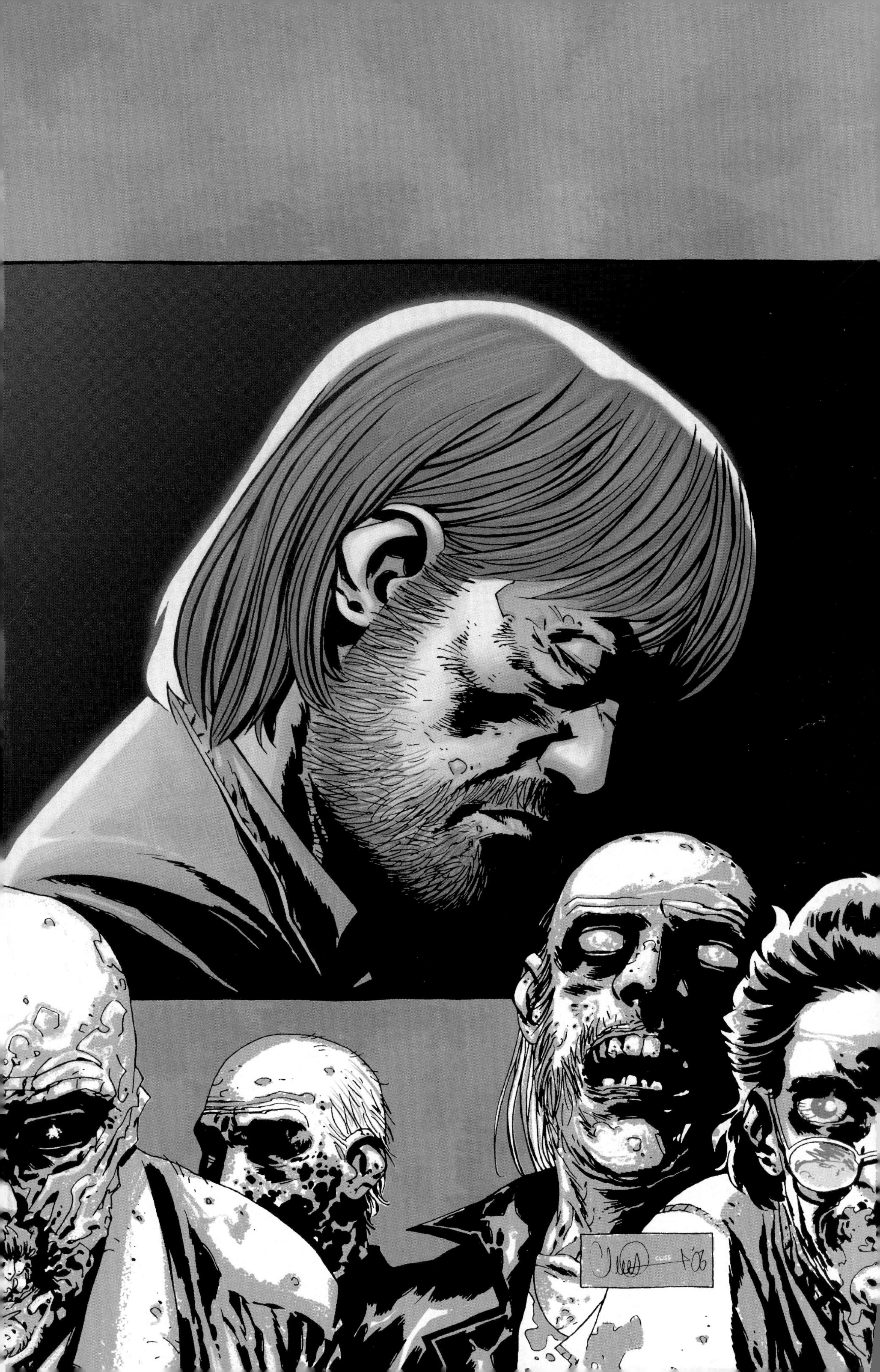

MORE GREAT BOOKS FROM ROBERT KIRKMAN & IMAGE COMICS!

KIRKMAN
OTTLEY
RATHBURN
PLASCENCIA
VOLUME 7

ROBERT KIRKMAN CHARLIE ADLARD CLIFF RATHBURN
THE WALKING DEAD
VOLUME 15
WE FIND OURSELVES

ROBERT KIRKMAN
THE
ROB LIEFELD
INFINITE
VOLUME ONE

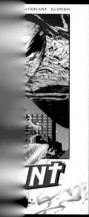

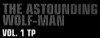

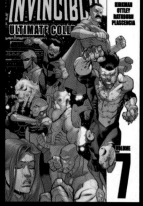

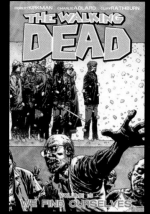

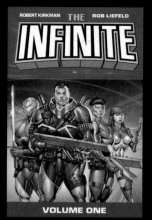

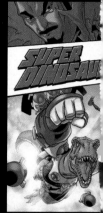

THE ASTOUNDING WOLF-MAN

VOL. 1 TP
ISBN: 978-1-58240-862-0
$14.99

VOL. 2 TP
ISBN: 978-1-60706-007-9
$14.99

VOL. 3 TP
ISBN: 978-1-60706-111-3
$16.99

VOL. 4 TP
ISBN: 978-1-60706-249-3
$16.99

BATTLE POPE

VOL. 1: GENESIS TP
ISBN: 978-1-58240-572-8
$14.99

VOL. 2: MAYHEM TP
ISBN: 978-1-58240-529-2
$12.99

VOL. 3: PILLOW TALK TP
ISBN: 978-1-58240-677-0
$12.99

VOL. 4: WRATH OF GOD TP
ISBN: 978-1-58240-751-7
$9.99

BRIT

VOL. 1: OLD SOLDIER TP
ISBN: 978-1-58240-678-7
$14.99

VOL. 2: AWOL
ISBN: 978-1-58240-864-4
$14.99

VOL. 3: FUBAR
ISBN: 978-1-60706-061-1
$16.99

CAPES

VOL. 1: PUNCHING THE CLOCK TP
ISBN: 978-1-58240-756-2
$17.99

HAUNT

VOL. 1 TP
ISBN: 978-1-60706-154-0
$9.99

VOL. 2 TP
ISBN: 978-1-60706-229-5
$16.99

THE INFINITE

VOL. 1 TP
ISBN: 978-1-60706-475-6
$9.99

INVINCIBLE

VOL. 1: FAMILY MATTERS TP
ISBN: 978-1-58240-711-1
$12.99

VOL. 2: EIGHT IS ENOUGH TP
ISBN: 978-1-58240-347-2
$12.99

VOL. 3: PERFECT STRANGERS TP
ISBN: 978-1-58240-793-7
$12.99

VOL. 4: HEAD OF THE CLASS TP
ISBN: 978-1-58240-440-2
$14.95

VOL. 5: THE FACTS OF LIFE TP
ISBN: 978-1-58240-554-4
$14.99

VOL. 6: A DIFFERENT WORLD TP
ISBN: 978-1-58240-579-7
$14.99

VOL. 7: THREE'S COMPANY TP
ISBN: 978-1-58240-656-5
$14.99

VOL. 8: MY FAVORITE MARTIAN TP
ISBN: 978-1-58240-683-1
$14.99

VOL. 9: OUT OF THIS WORLD TP
ISBN: 978-1-58240-827-9
$14.99

VOL. 10: WHO'S THE BOSS TP
ISBN: 978-1-60706-013-0
$16.99

VOL. 11: HAPPY DAYS TP
ISBN: 978-1-60706-062-8
$16.99

VOL. 12: STILL STANDING TP
ISBN: 978-1-60706-166-3
$16.99

VOL. 13: GROWING PAINS TP
ISBN: 978-1-60706-251-6
$16.99

VOL. 14: THE VILTRUMITE WAR TP
ISBN: 978-1-60706-367-4
$19.99

VOL. 15: GET SMART TP
ISBN: 978-1-60706-498-5
$16.99

ULTIMATE COLLECTION, VOL. 1 HC
ISBN 978-1-58240-500-1
$34.95

ULTIMATE COLLECTION, VOL. 2 HC
ISBN: 978-1-58240-594-0
$34.99

ULTIMATE COLLECTION, VOL. 3 HC
ISBN: 978-1-58240-763-0
$34.99

ULTIMATE COLLECTION, VOL. 4 HC
ISBN: 978-1-58240-989-4
$34.99

ULTIMATE COLLECTION, VOL. 5 HC
ISBN: 978-1-60706-116-8
$34.99

ULTIMATE COLLECTION, VOL. 6 HC
ISBN: 978-1-60706-360-5
$34.99

ULTIMATE COLLECTION, VOL. 7 HC
ISBN: 978-1-60706-509-8
$39.99

THE OFFICIAL HANDBOOK OF THE INVINCIBLE UNIVERSE TP
ISBN: 978-1-58240-831-6
$12.99

INVINCIBLE PRESENTS, VOL. 1: ATOM EVE & REX SPLODE TP
ISBN: 978-1-60706-255-4
$14.99

THE COMPLETE INVINCIBLE LIBRARY, VOL. 2 HC
ISBN: 978-1-60706-112-0
$125.00

THE COMPLETE INVINCIBLE LIBRARY, VOL. 3 HC
ISBN: 978-1-60706-421-3
$125.00

INVINCIBLE COMPENDIUM VOL. 1
ISBN: 978-1-60706-411-4
$64.99

THE WALKING DEAD

VOL. 1: DAYS GONE BYE TP
ISBN: 978-1-58240-672-5
$9.99

VOL. 2: MILES BEHIND US TP
ISBN: 978-1-58240-775-3
$14.99

VOL. 3: SAFETY BEHIND BARS TP
ISBN: 978-1-58240-805-7
$14.99

VOL. 4: THE HEART'S DESIRE TP
ISBN: 978-1-58240-530-8
$14.99

VOL. 5: THE BEST DEFENSE TP
ISBN: 978-1-58240-612-1
$14.99

VOL. 6: THIS SORROWFUL LIFE TP
ISBN: 978-1-58240-684-8
$14.99

VOL. 7: THE CALM BEFORE TP
ISBN: 978-1-58240-828-6
$14.99

VOL. 8: MADE TO SUFFER TP
ISBN: 978-1-58240-883-5
$14.99

VOL. 9: HERE WE REMAIN TP
ISBN: 978-1-60706-022-2
$14.99

VOL. 10: WHAT WE BECOME TP
ISBN: 978-1-60706-075-8
$14.99

VOL. 11: FEAR THE HUNTERS TP
ISBN: 978-1-60706-181-6
$14.99

VOL. 12: LIFE AMONG THEM TP
ISBN: 978-1-60706-254-7
$14.99

VOL. 13: TOO FAR GONE TP
ISBN: 978-1-60706-329-2
$14.99

VOL. 14: NO WAY OUT TP
ISBN: 978-1-60706-392-6
$14.99

VOL. 15: WE FIND OURSELVES TP
ISBN: 978-1-60706-392-6
$14.99

BOOK ONE HC
ISBN: 978-1-58240-619-0
$34.99

BOOK TWO HC
ISBN: 978-1-58240-698-5
$34.99

BOOK THREE HC
ISBN: 978-1-58240-825-5
$34.99

BOOK FOUR HC
ISBN: 978-1-60706-000-0
$34.99

BOOK FIVE HC
ISBN: 978-1-60706-171-7
$34.99

BOOK SIX HC
ISBN: 978-1-60706-327-8
$34.99

BOOK SEVEN HC
ISBN: 978-1-60706-439-8
$34.99

DELUXE HARDCOVER, VOL. 1
ISBN: 978-1-58240-619-0
$100.00

DELUXE HARDCOVER, VOL. 2
ISBN: 978-1-60706-029-7
$100.00

DELUXE HARDCOVER, VOL. 3
ISBN: 978-1-60706-330-8
$100.00

THE WALKING DEAD: THE COVERS, VOL. 1 HC
ISBN: 978-1-60706-002-4
$24.99

THE WALKING DEAD SURVIVORS' GUIDE
ISBN: 978-1-60706-458-9
$12.99

REAPER

GRAPHIC NOVEL
ISBN: 978-1-58240-354-2
$6.95

SUPER DINOSAUR

VOL. 1
ISBN: 978-1-60706-420-6
$9.99

DELUXE COLORING BOOK
ISBN: 978-1-60706-481-7
$4.99

SUPERPATRIOT

AMERICA'S FIGHTING FORCE
ISBN: 978-1-58240-355-1
$14.99

TALES OF THE REALM

HARDCOVER
ISBN: 978-1-58240-426-0
$34.95

TRADE PAPERBACK
ISBN: 978-1-58240-394-6
$14.95

TECH JACKET

VOL. 1: THE BOY FROM EARTH TP
ISBN: 978-1-58240-771-5
$14.99

TO FIND YOUR NEAREST COMIC BOOK STORE, CALL: 1-888-COMIC-BOOK